MELISSA K. MAGNER

OF THE Sun AND Sea

~THE COMPLETE DUOLOGY~

Illustrated by Viktoriia Davydova

ISBN-13: HB: 978-1-961249-00-4; PB: 978-1-961249-01-1; EBOOK: 978-1-961249-02-8, AUDIO: 978-1-961249-03-5

Library of Congress Control Number: 2025901341

Any references to real events, people, places, or things are used fictitiously. Names, characters, and places are products of the author's imagination. The realm of Elsudra is fictional and is not intended as a faithful representation of any one country or culture at any point in history.

Content Warning: *Of the Sun and Sea* is a fantasy duology intended for upper young adult and new adult readers (~17+ years old). It contains depictions of the following: grief, death, murder, gore, democide, suicide, purging, persecution, abuse, mental illness (including anxiety, depression, panic attacks, and suicidal ideation), violence, cursing, assault, torture, branding, mentions of forced sterilization, forced breeding, mass suicide. Please read with care.

Summary: After losing everything, a grieving young woman inherits an otherworldly power and becomes entangled in the fate of a dying realm. As her abilities awaken and her dreams of the sea grow stronger, she must confront the darkness both around and within her.

Front cover design by Bespoke Book Covers.

Illustrations by Viktoriia Davydova.

Printing edition 2025, United States of America

FOR MOM AND DAD

For helping me navigate changing tides
For loving me despite my storms
And for so much more

N
W
E
S
ELSUDRA
The Palace
The Belfry
Altus
The Antlers
Tolsea
NORTH
Lewes
Kalendus
WEST
Ulaex Mountains
Notts Mountains
EAST
Pirn
Sal
Tin
Admare Mountains
Inber
SOUTH
Candens Inlet
The Delve
Mossley
0 10 20 30 40
Miles

FOREWORD & ACKNOWLEDGMENTS

The first "book" I ever wrote followed a young girl stranded on a magical island after being swept out to sea by a tsunami. After showing it to my family, I said, "I'm going to publish this." Of course, seven-year-old Melissa had no idea what publishing entailed, and twenty-seven-year-old Melissa still has a lot to learn. The path I've chosen to walk is hard to define and constantly changing, but I owe its beginnings to my late grandmother, Patricia Kaspar. Her writing provided the foundation upon which I could debut with *Jinx*, a combination of our voices, before venturing out alone with *The Underground Moon*.

While I didn't end up publishing *Marina Oliver and the Island*, its essence exists in *Of the Sun and Sea*. Writing this series has simultaneously been one of the most challenging and rewarding things I've done, and I'm so grateful to those who have helped me make this a reality—including, but not limited to: my parents, Heidi and John Magner, who have encouraged me since the beginning and remain my biggest supporters. My sister, Jaclyn, who reminds me to go my own way in publishing, and who has listened to the run-down of this story several times and always offers hilarious commentary. My lifelong friend, Jack McCarthy, who was one of my earliest readers and whose unparalleled creativity and dedication helped shape Elsudra's magic system. My illustrator, Viktoriia Dayvdova, whose talent I am in awe of and whose illustrations so beautifully reflect this story. My editors, Cameron Montague Taylor and Rachelle Wright, whose expertise is invaluable. My narrator, Marissa DuBois, who brings care, nuance, and immense talent to every audiobook project. Peter and Caroline at Bespoke Book Covers, who are my go-to cover designers. My beta and alpha readers, especially Melissa Smith and Michael McCarthy, whose insights, comments, and suggestions I will always cherish. And, of course, the rest of my family and friends, who make every day, step, and breath worthwhile.

Over the last few years, I've learned a lot about my style as an author—most importantly, that I crave the freedom to write and publish in my own, somewhat unconventional way. It's why I include illustrations, why I lean into cross-genre fantasy, and why I decided to release the *Of the Sun and Sea* duology as an omnibus from the start. As an avid binge-reader, I love the idea of a cohesive narrative within a single volume: two books, one story. Readers can approach it as two consecutive books or as an integrated whole—regardless, the story is provided here in its entirety.

Please see the copyright page for content warnings. A glossary is included at the back of the book; while it can be used as a helpful guide, it is not essential to enjoy or understand the story.

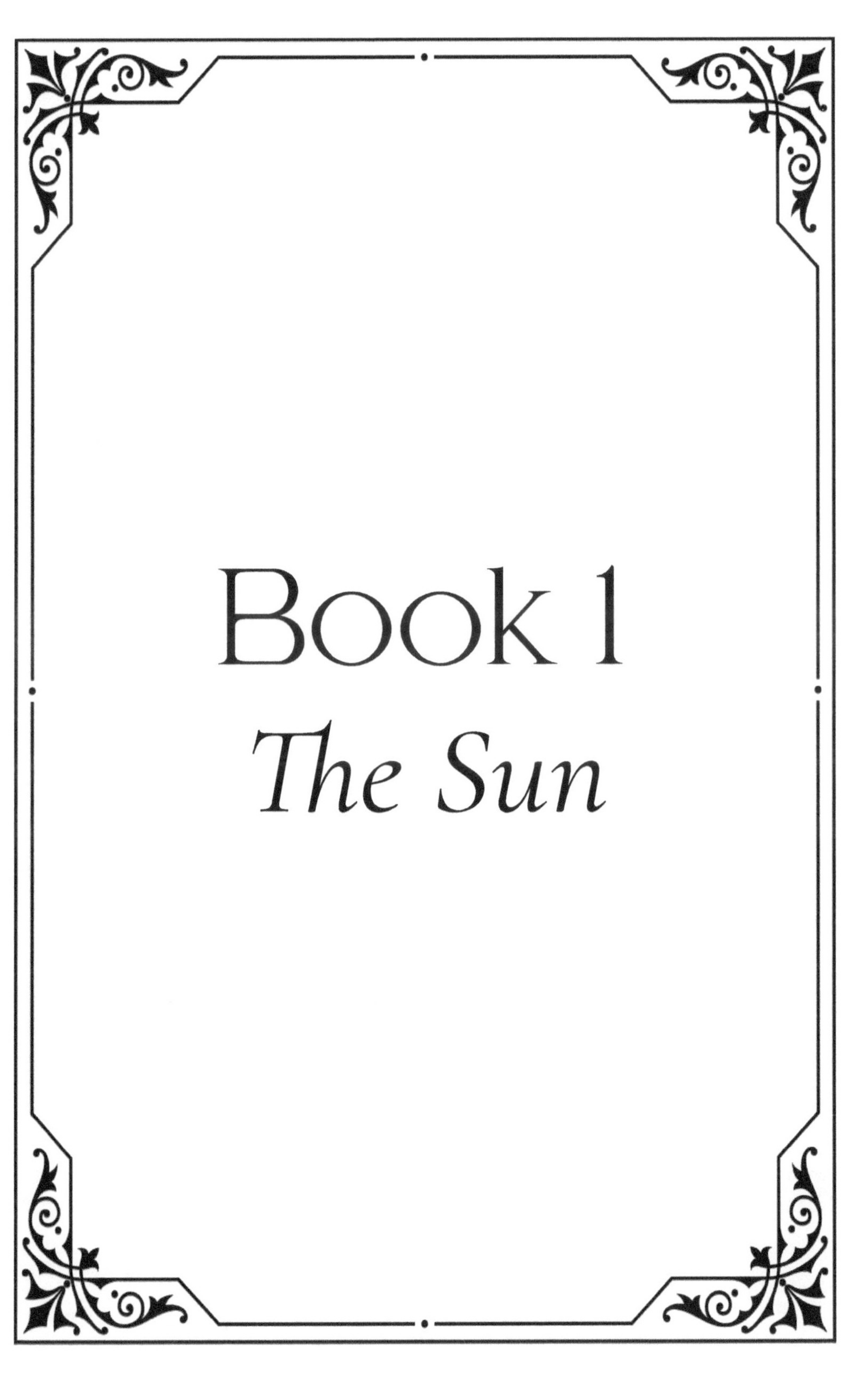

Book 1
The Sun

CHAPTER 1
Waves

The waves came to Marina in her sleep.

Sometimes, they were gentle—a blanket of glittering blue that ebbed with the tide. Other times, they thrashed and bucked like unbroken colts, mouths foaming as they crested. When she woke, they'd leave whispers of her name in their wake: *Marina, Marina, Marina.* She wasn't sure when they'd started, or if she had the ability to dream of anything else, but she didn't mind. Her waves were *hers,* and she saw no point in fighting them.

Every Monday at noon, when Gemma and Hank stopped by, she'd yearn for her waves more than ever. She'd imagine them washing over her, eating away at the residue of anger that clung so tightly to her tired frame. Her old therapist, who she'd seen on Gemma's recommendation, had said visualization was a form of meditation, then perkily added that there was no better form of therapy.

Marina had swallowed her response—if that were true, she wasn't sure what the hell she needed a therapist for—then canceled her future sessions.

Waves it was, then. Now more than ever, they kept her grounded as she tidied her living room and kitchen. One week without visitors could do a lot of damage, especially when Marina could hardly take care of herself, much less an entire house. But today was Monday, and Gemma would notice if things were messy, which meant Marina would have to endure an interrogation about her mood, if she wanted to try a new therapist, or if adding exercise to her routine would alleviate her depression. Well-intentioned as Gemma's advice was, it usually made things worse than they already were.

Gemma's *Heading over!* text with rows of heart emojis gave Marina an estimate of how much longer she had to clean and prepare to put on a happy face. It didn't help that her tears resurfaced as she folded her mom's handmade dish towels, opened the drawer filled with silverware they'd bought in Denmark, or passed her dad's office.

It hadn't always been like this. Once, she'd had a close circle of loved ones, and for someone like Marina—*a little cactus,* her mom always teased—that was more than she deserved. Maybe *that* was why everything had been taken from her—because she'd never deserved it to begin with.

Now, she only had Gemma and Hank. They'd never wanted kids, which didn't do wonders in curbing Marina's guilt. They had better things to do than help a nineteen-year-old fix the dishwasher or make payments her parents would've handled. But they insisted they wanted to help, and they stopped by weekly. Gemma would bring food, then send Hank off to do odd jobs around the house while she and Marina caught up on whatever Marina needed help with, which was usually everything. Right now, for instance, she couldn't remember where she'd put the laundry detergent. She scanned the cupboards, then slammed them shut. Like the rest of this place, they were empty.

She'd never thought her house was big, but on days like these, it could've been a mansion—a maze of rooms filled with stale air and memories—and she was the ghost at the heart of it. Mindlessly, she traversed the halls, tethered to the past, falling into the same endless cycle. She could never focus on one thing. A search for detergent became a trip to her parents' room, where their made bed sat untouched, which then switched to a walk around the kitchen, the counters littered with old mail. The only thing that brought her back was the donation boxes in the living room. If Gemma saw them, she'd grow suspicious, and since that was added stress Marina could do without, she hunkered down and pushed the boxes into her room. Once she got them out of sight, she returned to the laundry, abandoning the search for detergent and using dish soap instead. Detergent or soap; what was the difference? It didn't matter. Nothing mattered.

The only room she never cleaned was her dad's office. Perhaps she would if she could bring herself to open the door—to face the guitar that lay against his desk and know it would never be played again. But she didn't have the strength to do that. She never would. His office would remain the way he left it.

As she wriggled out of her sweats and put on something a touch more presentable, the burgeoning flame within her sputtered.

Three dead, but it should've been just one. It should've been the college student who'd *chosen* to drive shit-faced. *He'd* gotten into his car after taking God knows how many shots. Her parents hadn't.

Gemma's knock was as peppy as always, and Marina forced herself to smile before opening the front door. Her cheeks burned in protest.

The ocean breeze and sounds from the nearby beach struck Marina before Gemma's voice did. Though she did her best to respond to pleasantries as Gemma and Hank walked in, the sudden mustiness in the air distracted her.

"Did you just get up?" Gemma said through a laugh as she set a container of pasta on the counter. When Marina only grinned and edged over to the kitchen window, Gemma clicked her tongue. "You kids and your sleep schedules." She glanced at her husband. "Of course, Hank usually sleeps until noon too."

Hank didn't hear; he was too busy inspecting the dishwasher. "Still working?"

Marina nodded as she opened the window. "Better than it was last week."

"Good. Had a feeling it was a latch problem."

"It does me wonders to go on morning runs," Gemma said. "Once I'm finished, I have far less worries than I did before."

"Far *fewer*," Marina muttered, though she wasn't sure why she bothered. Maybe it just felt good to be a smart-ass in the face of unsolicited advice.

"Either way," Gemma said. "It might help. Exercise wakes me right up."

Exercise won't cure my kind of tiredness, Marina thought. When she glanced at the pasta on the counter, however, she forced a nod. "Good idea."

She resisted the urge to pull out a plate. If she seemed too eager, it would be obvious how little she was eating. She often wondered how much Gemma noticed and didn't comment on. Did she realize how rare a normal meal was to Marina? How she was a bit too thin, how her hair had turned brittle, or how her eyes were always glazed?

Hank was less of a worry. Even now, he was more concerned with the way the cabinets opened than he was with her. Gemma, however, seemed to see everything. She'd always had a rather astute look to her, from her tapering blue eyes to her styled hair. Marina often thought she resembled a canary: small and perky, taking in everything and unable to shut up. Like last month, for example, when Marina forced herself to go out for coffee and caught two older women staring at her.

"That's Luke and Stella's daughter," one of them had said. "The one Gemma knows. Can you imagine? One week into her sophomore year of college and her parents pass in an accident."

Marina had pretended like she couldn't hear them, but they spoke loudly.

"Such a tragedy. Gemma said she had no other family. Grandparents died a while back, and the parents were only children. Poor thing took a gap year because of it, but Gemma's worried she doesn't have plans to return. I can't imagine the grief."

"Well, who *wouldn't* be a mess after something like that?"

"Yes, but Gemma seems to think she blames herself."

She'd reined in her rage well enough, but in that moment, it snapped. Holding herself so straight her back hurt, Marina approached their table and sneered, "Next time you're talking about someone within earshot, at least have the decency to whisper."

She'd spun around and left before they could respond, then broke down the moment she got in her car. Gemma called her later apologizing, and Marina rattled off a few fake regrets of her own, only because she worried Gemma might not bring her food if she didn't show some remorse. Now, when asked how she spent her days, she lied. Most often, she'd tell Gemma she went out with friends, omitting the fact that she didn't actually have any. She used to, but after the accident, condolences became too much, and she'd stopped responding to calls and texts. Her old friends from high school and new friends from college had gone on with their lives, and now she was as good as a ghost to them. Fitting.

"Have you noticed the cabinet gets stuck halfway?" Hank asked.

Gemma shot him a look. "It's not a big deal."

Hank shrugged and went back to fiddling with it. With a dismissive wave of her hand, Gemma turned to Marina and softened. Only then did Marina feel tears pricking her eyes.

"I was out to lunch with some girlfriends the other day," Gemma said, obviously pretending she didn't notice. "One of them has a son your age. He's into music, like you. I told her I'd run it by you and see if you were interested in going on a date."

Marina had to hold back a laugh. Accident or no accident, dating sounded miserable. Since she figured it wouldn't be polite to respond with "I'd rather put out a campfire with my face," she shrugged and said, "That's sweet, but I don't think I'm into that right now."

Or ever. But that was something Marina could do without explaining.

"You're the only nineteen-year-old I know who *wouldn't* be excited about going on a date," Gemma quipped.

"You don't know many nineteen-year-olds," Marina said.

Hank's laugh turned into a cough when Gemma frowned at him.

"The offer's on the table. He plays the guitar, and I told my friend you sing. I figured you could get back into it." She smiled cautiously. "Maybe you could sing 'Landslide' again, like you used to with your dad. You always sounded lovely."

Marina's throat tightened. "I haven't sung in a while."

It had been her and her dad's thing. She sang, he played guitar. Nobody could replace him, but it was useless explaining that—useless to admit she'd never sing again because that was something she and her dad had shared. And now, because of her, he was gone.

When she was a child, she'd lie on the ground in his office, listening to him play Fleetwood Mac. Oftentimes, she'd hum along from her spot on the rosewood floor, which he'd put in because it was the same shade as her and her mother's hair.

A sob rose in Marina's chest, but she pushed it down. Gemma's gaze trailed off, and when it landed on the pot of daffodils on the table, she eagerly plucked the watering can from the sink and said, "I'll do it."

The silence that followed was welcome, albeit short-lived.

"I love that you've kept them around," Gemma continued. Marina had to stifle her groan. "Such a sweet nod to your parents. They kept a vase next to your crib, you know."

Gemma paused—perhaps because she realized she was rambling—but when Marina glanced at her, she saw Gemma looking at the letters next to the sink.

Oh God. Of *all* the things she could've forgotten to put away...

"Thirty thousand dollars to drunk-driving prevention?" Gemma pushed the letter aside, revealing several more of the same. *Shit.* "Twelve thousand to the animal shelter... fifteen thousand to ocean cleanup...ten thousand to the library..." *Shit, shit, shit.* "How much money are you giving away?"

"I just made a few holiday donations, that's all."

She hadn't, actually. The donations had started in September, a few weeks after the accident. They hadn't been so hefty at first, but now it was January, and time was of the essence. Gemma flashed a wide-eyed look at Hank, who muttered something about needing to check the toilet flapper before disappearing down the hall.

"But there are so many," Gemma said through an exhale, "all in the tens of thousands." She pushed another letter aside. "Ten thousand to an elementary school, twenty-five to mental health research..." She wavered, then gaped at the last letter. "*Sixty-five thousand* to a foster care organization?"

"You don't need to read them out loud. I know where I donated."

"But why?" Gemma put the watering can back in the sink. "I'm all for you making grown-up decisions with money—it's why I helped you become an authorized signer on your parents' account in the first place—but this is too much. You need some for yourself."

Agree with Gemma. Say you'll be mindful. Don't raise any more red flags.

"The way I see it, any one of us could die tomorrow," Marina bit back, then silently scolded herself.

Gemma's eyebrows narrowed. "Are you...are you okay? All this money, and only in the last few months. And you didn't tell me or Hank."

"I'm not going to off myself, if that's what you're worried about."

"I know," Gemma said, though Marina couldn't help but notice the relief in her voice. "But I'm sure it gets lonely in this house. And now that you're thinking about putting off college indefinitely..."

Marina rubbed her temples. "I can't deal with college talk right now or questions about where I'm donating, Gemma. Just leave it."

"I ask because I'm worried. It's noble what you're doing, but you'll be in a world of hurt if you give away too much."

Marina almost laughed. She was already in a world of hurt.

"I think we should check your bank statements and gauge where you're at," Gemma said. "I can help you. We can—"

"Thanks for stopping by," Marina interrupted, straining to steady her voice. "I bet you guys have things to do today."

"That's not fair. You can't blow me off when I express concern."

"I know what I'm doing. I'm very capable of making *grown-up* decisions."

"I didn't mean to sound condescending. It's just…I've never known you to be foolish with money. Your dad always stressed the importance of saving, especially given some of his clients…" Her voice faded, but it was obvious she was desperate to say something because she blurted, "I'm worried. The money, the house…you were doing so well before the accident. You seemed so happy."

"I wasn't happy. And I don't want to talk about this."

"I know some counselors who might be good fits. The first one may not have worked, but I'm sure the others would."

"Thanks for stopping by," Marina said again, this time more forcefully. She glanced at Hank, who now lingered in the corner of the room. "Great to see you."

Gemma hesitated but eventually scooped up their car keys and made her way to the door. "I'll text you," she said, patting Hank's shoulder as he passed. Tentatively, she added, "Love you."

Marina didn't acknowledge them as they left. She remained motionless, holding her breath until the roar of their engine faded. When she could no longer hear it, she swore into her hands.

Luke and Stella's once perfect daughter: perfect grades and manners, perfect life and future. How fragile those perfect things were. Maybe it was best, Marina figured as she lugged the watering can over to the daffodils. Best if Gemma and Hank didn't take time out of their day to stop by. Best to prove to them now that she didn't deserve their help and goodwill.

Tears welled in her eyes as she poured water onto the flowers, then placed the pasta in the fridge and retreated to the couch. As soon as her head hit the pillows, the urge to sleep pulled her under.

At least she had her waves. Even she couldn't push them away.

CHAPTER 2
The Emptiness Beyond

It was well into the night when Marina finally woke. Her head throbbed, but she got up anyway and checked her phone. As she suspected, she had a text from Gemma, which read, *Today was rough, but here's a reminder that we love you. Please call when you're ready.*

She lingered near her phone for a moment, then set it aside.

Some people rallied in the face of grief. They pulled together and stuck out the hard times, making conscious choices to do the right thing. She wasn't one of those people. Even when her parents were around, stoicism had never been her strong suit. A beast lived at the heart of her storms—a wild, broken thing that cowered and gnashed its teeth, lashing out when provoked and giving up just as quickly.

One day, one step, one breath at a time, her mom would say. It had been her attempt to keep Marina from spiraling, taking her focus from a thousand catastrophic futures to one manageable present. It helped, sometimes. Of course, taking a breath didn't always do it. Most notable was in ninth grade, when some little shit named Tony Hanson told her that if it weren't for her long hair, she'd be a four instead of a six. She'd taken her scissors, chopped off a section, and thrown it at him, grinning when he'd gawked at the locks of reddish-brown hair on his desk. Her mother, a hairstylist of over fifteen years, had handled it well. Instead of punishing her, she'd cut Marina's hair just below her shoulders, then topped it off with side bangs. Marina hadn't changed her hair since.

Those instances of acting out, however, were few and far between. She wasn't always so disagreeable, but nowadays, the venom was harder to control. It was made less of anger and more of pain—pain she'd always carried, but that had gotten so much worse recently.

The charity letters on the counter glinted under the pendant lights. She'd neglected to tell Gemma that she'd sent out several other checks this past week alone, all considerable sums. Of *course* Gemma had assumed the worst. Why else would a grieving nineteen-year-old make such massive donations?

Marina sighed and picked up her phone.

Love you too, she wrote back. After a moment's hesitation, she sent, *I appreciate you both. Don't blame yourself for my choices and know I haven't given up.*

She stared at the screen, unsure why she'd felt the need to say that. But questioning herself lately was useless, so Marina put her phone aside and returned to the couch, where she wrapped herself in blankets and blocked out the world. If there was anything she was good at, it was that.

⌒

Insomnia, Marina decided when she woke again, only plagued her at night. Usually, it lasted for only a few hours, but tonight was different. Though she closed her eyes, sleep wouldn't come. Still, the voices lingered. *Marina, Marina, Marina.*

They followed every crash of a wave. Sometimes, they were familiar, as though her parents were next to her, and other times, they sounded like strangers. The playful, gentle quips of a young man would morph into something just as playful but much more raffish. A woman's poised voice would soften into feathery whispers, and the warm, yet stern commands of a man would maintain their power but grow much colder. There were others too—that of a child, small and light, and a few more she couldn't make out. She never tried to, though. She just listened.

She remained between sleep and wake for an hour or so, then surrendered when the clock read four in the morning. She ate what little she could, then showered so long that she lost track of time.

She avoided the bathroom mirrors when she got out of the shower, only because she hated the girl who looked back at her. She had Marina's brown eyes and auburn hair, but the girl in the mirror was no more human than she was a poor imitation of one. Grief had leeched the color from her skin and the liveliness from her face, and her pronounced cheekbones, which she'd once thought pretty, had sunken in.

The house was still dark when Marina emerged from the bathroom. Though the kitchen shades were pulled back, no light came in. It had to be nearly five, but when she peered outside, stars gleamed amidst the onyx sky. Her towel still wrapped around her, she glanced at the clock in the living room, furrowing her brow when she read the time.

Four in the morning. Still.

She moved to the counter and picked up her phone. Gemma hadn't texted back, but that wasn't what Marina was looking for. All she could focus on was the time: four in the morning. Had she read the clock wrong when she woke? Was she really *that* disoriented?

She dug through the pile of clothes beneath the laundry machine until she found a clean sweater and a pair of leggings. She took extra time brushing her hair before checking her phone again. The time hadn't changed. Marina wavered, shifting her balance from leg to leg as she waited for a minute to pass. Nothing.

Go outside. The words—the *impulse*—lingered at the back of her head, but Marina ignored them.

She could hear the crash of waves from the closest beach flitting in through the window. Sometimes, she'd sit next to it, listening to the ebb and flow of the sea, remembering her childhood spent playing in the water and ignoring her parents when they told her to stay close to the shore. Something about the ocean had always called to her, and not just because of the waves in her dreams.

Go outside.

"Shut up," Marina said out loud. She cranked the window closed, then returned to her phone. The internet was out, and the time *still* hadn't changed.

Go. Outside.

In defiance, she scurried down the hall to her bedroom. Though she tried to ignore the temptation, she slipped on her shoes. Her parents had gifted them to her: rugged ballet-pink combat boots. A smile tugged at her lips as she laced them.

Girly and tough, her dad would say. *Just like my Rina.*

My Rina. My little Rina.

Her lips quivered as she lingered by her dresser, then turned to the bookshelf by her bed and brushed her fingers across the spines. Textbooks sat amongst epic fantasies, and poetry books rested on comics—her confidants these past few months, whom she turned to not for stories, but for comfort and answers.

For God's sake, Marina. Go outside.

She groaned, but this time, she didn't ignore herself. She glanced again at her books, then crept into the living room, running her hands along the walls as she went.

The clock still read four in the morning, and Marina didn't bother checking her phone again. Instead, she opened the front door and stepped outside.

At the first stroke of the ocean breeze, she yielded. The smell of sea oats and freshly weeded privet tinged her nostrils as she took the pathway leading to the shore. Though she had half a mind to fight it, she let herself fall further into her stupor.

One day, one step, one breath at a time. The words carouseled in her head as she took the wooden stairs down to the sand.

Echoes of stars danced on the sea, unpolluted by street lamps and headlights. A new kind of life existed at night, uncorrupted by beachgoers and screaming children. Every crash of waves lulled her further into calmness, and she couldn't fight it. But the night was alive with more than just stars. Beneath the sea, light danced—white and red, burning so brightly that Marina wondered if perhaps a sun was trapped within the waves.

What a silly thought. Strangely enough, it made her grin.

The air hummed, lulling her further into her trance. This place...it was so quiet. When she looked to the sky again, the stars were gone, their light snuffed out by glowing seawater. Head fuzzy, Marina turned to the hills.

But there were no hills. Not anymore. What had once formed a wall of rocky knolls and addled pathways leading to beachfront houses was gone, replaced by miles of sand.

That forced her out of her stupor. A gasp formed in her throat as she whirled to face the ocean, but it, too, had gone. No, not gone—pulled out so far that she could no longer see the waves. But she could feel them—the rumbling beneath her feet, the vibrations in the atmosphere.

Terror clawed at her as she stumbled back. She needed to get out of here—wherever *here* was—and to safety. She pushed herself to a sprint, her movements clumsy, but the world remained as it was: an endless expanse of sand lying flat beneath a starless sky.

More of that horrible silence followed, but it was different. It was cold and deadened, as though the world as she knew it wasn't a world at all, but the emptiness *beyond* worlds.

Running wouldn't do anything. Neither would calling for help. Nobody was here, and if they were, whatever was forming on the horizon would devour them too.

The ocean came into view from all directions. Though every fiber of her being screamed at her to fight, to run, to duck, to do *something*, she couldn't. Her body had given way, rooting her to the sand.

The ocean built on itself as it rushed forward, rising until it had formed a wall of blue. But there was something else—something in its depths that pushed it forward.

The foaming monsters before her weren't of this world, but she knew them all the same. Every inch of water, from the curling white-tipped crests to the cobalt underbelly, she'd dreamed of for the past nineteen years.

The waves were of her dreams, but this time, she was not dreaming. And when water fell from the lifeless sky, she felt every bit of its impact.

CHAPTER 3
No Fear

The cold was unbearable. It raked its claws across Marina's skin, tearing her senses to shreds. Her consciousness fluctuated, giving her relief when it faded only to return moments later and leave her writhing in salt-infested water. Time no longer felt linear, but when rocks brushed against her body, she no longer cared how long she'd been out.

She couldn't gauge the temperature of the ground, but it was warmer than the water, which was welcome enough. She lay with her cheek to the rocks, gasping and sputtering as she tried to collect herself.

Up. Get up, she commanded. She used her arms to push herself forward, reeling from the pounding of her head...and vomited on the nearest rock.

After willing the bile in her throat away, Marina gathered most of her senses. She tried to move her legs, but to no avail. They were numb, which made sense; the bottom half of her body was still submerged in the ice-cold water. Once she'd pulled herself to drier land, she scooted over to a rock and took in her surroundings.

What she'd first thought was a cave was really more of a cavern. Stalactites hung from the ceiling, some so long they touched the pool below. There was no way out except for an archway at the other end of the pool—probably only a couple hundred feet away but impossible to trek in her state. She flicked her eyes to the seawater at the center of the cavern, which glowed beneath the dripstone ceiling and gave light to the darkness.

She shouldn't be here. Not because she didn't know where she was—that was bad, yes, but even more inexplicable was that she'd survived a tsunami and freezing ocean water.

Trembling beneath the weight of her soaked sweater, Marina wrapped her arms around her body and dared to speak.

"Hello?" Her voice came out in a rasp. She could think of nothing else to say, so she repeated herself until she finally got her vocal cords working.

Her heart hammered against her chest, and for a fleeting moment, there was only fear. Fear of where she was and how she'd gotten there—fear of the unearthly waves that fell from the atmosphere. Her confusion escalated to full-blown panic, and she let out a sob before forcing it back.

No. She wasn't going to cry. She wasn't going to panic. She was going to find a way out of this cavern and back home—she had to be somewhere within the bounds of the coastline—and only then would she try to figure out what had happened.

She lifted herself onto the rock, cold radiating through her body. Like the waves that lapped against the shore, her breathing was choppy, and when she screamed a litany of curse words, the walls rumbled in response.

A voice followed, jolting Marina back. It sounded like a man, but when she turned to the archway, she instead saw two indistinguishable figures, dressed head to toe in skintight, armor-plated suits. Save for two mesh-like openings for their eyes, their heads were covered in helmets that made them look more like insects than humans.

The gasp that escaped Marina's throat hardly sounded like her, but it scared them too. They backed away, shooting each other glances Marina couldn't discern.

That's good. They seemed as confused as she was. But...who *were* they? She'd never seen suits like that. Hermetically sealed, inhuman—like they were dressed for Armageddon. At this point, she wouldn't be surprised if she *had* landed herself in some apocalypse.

One of the figures spoke again, but she couldn't make out what he was saying—not because of the ringing in her ears, but because he wasn't speaking English. He gave an order to his companion, and when the other figure turned and bolted, he did too. Marina remained where she was, frozen like a deer in headlights. Her mind was numb, and though she knew she should be thinking of ways to escape, she couldn't bring herself to move.

Idiot. Don't freeze now.

When the first soldier—or whatever he was—returned alone, she cursed herself for buckling under her fear.

"Please...don't" was all she could manage. As if *that* would do anything.

He seemed to sense the fear in her voice because he raised his hand to his neck and pressed a button. The helmet folded in on itself, retracting so smoothly and quickly that Marina blinked back her shock. The technology was clearly high-grade, but she focused less on the disappearing helmet and more on the head of the young man it revealed. As he approached, adjusting something in his ear, Marina could make out more of him. He was around her age, maybe a few years older, with beige skin and disheveled brown hair. He hardly looked dangerous at all. In fact, he was rather handsome. When she saw the dagger on his hip, however, her unease flared up.

"Please...please stay there," she said.

The young man stopped in his tracks and said something through a sheepish laugh. He set his dagger on a cluster of rocks, then took a hesitant step forward, his palm open. In it rested what looked like a hearing aid, so small that even when he pointed to his ear, she had to squint to see it.

He spoke again, and though Marina wasn't sure what overcame her, she scooted closer to him. Her fingers brushed against his gloves—she couldn't pinpoint the material, but it seemed just thick enough to allow for movement and protection—and stilled when she took the device. It couldn't be dangerous...not if *he* was wearing one.

Despite her uncooperative fingers, she managed to hook it around her ear and push the tube in. She almost wondered if she'd done it wrong. She couldn't feel it, and she wasn't sure how to turn it on...

"Did it work?" the young man asked.

Marina reined in a gasp. The sound was crisp. His voice filled her ears evenly, and she almost wondered if he'd known English all along and had just now decided to speak it.

"Is this a translator?" she managed. Whatever it was, it was probably off-market—the kind of high-tech gadget government workers used. That seemed logical.

The young man's eyes lit up. "A *working* translator, for the first time in years." Marina almost asked what he meant, but he spoke before she could. "I'm Pierce, by the way."

"Where in Georgia are we?"

Though the light in Pierce's eyes flickered, he held tight to it. "See, usually people respond with their name after that." He grinned, but upon realizing no answer was forthcoming, pulled his lips back into a line. "We aren't...whatever you just said."

"What city, then?"

"Not a city. We're in Elsudra." He lowered himself to a rock a few feet from her, fiddling with the baldric he wore over his armored suit. "What's your name?"

When the silence grew unbearable, Marina gave in and told him.

"And you're from a realm called Georgia?" Pierce asked.

She choked on a surprised laugh, then realized he was serious. "It's a state."

Pierce nodded as though he understood, and though Marina's head rang with thousands of questions, she didn't get the chance to ask them. The other suited man from earlier returned, and he'd brought a middle-aged man with him.

Pierce turned his attention to them as they moved from the archway to the other end of the cavern. When the middle-aged man neared, Pierce said, "Florin, I think it's—"

"I know." Florin rounded the side of the cavern in half the time Pierce had. The younger man—his face flushed as red as his hair—followed closely behind.

"Her name is Marina," Pierce said.

She regretted telling him that. Keeping her name to herself would've given her at least some sense of control. Not like it would've mattered; she was outnumbered anyway. They'd removed those horrible helmets, but their suits still made them look like wasps readying to sting. She opened her mouth, prepared to rattle off promises about keeping quiet, but Florin spoke first.

"Thank you," he said. He put his hand on Pierce's shoulder, eyeing the dagger on the rocks. "Good call. You can go to your post." He turned to the redheaded man. "You too."

Pierce faltered, still staring at Marina, wide-eyed. "Are you sure you don't need our help? She seems confused. We didn't expect—"

"Since your shift is starting soon, I'd rather you be at the southern border," Florin said, softly but sternly. "I've already alerted the others."

It only took another curt nod from Florin to get Pierce and the other young man moving. Pierce scooped up his dagger, then cast a hesitant glance at Marina.

"Nice to meet you," he said, then pointed to his ear again. "Keep that in, okay?"

Marina opened her mouth, but a response wouldn't come. Pierce didn't seem to have hostile intentions, but how could she be sure? His politeness could be calculated—meant to make her an unsuspecting target.

Head thrumming, she turned to Florin. He was muscular in the way of a hardened soldier, with a broad chest and stocky build. His cropped gray hair and beard stood out against his deep brown skin, and his suit had been adorned with strategically placed portable weapons. It was clear he could sense her discomfort because he kept his distance.

"Where are we?" she rasped. She gripped the rock beside her once more, rallying her strength as she stood.

"This place is called Elsudra," Florin responded. "We're at a secure, hidden location on the eastern coastline. Rest assured you're safe."

"How do I get home? I'm from Tybee Island...I can find my way back if I know where I am."

Confusion flashed across Florin's face. "You're in shock. Give yourself a few moments. When you're able, I'll bring you to the manor so you can get a fresh set of clothes and some food. After that, you can discuss your needs with the proper person. I'm afraid that person isn't me."

"The proper person? Who's that?"

"You'll meet him." Though Florin didn't seem intent on expanding, Marina eyed him until he said, "His name is Aeric. I'm not a betting man, but I'd wager he already knows what's going on."

"What *is* going on?"

Florin hesitated. "Aeric is more qualified than I am to help you make sense of things." A long, uncomfortable silence followed. Florin cleared his throat, then said, "We can head over when you're ready."

She could either go with him or stay here and freeze. Though the choice seemed simple, it required a good deal of thought and courage before Marina nodded and took her first step forward. Florin offered her his hand as she struggled to navigate the slippery rocks, but she mustered as much assuredness as she could before saying, "I've got it," and praying she didn't take a nasty fall.

The cold bit at every inch of her, making it impossible to think of anything else. Even her pressing questions came second to it.

The archway didn't lead outside, as Marina suspected, but instead to a massive cavern that had been made into a plaza. The rock that formed the ceiling and walls was buttressed by columns made from floodlight lamps, which cast blue and yellow light to the ground and stretched their shadows as they walked.

Though the plaza was large enough, nothing could stop the place from feeling cramped and stagnant. Even the fountain at the center didn't liven things up. Marina swept her gaze across the courtyard, where four stairwells stood equal distances apart.

"We'll head north," Florin said, pointing to the staircase diagonal to them. Marina couldn't tell if he was trying to sound gentle so as not to scare her, or if he was scared *of* her. Though she could hardly fathom why he would be wary, she couldn't help but notice the way he eyed her.

Marina looked up at the stalactites. "Are we underground?"

Florin nodded. "The manor's not far."

He was quiet the rest of the way. Though normally Marina would've thought the silence awkward, she was too preoccupied with the cold and her spinning head to care. Her body threatened to collapse as they took the stairs, and she couldn't tell if the knot in her stomach was due to hunger or fear. Either way, she needed to rest and eat something before she could pay mind to her muddled thoughts and emotions.

Not far, it turned out, was absolute crap. The staircase ascended multiple stories and branched into several hallways, all dimly lit. Florin continued straight, ascending until he reached a square of similar size to the plaza, which was empty bar a building fronted by grand pillars. The architecture made use of the cavern walls and uneven ground, and Marina had to find her balance as she climbed the perron. Florin held the doors open for her, and though she had half a mind to walk inside without questioning, her good sense brought her to a halt.

"It's safe," Florin said. "I promise."

What good were his promises? She didn't know him. But what else could she do? Turn around and head back the way she came?

Cautiously, Marina stepped inside. From here, it looked more like a manor. Elegant rugs spanned across alabaster floors, and the ceilings were painted with frescoes. Marina squinted at the images, but the lights were so dim that all she could make out were waves.

Waves...just like the ones that brought her here. Like the ones in her dreams.

Marina's blood grew cold. *No fear. Don't show fear.*

Hands clenched at her sides, she turned to Florin. "Will Aeric know how to get me home?" she asked.

The confusion in Florin's eyes dwindled, replaced with concern. He didn't have time to respond, however. A woman's voice echoed from down the hall, and with it, a person came into view. She had a youthful look about her, from her pale skin to her long, pin-straight hair, dark as the obsidian rocks in the cave. She didn't dress in armor, but instead wore wide-leg pants and a tiered shirt that hung from her plump figure, along with a lapis-blue band around her wrist that matched the color of her eyes. The band had a screen on it, much like a cell phone.

A phone. *That* would be nice to have. Hers was probably still on her kitchen counter. She glanced at Florin's wrist to see if he wore something similar. Sure enough, the same device rested atop his glove, but it was brown instead of blue.

"Hello there," the young woman said in a feathery voice. "I'm here. How are you, General Florin?"

General? Maybe this was some kind of underground military base. The answer seemed plausible until she remembered how confused Pierce had looked when she'd told him where she was from.

"All things considered, well," Florin said, his eyes darting between Marina and the young woman. "Can you take things from here? I need to speak with him."

"Absolutely. He's in his office." She beamed at Marina. "I'm so honored to meet you."

She waited for a moment, and it took Marina a little too long to realize she wanted her name. Only when she saw Florin open his mouth did she say, "Marina."

"Lovely. I'm Ismene. Are you comfortable coming with me?"

She looked nowhere near as uneasy as Florin. In fact, she almost seemed happy.

"Coming with you where?"

"First, to get you warmed up. You look freezing."

Marina's nod was immediate.

"Don't be alarmed if there's some minor confusion," Florin said to Ismene. "I'll speak to him about it."

Ismene furrowed her brow as Florin disappeared down the nearest hallway, but she quickly shook the look away. She guided Marina up a flight of curved stairs, above which hung sconces and a grand engraving. The engraving looked like a sun, but Marina couldn't be sure; it only had four rays.

"I scrambled to prepare your room the moment we were alerted," Ismene explained as they reached the second floor. "It's not finished, but it's comfortable."

Marina lifted an eyebrow. "Is that typical? To prepare rooms for...strangers?"

"Only strangers who made the sacrifice you did," Ismene said. "I just...well, I know I'm not supposed to ramble off my thoughts, but I'd feel so ill-mannered if I didn't at least thank you." When Marina frowned at her, she added, "For accepting the call, I mean."

I have no idea what the hell you're talking about, Marina almost said. But warmth, fresh clothes, and food may not be given to her if she made a fuss, so she held her tongue and followed Ismene to one of the doors closest to the staircase.

"There are three floors in the manor," Ismene said. "The first is open to anyone, while the second houses manor staff. There are also hallways designated for storage. The third floor, for all intents and purposes, is nonexistent. We aren't allowed there."

It took Marina a few seconds to find her voice. "What's all this for?"

"This place?" Ismene waved the band on her wrist in front of the door, smiling nervously when it clicked open. "We call it the Delve. Not just the manor, but the whole thing. It's meant to keep us safe—you included, now that you're here. We're indebted to you, Marina. I'm sure the choice wasn't easy."

She had no idea what choice Ismene was referring to, but she swallowed her questions and followed Ismene into the room instead, which was as uncanny as the hallways. Lancet windows overlooking the caverns offset ornate walls and furniture, and over the bed hung a half-canopy. It had a rather Gothic look to it, but like everything else here, there was something otherworldly about the style. It certainly wasn't how she would've imagined an American military base—not like she'd believed that explanation to begin with.

Usually, the peculiar nature of things would've unsettled her, but her attention shifted to the tray of food on her bed.

"That's for you," Ismene said. "Help yourself while I get the bathroom ready. Do you prefer baths or showers?"

"Showers," Marina whispered, but anything warm sounded heavenly. She wanted to ask more questions—to figure out what this place was for, where it was, and how to get home—but her hunger had become dizzying. As Ismene turned to the bathroom, Marina hastened to the tray and ate four muffins in about a minute, which probably wasn't smart.

No, it *definitely* wasn't smart. Her stomach revolted, and Marina sprinted to the bathroom, clutching the toilet as she vomited again. She was still heaving when Ismene knelt beside her.

"Exorsus, that was foolish of me," Ismene said. "I don't know why I left out that much. It slipped my mind it'd take a while for you to adjust after such a transition."

Exorsus? "What?" Marina choked. "What do you mean *transition?*"

The apprehensiveness in Ismene's eyes opened some kind of floodgate, and Marina couldn't stop herself. "Is there *anyone* who can tell me where I am?"

Ismene slowly helped her up. "There is," she said, "but it's not me."

"That's exactly what Florin said." Since the edge in her tone was impossible to release, Marina lowered her voice. "I don't know where I am, and I can't explain how I got here. I have no idea what choice you're talking about, but I never made one. I just need someone who can tell me what happened and how close we are to Tybee Island. Or give me a phone so I can call..." *Gemma and Hank.* "I know people who can pick me up," she added hastily. "I won't tell them about this place if it's a government thing. I promise."

Ismene's eyes fluttered. "You...you didn't mean to come here?"

When Marina shook her head, Ismene blinked at her and added, "Florin said there was some minor confusion. This doesn't sound minor."

"I understand if there are security measures you need to take, but I promise I won't tell anyone—"

"How about you take a shower first?" Ismene interrupted. Her voice broke, but she covered it up with a cough. "You're shaking."

Marina wanted to protest and demand answers, but the cold hadn't subsided, and she figured perhaps she'd have a clearer head when she didn't feel so terrible.

When she raised her hand to remove the translator from her ear, Ismene gave her a timid smile. "No need. It's waterproof."

Ismene started the shower, then promised Marina she'd be outside with a fresh set of clothes. By the time Marina placed her own clothes—which Ismene had offered to take to the washrooms—outside the bathroom door, it was hard not to notice how pale Ismene had grown. But Marina wasn't in the headspace to think about it, and at the first touch of hot water, her mind went blank. For now, all that mattered was bringing the color back to her fingers. The shower was gigantic, adorned with rows of buttons etched in unreadable symbols. They looked like letters, but not from any language she knew. Maybe they were military codes. Cautiously, she pressed one, flinching in anticipation when the shower filled with steam. It smelled like lavender, and as Marina ran her fingers along the other buttons, the tightness in her chest loosened.

She wasn't sure how long she showered, but once she got out and found a robe hanging by the door, she could move better. Still, her muscles were stiff as she cracked open the door and peered at Ismene, who had indeed brought a variety of clothes. As beautiful as the billowy pants and shirts were, Marina's eyes landed on her leggings and sweater, which had been dried, folded, and placed at the foot of her bed.

"Some of our staff used to work in textile manufacturing, so we have options," Ismene said. "I figured I'd let you choose."

Marina pretended not to notice the tremor in Ismene's voice. Instead, she slipped on her clothes from home, then took another muffin and forced herself to eat it slowly.

Ismene stared at her as she chewed. It was obvious she was struggling to find the right words. Eventually, she asked, "Where are you from?"

"Tybee Island," Marina said. "It's on the Georgia coast."

It was a failed attempt at clarification, clearly. Ismene only nodded, then said, "I'll take you to the dining room to meet Aeric. He can help you untangle things."

"Who's Aeric?"

"He's many things. Has many jobs, I mean, like all of us. He used to..." Ismene sighed through her nose. "It's a lot to explain."

Marina clenched her jaw but acquiesced. If Aeric was the only person who could explain where she was—though it was beyond her why it was so hard for Ismene and Florin to—then he was the person she wanted to see. Though that pesky knot burrowed into her stomach, she followed Ismene back to the first floor and down the hallways. Doors lined the walls, none the same size and all eerily lonely.

"What's your job?" Marina asked.

Ismene smiled, or, at least, she tried to. "I run the manor. Basically, I ensure affairs are running smoothly so Aeric can focus on other things."

She ran the entire manor? That was quite the undertaking for someone her age. What was she, twenty-six?

"How old are you?" Marina asked.

Ismene eyed her curiously. "I'm in the latter part of my second quarter," she said, as though it was some obvious thing Marina should've known. "Most of my time is spent here, which is nice, but it can also be a shame. There are some beautiful parts of the Delve. The gardens are my favorite. Them or the library."

Before Marina could respond, Ismene lowered her voice and said, "About Aeric. He can be...prickly. But what he lacks in agreeableness, he makes up for in his knowledge and talents. He and Florin have kept this place secure for quite some time. If anyone can fix this…potential error…it's him. There's no need to worry."

Marina didn't think the reassurance was meant for her.

The dining room doors were coated in silver, and the room itself was even fancier. Mahogany floors greeted ivory walls, which gave way to windows that let in light from the lamps outside. If sunlight made its way in, the room would look royal, but the artificial glow illuminating the panes made everything feel dead. By the time Ismene pulled out a chair for Marina and beckoned her to sit, her ears were ringing.

"We'll get this sorted out," Ismene said.

She was really forcing cheeriness, but Marina pretended not to notice. Instead, she nodded and did her best to maintain a sober expression. She scanned the table, barren except for a few goblets and an arrangement of stonecrop.

The gentle *click* of the closing doors made Marina flinch.

No fear, she told herself.

She needed to remain levelheaded, and if not levelheaded, then assertive. Whoever these people were, she wasn't one of them, and she'd make them send her home. She wouldn't freeze or show weakness. As foreign as this place was and as strange as the people were, they hadn't harmed her yet, which meant they may be more willing to listen than she'd expected.

Her thoughts scattered when the doors of the dining room opened, the mere sound of which was enough to signal it wasn't Ismene. As hard as she tried to stay calm, a gasp rose in Marina's throat as a man stalked into the room. He didn't so much as glance at her as he made his way to the head of the table, several chairs from her.

Good. Stay away.

When he sat, she dared to make eye contact with him.

He was in his early forties, if she had to guess—tall and thin, with sharp, saturnine features offset by wavy gold-brown hair that fell just below his ears. His face was pointed and seemed to have lost all color in the absence of the sun, if it ever had any at all, and his eyes were blue and cold. The wool of his overcoat glinted with crimson so subtly that Marina thought it was a trick of the lights. On his wrist was the same device Ismene wore, but silver instead of blue.

She wasn't sure how long it would take until he said something, but she refused to speak first. That, and she couldn't get herself to.

The man angled his chin, then picked up one of the goblets. When he flicked his eyes, the cup filled with wine, and the control Marina had clung so tightly to snapped.

CHAPTER 4
Ant Colony

Her head hit the table—hard.

She was only out for a second, maybe two, before the adrenaline roused her. The moment she regained consciousness, she shot out of her chair, clutching the table's edge as dizziness rushed in.

He'd...the wine...it had come from *nothing*...

"How did you do that?" she choked.

He raised an eyebrow, as though he was surprised she didn't know. "Sorcery."

Bullshit. "*How* did you do that?"

"How I just said."

She was going to be sick again.

"Wine won't hurt you," the man—Aeric, no doubt—said flatly. "Sit down."

"I've never seen that before" was all she could say.

"Sit down."

Marina lowered herself to the chair, balling her hands into fists to stop their shaking.

"Are you sound enough to listen?" he asked. She thought she saw shock in his eyes, but if she did, it disappeared quickly.

"Listen to what?"

"First, to my questions. What is your name?"

Prickly. Ismene had said Aeric could be prickly. Fair enough. She could too.

"Tell me why I'm here," she said. "You're Aeric, aren't you? Florin and Ismene said you'd help me get home, back to Georgia."

He gave her an unamused glance. "They said no such thing."

"They said—"

"That I'd answer your questions and help you understand where you are. But in order for me to answer your questions, I need you to answer mine. Beginning with your name."

Her mouth tightened. "Marina Oliver." More forcefully, she said, "Where am I?"

He ignored her. "Where are you from?"

"Georgia."

"No...no. What realm?"

His energy was even icier than his voice, and Marina tensed. "Realm?"

"That is what I said, isn't it?"

"Like...America?" Though she felt terribly strange saying it, an impulse urged her to add, "Earth?"

Aeric paused and looked off to the side. When he remained silent for too long, she blurted, "Tell me where I am."

"Elsudra." His eyes landed on her again. "I don't know what you expected when you accepted the Omnia. You obviously weren't going to stay in your realm."

The coldness that swept over Marina's body was different than the frigid seawater. This cold ran so deep that even fire would tremble at its touch.

"What?" she sputtered. "I don't know what that is. I've never heard of an Omnia, and I definitely never accepted one." She gripped the arms of her chair. "I didn't do *anything*, I swear. I'm here by accident. I was out on the beach, and there was..."

Light. Waves. A desolate landscape of sand and water. Now, everything was coming back, and fear reared its head.

"Please," she begged. "Tell me how to get home."

"I'm told two sentries found you in the sea cavern," Aeric said. "There's no way to get there from outside unless you make your way in from the ocean. The sea opened the doorway between your realm and ours, and it only did so because *you accepted the Omnia.*"

"I didn't...I just woke up there. I can't give you the answers you want. I don't *know* those answers."

"No," Aeric said stonily. "No, you clearly do not."

He stood, straightening as he approached her.

"What are you doing?" Marina demanded. She stood too.

"Getting the answers you can't give me."

Before she could protest, his hand was on her forehead, and she was back in her seat. And then, there were waves—thousands upon thousands of waves, swirling amidst her subconscious, strong enough to destroy civilizations and pure enough to build them anew. They thrashed and curled in an endless ocean—an ocean that lived within her. No...it *was* her. The waves in her dreams were but small parts of a wild sea, and here, they ran free.

She wasn't sure whose eyes she was seeing from: hers, Aeric's, or maybe nobody's at all. But she could see more than the waves; she could see memories too.

Every drop of water told the story of a girl whose storms made her different from most—not in ways that were unique or coveted, but in ways that reflected the flaws of her design. Her parents, above all, quelled those storms when they rose to the surface, and they loved her despite the fear she struggled to control.

Until the fear had taken them from her, and she blamed herself as much as that drunk college kid—hated herself as much as the idiot who took two lives with his own—then withdrew into the shadows so losing someone would never be an option again. She and her waves were safe in isolation.

But there was something else beneath her waves. Light. It had made a home in the water, merging with her spirit just as much as her body. The tsunami had brought it to her, then dragged her here. There was something else too—something that was neither water nor light. Was it another memory, or was it a piece of her dreams?

Marina, Marina, Marina.

She couldn't be sure. The voices were softer than they were when she was asleep, and they existed so far beneath her waves that even Aeric couldn't reach them. A thread of mist—which didn't belong to her, but to him—skimmed across the surface of her waves. When Aeric removed his hand from her forehead, the confusion on his face was evident.

"What did you just do?" Marina demanded. She wanted to stand—to run—but her legs wouldn't work.

He exhaled and returned to his seat. Marina watched him as he lowered himself into his chair, put his elbows on the table, and pinched the bridge of his nose. Eventually, he lowered his hands and said, "Prior to what I'm about to tell you, I must make three things clear. First, though you and your people may not know it, there are infinite realms beyond your own. Some defy natural laws as we understand them, while others—sister realms— look the same and have similar properties. Your home is loosely related to the one we're in now, which is why one could be forgiven for thinking they're the same."

Her head spun. "If this isn't Earth, why do you look human?"

"If anything, you look Elsudran. Our realm came before your own, and though it may be smaller, it's advanced in ways your people can only dream of."

If she wasn't so disoriented, the comment may have offended her.

"Why did Elsudra never contact Earth, then, if it's so advanced?"

"Why would we waste time doing that? Your realm has close to no magic, and your people are, by all accounts, primitive. Elsudra and Earth may be sisters, but that's by the loosest definition. Attempting to contact your people would be like traveling across worlds to visit an ant colony."

Marina's face flushed. "*You're* the ones underground."

He didn't react to that. "Second, magic is abundant in Elsudra. It has been since time immemorial, not counting the dead years, which ended"—Aeric paused, his gaze on her sharpening—"a little less than an hour ago," he finished, as though he, too, still had to process things.

Marina leaned back in her seat, determined not to pass out again. Dead years, the Omnia...what the hell was he talking about?

"Third," Aeric continued, "you've implicated yourself in a dangerous bid for power whether you're aware of it or not."

"I did not," Marina protested. "I'm here by accident. Please...let me go home."

"I didn't bring you here. How in the world would I get you home?"

"Tell me where Georgia is."

Aeric rubbed his temples. "Far away."

"What does that mean?"

"It means your realm is a distance away from Elsudra that even numbers can't measure," Aeric said, his already pale face now completely white. "You coming here was the result of a higher power—one even I cannot comprehend. *It* had the power to bring the Omnia back; *you* just happened to be the soul the Omnia attached to."

"No," Marina stammered. "No, no, no. That's not what happened."

"You obviously don't know what happened."

"*That* didn't!"

"You were supposed to accept it, and while it latched onto you—that much is indisputable—I cannot explain why you think you didn't have a say. I did not..." Aeric let out a shaky breath. "I did not expect that."

"It's a mistake." Desperately, she repeated, "I don't know what an Omnia is."

"*The* Omnia. There is only one, and it is not of your world—not of any world but the one you're in now. It is Elsudra's essence, born from a power even more ancient. Without it, Elsudra is little more than a dead realm, void of magic."

She'd only heard pieces of what Aeric had said—and even less of it had made sense— but somehow, she mustered enough nerve to say, "Magic doesn't exist."

"In your narrow worldview, maybe not," Aeric said. "But you're not in your world, and here, magic is our life force. I've very little knowledge of your realm, but I do know it resembles ours, even if it lacks magic as robust as Elsudra's. Have you ever asked yourself what sustains your world? What force makes the grass grow; what energy makes you age?"

Her jaw began to throb, and Marina wondered if she was going to pass out again. This was too much. She couldn't process it all.

"Magic *is* our world's energy," Aeric continued, "and the Omnia is *all* magic in Elsudra. It requires a host to sustain it, much like a body sustains a heart. What's of consequence for you to know is this: we sent the Omnia out of Elsudra to find a new, proper host for it—one both willing and able to apprehend it, bring it back, and aid us in our current plight. Now *you're* here, only you're not the person we expected."

"Then *take it back.*"

"I'm not powerful enough to do that."

Marina pointed at his wine glass. "You could do the thing you did with the wine."

"Summoning wine and severing the Omnia from someone's soul are two completely separate feats."

"You can't at least *try?*"

"Not unless you'd like to risk death. If I move wine from one location to another and lose a few drops along the way, nothing happens. But if I were to move the Omnia and lose a few drops of your soul or body in the process...well, that wouldn't end well for anyone, would it?"

Tears clouded her eyes. "I need to go home."

"What you need to do is stay calm. I didn't expect this, but that doesn't mean it can't be explained and remedied if possible."

"If possible?" Marina choked. "No, it needs to be remedied. Give it back to whoever had it before me. I don't want this thing..."

"I can't *do that,*" Aeric said, his voice low.

A dizzying mix of anger and fear overcame her. "Why not?!"

Aeric didn't react. He didn't even answer her. He simply took another sip of wine, as though she were a child in the midst of a tantrum he refused to indulge.

Marina put her head in her hands, desperate to block out the room.

The Omnia. It was inside her...*within* her, like her waves. What the hell did that mean? Had this happened when the clocks stopped back at home? This thing...had *it* been the voice she'd heard—the one that coaxed her outside? Had it brought her here? And why would it choose her when everyone was clearly expecting someone else? An ant colony... that was what Aeric had called her home. She was an ant to him. So what? He was crazy. This was all crazy. Nothing would *choose* her, and she wouldn't have chosen it back.

Slowly, she lifted her head and took a measured breath. "Why not?"

"Because the people who held the Omnia before you are dead."

A long, cold silence followed, and when Aeric spoke again, Marina couldn't discern the emotion in his voice. "They were the Keepers, in charge of hosting the Omnia until their reign ended and then passing it to their descendants. But a powerful and dangerous individual tried to take the Omnia for himself, and their line was cut short." Bleakness flickered in his eyes. "If this person had succeeded, he alone would've held the essence of our world and the core of our magic. Since he'd already had considerable magical talent to begin with, it would have been easy for him to establish himself as a supreme ruler."

He wavered, and only then did Marina realize what she was hearing: sorrow.

"But he failed," Aeric continued, and just like that, the sorrow was gone. "The Keepers realized what he was doing and took drastic measures to stop him. They sought higher guidance, which led them to believe they needed to sever their holds on the Omnia and send it out of Elsudra so it could traverse the sister realms until the right being accepted it—one who could help us overmatch the threat we face."

Marina knew she looked pathetic, sitting there slack-jawed and wide-eyed, but since speaking wouldn't remedy that, she remained as she was.

"This wasn't a decision made out of blind hope," Aeric said. "The guidance sought assured the Keepers that the being Elsudra needed would agree."

She had to say something now—anything. She settled on, "What?"

It was all she could think to say, and even then, she clearly didn't say it pleasantly, because Aeric's lips thinned. "I cannot fathom why it would have latched to you if you were unwilling," he said. "Unwillingness is a deterrent to wielding magic."

"I can't wield magic to begin with. Just take it back. Please. I don't want it. I need to go home." When Aeric didn't respond, she sputtered, "How did the Keepers sever their holds on the Omnia?"

After another painful bout of silence, Aeric sighed. "Until I can discern what happened, you'll have to stay in the Delve."

"You didn't answer my—"

He stood. "I've been tasked with protecting and fostering the Omnia's power. This is unexpected, but I'll figure it out. I'll call on you, and until then, you will reside in the manor and are permitted free range of the rest of this place. The only places you may *not* visit are the borders—you wouldn't be able to anyway; patrol towers line the top—and the third floor of the manor."

Tears burned Marina's eyes, and though she felt like a mewling child, she said, "When can I go home?"

Aeric didn't answer. He simply pushed open the doors and left her in silence.

CHAPTER 5
Minor Confusion

Numbness. That was all she felt after Aeric left, when Ismene came to fetch her, and long after. She'd felt it before. Sometimes, it was better than the storm that could exist in its stead. But this numbness was leaden, and when Ismene brought her back to her room, Marina didn't even take off her shoes before she climbed into bed.

"I'll check on you," Ismene whispered. "Tomorrow, maybe. Give yourself time."

Marina didn't respond. Instead, she stared at the walls as the bedroom door closed, then breathed until sleep consumed her and waves filled the void.

She wasn't sure how long she slept, but the floodlights outside were weak when she woke. It was hard to gauge time without the sun, and worse was the fact that this place felt as dead at midday as it did at midnight.

As hard as she tried to cling to sleep, her body wouldn't obey. Restlessness pricked at her fingers and toes. No, not restlessness. *Fear.*

She'd told herself not to let fear devour her, but she'd failed. And here she was, frozen beneath linens, hiding in a room that offered no protection. Marina supposed Ismene wasn't the only person who could unlock the door.

Freezing wasn't going to do it. She needed to flee. Unthinking, she slipped out of bed and creaked the door open, straining to listen for footsteps. When she didn't hear any, she stepped into the hallway, then followed the runner down the staircase to the foyer. She made it a point to walk with a purpose in case anyone was watching. Aeric had said she had free range of this place, so if anyone caught her, that would be her justification. She wasn't trying to escape; she was only doing what she'd been given the freedom to do.

Still, her heart was in her throat by the time she made it out of the manor. It was well into the night, if not early morning, and the cavern was so desolate Marina began to wish there were others around.

Go. Just go. Find the plaza.

Walkways bordered by metal railings passed over clusters of stalagmites, and where ceilings dipped, rocks yielded, obeying the confines of the cavern. Marina did her best to remember where she and Florin had come from, but it seemed like this place was made to be confusing on purpose.

She searched for markers to guide her, but they were all eerily similar. A few doors popped up here and there, attached not to any building but to the rock itself. Where they led, Marina hadn't the slightest idea, and right now, finding the stairs was her goal. From there, she could reach the plaza, then the sea cavern, which seemed her best bet. After all, if she'd come *in* through there, there had to be a way out.

If Aeric was right—if the ocean had brought her here—then perhaps it could get her out as well, and she could leave this parasitic power behind.

Thinking of an intangible force flowing through her made Marina so nauseous that she stopped to rest her head against the cool rock.

If the Omnia was the waves—the unearthly tsunami that defied the ocean itself—then it had never called her. It had *lured* her. Had it pushed her to give away her parents' money so she'd leave less behind? Had it come to her in her dreams night after night, year after year, only to steal her away when she was most vulnerable? And now what? Would it be the end of her, just as it had its previous hosts?

Don't spiral. Keep going.

In the silence, she could hear something rumbling within the rock. Water. She held her breath, following the sound until it grew to a burble at the stairwell's mouth.

Relieved, she took the stairs, not bothering to soften her steps now that the sound had grown louder. Water streaming down the walls merged into a waterfall, then pooled into a brook beneath a landing. How hadn't she noticed this before? Perhaps she'd underestimated the severity of her shock.

Though it was dark, the plaza was a welcome sight, and the sea cavern—which Marina found in seconds by following the sound of waves—glowed as it had hours before. She scaled the rocks as soon as she entered, skidding down to the water and plunging her hands into it.

"Home," she breathed, knowing it was stupid. "Take me home."

The water lapped against the shore.

Angrily, Marina submerged her arms. The cold stung her skin, but she didn't care. She'd welcome the feeling if it meant leaving this place and escaping the fate the Omnia's previous hosts had come to.

"Please," she begged. "Take me home. Give this to someone else. Not me."

She began to sob. Every last bit of numbness she'd felt earlier was gone, and now the storm in her chest pounded against her ribs. When it couldn't escape, it wrapped itself around her lungs so tightly that her words came out in wheezes.

"Please, please, *please*..."

Desperation reamed through her, and before she had time to get a handle on her thoughts, she'd already plunged into the water.

The cold was harrowing, but it didn't stop her. Neither did the heaviness of her clothing, which tightened the deeper she swam. She'd always been a strong swimmer, and if there was an underwater exit, she could get to it. But the water was much too murky to make out where it led, if anywhere at all. Marina surfaced, still sobbing and begging the water to respond.

"You brought me here!" she cried. "Take me back! *Please*, take me—"

She was cut short when something wrapped around her shoulders. Before she could register that it was someone's hands, she was out of the water and back on the rocks, gasping and shivering.

As her vision cleared, she braced herself for the wrath of whoever stood above her, expecting it to be Aeric and hating herself for cowering. Only...it wasn't Aeric.

As Marina blinked away the salt in her eyes, the figure of a young woman solidified. She was around Ismene's age, with angular features, tanned skin, and long raven hair. She wasn't wearing one of those terrifying helmets, but the suit she wore made it clear she was a soldier. On her hip rested a cutlass, its hilt the same carbon-black as her armor.

Marina didn't have it in her to apologize or explain what she'd been doing. She could barely control her breathing, which was so disjointed and shallow that it must've shocked the woman, who knelt beside her.

"Deep breaths," the woman said. "Focus on nothing else."

Stupefied, Marina obeyed. *One day, one step, one breath at a time.*

"Breathe."

And she did—one after the other, in and out, until her heart slowed and her lungs worked again. When she opened her eyes, the woman leaned back on her heels. "Better?"

Marina nodded, her head light. The world took a while to stop spinning, but once it had, her common sense returned.

Shit. How was she going to explain this? She was drenched and shaking, and she knew she must look ghastly. "I was just..."

"No need to explain," the woman said gently. "So you're the new host."

Marina let out a defeated sigh. "I've been told that I am, but I didn't choose—"

"I can tell. Only someone desperate to escape would brave that water. I hate to be the bearer of bad news, but any tunnels out of this cavern are too deep to reach."

Marina couldn't tell what the woman was thinking. Either she was good at hiding her emotions, or Marina was too out of sorts to decipher them.

"I'll keep this quiet," the woman said, "if you promise not to try to escape again."

"I need to leave. There's been a mistake."

The woman was silent for a moment. She rubbed her hands against her legs, and only then did Marina realize she was also drenched. When Marina's eyes widened, the woman only chuckled and said, "It's fine." She extended two fingers to Marina. "I'm Cal." When Marina blinked at her, Cal said, "Place two fingers on mine. Standard Elsudran greeting."

Slowly, Marina reached out and tapped her fingers on Cal's. "Marina," she said.

"You're a welcome sight, considering the last twelve dead years. Even if your reaction is...unexpected."

*Dead years...*Aeric had said that. "What are dead years?" Marina asked.

"That's how long we've been waiting for the Omnia to return—give or take," Cal said. "Dreadful business. We didn't realize how much we'd taken the Omnia for granted until it was gone." When Marina gaped at her, Cal shook her head and said, "Never mind that."

"No," Marina said, then softened her tone. "Tell me."

If she couldn't escape, then she'd learn, and maybe she'd know enough to get out of this mess.

"I don't want to be the reason you fling yourself into the water again," Cal said.

Marina grimaced. "I'm confused. Confusion overwhelms me."

A sad smile appeared on Cal's lips. "Someone else used to tell me that. Usually, she wouldn't stop until she got what she wanted." She stood, then pressed a few buttons on the device around her wrist—the same kind Ismene, Florin, and Aeric wore. "I'll escort you back to the manor." She offered her hand to Marina, who gave in and took it. Not like she had much of a choice.

"Are you a guard?" she asked as Cal helped her up.

"Kind of. I'm a scout, which means I sometimes leave the Delve."

"You go above?"

They maneuvered about the rocks, then stepped into the light of the plaza. The intensity of the lights had increased a bit. Marina wondered if that signaled dawn.

"Don't go getting any ideas," Cal said. "It's horrible out there."

"Why? What's up there?"

"Things you'd wish you hadn't seen."

A chill ran down Marina's spine, but before she could press further, Cal switched the subject. "There's going to be a lot of talk about you in the coming days," she said. "Few people had heard of your realm before, and news spreads quickly in the Delve."

Marina wavered. "People know there's been a mistake, then?"

"They've been told there's some minor confusion."

Minor confusion. Just like Florin had told Ismene—something to placate the masses so there was time to figure things out behind the scenes.

"Seems like you don't think the confusion is minor, though," Cal added.

Marina shook her head. "I'm sorry," she said again.

Cal's lips twitched, but she was remarkably good at staying poised. "I won't repeat it. Just be warned that others may act a little awestruck around you. Nobody here, minus Aeric and maybe Florin, has interacted with a host before. The Keepers were kept away from the public for everyone's good. To most Elsudrans, anyone with even a drop of the Omnia in their veins is akin to a god."

Marina went still. "Do *you* think that?"

"There's no such thing as gods. Not caring ones, at least." Cal wavered as they began their ascent of the northern staircase. "The dead years you asked about were the result of the Omnia's absence in Elsudra," she said. "People who used to be able to wield magic had no magic to wield, and natural laws stopped working."

"What does that mean?" Marina asked, keenly aware of how cold she was.

"It felt like time had stopped," Cal explained. "It hadn't, though; it was our world's energy that came to a halt, and as a result, life energy. We didn't age. Babies weren't born, children didn't grow, and people didn't pass on—not naturally, at least. Our world didn't change either. Food production stopped, which would've been catastrophic had our Elsudran needs not stopped too. But nature wasn't nature."

She spoke plainly, as though she looked upon whatever hell she'd endured with apathy. Still, the blood drained from Marina's face. Did years last as long in Elsudra as they did back home?

"I don't think it's hit us that the dead years are over," Cal added. "I don't think it's hit *me*. It's only been a day, but it's enough to make a person feel different. I forgot how good it feels to eat when you're hungry—almost forgot what it felt like to be hungry, or tired, or anything at all."

Marina's ears began to ring. Ismene had brought her food earlier today...was that the first food that had been made since the dead years started? Ismene hadn't *seemed* to think it was a big deal, though Marina supposed she'd been too out of sorts to notice anyone's emotions but her own.

Cal must have noticed her discomfort because she put her hand on Marina's shoulder.

"Beyond that stint in our history," she said, "I have a sneaking suspicion we aren't much different from your people."

"Except for magic," Marina whispered, then eyed Cal. "Are *you* magic?"

"Nothing but the Omnia *is* magic." Cal snorted and shook her head. "I don't have those talents. Only a fraction of the population does, and even then, most don't have much to show for it. You'd be better off asking Aeric about the specifics."

Marina's budding curiosity shriveled up. There was no way she'd do that. The water in the sea cavern was warmer than he was—and far less frightening.

Marina settled on a nod, then followed Cal back to the manor, where Ismene waited on the steps. When she saw them, she let out a hearty exhale and said, "Oh, Callina, you're a blessing from Exorsus."

Exorsus...Ismene had said that before.

"I wouldn't have realized she was missing until later this morning," Ismene continued. "Aeric would've had to send people out. I cannot thank you enough."

Marina's guilt returned, and with it, embarrassment. She almost said Aeric had given her free range of the Delve, but she held her tongue.

Ismene took Marina by her arm, patting her damp sweater as she tilted her head at Cal and asked, "Why were you by the sea cavern so early?"

"Ending my late-night shift," Cal said. Marina couldn't tell if she was being honest, but she shook the thought away when Cal turned to her. "Take it day by day, and give your memories time. They have a funny way of coming back to us."

She seemed certain—too certain. And yet, despite her urge to protest, Marina only nodded as Cal walked away.

CHAPTER 6
Mind Game

Ismene fussed about that morning, bringing Marina new clothes and a tray of foreign food that smelled like nutmeg and chocolate. She'd hardly realized how hungry she was until she started eating, but Ismene made her take it slow this time.

"I'm here to do more than simply make sure you're alive," she said when Marina finished breakfast. "I know this has all been...stressful. But I'm here to help if you need me." She watched Marina, doe-eyed. "Are you okay?"

Though the honest answer was no, Marina only nodded. It seemed to appease Ismene, but the worry returned to her face when she said, "Aeric wants to speak with you today. He seems to think time is of the essence."

Marina's stomach flipped. "I don't know how to convince him I didn't choose this."

Gently, Ismene said, "He believes you."

"He didn't give me that impression."

"Aeric's not very good at communicating his impressions, but he *is* committed to uncovering why the Omnia returned with you. There are many unknowns right now—for us as well as you—but you're safe here until we can figure things out."

Safe. What an empty word. She didn't feel it—not in a maze of caves with unfamiliar people, one of whom had the power to summon things with his mind and peer into the psyche of others. Not when her home was an immeasurable distance away. And definitely not when she faced the fact that, if she did return home, her misery wouldn't disappear.

"Your Keepers," Marina said, scanning Ismene's face for her reaction. "Why didn't *they* do something instead of sending their problem out to another realm?"

"The first Keepers were uniquely powerful sorcerers," Ismene said, "but that doesn't mean their descendants were. Keepers varied in magical ability like the rest of us, which usually meant they had nothing. And any abilities they might've had were curtailed by an oath they took. It..." She clamped her lips shut when Marina put her head in her hands.

If the Keepers had sent the Omnia out because they weren't powerful enough, what kind of person did they expect to accept it? Certainly not *her*. And...powerful enough for what, exactly? She locked eyes with Ismene and whispered, "Florin said the Delve was underground to keep us protected. And Aeric said someone was after the Omnia, which everyone seems to think *I* hold. That doesn't sound safe."

"Kieron," Ismene said. When Marina furrowed her brow, she added, "That's the name of the person after the Omnia."

"Aeric didn't tell me that."

After another bout of silence, Ismene said, "Kieron is far away, and he has no idea where the Delve is. He may be aware the Omnia is back due to his own abilities returning, but he doesn't know where it went or to whom it attached." She wiped her hands on her pants, then said, "Let's get you to Aeric so we can get this mess sorted out, okay?"

"Do you think he'll be able to find a way to sever the Omnia from me?" Marina asked, knowing—but not caring—that she sounded like a broken record. "That I can go home?"

"I don't know," Ismene said, fiddling with a strand of her hair. "I know that's not very confidence-inducing, but..."

"It's fine," Marina said. She wanted knowledge, and Aeric was clearly the best person to get it from, so she grounded herself with a breath and followed Ismene out the door.

The shadows that crawled up the manor walls beckoned her, and Marina wished more than anything to become one of them—to disappear into the darkness where she couldn't feel or think or be. It would be easier that way—*better*, even—to become nothing but shadow herself. The shadows on Earth had tempted her too, long before the accident. Afterward, she'd come close to taking the leap—succumbing to her storms and bidding herself a permanent goodnight. But she hadn't been able to muster the courage, so she'd turned to sleep instead. Now, even sleep wasn't an option. And so, despite the urge to sink into herself, Marina held her head high as she and Ismene approached a door at the end of a hall, which led into a dimly lit, yet strikingly elegant, office.

Aeric leaned against a marble desk, arms crossed and eyes emotionless. He nodded dismissively to Ismene when they entered. "I'll call you when we're done."

"Of course," Ismene said. She smiled at Marina, who couldn't bring herself to smile back, then scurried from the room like a timid mouse.

Though Marina's first instinct was to scoff at Ismene, she quickly realized she wasn't much better herself. It took effort to find the courage to make eye contact with Aeric, but she forced herself to anyway, defiantly searching her memories for something that would make it easier to project confidence.

Tony Hanson. Ninth grade. The memory of his expression when she'd thrown a chunk of her hair at him always brightened her mood. A shadow of a smile tugged at her lips.

"Ismene told me you returned to the sea cavern last night," Aeric said flatly. "I'll save you a second trip; you won't find your way out from there."

Marina's courage dissipated. What else had Ismene told him? That a scout had found her splashing hysterically in the water and begging it to bring her home? Cheeks flushed, she gripped the back of a chair, appreciating the distance it put between her and Aeric.

"I obtained a cursory understanding of the Omnia's presence within you through psychometry," Aeric said, "but only you can fill in the gaps. As I understand it, you seemed aware of the Omnia before it latched onto you."

Marina's lips parted before she spoke. "Ismene said you believed me—"

"I believe you *think* you were unaware," Aeric interrupted. "Why your awareness wasn't explicit, I don't know, but the connection was there—a tether that snapped into place when you wandered onto the beach."

Marina blinked at him. Maybe...maybe he was right.

No. He's not. A mistake's been made, but I'm not the one who made it.

Weakly, she asked, "Was the Omnia the tsunami?"

"No. It brought the Omnia to you and transported you here, but it represented the ineffable—something your mind made up to understand what was happening."

She wanted to protest—it had all felt so real—but stayed silent as Aeric continued. "The same is true of your spirit. We are limited in our ability to perceive the ethereal, so our minds construct images we can comprehend. Your waves *are* your spirit—your soul, your essence—and the light beneath them is the Omnia, which proves you hold it."

"The waves...like the ones in my dreams?"

Aeric paused. "Tell me about them." When she only stared at him, he gave her an irritated look and said, "Your *dreams*. I cannot access them with psychometry—not like I can with memories. I must rely on your word."

She had no idea what her dreams had to do with anything, but Aeric's tone was unwavering, so she gave in. Still, she made it a point to keep things vague. He'd seen more than enough in the dining room, and if her dreams were the one thing she could keep to herself, she would. She left out the voices—the familiarity of them, and how sometimes, they kept her company when the loneliness became too much—and instead focused only on the recurring waves. Aeric was silent long after she finished, processing what she'd said but showing no emotion.

When he finally spoke, his voice was as cold as ever. "I stand by the Keepers' belief," he said, "that the Omnia would return with someone of magical ability."

Marina's stomach twisted. "But I can't—"

Aeric put his hand up. "I'm not finished. Just because you couldn't wield magic where you're from doesn't mean you can't wield it here. I want to work with you to uncover this skill—to gauge where we're at so we can know how to proceed."

"What about helping me get rid of the Omnia so I can go home?"

"Have you forgotten what I told you, or did you choose to ignore it? In your current state, that would *kill you*, and if you die, we risk irreparable damage to the Omnia—the kind that could plunge us into eternal dead years. You haven't been trained in the ritual like the Keepers, and what's more, you lack the magical talent needed to protect yourself."

"So...there's a ritual?"

Aeric's lips thinned. "You're a remarkably bullheaded girl, aren't you?"

"It's possible, then," she pressed on. "I just have to know how to do it."

"If you wish to complete the ritual and die—which is exactly what happened to the Keepers at the end of their reigns—then yes, simply knowing it is all you have to do. But if you'd like to live out the rest of your days, you'd need magical prowess to protect you."

"If I try whatever it is you want me to," Marina said slowly, "will you help me learn the ritual so I can do it safely?"

"Let us see what you can do first."

That wasn't the answer she wanted, but Aeric didn't seem to be in the mood for pushback. "Magic is a mind game," he said, "and a fickle one at that. To wield it, you must demonstrate mastery over your thoughts and emotions. Even acts like summoning wine require a level of inner quiet, which allows you to craft a bridge between your spirit and the world around you."

Marina froze. Why did he have to remind her of the wine? Timidly, she said, "I don't know where to start."

"You haven't tried."

"How do you expect me to wield magic when I'd never witnessed it until yesterday? And how are you so sure I can? Because the Keepers told you so?"

"Because your essence is fluid, and fluidity yields interaction with magic."

She might've asked what he meant, had she not been hit with a wave of nausea upon yet another unnecessary reminder. He'd seen too much, and now he had the gall to suggest she find her inner quiet? What was she meant to do, *meditate*? She hated him for it, but what she hated more was the fact that doing nothing meant she was guaranteed to be stuck here forever. If she wanted a fighting chance at getting away from this nightmare, she'd have to try. And so, she swallowed her protests, lowered herself to the chair, and closed her eyes.

Meditate. It's not that hard.

The sea cavern flickered at the back of her head. Had that very water been part of the tsunami that brought her here? It was hard to piece together memories that seemed to have happened outside the bounds of time. How long had it been since she'd been taken? Had Gemma and Hank already realized she was gone, or would it be another week until they showed up to an empty house?

Gemma and Hank...she'd left them so horribly. Would she ever see them again, or was she doomed to stay here forever? And...stay here for what? What did Aeric intend to do with her? He didn't seem eager to take the Omnia back from her—quite the opposite, really. And what about Kieron? Did Aeric expect *her* to face Kieron? Was that why he was pushing all this so hard? What was he going to do? Force her onto the front lines of some battle or send her off to commit espionage, not because she could, but because she held this...*thing*? Maybe the Omnia really *would* be the end of her. Maybe *Aeric* would be.

"Stop."

When Marina opened her eyes at Aeric's voice, a tear rolled down her cheek.

"You're struggling to remain calm," Aeric said, "though I shouldn't be surprised, given the stunt you pulled last night." He shook his head, then sighed. "Try again. Don't let your emotions cloud your focus."

"My emotions? Can you blame me for having them, given everything?" Her chin began to quiver—even more so when Aeric remained silent—but she steadied it, closing her eyes again, fumbling in the darkness...and failing miserably. Now it wasn't so easy to hold back her tears. She tried to suppress them, but her shoulders shook uncontrollably.

Aeric inhaled through his nose. "We'll try again tomorrow."

Ismene was much more understanding. As she escorted Marina back to her room, she squeezed Marina's shoulder and said, "Keep trying. Tomorrow will be better."

Tomorrow, it turned out, was not better. Marina's head spun all night, and come morning, she hadn't gotten any sleep. She hoped her fuzziness would give her the emotional quiet Aeric wanted, but it only made things worse.

She couldn't tell if he was angry or disappointed; the ice in his eyes was too thick to discern the emotion beneath. He tried to have her forge a connection to her waves— something he seemed to think stilling her mind would help her do—but the fact that he knew about her waves to begin with unsettled Marina so deeply that she lost focus.

"Children learning magic do this," Aeric said through his teeth. "Like I said yesterday, your waves are a rendition of your spirit. They're within arm's reach, yet you refuse to extend your hand." He gave her a glassy stare. "You have all the tools available to you, but I cannot force you to use them."

"I'm not failing on *purpose*."

"You're not trying to succeed either. I don't think I've ever witnessed someone with such a strong spirit be so averse to utilizing it. To successfully perform Locus, you'll need a sturdy mind. If you wish to go a step further and survive it, you'll need to wield magic."

"Locus?"

"The ritual you're so obsessed with. If you want to escape the Keepers' fates and live out the remainder of your days, you'll need to shield your soul." He gave her a look. "And without a grasp on magic, your shields will be weak, if there at all."

Marina's heart fluttered. "Does that mean you agree to help me with...Locus?"

"At present, there's nothing to help you with," Aeric said. "You're useless."

"You're expecting too much from me," she snapped. A tiny flame sputtered to life within her. "Clearly, whatever guidance your Keepers sought was wrong."

When Aeric's gaze met hers, the flame died out, and Marina looked away.

"As unfamiliar as the concept may be to you," he said, "continue trying to still your mind. Until you shatter that barrier, you cannot move forward."

"To *Locus*," Marina said pointedly. She was doing this so she could get rid of the Omnia, not so she could fulfill the wishes of Aeric and whichever dead men forced this burden upon him. But it didn't seem to matter either way; Aeric didn't answer her.

⁓

A few days passed, all the same, and Marina began to feel her sanity unravel. Aeric was notoriously short with her, and his tolerance lessened every time they met. As kind as Ismene tried to be, Marina could see the anxiety in her eyes—the anxiety of knowing the savior she'd yearned for hadn't come. At night, Marina tried to lull herself to sleep with her mom's reminders: *one day, one step, one breath at a time.* But she'd never been very good at taking that advice, especially when she was scared.

She prayed Ismene was right—that they were safe in the Delve—but she couldn't be sure. Safe was already a foreign word to her, and here, it seemed impossible. What bad luck had brought her to this place? What cruel, morbid fate damned these people to a purgatory, only to strip them of hope when it ended?

In a better world, things would be different. She wouldn't have fallen so deep into despair—wouldn't have been overcome by the impulses to donate her parents' money or the brain fog that led her out onto the beach at four in the morning. She'd be home safe with the people she never should've lost. She wouldn't be here.

Ismene seemed to cling to optimism, but Aeric...Marina wasn't so sure. He was clearly desperate, but no amount of desperation on his part could change what he knew about her —what he'd gleaned that day in the dining room. Her waves weren't the only thing he'd seen. He'd seen the cowardly, unstable person she was, and the role she'd played in ripping her life to shreds.

Sometimes, when it rained in Georgia, she'd close the blinds and put headphones in to block out the noise. Other times, she'd listen, reminding herself that it had been raining when they'd died—when she'd called her parents sobbing from a coffee shop a few blocks from her dorm, telling them she couldn't do it anymore and she needed them to bring her home *now* because another night would be unbearable. They'd asked what was wrong— panicked, even though she'd done this a hundred times—and she'd hated herself even more because the answer was *nothing*. Nothing ever did happen to spur the episodes—nothing of any consequence, at least. They hit like sudden storms, some quick and evasive, others so destructive that they tore her insides out and made it impossible to take things one day, one step, one breath at a time, because good God, breathing was so terribly painful.

Even when the episodes subsided, she knew they'd come again—knew her descent into instability wasn't a matter of if, but when. They were predictable like that.

She thought she'd made a good decision choosing a college close to home, and after a rocky first year with crying spells at midnight in the dorm bathrooms, she'd pushed herself to do it again. For a while, her performance worked. She'd put on a happy face, even if it wasn't genuine—even if the episodes kept coming. Nobody knew how out of place she felt and how deeply she longed for home. How she could barely get through the days without crying for no reason, or how she wavered between medicating herself or just pushing through it because everyone *else* could go away to college. Why couldn't she?

And then a week into her second year, there she was, sitting outside a closed coffee shop and begging her parents to bring her home. Because that was the way her mind worked; time and time again, it took sparks of anxiety and set wildfires with it.

When her parents said they'd come, calmness had washed over her. She'd headed back to the dorms, and when her phone rang a few hours later with an unknown number, she was curled up on a common room chair and in oddly good spirits.

The accident had happened ten minutes from her campus.

She didn't possess the inner quiet Aeric wanted her to find. She wasn't brave, either. Or selfless, or heroic. Her single redeeming quality was that she was consistent.

CHAPTER 7
Enigma

After the fourth day of training, or maybe the fifth—not like it mattered, she failed anyway—Marina had grown so restless that she asked Ismene about the library. Ismene was elated that Marina wanted to get out of her room, and to help her find her way, she brought her a copper device identical to the one she wore around her wrist.

Ismene called it a voco—a populace device that reminded Marina of a phone in the shape of a watch, used for navigation, telling time, and all manner of communication. To send a message, all one needed to do was scroll through their contact list, select a name, and speak. Vocal messages could be translated into text, and vice versa, making it easy for anyone to send memos—formal and informal alike.

"I've programmed yours so you can reach anyone in the Delve," Ismene said. "If you need help, I'm a call away. I suppose I should've brought it to you earlier, but Aeric didn't seem to think it was necessary."

Marina couldn't help herself when she muttered, "I'm surprised you don't have to ask him if he thinks it's necessary I eat too."

Ismene pretended not to hear.

Marina fiddled with the device, her hands running over the dial and a reddish button on the side.

"That's the one button you *shouldn't* press," Ismene said quickly. "Not unless it's an emergency. If you happen to receive that kind of message, you'll know it."

"Has anyone ever used it?"

"Only once. One of our scouts got attacked and used it to call for help."

"What happened?" Marina asked, unsure if she wanted to hear.

"She ran into something dangerous up above. The alarm got others to her quickly, but they were too late to get her back to be healed." Ismene stared blankly at her feet. "It's the only death we've ever had here."

Marina considered for a moment. "I thought natural laws stopped working when the Omnia wasn't in Elsudra."

"There was nothing natural about the way that scout died."

Silence followed, cold and unnerving. Marina tried to ignore her churning stomach when she asked, "Who do *you* use your voco to communicate with?"

"Mostly manor staff."

"I meant for fun. You can use them for fun, can't you?" When Ismene only shrugged, Marina's heart sank. Gently, she added, "I bet *I'll* need someone to call."

Ismene grinned. "My line's always open." She folded her hands, then nodded to Marina's voco. "That's all there is to it. Just avoid the emergency button unless you're in trouble. Aeric would kill me if you set off a false alarm." When Marina's eyes widened, Ismene chuckled. "He wouldn't really, but it's a serious thing to set that off. With the threat of Kieron, emergencies are dire."

Marina nodded, praying the dryness in her throat away. She tried to focus on finding the library. Her voco functioned like the navigation system on her phone, which took away the anxiety of getting lost. Still, when she arrived in the western section of the Delve, her stomach was in knots. She reminded herself she was here for books—for knowledge that may bring her clarity. It did little to ease her tension, but it was better than nothing.

Unlike the northern floodlights, string lights illuminated the West. They hung from stalactites that dripped from the ceiling, the tips of the longest ones only several feet above the ground. When the lights dimmed, the ceiling probably looked like a weeping sky inlaid with milky tears.

Like the manor, the library protruded from the walls of the cavern. The canopy roof glinted with stained glass, and the pillars beside the entryway had been carved from the rock itself. Inside, books lined every open space, and Marina followed the prickets on the walls to a mural at the end.

It depicted a map beneath a sun, shining with lakes and rivers that feathered into the sea. From the fine print, it was clear the land was Elsudra—a single continent divided into four regions: North, South, East, and West, just like the Delve. The bodies of water weren't named like the regions and cities were, though. As she neared the map, she wondered if perhaps it was because they were all connected. They didn't only feed out to the sea; they fed into each other—every lake bound to a river and every river to the ocean. The cities and mountains glistened; in fact, the entire map carried a sheen. Marina reached up to touch the canvas, bracing herself for a tingle or a shock, only to feel nothing.

She wasn't sure what she'd expected. For a moment, she felt foolish for thinking it would've felt like anything. The pockets of magic that existed in this place kept her on edge, but her unease paled in comparison to her embarrassment. To these people, her curiosity would probably come across as primitive—no better than a caveman discovering fire. An ant.

She wrapped her arms around herself, then turned her gaze to the sun atop the mural. It had four rays, drawn to look more like waves than light. She stood on her toes to get a closer look at them, only to have her curiosity jolted from her when a stack of books fell somewhere nearby.

She gasped, and a familiar voice said, "Sorry!"

Marina tilted her head, then took a step toward the nearest turn of shelves and peered around the corner. A pile of books lay around a young man with messy brown hair. If his armor didn't give him away, the dagger on his hip did.

"You're Pierce," Marina said through a breath.

He rubbed a hand on the back of his neck. "This must seem like I was stalking you. I wasn't, I swear. I heard you come in and didn't want to freak you out, so I tried to be quiet. Didn't work, clearly."

"You didn't freak me out," she said, a little too eagerly.

Awkward silence followed, which Marina tried to disrupt by helping Pierce restack the books he'd dropped.

"What were you getting books for?" she asked.

"I like to take a couple whenever I'm on duty at the southern border. I'm usually the only one staffed there since it's so inactive." He shrugged. "It faces the coast, so what it lacks in action, it makes up for with a view of the ocean. Books help me pass time." He turned to Marina and smiled, light glinting in his vale-green eyes. "You look...less cold than when I met you. I take it you still have your translator."

Marina's fingers flew to her ear. She'd forgotten she was wearing it.

"I *knew* you were the Omnia's new host when they worked again," Pierce said, grinning. "Without the Omnia in Elsudra, magic-made technology shut down. We have staff from the East here, and it took us a while to get the hang of their dialect. Guess we forgot how heavily we'd relied on translators. Thank Exorsus that's no longer a problem." His grin turned tender. "Florin told us what's going on...the basics, at least. It seems like you're having trouble remembering things?"

Marina raised an eyebrow. Clearly, Aeric and Florin were pushing the narrative that her memories were to blame rather than their Keepers' judgment. Did they really believe that, or was it something they were saying to calm people down and make this all seem like a temporary problem?

"Maybe your memories will return sooner than you think," Pierce said hopefully.

He seemed so *sure*, just like Cal. Luckily, he didn't wait for a response. He glanced at the book in his hands, held it out to her, and said, "There are tons of history books here. Won't clear the shock, but they might help you make sense of things."

Marina took it from him, then flipped it open and frowned at the sheen.

"That makes it so everyone can see the words in their preferred tongue," Pierce said. "Prime example of magic *and* technology. Look." He pointed to the spine, where a dial the size of a penny was embedded into the tail. When Marina turned it, the sheen dissolved, and English letters turned into symbols.

She let out a timid laugh. That was actually pretty cool.

"The dial makes the magic 'stick' when you turn it on," Pierce explained. "Crazy what can happen when sorcerers and engineers work together."

"The map has it too," Marina said. She turned back to the mural, and though Pierce hesitated, he followed her and leaned against a bare wall.

She directed her energy toward studying the map, praying the distraction would help calm her. The North was the largest chunk of land, and on its coast, a glittering city had been painted.

"Altus is our capital," Pierce explained. "The books in this library come from there as well." He paused, then said proudly, "That's where I grew up."

"In the North?" When Pierce nodded, she asked, "What was it like?"

"Pretty similar to the other regions, minus small dialect differences. You can't tell where someone's from unless you listen to them without a translator. But Altus...Altus is unlike any city in Elsudra. It's perfect." His lips twitched. "At least, it *was* perfect, up until Kieron ruined it."

Right. Kieron. That was a reminder she didn't need.

"I need to sit," she said. Her ears rang as she made her way to a couch a few paces from the mural. When she lowered herself to the cushions, she put her head in her hands.

"Shit, I'm sorry. I didn't mean to overwhelm you."

To make him feel better, Marina tried to smile. "When's your shift?"

"Not for a while, which is good." Pierce knelt down next to the couch. "I'd feel terrible leaving you when you look like you're about to pass out."

"I won't." She decided not to mention that she already had once, albeit in the company of someone far less agreeable.

"Do you need water?" Pierce asked. When she shook her head, he let out a relieved breath. "Good, because I don't have any."

Marina chuckled, which surprised her. Not necessarily because it was unexpected, but because for the first time in a while, it was genuine.

"I shouldn't've mentioned Kieron," Pierce said. "Don't worry, you're..."

"Safe. I've been told that." *I just don't know if I believe it.*

"We all are. The Delve is hidden in the Admare Mountains, and now that the Omnia has returned, Aeric can further protect our entrances by casting glamours and shields."

"Glamours and shields?"

"Types of magic that hide and guard our entrances. The Delve is hard to find already, but now, it's as good as invisible."

Slowly, Marina stood and reapproached the map. "Where's the Delve?"

Pierce came up beside her and pointed to a small panhandle at the bottom of the eastern region, covered on all sides by a mountain range that spanned the coast and made its way to the south.

"Around here," he said. "The south side faces the sea, and the Admares surround the others. Like I said: safe. And not a bad place to be either. We've everything we need down here, and then some."

"I heard there was a garden."

Pierce brightened. "I can show you if you want."

Marina accepted, and before they left, Pierce brought her more books. He reminded her a bit of a puppy, bounding around the shelves and eagerly explaining where to find the best reading material. And to think she'd been scared of him at first. His armored suit no longer made him look threatening, though Marina *was* glad he wasn't wearing his helmet.

"Your realm is called Georgia, right?" he asked when they reached the plaza.

A hint of a smile appeared on Marina's lips. She was surprised he'd remembered that. "I come from a place called America. Georgia is a small part of that, but my home is really called Earth."

"What's Earth like?" Pierce asked.

"Sunnier."

"It's sunny above," Pierce said. "The Delve makes a bad first impression."

"Then maybe my home is similar to Elsudra, minus magic." Would her stomach ever *not* flip when she said that word? Softly, she added, "Aeric made it clear Elsudra is on another level compared to where I'm from."

Pierce rolled his eyes. "Sorcerers can be arrogant. Anyone born with magical abilities tends to have an inflated sense of self, but those who are really powerful look down their nose at everyone. Don't take it personally."

Marina chewed on her lip. "Where are the other sorcerers?"

"Either dead or in hiding." There was a surprising lack of emotion in Pierce's voice—the kind that came when bad news was the norm instead of the exception. "We *do* have a few healers here," he continued, "but most inclined people either died in the war or fled when they were targeted."

"Inclined?"

"Magically-inclined—people who have an inclination toward wielding the Omnia's magic," Pierce said. "Some people—like Aeric—are more inclined than others. They're also called sorcerers. But most Elsudrans with magical abilities are referred to as inclined."

"Are you...inclined?"

Pierce chuckled. "No. Very few people are." He shrugged. "Guess I don't blame Aeric for being pompous. If I were inclined enough to be considered a sorcerer—and not just a sorcerer, but the actual Sorcerer of the Court—I'd wear a damned medal."

Marina knit her brow. "What's a Sorcerer of the Court?"

"Elsudra's most esteemed sorcerer," Pierce said. He seemed shocked she didn't know. "If the Keepers hold the Omnia, the Sorcerer of the Court manages it." He nodded at the books she held. "Those should do a decent job explaining the basics. But I will warn you, it's a lot of Elsudran government crap. Pretty boring."

Not boring. *Horrifying.* She'd already known Aeric possessed magical talent, but she didn't realize the extent to which he did.

"Aeric became Sorcerer of the Court after Kieron," Pierce added.

Marina stopped at the mouth of the eastern staircase. "Kieron was Sorcerer of the Court too?"

"I figured you'd have been told that."

"I'm starting to think I've been told the bare minimum," Marina muttered. Aeric expected her to wield a power she didn't understand—didn't *want* to understand—with very little explanation as to why. He was clearly against explaining Locus to her as well.

"Tell me more about Kieron," she said. She was damned either way, but she'd be more damned if she was ignorant.

Pierce took a tentative step up the staircase. "He believes the Omnia should be held by the Elsudran who possesses the most magical talent, which means the Sorcerer of the Court would become Elsudra's all-powerful Keeper *and* ruler. It means *he'd* become that. He kept his ideologies under wraps for a long time, but our Keepers eventually found out he was planning to take the Omnia from them. Kieron was exiled to a dead realm, but..." Pierce pursed his lips, and for a moment, Marina wondered if he'd decided not to continue. "He got back," he finally said, "and for a while, things looked really bad. But just when it seemed like Kieron was about to take over Altus and reach the Keepers, they sent the Omnia out of Elsudra."

Marina rubbed at her chest as they came to the top. "So…Aeric *knew* Kieron?"

Pierce nodded, then hastily said, "But he's working hard to make sure Kieron doesn't achieve his goal. We may be outnumbered, but now that the Omnia's with us, we have an advantage."

That didn't make her feel any better.

In a whisper, Pierce added, "Some say Aeric's magical talent rivals Kieron's. Not like I'd know. Most people don't get the honor of speaking with the Sorcerer of the Court. Even if they did, the man's an enigma."

Before she could decide if it was smart, Marina muttered, "It's no honor."

Pierce tensed at her iciness but brushed past her comment. "I knew someone who had a talent for magic. He couldn't do much, but it went to his head anyway. What about you?" He fiddled nervously with his baldric but kept his tone playful when he said, "I mean…it's been confirmed you *do* possess the Omnia. Should I be worried?"

"I think you could do more harm to me with that dagger than I could do to you," Marina said. "I don't feel any different. Just…out of my element."

"That'll fade with time. And I'm here to help if you'd like." He paused. "But mostly, I'm sorry—about the confusion, your memories…all of it. And I'm *especially* sorry that I dropped a stack of books and scared you half to death. If I can make it up to you, tell me."

He was joking, but Marina took the bait. "Show me around the Delve." When Pierce blinked at her, she added, "It's intimidating."

It wasn't a complete lie. She *did* feel ill at ease learning the Delve's layout alone, but more beguiling than a guide was the fact that Pierce had access to borders, which meant he had access to exits. Though she wasn't intent on leaving the Delve—not yet, at least— she figured she should familiarize herself with as much as she could. Aeric wouldn't want her to know where the exits were, which made her all the more eager to find them.

"The gardens are the best place to start," Pierce said through a grin. "Of all the places in the Delve, they're the most beautiful."

CHAPTER 8
The Heroic Ones

The gardens were easier to find than the library. At the first bend of the eastern stairs, the cavern opened into a cloister garth surrounded by apartments that leaked white light from their windows.

For a moment, Marina forgot they were underground. Colored lanterns hung from stalactites like the string lights in the West, gifting reds, greens, blues, and yellows to the botanical gardens below. Small streams weaved through clumps of greenery and led to reflecting pools, where benches had been strategically placed.

Unlike the western side of the Delve, the gardens beckoned all manner of people. Some tended to flora, while others sat and talked. A few donned the suits of sentries, but most wore more casual clothes. One thing united them, though—they *all* looked her way. Marina remembered what Cal had said about Elsudran perceptions of the Omnia's hosts. Or, in this case, host. She was glad when a few people looked away, trying not to gawk.

"People usually like to spend their free time in the gardens," Pierce said, then paused. "That doesn't make you feel uncomfortable, does it?"

"No," Marina breathed, though she wasn't sure. There weren't many people to begin with—only a few groups and preoccupied stragglers—but it was jarring anyway.

"We can leave if it does," Pierce said. "They've been given orders not to bug you if it makes you feel any better. Florin said you'd need time to settle in."

Marina's face flushed. How much did these people know about her? And how sorely did she stick out? Skepticism followed her unease. Had Pierce been given those same orders? He *wasn't* bugging her, but she couldn't help but notice the way he brightened when other sentries looked his way. What were his motives?

"It's good to see others," she lied. "And you weren't kidding about the gardens."

"Breathtaking, aren't they? They weren't always like this, but some of our creative members of staff decided to spruce things up a little bit." He nodded to the lanterns. "Ismene had that idea. You've met her, right? Makes the place look lively."

Marina nodded in agreement. "You know Ismene too?"

"As well as I can. She works in the manor, and I'm at the southern border or the barracks. But whenever I do see her, she's in good spirits."

Marina glanced at some of the nearby sentries, her eyes landing on one with red hair. When his gaze shifted toward her, she looked back to Pierce and asked, "How do you like border patrol?"

"It's okay. Gets boring sometimes, but that's mostly because of my station. I'd probably have more to do if I'd finished my training and been an actual soldier when we came here, but beggars can't be choosers."

"What were you training to be a soldier for?"

"I wanted to follow in my dad's footsteps. He was a general—worked with the court and the Keepers like Florin did. The two of them were close."

"Your dad didn't come to the Delve?"

"He died in the war."

Marina's heart sank. "I'm sorry."

"He fought for a good cause," Pierce said. His voice shook a little.

They approached a cluster of thornapples, blooming white under ultraviolet lamps. Marina tried to observe them, but the redheaded sentry was still looking at her, making it impossible to focus.

"Is that your friend?" she asked Pierce. "The one from the sea cavern?"

Pierce kept his eyes on the flowers. "Boris is...more of an associate, really. He's stuck in limbo between being a scout and a sentry. Guess he's too much of a rookie to fit in with the other scouts, so he chooses to spend time with...them." He frowned at the thornapples, making it a point to avoid eye contact with the two sentries near Boris. "He has to do work the sentries can't do and the scouts won't do, like check up on border entrances and unused passageways to make sure everything's intact. He was heading to the southern border with me when we found you in the sea cavern." He grinned. "Gotta say, you have quite the voice on you."

Marina raised an eyebrow, then choked on a gasp when she remembered how loudly she'd cursed. "You heard that?"

"Just the two of us, if it makes you feel any better. Scared us shitless, only because we weren't expecting it. So we snapped on our helmets to take a look, only I think we may've scared you more than you scared us. Sorry about that."

She gave him a reassuring smile. "No hard feelings." Though she could sense Boris's eyes on her, she didn't look his way. Instead, she moved to another patch of flowers. "Are there entrances at every border?" When Pierce nodded, Marina blurted, "Can I see them?"

He laughed nervously. "Our job is to keep you safe, not to bring you closer to the surface. I'm not sure why you'd want to see them, though. The northern border is heavily guarded since it's most vulnerable, and the western and eastern ones aren't any better. The southern one, by contrast, is about as exciting as dog shit."

"Doesn't the southern border have a view of the ocean?"

"Its one perk." Pierce's lips twitched. "I'd take you, but Florin would kill me."

Marina opened her mouth, but before she could respond, she was cut short by the booming voice of one of the sentries. The voice didn't belong to Boris but to a robust young man with flaxen hair and shiny eyes.

"Pierce, my man!" the sentry said, his tone too friendly to be genuine.

Marina grimaced as he neared them, Boris and one other plodding along at his heels. All three wore their armor.

"Ocot," Pierce said, his jaw tight.

"May I ask how you, of all people, got the honor of speaking with our Omnia's host? And to think—you didn't even introduce her to your friends." He barked out a laugh, then extended his hand to Marina. "Pleasure to meet you."

Hesitantly, she reached out and tapped her fingers against his, remembering what Cal had taught her. It seemed to surprise him, which gave her a confidence boost.

"And she's familiar with Elsudran greetings," Ocot said. He rubbed the stubble on his chin, then grinned, showing his teeth. "Aren't you going to tell us her name, Pierce? Or does your friend have better manners than you?"

"Marina," she said before Pierce could respond.

"Marina," Ocot echoed. "Don't you think it's a little rude, Marina, that Pierce hasn't introduced us?" He snorted. "I'm joking. I already knew your name. Dane got it out of Ismene the first day you arrived." He glanced sidelong at the sentry next to him—a wiry young man with deep-set eyes—who shrugged and crossed his arms.

Pierce scoffed. "You sought out Ismene to bug her about the Omnia's host?"

"Didn't seek her out," Dane said. "Just happened to see her while I was headed to the northern border to report to Florin. Some of us have *real* jobs."

Pierce gripped the strap of his baldric. "I bet it gets taxing for her having to work under Aeric, run the manor, *and* entertain the questions of lowly sentries."

Marina tensed, but Ocot's smile widened. "Lowly only to some," he mused. He observed Marina for a moment. "Y'know, you're not what I had in mind."

Though Marina's instinct was to agree, she asked, "What did you have in mind?"

"Maybe a warrior, or better yet, an all-powerful sorcerer. You're...unexpected."

"The Omnia isn't known for being predictable," Pierce said coolly. "Our Keepers only forced it to be that way. I think it makes sense that it gravitated toward an unconventional being."

Marina didn't have time to mull over his choice of words. *Unconventional.*

"Pick up that insight at the southern border, did ya, Pierce?" Ocot crooned. "Can't imagine there's much to do there. Good on you for brushing up on history."

Marina had to bite back her scoff. Ocot wasn't intimidating. If anything, he was another Tony Hanson—an obnoxious prick who thought he held more power than he did. Still, she reined in her reaction. She wasn't about to proverbially throw her hair in his face —not when she didn't know him, or Pierce, or anyone else in the Delve. It would be idiotic to align too closely with *anyone.*

"Only we've heard that she doesn't remember accepting the Omnia," Ocot continued. "Hasn't shown any inclination toward its power, at least."

Marina shrugged, intent to seem unbothered. "I do things in my own time."

Pierce shot her a puzzled look, which Marina pretended she didn't notice.

Ocot studied Marina for a moment, then leaned back and laughed. When he straightened, he was beaming. "Unexpected *indeed.* But I like you anyway, Marina."

It wasn't a compliment Marina wanted to accept, but she gave him a nod anyway.

"Either way," Boris said, "she brought the Omnia back. And eventually, Kieron will be good as gone." He gave Marina a shy smile. "We should all be thanking you."

The others murmured their agreement, but Marina began to feel dizzy. Why was everyone so quick to believe she was the person their Keepers had wanted? More than that, why were they so eager to believe she'd agree?

"Boris tells me he and Pierce found you in the sea cavern," Ocot said. "Seems like you've gotten to know Pierce quickly. If you're ever feeling out of place, he's a good person to turn to. He knows what it's like to feel lonely."

Marina hardly heard him through the ringing in her ears, but Pierce bristled.

"Screw off, Ocot," he hissed. "Remember what Florin said about bugging her."

"I'm not bugging her. I'm bugging *you.* Last I recall, there aren't any rules about that, especially since your daddy isn't here to enforce them."

"Ocot..." Boris began, but Ocot dismissed him with a wave of his hand.

"I'm joking," he said, giving Pierce a hard slap on the shoulder. "We joke, don't we, Pierce?" When Pierce shook his head, Ocot leaned toward Marina and chuckled. "Well, one of us does. He's never had a sense of humor."

For some reason, *that* pulled her back. She couldn't help herself when she said, "Maybe you're just not funny."

Ocot's lips straightened, but he leveled and shook the sting away, elbowing Dane when he chuckled. "Pierce isn't doing you a kindness by showing you around," he said, his jest leaving him. "He's using you to heal his inferiority complex."

"Ocot, shut up."

The words didn't come from Pierce, but they sounded familiar anyway. Marina's heart skipped a beat as she turned to see Cal, who stood with her arms crossed and mouth pulled subtly upward.

Ocot drew back at her smirk, then droned, "Have you met Marina?"

Cal ignored him. "Don't you have a shift at the eastern border?"

"Responsible as always, Cal. I appreciate it." He glanced at Dane, his grin intact. "We were just headed there now, actually, but I couldn't pass up the opportunity to give my love to Pierce and meet our esteemed guest."

Pierce bristled, but Cal only turned to Boris. "And *we* have a meeting with Florin and a few others soon," she said, a touch gentler. "I expect you'll be there for that."

"He knows," Ocot said. "Careful getting too involved with others' jobs. You might fail to do your own, and someone may get hurt."

Cal's jaw tightened, but she didn't react. Ocot turned to Marina and said, "If you ever want a more competent tour guide than the one you have now, I'll happily oblige."

He and Dane left before Marina could respond, and Boris gave Cal a nod before following suit. Once they'd turned the nearest corner, Pierce smiled sheepishly at Cal and said, "Thank you, but I could've handled Ocot myself."

"Last time you handled him yourself, he gave you a broken nose," Cal responded. "The healers griped for days about the work it needed." Pierce sighed as Cal turned to Marina. "Good to see you again."

"You too," Marina said. Her voice was small. It wasn't that she was scared of Cal; she wasn't even embarrassed, which surprised her, given how they'd met. Cal's demeanor, Marina realized, demanded respect—a confidence even Ocot reacted to.

"You look good," Cal said. "Any memories returning?"

Marina shook her head. "I wish."

She wasn't sure why she'd felt the need to say that. Maybe she'd wanted to make Cal feel better. But the truth was simple: this was a mistake. A colossal, cruel mistake that put her and all of these people at risk.

If I believed in gods, she thought, *I'd probably think they had it out for me.*

"Patience is a joke, isn't it?" Cal said. "The more painful it is, the more necessary it is.

Hang in there, and we'll do the same." She nodded to Marina, then flicked her gaze over to Pierce. "I *also* have faith you'll be on time for your shift."

"Right," Pierce said quickly. "I was just about to head south."

Cal gave him a tight-lipped smile, then nodded once more to Marina and left as quickly as she came.

"It's rare to intrigue Cal," Pierce whispered. "She hardly talks to anyone."

Marina loosed a breath, thankful Cal hadn't mentioned the sea cavern fiasco.

"Sorry about Ocot," Pierce added. "He's a piece of shit."

"What did he mean when he warned Cal about not getting involved with others' jobs?" Marina asked. "He said something about someone getting hurt."

Pierce sighed through his nose. "We had a scout death during the dead years," he finally said. "Her name was Astra. Cal's younger sister."

Marina stiffened. Ismene hadn't told her it was Cal's *sister*.

"Part of Cal's job is tracking scout and sentry whereabouts and making sure nothing gets breached," Pierce continued. "She's supposed to report issues to the higher-ups, but she has a habit of trying to fix stuff herself. It came back to bite her because one day, she got distracted by a unit of scouts or something, even though she was supposed to be with Astra. You have to stay in groups on the surface. Going off alone puts you at risk for attack by…" He cut himself short, but Cal's words echoed in Marina's head: *Things you'd wish you hadn't seen.*

"Cal was aloof before that," Pierce said, "but now, she barely talks to anyone. Boris knew Astra well too. They were both younger scouts…spent a lot of time together. Pretty sure there was something between the two of them, but I'd never ask Boris about it. Cal goes easier on him, though, and I think that's why." He shook his head. "Ocot only said that to get to her. Out of everyone in the Delve, he's the worst. Dane's a close second, but he's more of a weasel than anything. And Boris…I don't know. Now that Astra's gone, I think he has nowhere else to go."

Silence lingered between them, and though Marina figured she probably shouldn't ask, her curiosity bested her. "What was Astra attacked by?"

Pierce tugged at one of his gloves. "Kieron's…foot soldiers."

It was obvious he didn't want to expand—that, and a terrible pit had edged into Marina's stomach—so instead, she asked, "Why did Ocot break your nose?"

"I dislocated his shoulder, but you don't hear anyone talking about that." Pierce crossed his arms when Marina didn't respond. "Ocot and I have done more damage to each other than either of us cares to admit. The healers aren't fond of us, especially since during the dead years, injuries couldn't heal without external intervention. No life energy means the body can't naturally fix itself, and there wasn't any magic in Elsudra either. We had to rely on technology to compensate."

Christ. She hadn't considered that. Given the circumstances, she couldn't blame the healers for disliking Pierce and Ocot.

"Anyway, he holds grudges," Pierce said, "and I rub him the wrong way."

"Why?"

Pierce's jaw tightened. "There's around two hundred people here, and every person earned their spot. But not me. I was a soldier still in training, but I came here anyway because I'm the son of General Tover, who begged the Keepers to let me come despite not being qualified." Though his cheeks flushed, he didn't turn away. "So many people died when Kieron returned from exile, and not just in Altus. It was brutal. His soldiers targeted members of the court and hung them around cities, their corpses branded with Kieron's sigil. When the dead years started and Kieron made it into the capital, my dad stayed behind to fight, but he didn't want me to. And when he told me I'd be granted a spot in the Delve, I fled as quickly as I could."

Marina's stomach soured. *This* was the man the Keepers couldn't defeat—the man who tortured and branded and executed. The man who was coming after what she held, and who Aeric wanted her to face, even if he wouldn't say it explicitly.

She wouldn't. She *couldn't.*

She didn't know what was worse: her gut-wrenching dread, or the ache that bore into her chest when Pierce's eyes watered.

"I knew talented soldiers who died because they didn't have a powerful family member to protect them," he said. "One of those soldiers was closer to me than anyone has ever been. And now he's gone, like the rest."

He scrubbed his hands down his face, clearly embarrassed. For some reason, all Marina could think to say was, "And...that was why Ocot broke your nose?"

"Nah. He broke my nose because I rammed his head into one of the barrack doors." When Marina let out a surprised laugh, a grin tugged at Pierce's lips. "He's always had a stick up his ass about me because of my dad and the fact that I'm here...among other reasons. If the others take issue with me, they don't say it out loud, probably because they're worried Florin will punish them. But Ocot's never been able to keep his mouth shut, and I'm shit at ignoring him."

"I'd choose you as a guide over Ocot, if it means anything," Marina said gently.

Pierce's lips parted. "It means more than you'd think."

For a while, they meandered the gardens, and as Pierce went on about the layout of the eastern side of the Delve, Marina let herself get lost in the colored lanterns.

Aside from the border up above, the East was a singular level used for storing food, in addition to providing extra housing for staff. After the botanical gardens had been put in, people had started using the space for socialization as well.

"We needed something to remind us of above," Pierce said. "We had the greenhouses, which nobody used during the dead years, but it wasn't enough. So the scouts dug up plants and brought them down here. It was a team effort, and after Aeric agreed, we spent a while making the garden. Gave us something to do in our free time...something more than thinking about what we'd lost. They didn't grow or anything, but they were pretty enough. It'll be nice to have them now, especially since we have to start using the greenhouses for food."

Though the technicalities of the dead years still disturbed Marina, it was what she'd learned about Aeric that piqued her attention. "He *agreed*?"

"We wouldn't've been able to if we didn't get his permission."

Marina didn't bother to voice her surprise.

"I'm packed with shifts these next few days," Pierce said as he walked with her back to the manor. "But when I get some free time, I'd love to show you around the Delve. I'll call you." He glanced at her voco, the eager look returning to his eyes.

Marina agreed, but she couldn't shake her returning skepticism. Why was Pierce so willing to show her around?

Ocot's voice rang in her head. *He's using you to heal his inferiority complex.*

So what if he was? Pierce had his reasons, and she had hers. If she was going to be forced to stay here, she'd learn as much as she could. Then maybe she'd be one step closer to getting home and ridding herself of the Omnia. Someone else could take it. Someone far more heroic.

Unknowns swarmed in her head, but she pushed them down as she returned to her room, thinking of the gardens and the lanterns that filled its rocky sky.

It was lonely in the Delve, and even gardens couldn't bring warmth to a place made to hide from the sun. But in the face of uncertainty, these people had taken dark caverns and filled them with flowers and light. They'd kept going despite the dead years—despite the fear. And as Marina nestled into an armchair by her bed and opened one of the books Pierce had given her, she knew who the heroic ones were.

CHAPTER 9
Unwilling Player

Modern Elsudra, Marina learned as she scoured her books, had been built on the number four. After the first Keepers came into possession of the Omnia, a new era was born, and Elsudra was divided into four regions. Though Elsudran minutes, hours, and days passed the same as on Earth, years only lasted one hundred and sixty days. Elsudrans split years into four seasons, each ten weeks long and named after a gem of the ocean—Pearl, Olivine, Aragonite, and Calcite—while weeks spanned four days. The year ended in a ceremony called Double Moon, where the usually moonless sky would boast two and people would celebrate as Calcite turned to Pearl.

Had they acknowledged holidays during the dead years? Marina couldn't imagine going twelve years without Christmas or Halloween. Of course, twelve years in Elsudra was only about five back home, which meant the dead years weren't nearly as long as she'd thought. But even five years of stagnancy sounded torturous.

It was hard to keep five on her mind, though, when Elsudra revolved around four. Even the government was made of four symbolic parts: the Omnia, Keepers, Sorcerer of the Court, and the court itself. Though the books didn't go into it, they mentioned that the nature of the Keepers' role removed them from society. Over time, they faded into the background until they were mere figureheads and vessels for the Omnia.

Pierce was right about the importance of the Sorcerer of the Court, but it seemed the court itself—a group of the wealthiest Elsudrans—had just as much say. Technology, parties, medicine...they controlled every ounce of Elsudra's magical infrastructure.

Other information piqued Marina's interest as well. Elsudrans didn't have family names, which made naming a child all the more important. With a population of a little over a million, names seldom repeated. They didn't seem to celebrate birthdays, and they didn't count ages, which made it clear why Ismene had been so confused when Marina had asked her. Instead, Elsudrans divided generations into developmental quarters: children in the first, teenagers and young adults in the second, adults in the third, and seniors in the fourth. Marriage wasn't a concept, which Marina found strangely refreshing, and the dead, rather than being buried, were sent out to sea.

Of course, no amount of knowledge could aid her work with Aeric. In his office, amidst the chill he cast over the room, Elsudra's history didn't matter. Only one thing did: her unending failures.

"With every passing day, we lose more of our advantage," Aeric said. He stood by his desk, clutching the rim like he always did when he was impatient. "I wasn't the only person who regained my abilities when the Omnia returned. You put us in an increasingly vulnerable position every *second* you refuse to make progress."

Marina dug her nails into her palms.

"I know you have it in you," Aeric said. "Your essence is exceptionally suited for interaction with magic, which makes me think we need to try something different." He straightened. "I want you to try mental shielding. It's basic but important. Anything from inducement of unconsciousness to dissolution of an essence is possible when a person doesn't shield, which is why even those who aren't inclined benefit from building strong walls around their mind and spirit. Soldiers practice all the time. They may not be able to breach the minds of others, but that doesn't mean they don't have rudimentary shields of their own. In your case, it may force you to obtain the inner quiet you're struggling with."

Marina eyed him hesitantly. "Shield against what?"

"Psychometry."

She froze. "No. Not that."

"When I say you're averse to improving, this is what I mean."

"I'm not. If I have the potential—like you say I do—I want to improve."

"Then *prove it*," he said through his teeth. "You seem to have convinced yourself there's no use in trying, and so, like a child, you sit in that chair and fumble about, then cry when nothing happens. The barrier in your head was built by no one but yourself."

"Do you think I enjoy failing?" she said, her voice breaking. "You know I want to go home. But how am I supposed to know you'll help me? Even if I do what you want me to, how do I know you won't push me to do more? Or worse, how do I know you won't force me to go head-to-head with that psychopath Kieron like your Keepers wanted?"

When Aeric tensed, she stood. "That's another thing," she said. "How do you expect me to move forward when I know so little? You wouldn't even tell me Kieron's name."

"I've told you the basics. Anything else would be unnecessary, and you overwhelm extraordinarily easily. I'd prefer it if you didn't fall further into hysterics." When she only glared at him, he pinched the bridge of his nose and added, "At the moment, I wouldn't have you go head-to-head with Kieron because you would lose, and then so would we all."

"But you would eventually."

Admit it. Admit I'm right. He'd told her in the dining room that the Keepers had wanted the right being to accept the Omnia—one who could help them overmatch the threat they faced. What was the threat, if not Kieron? And who was she, if not the person the Omnia had latched onto? *She* knew she hadn't accepted it, but Aeric seemed to think it was her memories that erred, not the Keepers.

He's wrong. I remember everything. And I'm not going to let him force me into this mess.

When Aeric didn't respond, she hissed, "Wouldn't you?"

"I don't know," Aeric said flatly. "The Omnia's return has not gone as any of us had hoped. But what I do know is what I've seen. There's potential in you, though I cannot say for certain why you're so unable to actualize it. Hence why I wish for you to shield against psychometry. It may be the push you need."

"I don't—"

"At this point," Aeric snapped, "you don't have a choice."

Marina flinched at the sudden change in his tone.

"You maintain your shields by keeping yourself centered," Aeric said, stepping toward her. "Do away with your emotions, visualize your spirit, and let your *waves* keep me out."

She opened her mouth, but he clearly didn't have time for her reservations. When he touched the back of her hand, Marina's heart dropped.

Waves. There were waves, just like before, and they were so inexplicably *her* that, for a fleeting moment, Marina almost wondered if she could manipulate them. But the fog that had slipped into her mind was suffocating, and even the ocean yielded to its presence.

Where was her body? She'd pull back her hand if she could, but her essence didn't have limbs. He could maintain his hold for as long as he wanted, which didn't scare her nearly as much as the fact that her memories—her life—existed beneath the water he so effortlessly skimmed across.

"You're letting me win," he said, removing his hand.

Marina's chin shook. The buzz that filled her head made it impossible to focus.

"Is your emotional capacity so stunted that even this upsets you?" Aeric shook his head. "Try again."

"No, I—"

The ocean flooded back into frame. If she could find her voice, she'd throw a thousand curses his way, but she was useless here. Useless...she was so useless. Her waves collapsed on top of the light, smothering it.

"You're self-sabotaging," Aeric said, and this time, when he removed his hand, Marina jerked backward and stepped away from him. "Continue down this path, and you risk damaging your spirit *and* the Omnia."

"I can't focus," she protested. Not here...not in this room, with him.

"You're not committed to focusing. You're more scared of success than failure."

"How the fuck would you know that?"

She recoiled as soon as she said it. Aeric, however, only responded, "Because your shields are weak. And when they are, I can see inside your head."

The day progressed painfully. Marina tried to read, but she couldn't concentrate, so she lay on her bed and stared at the canopy for a few hours instead. She seemed to be on a streak with uselessness, anyway; might as well keep it up.

When Ismene came in that evening with dinner, Marina couldn't help but notice she was acting even gentler than usual. She wasn't sure what upset her more: Aeric's anger, which could freeze the world over, or Ismene's pity.

Perhaps pity was more useful. Aeric was a lost cause. She couldn't get anything out of him, despite the fact he so freely dug around inside her head. But Ismene...

"Why didn't you tell me Aeric was Sorcerer of the Court after Kieron?" Marina asked.

Ismene let out a breathless laugh. "Who did you hear that from?"

"Pierce."

"Well, tell Pierce to keep his mouth shut. He'll ramble on about anything, and you're overwhelmed as it is."

"Some of that comes from how little I know."

Ismene bit her lip. "I suppose that information slipped my mind."

Or Aeric didn't want you saying it. Heat flushed through Marina's body, but she was careful not to let her emotions show. She needed to tread carefully if she wanted to seem genuinely curious. In a way, she was, but at this point, her curiosity was countered by an equal amount of spite. If Aeric wished to keep her in the dark, she'd find light on her own.

"My confusion is probably stunting my training," Marina said innocently. "I'd hoped you could clear a few things up."

She silently rejoiced when Ismene nodded. "I'm happy to help any way I can, Marina," Ismene said, "but I know very little about magic."

"Actually, I was wondering about Aeric's relation to Kieron."

Ismene fidgeted. "He was one of Kieron's students—chosen to succeed him. Since

Kieron was exiled before he could finish serving, Aeric took on the role early."

"Where was Kieron exiled to?"

"One of our sister realms is called Sundra," Ismene said. "Its people were wiped out many years ago. They'd experimented with contacting unrelated realms, but once they'd opened that door, they couldn't close it." When Marina tilted her head, Ismene continued, "The Sundrans were a curious people. They tried searching outside the sister realms to find out if other beings existed. They were successful, only...the things they found got *into* Sundra. The Sundrans launched a wide-scale resistance, but they lost, and eventually, there were barely any Sundrans left. Those who *had* survived faced a lifetime of oppression at the hands of the beings they'd let in—one where they were no better than livestock. So the Sundrans chose mass suicide instead, and their kind came to an end."

Marina gawked at Ismene. She almost asked *what* the beings the Sundrans found were, but she couldn't get her voice to work.

"After that, one of our Sorcerers of the Court, Brenna, created a one-way portal that flowed from Elsudra to Sundra," Ismene continued. "We'd known other sister realms existed before, but we'd never tried to reach them. Since Sundra was no longer occupied— not by Sundrans, at least—Brenna figured we could use it as an exile for our prisoners, which barred them from getting back here." She shifted nervously. "It was more a death sentence than an exile, truthfully. The Elsudrans we sent to Sundra knew they'd be killed by the same beings the Sundrans themselves were killed by. But 'exile' sounded more civilized than 'execution,' so that's what we called it."

But Kieron got back, didn't he? Marina watched Ismene closely, hoping her assessing gaze would hold more power than questions.

Ismene clearly hated silence. She fiddled with the hem of her shirt, then said, "Brenna was Kieron's predecessor. She was brilliant, if not a bit eccentric. She cared more about innovation than she did choosing the next Sorcerer of the Court. By the time she passed and Kieron came into power, the Sundran portal—Brenna's portal, we call it—had been up and running for years. When the Keepers discovered Kieron's plans to usurp, they sent him to Sundra, and..." Ismene's mouth started to form the name—*Aeric*—but she stopped herself before she could say it.

Marina was careful to mind her tone when she asked, "And...?"

"Aeric's a private man," Ismene said. "He was never like Kieron. He rarely attended the court's parties or socialized with anyone. Kieron did it all for show, of course, but Aeric was virtually nonexistent. I don't think I should..."

Her voice trailed off, and Marina silenced herself before she could say something that would draw even more attention to her impatience. She took a moment to consider, then rallied her pent-up distress and let it surface.

"I'm trying to understand everything," she said, her chin trembling, "so I can help." She leaned against the bedpost, finding that just like her lie, her tears didn't need to be forced. "I'd hoped if I understood more, my memories would come back."

Guilt careened through her, but she couldn't give up her act now. If her tears were going to come unintentionally, she might as well use them for her benefit.

"It's just...our history has been dark as of late," Ismene whispered. "You've never lived under the rule of Keepers. To an outsider, it might seem like we were blindly faithful to them. But we trusted our Keepers because we knew their sacrifice. They swore an oath that made them...not as Elsudran as the rest of us."

"I won't judge the workings of a world I'm not from, if that's what you mean."

"I'm glad to hear that, Marina, but you must promise me more than that. If I tell you what I'm about to, you *cannot* repeat it."

When Marina nodded, Ismene folded her hands and said, "Before the Omnia was cast out of Elsudra, and before much of the palace staff was sent to the Delve, our Keepers informed us that Aeric had been tasked with overseeing the Omnia's eventual return. In some ways, that made sense; he was the Sorcerer of the Court, and few could match his talent. But I won't lie when I say we didn't expect our Keepers' decision, for *Aeric* was the reason Kieron escaped Sundra in the first place."

Marina could feel herself pale, but she forced a deadpan expression.

"Somehow," Ismene continued, "Aeric manipulated Brenna's portal to create a path back to Elsudra. It took him years to perfect it, and when he did, Kieron—who'd managed to survive in Sundra—returned."

Marina's heart quickened, her neutral facade threatening to shatter with every beat. Pierce hadn't mentioned *that*. Of course, she probably wouldn't have either. The story damned Aeric, who clearly didn't want Marina to know what he'd done. And yet...why was he here? Why had he—the man partially at fault for the danger Elsudra was in—been given such a pivotal task? What did that mean for the Delve...for *her*?

"Brenna's portal was built in the palace itself, and when Kieron returned through it, he tried to secure himself a stronghold by attacking the capital," Ismene said. "The Keepers and the court were blindsided—*everyone* was—but Kieron ultimately lost the battle. He didn't have the numbers on his side, and his time in Sundra had made him weak. So he and Aeric went into hiding. Over the course of seasons, Kieron gathered strength and stirred up support for his ideology, amassing an army that could contend with the Keepers'. But just as Kieron started to occupy significant territory and set his sights on Altus again, Aeric returned to the capital. He sought counsel with our Keepers, where he exposed every last bit of Kieron's plan. And when the Omnia was cast out and we were sent to the Delve, we learned Aeric would superintend the Omnia upon its return."

Marina blinked at Ismene. "The Keepers *trusted* him after what he did?"

"I was wary at first," Ismene said, "but I've come to see Aeric's loyalty for myself."

"How can you know that for sure?"

Ismene lowered her voice. "There are rumors," she said slowly, "that before the Omnia was sent from Elsudra, our Keepers made Aeric swear an oath of his own—one that compelled him to protect both the Omnia and its host when the time came, as well as lend a hand in Kieron's defeat. Aeric knows Kieron better than any of us, and for some reason, he betrayed him. I imagine our Keepers could think of no one else fit for the job. So they sent out word that Aeric had been executed, and he fled to the Delve with us as Kieron closed in on the palace." She twisted her hair around her finger. "Magic in Elsudra was absent during the dead years. If Aeric truly wished to avoid this hypothetical oath, he could've ended things before the Omnia returned and his oath resumed. But he never did."

"That's a stretch," Marina said, ignoring the regret that flashed in Ismene's eyes.

"This is why I was hesitant to tell you," Ismene said. "It's a terrible story, laden with terrible mistakes...but we're not terrible people. *Aeric* isn't a terrible person. He could've forsaken us during the dead years."

"By checking out, you mean? That doesn't make him genuinely loyal; it means he was too scared to turn to death instead. Sometimes, even desperate people chicken out."

Something heavy curled up in her chest, but she ignored it.

After a pause, Ismene said, "Aeric and Kieron match each other in many ways, but I believe they're fundamentally different people. Aeric never wanted the Omnia, and it's clear even now he has no interest. In fact, I'd wager that out of everyone here, Aeric is the most determined to see Kieron fail. Remember that, Marina, and *please* don't repeat this."

There were so many things Marina wanted to say. If Aeric was the reason for Kieron's return, then he was also the reason the Omnia had to be sent out in the first place. The reason Elsudra was the way it was. The reason she was here to begin with. How could one possibly atone for that? She wanted to be angry—furious, even—but she was only scared.

She'd gotten the insight she was after, so it would do little to dwell on it. Besides, now the playing fields were even. Aeric had pried into her past, and she'd repaid him by doing the same. But with her new knowledge came a crushing confirmation: Aeric was an unwilling player in this game. He wasn't choosing this; he was being forced, just like her.

No fear, she commanded herself. *Push it away. Ignore it.*

But when Ismene left, Marina locked her door and wedged the vanity chair beneath the handle all the same.

CHAPTER 10
Terrible Company

Marina's sleep was restless. When she finally succumbed to the darkness, the waves in her head thrashed mercilessly. Her stomach coiled and soured with them, and by the time she made it to Aeric's office the next morning—her head ringing with what Ismene had told her—she felt like she had the flu.

Brave. Be brave.

She needed to show assertiveness—to prove to Aeric that she wasn't going to be made a puppet for his oath. It was harder to conjure bravery so close to him, though, and Marina hoped her fear wasn't noticeable. It probably was.

"I don't want to do psychometry," she said in greeting, figuring she might as well come straight out with it. She stood behind one of the chairs, her arms crossed.

"What you want doesn't matter."

She should've expected that. Callousness was the only language Aeric knew.

"It does if I'm the one training," she said. Her hands started to shake, so she dug them under her armpits.

"At the moment, you're not training. You haven't made any progress. Sit down."

"No." She could do this. She could stand strong...she could shun the fear and fight the urge to freeze.

"It seems you aren't comprehending the severity of this situation," Aeric said. "Would you prefer to face Kieron with no grasp on magic—not even shields to keep you safe?"

"I'd prefer not to face him at all," Marina retorted, "but you know that."

He took a stiff step toward her. "Kieron doesn't just use psychometry to obtain information," he said. "He tortures people with it. Tell me, Marina, would you *prefer* that to simple practice? Rest assured, I'm going easy on you. Yet you still find a way to whine about it."

"You're not listening—"

"Neither are you. Would you prefer a demonstration, seeing as though my attempts to underscore the threat we're facing pass unheeded?"

He didn't give her time to answer. The moment his hand touched hers, all she could see was an endless ocean, writhing as violently as ever. This time, however, the fog didn't hover above her waves—it dove beneath the surface to where a little girl stood at a crowded school drop-off, clinging to her mother's arm.

"I always come back, cactus. You'll have fun today."

The pictures were blurry, and the sounds were distorted.

The little girl shook her head violently. *"I want to go home."*

This was a memory—her memory—shrouded in water.

She could feel a sob rising in her throat, but her body was far away. Even worse was the fact that the fog was quick and elusive.

She was nine in her next memory, crying into an old flip phone her mom had lent her before she attended her first sleepover. Her friends had been to countless sleepovers. Why was it so hard for *her*?

"I changed my mind. Please...pick me up. I want to come home," she wept, the phone pressed against her wet cheek.

This was how it always went. Nine or nineteen, she could do very little without breaking down. The memories that followed confirmed it. Her most recent were particularly harrowing, for they were all the same: days spent lying on the couch, rotting in the emptiness of her home, and nights spent wide awake with nothing but grief to keep her company. Sometimes, when it became too much, Marina would get out her mother's old flip phone and beg her to come back.

The line would remain silent.

"These memories are mild compared to the alternatives."

Aeric's voice. Now she could see him, and she hated that even more. Marina didn't pull away this time. Instead, she buried her face in her hands and cried.

Coward, coward, coward.

She could always tell when she was shutting down. It became a physical thing as well as a mental one. The lights in the room, which she'd once thought dim, were now too bright. They hurt her head, just like every sound, movement, and texture.

Aeric wasn't just callous. He was cruel.

This is your fault, she thought. *You're the reason Elsudra is what it is. The reason I'm here.*

"Kieron will do worse if you're unprepared," Aeric said. "That's why it's essential we develop your skills—to protect you, if nothing else."

"What skills?" Marina choked. "I don't have any! And you won't answer me about Locus. I want to go home...I don't want to be here."

"You *are* here," he hissed, "no matter how much you fight it. All we can do now is move forward."

She dared to make eye contact with him. Had she detected desperation in his tone?

"How many times must we end these sessions with you in shambles?" he said. "Do you possess a modicum of self-control? Of discipline? How do you expect to progress if you so easily shatter?"

She couldn't respond to that—not without breaking down further and proving him right. Instead, she remained silent, her head numb.

Coward, coward, coward.

Aeric didn't summon her the next day. According to Ismene, even before the Omnia's return, he'd disappear once a week to discuss logistics with Florin. Now that he had his glamours and shields to reinforce, he was gone even longer.

Though Ismene mentioned it offhandedly, Marina considered it some of the best news she'd received since coming to this place. Even luckier, Pierce sent her a message that afternoon asking if she still wanted a tour of the Delve. Since her only other option was to obsess over what Ismene had told her in the silence of her room, she agreed.

Pierce had to make a trip to the barracks, so they planned to meet at the turn of the hour. Luckily, her voco helped her track the time. It told her the date as well: day two, week five of Calcite.

Back home, it was still January—nearly two weeks since she'd seen Gemma and Hank. What would they think? Would they blame themselves? She hadn't wanted them to. She'd told Gemma she hadn't given up.

Her heart sank. *Had* she been unconsciously aware of the Omnia? Was the text, just like her donations, a form of preparation?

No. It wasn't. She never would've chosen this.

Don't doubt yourself, Marina. You're not forgetting anything.

Since even an hour was too long to sit in her room and ruminate, Marina decided to pass time by touring the first floor. Besides, knowing the ins and outs of the manor could be useful, couldn't it?

As she meandered the hallways, studying the paintings and mirrors that lined the walls, she thought of the ocean. Pierce was lucky to have that view. She'd taken so much for granted back at home—the ocean included. Perhaps it would've done her well to spend her days by it. At the very least, it may've brought her some peace. Instead, she'd wandered around her house like a ghost clinging to memories—to a past she wished she could relive.

And now she was here, made to reckon with this power living inside her—longing for answers, only to find each one more terrifying than the last.

You'll see Pierce soon, she told herself. *He'll show you around the Delve. You can get your bearings straight, and eventually you'll know enough to get home. You will. Just take things in ones.*

It didn't matter that home was dark and empty. It was better than being here.

She sniffled to clear the tingling in her nose, then stopped at a console beneath a mirror where a vase of petunias sat. Someone must have recently brought them in because bronzed shears lay at the edge of the table. Marina ran her fingers over the petals, then turned to the mirror, expecting her tears to resurface. She'd awoken groggy from a night filled with crying spells, hating just how right Aeric was. She did shatter easily. And yet, the sorrow of yesterday had started to fade, and anger emerged in its stead. She let herself get lost in the feeling—in the power it gave her—only to regain her wits when she heard voices coming from a nearby room.

Though her good sense urged her to leave, she strained to listen. The voices were familiar. The first was strong but gentle, and the other was low and cold in a way that made Marina's limbs go stiff. Out of instinct, she grabbed the shears and tucked them into the shaft of her boot. She felt rather idiotic carting around shears, but it felt better to have them close. *Safer.* Tentatively, she took a step toward the room. The door was shut, but she could hear through it well enough.

"I can send more scouts out," Florin said. Scuffing sounded as he neared the door. Though Marina recoiled, she didn't move.

"Not yet." Marina held her breath at Aeric's voice. "For now, I'll have to head up there more often. If it gets worse, we'll increase numbers at the borders."

"They've never been this close. During the dead years, we'd only come across packs a few miles out. Do you think they can sense it?"

They clearly weren't discussing Kieron's soldiers.

"No," Aeric said. "We're too far below ground. If she were on the surface without diminution cuffs, I'd worry, but she's not. And the Delve insulates the Omnia's energy better than the cuffs could."

Marina didn't waste time trying to guess what diminution cuffs were.

"If anything," Aeric continued, "they're picking up hints of my glamours and shields, but they aren't astute enough to pinpoint where the magical energy is coming from. Not like trained sorcerers are, at least."

"And if a trained sorcerer *does* locate your glamours and shields, then what?" Florin pressed. "We'll be in a world of hurt if they find the Delve before something clicks with her—if she has the potential at all."

"Kieron has no idea the Delve exists," Aeric said, "and he thinks I'm dead. We have some advantage."

Silence followed. When Florin finally spoke, he lowered his voice to a whisper. "You all believed whoever returned would be able to wield the Omnia's magic. Now all we have is another Keeper, only this one's not Elsudran and nowhere near as likely to be of any help. I hate to doubt you and the Keepers, but I won't lie either, Aeric. I find myself increasingly convinced something went awry with their interpretations."

Interpretations of what? Marina strained even harder to listen to Aeric, whose voice was level when he said, "I know. This is an unpleasant surprise."

Her face heated. *For me too,* she thought.

"Now Kieron has his abilities back, as do you," Florin continued, "and the girl is unable to do what we expected. He may not know about the Delve, but he knows the Omnia is harbored somewhere. Elsudra is only so large, and we're outnumbered as it is. We need the Omnia's host at full power to have any hope of defeating him." He lowered his voice even more when he said, "And if he finds her..."

"The Keepers knew how to perform Locus," Aeric said. "That was what Kieron was betting on. She doesn't. If he apprehends her, her lack of knowledge about the ritual would be our buffer. He'd tread cautiously to prevent harm to the Omnia, and we'd have time to hit him back."

Of course. Aeric wasn't hesitant about her performing Locus—he was vehemently against it. Her ignorance was useful. In his eyes, there was only one path forward. And now, she was to be cannon fodder in a war she hadn't started—a pawn thrown around on a board she couldn't read, all to remedy the mistake *he'd* made.

"Only, we'd be dealing with severely depleted numbers due to attacks on the Delve," Florin said. "If we could forge allies elsewhere, it might help, but our intel on others is vague. At the moment, we're only certain about one place. And even then, we can't be sure of their willingness to help."

One place. Where was Florin referring to?

"So we'll keep watch," Aeric said. "I'll reinforce the entrances more often, and if the numbers get worse, we'll increase sentries at the northern border." There was another long pause before he added, "Her essence is like mine. I know she has the potential, and there's no debating she holds the Omnia."

Though Florin didn't sound confident, he only said, "I'll keep this quiet for now. No need to raise questions amongst my ranks unless things worsen."

Marina stepped back, wondering how fast she'd need to run if she didn't want to be seen, only to freeze as the door opened.

Florin stepped out first. He quickly masked his reaction to her presence, shooting a glance at Aeric when he, too, emerged. If Aeric was surprised, he didn't show it. He simply nodded at Florin, who eagerly accepted the dismissal. Marina didn't watch him as he passed her. She kept her eyes on Aeric, trying not to look like a deer in headlights.

"Any reason you're in this part of the manor?" Aeric asked. Normally, his tone would've made her shrink, but today, the flame within her was stronger than his ice.

"I was trying to find the second floor." Her lie was quick but sloppy.

"And the massive staircase next to this hallway wasn't obvious enough?"

It was hard not to take out the shears and stab him.

"The manor is very complicated, and my memory is about as good as an ant's," she said innocently. "You'll have to be patient with me."

He raised an eyebrow at her, which Marina figured was about as much of a response as she was going to get. Still, she reveled in her newfound vigor—fueled by a fire so intense that even Aeric drew back at its heat.

Emboldened, she blurted, "Do you mean to kill me? I thought about it a lot last night. You're never going to help me learn Locus, which by extension means you're never going to help me get home, even if I do learn magic. So what am I to you? A weapon of war? Do you *honestly* think I can help you defeat this Kieron person?"

Aeric sighed. "No. But you're what we got."

"Is that your justification for—"

"It is my justification," Aeric interrupted, "for trying whatever I can."

"Well, I'm done," Marina hissed. "I'm done playing these stupid mind games with you. I'm done trying to wield a power I never wanted, all so I can be thrown into a war that isn't mine to fight."

"This isn't a game you can quit," Aeric said, and a chill seemed to descend over the hall. "We're facing a threat who won't stop playing until he wins. *You* may have ample experience giving up, but now, other people are involved."

Her senses narrowed, and she began to see spots.

Don't, she told herself. *Don't say it. Don't betray Ismene's trust.*

"Did you consider those people," she said, caution be damned, "when you brought Kieron back to Elsudra?"

The silence that followed was painful, but Marina refused to back down. She almost wondered if Aeric hadn't heard her correctly, but eventually, he said, "You forced that out of Ismene, didn't you? Did you play on her sympathy? Use her weakness against her?"

Sympathy isn't a weakness, Marina thought. On second thought, maybe it was. Who was she to know anything about sympathy?

"If I hadn't detected the Omnia myself," he continued, "I would think there *had* been a mistake. Our Keepers believed someone noble would accept it. You're astoundingly far from it."

"That's a fine example of the pot calling the kettle black," Marina sneered, her heart racing. "If you hadn't altered Brenna's portal for Kieron, nobody would have to deal with this. *I* wouldn't have to deal with this. You may've sworn some kind of oath, but I never did, so don't act like I'm the one putting your people in danger."

"I've made it clear that regardless of whether or not you think you accepted the Omnia, you hold it," Aeric said. "I may be part of the reason it had to be sent out in the first place, but you being here was out of my control. Why it latched to a girl who can hardly resist the fear that permeates her every action is beyond me, but it did, so we must make do with what we've got—painful as that may be for both of us—and hope you don't make a mess of things like you did with your parents."

The words hit low and hard. Though she expected herself to blow up, her mind and body had gone still, and when she spoke, her voice was less than a whisper. "I'm not a person to you, am I? I'm something you can use now and let die later. Just a stupid Earth girl forced into a game you created. But if you lose, you'll know deep down it was *you* who fucked everything up."

She knew she'd done what she'd intended when rage flickered in Aeric's eyes. "Choose the words you use around me carefully. I've given you freedom in the Delve, and I can just as easily take it away. If you continue making my job harder than it already is, I see no reason why I shouldn't lock you in your room. With your current inability to wield magic, you'll be as useful there as you are anywhere else. Try me again, and I'll not think twice about leaving you with only your thoughts to keep you company." He paused, then added, "And what terrible company that would be."

Marina clenched her hands by her sides, her tongue burning with all the insults she wanted to throw at him. Instead, she turned away, ramrod straight, and left without saying a word.

CHAPTER 11
Daffodils

Marina had to mentally stomp on her anger to keep it from showing. Even as she greeted Pierce, who threw himself into a detailed tour of the Delve, she couldn't stop her mind from racing. For what it was worth, she salvaged some peace by thinking of ways she could kill Aeric. Hypothetically, of course, though the shears *would* make for a satisfying death.

Her mind was scattered, but she forced herself to take note of the Delve's layout. The barracks were in the West, a flight above the courtyard with the library, while the East was primarily for greenhouses, food storage, extra apartments, and the botanical gardens. The North housed the manor, additional barracks for generals and scouts, and an infirmary where the healers worked. The South was the smallest and most vacant, containing only storage and an old building used for training. Marina couldn't help herself when she peered up a flight of stairs that led to what she suspected was the southern border.

"I almost fell down that once during the dead years," Pierce said when he noticed where she was looking. "Would've been a disaster if I had. A broken nose is one thing; the healers had tools to fix that. But a broken leg? That would've required a shit ton of intervention. They'd have hated me even more."

He launched himself into some random story, and though Marina tried to listen, her attention flitted to a barred archway a few paces from the stairwell. She approached it hesitantly, giving Pierce nods so it seemed like she was following along, then peered inside. The tunnel was too narrow and dark to see farther than the bars.

Pierce said something else, but Marina didn't hear him until he came up behind her and said, "I know my story wasn't the most riveting, but if a hole in the wall is more interesting, I need to rethink my approach."

"Sorry," Marina said quickly.

Pierce chuckled. "That tunnel leads to an abandoned shaft. Funnels out of one of the southern faces of the Admares. At least, that's what Boris told me. He does checks on it every once in a while. Now it gets cut off halfway by glamours and shields. Guess we can never be too careful."

"Are there more tunnels?"

"I've heard of a few, but sentries don't have access to them. Not like they're very interesting. They're old, from what I've heard—hard to get through unless you're a good climber. The Delve was built over them as a hidden military base, and after that, a lot of the tunnels either eroded or were forgotten about."

Marina squinted into the darkness. "What were they made for?"

"Finding magic. Early Elsudrans—especially those in the East—were desperate for anything. Guess they hoped they'd hit an underground spring or something." He gestured to the tunnel. "They didn't find much. Everything leads to cliffs or dead ends. The sea cavern was the luckiest they got."

Marina blinked at him. "What do you mean, *finding* magic?"

He frowned. "Water was the Omnia's host before the Keepers."

When he realized she wasn't following, giddiness flashed in his eyes, as though her confusion was an opportunity. Excitedly, he said, "Elsudra was a water world long ago, like all the sister realms. When Elsudrans came about, they discovered that magic existed in the water and could be traced back to the sea. They believed it all came from the same source—one that made the ocean."

Marina's heart fluttered. The ocean...just like what had brought her here.

"My dad used to tell me about the different communities that lived in early Elsudra. Coastal ones had the most magical resources since they lived so close to water, but those near lakesides and rivers weren't far behind. Others took what they could, but some groups claimed entire coastlines and left others out to dry, literally."

"What do you mean?"

"Unlucky groups didn't have easy access to water, which meant they didn't have easy access to magic," Pierce said. "Fights broke out, and I guess eventually, some groups decided on less violent strategies." He cocked his head toward the tunnel. "Whoever lived in the Admares was probably barred access to the resources other communities had. Searching underground was their last-ditch attempt to find water."

Marina ran her hand over the bars. "What did people use magic for?"

"Medicine, protection, technology, growth...or, if a community was so inclined, destruction and war." The sides of Pierce's lips twitched. "Everyone had access to magic, but some people had more—a talent that didn't care which community they came from or what kind of person they were. They wanted to be close to water too, because it meant their abilities would be enhanced. There was even a ritual—Tempus, I think—that sorcerers in early Elsudra had to perform in water. I guess it was only a matter of time before people decided to centralize the Omnia's magic. Enter our first Keepers, who took the Omnia from the ocean and became its new hosts."

Marina frowned. She hadn't heard of Tempus before. "What did the ritual do?"

Pierce chuckled and shook his head. "I don't remember. Florin would be disappointed in me for admitting that. He's a stickler when it comes to soldiers studying history. Says the past is a predictor of the future." His smile grew doleful. "My dad used to say that too."

Marina wondered if perhaps that was why Pierce's eyes lit up so much when he told her of Elsudra—because it made him feel closer to his dad. Maybe, in some way, history meant to him what music meant to her.

Gently, she said, "Tell me more about the first Keepers."

Pierce tapped one of the bars with his knuckles, then motioned for Marina to follow him. "They were four of the best sorcerers in early Elsudra, and they did what no one had been able to do before. They came into possession of the Omnia, and after that, their bloodline acted as the hosts instead of water." He made a gesture with his hands as they descended into the plaza. "The Delve was built over the existing tunnels sometime during the era of Keepers. This is the first time it's been used, though. Florin says it was built specifically as a last resort. Nobody knew about it, minus the Keepers, who kept their knowledge of this place quiet until Kieron returned from exile and its use was warranted." He sighed through his nose. "Bet they thought *that* would never happen. But here we are."

Here she was too, even though she shouldn't be. Marina held back her grimace.

"How did the first Keepers take the Omnia from water?" she asked as they began their ascent on the eastern staircase.

"Beats me. All I know is that after them, magic was no longer a natural resource; the government controlled it, and Altus became the center of magical advancement. I wouldn't have wanted to grow up anywhere else." He broke into a grin. "They'd throw parties too, right at the palace. Since my dad was a general, I got to attend some. You'd never believe some of the magic-made technology there. I may not have been born inclined, but I sure did get to experience the things magic could do." His grin turned wistful. "Elsudra was really something before all this happened. I wish you'd gotten to see it at a better time."

Marina forced a smile. "That would've been nice."

"What are parties in Georgia like?" Pierce asked. When Marina only shrugged, Pierce said, "You'd like the ones we have here. The best one comes at the turn of Calcite to Pearl. We celebrate in the Delve, but it's nowhere near what it was in Altus."

"You celebrated during the dead years too?"

Pierce nodded. "It was more of a metaphorical ceremony. But not anymore—this year, I bet it'll double as a celebration for the Omnia's return."

Marina's stomach dropped. This wasn't something to be celebrated—not for her or them. When would these people realize they were celebrating a mistake?

The sound of trickling water grew louder as they entered the botanical gardens, and she let it take up space in her head. Thankfully, nobody else was around. At least they wouldn't run into Ocot again.

"When things get hard," Pierce said, "I think about celebrations in Altus. Small things like that keep me going—training with Florin, the view at the southern border, and dancing. *Especially* dancing. I have good memories of dancing back in Altus with someone special." He turned to Marina. "That very someone used to say small joys are the lights we use to find our way through dark times. I used to think it was silly, but it's helped, now more than ever." He sat at a bench surrounded by rosemary, and when Marina lowered herself beside him, he said, "Try it. Something's bugging you."

She tried to laugh off his comment. "Nothing's bugging me. I'm fine."

"You say that, but you don't look it." He nudged her. "C'mon, try."

Marina picked at her nails. "The sea brings me joy," she said softly. "I love books, and music...I used to sing while my dad played guitar." She chewed on her lip, then asked, "Who told you about small joys?"

Pierce eyed the rosemary. "Another soldier in training."

"A friend?"

"At first. And then..." Pierce's voice trailed off, and he inhaled through his nose.

Marina gave him a coaxing glance, and though he smiled, his lips quivered.

"I was the best in my class when I trained in Altus," he said. "It'd all gone to my head by the time I was in my second quarter. Then he came along. He was from the South—lived on a farm next to a river—and he was better than me at everything. He was faster, stronger, more agile...he even had some small talent with magic, which made him think the world of himself. Add that to the fact that he showed me up the first day he arrived, and it was like a slap in the face. I'd push myself beyond my limits because I was desperate to pass him up. And then, one day, I was practicing in some shitty training arena a mile from the palace because I didn't want anyone to know, and I sliced my hand with a scythe pistol. So I'm sitting there, cursing, and I hear...laughing. The asshole had followed me. But then he asked if I wanted to practice with him, and I said yes. He was the one who introduced me to dancing and tied it back to combat. I laughed when he first told me that was why he was so good—because he'd danced when he lived in the South. But then he showed me what he meant, and..."

This time, when his voice trailed off, he didn't regain it.

"And what?" Marina asked.

"And I fell in love with him. I'd never felt that way about anyone before. Later, I realized the feelings were mutual, and..." Pierce's throat bobbed. "The person I'd been jealous of—the one who was better than me at everything—became everything to me. We spent every moment we could with each other. But then Kieron returned from Sundra, and before the year had turned, I'd evacuated to the Delve. But not him. He and so many others didn't get the chance I did."

Marina let out a pained sigh. "I'm so sorry."

"It's done," Pierce whispered, though she knew he was far from accepting it. "I have to find some way to live with it." He forced a mirthless laugh. "I'm lucky Ocot doesn't know about that. It'd be another reason for him to judge me."

"I know he's an asshole, but judging someone for who they love is a dick move."

Pierce raised an eyebrow. "I meant he'd judge me because it's another example of why I shouldn't be in the Delve." He paused. "Why would someone judge people for who they love?"

She regretted bringing that up. "It's...something people do where I'm from." Hastily, she added, "Not everyone. Some people just make it their business to care about things that don't affect them."

Pierce considered for a moment. "That's...strange."

Marina shrugged, and though she almost swallowed her question, she asked, "Do Elsudrans care if someone *doesn't* experience attraction...to anyone, in any way other than platonic?"

"I don't see why they would," Pierce said. "None of that stuff carries any weight here. People love in different ways, and even idiots like Ocot have enough sense to mind their own business."

Marina almost laughed. That was probably the most refreshing thing she'd heard all day. Of course, her basis of comparison wasn't great, but she'd take any reason to look upon Elsudra more favorably.

Back at home, she'd only confided in her parents about her lack of attraction to others. It wasn't that she was ashamed of the way she was—which she often found ironic, given how much else she'd change about herself if she could—but rather that she feared people would pry or attempt to dissect nonexistent issues. That, and she'd never quite figured out how to explain things like aromanticism and asexuality without making it sound like she couldn't love at all. But she could love. She *did* love. Unconventionally, perhaps, but deeply.

Marina's heart sank. No—she *used* to love. And then she'd lost, and it had torn her apart so severely that she'd resigned to loving nothing at all.

"Ocot has a thousand problems with me," Pierce continued, "but that isn't one of them. He uses my dad as justification, but honestly, his issue with me has to do with an accusation I made—one he hasn't forgotten."

That piqued her curiosity. "What accusation?"

"It's...nothing important."

Since she didn't want to seem pushy, she shifted her gaze instead to a cluster of daffodils at the edge of one of the reflecting pools. When Pierce noticed where she was looking, he stood and extended his hand to her. Though she didn't feel like moving—all she wanted to do was fall into a deep sleep filled with waves—she got up anyway.

Guilt weighed her down as she walked. Pierce didn't deserve any of this. He was being so kind to her—the girl he thought was here to help his people. If only he knew what she'd said to Aeric. Then, maybe he'd hate her, and rightfully so.

As they approached the flowers, Marina asked, "What was the soldier's name?"

"I don't say it. Not anymore." Pierce's eyes met hers, dull as lead. "During the dead years, all I could think about was what had happened to him. It's hard to accept that he probably died, just like my father and so many others who weren't given the opportunity to flee. And with his minor talents in magic, he would've been an even bigger target." His face tightened. "When I get in my head with all of it, I think of memories that bring me joy. Most involve him. And his eyes...they must've been the most unique in Elsudra." He looked out at the gardens. "But he was practical," he said softly. "Would've wanted me to go on and not waste time mourning him. My dad would've felt the same."

Marina's chin trembled. "I'm sorry for it all," she whispered. "And I'm especially sorry that the Omnia didn't return with someone better."

"Why would you say that?"

Because I'm weak, she wanted to say. *Because Aeric looks at me like I'm an ant, and you should too. Because I'm not the host you prayed for, and I'm just as useless back home, and if Aeric forces me into this mess, I'm going to get your people killed, like I did my parents.*

Now she couldn't hold back her tears. When they fell, she yielded, too weary to care that she hadn't waited until she was alone. "I hope Gemma remembers to water them."

Pierce paused. "The...flowers?"

Marina nodded, then crouched beside the daffodils and put her face in her hands.

Everything swept past her—paralyzing, suffocating, drowning—until all she could do was cry. Pierce knelt beside her.

"I can't wrap my head around what I was brought into," she said. "There's so much talk of Kieron and how everyone expected some all-powerful sorcerer to come help fix things, and then *I* come. I can't even control myself, much less your Omnia." Her body shook—so hard she wished it would shatter and blow away into nothing. "My parents are gone because I couldn't control my fear. It eats away at me—leeching off my sanity, never letting me rest—and it took them from me too."

She held Pierce's gaze, expecting to see hate in his eyes—expecting to drink it in and let it chip away at the dilapidated string she held herself together with. But he only hugged her, and somewhere between her sobs and the sound of trickling water, the pain in her chest eased.

One day, one step, one breath at a time. Ones were easy. Simple.

She pulled back and wiped her cheeks. "You asked what else brought me joy," she said. "My parents did. They helped me find it when I'd lost it. And I lost it a lot."

"But you're still going, aren't you? Even if it's harder. Even if you feel like you can't. You're still moving forward." He leaned back and studied the daffodils. "If I have faith in anything, it's the power of our Omnia. Elsudrans may have made questionable choices with it, but it was never ruined. It's always been just as divine as the rest of our world. And if fate brought it to you, that must mean something."

The silence that followed was peaceful. Marina breathed it in, letting it wash over her until Pierce said, "The sea brings you joy, right?" When she nodded, he stood. "Screw the rules, then. Come with me to see the view from the southern border."

Marina's eyes widened. "Seriously?"

"You've been taken from your home, forced underground, and inundated with things that'd make most people lose it completely. It's the least I can do. I have a shift from dawn until late noon tomorrow. There won't be anyone to see us—the South is almost always empty, even more so that early. You can spend my shift with me."

There was promise in his voice, and Marina reeled at the sound of it.

Something like hope, though the feeling was old and unfamiliar, furled through her. She'd finally be able to see it—the waves, the sea, the *world*—even if it wasn't her own, and even if it was from far away. When she stood and embraced Pierce, she knew she'd given him a clear enough answer.

CHAPTER 12
Electricity

Marina returned to her room late that night after spending as long as possible with Pierce. She'd mostly used their time together as a way to avoid the manor—more specifically, to avoid Ismene and Aeric.

She agreed to await Pierce's call come dawn. If everything went according to plan, he'd relieve the sentry on duty before him, then meet her at the border stairwell. As excited as she was, Marina's restlessness wasn't because of anticipation. Instead, the events of the day played on repeat in her mind, and guilt followed suit.

What she'd told Pierce in the gardens was one thing. He may judge her, but what did she care? Besides, he'd told her a damning story of his own, so Marina did her best to ignore the shame that followed when she thought of her breakdown. But she'd implicated Ismene as well as herself when she'd run her mouth to Aeric, and worse still was the fact that her regret paled in comparison to her pride.

If Aeric could hold her mistakes over her head, she should be able to do the same to him. He deserved it. Ismene didn't, but Aeric wouldn't punish her...it would be needlessly cruel. Besides, Ismene had only told Marina what everyone but her already knew.

She shook the thought away. For now, the southern border would be her focus. She'd deal with everything else later.

Some hero she was, setting fires and then running from them.

She woke that morning to the beeping of her voco and Pierce's voice message, then readied herself and hurried from her room. She left her voco behind; she wouldn't put it past Aeric to have put a tracker in it, and the last thing she planned to do was get caught.

Lights wedged in the Delve walls helped her find her way to the plaza, then to the shadowy stairwell that led up to the southern border.

Pierce greeted her by waving her his way. "Keep your voice low until we get up there," he whispered as she approached. "These walls carry sound." He cocked his head up to the mouth of the stairs. "It's a bit of a walk. If you need rest, tell me."

Marina only rolled her eyes. Of course, it had been a while since she'd done anything active, and the climb wasn't easy. The stairs made their way up at a steep angle, and she hadn't realized how far they'd ascended until her ears began to pop.

Her stomach flipped at the realization that this would be the first time she'd seen Elsudra—not the Delve, but the world beyond. How similar would it look to Earth? Would the grass be as green and the sky as blue? Would the ocean look like the one from home?

By the time they reached the top, Marina's lungs burned.

"Told you it's hard," Pierce said.

Marina snorted as Pierce turned to the door atop the platform. It reached from ceiling to floor, and when Pierce put his palm to it, it slid into the rock.

"Is that magic?" Marina asked.

A smile tugged at his lips. "Just a biometric scanner. Wouldn't want a nosey staff member meandering around up here."

Though his tone hadn't been patronizing, Marina's face flushed. How was she supposed to know the difference between technology and magic in a place like this?

"Most of our technology doesn't require magic, if you'd believe it," Pierce said. "We would've been in a world of hurt during the dead years if it did."

They entered the doorway and trekked down a tunnel, then arrived at a pocket door that led into a semicircular chamber. It certainly didn't *look* like it was above ground. Metal curved alongside the wall opposite them, ending at a steel door nestled into the corner of the room. Marina approached a stand near the entrance, where Pierce had set his voco face-down.

"I do that every shift," he explained. "It checks me in and lets the command system know I'm on duty. Where's *your* voco, by the way?"

Marina pulled her sleeve over her wrist. "I take it off before I sleep. Guess I forgot to put it back on."

Pierce frowned, but Marina didn't wait for him to challenge her. Luckily, it was easy to sidetrack him. When she turned to a map on the wall depicting the Delve's borders, he bounded up beside her and eagerly pointed to the markings.

"Our borders are built into the mountain faces," he said. "That way, every border offers us a vantage point. That's why it was such a hassle to get up here."

"And you almost fell down those stairs?"

"You *were* listening," he said through a grin. "The stairs are steep and the walk is shit, but from here, you can see the ocean."

Marina's heart fluttered. "Where do you see it?"

Pierce gestured for her to follow him to the wall with metal coverings, then pulled a lever at the end. "Here."

The coverings retracted, but instead of another dark hallway or chamber, the glassy hue of panes came into view, and with it, the world beyond.

It was more than she'd expected. Clouds of rose and cream flitted across a periwinkle sky, feathering at the touch of the morning sun. From here, she could see both the snowcapped Admares and the sea, which spanned so far that the entire world looked like glittering snow and ocean.

Marina put her fingers to her lips and exhaled. It could've been Earth, if not for the sun—larger and redder than the one she was used to, but gentler. And yet, despite being another confirmation that she was in a foreign place, what struck Marina most was the beauty. She'd expected Elsudra to look different—ravaged, even—because of Kieron. The horror stories she'd heard hadn't mentioned a world this beautiful.

"This is..." Marina's voice faded. No words could do the view justice.

Pierce pulled a chair to the center of the room, then perched on top of it instead of sitting. "I love the view," he said, "but sometimes it feels like it's mocking me from out there, knowing I'm here and I'll have to go below again."

"It's cruel," Marina said as she turned to face him. Though she knew it was silly, she cast a glance over her shoulder to make sure the view was still there.

Pierce's voice was little more than an echo. "It really is."

Though the windows called to her, so did the steel door. She pointed to it. "Where does that lead?"

"Wanna see?"

"You mean you can use it?"

"Technically. It's supposed to be an emergency exit, so sentries have access even if there are rules about when to use it." A mischievous smile tugged at his lips. "But after you arrived and Aeric could glamour entrances and put shields up, I peeked outside. I'm not allowed to use my voco to bypass anything unless there's an emergency—not unless I want to send the command center into a frenzy—but I can still feel the breeze. I'll show you."

Excitement ran amok in Marina's chest as Pierce put his hand to a scanner next to the door. When it clicked and pulled back into the wall, frosty air tinged her face.

She'd missed the feeling more than she'd thought—the clean, crisp breeze caressing her hair and making her skin prickle. The tightness in her shoulders eased, and for the first time since coming to this place, Marina could take a full breath.

The world outside, free from towering cavern walls, sang with brittle wind. It was quiet this high up—but not stagnant like it was below. Up here, the silence was soft.

The Delve truly *was* hidden in the mountains. The door was wedged into bedrock, and the threshold ended at a drop-off. The landing below eased into another unforgiving slope that plummeted into shrouds of snow-covered foliage.

"How do the scouts get outside?" Marina asked.

"They don't leave from the south. It's a nasty drop."

Marina peered once more over the threshold. She could see more than just the drop below. Farther out, pines and firs skirted along ocean-facing cliffs. A few had grown on steeper precipices, their roots splayed as they struggled to hold themselves upright. The range continued for miles, and Marina's gaze followed the trees as they twisted into the hills beyond—to the rest of Elsudra, she supposed, if one were to walk far enough.

She closed her eyes against the breeze. "Thanks for bringing me here."

"You deserve the view."

She tilted her head at the doorway, opening her eyes just enough to squint at it. "I don't see any glamour."

"Well, they're not tangible. Glamours bend light so people outside can't see our entrances. You may be able to catch a glint or two if you focus your eyes a specific way, but it takes practice. I've heard leaning back helps, but it's never worked for me."

Marina put her weight on her heels and peered at the hills, her eyes still half-lidded. It wasn't until she angled her head that a ripple purled in the air—a subtle bend of light that moved with the breeze.

"I see it," she breathed. That hadn't been hard at all. In fact, it had been intuitive.

Pierce blinked at her. "Seriously?" He almost looked jealous, but he laughed it off. "You're better at it than I am, then."

"*This* hides the Delve?"

"Yep. Someone standing outside wouldn't see us, but we'd see them. They might be able to detect a shift in energy or a change in the light, but it'd take them a while—especially if they didn't know exactly where to look."

"And the shield's invisible too?"

Pierce nodded. "We can't see it, but we know it's up." He angled his chin at a circular device just above the scanner, then pointed to the blue light at the center. "These monitor our entrances and exits. The command center is full of them. Blue means everything's intact, shields included. If it turns red, we have a problem."

Marina looked back to the door. "How strong are the shields?"

"Depends on the sorcerer who made it, I guess. Since Aeric made this one, I'd say it's pretty strong. Strong enough to withstand conventional force, at least, and the magic of lesser sorcerers."

"Could anyone *sense* the magic?"

"From the outside?" Pierce shrugged. "Maybe, but they'd have to be a really good sorcerer to do that, and even then, they'd have to find this place first."

"What happens if you touch the shield?"

"Would you be surprised if I told you I've already tried?" Pierce chuckled and put his hand to it. "It's like touching a wall. Can't push it out any farther than this."

Marina tentatively put her hand out. It made an impact with what felt like hard air, which was the strangest sensation she'd ever felt. "How do vocos bypass this?"

"They're programmed so the shield recognizes them and people can pass through both sides without destroying the magic. Prevents the Delve from being compromised."

"Are everyone's vocos programmed to do that?"

"Only some of the brown ones. Brown vocos are for our military unit, kind of like how blue ones are for the manor. The vocos belonging to higher-ups—like scouts, generals, and sentries at the northern border—have the most privileges, which means they can do things other ones can't, like bypass shields."

"What about silver vocos?" Marina ventured. "What can those do?" When Pierce only frowned at her, she said, "Aeric wears one."

"Probably everything, then. But I doubt Aeric needs magic-made technology when he has himself."

Marina tensed. "What if people need to get out of the Delve? If not everyone has a voco that can bypass the shields, wouldn't that put them in danger?"

"The higher-ups would be there for them," Pierce said. He sounded quite confident about it, and Marina tried not to look too skeptical. "But I don't see that happening. Not with the security we have and Aeric's newest reinforcements." After a moment's thought, he added, "I promise, we cover our bases. The military unit even has trackers in their vocos so the command center can follow them."

"*Just* the military unit?"

"Yeah, just us." He chuckled. "Is that why you didn't bring your voco up here?" When she didn't respond, he nudged her. "Just enjoy the view, okay? Nothing's gonna happen, and you'll run yourself into the ground worrying as much as you do."

Marina let loose a sigh as she brushed her fingers along the shield. She focused on the cool air, acknowledging but not fixating on her worries. For as long as this door was open, she was determined to feel at least *some* peace.

It was an unfamiliar but welcome feeling. Her anger had burned off, leaving her with

a tired kind of tranquility. "If I could go outside," she said, her hand still on the shield, "I'd go to the ocean. It's—" Humming beneath her fingers cut her off, and she recoiled. "Is it supposed to feel like electricity?"

Pierce snorted. "What did I tell you about running yourself into the ground? You're already going mad."

"I'm serious."

His smile faded. "It's not supposed to feel like *anything*. Try again."

Her curiosity trumped her common sense. At the first touch of her palm to the wall of air, the buzzing returned, and with it, light—from the shield or her own hand, she wasn't sure. She let it flicker, inhaling sharply as it grew. She knew she should remove her hand, but there was something peaceful about this feeling. Natural, even. The lights danced beneath her palm, illuminating the air that swathed the threshold.

When they brightened, Pierce paled. "Maybe you should step away."

The anxiety on his face was enough to fuel her own. She wrenched her hand from the light, but it didn't fade. Instead, it flared up, jumping and dancing as though her presence extended beyond her touch.

"Shit," Pierce breathed.

"It shouldn't..." Marina grasped for an explanation but found herself mute as she watched the lights ricochet. It was almost as though they were devouring the shield *and* the glamour.

"Can you make it stop?" Pierce asked.

"I don't even know how I made it *start*."

"Shit, shit, *shit*."

"Shut the door," Marina choked.

Pierce swore, then stepped toward the threshold, and light exploded outward.

The brightness was so overwhelming that all Marina could think to do was grab Pierce's arm, eyes shut as she searched within herself—fumbling in the darkness for some sliver of power that would quiet the blazing around her. Only she didn't know what had brought forth the lights in the first place, and by now, they'd become their own being. They lashed about, violent and uncontrollable. All she saw behind her lids were colors, pulsing at every beat of her heart, and then waves, glowing as though they held the sun.

Though her eyes were still half-closed, she could see Pierce's figure. He'd twisted out of her grip and was falling forward, limbs flailing. She reached out to grab him, but her arms weren't working like they normally did.

It took her a moment to realize why.

She was falling too.

CHAPTER 13
Little Thief

Pierce was right; it *was* a nasty drop. It happened too quickly for Marina to register she'd hit the ground, but once she had, the unforgiving slope didn't let up. Branches materialized without warning, cutting her face as rocks bit her limbs.

The fall ended as soon as it began. She slammed into Pierce, who lay on the ground moaning. As the world stilled, Marina's eyes rested on a branch just above her where a bunting fluttered its wings and sang.

Though the frost beneath her made her fingers ache, Marina didn't move.

Outside. She was outside.

The momentary peace she felt was interrupted by Pierce, who sprang to his feet and cursed. Slowly, Marina lifted her head, then stood.

"We crossed the threshold," Pierce sputtered. "We can't get back up there."

Shit. The wooded dell they'd landed in had bad visibility; she could see nothing but trees and rocks. She inhaled through her nose, back aching and limbs throbbing. *Stay calm.*

"There's no way to reach the entrance again?" she asked.

"Not unless you can make it up the slope *and* scale the drop-off, which doesn't seem too fucking likely," Pierce snapped, then winced. "Sorry. I just...Florin will kill me."

"I doubt that," Marina said.

Her reassurance didn't work. Pierce swore again. "This is the kind of shit I could get thrown out for."

"Out of the Delve?" When he didn't respond, Marina's chest constricted. "This wasn't on *purpose.*"

"I know, but..." Pierce ran his hands through his hair. "What I was doing—opening the door to get fresh air and all that—wasn't exactly allowed." When Marina blinked at him, he added, "I figured since the shield was up, the old rules weren't applicable. But it wasn't meant to do that...the threshold's supposed to be nearly impenetrable."

"Do you think the command center was alerted?"

Maybe Cal had noticed. Pierce had said that was one of her jobs, wasn't it? Maybe she could help them.

"I don't know," Pierce said. Marina followed his gaze up the slope, but it was covered in so many trees that she couldn't see far.

"You *don't know*?"

"I mean, I think so," he said breathlessly, "but I don't work in the command center. Even if they did register a breach, it'd take them too much time to get down here. The South isn't meant to be used as an exit; it's there as a last resort. And this forest...it's a shit place to be. Way too much coverage." He put his hand to his forehead and rattled off another long list of curses. "We should move to another border's territory...somewhere more open. Staying stationary leaves us at risk."

"At risk of what?"

Pierce drew his lips into a line. "There are things out here, Marina—things brought back from Sundra by Kieron. If we stay put, we're bait."

Blood roared in Marina's ears, and she knew she wasn't thinking clearly when she said, "I thought Sundra was a dead realm."

"What do you think made it that way?"

This was a new kind of fear—not the kind she felt around Aeric, but that which turned her bones to jelly.

"We'll go east," Pierce said. "The land isn't as forested, and someone at the eastern border will see us."

"You're sure?"

"No. But I have more faith in the East than I do in the South," Pierce said. "If we had our damned vocos, we could sound the alarms."

"But wouldn't that attract danger?"

Pierce shook his head. "Vocos use a frequency only we can hear. Makes it a foolproof way to call for help." He groaned. "Not like it matters. Mine's clocked in, and you...I can't believe you purposefully left yours behind."

"I didn't know this would happen!"

"I know. Not your fault." Pierce put his hands up, then gestured for her to follow, muttering something about how he wished he had a gun instead of his dagger. Marina hurried beside him, sticking to his side and cursing herself for not bringing her shears.

The cold stung her skin as they navigated clumps of snow and towering trees. Pierce relied on his general sense of direction, which was the most he could do given that the glamours concealed any hints of entrances.

Once the trees had thinned out and they'd made their way to a ravine surrounded by walls of ice and rock, Pierce whispered, "How did you do it?"

Marina tore her eyes from the sky above them—now the powder blue of late morning—and stilled her breath. "I'm not sure."

"You just touched the shield...and that happened?"

"Pretty much." She wrapped her arms around herself. "I saw waves when I closed my eyes. And light." *The Omnia.* Marina shivered and clamped her lips together.

"So...you wielded magic. Which means you *can* interact with the Omnia."

Silence fell, softer than the faint spindrift of snow in the air.

"I guess," Marina whispered.

If not for the circumstances, she might've been just as proud as she was shocked, but she didn't have room to feel anything. The cold numbed her emotions, and Marina found it easier to focus on walking than on whatever lurked inside her.

The ravine widened into a montane forest that smelled of pine and wet bark. Here and there, frost turned into piles of snow, which they tried to avoid to keep their footsteps soft. Still, Pierce winced at the slightest sounds.

As beautiful as the mountains were, she knew she'd be a fool to get caught up in them. She tried to drink in the deep greens of the trees and the contrast of snow to sky—tried to let the sunlight warm her as much as possible—but she kept moving east, trailing alongside Pierce and praying he knew the way.

When her fingers began to ache, she asked, "How far are we?"

"Close, I think," Pierce breathed. "Not sure it makes me feel any better."

Marina's stomach sank when she realized she shared his anxiety about facing Aeric and Florin. Aeric especially didn't seem to be the forgiving type, accident or not.

But she'd shown an inclination toward magic—*she*, the unpleasant surprise Aeric seemed to have lost all patience with. If she'd shown a sliver of the Omnia's power, perhaps she'd show more, and...

She could get home. She wouldn't need Aeric. Her goals would be hers alone, and she could remove herself from this mess once and for all. If Aeric truly wanted to remedy his mistake, he could take the damn Omnia himself.

Only, this show of magic had been minor and more dangerous than useful. If it reared its head again, would it be just as uncontrollable?

"We're well past where my view at the southern border ends," Pierce said, "which means we're in eastern territory. We'll move slower now, but I don't want to stop."

Since they were shaking, Marina figured movement would do them well anyway. As they trekked another half mile to a grove of aspen, she kept her eyes on Pierce, dissecting every emotion on his face and praying his anxiety didn't turn to panic.

The grove was quiet. Clusters of snow formed at spindled trunks, but by now, both Pierce and Marina were too high-strung to admire the beauty.

"They should've seen us by now," Pierce said. "The borders surround the Delve. That's the whole setup. We're supposed to see *everything*."

"Should we head back to where we were?"

Pierce shook his head. "The trees will grow sparser if we keep going east, and our movement will set off sensors at the borders. The closer we are, the more the Delve can pick up on. Let's hope..."

His voice trailed off.

"Hope what?"

Pierce put a finger to his lips. Marina held her breath, listening to the breeze that rustled the leaves on the aspens.

"Ruemin," Pierce hissed.

"What?"

He grabbed her arm, and Marina turned to the nearest bunch of trees.

She heard them before she saw them.

Click, click, click.

And then they emerged, as though they'd come from the shadows themselves. The creatures must've been seven feet tall. Anthropomorphic and clawed, their arms were almost as long as their legs, and black scales covered their bodies. Their faces were somewhere between humanoid and alien: long and gaunt, with pointed chins and slits for noses, covered in red flecks that looked as though someone had set fire to their skin. Their claws were as sharp as their teeth and just as silver as their eyes.

There were five of them—ruemin—but even that felt like too much. Marina couldn't feel her heart as she watched those shining eyes take them in. Despite Pierce's strong, wide stance, she knew he was afraid, for *these* were what roamed Elsudra's surface—the beings that had wiped out Sundra and killed Astra. The beings Kieron had somehow gotten on his side.

The mouth of one stretched up. Marina supposed it was smiling as it croaked, "Two," followed by more clicking, so shrill and high-pitched that Marina and Pierce winced.

"No." *Click.* "One Elsudran." *Click, click.* "And a thief." *Click, click, click.*

Its words were slurred, as though its mouth wasn't made to speak the language—as though the earpieces she and Pierce wore couldn't fully refine the sounds. It must have

sounded similarly unsettling in Pierce's native tongue because he tensed as he unsheathed his dagger.

One ruemin tilted its head, then let out a shriek so bloodcurdling that Marina ducked and covered her ears. A prong-like appendage jutted from its throat—from all their throats—but Marina couldn't see clearly enough to make out what it was.

Another ruemin wailed, then looked at her and uttered a guttural whisper. "It's here." *Click, click.*

"Leave. Now," Pierce commanded. He couldn't hide the trembling in his voice.

Another screech followed—this time from all five and so loud that even Pierce raised his hands to his ears—as the ruemin narrowed in on them.

One pointed a long, bony finger at Marina. "Take." *Click.* The finger shifted to Pierce. "Eat." *Click.*

Panic coursed through Marina, but she was present enough to notice the change in Pierce's demeanor. It was as though he'd accessed some deep inner quiet that softened his fear and fueled the resolve in his eyes.

At the first lunge of a ruemin, Pierce pushed Marina out of the way. The air careened from her as she hit the ground, leaving her gasping as Pierce snapped on his helmet. She never thought the day would come when she'd be glad to see that helmet, but it seemed the ruemin were even more terrified of it than she'd been. As they recoiled, Pierce leapt at them, and one of the ruemin let out an ear-splitting wail. Violet liquid rained down onto Pierce, and with a cracking pull, he wrenched his dagger from its eye.

The other four screeched and doubled over, as though they'd also been stabbed, only... they hadn't. They recovered quickly—not a scratch on them—then started toward Pierce again, enraged. Pierce was quick, though; he evaded several swipes of claws, then thrust his dagger into the nearest ruemin's shoulder.

Again, *all* the ruemin screeched and recoiled.

Through blurred vision, Marina met the eyes of one ruemin, which broke from its pack and started toward her. She tried to stand, but it had her by her neck before she could move. Its scaly hand tightened around her throat, but she knew it wouldn't kill her —not when Kieron needed the power she held.

If the Omnia were to make another appearance, *now* would be the perfect time. She tried to will it forward, but she was grasping at nothing. The sea within her refused to answer her call. The absence of what had sprung forth so unpredictably at the border sparked fury in Marina that she couldn't contain. She tore at the ruemin's face, hoping to rip its scales off and let them curl under her fingers like wallpaper, only for another claw to wrap around her wrists and pin her hands down. In defiance, Marina let out the most bloodcurdling scream she could.

The ruemin lifted her and hurled her back to the ground, knocking the scream from her. A croak—no, a laugh—bubbled from its throat.

"Little." *Click* "Thief." *Click.*

Thief? She didn't have much time to process that; screeches sounded as another ruemin fell to the ground. Two...Pierce had killed two. The ruemin on top of her howled again, but as Marina tried to pull herself out from underneath, it regained its senses and caught her by her neck.

And then, the ruemin was gone.

It flew off her, crashing into a tree so hard the wood cracked. Blinded by fear, Marina could barely make out Aeric's figure as he tore into the creature from afar.

A stockier man came into view beside Pierce, and with a single stroke of his sword, Florin decapitated the ruemin that had knocked Pierce to the ground. The last ruemin screeched, then released Pierce and hurtled toward the trees before Florin could reach it. Aeric, who must've been yards away, made a wide gesture with his arms, and the ruemin collapsed—scales ripping from its body as though Aeric was flaying it himself.

The snow on the forest floor was now a mix of the ruemins' inky blood and bits of fabric from Pierce's armored suit. Though she couldn't control her limbs enough to stand, Marina managed to catch sight of Pierce.

He was alive. She might've cried, had her shock not been so intense.

Pierce rushed to her, splattered in ruemin blood. With a trembling hand, he sheathed his dagger and retracted his helmet. Florin followed close behind, softening when he reached out to steady Marina.

"Are you hurt?" he asked, helping her up.

Marina shook her head. From the corner of her eye, she watched Aeric, who stared at the ruemins' carcasses before approaching them.

"Florin..." Pierce started.

Florin only shook his head as Aeric said, "We head back. Now."

Pierce remained quiet all the way to the border, his face drawn. Every once in a while, he glanced at Aeric and Florin, then winced in a way that made one thing clear: the ruemin didn't scare Pierce half as much as the wrath of the men before him.

Though Marina expected herself to feel similar anxiety, the fear didn't come. All she could think of was the quiet sea eddying within her.

CHAPTER 14
The Paths We Choose

It took minutes to get to the eastern border. With a movement of Aeric's hand, the air rippled, revealing a doorway, which Florin whisked her inside of. Before she could gather her thoughts, Ismene had come to take her back to the manor. At first, Marina thanked the heavens Aeric hadn't punished Ismene for telling Marina about his history with Kieron, but her relief quickly gave way to dread. Ismene was quiet and solemn; she hardly even acknowledged Marina. Tempting as it was, Marina knew there was no point in pretending like she hadn't betrayed Ismene's trust to strike back at Aeric—despite having promised to keep quiet.

"I'll start you a shower," Ismene said when they reached Marina's bedroom, "and get you a fresh set of clothes." Her words were clipped.

Marina eyed her. "Ismene..."

Her voice faded as Ismene turned away, and she resigned herself to silence as she cleaned up and changed. She didn't notice the scratches on her face until she sat in front of her vanity. Maybe *that* was why Ismene hadn't confronted her; she looked horrible.

Little thief, the ruemin had called her. What else could it have been referring to, if not the Omnia? The ruemin were loyal to Kieron, and Kieron wanted what she held.

A bitter laugh simmered at her lips. Thief—as though she'd willingly taken the Omnia for herself. As though it wasn't what had stolen her. The words echoed in Marina's mind as she slipped her voco back on and followed Ismene to Aeric's office.

Pierce sat in one of the chairs by Aeric's desk, looking like a scolded child. Now that he'd washed, she could better see the damage the ruemin had done to him. His face was bruised—though she wasn't sure if that was from the ruemin or the fall—and his arm was bandaged. Still, he smiled at her as she lowered herself into a chair.

Aeric sat at his desk, elbows on the table. Florin stood beside him, the weapons on his baldric glinting. When the silence came to a fester, Marina broke it.

"This is my fault," she blurted.

Aeric glanced up as Florin turned to face Marina. Pierce shot her a look as well, but she ignored him. Instead, she continued, "I convinced Pierce to take me to the southern border. He said it was against the rules, but I pushed until he gave in."

Pierce stayed silent, but she could feel his gaze on her as she spoke. Florin stood straight-backed, a stony expression on his face, while Aeric remained motionless, disgust in his eyes. Whatever. He already thought she was selfish and manipulative; let him continue to think it. She had less to lose than Pierce.

"While we were up there," she continued, "I made him open the door. When I reached out to touch the shield, it reacted. I couldn't stop it." She swallowed, her mouth dry. "We tried to head east, but..."

"You wielded magic," Aeric said when her voice trailed off.

Marina locked eyes with him and nodded. As jarring as everything was, she couldn't ignore her pride, especially given the shock on Aeric's face.

"You know the rules, Pierce," Florin said, his voice low. "They're not loose guidelines you can simply *give in* to."

"I only meant to take her to see the view."

"Where was your common sense? Something as precious as what she holds needs to stay here. Not at the borders—certainly not near any glamours or shields."

"She's a person, not a thing to be locked away," Pierce whispered.

Though the sentiment brought her warmth, Marina eyed Pierce to keep quiet.

"She is the Omnia's sole host, which, for all intents and purposes, makes her as important as our Keepers, if not more so," Florin said. "And at the moment, she does not have the strength needed to protect herself and what she carries. You know how dangerous that is. If even one of those ruemin had lived, they'd already have found and alerted the others. The news would carry quickly."

Pierce nodded. "I'm sorry."

Though Florin softened, the edge in his voice remained. "For doing what you could to protect her, I thank you. But you ran into a small group of ruemin. Five is nothing compared to what you could've faced."

"I know." Pierce's voice was meek.

Before Florin could respond, Aeric said, "You can take Pierce to the barracks."

Florin nodded, then gestured for Pierce to stand.

Marina looked to Aeric. "Can I leave too?"

"No."

Pierce squeezed her shoulder as he passed. She watched Florin and Pierce as they left the room, then shifted to Aeric and repeated, "This is my fault. Pierce said it wasn't allowed, but I ignored him."

The lie hung heavy in her chest, only to plummet to her stomach when Aeric said, "Try again." When Marina gawked at him, he shook his head. "You're lying, and you're not very good at it. Pierce offered to take you up there, didn't he?" He sighed. "I don't care why you were at the southern border; I only care that you were. I made myself clear when I said there are only two places you can't go. The borders are one of them. Did you not consider that I may have good reasons why?"

"I wasn't thinking..."

"Clearly not. The presence of something as intense as the Omnia is noticeable to ruemin. They can sense it—especially in such a concentrated form—and it drew them to you. You interacted with my shield, even if unintentionally, putting the Delve *and* Elsudra at risk. All due to your inability to *think*."

Marina stared at him. Just like with Ismene, she couldn't get herself to apologize.

"What happened at the border is a flicker of your potential," Aeric continued. "That's precisely why you need to stay here as your skills evolve."

"You can't be suggesting what I think you are." When he didn't respond, her pulse raced. "I'm not training with you again. I'd rather feed myself to ruemin."

She couldn't believe she'd said that out loud, even if it was true. Those fire-faced demons seemed a better fate than being branded and hung by Kieron. From now on, her goal was hers and hers alone. She'd learn enough magic to perform Locus and get herself home. She had no clue how to do either of those things, but if magic had brought her to this place, it could remove her from it. She just had to figure out how.

"Fine." Aeric's voice was unsettlingly calm. Marina blinked at him, expecting him to say something else, but he remained silent.

That was it? He wasn't going to fight her on it—wasn't going to force her?

"But if you go to the borders again," he said, "you *and* Pierce will be punished."

"Fine," she echoed, then left before Aeric could change his mind.

↶↷

Instead of retreating to her room, she left the manor. As she headed to the plaza, her heart in her ears, she lifted her voco to her mouth.

"Pierce, it's Marina. Meet me in the gardens when you can."

She needed to know he was okay—that he hadn't lost his station, or worse. It didn't seem like Aeric was planning to kick him out. He'd let her off with a warning; Pierce probably got the same. Still, by the time Marina reached the gardens and Pierce's message came in, she was on the verge of tears.

"Will do," he said, "but I may be a bit. I hope you're okay."

Her sigh of relief was audible. She put her head in her hands and breathed to bring herself back down. It was hard to ignore the urge to claw at her skin in a desperate attempt to wrench the Omnia from herself.

Locus. That was what she needed to concentrate on—that and cultivating her abilities so she could perform it safely. If she'd managed to wield magic on her own, who was to say she couldn't do it again, and intentionally this time? She could do things independently, without the threat of Aeric looming over her and bending her to his will. If she improved alone and kept her progress under wraps, he'd be unable to fulfill the Keepers' twisted wishes, and she'd get out of here as soon as possible.

Coward.

So what if she was? She didn't owe anything to Elsudra.

But Aeric did. And yet, he'd given up so easily. Why? Now that she'd shown an aptitude for magic, she'd expected him to push even harder. She wished she could see into his head. Things would make more sense if she could.

Whatever. She'd take this win without fuss if it meant she was closer to getting home. For the time being, she'd avoid Aeric like the plague. Once she was good and gone—and she would be, soon enough—she wouldn't have to worry about him changing his mind.

Her thoughts fizzled away, leaving the ruemins' screeches on repeat in their stead. She thanked the heavens when they, too, silenced, only to realize someone was sitting beside her. Marina lifted her head from her hands.

"Nice early evening, huh?" Ocot said, a brutish grin on his face. He was chewing something—some kind of gum. "But I guess they're all the same down here."

Great. Of all the people she could've run into, it had to be *him.*

Marina didn't respond, but Ocot wouldn't take her hint. He turned to face her and uttered an exaggerated wince. "Look at those scratches. I heard about the ruemin. We all did. What a day. Something like this hasn't happened since one of our scouts got disemboweled up above. Unfortunately for us, Pierce still lives." He barked a harsh laugh at Marina's expression. "I'm joking. Don't tell me Pierce's lack of humor rubbed off on you. Where is he, by the way?"

"No idea."

A popping sound bubbled from Ocot's mouth. "I'd say I'm worried about his punishment, but I'd wager Florin begged Aeric to let him off, just like Tover begged the

Keepers to bring him here. I'll give it to Pierce. He makes his nepotism work for him."

Ocot had clearly meant it as a slight, but all Marina felt was relief. He was right: Florin would protect Pierce out of loyalty to Tover. Pierce would be okay.

"Y'know," Ocot continued, "if you'd wanted to see the view beyond the Delve, you could've asked me. The tunnel down south leads to a cliff facing the ocean."

"I thought sentries didn't have access to tunnels."

Ocot grinned, his teeth coming down hard on each other as he smacked his gum. "I have my ways." When she didn't indulge him, he said, "Boris and I drink down there when he's on duty. You should join us. It's a lot safer than the borders. Even if you screwed up one of Aeric's shields, you wouldn't be able to get out unless you knew how to climb." He chuckled. "And you don't strike me as a climber."

Marina grimaced. She remembered what Pierce had said: Cal tracked scout and sentry whereabouts, and she went easy on Boris because of Astra. It didn't surprise her that Ocot manipulated Cal's sympathy.

You're a hypocrite if you judge him for that.

"What do you say?" Ocot droned. Either his chewing had grown louder, or Marina was imagining it. Regardless, she wanted to strangle him. "How about you throw out the old tour guide and look to more competent friends in the Delve?"

When Marina simply rested her gaze on a row of striped carnations, Ocot crossed his arms and said, "Seems I'd have to find Exorsus if I wanted answers from you. I'll credit your mood to your run-in with the ruemin—"

"What's Exorsus?"

Another grin sprang to life on Ocot's face, and Marina wished she hadn't asked. "*Now she talks,*" he said. "How about this? If you agree to come to me instead of Pierce, I'll tell you all about Exorsus and whatever else you'd like to know."

Marina hesitated. How much did Ocot know that Pierce didn't, especially if he served at a more active border? What knowledge might she forsake if she turned him away? She tried to sound more curious than accusatory when she asked, "What do you have against Pierce?"

"I can't stand freeloaders at the best of times, and this is *not* the best of times." He picked lazily at his nails. "You know he only wants to get close to you so he can have the admiration that comes with knowing the Omnia's host, right? His dad and Florin knew the Keepers, and all he wants to do is be like them. Someone that selfish doesn't deserve your presence."

Marina's grip on the bench tightened. Ocot wasn't wrong—why *wouldn't* an Elsudran want to get close to the newest host of the Omnia, however temporary that host may be?

She couldn't blame Pierce. So why did Ocot's remark hurt so much?

Though it pained her, Marina forced a smile. "Alright. Tell me about Exorsus."

Ocot stared at her for a moment, as though he hadn't expected her response. "It's a creation myth. Hardly as interesting as some of the other things I know."

"Such as?"

Come on, you idiot. Tell me something useful.

Marina stifled her groan when Ocot shrugged. She was tempted to call him on it—to tell him how two-faced he was being, insulting Pierce for wanting to get close to the Omnia's host while doing exactly the same thing—but if there was a chance he *did* know something worthwhile...

"What about Locus?" she asked. "Ever heard of that?"

Silence followed. She'd expected as much. But Ocot wasn't *entirely* useless, Marina supposed. The southern tunnel could be her saving grace if things took a turn for the worse. Best to keep Ocot around, irritating as he was. If everything went to shit, the best ally to have would be one of few scruples.

"Maybe I'll take you up on that drinking offer," she said.

"Just say the word. But do everyone a favor and ditch Pierce. He's no good for you. No good for any of us." Another loud *pop* sounded.

Marina couldn't bring herself to respond—couldn't bring herself to stay a moment longer and listen to that awful chewing. She scanned the gardens, her heart singing when she saw a woman polishing her cutlass beneath a wisteria tree.

Ismene was right; Cal *was* a blessing.

Marina smiled at Ocot again, hoping it would come across as genuine, then slipped away. She let out a sigh of relief when he didn't follow.

Cal sat with her head bent to her blade, hiding behind curtains of hair. Though Marina had a feeling she made it a point to be alone, she sat next to her anyway.

"I hope you don't mind," Marina said when Cal looked up. "I'm trying to get away from Ocot."

She only got a nod in response, but it was good enough. Marina glanced back to the bench she'd left, which was now vacant.

Cal set her blade aside. "I'm surprised you made it back."

Marina put her hand to her face. "Does everyone know what happened?"

"Everyone knows we came very close to the worst-case scenario today." Cal pursed her lips. "That was stupid what you did, you know. You and Pierce both."

Marina winced. "I know."

"You almost compromised the safety of the Delve and the Omnia. I'd attribute your choice to ignorance, only I don't think that's the case. But Pierce...Exorsus, that boy needs to grow up."

"I promise I wasn't trying to escape," Marina whispered. She looked Cal straight on, and if only to emphasize that bit—because it was true, she hadn't been trying to do *anything*—she repeated, "I promise. And Pierce was trying to make me happy by showing me the view. He didn't know I'd..."

"Overpower a shield," Cal said when Marina's voice trailed off.

Head fuzzy, Marina nodded.

"You, more than anyone, need to be careful," Cal said sternly. "You carry something powerful."

A damn nuclear reactor, Marina thought.

"I just hope your ruemin run-in was punishment enough," Cal added. "You wanted to see the surface? You got it. You're lucky it's no longer the dead years. Do you know how wasteful it would've been for the healers to scour your body and use precious resources to fix every scratch?"

Marina's stomach flipped. It was horrifying enough to think about the ruemin, but the implications of the dead years got worse each time she heard about them.

After a moment of silence, she whispered, "Ruemin cry out when another gets hurt."

Cal softened a bit. "They're a little like aspen trees." When Marina raised an eyebrow, she chuckled. "Aspens have a single root system. Ruemin are the same—they're one entity, even if their root system isn't visible. They feel what the others feel, and when one eats, they all do." She shrugged. "It makes the business up above much more satisfying. I like knowing that each time I kill a ruemin, the others feel the pain too, even if it only lasts a few seconds. They may not know where the pain is coming from—they don't seem to have connected minds, from what we've observed—but I consider it a victory anyway."

"That's what you do as a scout? Kill ruemin?"

"We stayed away from them during the dead years—didn't want to risk unnecessary injury. We weren't always successful, though." Cal's lips twitched, but she regained her composure. "Mostly, we gather intel and make sure Kieron's forces aren't nearby. Now that the dead years are done, we gather food when we can. But every once in a while, there's cause for killing ruemin. Can't say I mind it much."

"What are your helmets for? The ruemin seem to hate them."

"The Sundrans made them before we did. We think they resemble what might've been a predator back in the ruemins' original realm."

Marina tensed. She had no desire to learn what kind of monster the ruemin, of all creatures, fell prey to.

"It's just a theory," Cal said. "The helmets don't prevent ruemin from attacking, but they freak them out. Gives us more time to prepare."

Silence followed, and Marina tried to forget the sound of clicking throats.

Cal sighed. "I could lecture you more—could tell you how horrible those things are. The population of Sundra used to be in the millions, but after years of fighting the ruemin, hardly any Sundrans remained. Those who did were completely at the mercy of the beings they'd let into their realm. When the ruemin realized their food source was running out, they tried to breed the Sundrans like animals. Eventually, the Sundrans decided self-inflicted extinction was the kinder way out."

This time, Marina's stomach didn't just flip; it dropped—so suddenly she felt like she was going to be sick. Ismene had said that Sundrans had turned to mass suicide to avoid living like livestock. This had to be what she'd been referring to.

Marina's nausea worsened when Cal added, "Somehow, I think Kieron might be worse. He's the only prisoner to have survived the ruemin, and nobody knows how. Now, they do his bidding and he makes sure they eat their fill." She paused, then said, "You're safe here in the Delve. You'd do well to remember that."

Marina nodded again, numb.

"You know," Cal said, decidedly gentler now, "if you're trying to avoid Ocot, the gardens aren't the best place to be. He and other sentries come here a lot."

"Are the others as bad as him?"

"Ocot is a singularly miserable creature," Cal said. "If you want to spend time alone, go to the sea cavern. That's where I go when I need to get away from people." When Marina blinked at her, Cal smiled knowingly. "It's better than the borders."

A wisteria petal broke from the tree, and Marina watched it fall. When it settled at the foot of the bench, she said, "Thank you...for calming me down that night."

Cal nodded, then went back to inspecting her blade. Though Marina wasn't sure why, she said, "I heard about your sister. I'm sorry that happened."

For a moment, she wondered if perhaps she'd been too brash. Cal, however, only shrugged. "When you're up above, you need to be prepared for that. Astra was. Me, on the other hand...not so much. But it's the way things are."

"Do you ever wish you could change the way things are?"

"Who doesn't?" Cal tucked a strand of hair behind her ear. "But it helps me to know I still have power over small things, like the choices I make." She turned her blade, which shined in the garden lights. "We may not be able to control the way of the world, but we can control the paths we choose." She stood and slipped her blade into the scabbard on her hip. "Just do us all a favor and choose to stay down here so you don't nearly fall into

Kieron's clutches the next time the Omnia does whatever it does. Because if he wins, we'll no longer have any paths to choose from."

Marina took a shaky breath. "Noted."

She wasn't sure how long she sat in the gardens after Cal left, but by the time the lights had dimmed, signaling night, her eyes were heavy. Still, she refused to leave. She couldn't bear not having heard from Pierce.

Florin will protect him, remember? Even Ocot said it.

Her mental reassurances didn't do much, and so she sat, desperately waiting for Pierce to arrive.

Breathe. One breath. Another. What could she choose in this moment? She could choose to remember her mother's words—to focus on her breaths until...

Marina's heart stopped when her voco beeped.

"Sorry for not calling sooner," Pierce said. "Can't meet today, but I'm fine. Can we meet tomorrow afternoon? I'll come to you at the manor. I have good news."

He was okay. Thank God, he was okay.

She responded in agreement, too exhausted to question him, and determined more than anything to get a good night's sleep so she didn't feel so awful tomorrow.

She could barely keep her eyes open by the time she made it to her room, but a tray of food—left by Ismene, of all people—roused her. Next to it, a note in pretty handwriting read: *Remember to eat today.*

Ismene. The person she'd betrayed, all to satiate her vendetta against Aeric. How could a person be so kind? So forgiving?

Perhaps she should apologize. Yes...she should. Even if she wouldn't take back what she'd said to Aeric in the hallway, she couldn't help but feel bad for Ismene, whose kindness had gotten her caught in the crossfire.

Tomorrow, Marina thought. *I'll apologize tomorrow.* That would be her first of many choices. The future was terrifying, and she hadn't the slightest idea what choices she'd need to make to ensure survival, but this next one was doable.

CHAPTER 15
Only Water

She'd planned to come right out and say it. But when Ismene came with breakfast that morning, all Marina could manage was, "You don't need to be my maid. If you tell me where the kitchens are, I can get food myself."

Ismene's lips twitched. "If you wish. First floor, right side of the manor." Her voice was pleasant, even when she was unhappy.

For God's sake, apologize. Why is this so hard for you?

"Ismene, I..."

"You don't need to say anything," Ismene whispered. "You've been dealing with a lot. I don't know what I expected when I told you about Aeric and Kieron."

The urge to agree and end the conversation was tempting. Besides, Ismene seemed to be the type of person to let it go.

Marina dug her fingernails into her palms. Though the words stuck to her throat, she said, "No. It's my fault. I'm sorry."

There. See? That wasn't so hard.

Still, when Ismene's gaze met hers, Marina wanted to disappear.

"He was furious I told you," Ismene said. "Said he'd have thrown me out if I wasn't so competent at my job."

Marina shifted awkwardly. "Well, that's good, though. The compliment, I mean."

She kicked herself for saying that. Nothing about this was good. Hastily, she added, "I hadn't planned on telling him. But he was pushing me, and then I overheard him and Florin, and I snapped. And then he—"

"My parents would do this," Ismene said. "They'd use dirt they had on each other to win arguments. And they'd abuse the trust of their daughters so they could add another point to their imaginary scorebook." Shame burned through Marina as Ismene continued, "I know choices like these are born out of anger and hurt, but we're all hurting here—each and every one of us. I wanted to ease your hurt, but all I did was add fuel to the fire."

Can you blame me for lashing out? Marina wanted to say. She'd been backed into a corner like a dog, then scolded when she bit. Her face heated, but when she remembered what Cal had said, she forced herself to choose the better path.

"I'm sorry," she said, and this time, her voice didn't sound so croaky.

Ismene smiled weakly. "I accept your apology, Marina. We're all trying to do what we think is best."

She said it genuinely, but the pain in Marina's gut only worsened. Ismene likely accepted every apology. What would she say to the others that clawed at Marina's throat and bubbled at her mouth?

I'm sorry I'm going to try to find a way to leave this place. I'm sorry I can't help you.

She'd probably accept those too. Regardless, Marina couldn't utter them.

She invited Ismene to come meet Pierce with her, finding measly solace when Ismene accepted as though Marina's betrayal was a distant thing of the past—something she was happy to forget. Was she truly so quick to forgive?

If anyone should hold the Omnia, it should be someone like her, Marina thought.

She'd hoped apologizing would lessen the guilt, but it had grown by the time they reached the manor steps where Pierce waited. He and Ismene exchanged pleasantries like friends who hadn't spoken in far too long, and as Ismene inquired about Pierce's injuries, Marina tried not to look as perturbed as she felt.

Luckily, Pierce was more talkative than usual, which gave Marina a much-needed reprieve. Apparently, he'd been removed from his position in the South—something he seemed strangely giddy about—and a few other sentries had been assigned his shifts.

"Ocot was one of them," Pierce said. He laughed. "Wish I could've seen the look on that dipshit's face when he got the news."

Something sharp nipped at Marina's lungs. Pierce would no doubt be upset if he learned she'd accepted Ocot's half-baked request at friendship...or whatever it was. Even though she knew she shouldn't care—*focus on getting home,* she reminded herself—she decided not to tell him.

"I bet he's upset," Ismene said. "Ocot treasured his station in the East."

"He'll get over himself. Technically, he still has it; he's just not there as often as he used to be."

"Still. Other sentries may not mind, but he's..."

"Obsessed with status." A muscle feathered in Pierce's jaw. "Anyway, it's not just Ocot

I'm happy about. Turns out I was removed so I could be given a better job."

That caught Marina's attention. She raised an eyebrow.

"Guess it occurred to Florin and Aeric that even in the Delve, it'd be a good idea to ensure your safety," Pierce said. "It's a precaution. Useless at worst, pivotal at best. With the Omnia's power coming to life, it's probably smart you're not alone, just in case another incident happens again." He monitored Marina's reaction as he added, "That job was assigned to me."

Marina gawked at him. "Are you serious?"

"I won't be with you all day," Pierce said quickly. "Aeric said you'd throw a fit if you felt like you were being watched constantly. Besides, in the mornings, I'm set to train with the scouts, which means I'll be getting more combat practice than most sentries."

Beaming, Ismene said, "What a delightful turn of events! Especially after your... mistake." She said it mildly, as though she was trying to lessen the severity of what they'd done. But it *had* been severe. Not being punished was one thing, but why was Pierce being rewarded?

"Why would they choose *you* after what happened?" Marina asked.

Pierce chuckled sheepishly. "It was Florin's idea. He said you wouldn't accept anyone else, and technically, it keeps me off the borders."

Marina remembered what Ocot had said about Pierce making his nepotism work for him. Maybe he did. But why should she care? At least he was okay.

"I won't act like a shadow," Pierce added. "I'm just happy we can spend time together."

Was he really? Or was he simply excited to have another excuse to get close to the Omnia's host, like Ocot had said?

If she played things right, though, maybe Pierce could help her learn about Locus. She didn't need to tell him her plan—she wasn't stupid enough to think he'd help her with it—but if he didn't *know*...

Marina considered for a moment, finding it both odd and endearing how anxiously Pierce awaited her answer. When she accepted, he and Ismene broke into smiles, and something warm flickered in Marina—something familiar, but far away.

Despite going on about her busy schedule, Ismene stayed with Pierce and Marina a while longer. She was good at keeping the conversation light, and when paired with Pierce's jokes, Marina felt like she was back home, speaking with friends. She remembered these kinds of conversations—the easy ones where she didn't have to plan what to say or flounder in silence. By the time Ismene returned to her work and Pierce suggested a trip to the library, Marina's spirits were strangely high.

Regardless, she couldn't let her emotions distract her. Besides, Pierce and Ismene didn't view her as a friend. They viewed her the same way everyone else did—a *host*.

She didn't fault them for it. If anything, it made it easier for her to focus on her goal. If she wanted to scout out magic-based knowledge, the library was the best place to start.

Pierce, thankfully, was more than happy to help.

"You started something up at the border," he said as he plucked a few books from the shelves. "Imagine how much more you could learn if you knew what to do."

It was good he was excited, she figured. At least her own eagerness wouldn't seem so suspicious.

"I trained with Aeric a little," she ventured.

Pierce looked up from the stack of books he held. "Will you continue?"

God, no, she wanted to say. *He's horrible and terrifying and would sooner sign my death certificate than show me mercy.*

"Maybe later," she said, straining to sound casual. When Pierce frowned, she added, "We hit a wall. And I'm..."

"Scared of him?"

Marina opened her mouth to protest, but Pierce chuckled. "You're not the only one," he said. "I almost passed out in his office yesterday."

She hadn't expected him to react so indifferently to that. A smile tugged at her lips. "I *did* pass out once. The first time I met him."

"I think Ismene may be the bravest person here, working with him so closely." He paused, considering, then said, "How about you train with me? I may not know all the technicalities of magic, but I bet I could find resources that'd help. Maybe you'll improve quicker than you think."

Marina nodded. "I'd like that." Then, carefully, she added, "Have you heard of Locus?"

"It sounds familiar, but I don't remember anything about it. Why?"

"Aeric said I should learn it," Marina lied. "If we could find information on it, I bet it'd help."

"Ah...okay. Well, I'd have to look."

Marina gladly accepted his response. It was better than nothing.

After finding a few books to settle down with, Pierce said, "What did Aeric suggest when you trained with him?"

Marina tensed. "Mostly just meditation, but I wasn't any good at it."

"It's a good place to start. We do it as soldiers all the time—helps us draw on our skills. I don't think there are many books on that...not here, at least. But I *do* remember

Florin having us read documents about the use of higher-level magic, and those included some helpful tips."

"What kind of higher-level magic?"

Pierce shrugged. "Remember how I told you Florin has his soldiers study up on history? Well, he made those of us in the Delve read a bunch of stuff about military involvement with magic. Guess it made sense, given everything going on. I told you, he's a real history buff, just like my dad. He has us study as much as he has us train."

"Did any of Florin's documents mention Locus?" She was grasping at straws.

"They might've. But we wouldn't be able to read them unless we got the go-ahead from him or Aeric. Rules of confidentiality and all that."

So *now* he cared about rules. Marina tried not to scowl.

"Luckily, meditation's an intuitive thing," Pierce said. "Give it a few tries and see what works for you."

Marina resisted the temptation to press him further. There was no way Aeric would let her access those documents, especially if they included information about Locus. Since pushing it too hard with Pierce would probably bode just as poorly, Marina gave in and closed her eyes, trying not to think about how horribly her last attempt at meditation had gone. But Aeric wasn't here now. The library was empty, minus her and Pierce, who sat in a corner surrounded by towering shelves.

Even if the silence was peaceful, Marina's head put up quite a fight. When she peeked at Pierce, she caught sight of his bruises, only to flinch as crimson-flecked faces flashed before her.

Kieron haunted her too, even more when she closed her eyes. How could this name without a face evoke fear so stifling? Every time she thought of him—of who he was and how he may be her end—the urge to learn Locus grew stronger.

The documents Pierce mentioned weren't the only things that appealed to her. What was on the third floor of the manor that Aeric didn't want her to find? Insight about Locus? A way home?

She wasn't sure it was a risk she was willing to take right now, but it was an option. A dangerous, unpredictable option, but an option nonetheless. Come the day she ran out of others, it may be her last hope.

For now, she'd try her hand at magic and maybe find a way to get the documents Pierce had mentioned. He probably wouldn't be much help with the latter, but his eagerness to help her train ignited her hope. Maybe—just maybe—she'd learn what she'd previously thought impossible. That was, if she could get her head straight. What was she supposed to be doing again? Right...meditation. How the hell did people quiet their minds? Hers wouldn't shut up.

"How's it going?" Pierce whispered.

Marina sighed through her nose. "I'm not getting anywhere."

"You will. Just be patient with yourself."

Though she appreciated his confidence, she couldn't hide her frustration. Pierce gave her an encouraging smile, then leaned forward and placed an open book on her lap.

"The Omnia is like a sun," he explained, and though Marina wasn't sure where he was going with this, she listened, because it was better than trying to meditate again. "Its light shines everywhere, but only some people can manipulate it. Even then, those people don't *possess* magic. They can just interact with what radiates from the Omnia itself, like a solar cell converting sunlight into energy."

Marina peered at the page before her, where a black-and-white illustration depicted tendrils of energy bursting from a ring at the center.

"But you're an exception," Pierce said. "You *do* possess the Omnia, and you have the talent needed to wield its magic. You have everything you need within you. Don't focus on becoming a meditation expert; just do what feels right. Pull on the waves you mentioned. And if nothing happens, so be it. It's about taking things slowly and finding peace in the chaos."

One day, one step, one breath at a time.

Though part of her resisted, Marina closed her eyes again.

Her waves. That's what she needed to harness. Aeric had said that as well, but around him, they were much too violent to control. With Pierce, however, her sea was calm, and somewhere in her mind's eye, she could make out the Omnia's light—bioluminescence that glowed beneath the water, teeming with energy as each wave came and went, washing away the unknowns and cleansing her with salt.

Though she wasn't sure where it would take her, she let her waves encapsulate her, then free-fell into them.

❧

Nothing more happened that day, but Marina didn't mind. She was making progress, even if minimal, and that was good. When she woke the next morning from a fitful sleep, the dread that usually greeted her didn't come. She stirred, groggy and content, as her waves played on repeat in her head. And when she opened her eyes, waves were what she saw.

They hung above her, a blanket of seawater rippling and curling under the ceiling, illuminated by the floodlights outside. For a moment, time seemed to halt, and Marina lay unmoving as she watched the yellow-blue tide glitter and swirl. Then she took a breath, and the water came crashing down.

Marina shrieked and rolled off the bed, though it didn't do much good; the water came from everywhere, drenching both her and every inch of the room. If the sight of floating waves hadn't jolted her awake, the cold certainly did. She raised her voco to her mouth and sputtered, "Ismene, I need help."

She was still shaking when Ismene arrived minutes later, breathless. The moment Ismene stepped onto the sopping carpet, she gasped. "What...?"

"Me," Marina breathed, wrenching herself off the ground and leaning against the slippery bedpost. "I did this." She brushed away the wet hair that clung to her face. "Waves. There were waves..."

Marina pointed to the ceiling. Ismene winced when she looked up, as though she expected more water to fall.

"I didn't mean to," Marina said. "It...it was there when I woke up. Above me, like I'd summoned it out of thin air."

"I don't think that's how it works." When Marina blinked at her, she said, "I only mean...you can't summon something from nothing. This may've come from the sea cavern." She put a hand to the glistening walls. "I'll alert Aeric. He'll know." When Marina paled, Ismene said, "You don't have to come with. Go see Pierce. And don't worry yourself over this. The staff will have it cleaned up in no time. It's only water."

~

Pierce brought her to the training ring that afternoon, which had been cleared out for the day. Marina's news thrilled him, and he spent a ridiculous amount of time pressing her for details. Though she was more unnerved than excited, she agreed to continue practicing meditation. Improvement, discomforting as it was, was her only way forward.

The southern building that housed the training ring was, at most, a dilapidated warehouse, but Marina imagined the sentries still got good use out of it. The ground was packed hard with sand scuffed about by morning training, and steel wire ran from the floor to the ceiling, forming a cage that made the ring look like a zoo.

It was intimidating to sit on the sand—to feel the divots beneath her fingers and think of the combat practice that happened here. Much to her relief, Marina's training wasn't so active. She and Pierce started with meditation, then turned to the books Pierce had brought, which they searched for anything that might be helpful. A few chapters discussed broad categories of magic, but none went into detail beyond that. Worse still, none of the books mentioned Locus.

"I looked," Pierce said. "I really did. But I wouldn't be surprised if information about

Locus is classified, especially if it involves the Omnia directly." He paused, then asked, "Why can't Aeric teach you?"

Marina's fingers tightened around a clump of sand. "It's...not within his expertise."

Pierce nodded absently. She wasn't sure if he bought that, but he didn't challenge her.

"Let's focus on water first," he said. "You summoned some last night, and I *know* it was because of your meditation. If you use that as a stepping stone, I'll bet you can work toward more deliberate magic."

"How are you so sure?"

"I knew someone who had magical talent, remember?" He said it jovially, but the light in his eyes dimmed all the same. "I may not know much, but my memory's not *that* bad."

Marina snorted. "I'll do my best."

A good five minutes passed with nothing. Her thoughts were particularly stubborn today. The seawater she'd woken to, the Omnia, Locus...every time one thought entered her head, two more followed. When Marina began thinking of her dad's guitar collecting dust, she swore and rubbed her temples.

"My head won't shut up. Again."

"Don't force it," Pierce said. "It's like quicksand. The harder you fight, the more you sink. Let the thoughts come and go, but don't pay mind to them. You won't get anywhere if you're at war with yourself."

That's who I'm always at war with, Marina thought.

She didn't say it out loud, though; she settled on a conceding nod instead.

Though her head buzzed just as loudly on her next try, she directed her focus not toward fighting her thoughts but simply acknowledging them. They came and went with her waves, rising and falling, cresting and curling. With every touch of water to the confines of her mind, briny residue remained—*don't think about Locus, just think about this moment*—only to be washed away by the next wave, and the next, and the next.

Her fear didn't budge; she'd expected that. Like the roaring sea within her, it had made a home in her mind long ago. But it didn't need to be fought. Not now.

There was peace in that realization, and it brought a rush of tears to her eyes. What else gave her peace? The ocean, like the one beyond the southern border. She let herself get lost in the memory—in the glittering water that surrounded snowcapped mountains, sleeping beneath the sun.

A soft pitter-patter on her skin brought her back.

Marina looked up, blinking through the droplets that clung to her lashes. She cupped her hand and reached out to catch the water, keeping her mind and thoughts steady as she whispered, "It's raining."

Pierce beamed. "*You* made it rain."

Marina let out an excited exhale of her own. She watched the water fall, still immersed in the tranquility she'd lulled herself into, and when she willed the rain to die down, it obeyed.

She put her hand to her lips, savoring the droplets on her skin. When she tasted salt, she furrowed her brow.

"This isn't rain," she whispered. Curiosity overtook her, and she pressed the tip of her tongue to the back of her hand. "It's seawater, like this morning." She wrinkled her nose, then broke into a smile when Pierce pulled her up and hugged her.

"You're a natural, Marina," he said, his eyes shining.

The weight on Marina's shoulders eased a bit. "I wouldn't say that." Offhandedly, she added, "It's only water."

"*Only* water? Are you kidding? You've taken a massive step forward."

She giggled. "Took me long enough. I've always been a bit of a late bloomer."

Pierce beamed. "If we keep practicing, there's no saying what you'll do."

Maybe he was right. She just had to keep her head down and focus—had to take things in ones and avoid getting bogged down by future worries. Though Locus hung over her head like an ominous shadow, she tried not to let it plague her.

One day at a time.

She spent the rest of the day with Pierce, and when she returned to the manor that evening, she even asked Ismene to show her the kitchens.

She knew her way around the Delve better now. That paired with the successes of the day left Marina in a calmer headspace, and when she succumbed to sleep, waves and voices greeted her.

Marina, Marina, Marina.

Though she still couldn't make them out, they sounded more familiar than ever. Perhaps some distant, buried part of her knew who was speaking.

Marina, Marina, Marina.

CHAPTER 16
High Places

As days blended together, things fell into a routine. Pierce met her outside the manor every day at noon, and they'd spend the next half hour loitering around the kitchens while they packed themselves food to bring south.

On her rare days off, Ismene joined them. She always brought a book with her, though she rarely read it. Usually, she preferred watching, her eyes wild with excitement when Marina showed any indication of magical ability.

It was unpredictable when the magic showed up. On the days Marina felt she'd mastered her emotions, she'd get nothing, only to have it flare up the next when she was considerably less focused. But as time passed, her control strengthened, and eventually, things like summoning water became easy. One evening in the gardens, she managed to coax a cluster of goldenrods into bloom, which left Ismene speechless and Pierce elated.

Though Marina oscillated between eagerness and nerves, she kept going. Power simmered within her, and the more she pushed herself, the better she could sense the presence in her dreams. Something was there, far beneath the waves—waiting, perhaps, until she was strong enough to call it forth.

Home, she'd remind herself when she grew anxious. *You'll find a way home.*

Of course, the dark hallways of home paled in comparison to the garden lights. In the evening, flowers bathed in splashes of color, and Marina stayed as long as she could to bask in the glow. Ismene would join her on occasion, and the two would meander the pathways and talk. Much like Marina and Pierce, Ismene loved reading. Horror, it turned out, was her favorite genre.

"*You* like horror?" Marina asked, dumbstruck. The lights had dimmed so low that their colors coalesced, glinting off Ismene's hair like bursts of the cosmos in a pitch-black sky.

"Of course," Ismene said. "Why? You don't?"

"I love horror. I just didn't expect you to."

"It's my guilty pleasure. There's nothing better than a good bloodbath." She paused, then added, "*Imaginary* blood bath."

Marina laughed. "Any recommendations?"

"I haven't been to the library in ages. Even coming here is a change. I didn't realize how long I'd been cooped up in the manor. Pathetic, isn't it?"

"Not at all," Marina said. Gently, she added, "I'll get some horror books for you next time I'm in the library. I'll try to find the gory ones."

"With *lots* of blood," Ismene teased.

When more people began to leave, Ismene decided to turn in as well. Marina almost went with her, but a burly figure a few yards away caught her attention.

It had been a week or so since she'd last spoken to Ocot, and at first, she'd planned on avoiding him. She hadn't ditched Pierce, after all—if anything, they'd grown closer—and she knew Ocot would badger her about accepting his stupid drinking invitation. She had no desire to trek those tunnels with him and Boris, but Florin's documents lingered in Marina's head. If anyone was brash enough to get them for her, it would be Ocot. She couldn't let this opportunity go to waste—not if there was a chance they might include *something* about Locus. It was a better option than trying to break into the third floor.

After making a casual mention about wanting to take another stroll through the gardens, she and Ismene parted, and Marina made her way over to Ocot. He stood with a small group of sentries, his back turned to her. Dane was with him, but the others, Marina didn't know.

Good God, what have I come to? Ocot was a can of worms she really didn't want to open, but what other choice did she have? Pierce wouldn't get those documents for her, and she couldn't bear not knowing what was in them.

Ocot held a bottle of alcohol in his hand, and when Marina tapped his shoulder— hating herself for stooping so low—the smell of booze tinged her nostrils.

He brightened when he turned around. Dane blinked at her, his brow knitted.

"Look who it is!" Ocot said. His words slurred a bit. Was that even allowed? The other sentries weren't drinking. And how had he even acquired an entire bottle of liquor?

She forced a smile. "Can I speak to you?"

Ocot took a swig. "Anything for a *friend*, Marina," he said, smirking at the others.

"Alone, preferably," Marina said. The sentries blinked at Ocot, and Marina gave them a polite nod so she didn't seem rude.

"About what?" Dane asked.

"None of your business," Ocot said, then began to laugh. He shoved his bottle into Dane's hands, then grabbed Marina's wrist and led her away.

Maybe this was a horrible idea. Still, she tried to sound confident. If she was already knee-deep in this pile of shit, she might as well go all in.

"I have a small favor to ask," she said. "I heard Florin had you all read documents about magic use in Elsudra as part of your training." When Ocot frowned at her, she added, "It makes sense. I bet sentries need a *lot* of knowledge, especially when it comes to the military and government and...all that."

She hoped her tone would rouse Ocot's ego, but he only snorted and said, "Who'd you hear that from?"

"I overheard sentries talking." That seemed believable enough. "Sound familiar?"

"Yeah."

When he didn't expand, she said pointedly, "Would you know where to find them?"

"Why?"

Marina swallowed her groan. "I'm looking for resources that'll help me wield magic, and Florin's documents may have information I need. It's part of my training."

"You want *me* to get them for you?" When Marina nodded, Ocot let out another harsh laugh. "Why not ask Aeric?" He grinned when she didn't respond. "I know the documents you're talking about," he said. "I'd have to jump through a lot of hoops to get them for you. And if I get caught carting off confidential material..."

"I'll remember my real friends here," Marina said, "especially as I improve. I'm sure the Keepers had trusted protectors they relied on. If the time comes when I need someone to stand by me, I'd pick people willing to take risks for the Omnia."

The words left behind a horrible aftertaste, which soured even more when Ocot's eyes glinted. But she needed those documents—needed *anything* that would help her get home.

Pierce and Ismene would be so disappointed. A rush of anger followed the thought. She couldn't—*wouldn't*—be led astray by sentimentalities. She didn't belong here.

Ocot frowned. "I'd have thought that honor would go to Pierce."

"Pierce deserted Altus. How do I know he won't desert me?"

I'm a horrible person. A horrible, cowardly person.

Ocot blinked at her, as though he hadn't heard her correctly. She held his gaze, and after a moment, he chuckled. "Smart," he said. "I worried when I saw you with him— thought he'd sunk his claws in before you had time to learn who he really is."

"I let him hang around. But I know who deserves my trust."

Her chest tightened so severely that she wondered if it would suffocate her. *This is life or death,* she told herself. *This is about you getting out. Don't think about anything else.*

Survival, it seemed, was a terribly selfish business.

And yet, she couldn't help but notice how easy it was to lie to Ocot. Perhaps it was because she wasn't scared of him. If only she felt this way about Aeric. Manipulating *him* wouldn't make her feel so guilty.

"What about joining Boris and me in the southern tunnel?" Ocot mused. "We bring some of the best drinks from the kitchens."

He couldn't be serious. He was still going on about that after what she'd offered?

"Sure," she said. "That too."

When Ocot smiled, the garden lights danced off his teeth. "I'll do what I can."

Marina's heart sped up. "Really? You're sure you can find them?"

"There's a classified storage room in the northern barracks."

"Can sentries access them?"

"Have a little faith in me, Marina. Scouts can, and I'm good friends with a scout."

Boris. He was going to implicate Boris in this.

"You're sure Boris will agree?"

Ocot patted Marina's shoulder. "Let me handle that. Like I said: anything for a friend. Especially those in high places."

High places. What a joke. If she were truly powerful, she wouldn't need Ocot to steal for her—wouldn't need to chase every tiny possibility in the hopes that one would lead her home. She'd be able to do more than summon water and manipulate flowers. She'd be far gone from this place, safe and alone, and the Omnia would be a distant memory.

Soon enough, she told herself.

⌒

She didn't hear from Ocot for three days, which sent her stress through the roof. She tried to use her heightened emotions as a challenge to achieve inner quiet, and though a month ago she would've scoffed at the idea, meditation helped. Pierce even suggested she practice mental shielding, which she was open to now that Aeric wasn't around to threaten her with psychometry.

Of course, it was hard to work with Pierce when she thought about the things she'd said. What if Ocot repeated them? She could claim she'd said it out of desperation, but that would do precious little to remedy the damage. She hadn't meant it. She *did* trust Pierce, and she could hardly blame him for what he'd done in Altus. She was doing the same thing now, wasn't she? Preparing to flee?

She pushed the guilt down, praying it wouldn't swell up and pour over. Still, she could feel it simmering—could feel it burn her insides whenever Pierce greeted her or shot her smiles during meditation.

Don't think about it. Just focus on your goal, she'd remind herself.

Pierce seemed to think things would happen in bursts, just like with the border and seawater incidents. For someone who'd been so adamant about not understanding the technicalities of magic, he certainly had no shortage of helpful tips. Even if they didn't all lead to tangible progress, Marina could feel their effects, and not just during the day. The murky waters in her dreams remained, but they were different. With every ebb current, the sea rose.

Marina, Marina, Marina. It was there, then it wasn't—that fleeting, dark glimpse. It beckoned her, and Marina listened. Watched.

It would've been the end of January back at home—Calcite's eighth week—when Ismene stopped joining them on her days off. According to Pierce, Double Moon was coming up, and Ismene had taken charge of preparation.

"She does this every year," Pierce said as they left the training ring one evening. "It's weeks away, but she insists on supervising the whole process. I feel bad for those who help her; she can have a real iron fist when she wants to. I bet she'll be even more uptight this time around. We aren't just celebrating a new year—we're celebrating a new era." He looked at Marina, his eyes alight, and it took a great deal of power on her part to smile.

"You should see the Delve—colored lights everywhere," he continued. "This year, I bet the plaza and gardens will be filled with food and drinks. Some people even brought instruments here, which they play during the ceremony. It isn't as grand as the festivals we had in Altus, but we make do." He leaned against a post, then undid his flask and took a sip of water before saying, "You'll come, won't you?"

Marina's stomach flipped, but she knew Pierce wouldn't be happy if she turned him down, so she nodded.

He broke into a smile. "You'll love it. There's a change in mood around Double Moon. Sometimes, I see people I haven't seen the entire year."

"Does Aeric come?" Marina asked cautiously.

"Never has."

Marina had to stifle her sigh of relief.

"You should see what it looks like above," Pierce said wistfully. "The moons are even more beautiful than our sun." He paused. "Does Georgia have moons?"

"*Earth* has one moon, but it's tidally locked, so it rises every night."

Curiosity sparked in Pierce's eyes. "I wish we could see ours nightly. It felt strange during the dead years—knowing the moons were taking their own course while I was stuck here." He looked down, smiling into his water. "But it gave me peace too. The moons kept coming, and I knew that somewhere beyond Elsudra, there was hope. You brought that hope back."

Why did he have to say that? This time, Marina couldn't fake a smile, but she didn't have to—Pierce's attention shifted when Ocot and Boris turned the corner.

Both wore their armored suits, but Ocot had rolled his sleeves up, exposing his arms. For some reason, it made him look like even more of a prick. Though Marina bristled when his gaze met hers, she tried to look as unbothered as possible—as though she hadn't just spent the entire day with Pierce.

Ocot eyed Pierce for a moment, then turned back to Marina and held up a satchel. "And here I was, planning to call you tonight and surprise you with the good news," he sang. Any confusion she thought she'd seen was gone. "What impeccable timing."

What horrible timing, Marina thought. Pierce blinked back his shock, then opened his mouth, but Ocot quickly said, "Not you."

He held out a satchel to Marina, which she eagerly took.

Holy shit. Had he actually...?

"You can save your gratitude for later," Ocot said. He held a flask of his own, which he took a swig of. It clearly wasn't water. "I know Pierce visits the South a lot, but why are *you* here?"

Marina's head buzzed, but Pierce spoke before she could. "What's in the bag?"

"Doesn't concern you," Ocot said. Boris looked like he wanted to disappear.

Pierce turned to Marina, expecting a response.

"A book," she said. "He recommended it."

Pierce looked hurt. "What book?"

Marina's grip on the satchel tightened. "It's—"

"Rude to be nosey," Ocot interrupted.

Pierce crossed his arms. "Where are you off to, Ocot? The *southern* border?"

Boris, clearly trying to diffuse things, chuckled and said, "You wouldn't believe how often I've been sent up there to do checks after what you two pulled."

Pierce ignored him. Eyes still on Ocot, he droned, "Sorry about your post change. I know you enjoyed the East."

Ocot's smug smile thinned. "We all have to pick up the slack when the lowest among us make mistakes."

"Thanks for the book," Marina said. *Just leave, both of you.* "It's getting late."

"What about *your* end of the bargain?" Ocot turned to her, and Marina wished she'd kept silent. "I'd love to have you tag along with Boris and me after my shift. Only rule is you can't bring your dog."

Pierce's eyes narrowed. "You invited her to the tunnels with you?" He choked on a laugh. "Can't imagine Florin and Aeric would be happy to hear how you spend your time. Shame nobody's told them yet."

"That's because nobody knows, minus the people I don't care about," Ocot said. "Go ahead, Pierce. Snitch on me. Bring Boris into this. Bring Cal into it. I'm sure that'd do your reputation good, considering everyone already thinks you're a pretentious, freeloading daddy's boy."

Boris shot Pierce a desperate glance.

"You have a shift, Ocot," Marina said, straining to sound calm. "And I have to get back to the manor."

"Don't tell me you're about to avoid me after what I've done for you." Ocot said it wryly, but there was an undercurrent of hurt in his voice.

"I won't," she said hastily. She caught Boris's gaze, and though the words clung to her throat like syrup, she managed a quiet "Thank you."

Boris responded with a timid, tight-lipped smile, and Marina's stomach sank. She wasn't sure how Ocot had managed to convince him, though maybe "convinced" wasn't the right word. Given the anxiety on Boris's face, "forced" seemed more fitting.

"What exactly *have* you done for her?" Pierce asked, eyeing the satchel. This time, he wasn't going to let up.

"Enough with the questions, Pierce," Ocot droned. "Aeric and Florin gave you a simple job for a reason. Go on. Run back to the manor like you ran from Altus."

Pierce's lips curled. "I'm surprised you aren't still in Altus, given your fascination with a certain ideology—"

Ocot's fist collided with Pierce's face before he could finish speaking.

Marina gasped, stepping out of the way with Boris as Ocot dropped his opened flask, dousing the stones in alcohol. Pierce stumbled back, and before he could straighten, Ocot punched him again, knocking him to the ground. He sputtered a few insults Marina couldn't hear, then wrapped his meaty hands around Pierce's throat and dug his knee deep into his gut. Pierce, for what it was worth, managed to hit Ocot square in the jaw.

"Ocot, he's not worth it," Boris said.

"Holier-than-thou piece of shit," Ocot spat. Pierce shielded himself, then struck Ocot again, this time harder. There was blood—Marina couldn't tell whose—and grunting as the two of them struggled for control.

"Both of you, *stop*," Marina begged. They didn't listen.

She shot a distressed glance at Boris, who side-eyed her as he said, "You've made your point, Ocot."

But Ocot kept going—and going, and going, and going. Pierce got in a few hits, but he wasn't going to win—not pinned to the ground like this.

Pierce's eyes began to flutter as Ocot held him in place by the neck, and when Marina realized they weren't going to stop—not on their own, at least—she reached out and grabbed Ocot. She wasn't sure what she intended to do—she didn't fool herself into thinking she had the strength to pull him off Pierce—but when her hand wrapped around Ocot's lower arm, something burst from her fingers.

She couldn't see it, but she could feel it—a burst of air so dense it made a crunching sound. Ocot hollered and tumbled backward, curses pouring from his mouth as his gaze darted from her to Pierce. Marina recoiled, eyes wide.

"Oh my God!" she said, then swore. "I didn't mean to..."

She remained frozen where she stood as Pierce heaved in gulps of air. She looked at her hands, then at Ocot, who gaped at her. Even Boris took a step away.

Ocot pulled himself up, wiping blood from under his nose as Pierce propped himself up by his elbows.

"Let's go," Boris said. It wasn't a command; it was a plea—one that made all the more sense when his eyes met Marina's. He could've been looking at a monster.

Good God, could that have gone any worse?

Ocot hesitated but gave in. He held his arm as he approached Boris, who shook his head and hissed, "You need to check yourself. You're too reckless when you drink."

Ocot waved him off, then turned to Marina. He glanced at the satchel, then back at her. "You're welcome," he sneered. He didn't sound like his usual self—didn't sound cocky or obnoxious. He sounded upset. Still, when he and Boris turned to the southern stairwell, Marina didn't watch them go.

"What were you thinking, baiting him like that?" she said, kneeling beside Pierce.

Pierce groaned. "I was thinking...that I was mad."

"So you weren't thinking."

"Don't lecture me." He sat up and rubbed his temples. "What did you do?"

"I...honestly, I have no clue. It was like I punched him, but not with my hand...with a burst of air." She winced. "That wasn't...I didn't...I hope I didn't break anything."

"I hope you did." When Marina gawked at him, Pierce scowled. "He'll be fine. It's not like it's the dead years anymore. He'll heal before he knows it and go right back to being an ass." He paused. "What did Ocot bring you?"

"It's just a book." When Pierce furrowed his brow, she added, "You know how Ocot is. He approached me a few nights ago, asking about my magic, then offered to bring me a book. I figured accepting would shut him up."

"Ocot doesn't read."

"Who cares?" Marina said, praying this conversation would end. "I doubt it's relevant. He just wanted to feel important. I couldn't say no."

"Yeah, you could've."

"I'm trying not to make enemies," Marina muttered. *That* was going terribly so far.

"You can't not make an enemy out of Ocot," Pierce said. "He's the worst of us. He'll do whatever it takes to get power and admiration, and there's no better way to do that than cozying up to the Omnia's host."

Funny, Marina thought. *I happen to remember him saying something similar about you.*

She sighed as Pierce said, "I'm serious. You need to stay away from him. He may like you right now, but the moment you double-cross him, he'll never forgive you."

"How did *you* double-cross him?" she asked, folding her arms. "You told me you accused him of something, and that's why he has it out for you."

Pierce sucked the air in through his nostrils. "I called him a Kieron sympathizer once, and he's had a stick up his ass about it ever since."

"You mean...you think Ocot *wants* Kieron to be in power? Is that what you meant when you said—"

"Forget it," Pierce interrupted, clearly annoyed. "It doesn't matter."

"Is that why he punched you? Is that what you were alluding to?" When Pierce didn't respond, she leaned back on her heels. "Pierce, why did you call him that?"

"If you're so concerned, why don't you ask Ocot yourself? Seems like you two know each other better than I thought." The words came out cold, and Marina bristled at them. Pierce took another deep breath. "I'll see you tomorrow."

He stood, wincing, then left without looking back. She debated following him and trying to justify herself, but since she figured that wouldn't do any good, she returned to the manor instead. Best to let him cool off on his own. For now, the documents demanded her attention.

The satchel was packed with tightly bound papers, and the folios had dials on their spines that meant they'd been magically altered to be read by anyone. More exciting than that was the sheer number of pages in each one—chock-full of text so dense that Marina hardly knew where to start. And yet, even as she settled down to read, with her bedroom door locked and the lights dimmed, her eagerness came second to the rock in her stomach.

CHAPTER 17
Hollow Victories

Marina's eyes burned. She'd spent the night reading, anticipation pricking at her fingertips as she turned every lustered page. Locus was her priority, but she reigned in the urge to skim. Anything could be useful.

There were lots of terms she didn't know, but she preferred those to the ones she did. *Delirium inducement* might have unsettled her had it not been listed next to a section on how seasoned sorcerers could cut into enemies so long as they were within eyeshot, like Aeric had done with the ruemin.

The documents weren't meant for sorcerers, though. If anything, they were meant for those seeking to defend themselves from sorcerers. Mental shielding was covered in detail, as was psychometry. Apparently, psychometry could only be conducted on people who were fully awake and aware, as any level of unconsciousness barred sorcerers from performing mental-based magic. In some cases, soldiers were said to have ended their lives to prevent valuable knowledge from being uncovered.

Those instances, however, were rare. Mostly, the military relied on armaments meant to help them outmatch magically-inclined adversaries.

Any damage a sorcerer could do wasn't much different from that of a knife, sword, or gun, and even then, it took a fair amount of talent and strength. But the threat of epidermal damage wasn't overlooked, and soldiers' armored suits were made with magical combat in mind. With the helmet on, the entire body was protected, and it would take even the best sorcerers some time to break through.

For a realm as small and unstained by war as Elsudra, they were certainly cautious. Document after document outlined wartime procedures, and it became clear to Marina how well the military anticipated and squelched civil conflict. The documents mentioned instances of regional squabbles, but most never lasted longer than a few seasons, owing to the government's insistence on keeping their military active and on retainer. Subunits of soldiers also policed cities, but for the most part, Elsudra was as peaceful as it was well-prepared. Until Kieron, of course. Nobody had anticipated the likes of him. Or Aeric.

The paper crinkled under Marina's fingers. The Sorcerer of the Court was supposed to protect Elsudra and the Omnia, not threaten it.

By the time she reached the history-specific section—Florin's personal touch, no doubt—her head had grown heavy, and the floodlights outside signaled morning. But she pushed on, determined not to sleep until she'd read everything. Fortification magic, the modernization of arms, the history of magic in government security, the military's involvement in rituals...

Rituals! Marina's heart quickened.

Military involvement in the Daughter Rituals has occurred since the days of early Elsudra. While related, each ritual serves a different purpose, and the role of the military is dependent on the one being performed.

Holy shit. Ocot really *had* come through.

Tempus, the ritual of guidance: Tempus is the oldest of the Daughter Rituals, dating back to before the first Keepers. Performance occurs in a dream-like state, offering divine but transitory interaction with higher powers. In early Elsudra, Tempus was most often performed during times of crisis; historical texts mention its use as communities sought guidance during periods of war, famine, and disease. A notoriously vague ritual, sorcerers avoided its use unless there were no other options. Furthermore, lesser sorcerers often failed in their attempts. Since maximal intimacy with the Omnia is required for Tempus to work, early Elsudrans performed it in water.

In the current era of Keepers, Elsudran law mandates that Tempus can only be used in times of dire need, as decided by the Keepers and the Sorcerer of the Court. Now obsolete to the rest of Elsudra, only the Keepers and Sorcerer of the Court take part in the ritual. While the Sorcerer of the Court orchestrates both Daughter Rituals to compensate for the Keepers' lack of magical prowess, only Keepers are partial to the guidance Tempus generates. This is due to their proximity to the Omnia as hosts, which other parties lack and can no longer achieve.

Marina remembered Ismene saying that while the first Keepers were uniquely powerful sorcerers, their descendants varied in magical ability—most having none at all. No wonder they needed the Sorcerer of the Court. Eagerly, she turned the page.

Attempts at psychometry consistently fail to give the Sorcerer of the Court insight into the ritual's guidance, which makes protecting the Keepers during this time integral.

She flew through the rest of the section. It was military-specific, and if there was anything she should be focusing on, it was the rituals. As fervently as she devoured the information about Tempus, it was Locus she was really after. When she reached its section, her heart all but stopped.

Locus, the ritual of movement: Locus relies on the autonomy of the performers, and as such did not exist before the era of Keepers, given that water was the Omnia's host. Newer and more volatile, it is performed at the end of the Keepers' lives as they transfer their quarters of the Omnia to their descendants. While the first Keepers' magical prowess helped them protect their spirits, later generations generally sustained fatal damage and passed in the weeks following Locus's completion.

Marina's stomach flipped. Aeric had said as much, but seeing it in writing solidified just how risky the ritual was. But *she* had magical prowess, and though acknowledging it still made her head go fuzzy, she'd take the anxiety if it meant Locus was an option. Regardless, her hands shook as she continued to read.

Since the transition is delicate by nature, Elsudra's military (most notably, commissioned officers stationed in Altus) operates at a maximum state of readiness while the ritual is performed.

More military specifics. Marina skipped ahead.

Locus is also permitted in the event a Keeper falls ill. In early Elsudra, the Omnia existed in bodies of water, all connected to the ocean. Now in a more contained form, illness on the Keepers' part poses a significant threat. On such rare occasions, the Altus Military District will...

A knock interrupted her focus.

She reigned in a gasp. Ismene didn't visit her in the mornings anymore—not since Marina had learned her way to the kitchens—and even so, it was extremely early. She rolled off her bed and buried the documents under the covers, her heart pulsating under her fingertips as she opened the door.

And then her heart stopped.

Aeric looked even more grim than usual in the scant light, though Marina supposed she didn't look much better given the all-nighter she'd pulled.

Oh, *shit.* Was this about what she'd done to Ocot? Why hadn't he just summoned her to his office? She hadn't seen him since after the border incident, and even that wasn't long enough.

"Hi," she said, though it came out more like a question, which was fitting because what she really meant was: *Why the hell are you here?*

She almost began rattling off excuses about what had happened to Ocot—best if she downplayed it as much as possible—but since she wasn't sure what Aeric wanted yet, she stayed silent as he brushed past her and into her room.

"I mean to speak with you about what happened with the sentry," Aeric said. His eyes weren't on her, though. They scanned the room, taking in every detail.

"That was involuntary," Marina blurted.

"So was the stunt you pulled at the border."

The floodlights beyond her window had started to brighten, and the waxy light that seeped into her room glinted off Aeric's hair. He lingered by her vanity, then opened one of the empty drawers.

"What are you doing?" Marina asked, eyeing the hallway. If she needed to, she'd bolt. She probably wouldn't get far, but if push came to shove, at least she'd have tried.

"What spurred that most recent show of power?" he asked stiffly.

"I...like I said, it was involuntary. I was trying to break up a fight."

"Yes, between those two dim-witted sentries. I realize why it happened; what I want to know is *how*."

"I can't tell you that." When Aeric's eyes met hers, she quickly added, "Only because I don't know. It was sudden and useless."

Nothing of any importance. Nothing you could use against Kieron.

"Not so useless," Aeric said. "That sentry had to leave his shift early and go to the infirmary. You fractured his radius."

Marina's eyes widened. "I...I didn't mean..."

"I know. You're not in trouble...for that, at least. What happened yesterday isn't the only reason why I'm here." He paused. "Where are the documents, Marina."

Not a question. A demand for answers. Her blood went cold. How had he realized so quickly? It hadn't even been a day.

When she didn't answer, Aeric said, "I'll ask you again..."

"I have no idea what documents you're talking about."

"Lying to me about the southern border didn't go over so well," he said, his voice low. "Are you really so daft that you'd try again?"

Perhaps she was. Desperation did that.

She held her tongue, commanding herself to stay silent. But even if her words didn't betray her, her eyes did. A knee-jerk glance at her bed was all it took for Aeric to catch on. She imagined she looked like a child caught with her hand in a cookie jar—pale-faced and hunched over—as Aeric pulled back the sheets and stared at the papers, his jaw tight.

God, she needed to work on her discretion—with this *and* her improvements in magic. If she failed to, she might as well give up on going home.

Marina cursed to herself as Aeric scooped up the documents. He straightened, beholding her with enmity so cold that she wrapped her arms around herself.

"If you're looking for instructions on Locus, you'll find no such information in these." His hand tightened on the papers, and like that, they were gone. No flash of light, no fading away...just gone, as though they'd never existed to begin with. Wherever he'd sent them, Marina knew she wouldn't get them back.

"The sentries that stole those for you have been punished for theft of confidential information," he continued. "How they thought they'd get away with it, I have no idea, though I find myself significantly less surprised by your recklessness."

Marina's breathing grew hitched. "You...you didn't kick them out, did you?"

"They've received a reduction in grade and are on probation for the foreseeable future. Luckily for them—and you—those documents were benign. Had they stolen more sensitive information, their stations would be the least of their worries."

"Boris was bullied into this," Marina said quietly.

"And the other was manipulated. By *you*." Aeric sighed, and only then did Marina realize how exhausted he looked.

She was exhausted too. Exhausted from fighting so hard to regain her old life, all while remembering how terrible that life had been.

Aeric must've noticed the defeat in her eyes because the chill that followed him lessened ever so subtly. And yet, his voice was as cold as ever when he said, "How many people must you exploit before you grow tired of your hollow victories?"

He didn't wait for an answer. Marina lingered at her door as he left, frozen.

No threats. No punishments. Perhaps it made sense. What *could* he punish her with when there was nothing left for her to lose?

Every victory here was hollow. When her magic improved, so did the precariousness of her situation. When she acquired information that may help her, she hurt others. When she fought for home—brass-knuckled and iron-willed—she only grew more hopeless.

There were no good options. Only slightly less horrible ones.

Pierce met her outside the manor. When Marina approached him, too numb to be uneasy, he said, "I heard what happened. What were you thinking?"

"I didn't lecture you about your fight with Ocot," she muttered. "Don't lecture me about this." When Pierce scowled, she added, "I thought the documents would be helpful with my training. Ocot *offered* to bring them to me." The lie hung heavy in her throat.

"If you wanted them so badly, you could've asked Florin or Aeric."

Marina crossed her arms. "We both know Florin would've had to report that to Aeric, and Aeric would've said no."

"Why? And don't tell me it's because he dislikes you. If those documents would've helped your training, there's no way he'd have turned you down. Which makes me think you were after something else."

Marina rubbed her temples. "I had no idea what was in them, Pierce. How could I have? I'm ignorant about everything else. That was part of the reason why I wanted them so badly. I hoped they could give me insight about the Omnia, or wartime magic, or *something* that'd make me improve quicker. But I didn't ask Aeric because like *you* said, I'm scared of him. Only I couldn't stop thinking about the documents after you'd mentioned them, and when Ocot said he could get them for me, I accepted. It was in the heat of the moment, and I regret it. I didn't even have time to read them."

It wasn't *all* a lie. And yet, even the untrue parts slipped off her tongue quickly—easily—and she hated herself all the more for it.

"It was stupid and short-sighted, and it's my fault," she continued. "I should've told Ocot to screw off." *Liar, liar, liar.* "But I was desperate for anything."

Pierce sighed. "It's just...Exorsus, Marina, we could've found something just as useful. Besides, you're already improving. Ocot can attest to that."

Marina studied his face. "And how do you feel about that?"

"About Ocot?" Pierce sucked on his cheek. "Will you think I'm a horrible person if I say he deserved the fractured arm and the demotion?"

"What kind of demotion?"

"He's stationed fully in the South now. And he thought part-time was bad."

"What about Boris?" She didn't want to ask but felt she must.

Pierce shifted. "He's had his duties as a scout...reduced," he said, obviously struggling to find mild words. "It's probably temporary. Both are on probation, but if they behave, I'm sure it'll end. Maybe this will be the push Boris needs to shed Ocot."

Marina pressed the heels of her palms to her eyes.

"Look, I'm sorry for getting pissy yesterday," Pierce said. "You know I have my issues with Ocot, and it turned into jealousy. But next time you need help, come to me. We have a good thing going, the two of us. Nobody in the history of Elsudra has ever had to learn magic as quickly as you, and you're doing brilliantly." He squeezed her shoulder. "You're my friend, and I want to be here for you however I can. We'll keep practicing, okay?"

Friend. The thickness in Marina's throat dropped to her stomach. He wouldn't be saying that if he knew what she'd said to Ocot about him. But she only smiled and nodded.

That was all she could do, after all: lie low and practice. She needed to be careful going forward. The more Aeric knew, the more likely he'd be to interfere.

So Marina practiced, chasing small victories, even if they were hollow. Whether or not she learned Locus—whether or not she ever got home—there was only one thing she was certain of: Aeric wouldn't be her undoing.

CHAPTER 18
A Lone Petal

It would have been around February at home when Double Moon came upon them, and the Delve was livelier than ever. Colored lights hung from every rock, and white rose petals littered the cobblestones.

The beauty lessened Marina's nerves, which was about the closest she'd come to relief since she'd seen Aeric. Their interaction with the documents hadn't been particularly traumatizing, but it had stirred up reminders of her first days in the Delve—and more than that, what she was trying to avoid: Kieron. Ruemin. Being forced into a war that wasn't hers to fight. Dying because of it.

She hadn't heard from Aeric since, thank goodness. She hadn't heard from Ocot either, but she did catch wind of rumors. Nobody seemed to get the story right. Some said he'd broken into classified storage on a dare, while others figured he'd been trying to impress the Omnia's host. The latter was more accurate, but none reflected the truth—that *she* was at fault for manipulating him, just like Aeric had said.

Of course, Aeric never set the rumors straight. As always, he remained absent, never emerging from the manor or mingling with the masses. He'd sooner have Florin do so, only Florin was just as silent. It wasn't until Marina learned Boris and Dane had distanced themselves from Ocot that she realized why Aeric and Florin weren't saying anything. They didn't want the Delve to see her as she really was: selfish, conniving, and cowardly.

"I doubt Ocot will come today," Ismene said on the morning of Double Moon. She fussed with Marina's hair, weaving blue ribbons into braids and starting over when it wasn't perfect. Marina didn't mind her meticulousness—it gave her time to read. Pierce had brought her a book on summoning, which she'd almost finished, even if she'd yet to summon anything herself.

"Everyone was already wary of him before he did what he did," Ismene continued. "Add that to the fact he nearly beat Pierce unconscious, and it's a recipe for disaster. Alienation does no one well, especially here."

Marina put her hand to her mouth and exhaled through her fingers.

Ismene went to pick out more ribbons, and before she could bring up Ocot again, Marina said, "I hear the Double Moon ceremonies in Altus were amazing."

"Oh, they were," Ismene said nostalgically. "You'll get your first taste of it here, but it's nothing compared to the capital."

"Did you grow up there?"

Ismene shook her head. "I was raised in a town called Lewes. It's in the North, like Altus, but nestled at the base of the Ulaex Mountains instead of by the sea. It's really quite quaint." She held a ribbon to Marina's hair, testing the color. "I came to Altus a season or two after Kieron was exiled to Sundra. His banishment stirred up anxiety and created an exodus at the palace, which meant there were vacancies young people like me could fill. Still, it took me quite some time to become head of the household department."

"That's impressive," Marina said.

"It was either that or become a teacher like my parents. Not that it's a bad profession, especially in Lewes. My city was known for churning out healers who worked in Altus."

Was. Marina pretended not to have picked up on that.

"My parents taught at Lewes's School of Medicine," Ismene said. "They weren't inclined, but they were smart as whips and knew everything there was to know about healing. Their students loved them." She laughed through her nose. "I wish I could say they held the same love for each other, but I think they enjoyed being in the classroom more than they enjoyed being home. Luckily, I had my sisters to keep me company." She paused, then whispered, "I never should've left them."

Her voice broke—subtly, but enough for Marina to know she shouldn't press.

Ismene chuckled sadly. "My youngest sister would call me all the time when I lived in Altus, asking if I'd seen the Keepers."

"Had you?"

"Exorsus, no. Only the Sorcerer of the Court and a few generals interacted with them. Perhaps some highly trained healers too. Nobody else had access." She considered. "Well, there was *one* palace worker who claimed she saw Four, but she was a known liar, so I took her story with a grain of salt."

Marina knit her brow. "Four?"

Ismene nodded and moved to Marina's bed, where she'd laid out a few outfit options. "Our Keepers didn't go by names—only numbers. The oath they took was, in part, a sacrifice. It wiped their identities so they'd remain uncorrupted—they'd have no familial ties and no selfish desires." When Marina only stared at her, slack-jawed, Ismene quickly said, "You never swore an oath, Marina. You'll retain your personhood." She put her hands on her hips. "Now choose an outfit and stop worrying."

That was a rather impossible ask, but Marina nodded. Back in Georgia, she would've chosen a dress, but she'd never seen any here. Perhaps Elsudrans didn't make them. She settled on a blue jumpsuit with palazzo pants and gossamer sleeves that swished when she moved, just like waves.

Ismene grinned. "How did I know you'd choose that one?"

With the outfit on and her hair bound in ribbons, Marina felt—for once in a very long time—beautiful. Clothing and hairstyles had stopped mattering recently, but today was different, and things had changed. She'd changed too. She'd gained back some of the weight she'd lost, and with it came more color—to her face, to her eyes, to everything.

As Marina and Ismene made their way to the plaza, memories of childhood days spent by the sea flickered at the back of her head.

You'll find a way to get home. You will. Strangely enough, the reassurances felt lost on her today. She was glad of it, though—glad to get lost in the excitement.

When Pierce saw Marina and Ismene from across the plaza, he beamed.

"You two are stunning," he said.

Ismene gave a little twirl. With her crimson outfit, her hair and eyes stood out even more. Pierce, too, had cleaned up nicely. Though his hair was untidy as always, he'd swapped out his usual tunic for something a little nicer. He kept his dagger on his hip, though it seemed he wasn't the only one.

Just in case. This place was run on just-in-cases—always preparing for the worst.

Marina pushed the thoughts away. Luckily, the spirit of Double Moon was contagious. Everyone wore colorful clothes that matched the lanterns, and like Pierce had promised, some people set up instruments near the fountain and began to play.

It had been months since she'd heard music, and though the songs were foreign, Elsudran instruments didn't differ much from the ones Marina knew. The sounds of string, percussion, and brass moved her in a way she'd almost forgotten.

She peered up at the banners hanging from the rocks, each one painted with a sun at the center—a sun with four rays, like the one that hung above the staircase in the manor.

"What's the sun for?"

Pierce followed her gaze. "It's not actually a sun," he said. Marina tried to ignore the amusement in his voice. "It's Elsudra's emblem, meant to represent the Omnia and the magic it radiates. The four waves coming from it symbolize magic as it was kept in check by our Keepers."

Marina studied it. "You said you saw sorcerers in Altus branded with Kieron's sigil," she said. "What does that one look like?"

"A terrible mockery of our own," Pierce muttered, then shook his head. "Try not to think about Kieron today. It'll only stress you out, and there's fun to be had." He gestured grandly to the people and decorations, and Marina acquiesced.

It turned out having fun was harder while being stared at. As Pierce, Marina, and Ismene listened to music and got drinks, the eyes never left them. The gardens weren't any better. She tried to pretend she didn't notice, but it grew difficult when people came seeking an introduction. Pierce and Ismene were good at cutting conversations short, especially when questions about the Omnia popped up. As uncomfortable as it was, especially when a bumbling greenhouse worker stopped to ask her about magic and if she'd improved, Marina did her best to seem at ease. She couldn't fault them for being curious, even though their questions bore a hole in her so deep that she slipped away the first chance she got.

If there was one thing caverns were good for, it was hiding. Concealed in an alleyway behind an arboretum, Marina counted the petals that littered the floor and strained to compose herself.

She sighed to the ceiling, knowing she should emerge soon to keep Pierce and Ismene from questioning her. As she moved back out to the gardens, however, a yellow petal hiding in a shadowy corner caught her eye. Where it had been uprooted from, she didn't know, but it stood out sorely amongst the sea of ivory.

She straightened, tilting her head curiously and checking to make sure nobody was around. Voices flitted from the gardens, distant and coalesced, and Marina blocked them out. She let her feelings come and go—let herself wade in the current without drowning in it. Then, using the ebb to guide her, she bent down and reached out her hand. Slowly, the petal drifted across the floor in a nonexistent breeze.

Calmly. Carefully. If her waves were tangible, they'd have extended beyond her, prodding the petal along the floor and onto her opened palm.

"That's cool," someone said.

Marina inhaled sharply and whirled around. Dane lingered a few feet away from her. When he eyed the petal in her hand, she closed her fingers around it. Couldn't she get *any* privacy here?

"I heard what happened with Ocot," he ventured.

Marina tensed. "Seems like everyone has," she said as she moved past him and back into the gardens. When she realized he was following her, she said, "I thought you two were close."

"Not close. We just work together. *Worked* together. Not anymore."

Well, he wasn't here; that's what counted.

"Ocot goes too far," Dane said as they came up to a table with drinks. Marina looked around for Ismene and Pierce, but she didn't see them. "What I mean to say is...I'm not like him. He forces people to do things they don't agree with. Boris, me...he just won't let up sometimes. But the things he's said to Pierce, I...well, I don't condone them."

He seemed pleased with his choice of words. Marina, however, couldn't find anything to respond with, so she simply nodded and took a sip of cider.

"I also wanted to say congratulations," Dane said, wiping his hands on his tunic. He really was searching for words. "You seem to be improving...with magic and all that, I mean."

Marina let out a silent breath as Ismene came up behind her and cast a skeptical look in Dane's direction.

"Just getting a drink," Dane said. He nodded at them, then said, "Happy Double Moon," before fleeing without a cup.

"What did he want?" Ismene asked.

"To let me know he doesn't condone Ocot's behavior." Marina eyed her cider. "Does this have alcohol in it?"

When Ismene nodded, Marina set her cup down. She was already nervous; she didn't need more reason to feel out of control.

Pierce, on the other hand, seemed to have treated himself to far more than just one drink. He bounded up to them, eyes bright. "There's dancing in the plaza! Who wants to join?"

Marina accepted, figuring it might help her shake off her nerves. The plaza was full of people clustered around the fountain, listening to the music. Some small groups danced what looked like a jig, which Pierce picked up quickly. Even Ismene, who stumbled once or twice through the moves, was more proficient than Marina.

"Not much of a dancer, huh?" Pierce asked through a laugh.

"More of a singer, really," Marina admitted.

Pierce broke into a beam. "Then sing something!"

"I didn't say I *do* sing—just that I'm less shitty at it than I am at dancing." She waved him off playfully, relieved when he didn't push her.

As the dancing grew looser and the tempo increased, Marina found it easier to keep up with Pierce and Ismene. She absorbed the notes that lingered in the air, savoring the trill in her chest at every crescendo. The music washed away the tension that wound her shoulders tight, rippling through her arms and legs until she felt like the sea itself. Her ribbons were the waves, and she was the tide. She harnessed the power of the ocean—every inch of water, from the murky depths to the ever-clear blues and greens. Though she was careful not to demonstrate anything publicly, she could feel the change within her, emotionally and spiritually.

The world that spun around her was one of lanterns and lights, and though she knew rock walls surrounded them and stalactites formed the sky, she felt closer to the heavens than ever.

⌒

When the floodlights were at their lowest, the lanterns glowed even brighter, splashing the cavern walls with color. The day had ended in a blur, and when the plaza emptied, Pierce escorted Marina and Ismene back to the manor.

"The one thing that would make this holiday better is if everyone could see the moons," he said as they took the northern staircase.

"That's why I don't pity the sentries who have shifts during Double Moon," Ismene said. "They're rewarded with the most beautiful view."

"What about cameras?" Marina asked.

Pierce shot her a crooked smile. "Cameras are used for security purposes. We attach them to drones sometimes, if that's what you mean."

"How do you take pictures for fun?"

"We don't," Pierce said. "But we *can* capture memories, which I'd argue is better."

He started rambling about an Elsudran device that could catch and reconstruct memories based on information input, then render them into moving images. He called it an anteactus—a device so intricate that even Pierce struggled to explain how they were made. That, and Marina was yawning too much to pay attention.

Eventually, when Pierce got into the types of instruments—some could only capture personal, small-scale memories, while others were used by the court as historical records—Ismene cut him off and said, "One day, you'll see the moons in person."

Marina smiled groggily.

"Hey, by the way," Pierce said, "Happy Pearl."

Ismene's eyes lit up. "And here's to a better year."

Marina tried to ignore the subtle glance they threw in her direction. They didn't have time to say much else, though—when they turned the corner closest to the manor, a clinking bottle froze them in their tracks. Leaning against a wall a few yards from the perron was Ocot, his face redder than usual. Marina's stomach dropped.

Pierce cursed, then muttered, "You've got to be kidding…"

"Ignore him," Ismene whispered.

Marina tried not to look in Ocot's direction, shame barreling through her veins. Instead, she rested her eyes on the festive banners hanging from the manor's entrance, each one painted with Elsudra's emblem.

Of course, it only seemed to anger Ocot more when she didn't look at him. When he spat, "Coward," Marina knew who he was talking to.

"You're drunk," Pierce said sternly. "Go back to the barracks."

"I want to talk to her."

"Ocot," Marina started, only to be cut off by his low laugh.

"This is your fault," he sneered.

He wasn't wrong. Marina opened her mouth, but Pierce spoke first.

"What, that you disobeyed rules to impress her?" he said. "Your idiocy is on you and you alone, Ocot."

Ocot bared his teeth. "Shut the fuck up, you hypocrite. Butt in again and I'll beat you unconscious." He turned to Marina. "You turned everyone against me…turned Dane and Boris against me. Got me demoted. Got me punished."

The words burned her tongue, but Marina forced them out. "Ocot, I'm sorry—"

"You don't need to apologize to him," Pierce interrupted. "He offered."

"Offered?" Ocot sputtered. "Are you serious? *Offered*, Marina? She *asked*."

Shit. *Shit*. Of course this had to happen now. Of course he had to confront her in front of Pierce and Ismene.

"Yeah, you tell yourself that, Ocot," Pierce replied coolly. "Tell that to everyone here, but nobody will believe you."

Marina swallowed. "I did," she whispered, knowing the guilt would eat her alive if she stayed silent.

Pierce blinked at her. Even Ismene, who'd been rubbing her temples, stopped long enough to gawk at Marina.

"I was desperate, like I said," Marina continued. "I just…might've led Ocot on a bit."

Ocot let out a hitched laugh. "A *bit*?"

Marina braced herself, expecting Pierce to go off on her. He beheld her with a look she couldn't discern, but when Ocot stepped toward them, the look disappeared.

"Need I remind you how clear Florin was?" Pierce snarled. "If *anyone* harms the Omnia's host, Aeric will use magic on them that dissolves their mind—makes them unable to communicate in any way—before leaving them to fend for themselves above ground. Does that jog your memory?"

Marina gaped at Pierce. Was he serious?

"You don't get to lecture me," Ocot snapped. "Not after your fuckup."

"Ocot, stop and think," Ismene said. "This isn't worth it."

Ocot stared at her for a moment, then turned back to Pierce, dismissing Ismene entirely. "Why does everything that happens to me in this shithole involve you?"

"Oh, *there* it is," Pierce said through a hoarse laugh. "There's the blame I was waiting for. I didn't manipulate you, dipshit. You got manipulated because you're an idiot. But you won't just blame the person who led you on—oh, no. You find a way to turn it on me too. Who better to blame?" His lips curled into a mocking pout. "You're mad because I'm everything you're not—because I had a happy family and my dad was a general, so you feel like I didn't earn my place here, but your family didn't love you, and I hurt your feelings once by implying you fancied Kieron's ideology. Sound about right?"

"Because you're a bootlicking shit who weasels his way into positions of power and safety," Ocot said, his knuckles white around the neck of his empty bottle. He glanced at Marina. "Even she said it—said you can't be trusted after fleeing Altus."

Marina's blood went cold as Pierce turned to her. She screamed a thousand silent curses, then opened her mouth, only to say nothing at all. There she stood, voiceless, unsure whether she should apologize or explain—unsure whether any of it would mean anything anyway.

"You said that?" Pierce whispered. His voice broke.

"I didn't mean it," Marina said. "I needed to convince Ocot, and it was the only thing I could think of." Desperately, she repeated, "I didn't mean it. I do trust you."

Now it was her voice that broke, and Ocot jumped at the opportunity.

"Ouch," he said, faking a wince. "I take it Pierce didn't know? Don't beat yourself up, Marina. You only said what everyone thinks."

Red flashed before Marina's eyes. "Fuck you, Ocot."

Ocot only laughed. "If it makes you feel any better, Pierce has been running his mouth behind your back as well. Want to know how your *oh-so-virtuous* friend has been spending his time lately?"

Pierce wrenched his eyes off Marina long enough to glare at Ocot. Marina couldn't help but notice him pale. Ocot noticed too, and a feral smile made its way onto his face.

"Pierce has been leading a double life," he said. "He's been following you around, pretending to protect you and help you learn magic while he reports everything back to Aeric. Your progress, the things you talk about...everything. *He's* the piece of shit who turned Aeric onto me and Boris."

Silence followed. The rage rippling around Marina settled, replaced by shock. "How would you know that?"

"I didn't—not until recently. If I had, I wouldn't have given you that bag with him lurking around."

"You're lucky I didn't tell Aeric what *else* you and Boris do," Pierce hissed.

Ocot's nostrils flared. "But I'm following the rules now, Pierce. Aren't you happy? What I just told her...*that's* not confidential knowledge." He shook his head. "Only you would evade punishment and be given a better job. Florin says he doesn't choose favorites, but he does all the time with you. And now I'm demoted because of a couple stupid documents, while you're prancing around as the Sorcerer of the Court's lapdog after putting the whole Delve in danger."

Marina's head began to buzz. *Idiot, idiot, idiot.* How could she have been so naive? She knew Aeric wasn't completely clueless about her progress, so why was she so shocked that he'd employed Pierce directly?

Or maybe it wasn't that she was shocked. Maybe it was that she was hurt. She knew Aeric only cared about her as a vessel for the Omnia, but some small, pathetic part of her had hoped that wasn't the case for Pierce and Ismene.

Idiot indeed. And a hypocritical one at that, given what she'd said about Pierce, and especially given her plans to desert this place when she could. Did Pierce know about that too?

"What have you told him?" Marina asked. Her voice sounded foreign in her ears.

"Nothing sensitive, I promise," Pierce said quickly. "It's just...he needs to know how you're improving. I can't do what Aeric can—don't know what he knows—and anything that slows the progression of your abilities hurts us in the long run."

So Pierce *didn't* know about her desire to learn Locus and go home. Maybe that made sense; Aeric obviously wouldn't have told Pierce her plans. Best to have Pierce think he was helping Elsudra, all while making *her* think she had a fighting chance at escape. She had to give it to Aeric—he'd found a way to sic a watchman on her, pulling her strings from the shadows. Even if Florin had vouched for Pierce after the border incident, it had been *Aeric* who'd realized he could use Pierce to his advantage.

And she'd been stupid enough to let him get away with it.

Head ringing, she said, "Did you tell Aeric I asked about Locus?"

She already knew the answer, but she wanted to hear it from Pierce.

"Yes...but he wouldn't tell me the details."

Marina looked to Ismene, who shrank. It was obvious she'd known too.

"Tough to be deceived by someone you think is your friend, huh?" Ocot said, that horrible smile still on his face.

"We are friends." Pierce turned to Marina, as though he expected her to back him up. "This doesn't change anything. I know you and Aeric didn't get along, but..."

His voice faded, and Marina almost laughed. *Get along? He means to send me off to die as soon as he can. Of course we don't get along.*

"I'm not choosing sides," Pierce said. "I swear it."

Yes, he was. Of course he was. He was Elsudran; what other side would he choose? Her survival mattered only to her, and though she wanted to hate Pierce for that, she couldn't.

"On the bright side," Ocot said, "it seems you and Pierce were made for each other. Neither of you has any honor."

Pierce snapped his head back to Ocot. "You're one to talk about honor. It's no wonder you fell for Marina's false promises—you'll take any power you can get. Everyone *else* may think your little stint back in Altus dabbling in fantasies of Kieron's reign is rumor, but I know better."

Ocot's voice was guttural. "Don't you dare insinuate that."

"I'm not insinuating." Pierce's inebriation, though less severe than Ocot's, had caught up to him as well. "You tried to hide it long enough, and you did a good job. But face it, Ocot: you love the idea of a single ruler. One Elsudran holding all the Omnia's power, maintaining his regime through conformity and erasing any semblance of dissent. Does that excite you, even now that you've seen our world go to shit? Are you so enamored with the idea that, minus one godly ruler and his chosen cohorts, nobody could look down on you? Is your desire for validation so strong that you'd trade away the freedom of others?"

"*You* started those rumors about me," Ocot barked. "You want me to fail. She wants me to." He turned to Marina, his face scarlet. "Tell everyone what you did. Tell everyone you made me get those documents. Set things right."

When Marina only stared at him, Ocot snapped. His bottle whizzed past her, narrowly missing her head and shattering when it hit the ground. "Tell them!"

Though she ducked, she still didn't respond. Her heart beat in her ears, stifling her voice.

Ocot glowered at her, writhing in the silence. "You don't deserve any of this."

Was it the Omnia he was referring to? She couldn't argue with that.

"Ocot..." Pierce warned.

But Ocot was already moving—lunging toward her—and in a burst of adrenaline, Marina twisted out of his way. Before Ocot could straighten and collect himself, however, Pierce tackled him to the ground. He dodged Ocot's cockeyed punches, then returned one with so much strength that two of Ocot's teeth clattered to the ground.

"Stop," Ismene pleaded. "You're acting like children."

Her voice could've been a whisper on the wind; neither Ocot nor Pierce gave her so much as a glance. Marina simply watched, her mind and body numb. She knew she should be grateful she was no longer Ocot's target, but she didn't care.

You idiot, she scolded herself. *You naive, weak-minded idiot.*

Ocot reached for a chunk of his broken bottle, but Pierce wrenched his hand behind his back before he could grab it. It was a victory, perhaps, but a short-lived one; Ocot kneed Pierce in the groin, making him lose his grip.

Marina turned to Ismene, and despite everything, said, "Get Aeric."

Ismene nodded furiously, raising her voco to her lips and hurrying up the perron.

Pierce swore as Ocot pulled him into a headlock.

Oh God, not again.

Even though Pierce got in a few punches, Ocot was bigger than he was, and he'd hit him in an unforgiving spot. Still gasping, Pierce rammed his elbow into Ocot's gut, who wheezed but didn't budge.

Energy sparked at her fingertips. Marina reached out and grabbed Ocot's arm, and...

Nothing. Ocot flinched in anticipation, then shoved Pierce to the ground.

"Not working, hmm?" he said, his eyes glossy. "I don't know why I ever believed you. You're useless."

Pierce was still heaving as Ocot approached Marina. She raised her hands again, only to be knocked to the ground with a punch to her stomach.

The air careened out of her. She hardly heard Pierce yell her name as Ocot piled on top of her, pinning her arms back as he sputtered, "You can't control it. You can't control anything."

Time slowed. As Pierce unsheathed his dagger, Marina closed her eyes, blocking out the feel of Ocot's sweaty hands on her wrists—blocking out everything but her waves and the light that simmered beneath them.

Her waters rose, and she opened her eyes so Ocot could see the storm within them. And then, she rallied her sea and let its power shoot from her palms.

This was no burst of air. This was something else—a lance brimming with electricity, popping and buzzing as it came at Ocot like a hammer. He went flying—five, maybe ten feet—then hit the ground with a grunt, his mouth foaming as he choked out her name.

Someone else was saying it too. Pierce. The floodlights flickered, as though she'd stolen their electricity for herself—as though she'd combined it with air, light, and an anger that burned so wildly she could scarcely feel it.

"Please..." Ocot begged.

"Marina, *stop.*" Pierce's voice. She blocked it out.

Her waves crested in her arms, and all their force shot from her outstretched hands. It was no more tiring than running, perhaps, and it felt good. Natural.

Heart beating in her ears and vision pulsing with every gust of power, she began to wonder if she could stop. Would it be like moving an arm or a leg, or would it require more effort? Did she even want to find out?

"You're crushing him," Pierce said.

"Please, please...stop..." was all Ocot could manage.

The blaze filled her mind and body, but the fear on Ocot's face had turned to pain, and something in Marina jolted. She let her power wane, only to let go of it completely when someone touched her arm.

She spun to face Aeric, her waves retreating, and only then did the exhaustion set in. Though Aeric watched her closely, it was impossible to tell what he was thinking. The surprise in Pierce and Ismene's eyes, however, was clear as day.

Lie low, Marina. Practice discretion with magic, Marina.

Apparently, she couldn't even do that correctly.

"Marina," Ismene breathed. "What..."

"I need sleep," Marina whispered. She looked to Ocot, still on the ground, then to Pierce, who stood frozen with his dagger in his hand.

She didn't want to think about this right now—about how stupid she'd been, and how no matter what she did, Aeric would always be ten steps ahead of her.

Ismene glanced at Aeric, wide-eyed. When he gave her no more than a stiff nod, she turned to Marina and said, "I can escort you."

Marina shook her head. "No...no, thank you. I know where my room is."

She had no idea how long it took her to climb the stairs to the second floor. Fatigue weighed her limbs down and her head was quiet. Still, she let her body take her where she needed, and when she got to her room, she slipped out of her clothes, then pulled the ribbons from her hair and let them fall to the floor. When she crawled under the covers, what had once been the knock of lingering thoughts grew to a pounding. Marina blocked it all out as she breathed, thinking of the lone yellow petal as she fell asleep.

CHAPTER 19
Cruel

Dawn came long after Marina woke, and as the lights outside seeped through her curtains, she gave up trying to avoid her thoughts.

She wasn't angry with Pierce or Ismene—not for their loyalty to Aeric. After all, why *would* they put her ahead of Elsudra's future? If she was angry with anyone, it was herself.

Maybe it was good she'd realized this. She'd let her guard down—a lapse of judgment that had dimmed her desire to go home. Now, that desire had been renewed. She'd needed this wake-up call.

Ismene called Marina down to Aeric's office that morning, which Marina had already mentally prepared for. She kept her expression neutral when she first entered, but her composure faltered when she saw Pierce and Ocot in the light.

They looked terrible—Ocot especially. The side of his face was black and blue, and the swelling on his lower jaw left his lips puckered and his face asymmetric. Pierce, too, had taken a beating—his neck was just as bruised as Ocot's face.

Ocot kept his eyes on the floor as she passed, but Pierce gave her a taut smile. She returned it with a nod—*unbothered, calm, collected*—and took a seat next to him, vowing this would be the last time she got called into Aeric's office. Ismene stood in the corner of the room, her face drawn. When the silence grew deafening, Ocot wrenched his eyes from the ground, swollen lips quivering as he whispered, "I'm...I'm sorry..."

"No." Florin's voice was raspy, as though he'd overused it on Double Moon. Ocot shrank into himself as Florin repeated, "No. You don't talk." He turned to Marina, an air of caution in his tone when he said, "Tell us what happened last night."

Marina looked to Ocot, who still refused to make eye contact with her.

"Ocot cornered the three of us, then attacked Pierce, who fought him back. When he came after me, I did what I could to stop him."

Ocot let out a hitched breath but remained silent.

"This is the last time," Florin said, his voice low. "I've heard of brawls you two have had in the barracks. I've been informed of previous fights. I let them go, even when you put a strain on our healers during the dead years—even when I asked myself why it was that everyone could follow the rules except the two of you." His jaw pulsed as he stared at Pierce and Ocot. "Perhaps I should've been harsher." When he turned to Ocot directly, his eyes narrowed into slits. "This has gone too far. I made it clear what would happen to anyone who tries to harm the Omnia's host, though I didn't think a sentry, of all people, would be vile and foolish enough to do so."

"I was...was drunk...wasn't thinking..."

Florin scrubbed his hands over his beard, then closed his eyes. When he spoke, it was clear he was straining to stay calm. "This is a pattern for you, Ocot," he said. "First stealing documents, now this. If you cannot control yourself—if you're more of a liability than an asset—then you do not belong in the Delve."

Ocot paled. They were going to throw him out—going to leave him to fend for himself amongst ruemin without the ability to communicate, just as Pierce said. All after she'd had him steal for her, only to let him flounder in the consequences alone.

Ocot looked to Pierce. "I'm sorry," he said again. "I was drunk..."

When Pierce didn't respond, he turned to Marina, trembling. "I'm sorry...I'm so sorry, Marina. I'd never...I didn't...I wasn't thinking..."

Tears spilled from his eyes as he faced Aeric, who sat at his desk with his usual icy expression. Even as Ocot got to his knees, desperate, Aeric remained emotionless.

"Please...don't do this," he sputtered. "It was a mistake. I'll never do it again. I'll never harm her, or even him." He pointed to Marina, then to Pierce, his hand shaking violently. "They'll kill me...the ruemin, they'll kill me..."

"There are people far worse than you who pose a threat to us," Aeric said. "How do I remain certain of the Omnia's safety if I cannot trust those sworn to protect it?"

"I promise," Ocot pleaded. When Aeric said nothing, he turned to Marina and put his hands up. "It was a mistake."

No, no, no. This wasn't right. Oh God, this wasn't right. Ocot may've chosen violence, but she'd pushed him to that point. Though the words tasted rotten in her mouth, Marina said, "Don't kick him out. Please."

The shock on Ocot's face was nothing compared to the others' expressions. Even Aeric lost his collected demeanor as he stared at Marina. Pierce shot her a look, but she stared ahead—not at Ocot, still on his knees, or even at Florin. Instead, she looked directly at

Aeric and said, "Please...let him off with a warning. He won't do it again." She faced Ocot. "You *won't* do it again, will you?" When he shook his head, she said, "Good. Because if there ever is a next time, I may not be able to control myself, and I may kill you."

It wasn't a threat—not really. At this point, she had no idea what she could do.

Ocot's head-shaking turned to nodding. "Thank you," he breathed, still trembling as he stood. "I won't...I promise I won't. I'm so sorry, Marina."

Marina squeezed her eyes shut for a moment, then said, "No...I'm sorry for coaxing you into getting those documents for me." She looked back at Aeric and Florin. Desperate, she repeated, "Please, show him mercy. Just this once."

Florin looked to Aeric, who waved his hand and said, "Fine. You can all leave. Ismene, stay behind. I have things I need you to do today."

Marina almost exhaled, but held her breath when Aeric said, "Ocot."

Hearing his name from Aeric's mouth was enough to make Ocot look like he was going to faint. He lifted his shaking head to meet Aeric's gaze.

"I want you to listen carefully."

Ocot uttered a sharp gasp. "I will, I will. I—"

Aeric held up his hand, and Ocot stopped halfway through whatever mewling promise he was about to make. For a moment, Marina thought he'd taken away Ocot's voice. Could he do that without touching him? She shook the thought away when Ocot muttered an apology under his breath. Aeric didn't need magic to silence Ocot.

"I said listen," Aeric said calmly. "An attack on her is an attack on the Omnia, which is an attack on Elsudra. If you so much as think of laying a hand on her again, I will not throw you to the ruemin." Ocot's mouth stopped moving as Aeric stood. "Instead," he said, his voice so cold it could crack ice, "I will kill you myself. Slowly. *Torturously.* Do you understand?"

"I understand," Ocot rasped out, then scurried from the room.

Marina felt Ismene's and Pierce's eyes on her, but she didn't stay behind. Instead, she turned and left as quickly as Ocot, who'd already made it to the manor door by the time she stepped into the hallway.

She was halfway to the stairs when Pierce caught up to her.

"Marina," he said, and though she wasn't sure she wanted to, she turned.

He was slower than usual because of his limp, and his voice was ragged when he said, "That's twice now you've covered my ass. You didn't tell them how I baited Ocot."

Marina only stared at her feet.

"Can we talk?" Pierce asked.

She lifted her eyes to his, then nodded. They made their way to a cluster of flat rocks beneath light-adorned stalactites, and though Pierce did his best to mask his pain as he walked, he winced when he sat.

"I don't have the energy to go farther. I got less than an hour's sleep last night." He tried to laugh but failed. After a moment's pause, he said, "Florin was furious." He looked up at Marina. "You did a good thing back there. Showing Ocot mercy, I mean."

"Yeah, well, the documents were on me. And the things I said about you to get Ocot to do my bidding...I'm sorry about that too. I was desperate, and I did whatever I could to get those documents." *Not like they helped much.* Her chin quivered, but she steadied it. Slowly, she sat, smoothed her pants, and said, "Which is why I understand why you did what you did. But I still think we should stop working together."

Pierce blinked at her. "Why?"

Though Marina knew she'd regret it, she whispered, "It's not just that Aeric and I don't get along. It's that I'm not the person Elsudra hoped would come, and I'm not going to try to be." Though something in Pierce's eyes shattered, she refused to look away. "I'm not learning magic so I can help. If I ever manage to wield the Omnia's power fully—if I'm ever strong enough—the first thing I'll do is sever it from myself and try to get home."

Pierce's voice was small. "*That's* why you wanted to learn magic? So you can leave?"

"That's what Locus is, Pierce. It's a ritual the Keepers used to move the Omnia to their successors. I don't know who I'd give it to...maybe Aeric, if I can." And though she felt like such a coward saying it, she whispered, "This isn't my fight."

Pierce was quiet for a long time. "If giving it to Aeric had been the right thing to do, our Keepers would've done that," he said finally. "But they came together and made a plan —one influenced by powers neither of us understand—and it led us to *you*."

Marina's face heated. "It's a cruel plan, Pierce. I don't care how they came to it. It's cruel to force the burden of your world onto a being from another."

Silence—again. When Pierce spoke, his voice was whetted to an edge. "Do you know what's really cruel? Being forced to live what feels like the same day over and over, never growing or changing. Do you know what it's like to not need to eat? To sleep? You start to crave the little inconveniences of life because they mean you're living. Why do you think they were called the dead years? We were corpses, the lot of us. But even then, we weren't safe from true death—weren't safe from being gutted and bleeding out, like Astra." He clenched his hands by his sides. "You'll never understand it. You'll never understand what it was like to hide underground in a shell of a body, where every injury had to be treated externally—where the risk of scouts leaving was tenfold, and where even healers grasped at straws because they no longer had their magical abilities."

Marina almost said something about how it was rich that he cared about the healers now, when he had a point to prove—how it hadn't stopped him and Ocot from beating each other up during the dead years—but Pierce didn't give her room to speak. Even if he had, her voice had deserted her.

"And the war," he continued. "*That* was cruel. When Kieron brought the ruemin back from Sundra and attacked the capital. When he fled into hiding after he lost and built his army, then began to take out anyone who was a threat—inclined and not inclined alike. When he made his way back to Altus and set the ruemin on anyone in his way, then hung what was left of their bodies around cities." His lips shook. "It was cruel when he burned books about magic so no one else had access to that knowledge. It was cruel when Ismene's family died because Lewes was targeted, and when my dad stayed in the capital knowing he'd never leave it. *Those* things were cruel, Marina. And so is your plan to desert us."

The words hung in the air, spiteful and cold. When Marina finally got her voice working again, it came out low. "The dead years happened because of your Keepers," she hissed. "*They* sent the Omnia out, and they wouldn't have had to if Aeric hadn't brought Kieron and the ruemin back to Elsudra. The entire war never would've started if it wasn't for him. How *dare* you act like I'm betraying you and your people when I never had anything to do with this in the first place?" Tears welled in her eyes. "I wish I was who you all wanted, but I'm not. You can't blame me for being loyal to myself above a world that isn't mine, the same way I can't blame you for being loyal to Elsudra above me."

Pierce rested his head in his hands. "I wondered why Aeric didn't like you," he muttered. "Now I know why. You're a manipulative coward who goes behind the backs of friends for your own self-preservation—who'd sooner flee than try to help."

A crack heaved down the center of Marina's chest. He wasn't wrong, but his bitterness at her will to live, of all things, stoked a fire so deep that its flame burned cold. Blood roared in her head so loud no number of breaths could subdue it.

"Just like you fled Altus," she said.

Pierce looked up, pain in his eyes, but Marina's vision was much too narrow to appreciate it. She turned and left, knowing if she didn't, the storm inside of her would seep from her veins and wreak havoc. She didn't go back to the manor. Instead, she hurried to the plaza and followed the cool breeze into the small archway between the southern and eastern staircases.

The sea cavern—just as dark and damp as it was when she'd arrived—beckoned her with every splash of seawater. She took the slope down to the edge of the pool, where she let herself fall to her knees and savor the quiet that lingered before she heaved out her first sob. And when she finally let the tears flow, she feared they'd never stop.

CHAPTER 20
A Strength

The glow of seawater, cerulean beneath the weeping stalactites, was more painful than it was beautiful. It reminded her of when she'd woken up here, writhing in the cold, only to come to the gut-wrenching realization that she was farther away from home than she could fathom.

Marina covered her mouth with her hands, muffling her sobs until they had the mercy to grow silent. Hunched over the pool, she let her tears fall into the water.

She could brave the waters again—she could swim as far as her limbs would let her— but the ocean would never help her get home. It hadn't the first night in this terrible place, and it wouldn't now.

"*You* brought me here," she hissed at it, unsure if she was speaking to the ocean, the Omnia, or something else. "I just want to go home. That's all."

Saying it made her cry harder. It was a lie, after all. She didn't want the emptiness— the quiet hallways and rooms she let collect dust. She craved the unobtainable, and even here—even now—she knew how foolish that craving was.

In a rush of rage, she curled into herself and let her power thrum in her body, then willed the water of the pool to follow. She shot her hands to the ceiling, pushing the water up until it hung like a funnel from the rocky sky. For one breath, then another, she kept it suspended, only to drop her hands to her sides and let it fall.

Part of her wanted to *feel* the bone-crushing impact of water the same way she'd felt the tsunami. She wanted it to consume her—to sweep her away and take her back where she belonged. But as it plunged to the rocks below, she shielded herself with her arms and watched the water cascade off the bubble of air she'd swathed herself in.

She belonged nowhere.

She leaned against the closest rock, despair melting into numbness. Why was she fighting so hard to survive when *this* was what survival was?

She brought her knees to her chest, her breaths quickening until footsteps ruptured her misery and replaced it with agitation. She expected to see Pierce, or perhaps someone assigned to bring her back to the manor, but it was Cal who stood a few rocks above her.

"This is usually where I go when I need alone time," she said.

Marina stood and wiped the tears off her face. "Shit, I'm sorry. I'll go."

"No, don't." She shot Marina a fleeting smile. "I recommended this place to you, didn't I?"

She descended the rocks quickly. When she came closer, the glow of the pool reflected onto her face, and Marina's embarrassment faded. Cal looked just as bad as her.

"One of those days," Cal said before Marina could ask. She lowered herself to a rock. "You look like you're having one too."

"Sometimes I think I have too many."

For a minute or so, they listened to the water lapping against the shore. Marina sat on a rock near Cal—close, but not uncomfortably so—then said, "I didn't see you yesterday."

"I take shifts during Double Moon so the sentries can get the day off."

"You don't mind?"

"I'm not fond of that many people, and I like to see the moons."

A few more moments of silence passed, and just as Marina began to fret about finding another way to break it, Cal beat her to it.

"The ceiling is dripping," she muttered. She glanced at the stalactites and held out her hand to catch the water. She didn't seem curious about it, thank goodness. She simply rubbed her palms together, then said, "So why are you here?"

"Needed time alone" was all Marina could think to respond.

"No shit. Why?"

She wasn't sure she could find an answer to that—not one that would suffice, at least. Instead, she shrugged and said, "What about you?"

Cal cast a longing look at the water before meeting Marina's gaze. "I'm missing her more than usual today. It gets harder around Double Moon."

Marina's heart sank. "I'm sorry."

"That's what everyone says."

"It's annoying, I know. But when I'm on the other end, it's all I can think to say."

"You lost someone?"

"My parents, in an accident. One that wouldn't have happened if not for me."

Through the corner of her eye, she could see Cal's demeanor change. For a moment,

Cal wavered, then whispered, "I blame myself for Astra too. Sometimes I don't know what's worse: the grief or the guilt."

"They're separate kinds of hell." Marina paused, then tried to smile when she said, "Take it day by day, right?"

"I hate to disappoint, but I don't take my own advice," Cal said through a bleak grin. "Sometimes it's easier to be miserable." She paused. "But hearing what you did to Ocot last night made me smile, even if only for a second."

That makes one of us.

"He isn't totally at fault," Marina whispered.

Cal frowned, but instead of pushing it, she said, "You seem to be improving with magic, though."

"I'm getting there." *For all the good it's done me.*

"Give yourself credit. Manipulating water to reach the stalactites? That's incredible."

Marina blinked at her, then laughed weakly. "Here I was thinking you didn't notice."

"Then you underestimate how many times I've been here."

Marina tried to conceal the ache in her chest by giving Cal a sympathetic smile. "If I'm ever here again and you're looking for alone time, tell me to screw off and I will. This place was your sanctuary before it was mine."

Cal returned the smile, and for the first time, Marina saw her composure fade away. "You remind me of Astra, you know. How you talk, how you act...that first night I found you here, I almost thought you were her." She chuckled. "Stupid, I know, because you look nothing alike. But she'd done what you did so many times. She'd had panic attacks here, especially when the dead years first started, and I talked her down from every single one."

Cal's chin wobbled, and though the gesture was uncharacteristic, Marina put her hand on Cal's shoulder.

"After she died, I had my own," Cal said. "Night after night, I'd see ruemin ripping into her, taking my sister away from me because of a mistake I made."

"It's not your fault," Marina whispered.

Cal rested her hand atop Marina's, and a few tears slipped out of her eyes. Though Marina tried to remain stoic—for Cal as well as herself—her throat had grown scratchy and her vision blurry.

"See, this is what I'm talking about," Cal said through a tearful laugh. "Astra was a sympathetic crier too. She felt so much, all the time. She just couldn't contain it."

Marina wiped her eyes. "I guess we share a weakness."

"It's not a weakness, Marina. It's a strength. Such an incredible, beautiful strength—to feel so deeply."

A kernel of light, which Marina once thought was long gone, brightened within her. Not by much, but enough for her to notice.

～

The light followed Marina back to her room that afternoon, and with it, determination. Her power flared up not when she did away with her emotions the way Aeric wanted her to, but when she acknowledged them—let them wash through her without drowning.

She could flounder all she wanted in guilt—hating herself for not being Elsudra's savior and scorning her desire to leave this place—but she *wasn't* a savior. The most heroic thing she could do was be honest with herself and move forward. If that meant braving the third floor, so be it. That was a risk she was more than willing to take.

If there was anyone in the Delve who'd have resources on Locus, it would be Aeric. More than that, it was Aeric who'd manipulated Brenna's portal to bring Kieron back. Who was to say she wouldn't find something that would bring her home? Was it an overly optimistic prospect? Yes, but she was more than desperate enough to chase it anyway.

Pierce didn't call her in the days following, but Ismene occasionally came in to check on her and ask if she needed anything. Marina did her best to put up a casual front, though she knew Ismene could see through it.

Luckily, when Ismene was uncomfortable, she talked, which was exactly what Marina was relying on. She wouldn't manipulate her again—she'd implicated Ismene enough—but when Ismene mentioned in passing one morning that Aeric was up at the borders for the day, Marina figured it was now or never.

Once Ismene had left, she slipped her shears into the side of her boot, heart pounding as she stepped out into the hallways, which felt larger and emptier than usual. She was improvising, but what else could she do? She couldn't ask for directions without raising suspicions.

The farther she was from the grand staircase, the narrower the halls became, and the pit of ice in her gut grew.

Keep focused on what you're trying to find.

It was the only thing that pushed her forward—knowing her risk would be rewarded if she found anything that could show her how the Keepers severed the Omnia from themselves. Still, she couldn't stop shooting glances behind her, making sure nobody had followed. A staff member would be easy enough to fool; she'd pretend she was lost. Ismene, perhaps, would see through her lie, but the likelihood she'd venture to this part of the manor was low. There was only one person she was worried about, and he was both quick to see through lies and slow to forgive.

Despite her rising pulse, Marina kept on, peering down dead-end hallways and into spare rooms until the second story straightened into a single corridor. There was no staircase, but there was a door—and it was locked.

Lungs tight and stomach in knots, Marina bent down to study the handle. A simple passage doorknob. Those weren't supposed to lock.

Eagerness pricking at her fingertips, Marina rested her hand on the knob and let her spirit—her *sea*—rise. She willed her choppy waves to her hand as she turned the knob, and...nothing.

Her first instinct was to kick the door, but that wouldn't do anything. Instead, she focused on herself. Her waves were chaotic, which wasn't a bad thing; it simply meant it was her responsibility to funnel them into something more effective. She hadn't practiced meditation for nothing.

She stepped back and inhaled, channeling the chaos into energy—into power that extended beyond herself. Then, she reached out and tapped the doorknob.

A snap sounded, and it wasn't until the door creaked open that Marina realized she'd broken something. That hadn't been her intention—in truth, she wasn't sure *what* she'd intended—but it had worked, and that was what mattered. Carefully, she peeked inside at a descending set of stairs.

Nobody had said the third floor was *above* the second—simply that it was a third floor. Pair that with whatever technology locked the door—whatever she'd destroyed, which didn't unnerve her so much as it pleased her—and it was obvious. Still, she tensed as she took her first step down, then another.

As the stairwell went on, it grew unnervingly out of proportion. Eventually, when it had become disorienting enough to make her dizzy, everything came to an end...at a wall of obsidian stone. Blinking in the darkness, Marina put her hand to the rock. That was it?

No, there was something...more. The energy around her had shifted. When Marina leaned back and squinted at the rock, a faint ripple of light caught her eye.

A glamour. Of course. Was there a shield here too? What was behind this wall that Aeric didn't want people finding?

She might as well try to bypass it. She'd overpowered Aeric's magic before, hadn't she? The only difference was she'd altered that shield from the inside. If there was a shield here, she'd be coming at it from the opposite direction.

No matter. She'd try anyway, and if nothing happened, there'd be no harm done.

This is so dumb, Marina.

She let the thought wash away. At this point, she was much too determined to turn back. The tide within her steadied, swelling from her bones and gushing to her skin. She didn't let it all out; she only needed a puddle of its power.

One breath. Another.

At first, nothing happened. But she kept on, directing her focus toward the rock and the waves within her. She imagined the metaphorical seawater at her fingertips, cresting and curling at her will as it washed over the obsidian. Slowly, the mental image became less an image and more a feeling—as though each breath brought her body closer to her spirit. When the center of the rock began to glimmer, she maintained a level head, silently reeling as the glamour faded, forming a hole big enough to fit through.

Marina's stomach flipped. *This isn't worth it.*

Yes, it was. She'd come here for a reason, and she wasn't about to let her fear turn her around now. In defiance, she stepped through the hole—through the *wall*—and when a new hallway came into view, a laugh bubbled at her lips.

Exhaustion followed soon after, and her laugh turned into a wince. She leaned against a nearby stalagmite, fighting hard to stay alert. She hadn't felt so tired at the borders, but that had been involuntary—a sudden burst of magic. Here, she'd had to pull from the deepest parts of herself.

The polished tile of the corridor before her had a tawny hue to it, but the walls and ceiling didn't look much different than the rest of the Delve. And yet, there were no lights or colored lanterns woven through the stalactites that hung from the ceiling, which made Marina realize how much of a difference they made. Life existed in the Delve; here, things were stagnant.

She took a few moments to collect herself, then started forward, her heart in her throat. As nimble as her steps were, she couldn't keep her shoes from echoing on the tile, which pissed her off about as much as it worried her. It was obviously by design—meant to call attention to intruders. She took great pains to silence her footsteps as she neared the maroon door at the end of the hall, and before her nerves got the best of her, she flung it open and stepped inside.

CHAPTER 21
Marionette

The room that lay before her wasn't grand, but it wasn't plain either. Bookshelves and ligneous tables lined the walls, and every open space was stacked with books and papers. Even the velvet chaise was covered in loose, crumpled notes.

If there was any beauty here, it was on the walls. Paintings even more stunning than the ones in the manor hung between bookshelves, each one full of so much color that Marina didn't stop herself as she moved toward them. She'd never been much of an artist herself, but there was a lure to these pictures that even an amateur could appreciate.

They were all impasto landscapes: forests beneath a night sky, sparkling seas, and golden suns. But despite their vibrancy, there was a solemn tone to each of the paintings Marina couldn't quite pinpoint.

Though she knew beyond any sliver of doubt that the room belonged to Aeric, it looked nothing like his pristine, painstakingly organized office. Here, things were haphazard, as though it took too much energy and time to pick up the scraps and right the toppled books. The sorry state of the room only made the paintings stick out more. How had he even acquired art so grandeur? Probably from Altus. She wouldn't put it past him to have taken them for himself.

Marina scoffed as she approached the chaise. The notes were written in symbols, much like the ones etched into the buttons on her shower. Elsudran letters; of course. She held a sheet up to the light of a wall sconce, scanning it for a sheen. Nothing.

The books, then. They had to have *something* readable. There weren't too many, despite the size of the shelves, but each one had a dial on the spine and a luster to the paper. She reached for one but froze when light caught the corner of her eye.

It came from the top shelf—from a wooden stand where a ring had been placed. The ring itself was a bit of an eye-sore. The center stone was the size of a marble, maybe larger, made to look like a plasma globe. At first, she thought perhaps that was where the light had come from, only to realize it wasn't the ring at all, but what surrounded it. The entire stand, in fact, was shrouded in a caustic network of lights—soft and gentle, like reflections at the bottom of a pool.

Marina stood on her toes to get a better look, then plucked a spare paper off the chaise and held its edge to the light.

A zapping sound ricocheted throughout the room, and Marina recoiled as the paper caught flame. It flitted to the floor, its edge alight, and before it could set fire to anything else, she smothered it with the sole of her boot.

As the embers died down, so did the wild beating of her heart.

Wonderful. Now he'll definitely know someone was here.

She'd think about that later. She'd made it this far, and by now, her curiosity was too overwhelming to ignore.

Breath in her throat, Marina turned her attention back to the books. Most were textbooks. She ran her fingers over the spines, then pulled a book titled *Sister Realms in Relation to Elsudra* from the shelf. Eagerly, she flipped through the pages. Realms like Sundra had whole chapters dedicated to their history and people, but when she finally found Earth, all she could find was: *But a small part of an otherwise barren realm, this ellipsoid planet is defined by its vast and rudimentary nature. Though Earth's biota resembles that of its fellow sister realms, even the most evolved inhabitants are unaware of their ocean's connection to alternate realms. They lack the acuity, technology, and magic to be of either considerable threat or benefit to Elsudra.*

"An ant colony," Marina whispered. She put the book back on the shelf. Even if there was more written about Earth, she didn't want to read it. Instead, she continued looking through the books until she landed on one with a cracked spine that read, *A Comprehensive History of Elsudra's Sorcerers of the Court.*

She pulled it from the shelf, smoothing the bookcloth as she hauled it to the nearest table and placed it on top of some scattered papers.

The book was gigantic—each page filled with pictures of and details about the Sorcerers of the Court. Stomach in knots, Marina flipped to the back. The last page wasn't as crisp as those before it. The parchment was creased and worn, as though someone had flipped to it many times and let it age beneath their fingertips. The text, however, hadn't faded, and she could clearly read the name that glinted beneath the paper's shine: *Kieron.*

She stopped breathing as she studied his picture. He wasn't some beast or demon, which seemed plausible given the stories she'd heard, but instead a man of middle age, with pale skin, an oblong face, and grizzled hair. Even his eyes—blue as the midday sky—didn't hold the malice she'd expected.

Marina soothed the pit in her stomach by pulling the shears from her boot and clutching them in her hand as she read.

Kieron's section didn't mention his exile. Perhaps no one had gotten around to updating the text. Aeric wasn't mentioned either.

Above Kieron, however, a woman with hollow cheeks and dark hair caught Marina's eye. Brenna—Kieron's predecessor and the creator of the Sundran portal. She had a far-off look to her, as though her mind was so active that she struggled to orient herself in the present. Had she realized who Kieron was before she'd chosen him to succeed her, or had she been too preoccupied to pay attention?

Marina's gaze drifted to Brenna's hand, which rested on her collarbone as though she'd wanted it to be pictured. Or perhaps it was that she'd wanted her ring to be pictured —large, gaudy, and made to look like a plasma globe.

Marina furrowed her brow, eyes trailing to the ring atop the shelf. Was that the same ring? It had to be—the two looked identical. But why did Aeric have it?

The text beside Brenna's picture didn't yield much insight, though it seemed Ismene had been right; Brenna *had* been eccentric. Her text detailed both her unconventional nature and her unmatched magical talent, even going as far to claim that she was, by and large, Elsudra's most talented Sorcerer of the Court.

Gingerly, Marina put the book back on the shelf, then scoured the rest of the titles. Perhaps there were no books about Locus. If the answers were contained in Aeric's handwritten notes, she couldn't read them; they hadn't been magically altered.

She stifled a groan as she scanned the rest of the space, but nothing stood out. Still, she spent a few more minutes circling the room to make sure she hadn't missed anything. At a serpentine table next to the chaise, a tortoiseshell box glinted in the light, and though Marina knew staying here longer than necessary was foolish, she approached it. She couldn't help herself. She'd come so far; she couldn't leave without looking at everything.

She clicked it open. There was only one object inside: a brass instrument that looked a little like a kaleidoscope—pretty, but otherwise unassuming. Her heart sank.

What did you expect?

She'd known going in that one of the possibilities was finding nothing, but it did little to curb her disappointment.

Fiddling with the shears in one hand, she plucked the kaleidoscope from the box and held it to the light, then pressed the lens to her eye.

There were no lights or colors, but rather a tunnel that somehow fit perfectly into the little device. The tunnel pulsed, then grew until it sprang from the instrument, enveloping the world around her...

Marina yelped and fell back, hitting the floor with her elbows. The shears clattered beside her, which she quickly grabbed, eyes wide and hands trembling.

The device rolled over to the leg of the serpentine table, where it clinked against the wood. Marina stood and neared it, then tapped it with the side of her shoe. Slowly, she bent down and picked it up, rotating it before raising it to her eye again.

Stupid as it was, she *had* to see what this thing was going to show her—what it could give her that books wouldn't. Though her good sense thrashed about in protest, she looked into the lens, clutching her shears with white-knuckled fingers as the tunnel materialized.

You can lower it at any time...any time...just for a few seconds...

The tunnel melted away, pooling into water—into a world that was, at first, ocean.

No...there was something before the ocean. It begot the sea, and thousands of realms sprang forth from the water, all of which looked and operated similarly. One of the smaller realms was born from a sliver of the sea that brimmed with light—with power, magic, and energy. *The Omnia.* Like a pulsing sun, it grew over the course of eons. Elsudra's ocean feathered into rivers, which widened into lakes, and the Omnia lived in them all—each body of water connected to the sea that surrounded the growing spit of land.

Here and now, Marina realized how small Elsudra was. She could hardly call it a continent. If anything, it resembled a large island. Compared to what she knew, the climates were mild and the seasons tame. But Elsudra's size didn't curtail its beauty. Silky blue mountains brushed against starry skies, and valleys burst with wildflowers. There were lifeforms too—animals and people. She could see them vaguely, as though she were looking through glass that blurred the figures until they were mere silhouettes.

Eras passed in seconds—eras when early Elsudrans discovered the Omnia's magic and realized a select few possessed varying abilities to wield it. Four of them had the most, which only made them want more. Marina strained to see them, but everything was blotchy. Was it her vision, or had someone tampered with the device? She swore she could see the sun's rays rising above the ocean, but the colors were so muted—the shadows so thick—that she could barely make out the four Elsudrans.

But then they emerged, and the shadows faded.

Light flickered in the first Keepers' eyes—the same light that had once existed in Elsudra's water. *They* held the Omnia now, and though Marina expected to feel their pride, all she felt was fear. She wanted to know what they'd done—what they'd seen—just as much as she didn't. Whatever stoked their fear was great enough to influence the rules by which their successors swore oaths to follow.

How long had she been here? Seconds? Centuries? She couldn't feel her arms and legs, but in the presence of so much knowledge, finding her body was an afterthought. She needed to see more, so she watched as those greedy, terrified souls crafted a new Elsudra with a more controlled kind of magic. No longer was their gift unfettered; now, it was contained and governed by the fear of what could be.

One, two, three, four. Every distant beat of her heart brought the taste of iron to her mouth, but she watched on.

Thousands of years of regulations and oaths, all of which pruned the nature of the beings who'd pulled the Omnia from water in the first place. Keepers came and went—some with marginal magical abilities, most with nothing—each paying a hefty price when they inherited their quarter. No names, no goals, no desires minus the good of Elsudra.

What were they, really—these beings who held the Omnia? They weren't gods, but they weren't fully Elsudran either. What a curse it was, to be nothing but Keepers—to give up one's selfhood for a few years of the same, only to raise descendants out of necessity rather than love. But those descendants were just as removed, and Marina wondered if they forgot the common desires of their kind—if they couldn't yearn for the love of family or friends, or seek out dreams they may've had, for their goal was singular: continuation of Elsudra—of the Omnia itself.

And so, they became reminders that the essence of Elsudra was alive and well, used lawfully by the people who'd found a way to harness it. Until, of course, it wasn't.

The figures before her were still silhouettes, but one was unlike the others. He wasn't a Keeper, but a Sorcerer of the Court—the acting link between Elsudrans and the Omnia. But his job was of little consequence to him. Even if he did it well, it was the Omnia that enticed him. So he devised a plan: he'd spin a blanket of rectitude, lure the unsuspecting fools to its warmth, and as they drifted off to sleep, reveal it to be a spider's web and suck them to a shell.

Kieron's plan had worked. Almost.

The Keepers turned to a ritual for help—Tempus, Marina realized—and a guiding hand pushed them to let go of what their ancestors had stolen. There was another ritual too—Locus, the riskier one—but they braved it anyway, and with Aeric's help, they severed the Omnia from their spirits.

Head pounding, Marina strained to focus, but the smell of iron and fear consumed her. Whose fear was it? Was it hers, spurred by the shadows around her? Or was it the fear of the shadows themselves—the fear they felt as they sent the Omnia out of Elsudra?

There was a voice...a familiar one...

"Marina."

The Omnia danced across sister realms, waiting to find somewhere it could settle—waiting for someone to protect it until it was no longer vulnerable. And yet, like a seed amidst a gust of wind, the Omnia itself didn't choose where to land. Something else did.

What was it? And why did it choose her?

"Marina."

Not me. I didn't...I didn't. I never asked, I never accepted...

But it had already found her, and she couldn't control where it landed.

"Marina."

Her arm...someone was grabbing her arm...

No, no, no, NO, NO, NO...

The world disappeared, but the grip on her arm remained, and she was yelling—begging for it to pick someone else.

"Marina."

The grip tightened. Marina gasped as the room came back into view and someone spun her around. Instinctively, she slammed the tip of her shears into their shoulder.

Aeric stumbled back, his usually guarded expression riddled with shock. Fear pulsated through Marina as he looked at the blood trickling from his wound, then straightened and wrenched the shears from his shoulder.

Marina clasped her hand over her mouth. Something seeped onto her fingers—her nose was bleeding, and by God, her head ached—and it took courage to make eye contact with Aeric. His shock had faded, though she wasn't sure if the rage that replaced it was much better. Aeric's anger was never explosive like hers. His was cold—a chill that burned more severely than any fire.

The shears tightened in his hand. He took a disgusted look at them, then tossed them to the floor. "I had two rules."

Marina eyed the shears as they clanked against the brass device, which she'd dropped once more onto the stone. "I thought you were at the border."

"I came back early," Aeric said. "Thankfully for you." The wintry blaze in his eyes flared up. "You *stupid* girl. I told you I had reasons for the rules I set." He strode over to the object and swept it up in one hand. "This is an anteactus—used to keep memories. This one contains the recorded memory of Elsudra itself. Absorbing that much information can cause irreversible damage to your mind."

Marina wiped the blood from underneath her nose. "I'm fine."

"The Omnia's power likely shielded you from the damage it would've otherwise caused," Aeric said flatly, "but you were bleeding and delirious when I found you all the same." He shook his head, then set the device down on the serpentine table. "Is it really so hard for you to follow rules?" He let out a long sigh, then stalked over to the chaise. With a flick of his hand, the papers and the anteactus flitted to the nearest table, leaving room for him to sit down and assess his shoulder.

"Apparently it is," he said when Marina remained silent. He put a hand to his wound, then observed the blood on his fingers. "You won't give up this hunt for Locus, will you?"

Marina shook her head, unable to find her voice.

"Tell me: even if you did learn it and successfully complete it, what would you do once you'd severed the Omnia from yourself? How would you get home? No portals have been made to your realm, and none ever will be." She met his gaze, willing her own to be just as icy. "What is your plan, Marina?"

"I don't know," she whispered, hating herself for admitting it. *But I'll keep pushing forward*, she thought, *because I have to. I'd rather die trying to escape than die fighting your war.*

Aeric nodded, as though he'd known that was her answer.

"What I do know," she added, "is that I'm not going to be your marionette and die trying to rectify your mistakes."

Aeric stood. "A marionette. A weapon of war. You play the victim very well for a girl who's caused her fair share of pain. Here you are, whining and scheming and breaking rules, while there are people above who may never know peace again."

"Well, you know who to thank for that."

"Yes, I'm aware of your disdain for me. Though I did underscore how much worse my predecessor is, did I not? At the moment, I'm one of the few people keeping you from him." A look she couldn't read flashed in Aeric's eyes. "If you continue like this, not only will you fail to learn Locus and get home, but you'll also never be strong enough to resist Kieron. He'll find a way to take the Omnia from you, then kill you as soon as he has what he's after. So I ask you, Marina: how much longer will you fight this pointless battle?"

Pointless. Was it really, or did he just want her to think that so she'd be more likely to bend to his will?

"I've learned some magic" was all she could think to say.

"Thanks to Pierce being my mouthpiece. Even so, fighting off a drunken sentry isn't a suitable way to measure your success."

Useless. Pointless. Maybe he was right. But the alternative—giving in and training for a fight she'd no doubt die in—was so unfathomable that she couldn't bring herself to accept it. Not unless she wanted to do away with what little was left of her hope. She couldn't match Kieron, just like she couldn't match Aeric. She didn't have it in her.

"It's better than nothing," she muttered.

"If a talented sorcerer challenged you, your progress would be akin to nothing," Aeric said. "If I attempted to breach your mental shields now, they'd likely be as weak as they were when you first arrived here."

Marina stopped breathing when he took a step closer to her. Her hands curled around invisible shears, only to silently curse when she glanced at them on the floor.

Her first instinct was to dodge him, but that wouldn't do much. There was nowhere to go. When he reached out his hand, something in Marina snapped. A great, violent current simmering beneath the surface of her waves reared its head, then furled outward, and Marina grabbed Aeric's wrist before he could grab hers.

Her waves flooded into frame and rushed toward a wall of fog. She'd never felt so in control before; even the light beneath the water bowed to her will. Electric and almighty, the Omnia was as much Marina as her waves were. She basked in its power as she rammed against Aeric's shields, forming fissures so deep he couldn't keep her out. She channeled her anger and fear into something as strong as it was wild, and when she broke through his shields, she saw what lay beneath.

Instead of an ocean, a labyrinth of fog swirled about Aeric's essence. It was heavier in some places than others, and its bite was cold. But since she wasn't sure she'd get this chance again, she flung herself forward.

She had no idea which memory she wanted to target, but she sure as hell wasn't going to let up. She careened into a distant, billowing cloud where a boy stood, surrounded by the haze. He was small and thin, and his wavy gold-brown hair fell in front of his eyes as he looked at a body. A tear rolled down his cheek, but he quickly wiped it away.

Like her own memories, the images were blurry and the sounds muted, but she knew who the boy was.

Aeric must've been six, maybe seven, and he stood over the body of a woman. Even in death, she was pretty, and her hair was the same shade as his. Marina couldn't help but wonder if her eyes matched Aeric's too.

Firm hands gripped Aeric's shoulders.

"Don't mourn her. You have a bright future to look toward."

The voice was strangely affable, and it was only when Marina got a glimpse of sky-blue eyes that she realized it was Kieron.

She wanted to see more, but Aeric was pushing her out—hard. He managed to wrench her from the memory, but his injury curbed his focus, and Marina's flurry of emotions formed a tsunami so powerful that Aeric couldn't stop her when she plunged back into the mist. At the moment, they were no more than spirits, grappling for power amidst a shadowy landscape of fog and invading seawater.

And *she* was winning.

In the next memory, Aeric was a little older, standing with Kieron in front of a portly, slick-haired man bound by chains.

"I can't," Aeric whispered.

Kieron got down to his level as the man in chains let out a muffled plea. "*This man hurt your mother*," he said. "*Will you watch as someone else avenges her, or will you take control and do it yourself?*"

Marina could feel Aeric's apprehension at war with his eagerness to please when he said, "*But our Keepers...*"

"*Are vessels for the Omnia. Beyond that, they're useless—nothing more than automatons who blindly follow the whims and wishes of the court. People like us don't have the luxury of being so naive.*" He clasped his hands. "*People are not good, Aeric; this man is not good. Will we forgive him and let him do to another what he did to your mother, or will we use our greatness to ensure he never does it again?*"

Aeric's nod was satisfactory enough to Kieron, who patted his shoulder. "*Today, we'll practice delirium inducement.*"

The man uttered another strangled cry, and the memory dispersed.

Pressure surrounded Marina as the fog closed in on her. The temperature dropped even further, threatening to freeze her in place, but she persisted, stumbling about until she saw a much older Aeric and Kieron.

"*Four knows*," Kieron hissed. He flicked his hand toward a desk full of notes, reducing them to shreds. "*The others will soon. They'll know I found their archives, and they'll realize what I've been researching. This is more than the hypotheticals we've discussed.*" He turned to Aeric, desperation in his eyes. "*But this could be a win for us if we're patient—if you promise you'll do what we agreed.*"

Aeric didn't falter when he said, "*You know I will.*"

He was taller than Kieron now, and his face didn't hold the apprehension it did when he was a child. And yet, the pain in his eyes made it all too clear that beneath his exterior, he was still the same wary young boy.

Marina wasn't the only one who noticed.

"*You became a son to me the day your mother died*," Kieron said as he put his hands on Aeric's shoulders. "*I don't say it enough, so I will now. You're more to me than my successor. Remember that as you play your part to the court charlatans and hypocrites who suppress the power of our world. Remember what can be.*"

A pang of warmth and sadness washed through Marina—through *Aeric*—as he glanced at the remaining notes scattered throughout the room, then destroyed them with a nod.

Now she was starting to get tired. As infinite as the Omnia's power was, her ability to wield it was limited. But she couldn't stop. The revenge that had first motivated her was gone, replaced by an insatiable curiosity.

She sidestepped every gust of haze that came her way, skimming through and past hundreds of memories as she hurtled forward. Fog darker than the rest hung ahead, and Marina gathered her strength before leaping into it.

Two figures stood in a grand room with marble floors and windows so tall they hit the ceiling. Aeric was one of them—the same age he was now—but the second man Marina had never seen before. Minus the man's pointed nose and pale skin, she could barely make out his features; he wore a gossamer veil that sheathed his face and fell to his knees, held in place by a corolla adorned with four towers of beryl. It wasn't until he spoke and moved that Marina realized how old he was.

"You understand what's been asked of you," he said. He didn't go to any lengths to make his command sound like a question.

Aeric's reply was curt. *"Nothing was asked."* The silence between them lingered until Aeric whispered, *"I understand."*

Marina thought she saw a glimpse of a smile from beneath the veil. *"I know this wasn't what you'd hoped for, but death would've been an easy punishment."* He turned to face the four thrones at the center of the room, only to be called back by the world beyond the panes. *"Between us,"* he said, his eyes on the distant hills, *"I don't think you deserved execution."*

"The other three didn't seem to think that."

The other three...was Aeric referencing the other Keepers? Was this man one of them?

Four, Marina thought when she looked again at the crystals on his headpiece. There were four...who else could he be?

The old man smiled again. *"Tempus gave us clear guidance. Whether or not you have faith in our interpretation, I'm hopeful for the future."*

"Of course I have faith in it," Aeric snapped. After a bout of uncomfortable silence, he lowered his voice and added, *"You're not a stupid man, Four, even if you were slow to see who Kieron really is."*

Though she'd known who Four was before Aeric confirmed it, Marina reeled from the shock anyway. She wasn't sure what she'd expected the Keepers to look like, but it certainly wasn't this. The veil that hung from Four's head obscured his features, making him look more like a ghost than a person. Did the other three look the same?

The mist condensed, swathing about the memory until she could hardly see or hear it. She felt like she was watching an old movie; the voices sounded like static and the room was blurry. She almost lost focus, but she refused to release her hold. She smothered the mist in seawater, washing away the distortion and hanging on despite her exhaustion.

"Some of us are still coming to terms with who he is." There was no judgment in Four's voice, but Aeric wilted anyway.

He'd always had a wan look to himself, Marina thought, but it was worse here. Even the flickering candlelight from the chandeliers couldn't bring light to his face. Most noticeable of all, however, were his eyes—filled with regret and the pain he held as a child.

"I hope you're right," Aeric finally said. *"About more than the Omnia's future host."*

"I hope so too," Four whispered. *"But I have faith in more than the guidance we obtained. I have faith in you."* When Aeric shifted uncomfortably, Four said, *"You don't like to hear that."*

"I don't understand it."

"Would you have preferred to swear an oath? To mar your spirit so severely that you live the rest of your life abiding by laws you never wrote? Of course, you'd have to consent to swear an oath for it to work, and we both know you'd sooner choose death." He chuckled. *"The voice I heard during Tempus...there was scarcely anything to interpret."*

Marina could've gasped had she control of her mouth. The rumors of Aeric's oath— they were all just that: rumors. Why hadn't he corrected them?

Four turned to Aeric and put a hand on his shoulder. Though Aeric tensed, he didn't move away.

"I didn't need to be told by some higher power to trust you. I always have." When Aeric bristled, Four said, *"I believe you're as much Kieron's victim as anyone else. Maybe more so."* He lowered his hand. *"The Omnia is gone, and Kieron will be here soon. I can only hope I'll meet the others in a kinder world than this. Whether the effects of Locus kill me or Kieron does, my time is at its end. So I look to you, and I think my hope is well placed."*

The silence that followed remained unbroken for some time, as though both men were too exhausted to fill it. It was then Marina realized that Aeric had stopped trying to push her out. Had she truly overpowered him? Though the notion gave her pride, with it came a second, far more uncomfortable realization: she was barely hanging on.

Absently, Four said, *"The voice I heard...it made me feel as though I was no longer an old man. 'What comes from the sea calls to the sea,' it said. And if I hadn't been sure of our decision before, I was then."*

Aeric's lips parted before he spoke. *"I fail to fathom what kind of being would accept the call of a world that isn't their own."*

Again—that shadow of a smile beneath the veil. *"Perhaps,"* Four said, *"the kind we need."*

The words evoked pain so deep that, at long last, Marina lost control of her waves.

As her consciousness and body became one, exhaustion swept in, ravaging her senses and rendering her limbs useless. She hit the ground, her head spinning.

Too far...she'd pushed herself too far. And yet, as loud as her ears rang and as dizzy as she'd grown, all she could think was…

"There was no oath."

She recoiled after she said it, expecting Aeric's rage to freeze the room over. But he was quiet—even for him—and when Marina's vision leveled out, she saw him sitting on the chaise with his head in his hands.

A few seconds passed, then a minute, and finally, Marina said, "Aeric."

He looked up at her—blood still dribbling down his shoulder and onto his coat—and though she'd anticipated *some* emotion, it seemed he had none left to give.

Marina collected what little there was of her strength and tried to stand, but her legs were as useless as they were that day in the sea cavern.

"Wait," Aeric muttered. "Wait for your energy to return. You overexerted yourself. As did I." After another beat of silence, he said, "For a beginner, that was perhaps the greatest show of psychometry I've ever seen. I expected something…but not that."

"Were you…*baiting* me?"

Aeric didn't need to respond for her to know the answer.

Marina pressed her palms to the ground, savoring the cool stone beneath her fingers. Cautiously, she asked, "Why did you lie about your oath?"

"Saying nothing isn't the same as lying."

She didn't have the energy to debate semantics with him—that, and her curiosity was elsewhere. In less than a whisper, she asked, "What did Kieron do to you?"

When Aeric didn't respond, she sighed. "I'm sorry I came here. It was a last-ditch attempt to find something that would get me home." Saying it brought tears to her eyes, but she blinked them away, then added, "I'm also sorry I stabbed you."

"I deserved it," Aeric muttered.

"Are you saying that because you believe it, or because you're too tired to argue?"

"Maybe both." He took a breath, then said, "This is good. You broke through my mental shields and surpassed my strength, even if your stamina needs work."

Marina winced. He was obviously still hell-bent on his original plan. It seemed all her attempts to escape were for naught. Her eyes began to sting again.

Aeric observed her before saying, "I know you didn't ask for this, so I'll make a deal with you."

Marina's stomach flipped, and though her limbs still shook with fatigue, she forced herself to stand as he did.

"Even if you didn't show it right away, you possess the aptitude needed to wield the Omnia's magic. If you let me help you cultivate it, I believe you'll improve remarkably." He wavered as he mustered the energy to say what he clearly didn't want to. "If you do," he finally said, "and if, by then, you still wish to sever your connection to the Omnia—and are, beyond any reasonable doubt, strong enough to withstand doing so—I'll help you attempt Locus."

Marina blinked at him. "But I thought—"

"I'm making a compromise with you," Aeric said, his words clipped. "I don't want you to do that, but since my way clearly didn't work, we must find some middle ground."

Marina looked at the anteactus, then at the bloodied shears. Aeric's deal was the closest to real, lasting peace she'd felt in a while. She didn't know the price she'd pay if she agreed, but she knew the cost of turning him down: she'd destroy any chance of getting home.

She glanced at Aeric's shoulder. "Will you have to see healers for that?"

"I can heal it myself. Not as well as the healers, but enough to suffice."

"I thought Sorcerers of the Court performed all magic better than everyone."

"We aren't gods. We cannot do what we don't train to do. It's our *ability* to wield magic that surpasses most." He paused, a kernel of unease in his eyes as he said, "Which brings me back to the deal I offered you."

Marina wiped some of the dried blood from under her nose, then asked, "What will happen to Pierce's job if I agree?"

"I'm sure Florin can find another for him."

"Not at the southern border," she said quickly. "He has a lot of talent. He should serve somewhere he can make a difference."

Though it still hurt to think of the things he'd said to her, she knew he'd said them out of anger and fear. She'd done the same, far too many times to count. Small as it was, she hoped her gesture would bring him happiness.

Aeric responded with a nod, and despite the pounding of her heart, Marina said, "I agree." She knew she should leave it there, but she couldn't help herself when she asked, "If I *do* get strong enough and choose Locus, how do I know you won't back out of the deal?"

Aeric straightened, frowning at his shoulder before he said, "I think, Marina, if you know anything about me, it is this: I do not back out of the promises I make."

And though she never imagined the day would come, she believed him.

CHAPTER 22
Endless Cycles

That night, Marina's waves churned and foamed, as haphazard as the rest of her psyche. Somewhere an immeasurable distance away, an abyss swallowed the ocean in mouthfuls. And her home...she could see her home, but it wasn't empty like she'd left it. People filled the halls, and they called her to them.

Marina, Marina, Marina.

Somehow, the home she saw was both of her past and her future—the way things were and the way they could be. But as she tried to get closer, it shrank away, stranding her in the middle of a stormy sea.

A watery hand tugged on the tether between her subconscious and the world around her, and Marina woke to the glistening of a thousand stars suspended in the air of her bedroom. It was as though the night sky shrank to fit between the walls, only to flicker into nothingness when she adjusted her vision. She wondered where they'd come from— what they meant—but quickly found herself preoccupied by anticipation.

Her agreement with Aeric was simple. Every evening, they would train. She'd been surprised when he'd told her to meet him on the third floor, only to realize he wanted to see if she could get in again. She already knew he wasn't an easy teacher, but remembering how horribly their previous training had gone made Marina feel sick. Would their work together be just as painful as before?

The emotions she'd gleaned from Aeric's memories only made her more conflicted. She'd expected him to be filled with rage, but Kieron had left him empty. It wasn't the wrath of a cheated man she'd felt; it was the despondency of an abandoned child.

When Ismene stopped by her room that morning—it had really become more of a social thing, Marina realized, but she didn't mind—she seemed happier than usual, and it didn't take long before she admitted that Aeric told her what had happened.

"Did he tell you the part where I stabbed him with shears?" Marina asked nervously.

"Not explicitly. But he didn't hide his pain very well."

Marina winced. "He said he could heal it."

"He's never been a good healer. It's one of the few areas of magic he doesn't excel in. Back in Altus, a servant accidentally slammed Aeric's hand in a door. People say Aeric healed it himself, but I've noticed he still struggles to write."

"What happened to the servant?"

"Nothing, minus a tongue-lashing from his superiors, I presume." Ismene paused, then said softly, "Aeric isn't as cruel as you think."

The image of that sullen child flickered at the back of Marina's mind, and with it, the promises he'd made—none at the behest of an oath.

"I don't know what agreement you came to," Ismene said after a few moments, "but Aeric seems hopeful. I didn't realize how strange it was to see him that way."

Marina only nodded. Ismene clearly didn't know about Locus, and Marina didn't have the heart to tell her.

"You should also know," Ismene continued, "that you're more to me than the Omnia's host. More to all of us. I mean it. We care about you because you're *you*—because you're so much more than the curse you were given. It wasn't supposed to be one, but that's what it became. Pierce understands that too."

A tingling sensation rushed from Marina's nose to her eyes. "I'm not angry at either of you," she said. "Aeric and I were at a standstill. He did what he had to do to move past it. But I owe you an apology. I doubted your faith in Aeric. For that—and for manipulating you to get dirt on him—I'm sorry."

"Bygones," Ismene said.

Marina smiled weakly. "I should speak to Pierce too."

Ismene gave her a knowing look. "Something tells me he's waiting on your call."

Marina's heart fluttered as she sat at the plaza fountain that afternoon, waiting for Pierce. She practiced manipulating the water as a distraction, but her mind was elsewhere, and the whirlpools she managed were small and sloppy.

"Those are nice." Pierce made no effort to hide the hesitancy in his voice, and when he sat beside her, he kept his distance. Marina wasn't sure if it was out of respect or timidity.

The tension hadn't burned off yet, and strained silence hung between them. Marina took a breath, then whispered, "Remember when you asked me to sing, and I said I didn't?

Well, I used to." She let the whirlpools fizzle out. "My dad had a guitar. We'd learn songs together, and I'd sing them. But after my parents died, I told myself that as long as his guitar remained unplayed, I wouldn't sing. I did it as some kind of punishment at first, but it became the only control I had over what happened."

Pierce leaned onto his hand. "What *did* happen?"

Marina took a breath, and despite her reservations, she told him everything. When she described the storms that took her parents from her, he didn't recoil or flinch.

"There were two storms that night," Marina whispered, her chin trembling. "The one they got caught in—the one with rain and that drunk college kid on his way home from a party—and the one that brought them there. I'll never forgive myself for the last one." A tear rolled down her cheek. "Even as a kid, little things worked me up. One moment I'd be fine, but if something set me off, my reaction would be so *intense*. Sometimes, I'd even get worked up for no reason at all, but the feelings would fade, even if they were always there, in my head. Doctors said it was anxiety. Depression. Obsession. Neuroticism. They'd throw around all these words...but my parents and I just called them storms. As I got older, I got better at working through them, but every once in a while, they would be too much. And the night my mom and dad died, that was what they were. Too much. Ever since then, I haven't sung—not because I don't want to, but because I won't let myself. Because I'm the one at fault for their deaths, even if it wasn't my car that rammed into theirs."

She scoffed softly. "Sometimes I wonder how much I really want to go home. But then I think about the Omnia and everything I *can't* do, and home seems safer, even if it's not the home I want. Maybe Elsudra would be better served if I wasn't in the picture."

A bout of silence passed, which Pierce interrupted when he wrapped his arms around her. When he pulled back, his eyes watered. "I trust you and Aeric," he said. "I know you'll make the right choices. But as for Elsudra being better without you...I'm not sure I agree. Because for the first time in ages, Marina, I finally feel like I'm home."

Marina's face crumpled. She couldn't figure out what she felt. Warmth, fear, longing... what did it matter? Pierce embraced her again, and for a while, they leaned on each other.

"I got stationed at the northern border," Pierce whispered.

Marina let out a surprised exhale, then released Pierce and studied his smile to make sure he wasn't joking. "You did?"

"On Aeric's orders. Even my voco got an upgrade. Would I be wrong to think that Aeric's orders were actually yours?"

Marina shrugged, unable to keep her own smile from tugging at her lips. "Consider it part of my apology. Especially after I used what you'd told me about Altus to manipulate Ocot. That was horrible of me to say. My desperation doesn't justify it."

Pierce's smile faded. "Horrible, maybe. But not untrue."

"It *is* untrue. What I said about not trusting you…that was all bullshit."

Pierce sighed. "Well, Ocot was right about one thing: I *can* be a hypocrite. After what I did in Altus…I deserved to get called out for that." Before Marina could protest, he said, "You were right. I fled Altus to survive, then judged you for wanting to survive as well." He pulled his knees to his chest. "I did the same shit to the man I loved. We used to promise we'd never abandon each other for anything. And I abandoned him." His throat bobbed. "When the war started, I said I'd sooner die than live under such a repressive regime. He disagreed—said he'd prioritize survival. I didn't react well, and when my dad told me of my place in the Delve, I didn't even try to secure his safety. I ran off to save myself—did exactly what I said I'd never do. And I broke the one promise I swore I'd never break."

Marina's chest began to ache, even more so when Pierce said, "Fear breeds hypocrisy."

She nodded, and for a while, they sat in silence.

Eventually, Pierce said, "I was happy when I learned you'd be working with Aeric. If you two cooperate, there'll be no limits."

Marina gave him a tight-lipped smile. "If we can set aside our differences, maybe."

"I think it's your similarities you should be more concerned with," Pierce said. When Marina scoffed, he put his hands up. "Work with him and report back. That's all I'll say."

More silence passed, marred only slightly by the fountain's trickling. She could tell Pierce was lost in thought long before he whispered, "Sometimes I wonder where the line is drawn between grief and guilt. We grieve the ones we love, but we punish ourselves at the same time. You don't sing because you blame yourself. I don't say his name because I blame myself. The cycle keeps going."

The pressure in Marina's throat plummeted to her stomach. How many people were in this endless cycle of guilt? Cal blamed herself for Astra, Ismene regretted leaving home, Pierce refused to say the name of the man he'd both loved and deserted. And even Aeric, who Marina had convinced herself was at fault for everything, had never pined for Kieron's reign more than he'd pined for his approval. How different was he, really, from the rest of the lonely people plagued by guilt—by this cycle? How different was she?

"It goes on until we break it," she said.

"When do we do that?"

"I don't know. I guess when we choose to. But we have to be patient with ourselves."

Pierce nodded. "Let's promise each other we will be, for both of our sakes. We'll take things day by day." He sighed, then wrapped his arms around his legs. "And today, I'm not ready to break my cycle."

Marina peered into the fountain. "Neither am I."

CHAPTER 23
Weak and Afraid

Though she left Pierce in a better headspace, Marina couldn't shake what he'd said about her and Aeric's similarities. She knew she should prepare to train, but instead, she spent most of the afternoon mulling over ways to prove Pierce wrong.

By the time she'd reached the hallway at the end of the second floor, she was already exhausted from the day's ruminations. She managed to ground herself—not perfectly, but it was something—and breathed as she turned the passage knob, preparing for the worst.

With a *click*, the door popped open. Marina let loose a confused exhale as she peered down the stairwell. She'd expected Aeric to have at least relocked it. Hesitantly, she descended, but the stairwell—strange and disorienting as it was—seemed no different than it had the first time.

Down, down, down. To the right, just a bit, though right seemed terribly like left, and at every slight turn, Marina flinched in anticipation. But there was nothing there. When she arrived at the wall of obsidian stone, her sigh of relief was audible.

She'd expected Aeric to have laid out some kind of magical trap, but everything was just as it had been yesterday. Though it took her some time to visualize her waves pooling at her fingertips, his glamour and shield eventually started to disintegrate.

It was like moving water: simple, natural, and peaceful. As the third floor's hallway came into view, euphoria bubbled up inside Marina. She figured Aeric was going easy on her—perhaps he'd taken a hint from their earlier trainings and decided to cut back a bit—but she didn't mind. At least she'd gotten through.

She reached the maroon door with a trill in her chest. Though her hands shook, she didn't feel too fatigued. That was good, wasn't it? Her head hurt a bit, but she supposed it was normal. As she reached for the knob, the pressure at the back of her head increased ever so slightly.

That wasn't a headache. Before she could whirl around, fog enveloped her essence.

Waves flickered into view, clear as ever. Marina could feel her stomach drop, but her body was far away.

Psychometry. That's what this was. And the fog...it was Aeric's. By now, she could pinpoint his spirit anywhere. She almost started to panic, but the fog didn't dive beneath her waves. In fact, it didn't do *anything*. It just hung there, waiting. But...for *what*? Her seawater grew choppy, as though it were thrashing about in protest. The fog remained.

Get out, get out, get out.

He wouldn't. Not until she pushed him out herself. Asshole. Didn't he remember how horribly she'd reacted to psychometry?

Obviously, he did; he was being cautious. Though her memories flitted underwater, he kept his distance.

One day, one step, one breath at a time. Confusion was okay. Anger and fear were okay. The feelings didn't need to be suppressed so long as her wit stayed intact.

As if in response, her waves settled. When they weren't so rough, she could see the light beneath them. It pulsed, then settled back down, like a sun bursting with solar flares.

The Omnia was so very powerful. But her waves were too. That power—that *emotion*—didn't die down when she smoothed her choppy waters. It just became easier to harness.

She and Pierce had promised each other they'd be patient with themselves, and that patience pertained to this moment as much as it did to others.

Patient, calm, at ease with her emotions—things she'd never been the best at but was learning to become. One day at a time. Aeric himself had underscored the value of stilling her mind...and shielding.

Shielding. *Of course.* That's what Aeric wanted her to do. He wasn't baiting her with memories; he was simply waiting for her to raise her walls on her own.

She'd practiced this with Pierce. Letting the sea within her rise into walls of water was easy; keeping them up was the hard part. She focused her energy on staying centered as she rallied her waves and swathed them around the border of her mind. As soon as she did, her surroundings came back into view. She turned and locked eyes with Aeric.

"I've told you this before, and I'll tell you it again," he said—but not harshly. "Mental shielding is one of the most important skills you can learn. Anyone can sneak up on you and make physical contact, which means they can break into your mind and access every ounce of your essence. It's up to you to keep them out."

With that, he opened the maroon door and strode past the threshold. Dizzy and breathless, Marina followed.

"How am I supposed to keep my shields up all the time?" she asked.

Aeric sat at one of the tables, where he picked up a pen and began making notes on some of the scattered papers. "Practice."

She lowered herself to the chaise. "I don't know if I have the strength for that."

"You do. You had more than enough strength to sense my glamour and overpower my shield. Most sorcerers wouldn't have been able to do that."

Sorcerer. Was that what she was—what she could be? Would it be enough to get her through Locus? Bemused, she asked, "You didn't go easy on me?"

She couldn't help but notice Aeric grimace. "The glamour and shield you pass through to get here isn't as strong as the ones at the borders. But no, I didn't. You have an innate ability to break through things. Protecting yourself is where you struggle—and what you need to train at."

Marina pursed her lips. "Well, right now, I need to rest."

Aeric resumed writing. "Then take a few minutes."

She sighed at the coffered ceiling, smoothing the velvet on the chaise with her hands and wishing she had Ibuprofen. Now she had a headache—a real one. There had to be some kind of magic that would ease her pain, but she supposed Aeric would be a bad person to ask given what Ismene had said about his healing abilities.

Marina turned to Aeric, who did indeed write far slower than the average person.

"Why don't you go to the healers?" she asked.

She could tell it took energy for him to tolerate her. "Because my shoulder isn't badly injured."

"I mean in general."

"I lack faith in others. I'm sure you understand."

She couldn't argue with that. She leaned back, resting against the arm of the chaise as the pounding in her head died down. Her eyes trailed off to the bookshelf, where those veiny rays of light cocooned the wooden stand.

"What's that?"

Aeric barely glanced at the shelf. "Not magic," he muttered. "Small laser beams."

Marina scowled—partially because it was yet another reminder how similar magic and Elsudran technology were, but mostly because she knew Aeric was well aware the lights weren't what she was curious about.

When he caught her gaze, he sighed. "A ring."

"Brenna's ring," Marina said pointedly.

His lips thinned. "How many of my things did you go through?"

"Not...much." When Aeric returned to his notes, she sat up. "Could you tell me more about the Daughter Rituals?"

"Are you resting or not?"

"This is how I rest."

He closed his eyes for a few moments, and just when Marina thought he wouldn't respond, he set down his pen and said, "Locus relocates the Omnia. Tempus generates guidance."

"I know that. I read about it in..."

He gave her an irritated look, and she cut herself off. Mentioning Florin's documents probably wouldn't go over well. "I only know the basics," she said, then added cautiously, "but I don't know how to perform it."

He knew which ritual she was referring to.

"You have a long way to go before Locus is a possibility," Aeric said. "It's a dangerous ritual for the giving *and* receiving party, but more so for the former. Separating the Omnia from something as delicate as a soul is bound to result in loss, so getting the Keepers through it alive was the priority. Failure meant catastrophic damage to the Omnia."

When Marina wilted, Aeric's tone softened. "I won't lie to you, Marina. Locus has never been done without damaging the souls of the givers. The first Keepers had enough magical prowess to survive it, but even then, it's said they lived out the remainder of their lives weak."

Weak and afraid. Had she more energy, Marina would've paid mind to the knot in her stomach. Was that destined to be her fate too?

"Both rituals have their downsides," Aeric added. "That's why they were regulated so heavily."

Though he obviously would have been content stopping there, Aeric gave in when Marina eyed him curiously.

"Tempus and Locus act as bridges between the Omnia and its mother deity," he said. "It's why they're called Daughter Rituals. They allow us to temporarily possess the power of what begot the Omnia and made the rituals possible in the first place."

Marina's brows narrowed. "The deity...what is it?"

"We call it Exorsus. *The beginning.* It created the ocean, which created the sister realms. We're all connected by it."

She'd suspected as much. Still, her stomach flipped. Exorsus was more than a creation myth; it was the link between Elsudra and home. Was it sentient, like the gods in lore she knew? Had it played a role in her coming here?

"Exorsus is ineffable," Aeric said before she could ask. "Even ancient texts allude to how little we know. We're limited, mortal beings, which is the very risk inherent in the rituals. While the guidance Tempus yields is inerrant, we may err in our interpretations." He looked to the side when he said, "Locus, on the other hand, is a game of souls and wills —one we never should've been able to play to begin with."

Silence fell. After a moment, he added, "The crux of Locus is autonomy. It relies on the consent of the giver and the receiver. In fact, *all* magic relies on will. That's why our training together failed when you first arrived. You weren't willing to wield magic—not around me, at least. I could feel your fear when we tried psychometry, and after the border incident, I knew my direct involvement would only set your progress back further."

"That's why you used Pierce," Marina said.

Aeric didn't respond, but she swallowed the urge to press him. Instead, she used the lingering silence to consider everything. Florin's documents echoed what Aeric had said, but if Locus wasn't possible when water was the Omnia's host—if it required the will of *both* parties to work—then...

"How did the first Keepers take the Omnia from water to begin with?" she asked.

"They found a loophole," Aeric said. "One that allowed them to cheat nature and bypass water's lack of autonomy."

"Do you know what the loophole was?"

"I have my guesses, but I don't know for certain." Before she could pry, he said, "The first Keepers did a thorough job covering up what they'd done. Any archives they left behind were accessible only to their descendants. Even the Sorcerer of the Court wasn't made partial to that information."

"Why?"

This time, Aeric's response was immediate. "Fear."

Marina's chest tightened. She'd seen the first Keepers' fear—*felt* it—when she looked through the anteactus. It was fear of an irreversible type—the kind that came from biting off more than one could chew. The words echoed in her head again: *weak and afraid.* A horrible end for those who were once so powerful.

"Whatever the first Keepers did, they didn't want anyone to do it again," Aeric said. "It was why their descendants made such severe sacrifices when they inherited the Omnia. Locus could only be used at the end of their reigns, and Tempus could only be used during times of calamity. Their oath made it harder to complete the rituals and distanced our kind from what the first Keepers believed we shouldn't meddle with."

Fear *did* breed hypocrisy, like Pierce had said. But what had they been so afraid of?

"In some way," Aeric continued, "the Keepers believed the best host for the Omnia was not Elsudran. It was the basis of their sacrificial oath, which not only bound them to strict rules, but also stripped them of their Elsudran identities to control for corruption. It seems like Kieron proved why that caution was warranted."

Marina thought of Four—of his gentle voice and the veil he wore over what she could only assume were kind eyes.

"In your memories," she said, "Four seemed so confident that sending the Omnia out of Elsudra was the right thing to do. But how did he know his interpretation of Tempus wasn't wrong? How did you know?"

Though she could see a terse response simmering in Aeric's eyes, he suppressed it. "Whether in early Elsudra or modern times, Tempus has yielded impactful guidance. I may not have experienced what the Keepers did, but I trusted them, and they trusted what they'd witnessed." He said it quietly—begrudgingly, even.

Marina kept her voice low, wary of Aeric's reaction. "Why do you think the guidance implicated you?"

"I don't know."

She put her elbows on her knees, then whispered, "If I'm ever able to remove myself from all of this, would you take the Omnia from me?"

Aeric's usually inscrutable mask cracked when he said, "Yes."

He didn't need to expand. He'd take it, but he didn't want it. Marina couldn't help but wonder if he was more averse to the Omnia than she was. Was that even possible?

"What if you didn't?" she asked.

"A heart without a body to sustain it won't beat—not for long, at least," Aeric said. "Regardless of what that body is—water, the Keepers, yourself, or someone else—the Omnia will be inactive and vulnerable like it was during the dead years. And if it's left untethered in Elsudra for long enough, the risk that any willing soul could steal it rises. That's why, if you decide to give it up, I'd have you give it to me before the worst could become a reality."

She knew what he meant by that—*who* he meant. "And what if I'm never strong enough to perform Locus? Will Kieron kill me?"

She braced herself for some patronizing response to her question—it certainly wasn't something a strong, noble hero would ask—but Aeric only said, "The last thing Kieron wants to do is damage what he's after, and if you die holding the Omnia, it will be endangered. He ran into the same issue with the Keepers."

"What was his plan, then?"

Aeric's voice was gentler than usual, as though he hoped it would lessen the blow when he said, "To cause pain."

Marina went still. "What do you mean?"

"Since Locus relies on mutual willingness, Kieron wouldn't have been able to receive the Omnia unless the Keepers all agreed to give it to him," Aeric said. "Kieron considered magically desecrating their minds, but since lack of capacity to agree doesn't equate to true autonomy, the only way Locus would work was if the Keepers agreed of sound mind to give him the Omnia. Likewise, a sturdy mind is essential during Locus; without it, the Omnia risks damage. That meant it was imperative the Keepers had full possession of their faculties while they performed the ritual."

Aeric's lips twitched. "Kieron knew if he continued inflicting collective pain against Elsudra through ruemin and war, the Keepers would weigh the cost of suffering with the cost of giving in. Painful as it would've been for Kieron to wait—to continue upping the stakes and hurting the world he wished to rule—a war of attrition would've been more painful for the Keepers. And Kieron wasn't against enduring pain if it meant winning. If he takes pride in anything, it's his tolerance for holding out until he succeeds. Nothing is impossible to him." Softer, he added, "Nothing but laying his ambition to rest."

Marina tensed. Had there been admiration in Aeric's voice? Affection?

"Why would *anyone* want to be the Omnia's host?" she whispered.

An unreadable look flashed in Aeric's eyes. "If the Omnia is Elsudra's metaphorical sun, then the magic that radiates from it is sunlight. If someone like Kieron—who already possesses substantial magical talent—comes to hold it firsthand, he'd be more than a conductor of magic. He'd be the sun itself."

The sun itself. In Kieron's despotic ideology, of course he was the only person fit to fill that role. But here and now, she held the Omnia, and she couldn't even shield properly.

The thought may have bothered her had it not been followed by one even more curious. If proximity to the Omnia enhanced magical abilities, then that meant...

"Have your abilities been enhanced since I've come here?" Marina asked.

"Somewhat. But the difference isn't glaring. Nobody loses their capability to wield magic if they aren't near the Omnia. Closeness simply makes its power easier to pull on. The only exception was during the dead years, when the Omnia wasn't in Elsudra at all." He paused. "Compared to what they were before the dead years, my abilities haven't changed since I worked with the Keepers. I've been close to the Omnia almost all my life."

Marina eyed him. "So has Kieron."

"Not anymore, thankfully."

Despite her better judgment, she echoed, "Thankfully." When Aeric shot her a look, she added, "Will you ever tell me what happened between the two of you?"

He answered her question with another. "Your plan is to strengthen your abilities so you can perform Locus safely, correct?"

Marina clamped her lips together before whispering, "I guess."

"Then I don't see what good that knowledge would do you. You'd no longer be a part of this."

The sharpness in Marina's chest turned into a burning, and though she opened her mouth to respond, it was too dry. When her ears began to ring, she rested her forehead in her hand.

"Don't faint again," Aeric said.

"I'm going to have a heart attack at nineteen because of this," she muttered. When she glanced up at Aeric, she added, "I'm only in my *second* quarter."

No response. She tried a different method. "Did you really want Kieron to succeed before you got cold feet?"

"I'll tell you what," Aeric said, clearly taking great pains to steady his voice. "When you manage to consistently keep me from overpowering and getting through your shields, I'll tell you what happened with Kieron."

"Another deal?"

Aeric nodded. Awkward silence followed, which Marina broke by pointing at the paintings on the wall. "Do you like art?"

Aeric didn't so much as glance at them. "Are you finished resting?"

"Where'd you get the paintings?"

"I painted them."

Her laugh was involuntary, which made the realization that he was being honest all the more shocking. Her eyes widened. "Those are...really good," she admitted, ignoring her creeping guilt. She'd so quickly assumed he'd taken them, not that he'd created them himself. "How did you learn to do that?"

His response was pointed. "*Practice.*"

She sighed when he turned back to the papers on his desk, then gave in. "Fine. I have enough energy to start training."

"Learning to wield magic is like using a muscle," he droned, picking up his pen. "If you do too much before you're ready, you'll hurt yourself."

Disbelief fluttered in her chest. "I don't have to train today?"

Though she thought perhaps she was imagining it, a smile tugged at Aeric's lips. "You already did."

CHAPTER 24
Something To Fight For

Though Aeric didn't sneak up on her again, the next few weeks were exhausting all the same. On one particularly rough day filled with continuous failures on Marina's part, he'd said, *I understand you're singularly neurotic, but can you not think of anything that would put you in a calmer headspace?*

Rather than shrink under his insults like she used to, Marina had coolly responded that yes, there was, then asked him to give her back the shears she'd stabbed him with so she could do it again.

Thankfully, not all their sessions were that intense, and when they were, Marina was glad of her newfound assertiveness. She wasn't as scared of Aeric as she used to be—not after getting to know him better. Sometimes, when he made snide remarks, she'd remind herself who *his* mentor had been and wonder how he hadn't turned out worse.

Aeric mostly had her work on shielding and meditation, but on occasion, he'd give her tips to achieve more tangible forms of magic. He even helped her refine skills she'd learned herself, like summoning and generating force. Despite her increasing stamina, however, keeping her shields up remained difficult. Magic wasn't a linear discipline, and Marina ended most sessions overwrought and exhausted.

She treated her frayed nerves with nightly trips to the gardens, where she'd meet Pierce and Ismene when they weren't busy. Marina even made it a point to stop by the library and collect books for Ismene to read on her days off. As it so happened, Ismene liked romances just as much as horror—the steamier the better, apparently. Though Marina didn't understand the appeal, she found some anyway. Whenever Pierce was around, he'd snatch the books from Ismene and read the obscenest passages aloud. Ismene never thought it was funny, but Marina did.

Sometimes, she'd even run into Cal, who seemed more than willing to set aside time to spend with her. Mostly, they'd sit under the wisteria trees, talking about nothing particularly deep but enjoying the conversations anyway. Simple as those moments were, they became the silver linings Marina needed to get through her days.

On a rare night when it was just Ismene and Marina—Pierce's shifts at the northern border were as unpredictable as they were long—the two settled down by a lily pond, telling stories about their homes. Though Ismene never mentioned the Lewes massacre outright, her eyes watered when she told Marina about her sisters, Raisel and Thora. Marina did her best not to pry—a courtesy Ismene extended to her as well when Marina told her about her parents. They talked until the white lights dimmed and only colors remained, then stayed a while longer as Ismene helped Marina align the Elsudran calendar with her own. It took time to get the exact date, but they eventually settled on it. Today was the first day of Pearl's sixth week—the second day of March back home. Marina even marked down her birthday on her voco's internal calendar.

"It's soon," Marina said. She'd nearly forgotten. "I'll be twenty. Back home, we make a special day out of birthdays."

"What did you do for yours?"

Despite the ache in her chest, Marina told Ismene about the strawberry-cinnamon cake her mom made every year.

When she finished, Ismene's smile faded. "Do you miss your home?" she asked.

Marina's lungs grew tight as she thought about the piles of unwashed clothes and rooms she refused to enter. She certainly didn't miss that.

Answering yes would be as much of a lie as answering no. It didn't help that the lure of Locus had fluctuated these past few weeks. It hadn't disappeared entirely; in some moments it flared up, but when it died back down, the flame that burned for the simplicity of home shone weaker than before. What good were things like simplicity if there was nothing more to it—nothing more than empty hallways and the rot of grief?

But then she'd think of Gemma and Hank, or of the unfathomable burden thrust upon her by mistake, and the little flame—hopeful and stubborn and laden with fear— would sputter to life once more.

After a few moments, Marina whispered, "I miss what it used to be."

Ismene nodded. "I miss what mine used to be as well."

The silence that followed was short-lived. Pierce bounded up behind them, startling them both when he said, "Exorsus, do I have *tea* for you two."

Marina snorted. She'd taught him some slang one evening in the library, and he'd taken an immediate liking to "tea."

"Spill it," Marina said, thankful to have moved on to a hopefully cheerier topic.

"I thought you were on duty," Ismene piped in.

"Just finished," Pierce said. "You'd never guess who came to the northern border as I was clocking out."

Marina's stomach flipped. She had a bad feeling about this. "Ocot," she breathed.

Pierce sighed. "Okay, fine, smart-ass. Yes, Ocot. Guess he found out Aeric and Florin were there, and this idiot interrupted them to beg for his station in the East back—apologizing, saying he'd do anything to prove himself, and almost breaking down when they dismissed him. I'm surprised Aeric didn't kill him then and there."

That certainly wasn't the lighthearted topic change she was looking for. Of course, it did nothing to stop her curiosity. "What ended up happening?"

"Aeric grew tired of his apologies and left, so Florin dealt with him. Long story short, Ocot's still stuck at the southern border."

Ismene cringed. "I feel sorry for him."

"Why? I spent the dead years in the South and you didn't hear me whining to Florin."

"It's less the demotion and more the isolation," Ismene said.

Pierce shrugged. "He had it coming."

"That doesn't mean he'll react well."

Marina remained silent, guilt gnawing at her. Once or twice, she'd debated seeking Ocot out to apologize again, but she couldn't do much more than she'd done that morning in Aeric's office, and no number of apologies would change the fact that he had attacked her. Magical prowess was one thing, but Marina doubted her power to sway the Delve's opinion on Ocot and his shitty impulse control. That, and it would come with admitting she'd had him steal Florin's documents...all so she could learn Locus and go home.

Pierce nudged Marina. "You okay? You look pale."

Marina forced a smile. "All good." And yet, even as she tried to join back in the conversation, Four's voice echoed in her head.

The kind we need, he'd said.

Wherever that person was, they certainly weren't here.

Marina swore and flattened her palms on the table. Her waves had fallen again, and Aeric's fog had swarmed into her mind. At this point, she was only a couple of failures away from giving up completely.

"You are masterful at making the same mistake an infinite number of times," Aeric said, leaning back in his chair.

"Thanks. Great pep talk." She crossed her arms. "If psychometry requires contact with the skin, I don't see why I can't just evade it."

"If you don't have enough stamina to keep your shields up, then you certainly do not have enough to outrun anyone who wishes to use psychometry on you," Aeric said. "Those skilled in magic can use just enough of their power to creep into your essence without you knowing, and by the time you are aware, they've already secured their hold. You'll be fighting an uphill battle after that—one you could've shielded yourself from." He tapped his foot on the leg of his chair. "There's a learning curve to magic, and it's inevitable you'll struggle more with some things than others. Sometimes, you'll experience bursts of your abilities, as you have, only to feel like you're back at square one the next day. Once you pass the curve, you'll make fewer mistakes."

When Marina sighed, Aeric said, "What you struggle with is your ability to follow through. Your confidence and willingness run in the same circle. When one wanes, so does the other, and your abilities take a hit."

Marina fiddled with a thread that had come undone from one of her sleeves. It was hard to fully commit when her goals had started to waver. A month ago, she'd been hell-bent on getting back home. Where was that determination now?

"What do *you* struggle most with?" she asked.

Aeric chuckled, which surprised Marina—she'd hardly seen him smile. "You tell me."

"Healing?"

"In my defense, I wasn't adequately taught." What little good humor there was in his eyes vanished when he said, "Kieron didn't think it was important, perhaps because he didn't possess an innate aptitude for it. Whatever didn't come easy to him, he deemed unworthy of his time. He was patient in many ways, but when it came to things he didn't understand, he'd grow angry and insecure, even if he didn't show it."

"Like me," Marina breathed, her stomach sinking.

"If there is anyone who is most *unlike* Kieron, it's you," Aeric said. "He wants to ascend to a godlike position. You want to get rid of the very thing he desires. Many people would not be as averse to power as you. But you're here." His tone was neither vexed nor weary. He wasn't addressing an unpleasant surprise, but something that perplexed him—a puzzle he couldn't fully solve.

"I'm here," she echoed. She folded her legs and put her elbows on her knees. "And I want to improve."

"Then there is one thing, beyond all else, you need to do," Aeric said, and the ice in his eyes thawed slightly. "You need to settle on something to fight for."

CHAPTER 25
Not Yet Whole

Several days passed, every night the same. In her dreams, the chasm beneath her waves rang with far-off voices. They competed for space, vying for her attention with every echo. Rather than choose, Marina simply listened. And listened, and listened...

On the morning of March eleventh—the second day of Pearl's eighth week—she awoke to a perky knock at her door, which her distorted senses almost made out to be Gemma. The knock sounded again, and Marina muttered something unintelligible before pulling on a robe and opening the door to Ismene and Pierce.

"Happy day of being twenty!" Pierce blurted.

Marina blinked as he hugged her. When she turned to Ismene and saw the strawberry-adorned cinnamon cake beneath a glass cloche, tears welled in her eyes.

"I don't know if it will taste the same as your mother's," Ismene said, "but the cooks seemed confident. Strawberries and cinnamon, right?"

Marina let out a breathless laugh, nodding as tears pricked her eyes.

Pierce chuckled nervously. "Is it normal to cry on birthdays?"

"They're tears of happiness," she assured him as she opened her door wider. "Thank you...both of you."

"It's no problem," Pierce said as Ismene set the cloche on the vanity. "I got to peek in the kitchen while the cooks made your cake. They all tired of Ismene and her fussiness with how it turned out."

Ismene elbowed Pierce. "I hope you like it."

Marina's chin wobbled as she pulled Ismene into a hug. "It's perfect. How did you know it was today?"

"I saw the date you put into your voco," Ismene said, beaming.

The cake wasn't too big, which made it a good size to divide among the three of them. Though Ismene seemed shocked that Marina wanted to share it, Pierce didn't object as he took a third and finished it in less than a minute.

The initial tang of spice brought with it the feeling of home, but the yearning that accompanied it wasn't as potent as usual. Maybe, here and now, some of that yearning had been filled.

"The foods in our realms are so similar," Marina remarked. "The names too."

"You can thank your translator for the names," Ismene said. "I'm sure they'd sound much different if we removed them. But yes, food is bound to be similar in all the sister realms. We were made the same, so I guess it makes sense that our bioevolutions would follow nearly identical trajectories."

Pierce grinned. "But Elsudrans *don't* have birthdays. This is a tradition we should take up." He turned to Marina. "Ismene tells me you make whole celebrations out of them?"

"Some more than others," Marina said, shrugging as she finished her last couple bites slowly. "I've always liked small-scale parties like this."

"And to think—you struck me as such a socialite," Pierce quipped.

Even Ismene giggled at that. Though Marina rolled her eyes, she couldn't help the grin that tugged at her lips.

"If I'm being honest," she said, "this is a way better twentieth than I expected."

She said it blithely enough so Pierce and Ismene wouldn't pry, but her heart sank all the same when she remembered how much she'd dreaded this date back at home. It was her first birthday since the accident—her first birthday without her parents. How would she have spent it in Georgia? The answer lingered at the back of her head: sleeping.

Marina glanced at Pierce and Ismene, then at the crumbs of cake and the room around her. The Delve was dark and quiet, hidden below a world even darker. But despite the nightmares above, there was hope and love and warmth here—a kind of solitude even the familiarity of home could no longer offer. It sprang from the rock walls, illuminating the garden and brightening the shadows—not because of the lanterns or the string lights, but because of the people. Perhaps, in some way, she was beginning to feel whole here.

She was late to training that night. After Pierce left for the northern border, Marina meandered the manor halls with Ismene, who—despite a few duties here and there—set aside a good portion of her day to spend with Marina. There wasn't much to do in the manor, but Ismene showed her rooms she hadn't yet seen, which Marina appreciated.

After making it a point to thank the cooks for the cake and taking her time with

Ismene before heading to the third floor, she'd fallen ten minutes behind. She knew Aeric would be cross, but strangely enough, she didn't care. She'd take his irritability if it meant finally feeling happiness, and not just the fleeting sort. She hadn't felt that way in a long time, and she'd do what she could to cling to it.

Still, when Aeric glared at her as she entered, Marina did her best to placate him by apologizing. It didn't work.

"Either be on time or prove to me you can properly shield," he said curtly. "You don't get to be late and unsuccessful."

"It won't happen again. It's just...today's my birthday."

Aeric didn't seem to care—either that or he didn't want to admit not knowing what birthdays were—because he simply said, "We'll begin."

Marina's stomach flipped, and she braced herself for the failures she'd become so accustomed to. Still, she harnessed her waves, steadying her mind as she extended her arm. The moment Aeric tapped the back of her hand, the sea flooded into frame. There, she floundered, grasping at whatever she could to raise her shields and keep them up.

When exhaustion threatened to disrupt her anchorage, she simply acknowledged its presence. Her stamina had been getting better. When she focused solely on keeping those mighty walls up, calmness settled in.

Of course, none of that actually got rid of the fatigue. She'd have to push Aeric out eventually, but she had no idea how. She didn't have the same impromptu power she'd had when she overpowered him the first time. At the moment, it took enough energy to keep her walls from collapsing at every touch of mist.

Aeric's endurance was better than hers. He'd mastered the learning curve she'd yet to overcome. What if she never mastered it? Maybe she didn't have the ability to, which would mean she'd never improve beyond trivial feats of magic. Worse, maybe she *did* have those abilities, but she'd fail to achieve them due to the insidiousness of her own mind.

When her walls fell once more, Marina refused to let her anxiety come to a boil. Instead, she looked at Aeric, winded, and said, "Again."

Though it seemed he had half a mind to insist she take a moment, he gave in.

It took energy to pull the walls back up, but she had the reserves; it was fear that depleted them. The ever-brewing storms at the back of her mind begged for attention, and though she acknowledged them, she didn't fixate.

Tiredness came quicker now that she hadn't given herself time to rest, but Marina didn't dwell on it. Instead, she noticed the feeling from afar, as though she were a distant observer—not fighting it, not pushing it down, not agonizing over its presence.

Raisel, Thora, Astra.

They didn't deserve to die before their world could be remade. Ismene and Pierce and the rest of the Delve didn't deserve the dead years. They didn't deserve to flee underground to protect themselves from the horrors above. Innocent people didn't deserve this.

The girl who'd arrived here three months ago had been too busy collecting the broken bits of herself to fathom anything but escape. But three months felt rather like an eternity, and now...now she was healing, even if slowly. Even if she wasn't yet whole.

It wasn't so horrible, perhaps, to be empty in some places—to not know if the cracks within her would mend. It was okay to take things one day, one step, one breath at a time.

This time, her waves didn't fall. Instead, they swelled outward, taking the fog around them by surprise, then smothering it and pushing it out. When Marina refocused on the world around her, she could still feel her shields—mighty walls of seawater that remained standing.

"Just now," Aeric said, "I remembered something Pierce told me you'd said."

Marina raised an eyebrow. "And what was that?"

A smile tugged at his lips. "That you were a late bloomer."

❧

March turned to April, and Pearl to Olivine, though not much changed in the Delve. Marina enjoyed the quiet monotony of her days, and though her shielding still took work, she'd improved enough to warrant focus on other skills.

She knew Aeric hadn't forgotten his promise, but she held out on bothering him about it. Strong as her shields were, they weren't perfect, so Marina figured she'd improve a little more before putting Aeric through what she knew he dreaded. She could extend him that courtesy, at least.

That didn't keep her from making guesses, though. Sometimes, she'd get so lost in her head with what she'd seen in Aeric's memories that she'd lose minutes or even hours.

Getting out of her room helped. Marina craved her evenings out, though every once in a while, she'd catch sight of Boris in the gardens and her guilt would run amok. It got so bad that one night, as she was waiting for Pierce to finish his shift, she plucked up the courage to approach him. He was alone, which made it easier. Still, Marina felt awkward as she maneuvered through patches of hyacinths and neared the wall he leaned against.

He fiddled absently with his voco, and Marina suspected it was rather jarring when she blurted, "I'm so sorry, Boris. I should've said it earlier. If there's any way I can make things right, please tell me."

A plaintive look made its way onto his face. "I don't think you can get me my position as a scout back."

"I can ask. I can *try*."

For a moment, he only stared at her, but when he opened his mouth to reply, someone cut him off.

Cal, more animated than Marina had ever seen her, smacked Boris's shoulder, grinning when he turned to her. She ruffled his hair, and though Boris shrugged her off, he smiled. The two certainly didn't look related, but in that moment, Marina wouldn't have been surprised if they were brother and sister.

Because of Astra, she thought. Her heart sank.

"Lucky me," Cal said. "My two favorite people in the same place."

Favorite? Did she really mean that? Either way, Marina couldn't help but grin.

Boris looked to Cal. "Uncanny."

"What'd I tell you?" Cal reached out and patted Marina's shoulder. "It's the way she smiles." When Marina let out a soft laugh, Cal said, "And the laugh. Exorsus, Marina. It's funny, because you and Astra couldn't look more different, but your mannerisms—"

Cal clamped her lips shut, her eyes flicking over to someone. A wave of dread washed over Marina when she realized it was Ocot, of all people, who'd snuck up on them. Ocot, who she hadn't seen in over a month—who she'd secretly hoped she never would, especially after the shitshow in Aeric's office.

The moment he opened his mouth, Cal said, "Boris and I have shifts. And Marina... I'm sure you have things to do."

Ocot's eyes met Marina's, and though she expected her guilt to flare up, all she could think of was his sweaty hands pinning her down as he spit in her face, his eyes filled with drunken rage.

"Just wanted to speak with Boris," Ocot said.

Hesitance was a horribly unnatural emotion for him. His lips had all but disappeared, and his once boisterous voice was now less than a whisper.

Boris paled. When it looked like he was about to give in, Cal said, "Boris is busy."

Relief settled onto Boris's face, and Cal gave Marina a nod before they left.

Maybe this was what it was like to have an older sister. Strangely enough, Marina didn't mind Cal's sternness—not when it gave her good reason to leave.

"I...overheard what you said to Boris," Ocot said before she could turn away. Marina silently swore. "About asking for his position back."

How close had he been? And how long had he been listening?

She let out a sigh. "I'd have more hope negotiating for you if stealing those documents was the only thing you'd done."

Ocot's lips quivered. "You know I was drunk. And I said sorry..."

"We both screwed up," Marina said. She took a step away from him. "But what you did on Double Moon...that's on you. I did what I could by keeping you from being thrown out of the Delve."

"But—"

"Please, leave it, Ocot." She shot him a desperate glance, then whispered, "I'm sorry," before turning and deserting him. Since she couldn't bear to stick around in the gardens and watch Ocot flit about like a ghost clinging to past glory, Marina called Pierce and had him meet her in the library instead.

~

Aeric was late to training the next day. Rather than fret about his absence, Marina instead took the time to observe his paintings. It was hard to believe he'd done them himself, but when she looked closer, she could see spots of darkness within the bright landscapes— shadows that clustered around trees and weaved throughout grassy knolls—and knew he hadn't been lying.

She hardly turned when he entered the room. "Now look who's late."

"Business at the borders."

That piqued her attention. "What kind of business?"

"Nothing concerning." When she shook her head at him to continue, he said, "There was activity past the Admare Mountains that Florin wished to inform me of."

"Ruemin activity?"

Aeric remained silent for a moment, as though he were contemplating the best way to answer. "No," he finally said. "Some of Kieron's forces were seen in the East."

When Marina stopped breathing, he added, "They were miles from the mountains' entrance, and they don't know this terrain like our people do. Furthermore, they don't know of the Delve. Kieron's troops are scattered throughout Elsudra—they aren't limited to the North. It's highly unlikely they'll find us."

"So...there's a chance they *might*?"

"Perhaps if they knew specifically where to look. Even then, all entrances to the Delve are hidden and heavily guarded."

Though Marina wasn't sure she wanted to hear the answer, she asked, "Could Kieron sense your glamours or overpower your shields?"

"He could," Aeric said flatly. "Others could too, if they were competent enough and worked together."

Though she'd expected that answer, it didn't stop her stomach from dropping. "But *I* sensed your glamours. And I overpowered your—"

"You are an anomaly," Aeric interrupted. "Lest you forget, you hold the Omnia. And it's clear that you're adept at sensing glamours—more than most. As for taking things down, I said it before: you have an innate ability to destroy things."

Had that been some underhanded compliment? On any other day, it might've warranted a response, but Marina couldn't bring herself to sass him back.

"Not all shields are made the same," Aeric continued, "and the ones at the border are about as strong as shields can get. But that doesn't mean they're invincible. They could be bombed, or destroyed by a powerful sorcerer, or wither away in my absence. My shields provide extra protection, but that does not make them infallible."

"But I thought you were one of the best sorcerers in Elsudra."

"Anyone's magic can be overpowered, the same way even the best warriors can be defeated and the most intelligent can be outwitted. My magic isn't indomitable. Nothing is." He sighed. "I didn't wish to tell you, because I knew you'd take the news and make it out to be worse than it is. We've detected Kieron's forces in the East before. They tend not to stay for long."

Though Marina wanted to ask more, she resigned. "I spoke to Boris today," she said cautiously. "I was wondering if...if maybe you'd consider giving him his position as a scout back." When Aeric's eyes flicked over to her, she added, "Eventually," hoping it wouldn't sound like a demand.

"You may be the Omnia's host, but you're in no position to decide such things."

"It's just...Boris is a good person, and—"

"He should have thought about his position before taking classified material," Aeric said, "just as *you* should have thought about the repercussions before sending sentries to do your bidding."

Anger followed her shame, making it impossible to hold her tongue. "I did that out of fear. I was trying to get out of here alive."

"Only to have your motivations waver now."

Marina scowled. "Things have changed."

"Such as?"

What was he getting at? Was he trying to have her admit that what once seemed like the only option now scared her as much as staying here? That home no longer appealed to her like it used to?

She'd dreamed of that possibility once—that she'd rid herself of this burden and come out unscathed. But those dreams were followed by evenings in the gardens, strawberry-cinnamon cake, and the names of those whose dreams had been taken from them.

Raisel, Thora, Astra.

And what of those who were still alive? What of their dreams? What of hers? What dreams would she be fulfilling if she returned home to nothing?

But if she stayed…if she managed to do the unthinkable and helped Aeric get rid of Kieron—which she *wouldn't*—what would happen after? Would she ever belong here, or would she be as much a ghost in Elsudra as she was at home?

Instead of answering, Marina said, "You haven't held up your end of our bargain yet."

Reluctance flickered in Aeric's eyes. "You want to know about Kieron and me. Fine; you've demonstrated consistency. But I have a counterproposal. If you keep me from breaking through your shields *and* manage to get through mine—which we both know you can—then I will not simply tell you what you wish to know. I will show you."

Marina tilted her head, then hesitantly lowered herself to the chair across from him. "You can choose which memories to show me?"

"As much as you can choose what to see. A strong sorcerer can guide a person through their mind as effectively as they can keep someone out."

She supposed that made sense. She considered for a moment, then said, "What if I'm not successful?"

"It's good practice anyway," Aeric said, as though he'd expected that question. After a moment, he added, "Our first deal still stands. I won't back out of my promise, however unnecessary and unpleasant it is for me."

Marina steadied herself and readied her waves. At the first touch of Aeric's hand, her walls of seawater came into view. They weren't particularly high, but they were up. They remained that way, despite the familiar haze and her own brimming exhaustion. She rallied the waters—not fully thinking or planning, just doing—and let the strength of the tide pulse out against the invading mist. Aeric wasn't intent on going easy on her, but the less she fought, the simpler it was to ward him off. When she didn't force things—when she moved *with* her waves—her strength better matched Aeric's. Maybe the peak of the learning curve wasn't as impossible to reach as she'd once thought.

When she gathered the strength to push against the mist once more, her waves didn't collapse or spill to the ground. They plunged forward.

The mist recoiled, but Marina didn't stop. She flooded past the boundaries of her own mind and into the fog.

One breath at a time. Breathe.

Though she expected him to, Aeric didn't push against her waves to try to force her out. Instead, the fog yielded, and she could've sworn it beckoned her to follow.

CHAPTER 26
What Could Be

Though she wasn't stumbling blindly through the fog like before, it took effort for Marina to orient herself. She let her waves carry her, observing from afar as the mist parted to reveal a dilapidated alleyway and the boy who ran through it.

Marina knew the moment she saw him that it was Aeric. He was young—five, if she had to guess. Elsudrans would say he was in his first quarter.

As a child, Aeric didn't dress in the stiff and tailored clothes he wore now. Instead, he wore a simple tunic and pants as colorless as the cobblestone around him.

Altus. This was Altus. She wasn't sure how she knew that; perhaps Aeric was telling her. But this wasn't the perfect city Pierce spoke of. The air was heavy and smelled sour, and the road was filled with potholes that Aeric expertly maneuvered. And yet, despite the sorry state of the houses and streets, Marina could feel the curiosity and excitement bounding through him. As he turned into a battered building and made his way up the uneven staircase, warmth flickered within him—the kind of warmth one felt when they were home.

He took a long hallway down to the door at the very end, then put his eye up to the lock and blinked it open. With a smile of smug satisfaction, he careened into the room beyond, then hopped onto a cot positioned under a semicircle window.

The mattress crinkled as he maneuvered past the woman on the bed and propped himself up enough to see outside.

From the window, Aeric could see more than just the slums of Altus. He could see everything. Beyond the thronging marketplace and blocks of shanties below, golden-crested buildings gleamed in the sun. If he squinted hard enough, he could even see the palace atop the far-off hill, its silhouette bordered by the ocean. That was where the rich lived—the merchants and generals who attended fancy parties and even got to speak with the Sorcerer of the Court.

The woman on the bed stirred, then put her hand on Aeric's cheek. *"Did you lock it?"*

Aeric slid off the cot and scurried to the door. With a glance in its direction, the lock clicked in place. His mother had pulled herself upright by the time he returned.

Had she not looked so frail, she would've been beautiful—*was* beautiful, despite the circles under her blue eyes and the scant color on her face. Her golden-brown hair fell in tangles to her waist, as though she hadn't brushed it in months. There was redness to her eyes too—the kind that lingered after crying too long and hard. But Aeric's mother smiled at him all the same as he stuffed his hands into his pockets and produced bronzed coins.

"They liked it?" she asked.

Aeric nodded, beaming as he curled up beside her. His mother looked across the room at stacks of pottery, which were charming despite having no color to them, then pulled him closer and kissed his head.

The fog thickened, and in a gust of nonexistent wind, it rose into the air and clouded the apartment, then returned to rest just as quickly. The setting was the same, but it was night. Light sprang from old lamps, and the stars outside were bright and clear enough to illuminate the floorboards. It was strangely peaceful until the figures materialized.

Aeric was the same age, sitting on the cot with his knees to his chest, watching his mother and the slick-haired man before her.

"I'm no longer doing that," she said.

The man only laughed. *"You have no other talents."*

She pointed a shaking hand at the pottery along the walls. *"I'm providing, which means I'm not taking clients. Get out."*

The man swore. *"Then why leave your door unlocked?"*

Aeric winced from where he sat on the bed, but his mother didn't so much as glance at him. *"Leave."*

The man—he looked familiar...where had she seen him?—stalked over to the ceramic vases and bowls. With one wide sweep of his arms, he sent them crashing to the floor.

Aeric cried out, and though Marina could clearly see the alarm in his mother's eyes, she only repeated, *"Leave. Now."*

She said it just like Pierce had when confronting the ruemin—loud and stern, but shaking all the same. The man before them may not have been a ruemin, but he was just as ravening. And like those silver-eyed beasts, he didn't leave.

The fog came together, and Marina only heard distant cries before the scene changed into a grand room of flagstone flooring and opened windows. Pillars lined the walls, and *he* stood at the center.

Kieron peered down his nose at Aeric and his mother, but despite his haughty, unbothered air, Marina couldn't help but notice the amused smile on his lips. He swirled what little wine was left in his goblet, glancing lazily at it as Aeric's mother spoke.

She was sick. Good lord, how terribly sick she was. Her skin had no color left, and her voice was frail. *"He's skilled,"* she said, *"especially for a child. Anyone I know who is inclined doesn't have half the talent he does."*

Kieron chuckled before saying, *"How many inclined individuals do you know, my dear?"*

"Not...not many. But if you'd see for yourself, you'd agree. He's self-taught and so sweet..."

Kieron made a gentle gesture, and she stopped talking as he bent down to Aeric's level and whispered, *"I gather you're quite gifted."*

Marina could feel the knot in Aeric's stomach as he nodded.

Kieron smiled at him, flashing his straight, white teeth. *"What can you do?"*

Aeric released his grip on his mother's hand and angled his head toward the crystal chandelier on the ceiling. He closed his eyes and focused on his breathing, and when he glanced again at the crystals, colors sprang to life and spilled onto the floor.

Kieron blinked in the light, then regained a sober expression. *"And?"*

The comment may've stung, but Aeric mirrored Kieron's lazy air as he pointed to the wine glass, which had already been refilled.

Kieron laughed, low and warm, as he eyed his wine. *"Manipulating light and summoning wine. For a child, this is impressive."* When Aeric's mother nodded, he said, *"We don't usually start training them until they're in their second quarter. Children tend to have a flimsy grasp on their developing abilities."*

Her chin quivered. *"I don't have that much time."*

"I see." Kieron clicked his tongue—strangely joyous despite the tearful woman before him—then said, *"In that case, I'd like to make a deal with you."*

Marina didn't notice the surrounding mist until the walls and floors were shrouded in it, and as the room faded, multiple scenes began to play at once. Some of them she'd seen before: Aeric stood over his mother's lifeless body in one, only to be swept away by Kieron, and in another, a paunchy man with oily hair begged for mercy. The realization hit Marina—that was the man who'd attacked Aeric's mother in her home—as Kieron's voice reverberated throughout the fog: *"Will we forgive him and let him do to another what he did to your mother, or will we use our greatness to ensure he never does it again?"*

There were other scenes too—new ones flashing amidst the old. In one, Aeric—who couldn't have been any older than ten—painted for the first time. He'd stumbled upon the canvases by accident, then hauled them to his quarters.

"We don't improve our magic by spending time frivolously," Kieron had said when Aeric asked him for paint. He patted Aeric's shoulder, his smile at odds with his tone. *"Get rid of the canvases."*

And though Aeric usually did what Kieron asked, he kept the canvases and found paint and brushes on his own—painting whenever he could and showing them to no one.

In another memory, Marina watched as Kieron taught Aeric to shield.

"Most people don't learn this until they're older," he said. *"But you're not most people."*

The comment stuck with Aeric. Kieron seldom offered encouragement, but the little he *had* said kept Aeric going as he trained. And yet, when Aeric shielded successfully for the first time as a teenager, Kieron's face remained blank.

"I know what I was doing wrong," Aeric said as Kieron folded his arms. Marina had never heard such emotion—such excitement—in his voice. *"I was too caught up worrying about you breaking through. But the less I fight, the easier it is."*

Kieron smirked. *"You're very confident for someone who took so long to learn it."*

Aeric's excitement vanished, and though Marina couldn't feel her body, she knew she was wincing.

"You said most people don't learn to shield until they're older," Aeric murmured.

"I also said you're not most people," came the terse response. *"I was starting to worry I'd overestimated your skillset."* There was no jest in his voice, but when Aeric didn't respond, Kieron tilted his head back and laughed. *"I'm teasing,"* he said, his eyes glistening. As he walked away, he muttered, *"Though you did take a ridiculously long time."*

Aeric only watched him go.

Over the course of memories, Marina realized Kieron was often like that—brutally condescending and more intent on leading with the stick than the carrot. His insults were sharp and his praise backhanded, and Marina wondered if that was why Aeric had been so cruel when they'd first trained together. Perhaps, in a way, it was all he'd ever known.

Most of Kieron's students withered in the environment. Of course, Aeric didn't know why Kieron agreed to teach magic to prospective successors; he'd already promised Aeric the job would go to him. Still, it was hard to see other students get Kieron's attention, and Aeric often had to remind himself that Kieron was simply doing his duties. Besides, Kieron clearly took no joy in it; rather, he'd comment on how weak-minded the younger generation was and how few of them deserved to be Sorcerer of the Court.

By the time Aeric was a few years into his second quarter, only ten students remained in the program. One day, from the corner of a classroom, Aeric watched as Kieron tested a peer's shielding abilities. The student—a gangly, horse-faced boy—had never been a particularly skilled sorcerer, but when he'd started staying after class to speak with Kieron about problems at home, Aeric's jealousy had swelled.

It was satisfying to see the smile wiped from the boy's face as he failed to keep his shields up. When he looked to Kieron for reassurance, Kieron said, *"I now understand why your parents are so disappointed in you."*

Some of the other students snickered, but Aeric remained silent. The boy blinked at Kieron, who dismissed him when he began to cry. One girl at the front of the room—tall and pretty with sea green eyes and plaited red hair—smirked as the boy left.

These memories...they were of Aeric's childhood, and it was with unease that Marina realized Kieron was in more of them than Aeric's mother. That boy raised in poverty grew to be a man surrounded by riches and power, yet he was more inclined to study in the dark than he was to play the games of the court.

"Ours is a lonely life," Kieron told Aeric the day he officially chose him as his successor. *"You'll soon come to see what blithering idiots the elite are. They piss away the Omnia's magic with their lust for luxury, and the Keepers are too blind to realize. But the common people are no better. They're ants—never questioning, never wondering what could be."* He put his hands on Aeric's shoulders. *"As esteemed as the two of us may be, we have no say as to how magic is used. We're the men behind the curtain, using our talents to oversee the Omnia, watching all its potential go to waste with these mindless middlemen and silk-stocking, high-society swine. And who suffers?"*

"People like my mother," Aeric whispered.

Kieron nodded. *"People like your mother."* His grin vanished. *"The virus she died from was curable had she gotten help earlier. But she couldn't, because she was part of the dregs of society. Our Keepers didn't care about her; they've lost touch with the rest of us."*

The memories began to flash before Marina even faster.

"You became a son to me the day your mother died," Kieron's voice echoed.

And then, the memories narrowed back into one, and the mismatched colors dulled into a soft purple. Light trickled in from the ceiling, not through any skylight or windows, but through crumbling stone walls. Guards were stationed at the sides of the room, and six others lingered near a semicircular archway.

Brenna's portal.

As hard as Marina strained, she couldn't see what lay beyond the archivolt. Blotchy figures hid in the bends of light, and Kieron stood before the portal's mouth.

She didn't need to see Sundra to feel the fear. Whether it was hers or Aeric's, she wasn't sure, but Kieron maintained his composure. His hands, however, curled beneath the leaden cuffs he wore. *Diminution cuffs,* she realized; or perhaps Aeric was telling her that. In a way, Kieron resembled a jinn—powers subdued by chainless shackles.

The Keepers stood near Kieron and the archway. She'd seen Four before, and though her eyes landed on him first, she studied the others as well—all veiled, all silent.

"Brenna would be distraught to know her brilliance was being used to exile her successor," Kieron sneered. When the Keepers didn't respond, he angled his chin at his cuffs. *"But that's typical of your kind, isn't it? You use others to exercise the magic you yourselves cannot, whilst stomping out anyone who challenges your fiefdom."*

The tallest Keeper, whose headpiece adorned a single tower of beryl, straightened. *"Is that not your goal?"* One asked. *"To create a new fiefdom where the only ruler is you, and no one is powerful enough to stomp you out? How different is that from what you claim to hate so much?"*

There was an edge to his voice, which the woman closest to him noticed. She raised a hand, her skin as dark as her raven hair, and said, *"You know your charges."* The crystals on her headpiece—one at the front and one at the back—caught a tendril of light. *"You know the treason you've enacted and the minority you've entranced,"* Two continued. *"Such crimes, especially committed by someone in power, are not taken lightly."*

Three, a bald woman with serrated features that protruded from her veil, murmured her agreement.

"Not such a minority." Kieron shook his head, and though his hands were bound, Marina could see the energy that jumped from his fingers as he broke into a low laugh. *"I did my best, but I cannot change the minds of those determined to perpetuate such a squandered system. You've all been bred and trained to march mindlessly forward and let the Omnia's power go to waste. And it's because of you that our realm will never reach the greatness it is capable of."*

Four turned to Aeric, sucking in a tired breath as he nodded at him. Pale as ever, Aeric approached Kieron, who barely regarded him as he turned to face the portal.

"I need no lesser sorcerer to escort me," Kieron hissed. *"I know where I'm going."*

The words evoked pain deep in Aeric's chest.

An act, he told himself. *Just an act.*

But Kieron was good at acting, and as he stepped into the mouth of the portal, giving Aeric no more than a glance, the pain didn't lessen.

Nine Elsudran years followed, each one lonelier than the last. Kieron's words were the only things that fueled Aeric's resolve: *You became a son to me the day your mother died.*

Aeric weathered those years, playing his part to perfection. He oversaw the Omnia, obeying the court's wishes as they sucked dry every last bit of magic they could. Esteemed healers, extravagant technology, lurid galas, and magical entertainment...they wanted everything, and while those in poverty clamored for resources, the court basked in luxury.

The memories came at Marina in batches, and though she was often watching multiple at once, she understood everything. It was like dreaming. Time moved differently during psychometry—quicker. Somehow, memories years long lasted only seconds, but

Marina experienced them all as though she'd been there in person.

Aeric showed her parties he never attended and wealth he never had. Kieron had always known how to blend in with the aristocrats, but since Aeric couldn't bring himself to mingle with the people who hoarded magical resources and left the rest of Elsudra out to dry, he hid in the shadows, disgust simmering until the feeling was all he knew.

Even if they held the Omnia, the Keepers didn't rule Elsudra. Neither did the Sorcerer of the Court. On paper, perhaps, Aeric oversaw the Omnia's magic, but in reality, he was at the beck and call of the wealthy. And so, hatred burning through his veins, he threw himself into getting Kieron back—into altering Brenna's portal so that one day, he'd no longer be alone amongst greedy patricians.

It was Four he had to be wary of—Four who'd caught onto Kieron's plans before the others did and sentenced him to exile. He grew close to Four, feigned ignorance and innocence, and when Kieron returned from Sundra, Aeric turned on the Keepers and fought alongside Kieron. But Kieron was weak, and the ruemin—having been driven close to extinction by the Sundrans all those years ago—were as few in number as the soldiers on Kieron's side. And so, they went into hiding—to bide time, rally forces, and wait for Kieron to recover before attacking again. Sundra had leeched the life from him, but Kieron didn't seem to mourn what he'd lost; rather, he had a strange affinity for the silver-eyed creatures he'd brought with him.

Marina felt as though she were watching events unfold through a zoetrope. Stilted images of war flickered in the fog, and there was regret...so much regret.

"I fear in the time I was gone, you became as idealistic as the Keepers."

She couldn't see Kieron's face, but she knew it was him.

"You fail to see past the ugliness of this war," he continued. *"If I let dissenters run free and fail to control the inclined, the Omnia will be vulnerable."*

Aeric's jaw tightened. *"You speak as though you already possess it."*

Silence followed, bitterly cold.

"Where's the man I shared my vision with?" Kieron said. *"Have these last few years made you weak?"* When Aeric didn't respond, Kieron shook his head, still shrouded in shadows as he whispered, *"You disappoint me, Aeric."*

The hollowness in Aeric's chest was impossible to ignore, and Marina could feel herself stifling a gasp as he removed his hand. Before she could ask why he'd pushed her out, he said, "I'd prefer not to relive some things."

Marina nodded, blinking to reorient herself. Though she wasn't planning to push him any further, it seemed she wouldn't have needed to. Aeric straightened a paper at the edge of the table, then said, "I was young when Kieron began speaking to me of his plans. In his eyes, the only person fit to possess and wield the Omnia was the Sorcerer of the Court. *He* was the only person fit. He rationalized his desire by pointing out the flaws in our system and spinning stories of a world where, minus one ruler and their chosen cohort of sorcerers, no one else would possess magical abilities. Complete homogeneity amongst the masses. What better way to prevent rebels from gaining power? Of course, Kieron was too tactful to say that outright. When he spoke of the future, he painted a world where the ruler acted as a link between the people and magic. He vowed to eliminate the court and the inequality they perpetuated. And he made sure to remind me that if not for their selfishness, unchecked due to the Keepers' passivity, my mother would still be alive."

Aeric pressed his fingers together. "In some ways, maybe he was right. In Elsudra, wealth is rewarded with magic, just as magic is rewarded with wealth, and the people outside that circle are left with very little. If not for my own abilities, I'd have remained in poverty, just like my mother. Kieron knew that; he knew who I blamed for her untimely death, and he was meticulous when it came to kindling that hatred." He paused, and though Marina could tell it was painful to say, he added, "But I'm not innocent either. I knew what would happen when Kieron returned from Sundra. Only I'd known very little of life without him, and..." Aeric cut himself off, then sighed. "There was a time I truly believed he viewed me as a son."

"What changed your mind?"

Aeric closed his eyes before answering. "Once Kieron had amassed enough strength to emerge from hiding, he sent ruemin and his forces out to kill inclined individuals, children included," he said. "He killed those who weren't inclined too—simply being perceived as a threat was enough to warrant death. Unless one was talented and faithful enough to join him, he wanted them gone. And when it comes to Kieron, few can prove their talent. Even fewer can prove their loyalty."

Marina swallowed her inhale. She wasn't surprised, but hearing about the reality of Kieron's war—especially from Aeric—chilled her to her core.

"Kieron was discreet when it came to the words he used," Aeric continued, "but his goals were clear: secure his position, ensure loyalty, and gain sole possession of the Omnia." Quieter, he said, "Kieron's body might've been weak when he'd returned from Sundra, but his resolve wasn't. If anything, it had strengthened. For a time, he tried to quell my reservations by offering me power. He knew he'd eventually need a successor—someone to hold the Omnia after him and continue his regime. He wanted me to fill that role. But when he realized I wasn't the dog he'd raised, he decided to get rid of me as well."

"He tried to kill you?" Marina whispered.

"Not kill," Aeric said. "One of Kieron's most loyal followers is an Altus healer known for his...unconventional methods. Kieron wanted him to subdue me using dissolution magic, which debases the mind and makes victims easier to control."

Marina blinked at him. "Like...a lobotomy?"

When Aeric didn't respond, she realized he didn't know what *lobotomy* meant. Since she knew he wouldn't admit his ignorance, she told him what it was. She wasn't sure why—she already knew the answer to her question—but when Aeric nodded, her stomach dropped anyway. For someone so eager to stomp out threats, she found it strange that Kieron would've gone to such lengths to keep Aeric around. Maybe, in a way, he *did* think of him as a son. She didn't voice her thoughts out loud; Aeric's eyes had grown shiny.

"I left when I realized his intentions," he said. "You know the rest." He cleared his throat, but his voice wasn't as steady as it normally was. "While Kieron obsessed over what could be for him, I remained hopeful as to what could be for us. I was a fool, as blind as those I scorned, and I'm paying for it dearly." He paused. "But so are you."

For a moment, Marina thought an apology was forming at his lips, but he shook it away. "There you have it."

She didn't respond immediately. Instead, she took in the weary man before her—the man she'd once thought uncaring and cruel. The mask he wore shielded the child beneath. Maybe it was similar to her own.

"What deal did Kieron offer your mother?" she asked.

Aeric shrugged. "I suppose he wanted her to uproot. My talent impressed him, and he saw it fit to train me early. In order to do so, he invited both my mother and myself to live in the palace. Her illness progressed quickly, and a few seasons later, she died. Kieron had me to himself after that."

For a long moment, the two were silent, and though Marina could think of thousands of questions to ask, only one came out. "What was her name?"

Aeric shifted in his seat. "Evren."

Marina drew her fingers along the grooves in the table as she sorted her thoughts. "I was no better than dead before I came here," she finally said. "And like you, maybe I was partially to blame."

One day, one step, one breath at a time. Every inhale skimmed across the top of her sea, smoothing those ever-turbid waves. Perhaps it was a kind of madness that overtook her now that she was reeling from her successes with shielding, or perhaps seeing him without that icy mask evoked a sorrow too familiar to ignore. Whatever it was, Marina didn't hesitate when she said, "If it's worth anything, I forgive you."

"I don't expect forgiveness."

"I know. But I forgive you anyway."

CHAPTER 27
Downfall

Unspoken harmony settled between them in the weeks that followed. In this new environment, her skills blossomed quicker than ever. Marina's mistakes became as rare as they were short-lived, and slowly but surely, she realized Aeric was right—the only thing getting in the way of her improvement was her own mind. Every time she convinced herself she'd hit the ceiling of her abilities, she'd falter, struggling against the barriers of her psyche, which tightened the harder she fought. But when she stilled her mind—not necessarily by wiping her thoughts away, but by acknowledging and accepting them—she'd shatter the obstacles before her and realize only she was at fault for creating them.

Aeric, too, was in better spirits than Marina thought possible. Of course, it took a lot to make him smile—and when he did, it was fleeting—but when Pierce told Marina that Boris had been reinstated as a scout, she knew it was Aeric's doing. Since thanking him would only result in a curt dismissal, Marina funneled her energy into training, which she knew was thank-you enough. As her skills grew, Aeric even had her turn to more complicated magic. He taught her how to break objects from afar and shield her body from attacks, and he even brought up basic glamour-formation.

"I told you it's like a muscle," Pierce said one evening in the training ring. She'd had him open his drinking flask, then filled it to the brim with water from the sea cavern, mostly to show off.

She'd tried filling it with drinking water before, but she hadn't been successful. In order to summon successfully, a sorcerer had to know exactly what they were summoning and where it came from. On top of that, Aeric had told her that anything she summoned couldn't pass through solid surfaces. The wine he'd summoned that day in the dining room had come from an unsealed glass in his office—one he'd already known the location of and could easily manipulate. Since liquids and gasses didn't have a fixed shape, he'd been able to bring the wine through cracks in the doors, the same way she'd summoned water from the sea cavern in her sleep.

Summoning happened quickly—so quickly one could be forgiven for thinking the objects had teleported when in reality, they'd moved across space at the speed of light. Being aware of surroundings, then, was vital. Neglecting to understand the path an object passed through could result in it slamming into something—or someone—which was why training most often occurred in designated, heavily safeguarded areas. Solid objects were even trickier, and lesser sorcerers avoided summoning them altogether.

Though Marina understood the rules, she'd been a little disappointed with all of summoning's limitations. When she'd admitted it to Aeric, he'd responded that the limitations were precisely what she should be glad of. If one could summon substances from anywhere and place them inside of anything they wished, what was stopping a sorcerer from filling a victim's lungs with water and leaving them to drown? She'd changed course pretty quickly after that.

"You just visualize the water passing from one place to another?" Pierce asked after she'd explained it to him.

"It's more like I bring it through *myself*." She nodded to the dagger on Pierce's baldric, which came loose from his sheath and danced in the air.

"Can you not—"

"Magic revolves around space," Marina said as it settled in her palm. "Inanimate objects can't move themselves, but *I* can move them, as long as I'm careful."

When the dagger disappeared, Pierce said, "You'd better bring that back."

Marina gave him a smile, then pointed to his hip, where it rested in its sheath.

Pierce let out a laugh. "Guess I'm lucky you didn't embed it into my chest."

"Well, that's because I like you," she teased.

"And why soldiers have such sturdy armor," he retorted.

Aeric had mentioned that as well. Summoning *could* be used in combat, if one was both talented and wily enough, but simply moving an object was different than making it do something. Breaking skin and bone was no more possible with magic than it was with brute force or weapons, but Elsudran armor was made with that in mind.

Pierce lay back on the sand. "You're a bona fide sorcerer now, aren't you?"

"Not really," Marina said, but she appreciated the compliment regardless. "I still need to work on my control. That's where my waves come in. They're the bridge between myself and what I want to manipulate. I either push them out"—she summoned a small, flickering force field at her fingertips, then let it pulse outward and fade on its own—"or bring them in. How much I can do depends on how much control I have over the magic that radiates from the Omnia...and myself." Softer, she said, "I'm still working on that."

"You'll improve faster than ever now that you and Aeric are getting along," Pierce said. "I bet you two match each other closely, being the savants you are."

She knew he'd intended that as a compliment too, but it made her uneasy all the same. Through a nervous laugh, she said, "Well, holding the Omnia gives me a leg up."

"Give yourself some credit. Your innate talent is there—that's a once-in-a-generation thing. If you'd been born Elsudran, your parents would've sent you off to Altus to study."

And I probably would've handled that as well as I handled college, Marina thought.

The thought was bitter at first, but another followed it. She wasn't the same person she'd been back in Georgia.

"It's strange," she said, more to herself than Pierce. "Since I've come to Elsudra, my dreams have changed alongside me. They used to be the same every night, but now, I can feel them shifting. Evolving, almost."

It was the first time she'd said it aloud. Pierce raised an eyebrow, but before he could respond, his voco chimed.

"Think it's Ismene?" Marina asked.

"She never calls me when she's working," Pierce muttered. He held out his wrist so they could both hear.

"Pierce, it's Boris. I...ah...wanna make sure I'm reaching you before I continue. Or that nobody else is listening. So confirm it's you...quickly, please."

Pierce stared at his wrist, unblinking. "Boris never calls me. Period." He lifted his voco to his mouth, then tapped the button eagerly. "This is him. Call me back."

He lowered his hand, and Marina whispered, "He. This is *he*."

Pierce shot her a glance, then looked back at his voco. "Seems strange."

"That's grammar for you."

"I mean the fact that Boris called me. And that he doesn't want anyone else listening."

The voco's beeping sounded before she could respond.

"Something's happened," Boris said. "I'm okay...Cal's okay...but we...*shit.* We're in the South. Are you near?"

Marina's stomach soured as Pierce responded. "In the ring. What happened?"

Within seconds, the reply came. "We're...we're by the tunnel entrance. I was checking it, and I let him come with me because he has a thousand times. A thousand times, and this never...it never..." Boris cursed, then said, "He just said he wanted to apologize. I messed up, Pierce. Cal and I...we messed up, and I was hoping you could vouch for us when we tell Florin since he and your dad were so close, and maybe he'll go easier on us if it comes from you." Again, he rattled off a litany of curses, and after a moment's silence, hissed, "It's Ocot. He's gone."

Marina stifled a gasp as Pierce shot to his feet.

"What does he mean *gone?*" she said, her voice low.

"I don't—" Pierce cut himself off. "Please don't say anything to anyone. Not yet. Let me alert Florin first."

"What about Aeric?" Marina whispered.

"We'll tell him. We will. Just let me figure out what happened. I don't want you running to Aeric without all the information." When Marina only stared at him, he said, "Boris knows Florin goes...*easier* on me." He cringed as though he didn't want to admit it. "He wouldn't be calling me if he didn't screw up. For his sake—for *Cal's* sake—just...wait here until I get back."

Marina barely had time to nod before Pierce sprinted to the exit, leaving her alone at the center of the ring.

Her head buzzed with possibilities, but they were all harrowing to consider, so she simply dug her shoes into little pockets of sand and wrapped her arms around herself. She'd never realized how cold the training ring was, but her face burned and her palms glistened with sweat anyway. Though she had half a mind to linger out by the border staircase, she stayed put, counting the minutes Pierce was gone. By the time she got to twenty, she couldn't wait any longer.

"Pierce," she said, her wrist trembling as she held her voco up, "I'm—"

The tone of an incoming message cut her off. "Head back to the manor. I've already alerted Florin, and he's told Aeric. I'll meet you outside your room when I can."

Marina lingered for a moment, but the silence of the arena had grown deafening. Staying any longer would be unnecessary torture. Though she had no intention of seeking Pierce out, she couldn't help herself when she asked, "Is he really gone?"

It wasn't until she reached the manor that his response came through.

"He's really gone."

It was agonizing to wait for Pierce, and the silence of her room wasn't much better than that of the arena. She had no idea how long she'd been alone for. Minutes seemed like hours, and though she tried to quiet her anxiety, her efforts went unrewarded.

When Pierce finally knocked, she all but flung open the door.

"What happened?" she demanded as he stepped inside.

"Ocot *planned* it," Pierce said. "He planned to pull a runner. He must've realized he had no future in the Delve…everyone turned on him after what he did to you. Ismene was right when she said he wouldn't take it well."

Pierce lowered himself to the foot of Marina's bed and rested his forehead in his hands. "From what I could get out of Boris, he was checking on the southern tunnel when Ocot showed up. Said he'd just gotten off duty or something like that, but it turns out he'd left his voco at the southern border to not raise suspicion. He started spewing off all these regrets to Boris, begging for a second chance…he even smuggled wine from the kitchens as some kind of peace offering. And like a fool, Boris gave in—figured a few drinks wouldn't hurt, because he felt bad for Ocot, like he always does. But Ocot spiked the wine. He'd received some hard-hitting shit from the healers after Double Moon—the kind of medication that's meant to help with healing but knocks you out in the process. Turns out Ocot slipped it into the drink, and once Boris was out, stole his voco and took the tracker out. But he knew he couldn't bypass the shield at the end of the tunnel without alerting—"

"Cal," Marina breathed.

"I told you she goes easier on Boris because of Astra and all. So Ocot spun some story about how Boris got drunk and hurt himself, and Cal must've gone down there to check because she knew if Florin was alerted, Boris's position would be taken away again, and there was no way he'd get it back after a second strike." He rubbed his temples. "You should've seen Cal. The side of her face is all bruised up."

Marina stifled a gasp. "Is she okay?"

"Could manage a coherent enough conversation when I spoke to her. He attacked her —overpowered her and knocked her out. With Cal out of the way and no one monitoring the tunnels, he took their weapons and used Boris's voco to bypass the shield. Now he's gone, and Exorsus can only guess what kind of head start he got."

Shit. *Shit.* Could she have prevented this? If she hadn't brushed him off that evening in the gardens…

"Food was taken from the kitchens too," Pierce added, "along with supplies from who knows where. He planned it…planned the whole thing."

"But…planned what? He was terrified when he thought he was going to be kicked out of the Delve."

"Only because he'd have been kicked out with no weapons, food, or ability to communicate. He has all those things now. The technicians remotely wiped the software from Boris's voco, but it can still access portals, which means once he finds the nearest town, he can get to Altus in a day."

"How far is the nearest town?"

"A couple days' walk from the Delve. Scouts are headed out as we speak, but Ocot already had an hour's head start...maybe more."

Marina's breath sawed out of her. "What...what if the ruemin find him? Maybe..."

Maybe they'll kill him. What a horrible thing to wish for. But oh, how she wished for it. If the scouts found his mauled body, she'd thank the heavens.

"If Ocot has information Kieron wants, the ruemin will spare him." Pierce shook his head, then sneered. "I knew he was a Kieron sympathizer from the get-go..."

Marina didn't hear whatever else he said. Her head had gone silent.

Kieron sympathizer. Was he really, or did he just think there was no better option? What did desperation do if not drive people to impulsiveness? Ocot wasn't the forgiving type. She'd known that, but she'd stoked his anger all the same. And now what? Would this be what killed her? What brought the Delve to its end? If he reached Kieron...

"Marina," Pierce said, and the room snapped back into frame. "Hey. You'll be okay."

"Not if Ocot gets to Kieron." She paused. "How did Florin and Aeric react?"

"I haven't seen Aeric. Florin was..."

"Scared," Marina said when he wavered too long. "You can say it." Pierce remained silent as Marina stood. "I need to find Cal."

"Why?"

"To make sure she's okay."

"You don't have access to the barracks or the borders."

"That's not where she is."

Pierce stood as well, nervously clenching his hands. "At least send me a message when you get back. Florin seems to think the manor is the safest place you can be. Something tells me a closer eye will be kept on you now."

Marina's stomach sank, even though she figured that would be the case.

The two of them scaled the manor staircase in seconds, then parted ways at the entrance. It was past noon by the time Marina reached the plaza, but in the sea cavern, it could've been night. The obsidian rocks shone in the glow of the pool, and though Marina was careful not to slip, she took the rocks down to the edge quicker than usual.

She wasn't surprised to see Cal sitting where they last spoke, but nerves coursed through Marina anyway. Maybe Cal didn't want to be bothered—maybe facing anyone was too much. Still, she lowered herself to the rock next to Cal, who gave her a little less than a side glance before saying, "I'm sorry."

"Cal, this is on Ocot." She searched for words, only to stop herself when she realized Cal's hair was drenched. "Did you...?"

"Screaming into the water helps." Her voice was broken, and when she turned to face Marina, the light from the pool illuminated the bruises on her face. "And cold helps with the nausea." She put her head in her hands and swore. "This is my fault. I've known for years that they drink in the tunnels, but I never said anything because…" Cal's voice trailed off, and when she spoke again, tears spilled from her eyes. "Because Boris used to do that with Astra. And I'd known about that too."

She wiped away the tears on her cheek with the back of her hand. "I knew how lonely Boris was after she died, and despite the shit person Ocot is, at least Boris had a friend. I figured it wouldn't do much harm if I didn't say anything because going for a few drinks every now and then is such a mild way to spend time, especially in a tunnel we hardly ever patrol. But if it had been anyone else besides Boris, I would've reported it…I know that. But I just…I couldn't."

She let out a pained exhale, then cursed under her breath. "Ocot called me and said Boris had passed out from drinking too much and hurt himself. And all I could hear at the back of my head was Astra telling me to check on him myself because Boris would be punished for drinking on duty." Her lips quivered. "Only Boris hadn't hurt himself at all. Before I realized he'd been drugged, Ocot attacked me. I *almost* managed to fight him off."

More tears fell down Cal's cheeks, and Marina had to press her wobbling lips together before she whispered, "This isn't your fault."

"It doesn't make me feel better to hear lies. Boris and I did exactly what Ocot wanted. Ocot knew Boris would give in and spend time with him, even if he's a pariah, and he knew just as well I'd go down and try to clean up their mess." She rubbed her temples. "He overpowered me, and next thing I know, I'm waking up next to Boris—both of us stripped of our weapons." She laughed mirthlessly through her tears. "I have a ridiculous number when I'm on duty. Ocot took everything. But my sword…it was Astra's. Now it's with him."

As hard as she searched, Marina couldn't find her voice. Even if she could, what would she say? That she was sorry? That they shouldn't worry? All equally empty responses—all equally unhelpful.

"The scouts won't find Ocot," Cal whispered. "He knows the tunnel system, and he has the skillset to get out of it. Exorsus, if *this* is the reason we lose this fight…"

"Don't say that. You don't know what will happen."

Cal didn't respond, and though the pit in Marina's stomach lodged deeper into her gut, she said, "Mistakes were made. We can't control where it leads us, but someone smart told me we still have control over the paths we choose. So that's what we'll do, if nothing else. We'll make the next right choice."

Cal chuckled tearfully. "The girl I met in these caverns wanted to escape the Delve."

"Not anymore," Marina said. She wasn't sure if that was the full truth. She wasn't sure there *was* a full truth. Things were so complicated that she couldn't decide which fate she preferred. But did she need to want one thing more than another? Could she not yearn both for her home *and* for the Delve's safety? The back of her throat began to throb, but she swallowed her tears.

"If you see Pierce before I do, give him my thanks," Cal said after a few moments. "He took on the burden of telling Florin, who probably would've responded a lot worse if Boris and I were the ones to do so. Mistakes like these are unforgivable." When she looked down at her feet, tears fell to her shoes. "I wouldn't be surprised if Aeric punishes both of us."

"Worse mistakes have been made. Aeric knows that better than anyone."

The shift in Cal's demeanor alleviated the tightness in Marina's chest.

"You were trying to help Boris," she continued. "You did what you did out of kindness. Ocot's manipulation doesn't change that." She glanced at the cerulean pool. "If you're to blame, so am I. I'm the reason Ocot and Boris got demoted. Those documents they stole..."

"You'd asked. Boris told me."

"Yeah." Marina's voice was less than a whisper. "I asked."

Because I was desperate and impulsive. And now so is Ocot.

"Astra always said that Boris's people-pleasing would be his downfall," Cal said. "Especially when it came to someone as domineering as Ocot. As for me...apparently mine is that I never learn."

Marina stayed silent for a moment. "And mine is fear," she admitted. Cal turned to her, a sober look in her eyes, and though Marina almost left it at that, she added, "But we haven't fallen yet."

Strangely enough, Cal smiled. "No, we haven't."

CHAPTER 28
Shadows and Sunlight

Aeric was an hour late that evening, and by the time he arrived, Marina had almost convinced herself he wasn't coming. Not bothering to hide her desperation, she asked, "Did you find him?"

Aeric shook his head, an unreadable look in his eyes. "We continue training anyway."

"What do we do if Kieron finds the Delve?"

"That entirely depends on what ends up happening."

"Worst-case scenario, then."

Aeric nodded at the crimson rug on the floor. "Move that to the side."

"Why?"

He gave her an impatient look in response. When she went to move it, he said, "Not with your hands. With sorcery. Even small acts contribute to long-term prowess."

Marina nodded, then calmed her choppy waves and extended a tendril of her energy to the rim of the rug, which curled up and onto itself as it pulled back.

You're improving, she told herself. *That's good, isn't it?*

No. None of this was good. Moving a rug wouldn't protect her from Kieron.

She swallowed her thoughts, which formed a heavy knot in her stomach, then peered at the floor. She had to clear her throat before asking, "Is it glamoured?"

Aeric gave her a tight-lipped, affirming smile that didn't extend to his eyes.

Before he could instruct her, Marina approached the stones, then kicked the rug to the side and knelt, placing her palms on the cool rock. If she squinted, she could see the sheen they carried, faint enough to be imperceptible to the untrained eye. There was a shield there too—a wall of compressed air only big enough to cover whatever it was hiding. She truly *was* good at sensing these things.

A breath. Mental shields up, waves calm. Even with the horror of today, her waves knew what to do. *She* knew what to do.

She bit back a gasp as the sheen flickered and the wall of air disappeared, revealing the narrowest spiral staircase she'd ever seen.

"That will take us out of the Delve," Aeric said. "It heads south, to the sea—away from where any attacks would be, which likely would come from the north, though the east and west are vulnerable too."

Marina glanced down the stairs, but they curved into the rock at such a sharp angle that she couldn't see where they led or how far they went.

"Another tunnel system?" she whispered, more to herself than Aeric.

"The manor was built over this tunnel specifically for evacuation," Aeric said.

"How would we get everyone through this in time?"

When Aeric didn't answer, she turned to face him. The realization dawned on her before she met his gaze, but she didn't have time to protest.

"You asked for the worst-case scenario," Aeric said. "Worst-case scenario means not everyone gets out."

Marina gawked at him. "But...what about Pierce and Ismene? What about—"

"If we're found, we'll have very little time to escape. We'd have to leave as soon as possible, which means we wouldn't have the luxury of rallying a big group. We'd only have time to take our first choices...if that."

"What would happen to everyone else? What happens to your shields if you leave?"

Aeric didn't need to answer; Marina already knew. They would fall, and the rest of the Delve would follow.

"How long would it take?" she demanded.

Aeric paused before admitting, "I can't be sure. Without me here to reinforce them, they'd weaken. And once I was far enough away..."

"How far?"

Dryly, he said, "Does it matter?"

"Yes. Would they even have a chance to escape, or would they be trapped down here as your shields erode and Kieron's forces get in?"

When Aeric didn't answer, Marina stood. "Who'd come with us?"

"Florin, myself, and anyone who would increase our odds of survival."

"As we go where?"

He closed his eyes, weighing, then said, "I've heard whispers of people who've made a similar hideaway by the Candens Inlet in the South."

Candens Inlet. Marina wondered if that was the "one place" Florin had been referring to when she'd eavesdropped on him and Aeric.

"Whispers by whom?" she asked.

"Scouts pick up more information the farther they stray from the Delve. They don't limit their expeditions to the East." Aeric tapped his fingers on the table. "I have good faith in the word of my scouts and officers, and it's been consistent throughout the dead years. A group of inclined people have found sanctuary in the wetlands that surround Candens Inlet. That's where we'd go as a last resort."

"So we abandon the Delve to seek out another group who we'd abandon just the same if another worst-case scenario happens?"

"What part of worst-case scenario gives you reason to believe our choices will be easy?" He paused, then added, "Perhaps Pierce could come, seeing as though he's skilled enough in combat to be useful."

"We can't abandon Ismene and the rest of the Delve as we flee somewhere else."

"Then I suggest you *practice* your magic," Aeric said through gritted teeth.

There it was—the icy tone that made the temperature in the room drop. Only now, Marina could sense the fear in it.

Though the manor was as empty as it always was, it had somehow grown quieter. Whether or not she was imagining it, she couldn't shake the unease that followed her as she made her way back to her room.

This is your fault. If you hadn't pushed Ocot to get those documents for you, none of this would've happened.

She sat at her vanity, swearing when she locked eyes with the girl in the mirror. Was she the same girl Marina avoided at home? Had anything changed, or had her heedlessness doomed these people like it had doomed her parents?

Fear was selfish. It prized survival over scruples and would sooner leave others out to dry if it meant one more day with a beating heart. Maybe it really would be her downfall. Maybe it would be the Delve's too.

Stop. Don't spiral.

Her hands began to tremble; she needed a distraction. She blinked at herself in the mirror. She hadn't realized how long her hair had grown since she'd come here.

It was good practice—a good *distraction*—to steady the waves within her, take her hair in her hand, and pull upon the Omnia's magic. She needed nothing but herself.

It was easier than using scissors and even more exact. She let her power pulse out from her fingers, severing small sections, just like her mother used to. As the first tendrils fell to the floor, Marina remembered the way the kitchen back at home would smell like hair products when her mother cut her hair.

Another section followed—it was as instinctive as moving a limb—and her mother's humming danced at the back of her head. She could do this. She was improving. She was learning things on her own and drawing on her internal resources like Aeric wanted her to. She could steady her waves when she was nervous, just as she did now.

One day, one step, one breath at a time.

Perhaps, if her mom were here now, she'd be proud. Marina had managed to recreate the style. Pride sparked at her fingertips as she continued cutting her hair, just like her mother used to. Just like Aeric had cut through the ruemin.

A sharp exhale escaped Marina's mouth as another section fell to the floor, followed not by memories of her mother, but of the tar-like blood that had stained the snow.

She stared at the clumps of auburn that littered the carpet, then gathered them with shaking hands. Would she ever have to do something like that? Would she have to face ruemin again, or worse, the man who brought them here?

The tightness in her chest returned.

Don't do this. You were doing so well today. You were calm despite everything...

It didn't matter. Not when the threat was what it was. Everything she was doing was futile. She wasn't meant to hold the Omnia.

No, no, no, Marina. Don't go back to that. Don't regress.

She forced her limbs to move as she took a shower and dressed for bed—telling her body to do things and following mindlessly.

Only the fear wouldn't wane, and it was becoming hard to breathe...

None of it mattered. Her thoughts didn't matter, her power didn't matter, *she* didn't matter; Ocot was gone, and she'd driven him away.

She couldn't breathe or think—couldn't see or hear—as panic's cold hands embraced her. The shadows within her pulsed, spilling out and over until she buckled under their weight, fighting and begging and praying for the storm in her head to retreat as she knelt on the ground. But even her waves couldn't help her. She needed to get *out*, and not just out of her room or the Delve, but out of her head. This was all too much...

She wasn't sure how long she remained on the floor, but somewhere between her labored breaths and muffled sobs, sleep rushed in to quell the panic. She clung to it, begging it to stay, because *that* was where she felt safe—cloaked in shadows, hidden from dangers she couldn't fathom facing.

Here and now, when it came to choosing between shadows and sunlight, the smartest choice was darkness.

CHAPTER 29
Barrier

Marina woke to an aching head and limbs so heavy she could barely move them to get dressed. Still, she commanded herself to go through the motions because she knew she had to—because there was nothing else she *could* do.

She was familiar with days like these. Days where the residue of fear turned viscid in her body, slowing her every movement until she chose instead to sleep.

Not today. The silent command brought about relief. Perhaps she *was* improving, and not just with magic.

Her confidence sprang to life even more when Pierce knocked on her door later that morning, and despite everything, gave her a crooked smile.

"Your hair looks nice," he said.

She did her best not to fixate on the circles beneath his eyes when she said, "I cut it."

"I'm surprised Aeric lets you have scissors."

"Funny. Turns out I don't need any."

Pierce snorted as he sat against the foot of her bed. "Convenient."

"I needed a distraction."

"Did it work?"

Marina only shrugged as she listened to the faint hum of the floodlights outside her window, then asked, "Have you heard anything?"

Pierce shook his head. "I was at the northern border all night. Aeric and Florin were too, but we all know it's useless to look for him."

She expected a rush of fear, only to be met with numbness. "Cal gives her thanks to you, by the way," she said, "for telling Florin."

Pierce smiled weakly. "I've known Florin since I was a kid. He and my dad may've been strict, but they were never unforgiving. Even now, Florin knows who's really to blame —and he knows even more that punishing Cal will only hurt us in the long run." He rested his head in his hands, his voice but a whisper when he said, "My dad used to say the worst threats come from the inside. Looks like he was right. Everything went wrong with Ocot, and now we're blind to the future."

"We're always blind to the future," Marina said, more to herself than Pierce. When he looked up at her, she said, "I don't know what's worse: the thought of a terrifying future, or of no future at all. But what I *do* know is that before I came here, I'd given up on mine. And now...something's changed." She laughed mirthlessly. "But I'm also scared shitless, and I don't know if that's better."

"It is," Pierce said. "It's better to feel something than nothing at all."

The lights outside flickered. Marina watched them sputter back to life before she whispered, "How do you know?"

"Because feeling something means you're still alive."

Aeric insisted they train in the dining room that evening. Since she couldn't bear to sit around in her room and spiral, Marina arrived early. She spent the first few minutes alone manipulating the stonecrop arrangement at the center. Pulling the water from the vase, exerting control over each flower...these small feats had become so simple.

It only took a movement of her eyes to put everything back in its place when Aeric entered, and Marina did her best not to tense at the fact that he was in a bad mood. Still, she couldn't help herself when she opened her mouth to ask about Ocot.

Aeric cut her off before she could speak. "We haven't found him. In the unlikely event we do, I'll tell you. There's no need to ask me every night."

Marina pursed her lips as Aeric sat at the table.

"Understanding and heeding your surroundings is as important in conveyance as it is in summoning," he said. "The rules are the same—however, you're moving *yourself* instead of something inanimate."

Conveyance. Marina raised an eyebrow. "So...like super-speed?"

"Semantics. You're not moving your limbs; you're transporting your body from one place to another. Obviously, the amount of space traveled affects the feasibility of the task, which is why you're to begin practicing in this room."

"Are you serious?" She glanced around the dining room. "I can't."

"You always say that, and then you do."

"But I've never done anything like that. What if it kills me?"

"Only you would think that." When she folded her arms, he sighed. "It won't."

"I've never seen *you* convey."

It was clear she was chipping away at his patience. Though he made no effort to hide his nettled expression, he answered her.

He didn't vanish—not really. He just...moved. One moment, he was sitting at the end of the dining room table, and the next, he was standing behind the chair at the opposite end, gripping the crest rail.

Marina wasn't sure what she'd expected, but she gasped all the same. "Motherfu—"

"Now you've seen it," he cut in, "and now *you* will try."

She remained still as he walked back to his chair.

"How far could someone go?" she asked after a few seconds.

"As far as they could walk. Perhaps a bit farther. Many limitations of magic are in sync with the limitations of one's stamina and strength, as you've realized. Having a spirit predisposed to magical interaction may give you a boost, but not by much. A sorcerer cannot convey from one region of Elsudra to another, the same way they can't walk that distance on their own in one go. We have portals for that."

"Are the portals up and running now?"

Aeric nodded. "Now that the dead years are over."

Marina paused, then said softly, "What about portals *between* realms?"

"Only one has ever been made."

"By Brenna."

Aeric angled his head at her. "Yes. Stop stalling."

"But that was a unidirectional portal," Marina said, her gaze coaxing. "How did you manipulate it to go *both* ways?"

"It wasn't the portal I manipulated. It was something that powered it."

"What do you mean?"

"Inter-realm portals are far more complex than intra-realm portals, and I haven't the time to walk you through the technicalities." Voice rigid, he repeated, "Stop. Stalling."

Marina sighed at the ceiling. "I don't know where to begin."

"Start with visualizing your waves. Your essence is the basis of all interaction with magic, and your ability to control it in relation to the Omnia is vital to your success."

Marina tapped the table anxiously. "Where do I go?"

"Somewhere in this room, preferably. Start small."

Another glance around the dining room stirred up her nerves. "If there are portals, why is conveyance necessary?" she asked. "Especially if you can only travel as far as you're able to walk."

"It would take me ten minutes, maybe longer, to go from here to the southern border by foot," Aeric said. "With conveyance, I can do it in less than a second. That, and it may be your only means of escape."

Marina hesitated. There was a fair amount of space behind the table she could aim for. Perhaps moving to the other end of the room was doable.

Breathe. Concentrate. Let your waves guide you.

She narrowed her attention on herself, becoming one with her waves and the power they held. If she let it, that power could bring her from one point to another. Aeric had said to start with her waves, which she supposed made sense, so she closed her eyes and imagined her body melting away into the endless seawater that comprised her spirit.

The ocean moved easily—freely—and so could she. When she opened her eyes, the room was blurry, almost as though every wall and ceiling was doused in water...

"Holy shit," Marina blurted. The room came back into view as her focus shattered. Upon hearing Aeric's sigh, she snapped, "Give me time. I get anxious with these things."

He leaned his head against his fist. "And with everything else."

"*That's* not helpful."

It took effort to block out his presence as she composed herself. She channeled every inch of her waves, acknowledging but trying not to fear the world blurring around her. When her head slammed into the window at the corner of the dining room, she realized she'd grossly overestimated how far she was going.

Hand on her forehead, she whirled around to face Aeric, who still sat at the table.

"You said it wouldn't kill me."

"Don't be dramatic. You miscalculated the distance."

Marina blew a wisp of hair out of her face, then turned her attention back to her waves and the distance between herself and the table.

She was bridging the gap; that was it. Anything beyond herself, her waves, and her destination was peripheral. The waves within her rose, narrowing into one great mountain of water and power that pointed in the direction of the table—no, of her chair—and swept her up with it.

Though her landing was shaky, she managed to get herself back into the seat of the chair. Gripping the arms to steady herself, she looked up at Aeric and grinned, breathless.

"You'll want to continue practicing," he said. "Anytime you remember, travel a short distance. After some time, you'll master your balance and improve your stamina, which will allow you to travel farther in a single go."

"I did it, though, didn't I?"

"You did it."

"And?" She swallowed, fervency at her fingertips. "You think I'm good enough?"

Her voice trailed off, but Aeric didn't jump to fill the silence. For a moment, he looked both at and beyond her, and Marina braced herself for some dismissive response. Which, of course, made it all the more surprising when he said, "For a non-Elsudran from a realm with effectively no magic, you've managed to successfully execute tasks that take most weeks to learn, if they're able to at all."

The heaviness in her chest lessened a bit. "Well, I *do* hold the Omnia."

"And I'm sure that helps. But so did our Keepers, and they couldn't do what you can. For some reason, you have the aptitude to interact with magic...when you're willing to do so." He paused. "In fact, with everything I've observed, I'd go as far as to say you only have only one glaring weakness."

Marina's grin dulled, and her grip on the arms of her chair tightened. He didn't have to say it for her to know what he was referring to.

"But," Aeric said, "having a weakness isn't detrimental. Being blind to it is. Whatever you do, do not forget what holds you back."

"If Kieron finds us, fear will be the least of my problems."

"Untrue. It would be all the more essential for you to keep it in check."

"How am I supposed to do that?"

The chill she expected when she locked eyes with Aeric didn't come. Had it thawed some time ago, or had she grown used to the cold?

"By remembering what protects you," Aeric said. "The Keepers knew how to perform Locus, even if they needed someone with magical abilities to orchestrate it—which meant once Kieron got them to agree, all he had to do was oversee the ritual to completion. You have the prowess, but your ignorance would buy us time."

When Marina bristled, Aeric said, "That's not a bad thing. It could be your saving grace. Kieron wouldn't dare rush you into Locus. He doesn't want to damage the Omnia—not when his goal is to hold it." He shook his head, a hint of amusement in his voice. "There is a massive barrier to Kieron's success," he said, "and it is *you*."

CHAPTER 30
Redwoods

Four Elsudran weeks passed, all uneventful. Marina spent her days honing her skills, mostly because she couldn't bear to let her thoughts wander.

One day, one step, one breath at a time, she'd tell herself in moments of panic. The advice seldom helped, but repetition mollified her better than anything else.

Since multiple units of scouts had been deployed to track Ocot and keep watch over the Admare Mountains, sentries picked up excess shifts. Marina rarely saw Pierce, and when she did, he seemed unable to speak of anything but details he'd gleaned from Florin—which, of course, were few and far between.

His anxiety was warranted, of course; as was Aeric's, whose patience was more strained than usual. Though he attended every session with focus and a slew of new things for Marina to practice, she couldn't help but notice the anxiety in his eyes—so deep-seated that even her successes didn't dull it.

Ismene seemed the most even-keeled, but Marina supposed she was simply better at smiling through her stress. When they ran into each other in the hallways or found some scant time to spend together, Marina tried to match Ismene's bubbly demeanor, only to fail when she remembered what Aeric had said.

Worst-case scenario means not everyone gets out.

She never dared mention it to Ismene, of course—Aeric didn't need to tell her to keep it to herself—but every time the two of them spoke, those words echoed in Marina's head.

So she practiced, then practiced more, finding solace in meticulousness.

She hadn't seen Cal in weeks, though she hadn't expected to. Cal had been one of the first to volunteer to track Ocot. Florin hadn't heard from their unit, according to Pierce, and when Marina asked him if it was normal for scouts to be out for weeks at a time, he only said, "They've never had reason to go as far as they're going now."

So again, she turned to practice. She stopped asking questions because at this point, the answers were the same, and hearing them from fearful, tired mouths was enough to rouse the storms in her head. They were hard enough to suppress as it was; she didn't need more reminders of how afraid she should be.

Sometimes, she thought of Locus—of what it entailed and how perhaps it was the smartest option—but she was far from adept enough to attempt it. Even if she was, would she turn to it? Every time she saw Pierce, spoke to Ismene, or passed a sentry, the roots that tethered her to this place strengthened. Whether those roots were made of guilt or hope, she wasn't sure, but something was keeping her here, even when fear reared its head.

The first day of Aragonite coincided with the first of May, and on its eve, Marina roamed the halls, practicing conveyance and pushing herself to go farther. Moving between two ends of a hall was easy, but taking corners and stairs tested her. When she began to think of home—she couldn't help but wonder how Gemma and Hank were doing —she switched into autopilot. Which, of course, resulted in her colliding into Ismene.

Marina gasped as Ismene gave a surprised squeak, then stumbled off to the side as her surroundings grew clear again.

"Sorry, Ismene," Marina said. "I was practicing..."

"Conveyance. I know," Ismene said through a giggle. "You slammed into one of the servants a week ago, didn't you?"

Marina cringed. She'd braved the staircase early—a stupid choice, really, since it had taken her a good half hour to gather the courage—only to overshoot the distance and careen into an elderly cook on her way to the kitchens. Thankfully, the cook had been more startled than hurt, but Marina escorted her to the infirmary anyway. She'd spent the rest of that day practicing shielding instead.

"You seem to be improving, though," Ismene added hopefully.

"Slowly but surely. I'm glad you weren't carrying anything breakable."

Ismene grinned. "Even if I was, it's good to see you practicing so often. Better still that you have such an affinity for it."

"Helps keep me busy," Marina said with a shrug.

"Busy is good." Ismene's smile grew strained, but she blinked it away and invited Marina to walk with her to the first floor. As they took the winding halls, Ismene spoke of the greenhouse's success in growing stubborn vegetables, and Marina pretended not to notice how hard she was trying to be optimistic.

When the subject turned to her recent lessons with Aeric, Marina tried equally as hard to keep the mood light. She told Ismene how he'd mentioned employing the help of the Delve's healers to teach her what he struggled with, and how she was beginning to understand the science behind glamours. He'd even told her about the different kinds of shields. Apparently, one of the more complicated kinds could be layered with magic that caused debilitating exhaustion when touched. No one could overpower those alone, which was why they were most often used in prisons.

Marina omitted that information, though. She made an effort to keep things positive, which seemed to work; when they came to the bottom of the manor's staircase, zest bubbled up inside of her. With it came hope, small and timid as it was.

It was a freeing feeling nonetheless—and short-lived. Just as they were about to turn a corner, a high-pitched ring coming from their vocos ricocheted through the foyer.

Marina shot a frantic look at Ismene, whose face had lost all color. As suddenly as the alarm began, it broke off mid-ring, stranding the two of them in the wake of its scream.

"Marina."

She wasn't sure if Aeric had been nearby or if he'd used conveyance. Either way, he appeared next to them so suddenly that Marina jumped.

"What happened?" Marina asked.

"The borders," Ismene said. "Are they…"

"They're secure." Aeric's tone wasn't dismissive; rather, it was riddled with fear. When his eyes met Marina's, her heart dropped. "But activity was detected near the northern border. Go to the third floor and stay there until I say otherwise. Ismene, you go with her."

He didn't have to say more. Marina grabbed Ismene's hand and pulled her up the staircase, then down the hallway to the third floor's door. Though her senses were jumbled, she steadied herself and her waves…

"Marina, Ismene!"

Marina snapped her head to the other end of the hallway, relief barreling through her when she saw Pierce. Though he was panting, he reached them in seconds. "Florin told me to come."

Marina only nodded, then put her hands to the door and let her waves do the rest. Pierce and Ismene fumbled about as they made their way down the stairwell, but they managed to keep up with Marina, who dismantled the shield quickly.

"Shit, you're good," Pierce breathed. Marina could tell it was his attempt to make her feel better, but it didn't do much. She'd give up her abilities if it meant not being Kieron's target. And if her suspicions were correct…

Stop. Just breathe. Don't focus on anything else.

When they reached Aeric's office, Pierce sat against the door.

"So *this* is the forbidden floor," he half joked. His smile quivered.

Too out of sorts to manage a laugh, Marina settled on a nod.

"What have you heard?" Ismene asked.

"As much as you two, I think," Pierce said. "Activity near the northern border sent everyone into a frenzy, and then I got Florin's call to come here. Nothing's been breached, if that's what you're asking. But I don't know the specifics."

"Maybe it's ruemin activity," Ismene said, straining to sound hopeful.

Pierce said what Marina was thinking. "That alarm wouldn't have gone off due to just ruemin activity."

Silence followed, and Marina's head buzzed violently.

"It'll be okay," Pierce whispered, though Marina had no idea who he was talking to.

It was a nightmare—waiting like this. As Pierce whispered to himself and Ismene took measured breaths, Marina stared ahead, wishing the world around them would disappear. But that was a child's wish, much like her prayers that ruemin would tear Ocot apart before he could betray them.

"We don't know this is them." Pierce looked at her when he said it.

Marina closed her eyes. She tried to access her waves—tried to smooth any turbulent waters—but found that the ocean within her wasn't choppy at all. It was stock-still, much like her head and body.

When Pierce's voco chimed with a message, Marina's eyes flew open.

"Come to the hallway." Florin's voice—weaker than usual. "Bring Marina and Ismene."

They obeyed, and though Marina steeled herself for chaos, or perhaps a slew of hurried orders, she was met with something else—something cold and despairing.

"The Delve is still secure," Aeric said before anyone could speak, "but I need you all to listen."

"Is it Kieron?" Pierce blurted, wincing when Florin shot him a warning look.

"Not exactly," Aeric said. Marina expected to feel at least *some* sense of calm, but her heart only stopped. There was more—so much more behind his eyes. "He sent messengers. They aren't powerful enough to get through the shields, which means they can't get into the Delve. But that doesn't mean we're safe, and it doesn't mean Kieron will remain in the North. As Florin and I prepare to proceed, you're to fall in line. We cannot entertain questions or moral quandaries, for we're no longer speaking of hypotheticals. Pierce, you'll accompany Florin wherever he needs you, and Ismene, you're to keep peace in the manor and placate anxieties, as we've discussed. Marina, go back to the third floor."

A thousand questions curled at Marina's tongue, only to die before they could be spoken into existence. A wave of lightheadedness rushed over her, rendering Aeric's voice a dull echo when he said, "It is vital, now more than ever, that you follow orders." He didn't look at Pierce and Ismene when he said it—he looked at her—and before she could say anything, he turned to leave.

Marina shot a desperate glance at Florin, Pierce, and Ismene, though she wasn't sure what they would do, and before she had time to orient her thoughts, she was on Aeric's heels. At the first turn of the hallway, she grabbed him by the arm and breathed, "What are you not telling me...telling *us*?"

"What did I say about questions?" Aeric hissed, and in one fell swoop, he'd broken out of her grip.

"Is this worst-case scenario?" Marina whispered. "What about Ismene? We can't leave her and the others to die."

This was Ocot's doing. It had to be. But even if it wasn't Kieron outside, he would come soon enough. Aeric intended to be long gone by that point, and now the threat was more inevitable than ever.

There could only be one reason Aeric wasn't telling her anything. He wanted to keep her in the dark until it was too late to protest—until she no longer had time to bargain for the lives of those in the Delve. If she didn't figure out what was going on *now*, she'd forsake her chance to save Ismene and the others.

Leaving the Delve or leaving Elsudra altogether...what was the difference? It was abandonment all the same, and with an unexpectedly clear head, Marina realized fleeing was no longer an option. She was equally as terrified as she'd been months ago, but something else trumped her fear. Something stronger. Aeric wouldn't give her what she wanted. Though she hated the thought, Marina couldn't help but wonder if getting past his shields would give her the answers she needed. Recent events were memories, after all, and she'd proven herself to be strong enough more than once...

"Don't even think it."

Her spark of hope froze as Aeric looked her dead in the eyes and whispered, "Go to the third floor, stay there until I notify you, and *trust me*. I'm not your enemy."

And then, he was gone. A surprised gasp escaped Marina's mouth—not because he'd used conveyance, but because he'd been quick to leave, even for him. Had he realized what she was planning to do? Was he worried she *could*?

She didn't stick around to give the matter much thought. Instead, she bolted back to Pierce and Ismene, her voice low and breathless when she said, "Where's Florin?"

Pierce blinked at her. "Staircase, probably. Just left. I have to head to the northern..."

Marina brushed past them, grimacing at the stagnant air that clung to the back of her throat. By the time she made it to the staircase, Florin was already at the bottom.

Instinctively, the world around her blurred. She took a steadying breath, then let herself pass by the staircase as effortlessly as water.

Mindful of the steps, of corners...

Florin's eyes widened when she stumbled in front of him. She caught herself, not caring how clumsy she looked, and blurted, "What happened?"

The bewilderment in Florin's eyes snuffed out, and Marina heard Pierce and Ismene gasp from atop the staircase.

"We're assessing the current situation," Florin said sternly. "When the time is right, Aeric will tell you what's needed. He's not looking to keep you in the dark."

Only that's exactly what he's doing.

Time was ticking, and her options were running out. But Florin must've been off duty when the alarm had sounded because he wasn't wearing his gloves.

Which meant his memories were only a touch away.

Was she really going to stoop that low? She knew what it was like to suffer through psychometry, but only now did she realize how desperate Aeric must have been that day in the dining room. Cooperating was a risk she couldn't take. Not now—not when it meant endangering so many lives, Ismene's included.

Pierce and Ismene had made their way to the bottom of the staircase now, and though she could feel them shooting her cautious glances, she didn't heed them. Instead, she steadied her waves, then whispered, "I'm sorry," before grabbing Florin's hand.

Aeric and Pierce hadn't been lying when they'd said soldiers trained with shielding. Marina's waves crashed against a fortress of redwoods that encased Florin's mind, but rather than let the magnitude of the trees deter her, she rallied her strength and slammed into the bark once more, searching for any weakness she could.

It was the environment that caught her off guard. Unlike Aeric's swift, evasive movements, Florin's were stilted. But he didn't have the abilities she did, and it was clear they were on an uneven playing field. She remembered Aeric saying that without magic, one's shields would be vulnerable, and as hard as Florin fought, he was very vulnerable indeed. Marina could feel him struggling to regain control, but he was failing.

I'm sorry, I'm sorry, I'm sorry.

Her waves curled as they grew, then plunged down onto the trees with so much force that even the sturdiest of Florin's redwoods couldn't hold her back.

One memory lingered on the outskirts, fresh enough to catch her attention.

Just this...this is all I need.

She'd regret this—she knew she would. But since she knew with even more certainty that she'd regret turning away, she let the memory surround her, praying Florin could sense her apologies.

CHAPTER 31
Blue and Green

The alarm sang its damning song again, but this time, the panic Marina felt wasn't her own. Florin hadn't been at the northern border when it rang, but by the time he got there, he'd already sent Pierce to find Marina and instructed a dozen more sentries to take their posts. He'd practiced this scenario—they *all* had—and things fell together so quickly that by the time Aeric arrived, only minutes had passed.

But no amount of preparation could stave off the panic. Weeks of restlessness melted away, replaced by a fear so primal Florin could scarcely feel it. This was the type of fear that prepared the body for a fight. He prayed it wouldn't come to that.

The view from the northern border was far from that of the southern one. Rather than the ocean, the north overlooked miles of mountains and trees. In late afternoon, the snowcaps sparkled—a beauty Florin usually let himself take in when he needed reminders of what they were fighting for. Now, even the view couldn't bring him peace.

Unlike the southern border, equipped with the bare minimum, this one was lined with technology Marina had never seen before. Sentries, scouts, and technicians huddled around a screen on a console, which a wide-eyed woman plucked from its recess.

"Three bodies are standing directly in front of the entrance," she said, struggling to steady her voice as she approached Florin and Aeric. *"They haven't moved since we detected them. Seems like they're confident the glamour is there, though."*

Florin's face tightened. *"How did they get this close without being detected?"*

"The radar identified them as ruemin," another technician said. *"They must've hidden in a pack. When we could finally make out Elsudrans, we sounded the alarm."* He paused, then added, *"But...maybe it's a good sign there are only three."*

It did nothing to ease Florin's dread. Even without the glamour, the northern border's entrance was well-hidden. In the rare event ruemin stumbled across it, it was coincidence. But Elsudrans...

"*We'll check,*" Aeric said.

Florin nodded in response. Of course, he knew just as well as Aeric that there was no plausible way three Elsudrans would've found the Delve—not unless they'd been led there by someone who knew its location.

Florin gave more orders to sentries, who rushed off to ready weapons, then unlocked a door at the corner of the room. It led into a passage tunnel lined by murder holes and steel doors equipped with biometric scanners. Light existed fleetingly, and the farther Florin and Aeric walked, the colder the air became. When they reached the last door, Aeric hesitated, so Florin unlocked the door himself.

Beginning at the glamoured entrance to the northern border, there was a stretch of land made by a trough in the Admares that ran over a mile long. He'd seen it many times, but today, Florin almost didn't recognize it, for it was littered in a sea of red and black.

Five ruemin had only been a nightmare, Marina realized. What lay before them—*this* was hell. They formed a tight line, some so close their scales touched. But Florin's focus wasn't on them. He'd seen plenty—*killed* plenty. Instead, he watched the three Elsudrans that stood a few feet from the entrance, still unable to see Aeric and Florin.

The first was a man in his early twenties, most likely—strikingly handsome, with a sharp jaw, warm brown skin, and dark hair. He wore a golden armored suit even nicer than the ones in the Delve, but he hadn't bothered to conceal his hands or face—a choice that might've been stupid had its message not been clear. The Delve wasn't a threat.

Marina didn't fixate on his armor for long, though. Something about his face made him stand out, but she couldn't pinpoint it. Maybe it was the arrogance etched into his features, which grew all the more noticeable when he smiled at the woman beside him and droned, "*He said you were one of the best. Said it all throughout the dead years. But here you are, struggling to even sense glamours.*"

The woman didn't respond. She was tall, perhaps around Aeric's age, with pale skin and plaited red hair. Her face drew the most attention—partially because of its beauty, but mostly because the left side was made of mechanized gold, as though her flesh had been cut away and replaced with sprockets and roller chains that moved when her jaw did. Her mouth and nose had been spared, but her eye hadn't; and yet, it hadn't been restored.

"*Or maybe there aren't any glamours to sense,*" the young man said pointedly, flicking his gaze to the beady-eyed soldier next to him—Ocot.

Marina could feel the urge to scream curling at the back of her throat—or perhaps it was Florin's rage she felt. She couldn't tell the difference.

Ocot was no soldier; he was a rat. Capital armor and fancy weapons wouldn't change that. His eyes glinted as he muttered, *"This is where the northern border is. I swear it."*

"Well, he's bound to be disappointed in one of you. Either you're a liar, or Safira isn't as talented as he thought. Reckon he'll remove her pardon?"

The woman with the mechanical face snapped her head toward the young man. *"Tread carefully."* Her voice was gravelly, and only then did Marina notice that, like her face, the left side of her neck was man-made. Perhaps her larynx had been replaced with something artificial too. *"It takes as long to sense a glamour as it does to create one."*

Did it? It had never taken particularly long for Marina. On any other occasion, that might've made her proud, but pride was hard to come by at the moment.

"If Ocot is honest, and Aeric's alive," Safira continued, *"I alone don't have the strength to get through the shields he's no doubt put up."*

"I am," Ocot said eagerly. *"You have my word."*

Florin and Aeric remained unmoving. How impressive it was, Marina thought, that they didn't bow to their anger—that Aeric didn't remove his glamour and shield to kill Ocot immediately. As stupid as the urge was, Marina couldn't help but feel it, especially when she glanced at Ocot's hip, where Cal's cutlass lay.

Conniving, manipulative coward. She wanted to scream it at him as much as she wanted to scream it at herself.

"You told us the Delve can sense bodies as they get closer. Can they hear us too?" the young man asked Ocot.

Ocot nodded. *"We have technology that picks up sound."*

A smile tugged at the young man's lips. *"We?"*

"The Delve," Ocot said quickly. *"Not 'we.' Not anymore. I'm not—"*

"A mix-up of words, then," the young man said, clearly enjoying Ocot's discomfort.

When Ocot nodded, the young man whispered, *"Don't be a traitor twice."*

Marina could feel the fire that curled in Florin's chest. They should've killed Ocot that morning after Double Moon. It would've been hasty—perhaps cruel—but that cruelty would've protected the Delve. And now...

"The energy is different here," Safira muttered.

The young man grinned, then looked up at the rock before them and raised his voice. *"We'd prefer you make this easy and grant us civil conversation, but if not, we'll call in our troops —they're not far out—and surround your hideaway. If we can't get through your shields, Kieron will make the journey and do it himself. He'd be happy to pay his old friend—who, until recently, he thought dead—a visit. You can imagine how eager he is to reunite."*

Aeric hardly reacted. *"Do you recognize him?"*

Florin shook his head. He'd trained hundreds of guards over the years, and though the young man did look familiar, he couldn't place him.

"*There's still the exit to the sea,*" Florin said. Though he knew the shield concealed their voices, he lowered his anyway.

"*They know the Delve exists and where the entrance is,*" Aeric said. "*We leave, they come back and slaughter the Delve, and we're blind to Kieron's next move. Better to speak with them, bide our time, and flee if there's no out.*"

Florin gave a nod of agreement, but despite the assuredness in his voice, Aeric didn't move. He kept his hands to his sides, his face drawn as he steadied himself and stepped toward the glamour. Though the ripple of light was subtle—Marina knew Aeric wasn't brash enough to remove the shields themselves—the young man noticed immediately.

"*There we go,*" he breathed, his grin returning.

Ocot's jaw slackened. "*I told you there was a glamour. They were watching us...*"

The young man put up his hand, and Ocot clamped his lips shut.

"*Thank you for accepting our invitation.*" The young man approached, putting his hands out to feel for a shield and chuckling when he made contact with it. Though Marina was tempted to study his face, her gaze flitted to his scarred palms. He'd been burned, but not randomly. The symbols on his hands looked much like the ones that decorated the Delve during Double Moon, but the wave-like rays of the Omnia curled in rather than out.

A mockery—just like Pierce had said. If the emblem of Elsudra depicted magic flowing outward, this one did the opposite, as though its power were being hoarded.

"*Naive of me to think you'd face us without protection,*" the young man said. He cleared his throat. "*My name is Ryder. The lovely woman beside me is Safira, but I imagine you know each other. You were both Kieron's students, and you worked together during the war, correct?*"

Safira. Florin knew that name well. She'd been responsible for taking down cities in her hunt for the inclined and anyone who dared protect them—a loyal servant to Kieron in every sense of the word.

Florin's gaze shifted to the young man. *Ryder.* The name sounded familiar too. He had to have trained in Altus.

When Aeric didn't respond, Ryder said, "*You don't need me to introduce you to Ocot.*" His lazy smile turned wily. "*It's strange to see you after thinking you were dead for so long. When you served as Sorcerer of the Court, your prowess for magic was greatly admired. Kieron admires it too. This is why we've come to extend a deal.*"

Neither Aeric nor Florin said anything as Ryder straightened. Though Marina couldn't help but steal glances at the ruemin standing motionless yards away, she tore her attention from them long enough to observe Ryder's face. It was his eyes that made him different, she realized: one blue and one green.

"Out of happiness that his successor is alive, as well as gratitude for safekeeping the Omnia upon its return," Ryder said, *"Kieron has found it in his heart to give you two choices. In my opinion, the answer is simple, but perhaps you'll disagree."* He shrugged. *"We hear the Omnia returned with a young woman—one who didn't wish to come with it. You can rest assured Kieron means this girl no harm. Give us the Omnia, and we'll grant you all amnesty. Refuse, and we'll have no choice but to view it as treason. We'll return with the full force of our military, destroy the Delve and everyone in it, and find the girl anyway. If, for whatever reason, we're unable to surpass your shields"*—he glanced at Safira—*"then Kieron will come and dismantle them himself. I'm sure you don't need me to specify that fleeing counts as a refusal, in which case, we'll track you down and massacre anyone you've sought sanctuary with. I need not tell you the things we do to dissidents. Your own side engaged in torture plenty; Safira can attest to that."*

A mirthless smile tugged at the still-flesh side of Safira's mouth. Aeric, however, only shifted his gaze to Ocot. The smugness on Ocot's face vanished the moment Aeric's eyes met his, and some of Florin's fear—and Marina's—turned to pride as he cowered.

"We chose our sentries based on physical prowess and abilities in combat," Aeric said, his voice whetted to an edge. *"Clearly, we didn't choose them on the basis of intelligence. How very simple-minded you are, to not think that the moment you left, we moved the girl to another location—one far away from the Delve, which we knew you'd come prowling back to."*

Florin refused to avert eye contact with Ocot, who gawked at them both.

"You don't think our Keepers and military planned for the possibility that one hideout may be compromised?" Aeric said. He shook his head. *"Of course you didn't. You have always been a fool, Ocot. Our mistake was not killing you before you could become a traitor as well."*

Cold—his voice was so cold that Marina couldn't help but remember the morning after Double Moon. Florin grunted in agreement, keeping an iron grip on his emotions. The Keepers had barely had enough time to send people to the Delve; he often wondered if the average Elsudran realized how close they'd been to defeat.

"Why was the rest of the Delve not made aware of alternate hideouts?" Ocot demanded.

"Those considered worthy were made aware. As I said, Ocot, you are a fool, and we do not trust fools with pivotal information."

Ocot began to object, but Ryder raised his hand, once again silencing him. For a long, agonizing moment, all Marina could hear was the breeze that skirted through the trees.

"There are no other hideouts," Ryder said. He met Aeric's gaze with an icy look. *"The Omnia's host is here."* The feral smile had vanished from Ryder's face, but he clung to his lazy confidence. *"She is here,"* he repeated, *"and you are lying."*

Aeric remained silent as Ryder leaned toward the shield and said, *"You have an hour to give her to us. Fail, and we resort to bloodier means. Happy Aragonite Eve."*

When he turned, so did Safira, with Ocot following at their heels like a cowering pup.

Florin watched as they retreated into the trees with the ruemin. When the last of them disappeared, Aeric concealed the entrance and shut the iron door. For one moment, then another, the two stood motionless in the dark.

Finally, Aeric said, *"We leave as soon as possible, and we don't tell Marina the technicalities of this conversation. She's already made her reservations about escaping clear."*

Florin grimaced. He'd sent out good scouts weeks ago to track down Ocot—scouts he'd likely never see again. But he'd prepared for this; he'd known it was a possibility. *"I'll gather our weapons and a small group,"* he said.

"Take Pierce too," Aeric whispered. Florin had already planned to—Tover's memory would haunt him if he left Pierce behind. *"He's a fighter and will increase our odds of survival as we seek out the group near Candens Inlet. And perhaps he'll lessen her rage."*

But not Ismene. Not those who weren't useful up above.

Florin's brow creased. *"How do you plan to get her to come?"*

"We'll tell her as little as possible." Aeric paused, and when he spoke again, there was pain—so much pain in his voice. *"And if that doesn't work, then with force."*

Whether that angered or scared her, Marina didn't know. As haphazard as her emotions were, they filled every ounce of seawater. When her waves began to thrash and convulse, she pulled away, worried if she didn't, she'd destroy every memory in her presence. She didn't know if she had the power to do that—didn't *want* to know—but she couldn't risk hurting Florin, so she withdrew her waves and finally found her hand.

Gray eyes filled with shock met hers as she regained her vision. Time really *did* pass differently in psychometry. Pierce and Ismene hadn't moved an inch, and she knew she'd only been in Florin's head for a few seconds.

"I'm sorry," she said again.

She wasn't sure where she meant to go as she hurried away from the staircase and to the door of the manor, but she needed space, and she knew Florin would tell Aeric—rightfully so—who would find her...

"I'll talk to her." Pierce's voice bounced off the walls. "I'll bring her back."

Florin said something else, but Marina didn't listen. Still, she slowed so Pierce and Ismene could catch up to her.

When she felt their presence a few feet behind her, she hissed, "I need...I need a few minutes. Somewhere hidden. Please."

Pierce and Ismene stared at each other, and for a moment, Marina thought they'd refuse. But Pierce gestured for the two of them to follow as he headed farther north—up past the infirmary, down a flight of stairs, through a hallway, then another—not stopping until they reached an alleyway that funneled into the bedrock.

"Whatever you did," Pierce whispered, "Aeric will find out."

"I know." Marina put her hands to her face. "I saw Florin's memories. I broke through his mental shields and saw what happened. He and Aeric...they plan to flee the Delve with me and a few others, but the rest they'll leave behind. Including you, Ismene."

Ismene's eyes widened. Whatever she'd known about worst-case scenario plans, it was obvious she hadn't known that she'd be among those left to die. How could she have? Aeric never would have admitted that to her—not when she served him so loyally.

"Aeric didn't want to tell me the choices he was given because he knew I'd fight him," Marina continued, "but the people at the border—who *Ocot* led here—said that if the Omnia wasn't handed to them within the hour, they'd come back with Kieron, overpower Aeric's shields, and massacre the Delve...which means everyone here who didn't escape would die, and even if they *did* manage to escape on their own, there's nowhere for them to go...not if we desert them like this, and the ruemin—"

"Slow down," Pierce said, shooting a quick glance at Ismene, whose eyes had started to water. "Who did Ocot lead here? What did they say?"

"One was a woman with half a mechanical face...Safira. She's one of the sorcerers Kieron pardoned to do his bidding, but she couldn't dismantle Aeric's shields. The other one must've been Kieron's main messenger, but he just looked like a soldier—a guy named Ryder—and he—"

"What was his name?" Pierce's voice was small and far away.

Marina blinked through her nerves, opening and closing her mouth long before she spoke. "Ryder...he said it was Ryder."

Pierce gripped her by the shoulders. "His *eyes*. What color were his eyes?"

Marina let out a gasp, her mind spinning. "One was blue, and the other was—"

"Green." Pierce released her slowly, hands trembling by his sides. He took a step back, then another, an unreadable look on his face. "They were blue and green."

Even Marina's fear, which she'd thought wouldn't let up, shrank in the presence of her confusion. She exchanged a wild glance with Ismene as Pierce crouched in a corner and pressed his forehead to the ground.

"Pierce?" Ismene whispered.

His breathing had grown hitched. "His name," he managed. "That was his name."

"Whose name?" Marina asked, but she knew long before Pierce said it.

And yet, all she could bring herself to do was gawk at Pierce, whom she'd never seen look so close to breaking, as he whispered, "The soldier I loved."

CHAPTER 32
Not Goodbye

Quietness had never felt so empty. Even in that void nestled outside time, home to only waves and sand, the quiet had been simple. Here, it overflowed with the ache of betrayal, which, combined with the danger above, somehow made the emptiness worse.

Pierce remained on the ground, murmuring. Marina was able to make out only a few words. "I don't...don't understand..."

"Maybe it's not him," Ismene said. "It...it could be a coincidence."

Marina's heart sank. How characteristically Ismene. She'd just been told she was going to be left for dead, but she jumped to console Pierce anyway.

Pierce ran his hands through his hair. "It's him."

More of that terrible silence followed.

"I don't understand," Pierce said. "He's inclined, but not enough to be considered a sorcerer. Definitely not enough to be useful to Kieron." He looked up at Marina, his eyes fluttering. "He's not safe from persecution..."

"He didn't show any magic," Marina said, her own voice barely a whisper.

"He'd hide it to protect himself. He's doing this to survive...he has to be."

Marina couldn't help herself when she breathed, "He seemed loyal to Kieron."

"No," Pierce said. "No...he's not...he's not."

Marina wished, more than anything, that she could offer Pierce comfort—that she could sit with him until the pain went away, even if it meant staying here forever. But no number of wishes would save them. Time was running out; she needed to make a decision.

Kieron's promise of amnesty meant little to her. At some point, the Delve would fall. But if she turned herself in now—if she tried to convince Kieron that all she wanted to do was go home, and that she'd be *willing* to work with him if he spared the Delve—more people could escape before the inevitable came to fruition.

Eventually, he'd realize she was bluffing—that she had no intentions of learning Locus for his sake, and even if she did, she was nowhere near competent enough to perform it yet—but by then, she would've done what she'd intended. Aeric would have less reason to leave so quickly, allowing more time to prepare and take the others with him.

Was it a desperate plan? Maybe. But it was better than knowingly leaving Ismene and the rest to die. Marina wasn't sure there would ever be a day she was strong enough to take Kieron down. Would this happen to every sanctuary they fled to? Would the time come when there was nowhere left to run, only to find she still wasn't ready?

But she could be ready now—just not in the way Aeric and the Keepers had hoped.

"Kieron won't hurt me," she said. "Not yet, at least. There's only one way he can take the Omnia, and he needs me alive to do it. But I can't. I'm the barrier."

"You can't be serious," Ismene said.

"Haven't you been improving?" Pierce added, desperate.

"Not enough for Locus. That's what he planned to make the Keepers do. But I don't know the ritual, and even if I did, he's too cautious to throw me into it right away. Not with the Omnia at stake." She wasn't sure Pierce and Ismene understood, but she didn't waste time trying to explain the intricacies. Instead, she continued, "If I convince him I'm already willing—that I want to get rid of the Omnia, and I'd learn Locus for him if he leaves the Delve alone—then I can buy you time. Aeric won't leave as quickly, which means his shields will stay up longer, giving you more time to prepare and take more people."

She'd be useless if she fled. She'd rather be useless to Kieron than useless to the Delve.

"There's a group near Candens Inlet," she said, her heart beating in her ears. "That's where they're going. If what Aeric has heard is true, they've created a sanctuary for people with magical abilities. They could be allies."

Pierce opened his mouth to protest, but Marina cut him off. "Even if I only give you one extra day to get more people out, it's better than nothing. But I'll need your help."

Slowly, Pierce stood and nodded. "You have it."

"Shouldn't we discuss this with Aeric and Florin?" Ismene asked, her eyes darting between Marina and Pierce.

"They won't agree," Pierce said. "You know that. If what Marina says is true, Kieron will run into a barrier with her. We can use that to our advantage, Ismene—for *your* sake and the sake of so many others here."

Marina took Ismene's hand in her own. "Let me make this choice," she begged. "I may not be Elsudran, but I have something that belongs to Elsudra, and I should do what I can for your people."

Especially since what I did to Ocot led us into this mess.

Pain guttered in Ismene's eyes, but she whispered, "Okay."

Marina's sigh of relief sounded more like a cry. "I need to get to the northern border—and through it—without being detected. We don't have much time. I'm sure Florin has already told Aeric what I did."

One breath. Then another. If this was going to work, she'd need to run on autopilot. Paying mind to her fear would paralyze her, and she couldn't turn back. Not now.

At one point, it had been unthinkable to stay. Now, it was unthinkable to flee—to let people die for her weaknesses, of which there were many. Her fear had stifled her progress with magic as much as it had stifled her judgment, and even if she'd changed, she couldn't take back those early days in the Delve when she'd manipulated, lied, and pined only for her own survival. She wouldn't let her fear stifle her now.

"I can cover for you," Ismene said meekly. "But I think Aeric may very well kill me."

"Tell him I'll never forgive him if he does. I want to see you again. Both of you." She steadied her voice when she added, "This is not goodbye."

Ismene's face contorted. "Not goodbye," she repeated.

She reached out and hugged Marina, who let out a small sob. When Ismene pulled away, her face was red and stained with tears, but she lingered only a moment before turning and scurrying off. She looked back once before disappearing around a corner.

Facing Pierce only evoked more tears, but Marina didn't waste time. She steadied her voice, then said, "Can you get me to the northern border?"

"I can get you inside, but I can't guarantee you won't be seen."

"All I need you to do is unlock the doors so I can get to Aeric's shield. The scanners recognize sentry handprints, right?"

Pierce nodded.

"Then I'll need your voco." When he blinked at her, she said, "I don't know how to put shields or glamours back up yet. Your voco will let me bypass both without putting the Delve at risk. I'll leave it behind before I slip out so no one can use it to get back in."

Pierce wavered, but only for a second. He took Marina's voco for himself, then put his onto her wrist. "Don't sell yourself short," he said as he fastened it. "You're more powerful than you think." He pulled her closer to him, then bent down so his face was directly in front of hers. "Remember that. And remember what I said about Ryder." He winced at the name. "This is an act. Use him, *please*. He can help you."

"Pierce..."

"I've never been surer about anything. Please, remember it...no matter what happens."

Marina nodded again, only because she couldn't get herself to speak.

"You'll be okay," he said. He was still muttering it as they made their way to the northern border staircase, taking the darkest and emptiest halls they could find. When they got as close as they could without standing fully in the open, Pierce surveyed their surroundings and said, "It's not going to be empty up there."

"I know. I can convey."

Pierce didn't press her further. "When the doors are unlocked, I'll ring you. The sentries and technicians up there will question me, if not alert Florin outright. I'll bullshit as best I can, but I can't stall forever, so be quick."

She half expected him to give her more warnings, but instead, he embraced her, so tightly his heart beat against her ear.

When he pulled back, tears ran down his face. "We'll go to Candens Inlet. We'll get more people, and we'll come for you. I promise. And you...please don't forget about Ryder. He can help you. And...and maybe you can help him."

His voice was fractured, deeply and severely. Could something that broken ever be repaired? Marina almost forgot her fear when her eyes met his, and she found herself fighting against the urge to tell Pierce not to leave. It took strength to stifle her sobs as Pierce pressed his forehead to her scalp and echoed, "This is not goodbye."

And with that, he left, disappearing up the mouth of the stairwell.

One day, one step, one breath at a time.

That was it. That was all she needed to do.

One breath. Another.

It was all she focused on, even as the minutes dragged. When Pierce's voco chimed with a message from "Marina"—"Go" was all he said—she stilled her mind and called upon her waves. The world blurred.

Breathe.

She flowed through pockets of space, vaguely aware of the Delve, then the stairwell and the northern border itself.

There were people there—people, muffled voices, and an open exit door.

Someone was arguing with the other sentries.

"...Florin's orders to open them. Ask him if you need to."

She almost stopped at Pierce's voice but turned back to her breaths and let his promise lull her into calm.

This is not goodbye.

If she fled, the goodbyes would be much more permanent. But here and now, she'd chosen her path, and she wasn't turning back.

Like a stream of water, she passed smoothly down the staircase and to the steel doors, cracked open just enough for her to get through.

When she reached the last one, she let her waves fizzle out as her surroundings materialized. She gave herself a second, if that, to regain the energy she'd lost and ground herself. Her relief at having successfully managed conveyance gave her the confidence she needed to pull the door open and fully face Aeric's shield—and the world beyond.

The sun was setting beneath the trees, and the kiss of cold air made her cheeks go numb. Just like at the southern border, the shield was no more than a wall of air, yet somehow strong enough to keep people out. For now, at least. The glamour rippled subtly in the evening light, but its presence didn't matter either way. They'd already been found.

One day, one step, one breath at a time. Marina placed Pierce's voco against the shield. It was intuitive—like running a barcode through a scanner—and far less taxing than using magic. When the voco vibrated, the shield parted just enough for her to slip through.

Raisel, Thora, Astra.

They deserved a better world—one they'd never get to see. And so, for all the people still around to see it, Marina slipped off Pierce's voco, put it on the ground, and stepped past the threshold.

Once outside, she instinctively turned back toward the Delve. All she could see were rocks and snow. She didn't search for any glints of light; instead, she turned and began walking the only way she could go: forward.

She sheathed her hands in her sweater, quickening her footsteps and blinking as her breath materialized before her. Did Aeric know what she'd done yet? The command center must've registered the breach of the northern shield.

She couldn't bear to think of it, and since she wanted to stay as invisible as possible, she conveyed to the mouth of the forest. She landed shakily beneath a tree, but kept on, repeating the names at every step.

Raisel, Thora, Astra, Evren.

Like the rest, Aeric's mother deserved a better future than she'd gotten. The same was true of Pierce's father, General Tover, who'd died fighting for a world he'd never see.

The forest grew colder as she walked, and when the sun's rays no longer peeked through the trees, she stopped.

Raisel, Thora, Astra, Evren, Tover.

"I'm here," she said, her voice so hoarse it hardly sounded like her. "If he wants the Omnia, you'd better come now because—"

Rustling in the trees cut her off. Marina grew still, breath in her throat and heart in her ears. Eventually, the sounds grew clearer, and Marina could make out what they were.

Click. Click. Click.

"Little girl." *Click, click.*

Little thief.

Marina whirled to the side, swallowing her shriek when a face eddied with black and red scales met her straight on. More ruemin came into view, their silver eyes glistening.

"Alone." *Click.*

"Yes, I'm alone." She could hardly hear herself through the ringing in her ears.

Take me to them and be done with it...

One of them pulled its mouth into a large, silver smile. "No trick." *Click, click.*

"No. Not a trick," Marina croaked.

Silence followed, interrupted every few seconds by the *click, click, click* of the ruemins' nails and throats. Finally, one reached out and wrapped its long fingers around her arm.

She wanted to pull away, but she couldn't move, so she let them lead her deeper into the forest, her limbs stiff and cold.

The names no longer came to her. Even as the trees faded into a clearing where a small fire burned on and a small group of people sat, Marina let her mind flit far away, finding comfort in detachment.

Ocot all but jumped from his seat, pointing at Marina as his mouth opened and closed like a fish gasping for air.

"Here...that's...she's here," he finally managed, and only then did Safira come into view behind him.

The soldiers close to Ocot quailed as Safira passed them, though it seemed Ocot was either too daft or shocked to do so himself. Safira didn't acknowledge them as she approached Marina and the ruemin, and with a swift flick of her hand, the grip on Marina's arm loosened.

"I didn't...didn't lie," Ocot sputtered as he rushed beside Safira. "They didn't move her. She was always—"

"Thank you, Ocot," someone else said. Marina turned to Ryder, who'd come up beside her as quietly as the ruemin had.

Ryder. Pierce was so sure about him. She wasn't, but for the sake of her friend, who'd lied and stalled and broken rules for her, she promised not to decry him just yet. After all, if it was true he was hiding magical abilities...

"So this is the girl Ocot told us about," Ryder said, his eyes taking her in intently, as though even he couldn't fathom how close he was to the Omnia.

"You came alone?" Safira asked.

Marina dared to look her in her remaining eye. It was the color of sea glass, shining in the fire's light as vibrantly as the golden half of her face.

"Yes. I came alone," Marina said slowly.

Ocot made a sound that resembled a laugh. "Why?"

"Because I'm willing to work with Kieron," she lied, making sure Ryder and Safira heard—making sure everyone did. "If he leaves the Delve alone, I'm more than willing to help him take the Omnia. All I want to do is get rid of it and go home."

Ocot's eyes fluttered as though he wasn't sure what he was seeing and hearing was real. Safira, on the other hand, showed even less emotion than Aeric. And Ryder...Marina couldn't tell if he was suspicious or amused.

"I don't reckon Aeric will be happy with that," Ryder said, eyebrows raised.

"Probably not. That's why I'd suggest we move things along."

Ryder let out a surprised exhale, as though he hadn't expected her gall. In truth, it hadn't been intentional, but at that moment, she was more than thankful for the edge fear gave to her voice.

"True." Ryder cocked his head toward Safira and gave her a coy smile.

The urge to cower was overwhelming, especially as Safira reached out to touch the side of Marina's head. Her hands weren't mechanical. In fact, minus the burns on both palms that mirrored Ryder's, her skin was soft.

Of all the things she could've done, Marina glanced to Ocot's hip, where Cal's cutlass glinted in the fire's light. Perhaps the adrenaline rushing through her dulled her good sense, for it was more a knee-jerk reaction than anything when she said, "That's not yours."

Before Ocot could respond, Ryder looked to Safira and cleared his throat.

Safira barely glanced at him. "She's telling the truth. She came alone."

Marina turned her attention back to Safira, and only then did she sense the presence of something foreign in her subconscious. It was light and airy, like Aeric's fog, but when she focused harder on it, the chalky burn of smoke made her recoil.

As jarring as it was, it came second to far more harrowing realizations: Safira hadn't needed to use a full gust of smoke—a mere feather had done her bidding, and her presence in Marina's mind had at first gone unannounced. And because of Marina's fear...

"Your shields aren't up," Safira said, her voice as dizzying as the fumes that coiled in Marina's essence.

It was a last-ditch effort to raise her shields, but it wouldn't have made much of a difference. By the time Marina had called the waves within her to action, smoke-induced sleep had already taken hold.

CHAPTER 33
Mask

Where the waves kissed the sand, a young girl—no older than seven, though her youth didn't extend to her eyes—stood silently. She twisted a strand of auburn hair around her fingers, counting the waves as they crashed to the shore.

One, two, three, four...

Sometimes, she'd imagine jumping into the ocean, then swimming as long and as far as she could. It was quiet underwater, and there, her mind could rest. The other children seemed to thrive on the sand—in the chatter and laughter of midday, building their castles and chasing seagulls. On occasion, she'd watch them too, but she'd always turn back to the waves. At night, they'd come again, whispering lullabies of their own: *Marina, Marina, Marina.* And she would do what she always did. She would watch.

Somewhere in the waters of Marina's subconscious, a force too large to contain lingered. When the rising sun's rays brushed atop the sea, it awakened—a doorway that led nowhere and everywhere all at once.

We named you well. Her mom's voice. *I think you come from the sea.* She'd always say that when Marina spent hours at the beach, standing on the edge of water and land.

With her voice, love came emanating from the darkness. It smelled like strawberry-cinnamon cake and sounded like freshly tuned guitar strings. But there was a different love too—a newer kind, filled with laughter and lights and small joys. She wasn't sure she could choose between the two, so she simply watched.

Maybe this was where she'd stay. It was as quiet here as it was underwater, and she wouldn't mind watching forever. Here, she could be as powerful and silent as a god—seeing everything but never engaging, never making choices. But reality was not so sweet. With the force of a tsunami, the darkness receded, pulling her into the light.

No, no...let me stay here, where it's safe.

Her pleas were useless. As blurry surroundings materialized before her, Marina braced herself for the worst. Only...the worst wasn't there.

Soft light flitted in through a bay window at the far side of the room, bordered by gossamer curtains that were lined with beads. From where she lay, she could see glimpses of the ocean outside. She propped herself up on her elbows to scan the rest of the room. Walls of gold and seafoam met ivory floors, and silver fragments on the ceiling glinted in the light. It took her a few seconds to realize they were pieces of mirror, made to look like a watery mosaic above her. She almost let herself get lost in their depths, but the world beyond the window called to her, and she yielded. Inelegantly, she pulled herself from the bed, pins and needles running up her legs.

The bench beneath the window welcomed her, and she all but collapsed onto it as she gripped the windowsill and pulled herself up just enough to see outside.

The ocean was everywhere. Her room must've been built into the side of a cliff because the windows dropped straight off into a mouth of jagged rocks hundreds of feet below. She could barely make out the waves that slammed against the cliff's face, but if she listened hard enough, she could hear them crash.

For a few moments, she leaned against the sill, soaking in what little she could of the world, then raised her hand to the glass. She could break it if she wanted to—break it and jump. What would Kieron do then?

She kept her hand on the glass, her skin prickling at the sun's warmth. A ripple in the air caught her eye, but before she could study it, dizziness rushed in.

Marina recoiled and stumbled off the bench, ears ringing. Tremors shot up and down her limbs so severely that her knees buckled, and she sank to the ground. The floor was cold, which was a godsend because she was terribly nauseous. Since she couldn't gather enough energy to make it back to the bed, she stayed where she was, head in her hands.

Aeric had told her about these kinds of shields—the kinds used in prisons—but she hadn't expected them to feel like *this.*

"I was going to warn you not to touch the windows, but you beat me to it."

Panic sent a shockwave down her spine, and Marina twisted to face the corner of her room, where a guard in a golden armored suit leaned against a clamshell dresser.

"The whole room is shielded," Ryder said. "Touch the windows or door, and *that* happens. They send your nervous system into a frenzy."

He can help you, Pierce had said.

She knew Pierce wasn't a liar, but that didn't mean Ryder was trustworthy. People could change, after all, and Ryder's lupine smile did him no favors.

"Safira must've done quite the number on you. We got here yesterday, and you *still* didn't wake up. He's starting to get impatient."

Marina's dizziness, which had just started to subside, returned with vigor. Safira had gotten in her head so effortlessly that she could've taken whatever she wanted. Thankfully, all she'd done was confirm Marina was alone. Perhaps she'd wanted to get going as soon as possible—whatever the reason, Marina was glad Safira had rendered her unconscious. At least her memories had been safe.

But now she was awake, which meant psychometry was possible—and Kieron, no doubt, would try it on her. She couldn't make that mistake again. Though her shields were shaky, she raised them as Ryder approached her like a fox stalking its prey. When he reached her, he pulled off one of his gloves and extended a branded palm. Marina knew it was purposeful—a power play of some sort—but that didn't stop her from drawing back.

"Up and at 'em," Ryder said. "He's eager to meet you."

Raisel, Thora, Astra, Evren, Tover. She had to be brave—for them and the others.

"You're supposed to escort me?" She stood on her own, slowly and shakily.

"Someone is."

Breathe. One breath, then another...

The smile remained on Ryder's face as he crossed the room, opened the door, put his voco to the air, and bypassed the shield.

Marina curled her hands into fists as she crossed the threshold, but she forced herself not to react when Ryder cocked his head at her to follow.

Just like the bedroom she'd woken up in, the rest of the palace was heavenly. Marble covered the floors and walls, as expansive as it was clean. Every corridor was open to the elements, and a salty breeze laced with the caws of sea birds danced across her skin. It carried memories of Georgia—so poignant Marina stopped walking.

"Better than a hole underground," Ryder drawled from behind her. Either he was masterful at sneaking around, or she was too disoriented to be aware of her surroundings. She jerked away before he could touch her.

"You're skittish, aren't you?" he said, amused. "That's not a trait I would've expected the Omnia's new host to have."

Unpleasant surprise. Useless. In this case, Marina hoped she would be. When Ryder chuckled, she bit her tongue, fighting hard to keep her eyes on the floor. If she met his gaze, would she give something away? There was no such thing as being too careful here, even if Pierce trusted Ryder.

Pierce...did Ryder even know he was alive? And if he did, would he care?

Marina forced herself to move. It wasn't until they'd taken the fourth or fifth flight of stairs that she realized her shields had fallen.

Shit. Come on, Marina. Shields up.

Ryder was silent as they continued through hallways and past mezzanine balconies that looked down even more marble stairs. Wherever they went, there was light, as though the palace was made to feel like part of the hill it sat on. But beyond the grandeur, what Marina noticed most of all was the emptiness. It hung in the air and crept up the walls, nestling deep into the foundation of the palace. At one point, perhaps, these halls had been filled with people, but now, they were as deadened as the ones back in Georgia.

The hallways opened into a courtyard made of marble so blue it looked like they were walking on water. Pillars resembled waterspouts, and archways imitated waves, all laced with golden veins that danced in the sun. A fine place to hang bodies, Kieron must've thought, because dangling from every archway's crown was a corpse so severely decayed Marina couldn't make out their features.

Feigning aloofness was impossible now. She stopped in her tracks, cringing away from Ryder when he gestured for her to keep up.

"These young soldiers were responsible for an assassination attempt at the beginning of the dead years," he said, no longer smiling. "Kieron had them flayed and hung up here. Guess they were like trophies to him—never decomposing, never wasting away. Not until the Omnia came back, of course. A season or two ago, the smell was so bad you couldn't pass this place without gagging."

Marina's head began to spin, and she clasped her hand over her mouth.

"You can't see their sigils anymore," Ryder said, shrugging. He put his hand to his forehead and flashed his palm at her. "Shame."

Marina's chest began to tingle, followed by her head, and though she didn't remember falling, she hit the floor so promptly even Ryder looked shocked.

The impact jolted her back to consciousness, and she had enough energy to shrug him off when he pulled her up.

"C'mon. Stand tall. First impressions matter."

How quickly would his smug demeanor change if she said Pierce's name? She'd like to see that—to be the reason his mask crumbled, if it was a mask at all. But she'd run her mouth before and reaped the consequences, so Marina straightened, put on a mask of her own, and resumed walking. Every step felt like she was wading through ankle-deep mud, but she pushed on until they reached a stained-glass door grander than any other in the palace. The colors were so vibrant that the door could hardly contain it, and the marble tile sang with motley bits of light.

She knew the door led to the throne room before Ryder pushed it open, but in that moment, she no longer felt fear. Maybe it had been knocked out of her. Whatever the reason, she was glad to be disconnected from her body as Ryder took her by the elbow and led her inside.

The throne room looked the same as it had in Aeric's memories. Windows surrounded the room, panes shining with every glint of sunlight. And yet, as grandiose as everything was, the world beyond was even more so. No longer was the view solely of the ocean; next to it, multicolored rooftops formed a city. The closest were mansard roofs made of marble and slate, but if she looked hard enough, she could see clusters of shanties in the distance. Was the apartment Aeric had grown up in among them?

She wished she could look upon Altus forever. She'd count every ivory veranda if it meant distracting herself from the horrors in front of her. But as Ryder tugged her sleeve, she took a breath, repeated the names to herself, and braved the nightmare she'd once hoped she'd never have to face.

Perhaps the throne room *wasn't* the same as it was in Aeric's memories. There were no longer four equally spaced thrones at the center, but instead a single dais. Safira stood to its left, the golden half of her face glowing like the panes in the room. The Elsudran cloak she wore came up to her chin, concealing both halves of her neck, but her face was fully in the light, which made the subtle upward curve of her lips impossible to miss.

Beside Safira was a smaller man who Marina couldn't pinpoint. She supposed he was another sorcerer Kieron had pardoned. Whatever his role was, he certainly wasn't a soldier; he had a feeble build and was a good two decades older than Florin. He was relatively harmless-looking—tawny-brown skin, gray hair, and a thin face—but his eyes were different. They swarmed with a curiosity that made Marina's skin prickle.

She may have observed the man longer had she not caught sight of Ocot standing on the opposite side of the dais, fiddling with the carbon hilt of Cal's cutlass and looking insufferably pleased with himself. There were a few other guards, but Marina didn't pay attention to them. Instead, she glanced at Ocot's freshly branded palms.

He must have noticed where she was looking, because his free hand flew behind his back, and the one on Cal's sword tightened.

I hope it hurt like hell. What little gall she had snuffed out, however, when she looked to the throne atop the dais and saw *him* sitting there, smiling at her as though she were an old friend.

She knew that smile; she'd seen it in Aeric's memories. Kieron possessed the same slippery charm she'd witnessed before, but despite his well-groomed if not rather plain appearance, he didn't look the way she remembered. Upon closer observation, Marina could make out the waxy hue his skin carried—the tired look in his sunken eyes—and she knew immediately that these changes hadn't occurred in Elsudra.

"Welcome," he said warmly. "My dear, it is an honor to be able to meet you in person."

Shields up. Keep your shields up.

She kept her hold on them, even as Kieron stood and descended the dais. Everything from his smile to his clothes, which were as well-tailored as Aeric's but less stiff, suited the debonair part he played so effortlessly.

"I wish we'd met sooner, for both our sakes," he said. "It's despicable to know you've been suffering underground all these seasons when you didn't consent to come to our realm." He paused, the gleam in his eyes growing, and he took her hands, running his unbranded palms over her fingers. He smiled at Ryder. "Thank you for escorting her."

Ryder responded with a nod before joining Ocot next to the throne. Though Ocot shot him a glance, Ryder ignored him.

Marina braced herself, praying her waves withstood whatever came at her, only for... nothing. Kieron removed his hands, then gestured to those in the room.

"You know Safira and Ryder, of course," he said. "This is Vaughn. He's one of the most esteemed healers in Altus, if not all Elsudra. A real pioneer in his field."

The small man didn't so much as smile in response, but his eyes shined. Aeric had mentioned a healer loyal to Kieron...was this him? She didn't have much time to think on it; Kieron put his hands on her shoulders, the sides of his lips raising when she flinched.

"I haven't been this close to the Omnia in far too long," Kieron said. "It's more invigorating than I remember." He sighed contentedly. "I'll say it again. Welcome to Altus —to Elsudra—even though the choice to be here wasn't your own. I have so many things I wish to ask you, Marina. Is that your full name?"

"Marina Oliver," she said, or tried to say, but her mouth had gone dry. She wasn't sure why she'd told him her last name. She knew it didn't matter, but for some reason, his gaze had wrenched it out of her.

"Exquisite thing, to live in a realm with such a variety of names. I once read that the Sundrans had *six* each." Kieron's smile turned into a beam. His teeth weren't white like they were in Aeric's memories; they'd turned a grayish purple, as though they'd been stained by wine. "Well, Marina Oliver, it's a pleasure to meet you. I'm sure you're still disoriented from the trip here, so I'll let you rest, but please, join me for dinner tonight. I meant what I said; I have *so much* I wish to ask you."

Pleasant as his tone was, she knew the invitation wasn't a request. Kieron nodded— not to Ryder, but to Ocot—and said, "Please escort our guest back to her room."

Ocot jumped at the recognition. As he approached her, Marina turned to Kieron and blurted, "I wanted to talk to you about the Omnia." *Act calm—like you want to be here.* "I'm willing to—"

Kieron smiled and put his hand up. She knew that gesture; he'd done the same to Evren when Aeric was a child. He'd done it to Aeric too, more times than she could count. Calm, dismissive—as though he knew he was in control. Though Marina tried to hide it, her face heated.

"You just arrived," he said. "Please, rest. We'll have all the time in the world."

What happened to the impatient man Ryder mentioned? This was probably one of his mind games. Whatever it was, Marina yielded to it. Coming across as docile was safest.

Ocot lingered at her side, obviously unsure whether he should touch her. Marina saved him the misery of making a choice—saved them both the misery of it—and headed toward the door on her own.

Shields up, shields up, shields up. And yet, no attack came.

She kept her eyes down at first, but the farther they walked, the worse the silence became. When the memory of those ashy, purple teeth flashed at the back of her head, her composure nearly broke.

"Why, Ocot?" She couldn't hold the question in. Still, she said it calmly—curiously, even though she knew the answer—determined to keep her mask up.

Ocot's jaw feathered. "My time in the Delve was at its end, thanks to you."

"I saved your life the morning after Double Moon." She came to a halt, daring him to look her in the eyes.

"You were the one who put my life—my station and status—in danger. Then you went and bargained for Boris's reprieve and left me out to dry." His nostrils flared. "You backed me into a corner, and you screwed yourself while you did it. Now *move forward.*"

Marina's nails bit at her palms, but she forced herself to smile. "Screwed myself? This could be my chance to get rid of the Omnia. Maybe I should say thank you."

She didn't wait for a response. She continued walking, silent until they reached her room, and when he opened the door, she passed the threshold without a fuss.

When he shut it, Marina counted the seconds, waiting until she knew he was long gone. Only then did she let out a tearless sob. She'd be damned if Ocot, of all people, was the reason her mask fell.

CHAPTER 34
Embers and Water

In the Delve, it had been easy to give herself to darkness. Here, the light fueled her. She familiarized herself with the bedroom, and when she finally worked up the courage, she opened the door. She anticipated the shield before she touched it, but since she couldn't turn away without trying, she put her palms to the wall of air, took a breath...and nearly buckled when her limbs began to shake.

Marina recoiled, fighting against the dizziness. When it faded, determination coursed through her once more, and she put her hands back on the shield.

Come on. If the Omnia could give her a boost with Aeric's shields, couldn't it help here? Maybe not. These were more sinister kinds of shields: unidirectional, sickeningly painful, and meant entirely to keep her in.

Though Marina tried one more time for good measure, she was so lightheaded she couldn't see clearly. She shut the door, but rather than hide away under her covers, she retreated to the bay window and collected herself.

Come dinner, she'd stick to her plan, milking her lies until she could no more. All she had to do was play the part of the girl who'd come to Elsudra. She may not be that girl anymore, but bits and pieces of her remained, and they'd be easy to pull on.

Unsurprisingly, it was Ocot who came to fetch her that evening. Since she'd expected it, she wasn't caught off guard when he flung the door open. He was really savoring this. He watched her raptly as he bypassed the shield, but Marina simply strode past him and said, "Next time, you knock. Understand?"

He only snorted in response.

As they walked, Ocot made it a point to fiddle with his new voco. He twisted the dial between his thumb and forefinger, then held it up so the screen caught the light.

"These are like the ones at the Delve," he said. "They removed the bells and whistles on my old one after you got me demoted, but here, I can bypass any shield I want."

"You mean whenever you're given an order to do so."

Ocot shot her a hateful look, but she ignored it. Instead, she watched the sea beyond the terraces, now tinted pink by the setting sun. The shadows in the Delve may have been safer, but nothing could match the lure of sunlight. Its touch soothed her, and for a moment, Marina wondered how Ocot would react if she apologized—*really* apologized. Would he have apologies of his own, or was he beyond regret?

Of course, she wanted to apologize just as much as she wanted to kill him for putting the Delve in danger. The conflict came to a boil inside her, fizzling out when they arrived at the doors to what she suspected was the dining room. Marina's composure slipped as they approached.

Suddenly, Ocot wasn't so quiet. "Aren't you going to thank me for escorting you?"

Apologizing no longer seemed as attractive an option. Marina's fingertips heated, then began to buzz with white light. When Ocot paled, she pretended it didn't surprise her how quickly she'd summoned the energy.

Her heart beat in her ears as she turned on her heel and entered the dining room herself. As much as she wanted to threaten Ocot, a quieter show of power seemed smarter.

She refused to look back as she approached the grand table at the center of the room. *Keep walking. Don't stop. Breathe.*

Unlike Aeric, who'd wanted their first few meetings to be brief, Kieron was obviously intent on drawing the ordeal out as long as he could. An alabaster table laden with food and drinks beckoned her, and it was only then Marina realized how long it had been since she'd eaten.

Kieron grinned at her and stood, then pulled out her chair and gestured for her to sit. Yet another way he and Aeric differed—when they'd first met in the Delve's dining room, it had seemed like Aeric couldn't get far enough away from her. As much as she'd hated his callousness, she'd take that over...whatever this was.

Kieron looked to Ocot, who'd followed her into the room. "Stay a moment. I'm sure Marina would feel more at ease having a friend here."

Marina lowered herself to the chair, her eyes on Kieron as he glanced from her to Ocot, then back to her. Amusement flashed across his features as he sat, and Marina turned her gaze to the beveled glass ceiling, silently praying this would be painless.

"If it's of any solace," Kieron said, "I also understand what it's like to be betrayed."

Ocot hovered by the door, his face red. Though Kieron pretended not to notice, the corners of his lips tugged upward.

"Eat and drink," he said to Marina. "It takes even the strongest minds time to recover from induced unconsciousness, and I'm sure Safira's magic takes a heftier toll." He pointed to the glass of water before her. "I'd be a fool to poison you."

She knew that, but she couldn't help her hesitance. It took an extra bout of courage—and logic—for her to drink. If not for her overwhelming thirst, she may have resisted.

"I chose to come here," she said when she set the glass down, "because I think you can help me."

Kieron leaned back, his eyebrows raised gibingly.

She pushed on, though she found it hard to steady her voice. "I know you've been told I don't possess the Omnia by choice. That's true. This has all been a mistake. Aeric didn't want to believe that, so he made me learn magic anyway. He told me if I learned enough and still wanted to get rid of the Omnia, he'd help. But he refused to teach me Locus." She monitored Kieron's face, but his smile only widened.

She tried to ignore it. Almost any lie was believable if the liar was confident enough. "I don't know if I can trust Aeric," she said, "because his goal is at odds with mine. He wants me to be a weapon. I want to get rid of the Omnia and go home."

"And how do you think I can help you, Marina?" Kieron said, still smiling at her like she was an idiot.

"You want the Omnia. I don't. I have no loyalties here. I'd be more than willing to learn Locus and move the Omnia to you if you agree to spare the Delve and those in it."

Kieron's teeth—more silver than gray in the evening light—shined like the ruemins'. Marina strained to look calm.

"No loyalties?" he mused. "Why would a girl with no loyalties barter for the Delve?"

"I may not be loyal to Elsudra or Aeric," she said, "but there are people in the Delve I care about. If they're safe, I don't care who holds the Omnia."

Kieron went silent for a while, but Marina kept his gaze, even though it pained her. Energy flashed in his eyes, strangely youthful despite his otherwise sickly appearance and the fact that he seemed to be well into his sixties. When he spoke, he sounded like he was fighting a laugh. "Please, eat."

Since he probably wouldn't take kindly to refusal, Marina gave in to her hunger. She took a plate filled with vegetables, and though all she wanted to do was scarf it down, she forced herself to eat slowly.

Kieron took a sip of his drink. "I've heard a fair amount about you," he said, "but it's all rather wanting. Our mutual friend was generous with the Delve's information, but he's also exceedingly self-obsessed, and everything he said revolved around how you and the Delve wronged him. I don't care about that. I want to know about *you*—about what you think brought you here, even if it was a mistake."

He didn't glance at Ocot, but Marina did. Though Ocot remained quiet, she could see his grip on Cal's cutlass tighten.

"Ocot's right," she said. "I did wrong him...out of desperation to learn Locus and find a way home."

"And you think *I* will help you get home?"

Silence. Marina lifted her chin, then said, "I don't even know if going home is possible anymore." Despite her best efforts, she couldn't keep her voice from breaking. That bit was true, after all. "But," she continued, "even if I can't, giving up the Omnia would still be a victory for me. I don't know why I'm here or what went wrong, but it doesn't matter. As long as my friends are safe, I'm more than willing to help you."

"You said that." He didn't say it accusingly; in fact, his voice was gentle. He peered into his drink for a moment. "It was a disgraceful thing our Keepers did. They should've kept the fight in Elsudra. Instead, they gambled with a power that never should've been gambled with. And who suffers, if not the innocent?" He exhaled through his nose and shook his head. "I do believe you're right about one thing: Aeric wouldn't have helped you learn Locus. For all his talent, he's a troubled man who cares more about fulfilling the Keepers' wishes than ensuring the wellbeing of the soul implicated in a conflict she has no ties to." He observed her for a moment. Then, as good-humored as ever, he said, "You don't know how happy I am you're willing to collaborate. I feared the day our Omnia would return—who it would bring with it—but what a pleasant surprise you are."

The food in Marina's mouth began to taste like lead.

"As I'm sure you understand, though, trust is required in collaboration," Kieron continued. "I'll gladly honor your wishes if I can be sure you'll honor mine."

He reached out—he was going to touch her hand—and Marina recoiled.

She'd known this would happen. Aeric had threatened her with it. Even if Kieron didn't intend to harm her, the things he'd see would damn her all the same, unless she could shield successfully. She'd done it with Aeric; she could do it here. Couldn't she?

Kieron chuckled. "Just psychometry. Nothing painful."

"I know," Marina breathed, "but I could just tell you what you want to know."

"Better for me to see myself. Memories have two parts: objective reality and subjective interpretation. Psychometry allows us to see the former as an unbiased third party, which means it's more effective than relying on word alone. That's the beauty of it—that, and it's incredibly quick." He smiled at her. "If you're being honest with me, which I'm sure you are, this will confirm it. In fact, it may give me even *more* information about your role in this mess, which could help us both."

She couldn't do this.

You can. She just had to put what she knew to use. With enough control, perhaps she could even guide Kieron to see the memories she wanted him to see—shielding some while showing others, as Aeric had done. Only that required far more practice than she'd had time for. She could shield, perhaps, but she hadn't yet mastered the nuances.

"You agree, don't you?" Kieron asked, his tone as condescending as ever. How had Aeric withstood it for so long?

Her voice was small. "About what?"

"About trusting each other." He folded his hands. "I do this with everyone who works closely with me. It helps ensure that those I surround myself with truly value Elsudra. You can appreciate why that's important, I'm sure."

Marina blinked at him. If that was the case, he would've used psychometry on Ryder —would've seen his essence and had him killed. But Ryder was very much alive. That didn't make sense. Regardless, she didn't have much time to consider. Kieron reached out his hand again, and Marina recoiled once more.

"It's just...psychometry is an invasive way to get information," she said. Was her mask crumbling, or could she hold out a little longer? Perhaps he'd never believed her at all, and this was all for naught.

How many days had it been since she'd left the Delve? Had Pierce and Ismene been successful in bargaining for more lives to be saved? Hastily, she added, "You didn't answer about the Delve. Trust goes both ways."

Kieron's eyes glinted. "I promised them amnesty if I was given the Omnia. I haven't been given it yet."

Of course he'd chosen to word it that way. She wrapped her fingers tightly around the edge of her chair. "I've agreed to give it to you."

"Then you have nothing to worry about."

She scanned his face, but she knew she'd never be able to tell if he was lying. He seemed to pick up on her skepticism, though, because he reached into his pocket and pulled out a circular device with a blue light at the center. He placed it in front of her.

She'd seen that device before; Pierce had shown it to her at the southern border.

"Safira synced this with the Delve's northern shield so we'd be alerted when it faded," Kieron said. "Honestly, we were waiting for Aeric to flee with the Omnia so we'd know to send our troops into the Delve." He tapped his nails on the device, and though the sounds weren't similar, Marina couldn't help but think of the ruemin again. "But the Omnia's host is generous," Kieron continued, "and the Delve is still standing."

Marina stared at the blue light. She wanted to believe him. Besides, why else would he have that device so close?

Kieron put it back into his pocket. "That's the most I can do for you, I'm afraid, but I hope it brings you peace." His grin tightened. "Now it's your turn."

Her stomach soured, and though she wasn't sure why—perhaps because he was the only other person in the room, or perhaps because, in some twisted way, he reminded her of the Delve—Marina glanced at Ocot.

Kieron turned to look as she did, then let out another exaggerated chuckle.

"Is this what unsettles you?" He turned back to face her. "I guess it makes sense part of you feels betrayed, especially if you worry about the safety of your loved ones." He cocked his head toward Ocot but didn't look at him directly when he said, "Come here."

Ocot hesitated, but eventually approached the table, his eyes wide and uncertain.

"I appreciate your service to Elsudra," Kieron said, "but I believe you owe Marina an apology. She has earnestly admitted her wrongdoings. You haven't."

Ocot stared at his feet. "I'm sorry, Marina," he rasped.

Kieron raised his eyebrows at her. "Do you forgive him?"

Marina's throat had gone so dry that she couldn't manage a response.

Kieron clicked his tongue. "Treason is a wound that cuts deep." He turned to Ocot. "I'm glad you're comfortable here, and that you trust me enough not to wear your helmet."

Ocot blinked at Kieron, who leaned back in his chair and made a motion with his finger—so imperceptible that Marina hardly noticed it. For a second, the room was silent.

And then the blood began to run.

It spilled onto Ocot's armor, staining gold with red, and for a moment, he simply watched it fall, as though he didn't think it was his own. When the realization dawned on him, he clawed at his neck—at the soft tissue just below his chin where his armor stopped, which had been gouged open so deeply that the blood ran more purple than red. He stumbled back, fingers dancing over the gash as he gasped and wheezed.

A strangled cry escaped Marina's mouth as Ocot collapsed to the floor, the bottom half of his armored suit dripping with urine. There he lay, writhing in a pile of blood and piss, until his body twitched for the last time.

Kieron took another drink from his goblet, long and slow. When he set his cup down, he made a gesture to her with his hand. "Your turn," he said.

She couldn't look away. The panic in Ocot's eyes was long gone, replaced by vacancy.

He's dead. He's dead. He's...

"Marina," Kieron said. "Any day now."

Numbly, she extended her hand, as though she could no longer control her limbs.

He's dead. Ocot's dead.

Unlike Aeric, Kieron's grip was warm. It made sense, though; his essence wasn't fog that could freeze oceans over. It was *fire*.

Her shields—she needed her shields; needed to still her mind, or else they wouldn't rise. When had they fallen?

She couldn't still her mind. Not after what Kieron had done to Ocot. Not after what Ocot had done to the Delve. And what about what *she'd* done?

Breathe. One breath. Another. He's dead.

She couldn't breathe either. With Kieron's flames came smoke even more suffocating than Safira's. The fire blazed atop her tides, turning the water red.

The young girl who watched the sea flickered into view, followed by years of storms, culminating in the phone call she never should've made and the months that followed. Then there was light—light, waves, and a sea cavern—and after that, Marina focused less on her memories and more on her resignation. Was she doomed to always fail?

And yet, as the early days in the Delve flashed before her, she almost didn't recognize herself. The girl who'd once avoided mirrors and slept to keep her pain at bay had changed. Not entirely, maybe, but it was something.

Marina, Marina, Marina. The voices were distant but personal. She wasn't even sure if Kieron could hear them. They belonged to *her*, and they gave her strength.

"We haven't fallen yet," she heard herself say.

Cal's smile followed—warm and hopeful. *"No, we haven't."*

For some reason, of all the memories that had flashed before her, that one snapped her into action. And so, before her memories became too revealing—before they betrayed her with Aeric's talk of Candens Inlet, what Pierce had said about Ryder, and her own plans—Marina roused her waves and directed them toward the flames on their surface. One by one, swells of glowing seawater collapsed onto the fire until it flickered out—until there was nothing but embers and water. And when the last of the sparks flickered in protest, she smothered them with vigor.

Her withdrawing waves gave birth to the room around her, and Kieron—hard as he tried to conceal his bewilderment—could only blink. When Marina refused to look away, he broke into his usual wide smile and laughed.

"Masterful," he said. "I'd ask who taught you to shield like that, but I already know."

Kieron leaned back, resting his chin in his hand and splaying his fingers over his lips. If she didn't know better, she would think he didn't notice Ocot's corpse on the floor.

"I certainly have a lot to think about," Kieron said. "I'll be honest: I find myself feeling sentimental. Seeing Aeric after thinking him dead all these years is enough to make me regret how we ended things. And you...well, you're more of a puzzle than I expected. But that's a problem, isn't it? You don't know what you want, and what's more is you don't trust yourself. And if you don't trust yourself, how can you expect me to?"

Marina's heart hammered against her chest, and her head spun.

"Bold move," Kieron continued, "using Locus to coax me into leaving the Delve alone. But your emotions precede you. You don't think you *could* perform it, if that was even your intention to begin with." His lips twitched. "I think you could," he added, "if it means anything. It isn't your skillset that needs work, Marina. It's your confidence."

That wasn't advice; it was mockery. He was mocking her. Marina's face reddened, and she hardly sounded like herself when she said, "It was my intention. It *is*. I promise. I'm willing to learn Locus. I don't *want* this—"

"It's not that I don't believe you," Kieron said. "I think you're incapable of telling genuine lies because you don't know the truth." Marina flinched when he stood. "Let's meet again for dinner. How about tomorrow?"

His smile didn't waver when she remained silent. Instead, it widened as he strode to her chair, bent down, and said, "I'm invested in your future. I'd like to see you put those storms in your head to rest, and I believe your internal suspicions are correct—not necessarily about Locus, but about this entire mix-up. You *are* a ghost in Elsudra. You'll never belong here, which makes what our Keepers did so deplorable."

The weight that settled on Marina's chest was unbearable. A ghost...and not just here. In Georgia too. A ghost drowning in pain, looking for hope in all the wrong places and sending others to watery graves of their own when she failed. Marina's eyes burned as she glanced at Ocot's body.

"But that doesn't mean you're useless," Kieron added. "In fact, when all is said and done, I think the two of us will be very good friends."

And then, he was gone. She didn't get to ask him what he meant by that or what he intended to do with the Delve; the silence numbed her.

She wasn't sure how long she remained in the dining room—alone, minus Ocot. When Ryder's voice sounded from beside her, she was too weary to react.

"I'd prefer it if you stood yourself," he said. "Carrying people around isn't my job."

She thought she detected tenderness in his voice, but perhaps she was imagining it.

Ryder's eyes flitted to Ocot, but he said nothing. He simply took Marina's elbow, knowing she wouldn't walk unless someone pulled her, then led her down the halls.

She didn't bother to memorize the turns. Each one was the same, after all: marble floors, ivory stairs, and a view of the world beyond, which she felt farther away from now than when she was underground.

CHAPTER 35
Small Joys

That night, Marina's waves returned in full. Somewhere deep in her subconscious, the abyss beckoned her, as dark and limitless as ever.

Marina, Marina, Marina.

Nobody came for her in the morning or afternoon—not even to bring her food, which she suspected was part of some stupid ploy to ensure she was hungry enough to willingly attend dinner. As if her unwillingness would've mattered.

To distract herself from her hunger, Marina forced herself to shower and change her clothes so she wouldn't look as miserable as she felt. As hard as she tried, though, she couldn't stop replaying the events of the prior evening. Visions of marble stained with blood flickered at the back of her head, followed by Ocot's vacant eyes and Kieron's smile.

Sleep blessed her as the daylight faded, breaking only when she sensed the presence of someone standing above her. When she caught glimpse of two distinctly colored eyes, she rolled to the side out of instinct and nearly fell off the bed.

"Guess you're stuck with me now," Ryder said.

Marina cursed at him as she slid off the mattress, finding little solace in the bed that stood between the two of them.

Ryder only laughed. "Are you ready, or do you need a few more minutes?"

"What the hell would I need a few more minutes for?"

"Maybe to brush up on your sunny demeanor."

Marina didn't know which urge was greater: to punch him or to mention Pierce. Both would probably knock the smile off his face, but short-lived satisfaction wasn't worth the cost of impulsivity, so she remained quiet all the way to the dining room. Ryder did too.

When they reached the entrance, an icy rigidity overtook her muscles, rooting her in place. Thankfully, Ryder didn't taunt her like Ocot had. He simply pushed open the doors, guided her to her chair, and left.

Kieron hadn't arrived yet. Marina couldn't help herself when she stared at the floor where Ocot's body once lay. There was no discoloration or stains, no remnants to suggest he'd ever been there in the first place.

"Like a rat in a trap."

Marina tensed. Kieron had clearly used conveyance to perturb her, which made her all the more intent to seem unperturbed.

"But that's the weakness of rats," he droned. "They might be good at surviving for a time, but they're overcome by myopia—always focused on the food in front of them, never seeing the trap they've walked into."

Was he talking about Ocot or her? Desperation had led them both out of the Delve—a different kind, but desperation all the same. Ocot's had gotten him killed; would hers backfire just as horribly?

Shields up, shields up. He's not getting through again.

"I *am* still willing to work with you, you know," she breathed, because she could think of nothing better to say, and maybe she could still convince him. "I meant what I said. If the Delve is left alone—"

"Marina, stop," Kieron said patronizingly. "You don't know what you want. I may not have seen all your memories, but my dear, I could *feel* your conflict. You're lost and afraid, and it's obvious coming here was your attempt to appease me and buy your friends time." The creases in his cheeks deepened. "I empathize with that. You yearn for the safety of your friends; I yearn for the safety of the Omnia. But I've already made my promise to you. Will you keep harping on it like a child, or will you return the favor?"

She could feel herself shrinking. This was Kieron's strength—he could make a person feel like nothing. He'd done it to Aeric, and now he was doing it to her.

"I told you I would," she said through gritted teeth.

"No more lies, Marina—to me or yourself. Let's be honest with each other. I'll go first: I'm not interested in Locus."

"What?" The word sputtered inelegantly from her mouth. Kieron let it hang between the two of them, basking in her shock. It didn't make sense. Locus had been his goal with the Keepers—a goal he was willing to suffer for. He'd been betting on it; Aeric had said as much. And she'd been betting on *that*.

"Truthfully, I've never liked the ritual," Kieron said. "The Omnia wasn't meant to be moved between hosts, no less by the hands of fallible beings. But Tempus...I'm very fond of Tempus."

Tempus? "But that's a ritual of guidance," Marina said. "I don't see how—"

"Your dreams," Kieron interrupted. "You've had them since birth, haven't you? And yet, in one of your memories, you mentioned them changing since you came to Elsudra. Did Aeric know this?" When Marina only stared at him, he whispered amicably, "Forgive me; you cut my psychometry short and left me with gaps to fill."

Strangely enough, she didn't think he was going to try again—not after he'd been so forcefully pushed out. Still, she kept her shields high.

"I...I never told him," she said.

"But he was aware of your dreams, at the very least. He noticed something the first time he used psychometry on you, even if he couldn't push any further. It unsettled him. I could tell by the way he acted afterward." Kieron chuckled. "The thing is, *I* have insight Aeric lacks, and that's why your dreams are of such great interest to me."

Marina pressed her lips together. She wasn't sure where this conversation was going, and she was afraid anything she *would* say might accidentally damn her. Instead, she kept quiet, trying her best not to react.

"The first Keepers were diligent when it came to keeping what they'd done a secret," Kieron continued. "Only their descendants knew, then swore oaths never to speak of it. I had to steal their archives to figure it out. It was one of the riskier decisions I've made, but I'm not opposed to risks if they get me what I want, and this one did. I uncovered what the Keepers had kept hidden for centuries. The first of them didn't need Locus to take the Omnia from water. Not when they could use Exorsus itself."

Exorsus. The deity even Aeric didn't understand. *The beginning.*

"You're wondering how they did it," Kieron said. He enjoyed her confusion, she realized. Reveled in it. "I'll give you a hint. They were guided."

She paled when it hit her. What could guide them, if not the ritual of guidance itself?

"My problem," Kieron continued, "is that I don't know what Tempus showed them. I know they used it, just like I know they used the Omnia to access Exorsus, much like a key. But I was exiled before I could find out where Tempus led them—where Exorsus *is*. And the last Keepers destroyed the rest of their archives when I returned from exile. That's why I need you."

Marina's head spun. She'd never heard Exorsus referred to as a place—as something that could be found. And what was Kieron implying? Did he expect her to do what the first Keepers had, however the hell they'd done it?

"But I thought Tempus could only be used in emergencies," she said, fully aware of how little she knew—how desperate her choice to come here had been.

And Aeric...Kieron had withheld this information from him, no doubt. How stupid had she been to work entirely off what Aeric told her? To cling to Locus as tightly as she had months ago, even if it was for a different reason?

"Only in the era of Keepers," Kieron responded. "That was a modern regulation—part of the vow they made, meant to keep them from doing what the first of them had done. Their oath went a step further and forbade them from using Tempus—or any methods—to find Exorsus itself. The first Keepers were nothing if not thorough."

A loophole. That's what Aeric had said the first Keepers had found. No...it hadn't been a loophole at all, but a manipulation—an exploitation of a ritual used in times of need, all to satisfy their wants.

Judging by the fear they'd felt after—the fear she'd felt in the anteactus—they'd paid the price of their greed. Only...what about Exorsus had scared them so much?

Kieron folded his hands. "When it came to the Keepers, I quickly realized that I, too, would have to bend to their limitations. They *couldn't* use Tempus to find Exorsus, which meant my only option was Locus—fickle and dangerous as it was. But not anymore." He smiled. "You came here thinking Locus was the only way I could take the Omnia from you. If you were a Keeper, you would've been right. But you're no Keeper, are you, Marina?"

No, I'm not. I'm far less—far worse. And I've made a horrible mistake.

It was painful to keep her mask up. How did Aeric do it? She'd been in his head; she'd felt what he felt. How was he always so aloof? She'd never been good at that. But now... now she *needed* to be.

"Still," Kieron said, "it was noble of you to come, and who can blame you for not having sufficient information? Even if Aeric had suspicions about what the first Keepers did, he wouldn't have told you. He didn't want you performing Locus; he definitely wouldn't have wanted you running off in search of Exorsus."

Mouth dry, Marina said, "But I've never learned Tempus, and even if I had, there's no way I could find Exorsus. I can't—"

"What did I say about your confidence, Marina? This is your issue; you underestimate yourself. That's what brought you here. You've convinced yourself you can't do anything of consequence, and you keep on with those lies—to yourself, and to others—out of fear." He watched her closely when he said, "But the thing is, you don't need to learn Tempus. You already know it."

Marina, Marina, Marina. The voices echoed at the back of her head, rising and falling in tandem with her waves, both a part of her essence and part of something different— something deep and ancient.

"You've sworn no oaths and made no sacrifices," Kieron said. "You're free to do as you like, and your unconscious knows it. You've been performing Tempus since you came to

Elsudra. You yourself admitted that your dreams have been evolving since your arrival, and while I couldn't witness them, their presence was overwhelming all the same." He leaned back in his seat. "Psychometry has limits, I'm afraid, and dreams are fickle things. They're an entirely separate level of consciousness. Even the best sorcerers can't push that deep."

Psychometry cannot discern Tempus's guidance, Marina remembered. And Aeric had told her dreams couldn't be accessed with psychometry. The darkness beneath her waves he'd tried to reach in the dining room...he hadn't been able to, just like Kieron said.

Kieron laughed, mostly to himself. "Though I suspect even if psychometry gave insight into dreams, Aeric wouldn't have risked it with you. Not given your...temperament." Before Marina could process the jab, he continued, "But I'm not Aeric. I believe pushing people beyond their limits encourages growth. I'd like for you to do just that. Observe your dreams—challenge yourself to peer further into them and tell me what you see. With enough effort, Tempus will be your guiding light to Exorsus. And you will be mine."

Exorsus. The word hung in the air, as did what Aeric had said: *the sun itself.* If Kieron found Exorsus, he wouldn't need to gamble on the unpredictability of Locus. Of *her.*

She couldn't imagine the light beneath her waves merging with the fire of Kieron's spirit. What kind of power would he possess? And what would it make him: ruler or god?

"Intimacy with the Omnia is integral for Tempus to work, and lucky us, you hold the entire thing," Kieron said. "Let your intuition guide you. Open yourself up to what your dreams are trying to say." Wryly, he added, "I wouldn't want you to feel rushed, of course. I'll be sure to give you more than enough time to find your footing. When we meet next, I expect you'll be a fountain of insight."

There's no us in this. Still, she made it a point to lock eyes with Kieron as she nodded.

She didn't need to give up on her plan. If her dreams truly were a performance of Tempus, then Florin's documents had been right: it *was* a vague ritual. She could use that to her advantage.

"If I do," Marina said, *and I won't,* she thought, "will you leave the Delve alone, like you promised?"

If she wanted to be believable, it was best to keep pretending like *she* believed *him*—that she had a reason to perform Tempus. She'd placate him as long as possible.

Kieron reached out and warmly squeezed Marina's wrist. She tried not to flinch—*shields up, shields up*—but given the smile that tugged at his lips, she knew she wasn't doing a good job.

"If you help me find Exorsus, I'll do more than that," he said. "I'll help you get home."

Yearning flickered to life within her, and with it, a momentary desire to change course. But hope wasn't always reasonable; it could deceive just as much as fear. He'd never help her get home. And even if he did, would she accept? *Could* she?

She kept her gaze on Kieron when she said, "I'll do it."

A tiny, optimistic voice at the back of her head reassured her this was still worth it. It had been a few days since she'd left the Delve. In that time, maybe Pierce and Ismene had done what she'd asked, and when Kieron's technology registered disintegrating shields, they'd be far enough away—with more people. And yet, another voice wondered if her choice hadn't been heroic at all, but just as myopic as Ocot's. Even if Pierce and Ismene successfully bargained for more lives, they couldn't save everyone. When Aeric's glamours and shields fell, people would die. It was inevitable.

But she was here; there was no turning back. Even if she could, she wouldn't, because then she'd know people were dying for her cowardice and mistakes. She'd be a deadweight. In Altus, she had some measly sway. Didn't she?

Kieron removed his hand. "What did I tell you?" he mused. "I think the two of us will be very good friends indeed."

Yes...she did.

Still, after Kieron left and Ryder came to fetch her, Marina had to fight to keep the regret from consuming her.

This was no different than Locus. She could still stall him. She could.

"You're very quiet," Ryder said. He was toying with her—it was obvious.

Marina didn't react. "Think he'll ever trust me enough to let me walk back to my room on my own?"

Ryder's metallic armor glinted in the light of the setting sun, which made him look all the more arrogant when he smiled lazily and said, "Don't count on it."

"He seems to trust you enough. Ever worry you'll be next anyway?"

Ryder didn't look at her, but she knew he was aware of what she meant.

"No," he responded flatly.

"I bet Ocot would've said that too." If he wanted to rile her, she'd do the same to him.

"It's a good thing I'm not Ocot, isn't it?" Ryder said through a smirk.

Marina paused, Pierce's words ringing in her ears. *He can help you.*

That was only true if Pierce was right about Ryder's allegiance being an act. As much as she wanted to take his word for it, she couldn't. The dead years were a long time to pretend. How far could someone go before they passed the threshold of reality and fiction —before the charade they performed became their truth?

"Kieron must trust you a lot if he sent you out to the Delve," she said, squinting in the light that flooded into the halls. She almost asked him how old he was but remembered he wouldn't have an answer. He was probably only a few years older than Pierce. "You're very young to be Kieron's glorified messenger."

Ryder snorted. "I'm not his messenger."

"Then what are you?"

"I don't give a shit about titles."

Marina glowered at him. "It seems weird that of *all* the guards Kieron could've chosen to serve him so closely, he chose you. You must've still been in training."

"Age and experience don't matter when you out-perform everyone else." The roguish smile reappeared on Ryder's face. "You have a lot of questions for someone who was so short with me earlier. Why do I get the feeling you're not genuinely curious?"

Marina ignored that. "How many people does he have working for him?"

"Planning to stage a coup, are you?" When she didn't answer, he laughed under his breath. "There are more of us than you'd think. I have a feeling the Keepers would've been devastated to know how many people had grown tired of their rule. As for the court...they didn't care until they were the ones being slaughtered."

Marina's stomach dropped.

"Bet it didn't seem that way in the Delve, did it?" Ryder said. "I hate to be the bearer of bad news, but your friends were all parrots for the Keepers. None of them possessed a single shred of original thought."

He held open a door for her, and only then did Marina realize they were back at her room. Instead of stepping over the threshold, she leaned against the door.

Ryder lowered his hand, then began to fiddle with the weapons on his baldric. He had a few—a brass gun, a spear-point blade, and a sword with a fuller that glowed in the light —but it wasn't until his fingers brushed along the hilt of his dagger that Marina's emotions grew overwhelming. Pierce did that, and now, he was all she could think of. Tears began to prick her eyes.

Keep your mask up, Marina. Keep it up. But she couldn't, and Ryder noticed.

"Chin up," he said, smirking. "Things like that can make a big difference."

The whirlwind of emotions within her settled. "That reminds me of advice I was given by one of my friends in the Delve," she said slowly. "It wasn't his advice—he'd heard it from someone he loved—but I'll never forget what he told me."

Ryder's smirk faded, replaced by an expression she could only assume was skepticism. "Oh? And what's that?"

She made herself smile, even though it was painful. "That sometimes, small joys are the lights we use to find our way through dark times."

Ryder's eyes widened, but before he could open his mouth, she'd already stepped into her room and shut the door.

CHAPTER 36
The Winning Side

Dawn tinted the world with violet, and Marina woke to light filtering in through the curtains. She thought she'd heard the door open, but she groggily chalked it up to the crash of waves outside.

She hadn't tried to decipher her dreams last night. If anything, she'd actively ignored them—the voices, the darkness, all of it. She'd make up some bullshit to appease Kieron, feeding him lies in dribs and drabs. She would be his barrier, just like Aeric had said.

Confidence flickered to life in her. It was fleeting and softened by her drowsiness, but Marina clung to it. Darkness rushed in again, and she yielded, halfway back asleep when someone gripped her by her shoulders. The darkness receded, and Marina gasped.

"Who did you hear that from?" Ryder snarled.

He pressed his dagger to her throat, and though it surprised her, Marina let out a laugh. Now she was fully awake. "Who do you think?"

"I want to hear the name. Say it."

"Move your dagger, Ryder. We both know you're not going to use it."

She spoke calmly, and she wondered if it was hysteria that gave her courage. Whatever it was, it only seemed to rattle Ryder more. He lost all composure, and his voice shook when he demanded, "What have you told Kieron?"

Marina wrapped her hand around his wrist. "Nothing." She tightened her grip, then let a generous amount of white light curl at her fingertips.

Ryder jerked his hand away. Clearly, he was desperate enough to remain near her, and he made no attempt to soften his tone when he said, "What about what he saw?"

"He didn't."

"I know the lengths he goes to when he wants information. How do I know he didn't witness something that would put me in danger?"

"Because I forced him out before he could. He has no idea about your abilities. I don't even think he knows much about Pierce. Those weren't the memories he focused on."

Ryder inhaled and lowered himself to a chair.

"He's doing well, if you want to know," Marina said, sitting up.

"I don't." The words were cold. "I want to know whether you'll tell Kieron something that'll get me killed." He laughed mirthlessly. "That would be hilarious. I survived the dead years, gained Kieron's trust, and managed to hide any indication of my abilities upon the Omnia's return, only to die because Pierce ran his mouth."

Marina bristled at the resentment in his voice. "He didn't run his mouth."

"If that were true, you wouldn't know what you know."

For a moment, she eyed him, then hopped off her bed.

"I have no plans to tell Kieron anything," she said. "Yet."

Ryder stood, slipping his blade back into its sheath before taking a few steps toward her. "You're shit at acting."

Marina tensed, but she was determined to win this standoff. She raised an eyebrow, then said, "Kieron would have been able to detect your essence through psychometry. How did you keep it hidden?"

Ryder straightened and smiled at her. "I noticed you didn't eat dinner last night."

She hadn't expected him to tell her, but she hadn't expected that either. She blinked at him, unsure how to respond.

"I'll have the servants bring you some," he continued. "I can't say the next time you'll be leaving this room."

Whatever fear he'd let slip had disappeared, replaced by his usual lazy roguishness. When he cupped Marina's face with his hands, she was too shocked to recoil.

"You don't need to threaten me to get me to do favors for you." He winked at her, chuckling when she stepped back, then left as quietly as he came.

৩

Ryder stayed true to his word. Every morning, a meal large enough to last the day would be brought to her by servants—all of whom never spoke and kept their eyes on the ground. They never entered either; they simply knocked, waited until she opened the door, then slid a tray of food past the threshold and hurried away. As if she could do anything to them from behind this god-awful shield.

On the bright side, she had plenty of time to think about what she'd tell Kieron—or perhaps, more fittingly, what she wouldn't. Every night, the chasm beyond the waters of her subconscious called to her. She tried not to listen. The more she ignored her dreams, however, the more exhausted she woke, as though turning such a deliberate blind eye physically taxed her. She'd never fought her dreams; even back at home when they were all the same, she'd welcomed them nightly. But she wasn't home.

You'll never belong here, Kieron had said. Marina tried not to think about that. Of course he'd say that to the person standing between him and the Omnia, but he hadn't said it maliciously. If anything, he'd said it offhandedly, as though she'd be a fool not to know it. She'd told herself the same thing before. Why was it so painful to admit now?

Perhaps because now, she knew Elsudra—because she knew its history as well as her own. She'd started tracking time in Elsudran weeks; it was just as much Aragonite to her as it was May. What did that make her? Elsudran? Human?

Maybe it made her nothing. A ghost.

Eight days followed, all of which she spent alone. She had a feeling Kieron wanted her to go mad in the silence of her room, which, despite everything, Marina found comical. In that way, he'd underestimated her. She was more than used to isolation.

When Ryder finally came to fetch her, she was in the middle of shielding. Even if Kieron couldn't see her dreams, that didn't mean he wouldn't resort to psychometry again.

The first thing Ryder said when he entered the room was, "Should I be worried about information you might share today?"

Today...Kieron wanted to speak with her today. Marina's stomach coiled. She'd practiced what she was going to say, but she didn't know how he'd respond.

Get up. Act confident.

Marina rose from her chair and headed to the door. "Not today."

Through a taut smile, Ryder said, "Glad to hear it."

He didn't ask her again as they made their way through the halls—not like she expected him to. She *had* expected him, however, to mention Pierce, but he didn't. In fact, the only time he spoke was when she took a turn in the direction of the dining room, and even then, he wasn't fully vocal—he simply *tsked* at her, as though he were redirecting a lost dog. Had she not been so caught up in her unease, it would've irritated her.

Though she wanted to ask where they were going, she stayed silent as they took one of the hallways outside to a crenellation overlooking the ocean. Like so much else in Elsudra, the style was both modern and archaic, but it was neither the sea-stone walls nor the swallow-tailed merlons that piqued her interest. It was the air.

If the breeze that danced through the palace hallways entranced her, this left her hypnotized. She could feel every gust of wind—every touch of sunlight to her skin, which was much warmer than it was in the Admare Mountains. A few birds perched on turrets, their caws in sync with the crashing waves. Lucky them; they could fly away at a moment's notice. If she had wings, she'd join them, but even Elsudra's magic couldn't offer her that kind of hope. The only control she had was over herself, so she willed her face into cold neutrality as she and Ryder approached Kieron.

He stood next to Safira, who regarded them with the same aloofness. Though her eye landed on Marina, there was no emotion in it. Kieron, however, broke into his usual smile when he saw them. In the afternoon light, his skin was as waxy and discolored as ever. If he stayed out long enough, Marina thought, perhaps it would melt from his face.

"What of your dreams?" he asked as he approached. "You've had quite some time to decipher them."

"They're hard to explain," she said.

Stay calm. You've practiced this.

"Try your best."

Marina looked out at the sea. "There are waves, which I've seen all my life. And... there's something else. It's different from my essence...but too murky to make out."

There. That was vague enough.

"Let's try that again," Kieron said. "I want to know what you saw as much as I want to know what you *felt*. What you *heard*."

Marina, Marina, Marina.

"I didn't hear anything. But I'm still getting the hang of everything."

Kieron sighed. "I expected this, but I'm still so disappointed that you've chosen to lie."

Though Marina's stomach dropped, she forced herself to speak evenly. "I'm not lying. It took me a while to grasp magic back in the Delve too. But I did, and I will with this. I just need a little longer. But I'm listening to my dreams...I promise."

"You don't need to listen to hear voices during Tempus," Kieron said. "They make themselves known. It's an intuitive ritual. You think because I'm not a host—because I can't directly witness Tempus—that I know nothing about the ritual? That I'll be satisfied with feigned incompetence? Every Sorcerer of the Court learns how to facilitate Tempus to help the Keepers in case they need to perform it. Lest you forget, *I* was a Sorcerer of the Court." He sighed again, this time slower. "I hoped my offer to help get you home would motivate you."

She hated how the word—home—stopped her in her tracks. Hated how it made her determination waver and her good sense fade.

It's an empty offer. Don't fall for it, she told herself. *And even if it's not, there's no home for you to return to.*

But Gemma and Hank mattered, didn't they?

Just as much as Pierce and Ismene. Just as much as Cal, Florin, and Aeric.

"Clearly," Kieron said, "it didn't. If this is a fire you want to start, then by all means, lie."

"I have no reason to lie," Marina pressed on. "I don't want the Omnia. You know that. You *saw* how hard I tried to learn Locus. And I'm still willing—"

"First, I'll send my troops back to the Delve," Kieron interrupted. "It would be an inconvenience, to be sure, and I'd hate even more to go myself. But if that's what this calls for, I'll make the trip."

He wasn't even listening. He didn't believe her.

How many days had it been since she'd left the Delve? Fourteen? Maybe more? She'd managed to string him along for nearly fourteen days before he called her on it. That was something, wasn't it? But she still couldn't give up.

"I'm not lying," she said. "Just give me more time. Tempus, Locus...I'll do either. I need to find my footing, like you said."

"After I take them out," Kieron continued, "I'll go after every rebel base in Elsudra. I may've been blind to the Delve, but believe me when I say I'm well aware of others." The darkness in his eyes leaked onto his face, and though he smiled like he always did, his lips twitched. "I'd appreciate your help, Marina, but if you don't provide it voluntarily, then obtaining it in other ways is fine with me."

She tried to ignore the fear that bore into her veins, but her mask was crumbling, and Kieron knew it.

"I've been in Elsudra for five months," Marina protested, "and in that time, I've never been able to decipher my dreams."

"You haven't tried yet. You've only watched. To be successful, you'll need to be more than a watcher. More than a listener too." He straightened. "I hope you take what I'm saying to heart—for the Delve's sake, if not your own."

She dug her nails into her palms. "Threats won't make me any quicker."

"Not threats," Kieron said. "Promises."

A glance was all it took for Ryder to pull her away.

For half a second, maybe less, Marina wondered what would happen if she tried to kill Kieron, here and now. Could she even do it? And if she could, would he anticipate it, or would she get some damage in before Safira was on her—before Kieron himself blocked her attack and punished the Delve in her stead? If the Delve wasn't *already* gone...

"Is he being honest about the Delve? Is it still standing?" Marina asked Ryder as they neared the hallway to her room. She'd been silent most of the walk back; her ears were ringing too loud and her head was numb.

She braced herself for a condescending response, but Ryder said nothing. Somehow, that was worse.

She tried another method. "Would you attack it if Kieron ordered you to? Even if you knew Pierce was there?"

React to his name. Show me something.

Again, he didn't answer, and something in her broke.

"Ryder—"

"What makes you think I have any desire to spare the Delve?"

On second thought, she would've preferred it if he'd remained quiet.

"Not the reaction you were expecting?" Ryder droned as they neared her door. "My apologies. War is heartless. Your friend knows better than anyone that some people aren't fortunate enough to be saved."

"He means nothing to you?"

"Pierce means as much to me as I meant to him."

Her legs gave in when he nudged her forward, and she stepped into the cool darkness of her room.

"He regrets it," she said. "Every day. It causes him so much pain."

Ryder's jaw tightened. "Good."

An ache careened through her.

"Congratulations on your performance, by the way," Ryder said. "For a second there, you had Kieron thinking maybe you *were* the scared, useless girl Ocot told stories about."

A glimmer of light caught her eye, but Marina refused to blink.

Ryder leaned against the doorframe, only inches away from the shield. "You might've been daring enough to come here and string Kieron along for a few days, but in the end, it won't matter. And if you keep up the incompetent little girl act, Kieron won't treat your friends as kindly as he has treated you." His expression cracked, revealing what she could only interpret as despair.

Her head spun, and she knew her emotions had bested her when she hissed, "Whose side are you on?"

Ryder grinned through deadened eyes. "The winning side."

CHAPTER 37
Quid Pro Quo

That night, Marina did as Kieron asked. Not deliberately, perhaps, and certainly not for him, but because some unconscious part of her couldn't resist. What Kieron had said about being a watcher—about being more than one—awakened something in her, and she couldn't help but wonder where her dreams would lead her if she chose to follow.

Maybe it was the whispers following each wave that beckoned her, or perhaps it was the darkness beneath the water—the darkness of countless possibilities, all as real as they were unwritten. At the first touch of sunlight to the sea, she could reach them.

As she swam deeper, the water grew heavier, but she kept on until the darkness pulsed outward and encompassed every echelon of existence. And then, there was no ocean—no nothing, except the everything before her.

For all its limitlessness, however, she was markedly limited. No matter how far she swam, the darkness stretched farther, until she resigned to exist within a small patch of it. *Her* patch—the one minuscule part of unending possibilities that comprised her existence.

Even then, it exerted her immensely, and Marina woke trembling and drenched in sweat. When her shivering grew uncontrollable, she ran herself a scalding shower and replayed her dreams in her head. Perhaps she wouldn't need to lead Kieron astray on purpose. It seemed she'd be unable to decipher them even if she wanted to.

But Kieron didn't send for her—not for another five days.

This time, it wasn't as easy to be alone. When Ryder entered her room on the morning of the sixth, Marina was well in the throes of paranoia.

"What took you so long?" she demanded.

Ryder raised an eyebrow. "You *want* to see Kieron?"

"I want to know why *he* hasn't wanted to see me." When Ryder raised an eyebrow, she added, "I'm as eager to get rid of the Omnia as he is to take it, you know."

"Oh, drop the act, Marina," Ryder said. "It's getting annoying." He observed her before adding, "We've been experiencing security issues. He's caught up in that."

Marina gawked at him. "What kind of security issues?"

Maybe someone's come for me...Aeric or Florin or...

Ryder laughed. "Pierce won't rescue you. I'd blame his character, but in this case, it has more to do with the fact that it'd be a suicide mission." He paused. "Is that really what you were thinking? Aeric isn't that brash, and Pierce cares more about himself."

Marina's chest hollowed, leaving behind a void she could only fill with anger.

"Do you think Kieron's sick and that's why he's so desperate?" she said. "He certainly looks it." She pretended to wince. "Wouldn't that suck—your winning side loses because Kieron keels over and dies before he can take the Omnia?"

"Why don't you ask him? I'd love to see his reaction." Ryder chuckled when she didn't respond. "Thought so."

He didn't say anything else as he led her to the throne room, but she didn't care; she couldn't find it within herself to speak either. Instead, she mulled over what she'd say to Kieron. Would he believe her if she told him she'd tried Tempus but still didn't know? The incompetent little girl act, it seemed, was no longer an act.

The sunlight wasn't as direct in the morning, but the door to the throne room was as beautiful as ever. Pastels splashed the marble floor, and Marina let herself get lost in it before familiar sounds brought her back.

Click, click, click, click.

Four ruemin stood next to the dais, watching the room with glazed eyes, and Marina reined in a gasp. If they noticed her as she entered, they didn't react. They stared ahead, the appendages on their throats opening one moment, then clicking closed the next.

The brush of Ryder's fingers against her arm—intentional or not—grounded her as she neared them. Kieron wasn't present; only Vaughn was. He watched the ruemin quietly.

Marina almost turned to Ryder to ask him why she'd been brought here, but he spoke before she could.

"Are they sleeping?" he asked Vaughn.

Marina swallowed her questions as Vaughn side-eyed her and Ryder, then said in a low, breathy voice, "Coming out of a daze." He paused. "I find them fascinating. It took me a great deal of work to sensitize them to my sound. They can't hear all frequencies, but they remember the ones they *can* hear. I've become quite adept at knowing when and how to call them." Absently, he smiled and added, "Strange things, they are."

Ryder knit his brow. "Murderous things."

"*Living* things," Vaughn corrected. "A condition of their living is to consume, and so they kill, then breed so they can consume more. They are not so different from us." His gaze shifted to Marina, then lingered like a hawk studying its prey. "Another strange thing: how a girl from a distant sister realm came to hold the magical essence of Elsudra. Has it changed you?"

Marina glanced at Ryder, then back at Vaughn. "I don't...I don't know."

"We've theorized about what would happen to a non-Elsudran in possession of the Omnia," Vaughn said, "but it was baseless conjecture. Now, it's not so baseless. Do you mind?"

Marina blinked at him, unsure what he meant. When he reached out and brushed his fingers along the tips of her hair, she found herself unable to recoil. Instead, she shot a baffled look at Ryder. Vaughn didn't react, but the curiosity that danced in his eyes made the hair on Marina's neck stand on end.

"How did you end up working for Kieron?" she asked. *Anything* to diffuse the silence.

Vaughn took his time before he spoke. "I worked many years in the palace," he said, the side of his face crinkling, "but the other healers didn't appreciate what I brought to the field. So I moved to the outskirts of Altus, where I conducted research on my own until Kieron persuaded me to work with him."

Silence settled like a thick blanket over the room, and though Marina expected to feel relief when it ended, her stomach only sank further.

"*Four* of them?" Kieron said, chuckling as he approached. Safira followed behind him, her heels echoing on the marble.

"A symbolic display," Vaughn replied.

Marina could only assume he was referencing the Keepers. But why were ruemin *here*? What was Kieron planning to do with them?

Kieron chuckled again. "You can go, if you've got things to do."

Vaughn nodded once more at Marina before turning and leaving. She almost watched him go, but the ruemins' silver eyes kept her attention.

"They'll be out of it for a bit," Kieron said. "Just until they recover. You understand what that's like."

He stood beside her now; Ryder had made room for him. Marina tried to conceal her wariness as she eyed Safira, who gave her a dry smile.

"What's this for?" Marina whispered, refusing to look Kieron straight on.

"They're tricky creatures," Kieron said. "Hard to communicate with and even harder to control. You leave them unchecked for too long and they get unpredictable. But they can follow rules if they're adequately rewarded, and I know how to reward them." His eyes shined. "Let's hear it. What headway have you made?"

Breathe. Stay calm.

She licked her lips, straining to control her voice. "I tried. I just...I have no idea what I'm seeing. There's darkness and water and—"

"You've already told me this."

She dared to look him in the eyes. "That's all there is."

The voices, the possibilities, the everything and nothing...

"No, it's not. There's more." When she didn't respond, he said, "Is this what it's going to be like?"

"I don't know how to convince you I'm telling the truth." *The partial truth...that's still truth, isn't it?* "You were right. I *had* just been watching. But now that I realize what I can do, it'll take me a while to do it."

"It's hard to trust you," Kieron said. "But I think I have the means to change that."

He smiled, and only then did Marina realize Ryder had left. He wasn't gone for long, though, and when he returned, it was with four other guards, all as silent as he was. But it wasn't the guards who caught her attention—it was the five people they escorted into the room. The first was a middle-aged woman with gray hair, followed by a short man and a young woman with cold eyes. Behind her limped a man even younger, and behind him...

Marina's body went numb.

Cal.

*No, no, no...*how had this happened? Why were they here? They weren't wearing the Delve's armored suits; theirs were tinted gold, as though they'd stolen ones belonging to the palace. They didn't have any weapons either—they'd been stripped—and their vocos were gone too.

Cal glanced at Marina, but she didn't say anything. Her face was covered in specks of blood—was it hers or someone else's?—but the enmity in her eyes was as clear as ever. She directed it at Kieron, who beamed as he beheld her.

"It seems these five were attempting something of an undercover rescue mission," he said, as though it was all a joke to him.

Security issues. That was what Ryder was referring to.

"They train them well in the Delve," Kieron continued. "They're as skilled as they are hard to break. I had to resort to more invasive methods to get what I needed." He faced Marina, his eyes alight. "Would you believe they came of their own accord—that they weren't given orders to do so?"

Though the ruemin didn't move, the presence of the scouts roused them from their daze. They eyed them hungrily, as though they were waiting for Kieron's orders. How had he come to exert such control over them?

"I would've killed them all immediately," he said, "but I recognized this young lady from your memories. I thought you'd like to reunite." He looked at Cal, then Marina. "I'm going to ask you again to describe your dreams, and I warn you not to be coy with me."

This couldn't be real. Cal hadn't been in the Delve when Marina left. When did she return? What did she return *to*?

Marina's voice sounded muffled in her ears when she said, "I see exactly what I told you. That's it. Endless darkness and ocean, and it's all so expansive that I can't comprehend it. I'm *trying*."

It's the truth. Believe me. Please, believe me.

Her mask was gone now, if there'd been anything left of it to begin with. And her plan...that was gone too.

Did they leave? she wanted to ask Cal. *Did they take as many as possible?*

Did it matter? Did any of it? Now Cal was here because *she* was.

"The word 'ruemin' comes from Sundra," Kieron said. "It means unwelcome visitor. But I have to disagree. They're very welcome here."

He clicked his tongue in tandem with the ruemin. *Click, click, click.*

"Their food has to be alive while they feast," he continued. "Dead bodies are useless to ruemin; it's *souls* they're truly after, not flesh. And once the body dies, the soul follows suit." He stepped closer to Cal. "Once a ruemin has devoured a spirit, it becomes part of their larger entity. It's a withered version of what it once was, perhaps—hardly capable of satisfying them forever—but the ruemin hoard it all the same. The Sundrans discovered that the hard way."

Marina was so out of sorts that she could hardly process what he'd said, but she clung to her sanity when she repeated, "I'm *trying*." Desperately, she added, "How do you expect me to know a ritual that only seasoned sorcerers could perform—that the Keepers couldn't even do unless the Sorcerer of the Court helped? I need time to figure it out."

Kieron inhaled, long and slow. "Patience has been hard to come by lately. Exile, the dead years...it's torturous business. Not to mention all the years I served as Sorcerer of the Court." He shrugged. "Luckily, I learned so much while I slaved away for the Keepers and the court. This might interest you: with every act of magic, one is drawn closer to the Omnia, as though actualizing what shines upon us closes the gap between ourselves and the source of our magic—and subsequently, the source of the Omnia itself."

He met Cal's eyes, then turned back to Marina. "Performing magic pulls on the tether that links the Omnia to Exorsus," he continued. "The more powerful one's magic, the closer they are to the Omnia, and consequently, its creator. *That* was why only the best sorcerers could perform Tempus and why the Keepers needed the Sorcerer of the Court's help—why, as your magic progressed in Elsudra, your dreams changed. You have every tool at your disposal, Marina. So stop with the excuses."

He positioned himself behind her, and a tremor shot down Marina's spine as he said, "How about a quid pro quo? You've had five days since we last spoke to try. I'll give you five more. If, on each one, you come to me empty-handed and blame your incompetence for your failures, a scout will die. If you decide to work with me and do what I know you can, I'll spare them." He straightened. "Those are your choices. I know which one I prefer."

He moved away from Marina, then nodded at one of his guards, who escorted the woman with gray hair over to the ruemin. There she stood, shackled and shaking, beneath silver eyes and clicking throats.

Kieron clasped his hands. "Today is the first day. I'll ask you again, Marina. What are your dreams telling you?"

Her vision blurred, then cleared. "Please, believe me," she pleaded. "I don't want the Omnia...I never have."

Kieron pursed his lips. "Anything else?"

The voices...she should tell him about the voices. But what if that gave something away? She wasn't sure what, but she couldn't be too careful.

But the scout...she'd die. She'd die, and so would the others. So would Cal.

And if she led him to Exorsus? What then?

Marina opened her mouth, but nothing came out. There were no good choices. Aeric was right: every victory was hollow.

"I'll take that as a no." Kieron nodded to the ruemin. "Enjoy."

There was no time to process—no time to prepare. The ruemin lunged forward, and then there were screams, so tortured even Cal's stony demeanor broke. A cry escaped her mouth as the scout with gray hair fell to the ground, splattering the marble with blood.

The three other scouts might have screamed too, but Marina couldn't be sure. She couldn't hear much through the ringing in her ears.

Kieron's voice, however, was loud and clear. "That's on you."

Light from the stained glass reflected off the ruemins' scales as they bore into their victim, and Marina braced herself for more blood.

It's on me. This whole thing was on her. It had been from the beginning. She'd doomed these people the day she'd arrived in the sea cavern.

The ruemin clicked ravenously as they circled the body. It took them a while to break through the armor, but once they did, they tore the scout's limbs from her torso. When she was no more than flesh and blood, they prowled from the room with her remains, leaving a pool of red in their wake. Kieron admired it before turning back to Marina.

"Four more days," he said. "I'll save the best for last."

When he glanced at Cal, something in Marina broke—something so deep that she didn't care about her fallen mask. To hell with it.

She wanted Kieron to die. She wanted his bones to tear from his body, like the scout —wanted him to drown in his own blood, like Ocot. She wanted to be the one to do it. It would feel *good.*

She raised her hands, and from her palms careened bursts of light. They catapulted toward Kieron, voltaic and crackling, and for a moment, there was shock in his eyes. *Fear.*

And then the fear was gone.

With a single movement of Kieron's arm, the light went sideways, humming as it hit the marble and died down. Cal and the other scouts jumped as Safira raised her arms, but Kieron only laughed.

"Good try," he said, breathless. "But I caution you not to try again."

Where was the fear she'd seen? She yearned for it to come back. She wanted him to fear her as much as she feared him. It was a horrible, hateful feeling, but she didn't care.

"You *psychopath,*" she spat.

That made Kieron smile—not in his usual, fake way, but as though he actually found it funny.

"*There's* the Marina I was waiting for," he said. "I'm so pleased to finally meet you."

She almost tried again, but the electricity at her fingertips fizzled out when her hand began to burn. It was quick but searing, and Marina gasped as Safira hissed, "Don't be impulsive."

Marina glanced at her skin—red, but not broken—then lowered her arms.

"Sound advice," Kieron said. "I don't want to put diminution cuffs on you. They'll affect Tempus, and that's no good for either of us. But if you lash out again, I may have to."

He took a step toward Cal, monitoring Marina's reaction. When she only stared at him, helpless, he grinned. "What is your name, my dear?" he asked Cal. "My memory isn't as good as it once was."

He waited patiently for her answer. When the silence grew unbearable, Cal gave in. "Callina," she rasped.

"Callina," Kieron said, drawing out the name. "*Now* I remember. But your friends call you Cal, don't they?" Though he looked at Cal, Marina knew he was talking to her when he said, "You know, I had to convince Vaughn to work for me. Such a brilliant mind—if not for him, Safira wouldn't be here—but he was disenchanted by our government and thought I'd bring more of the same. It took me years to convince him, but I did, all by giving him an offer that proved my reign would be different." He uttered a satisfied sigh, still looking Cal in the eyes. "When Vaughn's medical experiments pass away, he keeps a lock of their hair as a reminder of what he learned. The other healers didn't like that, but for Vaughn, I daresay it's a sign of respect."

He took a tendril of Cal's hair in his fingers and studied it. Marina had to give Cal credit: she stood ramrod straight, unflinching.

"The others are for the ruemin," he said, "but I would like to keep our friend Cal for Vaughn. What do you say?"

His voice was muffled. In fact, everything was. Even the light and shapes in the room blended together until they were no more than blobs. Marina didn't register that Kieron was standing right in front of her until he snapped his fingers.

"I trust you'll try harder tonight," he said, then nodded to Safira. "Please show our guest back."

Safira, not Ryder. Maybe that was Kieron's way of warning her against using magic again. Safira, no doubt, was more than equipped to fend off magical attacks. But even if Marina had wanted to attack Safira, she wasn't sure she could. Her waves had deserted her.

Marina hardly remembered the walk back to her room, and Safira wasn't one to make small talk. When the door of her room shut, Marina fell to the floor, wrenching out a sob and waiting for her tears to come. But they'd deserted her too.

CHAPTER 38
Ineffable

The next day, the short man died. She'd tried the night before—not only to see more, but also to concoct an explanation that would make Kieron happy. It wasn't enough. She failed again the day after, and the limping man's leg was torn from his body before the ruemin devoured the rest of him.

She could feel herself breaking with every scream and the clicks that followed. But the harder she strained to decipher her dreams, the more darkness she encountered.

On the fourth day, when the woman with cold eyes stood before the ruemin, Marina gave in and told Kieron about the voices. He listened intently, and just when she thought she'd placated him, he told her it wasn't enough, and the ruemin took a fourth victim.

Marina couldn't bear it. All she wanted to do was get out of her body, because she couldn't live with the fact that she'd played a role in the deaths of innocents.

It's on me.

Would it have mattered if she *had* given him something useful? Or would those four scouts have died regardless once he came into possession of the Omnia, along with her and everyone else she knew?

What was the difference? It would all be on her anyway. Kieron made it a point to remind her of that, then added that Vaughn was eager to meet Cal.

Marina tried again later that day—hopelessly, desperately—but sleep didn't come easy, and her dreams were all the same: sunlit waves and darkness.

The darkness. *That* was what Kieron wanted. It defied what Marina knew—existed outside of time and space—and she wondered if she'd ever understand it.

She was sitting by the bay window when Ryder came in, listening to the ocean and mulling over her dreams as the sun set. His visit surprised her; after she'd tried to attack

Kieron, Safira had been tasked with escorting her to and from her room. But when Ryder sat at the foot of her bed and sighed, Marina knew he'd come of his own volition. She glanced at him, then rested her elbows on the windowsill and turned back to the sea.

Ryder's voice was strained when he said, "Aren't you going to ask why I'm here?"

Marina only shrugged, her eyes still on the water.

"Are you even trying?" Ryder asked.

Any responses she may've had to that didn't come. She listened to rustling from across the room, only looking at Ryder when he sat beside her.

"Answer me," he said.

"Why do you give a shit?" she breathed. As if he cared about those scouts. He'd said it before: he was on the winning side. Clearly, they weren't.

"Because I think you're self-sabotaging, even if you don't know it."

"Are you an expert on Tempus?" She didn't have the energy to sound sarcastic.

"No. But I'm an expert on self-sabotage. And you're doing it."

Marina's lips quivered. Maybe she was. Maybe the resistance she was encountering was entirely her, which meant she couldn't blame her obscure dreams for her failures. Though she knew she was grasping at straws, she said, "Pierce told me you could help me."

Maybe you can help me now. Please...help me.

Ryder scoffed. "How very in character of him. He won't come rescue you himself, but he expects me to drop everything and help you escape."

Well, it wasn't a no. But it didn't make the bitterness in Ryder's voice any less painful.

Softly, Marina said, "I don't think you know how guilty Pierce feels."

"Guilt is useless."

Marina's chest hollowed. Yes, it was. It couldn't turn back time or right any wrongs. It couldn't bring back the dead.

"That saying about small joys...I've no idea where I heard that," Ryder said. "Probably from the kids I grew up with. But I do know Pierce is the only person I've shared it with." He lowered his voice. "I looked for him when Altus fell, you know—stayed behind because I thought I could find him and we could get out together. There were bodies everywhere... some I knew, all branded with Kieron's sigil. He loves his theatrics." His fingers curled to hide his palms. "But when I couldn't find him, I realized he'd fled before the battle was lost. I had no idea where he'd gone, but what I did know was that he'd gone without me. Tover was killed fighting, and when I heard of his death, I put two and two together and realized he'd probably secured Pierce's safety." He laughed mirthlessly. "Only, nobody knew about the Delve until Ocot showed up. And I didn't realize *that* was where Pierce had run to until you repeated that stupid saying."

Marina swallowed through the stickiness in her mouth. "Why *are* you here?"

"Because I never answered your question," Ryder said. "You asked how I kept my essence hidden from Kieron so he couldn't detect it. Here's your answer: I didn't."

She shifted to face him. "What do you mean?"

"I fought on the Keepers' side when Kieron returned from Sundra—then again when he attacked Altus a second time after seasons in hiding," Ryder said, making sure she heard every word. "It was only *after* the Omnia was sent out—after he'd already taken over the capital—that I got in with him and pretended I'd been loyal all along. Because of the dead years, psychometry wasn't a threat, and I was safe. But I knew the day would come when Kieron regained his abilities, and it wouldn't matter how loyal I'd been. He's too paranoid *not* to use psychometry." A muscle feathered in his jaw. "I might've been the only Elsudran who didn't want the dead years to end. Because when they did, Kieron could figure out who I was...what I could do. I knew he wouldn't sift through my memories—he had other soldiers to check, and that amount of information would damage even Kieron's mind—but he'd see my spirit, and he'd know I was inclined. So I prepared. I was Kieron's ruthless soldier, devoted to my supreme ruler. I arrested, tortured, and killed for him...and in the shadows, I changed myself. When the Omnia returned, I sabotaged every last bit of magical ability I had—altered the parts of my essence that made me who I was. And when Kieron looked in my head, he didn't see who I used to be, but who I was for him."

Shadows dimmed his eyes, and though Marina searched for the words, she couldn't find any. She remembered Aeric warning her about the damage self-sabotage could do, but she hadn't thought someone could do *that*. Had Ryder damaged himself beyond repair? Was that the path she was headed down? Was it all inevitable?

You're spiraling, she told herself. *Stop.* She didn't care enough to listen. Eyes glazed, she turned back to the window, but Ryder took hold of her chin and forced her to look at him.

"Hey," he said. "I'm not saying you're going to do what I did, but you *are* weakening yourself, which is what Kieron wants. He's playing a balancing game right now. Eventually, he'll have you right where he wants you: powerful enough to help him find Exorsus, but so broken that you don't pose a threat."

When he lowered his hand, Marina said, "What's your point?"

"Just. Don't. Sabotage. Yourself," Ryder said through his teeth. "Because if you do, we lose our advantage."

"We? Didn't you say you were on the winning side?"

"I never said which side that was," Ryder retorted. "After you attacked Kieron, I couldn't help but wonder if maybe the tides could change."

Anger flared in Marina's chest. She didn't mind her tone when she snapped, "So you'll just hop from side to side depending on which one you think will win?"

Ryder only shrugged.

She opened her mouth, but there was nothing she could say to that. She'd been selfish in the name of survival before, so she could hardly blame him. Voice low, she said, "I'm not sure what you've been seeing, but to me, it seems like Kieron is winning."

"Dunno, Marina. Call it a hunch, but I think your outburst surprised him. Surprised all of us. It may not have seemed like much, but he hasn't been caught off guard like that in a long time."

She gave him a skeptical look. "Is that why you're badgering me about self-sabotage? Because I surprised you, and now you think maybe it'd be smart to play both sides?"

Ryder chortled. "Or maybe, despite your blackmailing and your sparkling personality, I feel..." He cut himself off and shook his head. "I know Kieron. The more ruthless he becomes, the more desperate he is. And he seems pretty desperate right now." He stood. "I'm not going to pretend I have advice about Tempus, but Kieron's motives go beyond it. He wants you to be a shell of a person when he's done with you. Don't let him win."

Shell of a person. She'd been that before, back in Georgia.

"Ryder," Marina said as he approached the door. He turned, an eyebrow raised, and though she wasn't sure what overtook her, she asked, "Can a sabotaged spirit ever heal?"

Ryder paused, then took a few steps closer to her. "Nobody is damaged beyond repair. I used to think my abilities were gone for good, and I was better off for it. But then you came to Altus, and I started to try again. Not enough to be noticed, but enough. Maybe it's subconscious, or maybe it's because I'm closer to the Omnia than I've ever been, but..."

"But what?"

Ryder inhaled steadily, then took off his glove and held his hand up. His once dry skin glistened with water, and when he flicked it onto her, breathless, Marina gawked at him.

"Anyone can heal," he said, "if they find something worth healing for."

The past few nights, Marina had cried herself to sleep, consumed by grief. But what Ryder had said—what he'd shown her—gave her hope. Not the kind that could win wars or bring about miracles, but a softer, gentler kind.

She still didn't know what she'd say to Kieron or how she'd bargain for Cal, but that night, she let her dreams lead her deeper into darkness's territory. There, she was small and insignificant—a limited, mortal being floating across an expanse of potential, unshackled by time and location. It was what Aeric had said: *ineffable.*

She repeated the word to Kieron the next morning, praying it would sway him.

It didn't.

"Ineffable," he droned, then turned to Ryder. "Fetch the scout from the prisons and bring her to Vaughn, please."

Fear sawed through Marina when Ryder turned to leave.

There had to be something that would stop him. She couldn't break...she couldn't let him do this. Not to Cal. Not to her.

"What do you want to hear?" she snapped. "My dreams have given me nothing but what I've told you. Are you going to keep killing until you realize I'm telling the truth?"

Kieron's eyes shined. "Truth for you, Marina, is such a fragile word."

"Nothing I've said has been a lie."

For some reason, that seemed to amuse Kieron. He chuckled, watching the morning light dance on the marble, then said, "Did you know Aeric paints?"

The buzzing in Marina's head died down as she blinked at him.

"He picked it up as a child," Kieron continued, "and because I cared for him and his education, I told him to abandon it. He was too gifted to waste time smearing colors on a canvas. And although Aeric never brought it up again, I knew he was still painting, even though I'd told him not to."

He lowered his voice. "The thing is, Marina, lies of omission offend me just as much as outright lies. Maybe more so. And unlike Aeric, it isn't just me you're lying to with your silence. You're lying to yourself too. And that, I think, is the most offensive of all."

As hard as Marina tried not to give him a reaction, she knew he sensed her wariness—and he drank in every ounce of it.

"But patience is important," he droned, "and what's more is I believe you're a very sick girl with *very* poor control over her mind. So I will give you another try, even though I've given you more than enough already. But no more omissions, for everyone's sake—your friend's most of all."

It's on me. The deaths of those scouts...they were all on her. Whether her incompetence or resistance was to blame, Marina had no idea, but the ruemin had feasted because *she'd* been incapable of deciphering what was right in front of her.

"The darkness is everywhere," she said, her voice not much more than a whisper. "It's everywhere and nowhere, and it holds everything."

No space...no time.

"It doesn't have a location," she continued. "It exists wherever I am, but no matter how long and far I swim, I'll never be able to reach all of it. It's like I can only access the darkness that makes up my existence, but there's an infinite amount in all directions."

Emptiness. The emptiness beyond.

"I was somewhere similar," she said, "when the Omnia latched onto me. There was no time...no space. It felt...empty."

Kieron angled his head at her. "And?"

Marina's heart thrashed in her ears. Was she mollifying him? What would it mean if she did? Would he leave Cal alone, or would she meet the same fate as the others?

Vaughn, Marina thought, *may be an even worse death than ruemin.*

The hunger in the ruemin's eyes was nothing compared to the morbid curiosity in Vaughn's. The way he looked people over—the way he'd touched her hair...Marina could scarcely imagine what he'd do to Cal. Though every bone in her body fought against it, Marina kept talking, praying it was enough to satiate Kieron, even if it was vague. Even if it was useless.

"When the sun rises over the ocean, it can be opened," she said. "Like a doorway that leads to the darkness. But the darkness isn't a place. Not really."

It created every place.

How much more should she say? She was playing as much of a balancing game as Kieron—only hers was more precarious, and she had no idea if she was succeeding.

But she knew what would happen if she failed. She'd already failed—four times. The fifth would be on her too, all because of things she *didn't* say.

When Kieron turned again to Ryder, fear bleated through Marina's veins, pushing her further into compliance.

"It's not above, or below, or within," she rasped. "It's *beyond* the sea."

Let this save Cal. Let me do what I couldn't—wouldn't—for the others.

It was still vague enough, wasn't it? Even she didn't fully understand what she'd said—what she'd seen.

Though Kieron didn't say anything, his lips edged into a smile.

Had he broken her, just like Ryder warned he would? His threats—his *promises*—were the strings he used to pull her. She'd never been more of a marionette than she was now.

Kieron looked to the side, considering. Finally, he said, "You just bought your friend another day."

CHAPTER 39
Little Cactus

Whatever Kieron was thinking, he didn't tell Marina. Instead, he had her brought back to her room, and she was left in silence once again. If Ryder had come, she may have asked him what she'd done—if she'd been so desperate to save Cal that she'd stumbled over the blurry line she was trying to walk. But he didn't—no one did—and for the rest of the day, Marina felt as though a gauzy veil hung over her mind. She'd been so certain Locus would be Kieron's barrier, and for what?

For failures. For four innocent deaths, and perhaps a fifth, soon enough.

She might've bought Cal another day, but with it, she bought Kieron more means of extortion. Maybe that was what he'd planned all along—to kill those four scouts and work up to his grand threat, having her crumble right when he wanted her to.

It brought her solace to wonder if maybe Kieron would've killed the scouts no matter what—that she couldn't have made a difference either way. Shameful as it was to pray their fates were inevitable, it was the only thing that kept Marina from breaking completely.

But the words circled in her head anyway. *It's on me.*

Safira came for her before dawn, silent as she led Marina outside and down a perron facing the beach.

Marina couldn't get herself to speak in Safira's presence, but she supposed it was smarter to keep quiet. Safira didn't seem the type to be bargained with.

What had happened to her? Ryder had mentioned torture, but not by Kieron's side. Could people fighting against such an oppressive regime really be driven to do such heinous things? What did that make them: good or bad? Was there such a thing?

Head fuzzy, Marina turned to the waves, which stretched in both directions as far as she could see. The ocean was gentle so early in the morning—a flat, blue landscape beneath wispy clouds. It had been so long since she'd been this close to the water. Under better circumstances, she would enjoy the dewy feeling the breeze brought to her skin. But when her feet hit the sand, hands wrapped around her shoulders, and Marina checked to make sure her shields were up.

They were, thank goodness, but she flinched anyway. Kieron was deliberate with his conveyance, just like everything else.

"The ocean air suits you," he said. Marina pivoted to glance at Safira, who'd already begun walking away.

"I've asked a lot," Kieron added. "But if you help me today, one last time, I can return your generosity tenfold."

Can. Not *will.* But she'd never believed him to begin with, and his word choice didn't unnerve her. Not as much as whatever he was leading to.

"Why are we here?" she asked, trying to sound calm.

"I fell into a trap characteristic of our kind. I treated the *ineffable*"—he said the word pointedly—"as something to be understood using natural laws. But you've provided me with valuable insight: what we're looking for is *beyond*, and this is how we get to it."

One after the other, the waves fell. Marina tried to breathe with them. "The ocean?"

"The darkness beyond the sea—accessible at the touch of the rising sun. Isn't that what you said?" Kieron watched a few waves hit the shore before saying, "You filled in the gaps of my knowledge beautifully, and now we can put what we know to use. Complying won't reverse the deaths you're already responsible for, but it's better than nothing."

Marina's heart staggered. *He's trying to upset you. Don't let him.*

She made every effort to wipe the emotion from her face, then said as evenly as she could, "Cal is okay?"

"For now." Kieron stepped toward the water, gesturing for her to follow. "Like I said, you have every tool at your disposal. There's no one more apt to do what the first Keepers did than you, Marina."

What bitter irony. She'd come convinced she'd be Kieron's barrier, only to be his key instead.

Comply, she told herself. *For Cal.*

And then what? Watch her die anyway when Kieron got what he was after?

"But I'm not the first Keepers," Marina said. "I can't find Exorsus."

"I disagree. In fact, I believe it will be even easier for you." He gave her a nudge so she stood on the foreshore. "The first Keepers didn't hold the Omnia when they called to Exorsus. They had to work harder to manipulate it. Their archives were vague, but they *did* detail seasons of work to steer its power in their favor. Now I realize it was the sea—or, more precisely, the darkness beyond the sea—they were trying to reach." Another nudge, this time deeper into the water. "But unlike the first Keepers, you *hold the Omnia.* Do you understand how much of an advantage that gives you? How close you already are to Exorsus, by virtue of what you possess?"

Marina blinked away the salt in her eyes. "I can't."

"I'd like you to do something out of the ordinary," Kieron said. "I'd like you to try before telling me you cannot."

The water lapped against her knees, its spray making the air smell of salt and seaweed.

"Like an early Elsudran, you will forge a connection between yourself and the sea," Kieron said. "And in doing so, the Omnia will find its mother. Let it do the talking. You are no more than its vessel."

Vessel. Host. A temporary bearer of what she'd never asked for, known only in relation to what she held, not who she was. And when she released her hold on it—when Kieron took it from her and held it himself—she would be nothing at all.

Marina stepped deeper into the water, her eyes flitting to the horizon. Feathery rays of the sun had indeed started to rise, casting a reddish tint onto the water.

She couldn't do this.

From beside her, Kieron sighed. "More incentive?"

He took her wrist, then reached into his pocket. He pulled something from it—a lock of ebony hair—which he placed into Marina's palm.

She could feel the blood drain from her face as she raised her eyes to Kieron and hissed, "You said Cal was okay."

Kieron drew out his words when he said, "She is. *For now.*" His lips curled. "If you do as I'm asking, she'll stay that way."

Marina's fingers curled around the tendril of Cal's hair. "Will she?" she choked, her throat so tight she could scarcely breathe. "Or will you kill her like you killed the others, regardless of what I do?"

"Instead of focusing on what you don't know, focus on what you do," Kieron said. "Cal *will* die if you do nothing." He put his hands in his pockets—lazily, indifferently—and when he spoke, his voice was smooth. "Don't blame me for the other scouts. You forced my hand."

It's on me.

A spasm of impatience crossed Kieron's face when Marina didn't move. "I must warn you," he said through a sigh, "that as much as I respect Vaughn, his experiments are of a macabre sort. I don't think either of us wants to see Cal subjected to that."

A wave of nausea rushed through Marina. The ocean current did her no kindness; if

anything, it made the sensation worse, and her knees almost buckled. She forced herself to stand straight, breathing alongside the waves.

One day, one step, one breath at a time.

Cal was only the most recent and tangible of Kieron's threats. Here and now, she had two paths to choose from: refuse or comply. If she chose the former—if she let Cal die by doing nothing—it wouldn't end there. Kieron would go after the Delve, then track down Pierce and Ismene and Aeric.

But if he came into possession of the Omnia, he could very well do the same.

It was paralyzing—a quagmire with no means of escape. All she could do was choose the most immediate path—the simplest step—and do her part to keep Cal from Vaughn.

Her feet sunk into the sand the farther she walked, and when the tidewater was up to her waist, she braced herself for the chill and submerged.

The quietness underwater matched the numbness in her head. There was no sound sweeter than the acoustics of the sea. If she didn't need to breathe, she'd stay here forever.

How far did the ocean span until it reached her home? What channels did it take to cross realms—to connect worlds made by the same creator?

Maybe she was closer to home here than anywhere else. Closer to Georgia, the Delve... all of it. Closer to Exorsus. She could feel a power stirring in her chest, and with it, a wild sort of desperation.

She stood, drenched in water and smelling of salt. By now, the upper rim of the sun had made its way above the horizon.

"Try again," Kieron said.

She only looked at him.

Maybe there was a third path. Safira wasn't here now—nobody was, minus Kieron and her. Maybe she could end this.

She hadn't imagined Kieron's fear; Ryder had noticed it too. In some way, he *did* fear her. Maybe the Omnia did give her an unprecedented advantage. Maybe...

"Have you wondered why it was you the Omnia inhabited?"

Kieron's question brought her thoughts to a halt.

"You perplex me, Marina, more than most," he said, "and I've encountered my fair share of mysteries." If she saw unease in his eyes, it was fleeting. "At first, I thought the Omnia had gravitated to you because your spirit resembles its original host. But I don't think that's it. I think the truth is more humbling: the last Keepers' interpretation of Tempus was wrong. The Omnia didn't wait to be accepted by a powerful being like they believed it would. Instead, it settled on someone as unable to accept as she was to refuse— a little cactus who couldn't withstand storms, and who, in many ways, was as lost as the

Omnia itself."

Little cactus. Her mother's voice echoed in her ears, and Marina's fleeting strength faded. It didn't unnerve her that he'd heard it in her memories, but that he'd remembered.

Of course he had. Kieron remembered everything. Saw everything. He'd seen the flicker of determination in her eyes, then jumped to snuff it out.

Salty water clung to her lashes, and Marina couldn't tell if it was ocean mist or her own tears. She didn't want to believe what he was saying—she knew he was trying to chip away at the measly confidence she'd salvaged—but that didn't mean he was lying. She'd tried so hard to accept that this was a mistake, but maybe it wasn't.

Her chest tightened. She and the Omnia were ghosts in their own ways, cast away by tragedy and desperate to find a home.

A ghost. That's all she was. Nothing.

Spots eddied her vision. *No, no, don't break down. Not now. Come on, Marina.*

Too late. It was always too late.

Dread washed in, pricking her fingers and toes, so cold she began to shiver. And her heart...it was going to cleave in two.

Good. Let it. Let it die, because she was failing. She always failed.

Kieron put his hands on her arms. "If you try anything other than what I'm asking," he said, an edge to his voice, "your friend will die screaming. There are winners and losers in every game, Marina. People like you always break."

People like me. People with storms in their heads. People who fought for every breath—who took one step forward and several back because they'd been born wrong. Because the cracks within them were so deep that no number of days, steps, or breaths could fix them.

She'd tried—and not just in Altus. She'd tried in the Delve to put the broken pieces of herself behind her—to take things in ones and make the next right choice. And for a while, she'd thought maybe she was a different person. A braver one.

But she was wrong. Wrong to think she could ever change, or belong, or be anyone but who she'd always been. Wrong to think coming here would save anyone.

She could put herself back together after every storm did its damage. She could convince herself she was correcting the mistakes she'd made.

It wouldn't matter. Not for her parents. Not for the Delve. Not for Cal. Not for her.

She knew Kieron wanted to lead her into a spiral. This was *exactly* what he intended: to dredge up as much doubt as he could, knowing she was the type of person to crumble under it. Well, he certainly had her pegged. Wasn't that what she was? Consistent?

Slow and quiet, she turned away from him and let the water pull her under—a puppet to the tide, which prodded her back and forth.

In the cobwebs of her memory, that seven-year-old girl flickered into frame, face blank as she counted every wave that crashed to the shore. *One, two, three, four.*

With her eyes closed, the waves around her and the waves within felt much the same. They were all she needed—all the Omnia needed to coax its creator out of hiding.

What came from the sea called to the sea, just like Four had said.

She was more than a conductor of magic. She could feel the Omnia's power as it curled at her fingertips, kissing the water around her. For what felt like seconds and hours and no time at all, the world paused, and Marina wondered if she was still her. Maybe, in this moment, she'd become the Omnia itself, back in the salty water of its birth.

When Marina opened her eyes, however, she was no longer underwater. Somehow, the sea had retreated, and she sat on the sand, her hair and clothes clinging to her skin as her gaze landed on the curling wall of water before her.

For a moment, Marina thought it looked like a tsunami, but the undulating, seismic wave didn't move at her, or in any direction at all. It only pulsed—outward and inward at the same time—morphing the water into fractals. Where the water came together, there was a crevice—a fissure leading into the darkness beyond.

Exorsus.

"Yes," Kieron said as she stood. "Yes, *yes.*"

He repeated it to himself through his teeth, wild with excitement. Marina fought to keep her balance as she tried to peer into the abyss—tried to understand it.

When Kieron raised his hand, Marina realized he was shaking more than she was. Still, he reached out, eyes wide as his fingers brushed against the darkness.

And then, he gasped and recoiled.

Marina might've gasped too had she been able to find her voice. A spray of foam burst from the fissure's mouth, as though it were spitting him out. Though Kieron removed his hand, Marina caught sight of his skin, which seemed to be atrophying. His fingers had turned gray, and though the damage didn't spread, it didn't fade either.

Kieron's mouth opened, then closed, then opened again. When the surprise on his face turned into desperation, he lunged forward once more, his hand out.

This time, the damage reached his knuckles. Before it could lick up the rest of his hand and down his arm, Kieron lurched backward.

He couldn't get in. It was as though Exorsus...the darkness...rejected him. But why?

Who cares? A laugh rose up in Marina's throat. Confusion be damned; he was *failing.*

"No." Kieron's voice was cold. Even when he'd threatened her, he'd never sounded like this. There had always been an undercurrent of slippery charisma and theatrics. Now, he was a wholly different man.

When he grabbed Marina's wrist, the trill in her chest dissolved, and she tried to pull back. But Kieron was stronger, and he forced her arm out until her own fingertips brushed against the darkness. She braced herself for pain—for her fingers to decay like Kieron's—only to feel nothing.

She wasn't sure what she was touching. It was thicker than air, but too ephemeral to be tangible. Even more bewildering was the fact that her hand remained unscathed.

If she hadn't been so awestruck, Marina might've felt glee. She no longer cared about her own failures—not when witnessing Kieron's was so satisfying.

You failed, she wanted to say—to sing. *You failed, just like me.*

Kieron grabbed her shoulders, and the waves began to fall. Marina never saw them hit the sand, though; they were back in the palace before she'd even realized they'd left.

Of all the things she could have fixated on, Marina found herself wondering how he'd so effortlessly conveyed the two of them. The walk back up to the palace was by no means easy, but despite his usually wan features, Kieron hadn't broken a sweat. Perhaps she'd been smart to resist the urge to attack him. Regardless, her relief disappeared when she hit the ground and realized she'd crossed the threshold to her room. Before she could process what had happened, the door slammed shut.

Kieron was gone. He hadn't told her what happened, or why it had—hadn't so much as expressed his anger or shock. Marina's euphoria turned to horror when she remembered that she wasn't his only prisoner.

No...oh, God, no. His failure wasn't her doing, but Kieron was the type to punish her anyway—to punish Cal. He hadn't given her an explanation—no speech sprinkled with self-justification, no threats, no ultimatums, no *nothing.* Perhaps that was the worst reaction he could've had, because now she was left in the dark, free to imagine what he'd do. What he'd have *Vaughn* do.

Marina swung open the door and threw herself at the shield.

"I *helped* you!" she screamed. She cried out again, pounding her fists against the shield. Each touch made her lightheaded to the point of nausea, but she didn't care. She was trembling now—from the cold of her drenched clothes or the heat of her anger, she wasn't sure. She staggered back, facing the shield and squeezing her eyes shut as an unbridled streak of light careened from her hands, larger than the one she'd hurled at Kieron. It hit the shield with a popping sound, then faded. She hurled another current of light at it, and when that didn't destroy the shield, she tried again. Again, again, again...all for naught.

"I helped you find it!" she yelled in empty-handed fury. "I did what you said!"

But Kieron didn't answer. Nobody did, just like she'd expected.

CHAPTER 40
Miracle

She spent the next several hours obsessively washing the saltwater off her clothes and making sure the leather on her boots hadn't been ruined. It was the closest thing to control and distraction she had, but it didn't stop her thoughts from wandering.

Kieron wouldn't hurt Cal. If he couldn't access Exorsus and take the Omnia the way the first Keepers had, he'd be back where he was with the last of them. He'd need Locus, even if he didn't want to use it. He'd need *her*. And he knew she wouldn't cooperate unless he held something over her head. Hurting Cal right now would be idiotic.

Though she thought she never would, Marina longed for Ryder's presence. She wanted to ask him what had happened—if Cal was okay, and why Exorsus had rejected Kieron. But Ryder never came.

As morning turned to noon, then evening, Marina began to wonder what Ryder would say if she asked him to help her escape—more than that, if she offered to vouch for him when they found the others. Would he agree, or would he reckon his odds of survival were better in Altus? Would he help Cal too, or would he refuse? She wouldn't be able to leave without Cal, but Ryder helping with that seemed too good to be true. She'd need to give him good reason to believe such a risk would be worth it, and even then, she wouldn't blame him for turning her down. Kieron wouldn't kill her if she tried to escape, but he'd certainly kill Ryder.

When the sun set, a knock on her door had her up and braced for anything, hoping it was Ryder, but knowing it wouldn't be. It wasn't Safira either.

Kieron used his voco to bypass the shield when she opened the door, and when he smiled, it didn't reek of his usual manipulative charm. It was genuine.

She'd told herself not to expect anything—to be ready for whatever he'd throw at her

—but still, she gawked as he gestured for her to follow and said, "I have good news."

Marina stepped over the threshold, forcing herself to stand tall. She glanced at his hand—at his fingers—but a glove covered the damage Exorsus had done.

She wasn't sure if that evoked pride or horror. When she remembered Vaughn, she blurted, "I need to know if Cal's okay."

"She's fine," Kieron said, his smile twitching. "But if you ask me again, she won't be."

When Marina acquiesced, the smile crept back onto his face.

"Do you know how I survived Sundra?" he asked as he led her down the hallways. Marina knew it was a rhetorical question more than anything else, but she still shook her head—which made Kieron's smile broaden. "Quid pro quos," he said. "It's the language our kind responds to: give and take. The ruemin respond to it too."

When they reached the crenellation, Marina looked out on the twilight, desperate for anything to focus on that wasn't Kieron. Whatever this had to do with Exorsus, she wasn't sure, and Kieron's demeanor unsettled her even more than what he was saying. After what had happened, how could he possibly hold to such confidence?

"I did exactly what you asked," Marina said as Kieron leaned against a merlon.

"Of course you did," Kieron said, peering through the embrasure at the sea. "In a way, the fault lies with me." He sighed with the breeze, keeping his gaze on the ocean when he said, "You've been in Elsudra long enough to learn about the ruemin—about how they're... made differently. They're our only look at unrelated realms. They can teach us so much if we're willing to learn. They're resourceful creatures that never let their prey go to waste— connected in body, but not in mind, and able to understand the tongues of other species. The souls they consume give them the energy they need to propagate—to sustain their kind and continue consuming. But here's something most Elsudrans don't know: ruemin *can't* die of starvation. They may meet their end at a blade or at the hands of a sorcerer, but hunger isn't a death sentence to them. It's just suffering. If they were trapped in a realm without food, they'd starve for an eternity. Cruel, when you think about it."

Marina eyed him, resolving not to react until she knew where he was going with this.

"The Sundrans knew this," Kieron continued. "Their war with the ruemin had driven both sides perilously close to extinction. Only a couple hundred ruemin remained, and even fewer Sundrans. When the ruemin overpowered and began breeding their kind, the Sundrans decided to annihilate themselves, stranding the ruemin in a realm void of souls to eat. By the time Brenna made her portal, the ruemin were desperate." He chuckled mirthlessly. "Our Keepers and court loved the arrangement. They could send their biggest threats to die, then tell the public it was exile and keep up their righteous facade. It was a rare thing to be exiled—and painstakingly orchestrated too. To prevent the possibility of ruemin trying to breed Elsudran exiles, prisoners were sterilized before passing through Brenna's portal."

It was harder to conceal her reaction now. The disgust that barreled through her veins and the conflict that followed were overwhelming.

Kieron stared at Marina, unblinking, when he added, "That was the least of what was taken from me. Everything I had—my magic, my power—was stripped from me in Sundra, and all I could do was wait for Aeric to get me home. I could've given up; I could've let the ruemin feast on me like they had every other Elsudran exile. But instead, I approached them as though they were allies, and I offered them a deal. A quid pro quo."

He folded his hands, running his fingers along the seam of his glove. "The way I saw it, the ruemin were in a bind. Even when they had access to food, wide-scale resistances like the kind the Sundrans had launched resulted in ruemin not only losing mass amounts of their food source before they could feast on souls, but also losing their own numbers. I promised them that if they spared me, I'd bring them back to Elsudra and provide them not just with the occasional prisoner, but with an entire subpopulation—one comprised of inclined Elsudrans and anyone else who posed a threat to the Omnia."

To the Omnia or to you? Marina thought, but she didn't dare say it out loud.

"If the ruemin exercised restraint and did my bidding," Kieron said, "they wouldn't have to worry about armies attacking them—*killing* them, driving their species even closer to extinction. My soldiers would stand down, and when I took power, I'd give the ruemin access to a select food source—one ripe for the picking."

He leaned toward her. "You said it best, Marina: trust goes both ways. We've entered a mutually beneficial partnership, the ruemin and I. They use me to ensure they don't face resistance in Elsudra that eventually cripples them, and I use them to help stomp out those who seek to get rid of me and, consequently, endanger the Omnia itself."

He spoke as though he already held the Omnia, Marina realized. In some twisted way, she wondered if he really *did* view himself and the Omnia as the same thing—if he believed his existence was inherently tied to the Omnia's safety.

"I don't fool myself into thinking the ruemin are truly loyal to me," Kieron said. "They'd kill me in a second if I couldn't supply them with food. But they know that if they kill me, my armies will turn on them. And if they kill my soldiers—if they eat those I haven't given them permission to—I will attempt to kill them. The ruemin are smart creatures; they don't want Sundra to happen again. They know that if they help serve me, their food will never run out. Inclined Elsudrans will always be born, after all, and an apt ruler knows traitors are an ever-growing weed that must be continually pruned."

Marina surprised herself when she mustered the courage to ask, "And what happens when you die?"

"At one point, I'd intended for Aeric to take the Omnia from me and uphold my bargain with the ruemin. But he showed me his true colors. Thankfully, I have Safira." He sighed. "She would've been my successor, had Aeric not been. Perhaps I should've chosen her from the start. When I die, she will take my place as the Omnia's host, then find a new inclined child to succeed her—one she will pardon the way I pardoned her, then raise the way I raised Aeric."

She'll brainwash them, you mean, Marina thought. Again, she held her tongue.

"The cycle will continue," Kieron said, "and the ruemin will remain placated. I told them this in Sundra; I promised their eternal protection. But they needed more insurance."

He turned his gaze back to the sea. "Elsudran portals don't recognize ruemin, you see. They can't get through unless they attach to beings like you and me. The ruemin wanted to make sure I had the means to bring them to Elsudra—that I couldn't leave them behind without endangering myself. And so, to bind myself to my promise and prove its worth, I made a sacrifice: I offered them a piece of my soul. And they accepted."

Kieron straightened, still smiling with his teeth. They'd been so white in Aeric's memories, and his face...it was different now. What was he? Alive, or something less?

"Our kind cannot live for long without their full essence," Kieron said. "When the Keepers used Locus to sever their ties to the Omnia, pieces of their soul went with it, and they died soon after. I find myself in a similar predicament now, which was what the ruemin intended. I rely on them to sustain me, which meant there was no way I could abandon them in Sundra."

His smile widened, and Marina nearly choked. The wine he drank wasn't wine. It was darker—thicker.

"You look appalled. I can't blame you. But ruemin hold on to the souls they devour, remember? My own exists in their blood, defunct as it may be. With but a daily glass, I can keep myself from withering away." He gave her a coaxing look. "Except for Vaughn and Aeric, you're the only one who knows. And I tell you this because I trust you, Marina."

To stop the world from spinning, Marina closed her eyes. Why the hell hadn't Aeric told her this?

Because it would've made her even more scared than she already was—to know how much of a bond Kieron and the ruemin had, and how loyal they were to him. Because she was already grappling with holding the Omnia and all the threats that came with it. Aeric probably left this out for her own peace of mind.

More to himself than to her, Kieron said, "I imagine bits of the Keepers' souls passed to their descendants when they handed over their quarters of the Omnia—especially since they couldn't shield as well as me and you. Had they taken a page from my book perhaps, they could've made up for Locus's damage. But drinking the blood of one's successors is frowned upon, which was why Locus had such fatal consequences for the giving party."

Marina blinked at him, at a loss for how to respond. But Kieron didn't seem to expect a response; he was still watching the sea.

"I survived Sundra because of this quid pro quo," he said. "But I didn't realize how much my sacrifice had hindered me until this morning. Exorsus is a life-giving entity; it's the reason for our ocean and realms, and of course, the Omnia itself. It's the reason for us too—for our *spirits*." He chuckled. "Elsudran children are told that each of our souls is a gift from Exorsus—that even those with marginal magical abilities or nothing at all are divinely made. But when I was a boy, my father told me that notion was pushed by the ordinary to make themselves feel like they mattered. 'Exorsus made you great,' he'd say. 'It made you *better*.'" His smile faded. "There's a cruel irony to it all—to be rejected by the thing that made me who I am. But if Exorsus makes our souls, then as I'm sure you can guess, our souls are what it recognizes. And as it so happens, I've forsaken part of mine."

If she looked at him much longer, the reality of what he'd said would hit her. Since it was much too sickening to stew on, Marina stared out at the ocean instead—at what she knew was beyond it, which seemed as averse to Kieron as she was.

Breathe. One at a time. But the churning in her gut wouldn't go away. When Marina felt Kieron shift toward her, she dared to look at him again—her mouth and throat dry.

Even if Aeric had known about Kieron's dependence on the ruemin, he clearly hadn't anticipated the consequences of Kieron's sacrifice. As of this morning, even *Kieron* hadn't known. But now he did. What did that mean—not for him, but for her?

When her voice obeyed her, Marina said, "I still don't understand—"

"How this could result in a favorable situation for you," Kieron said. "I know." A seagull flew overhead, which he watched before saying, "It wasn't until I stole the Keepers' archives that I realized why they feared Exorsus so deeply, and it has to do with the Daughter Rituals. Tempus and Locus do what Elsudrans cannot but what Exorsus can. And yet, despite all it made, Exorsus doesn't meddle. It doesn't do; it simply is. But if an autonomous individual accessed Exorsus, they would have the power to manipulate what our creator simply watches over."

Her breathing sharpened. "They'd have the power to control *everything*?"

"Nobody can control everything, hard as we may try," Kieron said through a chuckle. "We are, each of us, restrained by our mortal natures. You said that despite the infinite darkness in your dreams, you could only access a small portion of it—the part of the darkness that comprised your existence. You're a product of your realm, and your realm is a product of Exorsus. In the grand scheme of things, you're but one of Exorsus's many creations, and an infinitesimal one at that. Which means if you came into this power, you would have the ability to alter space and time, but only as it pertains to you. Not omnipotent, perhaps, but powerful all the same. That's what our first Keepers did when they took the Omnia for themselves."

And what they were so terrified of. That was the fear she'd felt in the anteactus—the fear of mortals with the power of gods, terrified not by what they could do, but by what others would if they were given the chance.

Marina dug her fingers into her palms. "You don't expect me to—"

"Give me the Omnia? I'd appreciate that, but I'm not foolish. Grand and bright as my ambitions may be, they don't blind me." He took her hands in his, amusement flashing in his eyes at what Marina could only guess was his realization that her shields were up. "You don't want me to become the Omnia's host, and yet you don't want it yourself. Such a conundrum for an already mentally handicapped girl." He said it pointedly, knowing the words would land like physical blows. "But what if there was a way to take away this burden—to make it so you don't have to make the choice at all? And what if, in doing so, you could bring back what you've lost?" When she remained quiet, reeling from dizziness, Kieron added, "If you were able to alter your own life—your own timeline—what changes would you make? Is there anything you'd stop yourself from doing? Any calls you'd prevent yourself from making?"

That rainy night outside the coffee shop flickered at the back of her head.

Though Kieron lowered his voice to a whisper, he made sure she heard every word when he said, "If you hadn't made that call, who would still be with you?"

Marina's vision blurred. "You don't mean..."

Kieron's nod was so subtle she could hardly process it. By the time she had, shock had already settled in, stirring up so many nameless emotions that her head began to spin.

The past few months no longer mattered. Everything she'd built here—from her burgeoning abilities to the home she'd made for herself in the Delve—had been built in the shadow of what she'd lost. Returning to an empty house was one thing; the lure of that option had faded long ago. But returning to her old life—the one before that boy got into his car...before she'd cracked under the pressure of her storms and made that call...

"My parents." Her voice was faraway.

Again, Kieron nodded. "It's clear to me why the Omnia latched onto a being as lost and isolated as it was, and why you unconsciously accepted it. But in a better world, you never would've given it a reason to find you in the first place."

A tear slipped down her cheek. Gentler than ever, Kieron said, "The world has been unkind to you, Marina. You've been asked to make choices that never should have been yours to make. Know when I ask you to make this final choice, I don't do so for me, but for you—so the burdens unjustly thrust upon you disappear, and the people you've lost return in their stead."

The flicker of anger she would've felt at that—he was bullshitting her; Kieron *never* asked for anyone but himself—was nowhere to be found. There was only longing.

Aeric had been right, and though she hated to admit it, so was Kieron. Maybe she *had* unconsciously accepted the Omnia, at least in some manner of speaking. Maybe there didn't exist a being who would deliberately accept the burden of another world—who would forsake their home and shoulder the responsibility of carrying this weight.

The Omnia was of Elsudra—not of Earth, or Sundra, or any of the other realms made by Exorsus. Whatever the Keepers interpreted during Tempus had resulted in an error; for some reason, she happened to be the closest thing to a willing host the Omnia could find. Of all the sorry people in the sister realms, she didn't know why it had to have been her, but if she could change the Keepers' mistake *and* fix her own...

"My parents," she repeated, still not fully present. "They'd be back. With me."

"As they always should've been."

"What about the Omnia?" she whispered. What would happen to it? Did she care?

Of course she did. She still cared for Pierce and Ismene and the rest—for their safety. But her parents...

"It's no trivial feat to change time," Kieron said. "If a single person meddles with the events of their life, everything connected to them changes too." He lowered his hands. "The prophesied host that Tempus guided the last Keepers to was, by virtue of our timeline, always going to be you. But if you were to take away the conditions under which the Omnia latched to you—if your soul wasn't some broken, displaced thing that unwittingly accepted—it never would've settled. You would've disrupted the natural timeline, which would render their ritual ineffective. For all intents and purposes, the host they were so sure of would no longer possess the attributes that made her the host to begin with. You'd be erased from Tempus, and the Keepers would be left without the answer they so desperately sought."

Marina's chest caved in. If not for Tempus, the Keepers never would have sent the Omnia out of Elsudra. Which would mean...

"You'd have more time to seize the Keepers," Marina breathed. *And get them to perform Locus for you.*

"I'd be unaware of all of this—like everyone else. You'd disappear from our timeline, back where you belong, and the Keepers would do what they could to keep the Omnia from me. The only difference is they wouldn't cheat. It'd be a fair game, and nobody can complain about that."

When she hesitated, Kieron said, "Let Elsudrans fight this battle. You've just been presented with a miracle. Take it. Give your life meaning again. Belong somewhere with people who love you for who you are, not what you hold. That's what you want, isn't it?"

Marina's chest began to tingle. It'd been the only thing she'd wanted since August, but since it was impossible to get, she'd resigned to wanting nothing, and then, after some time, wanting other things, like the safety of a world she barely knew. Those things still were important...so why did the choice feel so damned easy?

Because she was a selfish coward, that was why. Because she'd rather go back to that rainy night outside the coffee shop and stop herself from making the call—because it was easier to forget Elsudra and instead use Exorsus to reinvent her life back in Georgia.

"Think of it this way," Kieron said. "You aren't giving me the Omnia; you're giving up the reality in which you came to possess it. Who will take it when the circumstances of time have changed...well, no one can say for certain."

The ache in Marina's stomach grew until it gnawed at her limbs. Maybe it would be best for everyone if she'd never held the Omnia. Best if Kieron took power swiftly, causing fewer casualties. After all, this was a fight for Elsudrans. She wasn't of this realm, and even if she was, she lacked the bravery and self-assuredness she'd need to be of any help. She'd proven that to be the case many times over.

Or maybe...maybe Kieron wouldn't succeed. Maybe when Tempus failed to give the Keepers what they sought, *Aeric* would step up and take the Omnia from them before Kieron could. He'd be unstoppable with it, wouldn't he? He could do what she couldn't; he could take Kieron down and end the threat once and for all.

Maybe Pierce and Ismene and the rest would find a way to live safely. Maybe Cal would never fall into Kieron's clutches...she'd never suffer the way she suffered now.

Maybe. But what could she rely on if not maybes? If there was even the sliver of a chance she could get her parents back—her old life, void of the destruction she'd caused— she couldn't refuse.

Coward, coward, coward.

She'd expected the words to be harder to get out, but there was no reluctance in her voice when she said, "I'll do it."

CHAPTER 41
Plagues and Storms

The crash of waves beyond the bay window beckoned Marina as though Exorsus itself was calling to her. Like a ghost bound to the past, she listened.

Kieron showered her with promises of the life she'd regain, then left her to her room. It was a reminder, no doubt, that she was still his prisoner, and she'd stay that way until the sun rose—until she made her final choice in Elsudra.

It was better to do things this way than have Kieron resort to the violence she knew he was capable of. Pierce, Ismene, Aeric, and the rest would have no one to be angry with because they'd have never known her. And she wouldn't forget them...not really. There'd simply be nothing to remember.

You're not giving the Omnia to Kieron, she reminded herself for the umpteenth time. *You're preventing yourself from receiving it. Besides, Aeric will have the chance to take it himself to protect the Keepers.*

He wouldn't. She'd seen how horrified he was when he'd considered becoming its host, and not because of its power, but because of the man he'd have to challenge. Perhaps, out of everyone in Elsudra, it was Aeric who was most terrified of Kieron.

She tried not to think about that. Kieron was right, after all. This was a fight for Elsudrans, not for her, and no matter how hard she tried, she'd never be more than a vessel to them. Reversing things was the only way to correct the mistake the Keepers had made.

And her parents...that possibility was more than a miracle.

A fresh storm brewed within her—one of euphoria, guilt, despondency, and relief. It was a dizzying mix, and it left her emotions blunted and her senses frayed.

At some point, she'd fallen asleep on the bench beneath the bay window, and when she woke up to the sound of her door, she didn't bristle like she usually did. Instead, she sat up, blinking in the dim light as Ryder's figure grew clearer.

Why was he here?

He flicked on a lamp by the armoire before approaching her.

"I wasn't sent by anyone," he said. "Except maybe my curiosity." He sat beside her, smoothing his pants with his hands. "I saw Kieron a few hours ago. He was happy...and not in his usual, fake way. *Truly* happy. And I didn't ask because it's not my place, but..." Ryder shook his head. "Maybe I shouldn't be here."

"I'm glad you are," Marina said gently. She'd said it to put him at ease, only to realize she *was* glad of his presence. She didn't know how to feel about that.

"I assume you know why he's happy?"

He wanted an explanation. Marina tensed, pausing long enough for the restlessness in Ryder's eyes to turn to fear. He tried to play it off with a laugh, but his voice shook when he said, "It's not fitting for a glorified messenger to be left in the dark."

What was she supposed to tell him? The truth? That would go over horribly. But even if Ryder didn't know the specifics, he was obviously onto something...and he cared. Kieron's ruthless guard—who'd made a place for himself in Altus and played his part so convincingly—cared enough to come here, and now more than ever, it was obvious he didn't like where things were going.

"You're going to be fine," Marina said.

Would he? Flawless as his act was, she wasn't sure it would be sustainable. Judging by the look in Ryder's eyes, it was clear he was thinking the same thing.

"That's not an answer," he said.

No, it wasn't. The answer was much too loathsome to put into words.

Silence hung between them, and when it began to fester, Ryder said, "Would you like to visit Cal?"

Marina's lips parted, but since she wasn't sure she'd heard correctly, she said nothing.

"Yes or no?" Ryder asked impatiently.

"Why would you offer?" she asked. Was he being sincere? Could he really bring her to see Cal? And if he could, why *would* he?

"That's still not an answer."

Marina's chest tightened, and in the wake of an exhale, she whispered, "Yes."

"Good. I'll get you diminution cuffs. Ruemin patrol the prisons, and I don't want to risk any sniffing out the Omnia."

"What?"

"They suppress your essence and your abilities so—"

"I know what the cuffs do," Marina interrupted. "But why are you taking me?"

Ryder only responded with a tight-lipped smile, then slipped from the room. For ten, maybe twenty minutes, Marina racked her brain on all the reasons Ryder could have for taking this kind of risk. He wasn't allowed to let her out of her room—not unless Kieron gave an explicit order—and Ryder didn't strike her as the type of person to take mindless risks...not unless they'd benefit him. How could this possibly benefit him?

Her head was spinning by the time Ryder returned with the cuffs, no different from the ones she'd seen in Aeric's memories. If Kieron couldn't overpower them, she certainly couldn't. She had half a mind to recoil when Ryder grabbed her wrists, but they were in place before she could protest.

"Rules are as follows," he said. "Don't try to wield magic while these are on—it won't work, and it'll tire you out—and stay with me. We're going to do this quickly and quietly, understood?"

Marina nodded. "But why?"

"No questions either. We're going now, before I change my mind."

All Marina could do was blink back her shock as Ryder gestured for her to follow. "Kieron spends his time in the Pale Tower at the far end of the palace, but I don't know where the others are. Keep your head down, and don't react—*especially* to the ruemin."

Was she really doing this? Was he? If they were found, nothing would happen to her, but she couldn't say the same for him.

But Ryder didn't seem to be in the mood for pushback, and he'd clearly made up his mind, so Marina stayed silent as he led her out of her room. If this was her only chance to see Cal, she had to take it. So what if they would forget each other come tomorrow? The sun hadn't risen yet, and Cal still rotted in a cell.

Beyond the balconies and terraces, starlight danced on the ocean. Marina hadn't thought it possible, but the palace was even quieter at night than it was during the day, which made it hard to muffle their footsteps. It was even harder not to feel like someone was watching, but every time Marina glanced over her shoulder, she saw nothing.

The starlight faded as marble turned to common basalt, and by the time they'd completed their descent, the palace looked horribly unlike itself. At first, Marina thought perhaps this area had simply been neglected, but as they passed cracked walls and toppled columns, it looked more like a storm had ransacked the basement. This couldn't be Kieron's doing, could it? Whatever it was, she knew better than to ask Ryder; even their breathing felt too loud.

Eventually, they reached a central chamber, empty except for two stairwells. Though Ryder turned to the right, Marina mindlessly peered down the stairs to the left. When Ryder noticed, he yanked her toward him.

"Stay with me," he hissed.

She fell into place, following Ryder to a door surrounded by locking lugs. Carved into its face was a scanner, which he waved his voco under until the lugs came undone and the door retracted into the wall. Marina caught a glimpse of a second scanner on the other side of the door, and she couldn't help but wonder if it unlocked for ruemin too.

"Look at your feet and follow me," Ryder whispered.

Breathe. Walk. The little commands helped enough to get her moving. She made sure to stay as close to Ryder as possible without stepping on the backs of his shoes, doing her best to walk quietly. Every once in a while, faint *clicks* echoing in the tunnels sent dread careening through her, and she'd hold her breath until they died back down.

Some of the corridors had manholes in the ceiling, which Marina glanced up at as they walked. She squinted to make out the bars that sealed them, but the darkness made it impossible. How Ryder managed to navigate these tunnels was beyond her. She couldn't help but wonder how many times he'd been down here.

At one turn, Marina thought she saw movement above her. When she focused on it— it was coming from one of the manholes—Ryder's arm jutted out and slammed into her.

She knew immediately to look down, and she was glad she did; she had no desire to see the lone ruemin slinking past them.

Click. Click. Click.

If it noticed Ryder, it didn't react. The gold of his armored suit marked him as off-limits, and Marina was grateful to be pressed up against him as the beast passed.

She watched the floor as it walked, glimpsing at its taloned feet before closing her eyes and praying the cuffs worked. She could see those creatures a thousand times, but she'd never get used to them—not when every glint in their silver eyes reminded her that death was looking back.

Once it turned the corner, Ryder resumed walking, exuding confidence she knew he didn't feel. By the time he stopped underneath one of the manholes, Marina had lost count of the number of turns they'd taken. He waved his voco over a scanner, and when the manhole's grated seal moved to the side and a ladder lowered, he said, "Five minutes."

Ears ringing, Marina grasped a cold rung. She was too out of sorts to think about caution, or where she was going, or why Ryder, notoriously pragmatic as he was, had decided to be so unpragmatic for her. Instead, she climbed, blinking in the darkness as she pulled herself through the hole and onto flatter ground.

The cell was windowless, with a single light lodged into the ceiling line. Minus a food slot near the base of one of the walls, a sleeping bench, and a basin, it was empty. Marina almost didn't see Cal at first, but when she caught sight of her on the bench curled toward the wall, the pit in her stomach grew.

And she'd thought *she* was a prisoner. Cal's armored suit had been taken away, replaced by a measly tunic and pants. She didn't even have a blanket. She'd wrapped her arms around herself, but she was still cold when Marina reached out and touched her.

She braced herself as Cal turned to meet her gaze, expecting her to startle. The blank look she received, however, was worse.

"Am I hallucinating?" Cal whispered.

"No," Marina breathed. "No...you're not. It's me."

Cal narrowed her eyes, then sat up. "How did you...?"

"Ryder," she said. "He brought me to see you."

Meekly, Cal rasped, "Why?"

"I don't know," Marina admitted. "But I'm here." She took Cal's hands in her own, hoping to warm them. "Are you okay?"

"Cold and tired, but not dying," Cal said. Her voice shook. "I could've sworn we had laws in Elsudra about the treatment of prisoners."

Marina's heart sank. "I'm so sorry."

Cal was silent for a moment, then let out a weak sob. "Why did you leave?" She brought her knees to her chest. "Kieron told us you came yourself. He said you didn't want to be saved." Marina's chest caved in as Cal repeated, "Dammit, why did you leave?"

"It's complicated," she whispered. "It's not that I didn't want to be saved. I thought I could buy time because—"

"*You* weren't supposed to make those choices. Aeric and Florin were."

"I know," Marina said. She wondered if she'd ever outlive her guilt—if even when she no longer remembered Elsudra, some small sliver of self-hatred would still gnaw away at her. "But I couldn't flee...not when so many people would've been left behind. I had leverage." *At least, I thought I did.* Desperately, she added, "I had to try."

Cal put her head in her hands, running her fingers through her hair, which was so matted Marina couldn't tell where it had been cut.

"Cal," Marina said—pleaded. When she didn't answer, a floodgate opened, and through her tears, Marina whispered, "Why did you come here?"

"Because *I* had to try. When my unit got back to the Delve, we realized what had happened. So I pushed them to come to Altus." She let out a shaky gasp. "I failed too...and now they're dead."

"That's not your fault," Marina said. She repeated it, knowing whatever she said would be useless because no number of words could turn back time.

Exorsus can, she thought. It could take this all away—all the pain and regret.

Only to replace it with more.

She pushed the thought down—down where the rest of her disgrace lay, writhing within her and clawing at her insides.

"They're dead," Cal whispered, tears falling to her lap.

Marina opened her mouth, searching for some consolation to offer Cal, only to have her reassurances ripped from her when Cal muttered, "...and the Delve. It's gone too."

Marina stared at her.

One, two, three, four seconds passed.

Gone. The word bore into her chest and gut, stirring up storms as it wreaked its havoc. The first words Marina uttered were incoherent, but she tried again—and again, and again, until she could finally manage, "When?"

"I don't...don't know," Cal said. "A few days before my unit got back, I think."

How long after I'd left? Did I give them time?

So what if she planned to reverse everything tomorrow? She could wipe every remnant of this reality from the world, and it still wouldn't matter. It wouldn't take away the fact that here and now, real people had felt real fear as they met their ends.

She'd known this would happen—known Kieron wasn't a man of his word, and eventually, he'd do what he'd always intended. What she didn't understand was why he hadn't said anything, unless he'd planned on using the Delve as leverage until he could milk it no longer.

"It was how we knew you were in Altus," Cal continued. Tears rolled down her cheek, and when she wiped them away, the grime on her face smeared. "They'd left a warning to anyone who'd come after the Omnia." She bit back a sob, then said, "They put bodies out to rot in the sun. Winning sides do it to losers during war as punishment, so their bodies will decay before they can be cast out to sea."

This time, Cal couldn't hold back the wrenching sounds that came out of her. She cried into her hands, her hair falling in clumps over her face. As her breathing shallowed and her body began to shake, Marina put her arms around Cal and whispered, "Deep breaths." Her chest threatened to cleave in two, but she ignored it. "Think only about your breathing. Nothing else." Cal's sobs died down bit by bit.

It seemed to help. When Cal could finally control her voice, she rasped, "We tried to identify the bodies. There weren't...weren't as many as there could've been."

Relief sluiced over Marina in waves. "You...you think people got out?"

Cal nodded, sniffling. "I didn't see Aeric or Florin. Didn't see Ismene or Pierce either."

Marina let out an exhale that sounded more like a cry. She didn't know what to think or how to feel—or if any of it would matter—so she yielded to her visceral emotions and let them take their course.

She'd done something right, even if she'd forget it. She hadn't completely failed.

"But Boris," Cal said, and Marina's stomach dropped. "He…"

Marina wasn't able to make out the rest.

"Oh, Cal." The words left Marina's mouth in a breath. "I'm so sorry."

Tears pricked her eyes—of sorrow and grief, perhaps, but mostly of feral anger. Kieron was a plague. Wherever he went, people died, and if it was Boris today, it would be Pierce and Ismene tomorrow. And Aeric…one day, maybe it would be him too.

But perhaps she was no better. Even if she didn't intend for people to die, she brought them to their graves anyway. Kieron knew what he was doing. He meant it. But the destruction she brought was a product of her storms, so violent and unruly she couldn't contain them. When there was no more room for them to do their damage, they burst from her body and swallowed others in their wake.

Plagues and storms…did the difference matter? Was it worth it to wonder?

"You shouldn't have come," Marina said, praying the whirlwind within her didn't get any worse—terrified it would overtake her like it always did, but this time, she wouldn't recover. "Kieron couldn't move forward, and Pierce was going to push Aeric and Florin to gather people beyond the Delve so they could come for the Omnia."

"The Omnia?" Cal choked on a tearful, mirthless laugh. "I don't give a shit about that. I came for *you*. Astra is gone, and now Boris, and…and I care for you like I cared for them. I can't lose you, Marina. You're not a host to me…you're my friend."

Her words were still a jumbled mess, but this time, Marina heard every one of them.

And her storm settled.

Not a vessel. Not a host. Ismene had said something similar, hadn't she?

She didn't know what to say—didn't know if any response would do her emotions justice, so instead, she embraced Cal. She knew Ryder was waiting below, but here and now, it was just the two of them. When Cal's arms wrapped around her, time slowed, and all she could do was listen to the beating of their hearts, thinking of how real this moment was, and how unfathomable that she'd soon forget it.

There was so much she should be scared of—so much she had been scared of moments ago. Kieron, Exorsus, the consequences of the path she planned to choose…all terrifying.

And yet, in this moment, the only thing Marina feared was letting go.

CHAPTER 42
Leave the Loss Behind

The sky was indigo when she emerged from the prisons, and the stars had started to dwindle. Marina's head buzzed all the way back to her room. It wasn't until Ryder shut and locked her door that she asked, "Did you know?"

Of course he did. But why hadn't he told her the Delve was gone? Had he wanted Cal to do it? And if that was the case, what was his reasoning?

Ryder slowly unlocked her cuffs. Once they were off, he said, "It happened a few days after you came here."

She expected to react more severely to that, but all she felt was numbness. Perhaps it was because the hole in her stomach was already there, and nothing could make it larger.

"Did you go?" she asked.

Ryder nodded. "So did Kieron."

"Was this before or after he threatened me out on the crenellation?"

"Before."

Marina closed her eyes and sat at the end of her bed.

"But," Ryder said as he sat next to her, "you still succeeded. They had an extra week—even more—to evacuate. Because *you* refused to flee."

When she didn't open her eyes, Ryder put a hand on her shoulder and said, "I need to know you're listening. Kieron meant to attack the Delve, but it was Aeric he had it out for. He'd left troops behind to keep an eye on things, but once he knew for sure where the Delve was—and that Safira couldn't dismantle the shields on her own—he was quick to go himself. I don't think you understand what a risk that was for him; he hasn't left the palace since the dead years started. But he seemed as desperate to find Aeric as he did the Omnia. Only, when he got there, Aeric was gone—along with nearly one hundred others."

That got Marina to open her eyes. "One hundred?"

She'd known she'd done *something*...but she hadn't expected that number.

"Maybe more," Ryder said. "Ocot had reported around two hundred personnel, but we were met with less than half."

She wasn't sure how to feel about that. Had those people chosen to stay behind, or had they been left? But...one hundred. One hundred people got another chance.

And they were waiting on her to find them.

Coward. The voice at the back of her head screamed it so harshly that Marina flinched.

"I looked for him," Ryder said, and Marina knew he wasn't talking about Aeric. "But I didn't see him either."

Cal had said that too. Of course, that was what Ryder was banking on. He wanted Marina to know how many people had escaped—that Pierce and the others were safe.

But she wanted to hear him say that, so she looked him straight on and asked, "Why did you take me to see Cal?"

Ryder sighed at the ceiling. "Because I may not know exactly what's going on, but I know Kieron, and in a way, I think I know you too. You've come to an agreement...one that's made him happy. So I wanted to remind you what you're fighting for."

Marina stared at him. For the first time, Ryder lowered his mask—not fleetingly or accidentally, but *truly* lowered his mask for her to see the fear in his eyes. And she knew, if she hadn't already, that Pierce had been right.

"I have hope for a world that doesn't include Kieron," Ryder whispered. "I didn't used to...but I do now. And maybe that's worth fighting for. Worth healing for."

Marina's heart sank. She never would've needed to convince Ryder to help her—not when he'd already convinced himself. Not when he'd already decided this was a risk he was willing to take. He'd come to that conclusion on his own, and yet...

What about her parents? *A miracle,* Kieron had said. She couldn't let some misplaced pipe dream pull her away from them.

She hated herself. She'd hated herself long before coming here, and then some of that hate had faded, and now it was back. One hundred people saved, and for what? For her to flee, like she'd told Aeric she wouldn't do? For her to strip those like Ryder of the hope they were willing to fight for?

Ryder braced his hands on his knees, then stood. "I've done all I can do," he said, more to himself than to her.

"Thank you for taking me to see her," Marina said as he neared the door.

For a moment, Ryder's eyes lingered on the floor, where pools of starlight danced. When he finally looked up at her, his mask reappeared. Through a grin, he said, "Turns out

I'll do favors for you even when you don't ask."

Marina stood and leaned against the bedpost. Though her mouth moved before her brain—and though she wasn't entirely sure why—she said, "I'm glad. Because I need to ask you something now."

Ryder raised an eyebrow, and Marina calmed herself—*one day, one step, one breath at a time*—before saying, "Would you do me one more?"

⌇

The night stirred up a mild storm, and come dawn, the sea beyond the palace was as restless as Marina's head. Ryder had left her in the small hours, and though she'd tried, she hadn't gotten any sleep. Instead, she'd gazed into the mirrored ceiling above her bed, strung between choices and overcome with contingencies.

She almost wished Ryder hadn't brought her to Cal because she'd already felt like a horrible person before. Now she felt like a monster. He could agree to all her favors, no matter how outlandish. Was she so cowardly that she'd wipe them all away in Exorsus? Was she so cruel that she'd turn her back on his kindness—on his hope? And if she did, would she remember the path she chose, or would she wake up in the world that was taken from her, surrounded by the people she'd once mourned?

"Now's your chance," Kieron said when they reached the water. "Leave the loss behind and seize what once was an impossibility."

Leave the loss behind. That was all she was doing. In its own way, perhaps it was noble.

Waves simmering with seaweed battered the shore. The reddish tint of first light did nothing to warm the water, which was almost as cold as it had been in the sea cavern. Still, Marina didn't flinch as she submerged. She pushed away the discomfort, refusing to acknowledge the heaviness of her clothes—her limbs and lungs and the gaping hole in her gut—as she pushed the waves within her forward. She could imagine them kissing the water, and when they did—*one, two, three, four*—the sea pulled back.

How small the Omnia seemed in comparison to this. How powerless it was in the face of its creator. It was only when she beheld the darkness that fear pulsed through her. Would it pull her in and devour her so that she became nothing as well?

She wavered, but Kieron gripped her shoulders, pulling her up and prodding her toward the void beyond the sea. When they stood only inches from it, he put his mouth next to her ear and whispered, "Leave the loss behind, Marina."

Numbly, she stepped forward, then reached out and tried to grasp at the shadows, but they were neither here nor there—created not by lack of sun but by nothingness itself.

Leave the loss behind, she repeated to herself, and she stepped into the darkness.

CHAPTER 43
The Girl and the Sea

At first, there was silence. When she began to wonder if it had no end, voices roused her—soft, airy, and ever so familiar. Since hearing was the only sense she had at the moment, she listened, and slowly, the voices grew louder.

Marina, Marina, Marina.

They were clearer than they'd ever been, and they struck a chord so potent they evoked tears. Tears...she could feel them, which meant she had eyes. Now she could see, and shortly after, she could touch as well. She flexed her fingers, then ran them over the rock in front of her. It was cold and wet, like the rocks in the Delve's sea cavern.

She blinked as she took in her surroundings, and for a moment, she wondered if she truly *was* back in the Delve. But as her surroundings materialized and her vision cleared, her flicker of hope faded. If this place was anything at all, it was a tunnel. She wasn't sure which way it led—forward, backward, down, or up—but there was nowhere else to go, so she followed it.

After walking for some time, Marina began to think that it wasn't *leading* anywhere, the same way it wasn't really a tunnel at all. When she touched the water on the walls, she remembered what Aeric had said: the tsunami had been her interpretation of forces beyond her comprehension. This was much the same. Only it wasn't a tsunami that surrounded her; it was Exorsus. At that realization, the tunnel came to an end.

One day, one step, one breath at a time. Keep going.

The rocks beneath her feet turned to water, and the world followed, morphing into a blanket of onyx that spanned endlessly in every direction. There was darkness, but there was also light, and as Marina stopped in the water—puddle or ocean, she couldn't tell— stars flickered around her.

She'd woken to stars like these back in the Delve, but they'd been so transient she hadn't the time to observe them. Here and now, she could, and only then did she realize the glimmers of light weren't stars at all, but dust, glowing with so many colors she could hardly drink them in fast enough.

Marina, Marina, Marina.

The dust fell from above, then faded when it hit the water, consumed by nothingness so exhaustive even darkness didn't dare touch it.

Slowly, she tilted her head upward and swallowed her gasp.

If nothing was below, then everything was above. Though the ceiling was as endless as the floor, it wasn't void of color and light; it *was* color and light, split by water and moved by her gaze. She couldn't explain why or how, but it knew her—acknowledged her, as though it had eyes of its own. The ripples slowed, then came together and descended in a waterspout. Instinctively, Marina reached out her hand. As the water caressed her skin, the nothingness below faded until she was standing on water so calm it looked like a mirror. But it wasn't her reflection she saw. It was home.

Carefully, Marina knelt to the ground, worried the world beneath her feet would break if she moved too quickly. She pressed her palms to the water, then lay face-first against the surface. The movement of her body didn't create waves; instead, the water hardened into something that was neither air nor glass, so wafer-thin that a single step would be all it took to break it.

Somehow, she'd risen to her feet—or maybe the world had shifted and brought her to a stand itself—and she was no longer surrounded by water, dust, and light.

She was home.

It wasn't a permanent thing, this sliver of time and space, but a glimpse at what could be. The lines and edges that formed her living room solidified only when she stepped closer to them, but the smell of strawberry and cinnamon burned through her.

Breathe. One more. Another.

Who had she been in this house? She longed for the familiarity of old as much as she feared what it would bring. Moving backward meant erasing pieces of herself—pieces that had healed without her awareness. Who would she be if she altered that rainy night in late August? Who was she now?

Eyes gummy, she turned down the hallway and neared her dad's office. Her heart pounded as she grasped the knob, but she did what was once unthinkable; she pulled open the door and stepped inside.

Silently, she crossed the room to his guitar, which lay against his desk. Her hands shook as she ran her fingers over the frets, then strummed the strings. The sound careened through her, and she breathed with it as she placed her palms on the soundboard.

She'd spent so long operating under the rules of her own oath—to never sing and never love—but she'd gone and loved anyway. It had crept up on her, and she'd broken one of her vows without even knowing. She'd *chosen* not to waste away. With quiet curiosity, Marina realized where that choice had been made.

Here and now, perhaps she could break another vow.

When she opened her mouth, the usual weight on her chest lifted. Slowly, she pressed her forehead to the guitar and closed her eyes.

And for the first time in months, Marina sang.

She'd almost forgotten what it felt like to soar over high notes and dip into lower ones, but she remembered every word to "Landslide," and she knew her dad would've been proud.

Marina, Marina, Marina. Her parents' voices echoed in her ears.

The girl back in Georgia who'd hated mirrors and slept her days away never would've imagined the changes she'd undergo in Elsudra. She would've scoffed at the idea of fighting—of having something to fight *for*. But now, she did. Wasn't that what Aeric had wanted her to do?

Settle on something to fight for.

Had she already found what she was looking for, here in Elsudra? Had she already found her home?

She'd thought she was fighting for home when she came to the Delve, but all she was fighting for was a place. Home wasn't a place; it was people. It was her mother and father, yes, but it was also Pierce, Ismene, and Cal; Florin, Aeric, and maybe even Ryder.

Marina, Marina, Marina.

It was *their* voices she'd heard—the voices of her friends, so intimate she could've known them her entire life. Since birth, they'd existed in her waves—memories that hadn't been formed yet. There were others too, and even though she couldn't recognize them now, she knew one day she would. In Exorsus, she hovered beyond everything that ever was and would be, only to realize just how small her own existence was.

Small, perhaps, but not insignificant. Every voice she heard meant the world to her, and for the first time, it didn't scare Marina to admit she had friends in Elsudra who she loved. They were home to her. And maybe...maybe she was home to them too.

She didn't want the song to end but knew it must. When she finished, she bid her dad's guitar a tearful farewell, then stood and opened her eyes.

The office was gone. She stood atop wooden stairs—the ones outside her house that led to the sea—and every step was covered in thousands of yellow petals.

Daffodils, she realized as she scooped one up.

She glanced back to where her house would've been, only to be met with sand and emptiness. The sky was empty too—so dark it looked like ink spilled on paper. Down the stairs, the ocean glowed like it did the night she left her house. When she reached the shore, still littered with petals, there was quiet.

She remembered this quiet, but she didn't fear it.

Gradually, the world shrank until the stairs, petals, and sand were gone—until there were only rising waves. Marina couldn't help but wonder if *she* was doing this. Was some subconscious part of her orchestrating what she saw?

The waves parted, forming two monstrosities that hung before her, unmoving. Lightheaded, Marina turned to the first one, where a bleary image of an island came into view. No, not an island: Elsudra. In a palace atop a hill, four veiled figures came together to perform Tempus. They begged Exorsus to guide their hands and help them protect the Omnia, but they were met with silence, for Exorsus never answered. It only watched.

She wrapped her arms around herself as she turned to the second wave, where a girl stood by the ocean. She'd seen this before too. The image flickered, and the girl was older, sitting on a curb outside a coffee shop in the midst of a summer storm. She'd let herself slip that night, causing damage much too large to fix.

But not here. Here, she could fix the mistake she'd made—erase it from every cranny of the universe. Like dominos awaiting a push, the waves stood stagnant.

Leave the loss behind.

She stepped toward the second wave but stopped.

If she were a god, she'd take away her storms and make herself invincible. But she wasn't. And Exorsus wasn't a god either—not really. It was a maker—one that crafted the bones of Elsudra and its sister realms, then watched over its creations like an absent parent. Never wanting. Never feeling. Only watching.

At one point, she'd wanted to do the same. She'd wanted to stop feeling because that was easier. It made her less human, and being human was far too painful for someone like *her* to endure. But then, she'd endured it. She'd endured pain and loss, love and hope. And she hadn't crumbled.

Though it would be easy to exist like this forever, never having to choose one path over the other, she knew she couldn't. She wasn't made that way. She was made to make choices, even if they were painful, and to accept their consequences.

Here she stood, beyond time and space, as bound to her essence as she was outside of Exorsus. She couldn't get rid of her storms, just like she couldn't get rid of her human nature. There was no changing how she'd been made. Only...maybe she didn't need to be changed. Maybe her storms just needed to be weathered.

The girl outside the coffee shop who couldn't think and breathe past her own pain wasn't someone she could bear to be anymore. If she chose that path, who would she be saving? Who would she be *dooming*?

Elsudra didn't deserve to be abandoned. They didn't deserve to have their hope stripped from them. But what of her parents? What of Gemma and Hank?

Leaving the loss behind was impossible. No matter what she chose, *someone* would lose. But here in Elsudra, she'd become someone who had the capacity to do good in the world, even if that world wasn't her own. She had the capacity to help, even if she wasn't all-powerful. That was what the Keepers had wanted, wasn't it?

And she *could* help.

Your essence is exceptionally suited for interaction with magic. She'd ignored Aeric when he'd said that; she'd been too overcome with fear to listen. But maybe he was right. After all, it was she who could access Exorsus—who could ignite fear in Kieron's eyes and break the mask of confidence he'd spent so long perfecting. She could pinpoint glamours quicker than most trained sorcerers. She could break through shields—physical and mental—in mere seconds. And even the things she'd struggled with, she'd learned. She had the aptitude Aeric said she did; she only faltered when she underestimated herself.

But her old life called to her too, and Kieron's voice echoed in her head. *You'll never belong here.*

He was wrong. She did belong here—with the family she'd found.

Elsudran or human...she'd once thought staying would make her neither. But she'd been wrong; it would make her *both*. And her parents...maybe they'd understand her choice to move forward instead of back.

In response, a small but stubborn flicker of affection warmed her. With it came the smell of strawberry-cinnamon cake and the sound of guitar strings, and she knew her parents would be proud—proud she was choosing the kind of life they'd always hoped she'd find the strength to live.

The walls of water were closer than ever now. One step would do the trick. The flicker of warmth within her swelled into a flame, and she looked to her old home—to everything that was and could've been—and smiled through tears.

"I love you," she said.

Then she turned away, faced the wave that held Elsudra, and submerged.

She became part of the sea itself—part of Exorsus—and from the precipice of what was beyond, she found the last Keepers and listened to their cries for help. Silence followed, but Marina didn't wait for some all-powerful being to break it. Perhaps they didn't exist. Here and now, there was only her.

"Out," she said. "Send the Omnia out of Elsudra."

The Keepers hesitated—was their interpretation of Tempus correct?—and she sent her assuredness unto them. It told them what words couldn't: the Omnia would find someone willing and able to help. *She* would find someone. If she was strong enough to stay afloat amidst her storms, then she was strong enough to do this.

"Send the Omnia out," she urged again. "Protect it. When it finds the right host, it will come home." When the Keepers' hesitancy waned, she added, "Let Aeric oversee the Omnia's return. He's made mistakes, but he'll atone. He's the most loyal Elsudran there is."

Though she could feel their uncertainty flare up again, it died down just as quickly.

The Keepers' choices weren't hers to sway, perhaps, but Tempus changed that. The ritual connected them to her, and in this void beyond the sea—outside of time and space—their paths aligned.

"What comes from the sea calls to the sea," Marina said, remembering Four's words.

The Keepers sensed her reassurance, and they obeyed. With Aeric's help, they severed the Omnia from their souls, and before it could remain untethered for too long, Marina directed it to the sea—to the sister realms connected by the ocean. Like a pappus cast from its seed head, the Omnia flitted aimlessly, unable to choose whom or what it inhabited.

That was fine; she'd make the choice for it.

Decades and seconds didn't exist in Exorsus. Time wasn't linear—not really. It was a blanket, a tapestry of events woven together. And Tempus...it had never given Elsudrans answers as much as it had let them peer into an interconnected future.

In that way, Florin's documents were wrong. Tempus wasn't a ritual of guidance.

It was a ritual of *time*.

The landscape condensed, and Marina found the version of herself who was as lost as the Omnia, but who held just as much potential, even if that potential was slower to come about. She floated above, within, and beside herself as she slept, knowing the day had been hard—knowing she'd turned Gemma and Hank away, only to hate herself even more after. This was the girl who'd arrive in the Delve, and she wouldn't make things easy—for herself, for Aeric, for anyone. But she'd do what she'd once thought impossible: she'd start to heal. The pain she carried could never be put down, but she'd find a way to move forward in spite of it.

She roused herself from her sleep, then whispered, "Go outside."

She said it one, then two more times, but tried to be patient with herself, just like she'd promised Pierce. She gave herself time to say goodbye—to soak in the nostalgia of her books and bedroom, to put on the shoes her parents had given her—but she knew if she didn't push herself, she'd linger there forever.

"For God's sake, Marina," she finally said. "Go outside."

Finally, she gave in, and Marina watched herself descend the stairs to the beach. Of course, it wasn't really a beach; nothing here was as it seemed. Even the light that danced atop the water had never truly been light. It was the Omnia—unfathomable, intangible, and brimming with the power of the sun. With a firm, guiding hand, Marina pushed it toward herself.

The Omnia was magic and energy in Elsudra. *Momentum.* It moved the realm forward, one day, one step, one breath at a time. It facilitated the ebb and flow of waves, sculpting the paths of rivers that wound through valleys and spurred the growth of trees and life. It enacted change.

Holding it had changed her. No—*choosing* to hold it had.

One day, perhaps the Omnia would return to its original host. Until then, she would protect it. And even when she no longer hosted the Omnia, her spirit would remain as it had always been: a sea, set alight by the eternal radiance of change.

The sea—*her* sea—brightened with the power of a mighty sun, and Marina almost pitied the girl before her, who watched the rising waves with wide eyes. But it didn't deter her. She controlled every ounce of seawater—pulled it from the deepest parts of her spirit, creating a tsunami so mighty it had the power to transcend worlds. She pushed it toward herself, and as her waves fell from the sky, the girl and the sea became one.

She didn't know where this path would take her or how she'd fare, but the unknowns didn't scare her like they used to.

After all, amidst a thousand mysteries, she knew one thing for certain.

Time and time again, *this* was the path she'd choose.

CHAPTER 44
Puppeteer

The first thing Marina saw was the sun. In the midst of clearing fog, light soaked the world in reddish gold, so divine that even the ocean couldn't compete. Rays caught in a spindrift curled about her head as she stood and realized the sun hadn't yet finished its ascent. It made sense, of course; she'd spent as much time in Exorsus as she had no time at all. But now she was back, and she knew to brace herself.

Kieron was quicker. The moment she stood, the world turned on its head, and Marina went with it. No...that wasn't it. She'd been pushed to the ground.

Instead of hitting the sand, she hit the marble floor of the throne room, rolling out of the way as a lance of energy slammed to the ground and sent the lights above into a frenzy. She shot up, then rallied her waves and returned the attack, which Kieron easily deflected.

"You idiot," he snarled. "Do you know what you've done?!"

"I know what I did." Her voice was calm, and she reveled in it.

Another blast came her way, and Marina shielded herself with hard air. But the blast still knocked her off her feet, and before she could stand, Kieron had her by her collar.

"Do you know who you've defied?" he roared. "I'm a different breed. I shine with everything Elsudra has to offer—with the power that makes our world what it is."

He released her, then stepped back, his face white. "So Exorsus is out of the question," he muttered, delirious. "Fine...that's fine. I'd planned to take the long and painful road with the Keepers; I'll take it with you too. They knew how to engage in Locus without dying mid-ritual. You're younger and more powerful than they were...you'll learn. Isn't that what you whined to Aeric about—what you begged him to help you with?"

"I'll never agree to perform it," she said calmly. Truthfully, she didn't know why she was so levelheaded. Perhaps her fear had yet to catch up to her.

Kieron laughed so hard that the skin around his eyes looked like it was going to snap off. "Of all the wills I've broken, yours will be the easiest. Omnia's host or not, you're the same weak-willed hysterical mess you were when you got your parents killed."

Was she? It seemed he was the hysterical one. He was the one who'd failed.

"Why did fate choose *you*," he asked, "to hold power made by a god?" She wasn't sure if he was really talking to her—wasn't sure if he was all there at the moment. "You are unfit in every way—defined by loss and plagued by fear."

He beheld her, his gaze a cold fire. She eyed the opened throne room door, but instead of bolting, she returned his stare with all the confidence she could muster.

"Fate didn't choose me," she answered. "*I did.*"

It took a moment for what she'd said to sink in, but once it did, Kieron lunged at her, his finger in her face. "I'm going to kill Cal," he hissed between his teeth. "I'll kill her, then I'll find your friends and kill them too—one by one until you *beg* me to help you perform Locus. And when you've finished, I'll kill you as slowly as I killed Four." His hand shook, but he kept it pointed at her. "You think I can't hold out until I get what's mine? That I can't break you down until you comply? The Keepers thought that too. They thought I wouldn't get this far. But here I am. I've achieved things most people only *dream* of."

At Cal's name, the fear she'd anticipated flared up. Still, her voice was even when she said, "Except for taking the Omnia."

"Shut your fucking mouth," Kieron barked. "You want to let the scum of Elsudra rise up and share this power? Then you'd better be able to defend it."

He grasped the sides of her head, and when an inferno of red and white flames came into view, Marina knew what he intended to do. The flames collided with her walls of seawater, their force overwhelming. She rallied the Omnia's magic and her own stamina to fend him off, but his attempt at the dinner table had been child's play compared to this. Kieron's anger fueled him, and he was so close to her he could've been holding the Omnia himself. Proximity strengthened him—she knew it did—but what else could she do if not fight with all she had?

Her shields shook. When a single flame broke loose from the rest and slipped past the seawater, Marina felt her heart drop from afar.

Kieron couldn't see things clearly, but he was edging his way in, and he targeted her most recent memories. Exorsus flashed before them, a mass of ill-lit images. Her eyes were Kieron's, and his were hers; if he got in any further, the images would sharpen, and who knew what he'd be able to do? Perhaps he'd induce delirium or render her unconscious so she couldn't fight back. She couldn't let him. She'd come so far.

Raisel, Thora, Evren, Tover, Boris, Astra. She had to be strong for them.

Normally, at the first indication she was failing, Marina would've given up. She didn't have that luxury anymore. Instead, she pulled every ounce of seawater from the deepest parts of herself and doused the flame, pushing it back out and into the conflagration that surrounded her mind. Kieron's fire sputtered in protest, then licked up her shields and searched for another weak spot. He found nothing.

Maybe she matched him more closely than she'd initially thought. Though she'd never considered it before, Marina couldn't help but wonder if Kieron had never been Elsudra's strongest sorcerer. Maybe he'd simply made everyone think he was by forcing those around him to shrink in his presence. It took skill to make someone like Aeric shrink, but Kieron had done it, year after year. He'd done it to her too, all so she wouldn't be a threat.

She wouldn't shrink now. Her waves swelled with the force of a thousand tsunamis, knocking him off balance. She could feel his fire retreating, and then...

Kieron pulled back, stupefied. Had *she* done that? She braced herself for another attack, but Kieron was preoccupied with the blood oozing from his torso. Flabbergasted, Marina looked to the throne room's door, where Ryder held a rifle out in front of him.

A feral look overtook Kieron. He extended his arms to the side—the way Aeric had when flaying the ruemin—and Marina's body acted automatically. The room blurred, and when she reached Ryder, every shred of power within her erupted.

Power sluiced through her, swathing the two of them in something that was more than a force field of air—something that came from so deep within her that she hardly needed to control it. Whatever surrounded them—air, electricity, or something else—sent Kieron's magic ricocheting. He recovered quickly, then sent another shockwave her way. It collided with the force field she'd created, so intensely Marina's body almost gave out.

Please, she begged the Omnia—the ancient, beautiful, radiant power. *Please help me.*

A wave of strength washed through her, answering her call. But it wasn't the Omnia. It was *her.*

Every inch of her body burned as deeply as her emotions, but she didn't stop.

Do not forget what holds you back, Aeric had said.

Fear. It did more than hold her back; it was her puppeteer. It orchestrated her every thought and movement, and like a compliant marionette, she played the part it wanted her to—lashing out when it gave the order, then freezing just as suddenly. On and on she danced for it, a prisoner to the strings she was bound by, finding it easier to submit than fight back.

No more. Strong as her puppeteer was, she was stronger.

Her blood sang with the magic that coursed through it—the power of the sun itself, wielded by the sea within her. The sea that *was* her. In this moment, she was no more human than she was of the sun and sea, thrumming with a force that couldn't be contested and brought to life by emotions she'd once fought.

Now she accepted them—every single one. The grief, anger, and fear; the love, longing, and hope. Every emotion was hers, deeply and intimately, and she cherished them. They gave her life and fueled her power, and she'd never deprive herself of them again.

Kieron, for what it was worth, managed a few blows to the energy surrounding her and Ryder, but whatever Ryder had shot him with depleted his reserves. When Marina noticed the vapor coming from Kieron's torso, her power faltered, but it didn't wane—not until something hit her from behind.

This time, it was Ryder who lunged at her. The air careened from her lungs as she hit the ground, heart leaping to her ears. When Safira's figure materialized before them, Marina almost felt guilty for assuming the worst.

"Not gonna kill you," Ryder said as he snapped his helmet on.

The fear on her face must've been obvious, but she didn't waste time apologizing—not as Safira curled her hand. What felt like a thousand electrical currents careened across Marina's skin, disorienting her long enough for Kieron to convey in front of her. He didn't use magic; he simply struck her across the face so hard she hit the ground again.

"Aeric did his best," he sneered, "but it'll never be enough. When this is over and the traitors are dead, he'll realize how severely he erred."

In his raving state, Marina realized, Kieron spoke of *Aeric*. Not her, or Ryder, or anyone else who'd wronged him, but Aeric. She didn't have time to let that thought settle in. Safira faced Ryder, golden light lining the metallic half of her face.

"Traitor," she hissed, raising her arms.

Marina wasn't sure what Safira intended to do to Ryder now that his armor covered him. If she couldn't target his skin, perhaps she'd crush him with a lance of light, like Marina had nearly done to Ocot. How long could Elsudran armor hold out under that kind of force?

Either way, Ryder didn't recoil, and Marina could hear the smirk in his voice when he said, "In more ways than one."

It seemed to confuse Safira, if only for a second. When Ryder hurled his own burst of light at her, she swore.

It was small, but blinding—as though a piece of the sun had fallen from the sky and landed in the room. It didn't slam into Safira or cause any damage, but the shock it evoked was useful enough. Kieron said something she couldn't make out, but before he could attack Ryder, Marina sprang up, wrapped her arms around Ryder, and let the room blur.

She'd never conveyed *with* someone, but if Kieron could do it, so could she. She had no idea where she wanted to go—they needed to get out of the palace, but the maze of halls was still foreign to her—so she focused less on precision and more on escaping.

She was more thankful than ever for the palace's opened hallways and doors because she was able to put good distance between them and the throne room. She brought them to an empty corridor—one of hundreds in the palace, which she hoped Kieron wouldn't find—but before they could get moving again, Ryder retracted his helmet and vomited on the floor.

Marina gasped. "Sorry!"

"Not you," he sputtered. "Exerted myself...too much. Used to be able to do that."

Somewhere in the midst of Ryder's adrenaline, a dash of pride made its way onto his face. When he straightened, however, it disappeared. "We need to get outside."

"What about—"

"*Now,*" Ryder hissed. Though he was weighed down by fatigue, he moved quickly. He grabbed Marina's hand, pulling her alongside him with so much momentum she nearly stumbled. "That bullet will hold them up," he added breathlessly. "Safira will have to help him get it out...it'll poison him if he waits. We have time."

Marina nodded frantically, taking great pains to push down the urge to question him. If there was ever a time that warranted trust, this was it.

The sound of distant shouting sent thronging fear through her—how had Kieron mobilized his troops so quickly?—but if anyone knew the ins and outs of the palace, it was Ryder. A side door leading to one of the parapets got them outside, and the two of them crouched as they ran, concealing themselves behind the merlons.

Marina lifted her gaze to the sky, now aswirl with more than just clouds. Yellow and white burned above, as though the sky itself had been set on fire.

Ryder swore—"Down...stay *down,*" he warned her—then turned into one of the towers at the end of the parapet.

It was less a tower than it was an uneven and dimly lit stairwell, and someone stood at the bottom, pressed against the wall with a bag in her hand.

"Cal!" Marina whisper-shouted.

Cal tilted her chin at Ryder. She wore a baldric adorned with just as many weapons as his, and an armored suit just as gold. "The guard said he owed you a favor."

He'd done it. He'd actually done it. Marina opened her mouth to thank him, but since Ryder wasn't in the mood for sentimentalities—that, and they didn't have the time—she simply gave him a nod as he put his voco to the tower door.

"Soldiers will be swarming every battlement in less than a minute," Ryder hissed. "You two need to follow me and stay close. We're getting out of this damned city."

CHAPTER 45
Astra

The sound of the lock coming undone was sweeter than any music. Silently, they made their way down a set of tunnels and narrow staircases. Ryder seemed certain enough of where he was going...until he came to a halt at the end of a stairwell.

A lone guard blinked at them in the darkness, and for a moment, there was silence.

Marina wasn't sure what broke it: the guard's voice, or the cracking sound his neck made when Ryder dug a blade into it.

The guard hadn't known what had happened until his blood began to spill. It was quick, though; Ryder wedged his dagger straight into the guard's jugular, and as the young man fell to the floor, blood pulsing, Marina wondered if Ryder had intentionally given him a quick death.

"Keep going," Ryder commanded, and Marina refused to look at the guard's body as they passed—refused to wonder if Ryder knew him, or if he cared. Instead, she looked to Cal's hip, where Astra's cutlass rested. Knowing she'd gotten it back—knowing Ocot's thievery hadn't robbed Cal of the chance to keep a bit of her sister with her—was enough to keep Marina sane as she stepped over what was less a guard and more a bloody pile of flesh and armor.

The tunnels widened into an antechamber, which led to another door that Ryder dismantled with his voco. When he opened it, the smell of fresh air and salt washed over them. They took the nearest flight of stairs down to a courtyard encased in yew trees, stopping only when a figure emerged from beneath one.

Vaughn was alone, but Marina didn't underestimate the calmness in his eyes. Instead, she steeled herself. Ryder and Cal snapped on their helmets, concealing any remaining bits of skin, and Marina thanked the heavens Ryder had managed to find Cal an armored suit.

Vaughn wouldn't hurt the Omnia's host—not severely, at least—but he'd certainly hurt Ryder and Cal. Even now, his gaze shifted between the two of them hungrily.

"How disappointing," he said airily. "It won't bode well for his mental state to know there was a traitor among us." He smiled at Ryder. "I haven't had such a handsome subject in quite some time."

Instinctively, a lance of light shot from Marina's palms. Though perhaps not the most effective method, it was the most trusted, but Vaughn deflected it as smoothly as Kieron had. He shot his own back at her, which she—along with Cal and Ryder—evaded. Before Marina could return the blow, spindle-like pain ran up her arms. It was like being stabbed with needles, and though it only lasted a second, it caught her off guard long enough for Vaughn to throw something else at her—not a lance of light, but a cluster of shadows. Like fresh tar, they purled over the stones and pooled at her feet, sending her to the ground.

A cracking sound exploded from Ryder's gun, but unlike Kieron, Vaughn was fully present. He shielded against it, then sent more shadows toward Ryder. As they closed in, another bullet grazed Vaughn's arm.

The shadows recoiled as Cal sent another bullet Vaughn's way, which he swathed himself in air to shield from. Vaughn clearly wasn't the fighting type; rather than launch more attacks, he reached into his pocket and pulled something from it—something long and pronged. Marina didn't know what it was until he put it to his lips and blew.

An inhuman screech filled the courtyard, so harrowing that Marina's hands flew to her ears. As terrible as it was, it paled in comparison to the clicks that came after.

Dread coiled in Marina's stomach as she remembered what Vaughn had said about the ruemin knowing his sound. They viewed him as an ally, no doubt—someone they'd protect. Vaughn blew again, still wrapped in his protective bubble of air, calling the ruemin as though he were one of them.

When Vaughn inhaled for a third time, Marina snapped.

Her waves were choppy, white-tipped, and unforgiving. A lance of white light cut through Vaughn's shield, and as he stumbled back, dumbstruck, Marina widened her arms and mirrored Aeric's movements as closely as she could remember.

The crack of breaking bone sounded throughout the yard, followed by the ripping of flesh. It happened so quickly that Marina hardly believed what she'd done until she saw Vaughn's arm on the ground, still holding the ruemin's appendage between his fingers.

She'd ripped his arm off clean, as mercilessly as Aeric had when he'd flayed the fleeing ruemin. She hadn't killed Vaughn—he was still breathing—but as he slumped to the ground in shock, Marina knew he'd bleed out soon enough.

She couldn't bring herself to feel pity for him—couldn't bring herself to feel much of anything as she staggered backward, overcome by a wave of exhaustion. Air careened from her lungs as her body met stone, and though Ryder pulled her up, her legs refused to work on their own.

"We need to go *now*," he said between his teeth.

Marina shook her head—she couldn't even breathe, no less run—still gasping for air as Ryder forced her forward. Cal came up on Marina's side and helped Ryder hoist her up, her voice low when she said, "What happened?"

"She hurt herself, that's what," Ryder hissed.

"You're welcome," Marina breathed. She glanced at Vaughn, who lay motionless as the blood from his severed arm stained the tines in his hand.

"You still have limits," Ryder warned, his grip on her relaxing as she regained control of her legs.

The courtyard narrowed into a flight of stairs that twisted around the side of a hill. Below the vibrantly lit sky, rooftops danced with firelight—as untamed as the howls in the distance. The adrenaline that followed replenished Marina's energy, and she picked up her pace. Horrible as the sounds were, she was almost grateful for them; they got her moving.

As thankful as she was for her adrenaline, the panic that followed wasn't as useful. It ran amok in her chest, meddling so severely with her balance that when the scaled body of a ruemin jumped into view, she nearly fell into its arms. Luckily, if she had, it wouldn't have mattered; the ruemin was dead the moment it landed in front of her. Cal's cutlass made contact with its neck, and in one fell swoop, she severed its head from its shoulders. The sight may've evoked relief had it not been for the shrieks Marina heard in response.

Cal swore, and Marina raised her eyes to the merlon above to see a dozen more ruemin perched on the battlements like gargoyles. They hesitated as they recovered, necks craned and mouths wide as though they were too scared to attack.

The helmets, Marina realized. *Thank God.* But the ruemin weren't easily dissuaded creatures, and when one lunged forward, the others followed. Their talons wrenched dirt from the hillside as they plunged to the stairs, landing as solidly as cats.

The one in front lunged at Marina, but before it could get more than halfway into the air, she stopped in her tracks and opened her arms, flashes of merciless waves behind her lids. The ruemin collapsed, its skin coming undone from its body.

The others bellowed, curling into themselves as though they too had been flayed, but despite her pride—she'd done exactly what Aeric had, just as seamlessly—Marina couldn't fend off the exhaustion. She wasn't used to this kind of magic, and even her confidence couldn't make her invincible.

"Exorsus, Marina," Ryder groaned.

Blinding dizziness swept in, and she could feel herself falling before she took her first stumble. Someone gasped—it might've been her; she wasn't sure—but before she hit the ground, arms wrapped around her.

Cal righted her quickly, then turned and shot another ruemin square in the head. Again, the ones around it howled, giving Cal just enough time to sling her arm around Marina's waist and get a head start.

Idiot, idiot, idiot. Drunk on adrenaline, she'd crossed the line between confidence and brashness, unable to learn from her first mistake. She could've saved her energy and conveyed the three of them to the bottom of the staircase. She'd already depleted a great deal by attacking Vaughn; how in the world had she assumed she'd flay a ruemin and make it out with her energy still intact?

"No more," Ryder barked. "Next time, *think* before you act."

If there *was* a next time...

Marina only nodded as she struggled to keep up with them. Her chest ached as badly as her throat burned, but she continued despite the pain. Anything would be better than being caught by ruemin...by Kieron.

Before they reached the bottom of the stairs, Ryder made a sharp turn into the side of the hill, waving his voco in the air to unlock the door at the bottom. The *click* it made was far more pleasant than the ones behind them, but the sound only seemed to rouse the ruemin further. They careened down the steps, screeching and clicking and digging their nails into stone, but Ryder managed to open the door and get the three of them inside before the ruemin could reach them.

He slammed the door shut, then locked it with his voco, but the ruemin didn't stop there. They pounded on the door, their distorted shrieks coming to a crescendo. Nails met metal as they clawed to get in—to kill, to eat, to bring the Omnia back to Kieron.

How long would the door hold out? One ruemin on its own probably couldn't get through, but a dozen of them—maybe more—would eventually.

The stone beneath their feet turned to water as they made their way through tunnels that mirrored those in the prisons. These channels, however, were smaller—meant to function as passageways.

"Keep on," Ryder commanded in a whisper. "If we take this long enough, it'll bring us to the outskirts of Altus. And Marina, I'm serious. Stop overexerting yourself."

Marina gave him a murmur of agreement. Blinking in the darkness, they trekked forward until the path evened out and the puddles shallowed. Ryder held his arm out, then flicked on a flashlight built into his voco. The light wasn't powerful, but it did the trick, and they continued walking until the sound of ruemin banging on the door became distant thunder. And yet, when the sound stopped, Marina felt no relief. Her gut coiled in the silence, which shattered moments later when a crash echoed through the tunnels.

Ryder cursed. "They're in. *Hurry.*"

The water sloshing about their feet was impossible to silence, but it made the ruemin easier to detect too. They were a couple tunnels behind, but Marina could still hear them splashing. Their nails raked along the walls as they moved, their throats popping and clicking. Marina made it a point to focus on her steps—quick and quiet, that was all that mattered—but as the clicking grew louder, she couldn't help but prepare for the worst. If they were found, would she be able to run? Even now, quickly *walking* drove her to lightheadedness. How stupid had she been to push herself so hard?

Even if she had the strength to convey, she'd have no idea where to go. The tunnels were a maze of stones and darkness festooned with cobwebs. Ryder set his flashlight to its lowest setting—without it, they'd be utterly blind—but even then, Marina feared the light would give them away. Still, she stayed silent as they pushed forward, gathering her energy as best she could.

After a while, Ryder whispered, "We're close. A couple hundred yards should do it."

That wasn't too bad...a couple hundred yards until they were out of these tunnels and farther from the palace—from Altus. And the ruemin...their clicking had faded. That was good; they hadn't detected them.

Scant light illuminating the walls signaled they were close. Eventually, Ryder didn't need the flashlight to see down the bore. He angled his head back at Marina and Cal to nod at them—to reassure them that they were getting out...

...then froze at the high-pitched ring that filled the tunnels. Marina had heard this sound before, back in the Delve on Aragonite's eve.

Ryder swore and wrenched his voco from his wrist, then hurled it into the nearest puddle and stomped on it. The alarm kept on.

"Your voco?" Cal said through a gasp.

"I got rid of the damned tracker," Ryder snapped. "They must've set off the alarm..."

Panic swarmed in, making it hard for Marina to keep a grip on her senses. Hadn't Pierce told her voco alarms rang at a pitch undetectable to ruemin? This didn't sound any different; maybe they couldn't hear it.

Cal seemed to be thinking the same thing. "What about the frequency?"

Ryder shook his head, swearing as he unsheathed his dagger and slammed it into the voco's face. When the screen cracked open, the alarm silenced.

"Kieron set these off," he said between his teeth. "He must've had the alarms remotely altered. He *wants* them to hear."

Marina prayed Ryder was wrong, but she knew as well as he did that Kieron would use whatever he could to keep them from escaping the city. They began moving again, but they only got a few yards before the sound of moving water became a roar.

And the clicking...it was louder than ever.

They broke into a sprint—apparently, she *was* able to run when she was desperate enough—but even at their fastest, they couldn't outpace the ruemin. Though she knew her energy was dangerously low, Marina had half a mind to grab the two of them and convey as far as possible. Before she could, however, Ryder stopped in the middle of a tunnel and shot behind them with the same gun he'd used on Kieron.

His aim was impeccable, as was his planning. The bullet hit the nearest ruemin in its throat, causing it—and the others—to keel and shriek, those horrible clicks now an eddy of retching. As one came to a halt, so did the others, falling over each other and grasping at the tunnel walls with shiny fingers. A few continued on despite their state, but as dense vapor rose in the air, they, too, weakened.

The poison the bullet held was as quick to activate as it was long-lasting, and like bugs writhing under repellent, the ruemin jerked and contorted. Marina's hope flickered to life, only to have it wrenched from her as they passed a fork in one of the tunnels...

...and a mass of scales and teeth sprang forward.

She was on her back before she realized where the ruemin had come from, her head submerged in a puddle which, all things considered, she was grateful for—it buffered the impact her skull would've absorbed had she hit dry ground.

The ruemin held her arms down as it let out a bloodcurdling shriek, the tines on its neck opening so wide that she could see the inside of its throat, which was laced with black veins and filmy saliva.

"*THIEF!*" it roared—*CLICK*—and just as it went to hoist her up, something wet and warm rained down on her face.

Cal stood above her, her cutlass dripping with the ruemin's blood. The shrieks of nearby ruemin ricocheted throughout the tunnels as Cal pulled Marina up. Though her head spun and the urge to faint was overpowering, she continued on, hastening until she could see light—only yards away.

The door at the end of the tunnel was bolted shut, but the window at the top let in sunlight. But without Ryder's voco...

"I can't bypass this," Ryder said, throwing himself against the door in some delusional attempt to break it.

Marina peered out the window—it wasn't glass, but something more resilient, like the stretched acrylic used on airplanes—then put her hands out in front of her.

Ryder's voice echoed in the tunnels. "You're going to hurt yourself…"

No more than she would if they didn't get out of here. She ignored his protests, which died down as she stilled the waves within her—the calm before the storm—then snapped them into action.

A burst of energy catapulted toward the window, hitting it with the strength of a tsunami. The window was made well and put up quite the fight under the pressure she threw at it, but she pushed on as hairline cracks began to form.

Somewhere in the distance, Marina heard Cal swear as a herd of ruemin screeched.

How many *were* there? They'd taken a handful out, perhaps, but that didn't do much —not when one ruemin's calls summoned several more.

The last stretch of the tunnel was long, but the ruemin were fast. Once they turned the nearest corner, they made a beeline for their prey.

Ryder and Cal turned their backs to Marina, preparing to fire at the stampede with what bullets they had left.

Raisel, Thora, Evren, Tover, Boris, Astra.

She had to get out for them. She had to find Aeric and the rest, had to get Ryder and Cal to safety…

Her vision blotted with colors, but Marina didn't yield. With a gasp, she threw even more power forward, ears ringing so loudly she could barely hear the crack the door made as it flew outward.

The world was spinning too furiously for her to maintain balance. As the door hit the ground, so did she, her hip taking the brunt of the fall. In an instant, Ryder had her on her feet, and they stumbled out of the darkness and into the light.

But the ruemin…they were still coming. Marina turned to peer into the mouth of the tunnel, where flashes of silver glinted in the darkness.

They couldn't outrun them. Not like this. Even if she'd had more energy, the ruemin would still be faster. Eventually, they'd catch up.

And the exhaustion…it was overwhelming. She knew she was a dead weight already, but the urge to shut her eyes and rest was so strong she couldn't stop herself from obeying.

Ryder snapped his fingers in front of her face. "Stay with us. We need to move."

"They'll get to us anyway," Cal said. She handed Ryder the bag she'd been carrying. It had weapons and food in it, Marina realized. But why was Cal giving it to him?

Through bleary eyes, Marina watched Cal fiddle with her baldric and take off one of the weapons—a gray shell. Her finger rested on its pin.

"Unless the tunnel goes down, they're going to reach us," Cal said. "This takes seconds to go off, but it covers a ton of ground. Find a place to hunker down or you'll get hit."

The pit in Marina's stomach jolted her awake. "No," she breathed. "No...no, Cal, that's not supposed to happen. You're not supposed to—"

"Those are *last resort* bombs," Ryder protested. Only after he'd said it did concession glint in his eyes—concession Marina couldn't bear to see.

"Don't do this," Marina pleaded. "Come with us. We'll run...I promise, I can run."

"They'll reach us," Ryder whispered. Though Marina's instinct was to hate him for being so unquestioning, she knew *she* was the fool. As the mouth of the tunnel echoed with screeches—louder and louder—she let out a broken cry.

"We can outrun them," she said hopelessly. "I'll get my energy back. Please..."

Cal placed her hands on the sides of Marina's head. "Let me do this," she said, her eyes watery. "Please. Let me do this, Astra."

Everything silenced—every roar in the tunnels, every heartbeat, every breath—and despite the horrible feeling that rose within her, twisting around her organs and squeezing the life out of her, Marina gave in. The human emotions would come later. Now, she could only nod as the name rang in her head: *Astra.*

As Cal turned to the tunnel, Ryder said, "We'll bring him down."

Cal smiled through her tears as she passed the threshold. The darkness swallowed her, but glints of light springing from the blade of her cutlass—of *Astra's* cutlass—remained.

Though her legs had turned to lead, Marina forced herself to keep up with Ryder as they staggered down a slope of tightly packed dirt and stray branches, then ducked behind the largest rock they could find.

Ryder wrapped his arms around her, holding her so tightly that when the bomb went off, she could hardly feel the vibrations that coursed through the soil. Somewhere not too far away, a tree came crashing to the ground. Even the maple above them shook, shedding clusters of leaves from its gnarled branches. Marina watched as they hit the ground, counting those that fell closest to her.

One. *Raisel, Thora.*

Two. *Evren, Tover.*

Three. *Boris, Astra.*

Four. *Cal.*

CHAPTER 46
Silver Lining

The outskirts of Altus were littered with old houses. They weren't as nice as the ones close to the palace, but nowhere near as dilapidated as the slums. Cobbled sidewalks narrowed into stairs that weaved between the residential units, leading to what Marina could only guess were restaurants or smaller city buildings. What drew her in most was how similar the architecture was to that in the Delve.

She might have been more entranced by the sleeping rows of houses and lantern-lined sidewalks had she not been so numb. It was a battle to keep her energy intact and her mind off Cal, but she was thankful for Ryder, who seemed vigilant enough to keep an eye out for both of them.

Both of them. Not all of them.

The lights in the sky clustered around the distant palace, and Marina figured the commotion had probably driven people to hide in their homes—either that or they were never out much in the first place.

"Portals are close," Ryder said. "They'll take us out of the city. But guards still patrol this area, so stay alert. We need to find working vocos."

Marina nodded. She figured they needed working vocos for the portals, but she didn't seek confirmation. She couldn't find the energy to speak.

"Do your best to stay out of sight," Ryder added. "You're bound to stick out covered in ruemin blood."

Marina looked down at her sweater. The once violet blood had dried into an ugly shade of seaweed, and when she realized how much of it covered her, she made a beeline to the nearest alley and vomited.

Ryder came up behind her, sighing impatiently. Though she tried to recover quickly, the nausea wouldn't let up, and she knew it was due to more than the remnants of ruemin that stained her clothes.

"Hurry up," Ryder said. "We need to—"

"Everything okay?"

The unfamiliar voice sent a wave of panic through Marina. She heard Ryder swear under his breath, then leave her side.

"All good," he said. She watched him through the corner of her eye as he slid off his gloves and held up his palms to the two guards who stood at the other end of the street.

The first was a blond woman who wore her hair in a braid. Though she knew it wasn't Safira, Marina couldn't quell her nerves. The style was similar, and the woman was equally as tall. Beside her, a more cautious man glanced at Ryder, then at Marina, his gaze shifting between the two of them.

"Doesn't look good," the woman said.

"She had a run-in with some ruemin," Ryder replied. "I'm helping her get back home. Heard any news from the palace?"

"Only that the city's on lockdown," the woman said. Marina righted herself, trying to look as unsuspicious as she could—an unfortunate civilian caught in the crossfire of all the havoc—but the woman took a step toward her. "You okay?"

Marina nodded. "Just...heading home."

Either her acting was horrible or the woman had already caught on, because she eyed the man next to her, then tilted her head at Ryder. Before she could say anything, however, Ryder already had her in a headlock.

One twist was all it took for the woman to collapse to the ground, eyes vacant. The second guard swore, and as he went to unsheathe one of the weapons on his baldric, Ryder tackled him to the ground. He was a little late—the guard had already managed to pull out one of his daggers. Not the most effective weapon, but suitable for close combat. At the very least, the guard hadn't had time to snap on his helmet.

Instinctively, Marina raised her hands, only for Ryder to hiss, "Don't you dare!"

Okay, fine. He didn't want her to help—didn't want her to waste any more energy. Though she bristled, she realized it was a smart call. She hardly had any left to waste.

In an instant, Ryder was on his feet, his own dagger in hand. He clearly didn't want to attract more attention by use of gunshots, but he also wanted this to be over quickly. As the guard wrenched himself to his feet, Ryder was on him again, blocking the jabs that came his way with ease. It really *was* like dancing. If Pierce had been excellent at combat, Ryder was phenomenal. Somehow, he knew to parry before the guard struck, light rippling off his blade as metal met metal. He scraped his dagger against the guard's breastplate, and when the guard went to block him, Ryder jammed his knife—which he'd managed to draw and keep hidden—into the guard's eye.

A second quick death—this one less clean. Though he was dead the moment the blade met his skull, the guard's legs still moved as he stumbled backward and fell to the ground, his head hitting a jagged patch of stones.

A wet *crack* sounded as Ryder wrenched his knife free. "Look at that. A silver lining."

He lifted the young man's wrist and took his voco for himself, then nodded at the woman's body and gestured for Marina to do the same.

She rushed to the woman's side and, with uncooperative fingers, managed to get the voco undone. Once it was around her own wrist, she breathed, "Sorry."

"Actually, this worked out," Ryder half joked, plucking a few of the weapons from the guards' bodies. Still, the nervousness in his eyes didn't wane until they'd trekked farther west, using alleyways to conceal themselves. Marina followed closely, praying no curious city dweller decided to open their window and report suspicious activity, then praying even harder she'd find a way to wash soon. Though she knew it was silly, she found herself unable to focus on anything but how dirty they were. Perhaps it was best; it distracted her from thinking of Cal.

As the walkways and houses thinned out, untamed trees sprang from the ground and shrouded the sky. The western side of Altus evolved from city to forest, which Marina was thankful for. It was uninhabited out here, and the foliage hid them well. Trees covered the horizon, but every so often, they'd part to reveal what lay beyond. Just south of them, Marina could see the faint outline of a bell tower, which she assumed belonged to the city. She'd never heard it ring, though.

Ryder took Marina's voco from her, then fiddled with both of them to get the trackers out. They were no bigger than button cell batteries, and the moment he removed them, he crushed them beneath his feet.

"Sorry for the long walk," he said after some time. "Portal systems at the center of the city would've been too big a risk."

Marina only nodded. It seemed nods and one-word answers were all she could manage for now. They walked quickly, but not so fast as to draw attention. Still, Marina couldn't keep herself from glancing behind them, half expecting to see ruemin hiding in the trees.

"We won't run into any," Ryder whispered when he realized what she was doing. "And even if we do, ruemin can't get through portals."

When Marina furrowed her brow, he said, "Portals only recognize beings from the sister realms. They'd have to attach to someone to get through." Then, quieter—as though he was trying to reassure himself—he added, "We'll make it."

Eventually, the walkway led to a circular courtyard, empty minus the two of them. At its center was a fountain, but it had been turned off. If it were active, Marina thought, it would look just like the Delve's. In fact, the entire layout of the courtyard mirrored the plaza, but rather than four staircases at each cardinal direction, segmental arches had been built, each made to stand on their own. Marina peered through the nearest one, but there was no bend of light—only the forest beyond.

Ryder gestured for her to come to the fountain, and when she reached his side, he said, "We need to figure out where we're going."

"What do you mean?"

He nodded to a pedestal built into the side of the basin. When he tapped his voco on the screen embedded in the rock, it came to life.

"City lockdown means civilians can't access portals," he said, then grinned wryly. "But the vocos we have don't belong to civilians." He tapped the screen the way one would a phone, then looked to Marina. "If we're trying to find Aeric and the rest, I'd wager you're the only one who'd know where they are."

She bit her lip. Though the first thought that passed through her head was Candens Inlet, her words didn't follow suit.

"The Delve," she said. Ryder opened his mouth, but she cut him off. "I only *think* I know where they went, and if Aeric left something behind, I want to find it before we blindly head off somewhere. Plus, if we *are* being followed, it's better to go where others won't be attacked."

"Are you sure Aeric left something behind?"

"That's what a cautious person would do. It's what *I* would've done."

"A little risky to assume he would've done the same thing, isn't it?"

Marina's answer was immediate. "No, it's not. Even if he didn't think I'd make it back, I wouldn't put it past him to leave something just in case."

Ryder sighed. "Fine, but I don't want to stay anywhere for longer than a single night. If we aren't constantly moving, the chances we'll be found increase exponentially."

He turned back to the screen, then pressed the corner and waved his wrist over it. Instead of asking Marina, he grabbed the wrist she wore her voco on and made a similar motion with it. She watched as he navigated the map now projected on the screen.

"They had that same map on a mural in the Delve," Marina said, mostly to herself.

"Who would have thought that Elsudra would be filled with Elsudran maps?" Ryder muttered. Marina gave him a look but stayed silent. She couldn't tell if he was teasing or being condescending, but she didn't care enough to find out.

She didn't watch as Ryder selected a destination. The screen was buffering, and he'd started to get flustered, swearing at it when it didn't respond. She figured it'd be best to give him space, and she trusted him enough to let him make the choice.

Finally, he got it working, and as the easternmost portal came to life, the view of the forest behind it blurred, replaced by air that rippled in the light. Though Ryder muttered something to himself about how the portals used to work faster, he didn't complain for long. He gestured for Marina to follow him into the mouth of the archway, then said, "If we ever return here, do me a favor and put me out of my misery."

Once again, she couldn't tell if he was joking.

∽

Ryder chose a town called Pirn—a rural settlement nestled in the foothills of the Admare Mountains. He seemed to think it was isolated enough to avoid an influx of Altus guards or anyone who would pose a threat, but he still warned Marina to stay alert.

"This is as good as it'll get if we want to gather ourselves before we head to the Delve," he said as they entered a tiny inn. It was pressed so close to the base of the Admares that it almost looked like it had been built into it. "You're sure that's where you want to go?"

"I'm sure," Marina said curtly.

"Just checking." He shrugged, then added, "There aren't any portals in the Admares, and the terrain isn't the kindest. It'll take around three days, not including possible hold-ups by ruemin or time we'll waste if you lag behind."

"I'm *sure*."

Ryder acquiesced, then sauntered into the inn, his confidence springing to life as he held up his palms to the old man at the front, who gave them a room for free. When he thanked Ryder for his service, there was unease in his eyes, which made it obvious his gratitude wasn't genuine. Marina almost felt bad for the man, but she thanked the heavens anyway that Ryder was still able to look and play the part of one of Kieron's soldiers. Luckily for them both, he'd had ample practice.

"Aren't you worried that man will hear the news and suspect us?" Marina whispered once they'd settled into their room—a measly thing with two cots, no windows, and a tiny hallway leading to a bathroom even smaller.

Ryder slipped off his shoes. "If you're going to shower, do it, or I'll go first."

"You didn't answer me."

"No, I'm not worried," Ryder said. "Pirn is piss-poor, and piss-poor towns care more about evading ruemin and hostile travelers than they do news from Altus. The man out there is scared of Kieron's soldiers, and he thinks I'm one of them. Even if his voco picks up an alert, he'll be too busy cowering at my presence to even *think* we're of interest."

It sounded arrogant, but Marina knew he was right, and it gave her as much hope as it could. When Ryder commented once more on the ruemin blood she was covered in, Marina pushed everything else away and left the room to shower.

There was something magical about water, even in its simplest form. Though the shower was old and the temperature barely got above lukewarm, Marina cherished every second spent washing away the film on her hair and skin. She even ran her clothes under the water—it didn't do much, but it was better than nothing—and when she returned to the room and swapped with Ryder, she forced herself to focus on cleaning her shoes.

For all the peace water and cleanliness offered, it couldn't patch up the hole inside of her. At first, she thought maybe she was hungry, but after finding an apple in Ryder's bag and taking a few bites, she realized that wasn't it, so she resumed cleaning her boots.

Don't think about anything else. Just clean your shoes.

But the hole was growing larger. Now that she wasn't thinking about escaping Altus or finding shelter, she finally had room for emotions.

She didn't regret the choice she'd made in Exorsus—she *couldn't*, lest she sought to destroy herself—but the things that had happened after...

A tear fell onto her boot, and she used it to wash away some of the grime. Another fell, and she did the same, desperate to bring back the ballet-pink color. It seemed to be working, but she couldn't be sure. She couldn't see much of anything because she was crying—sobbing onto her boots and desperately wishing the tears would fill the hole, only to cry harder when she realized they wouldn't. She set her shoes on the floor, then curled up on her cot, the heels of her palms pressed against her eyes.

They'd been so close. *Cal* had been so close.

Let me do this, Astra. The words rang in Marina's head, and she cried harder—for Cal, Astra, Boris, and all the others.

She didn't feel Ryder's presence until he sat beside her, his hand on her shoulder. When she kept crying, he whispered, "We're safe. We got out."

"Cal didn't," she wept. "And what about what I did?" Now everything was coming back, all at the same time. "I think...I might've killed Vaughn." She had no idea if that disturbed her, which upset her even more. "And those scouts," she continued, her words jumbled. "And then I just let Cal go into that tunnel. Who have I become?"

When her sobs finally died down, Ryder said, "Who you had to be."

CHAPTER 47
The Sun Itself

When Marina woke, Ryder was already up, packing their bags.

"Hope you like hiking," he said, grinning hesitantly as she sat up.

She returned his smile with a groggy one of her own. Her dreams had been different. The waves were still there, but less intense than ever, as though they were making room for something else.

"Feeling better?" he asked.

Marina nodded. "Good enough to get going."

The old man wasn't at the front desk, thankfully. Before they left, they nabbed some food stocked at the corner of the entryway, but there was next to nothing of sustenance—a few bags of packaged berries and some nuts. They also found a spare coat in the cloakroom; Marina figured it belonged to the old man, but she didn't protest when Ryder took it for her. Temperatures would drop the closer they got to the Delve, and while Ryder had his armored suit to regulate his body heat, Marina only had a sweater.

The base of the Admare Mountains was gently sloped, but after a few yards, the trail faded out, and Marina knew this wouldn't be the kind of hike she was used to.

"You said it takes three days to get to the Delve?"

"Give or take half a day," he responded, "depending on how quickly we move. Luckily, the glamours and shields won't be intact, so it should be easier to find. And if we run into any ruemin..." Ryder patted the weapons bag he'd attached to his baldric, then grinned smugly. "How's your energy?"

"Better. I won't be useless."

"Good to hear. I want to be quick. We're ahead of anyone who'd come after us, but we need to lie low and keep our guard up." He paused. "I assume you know of any secret exits in the Delve, just in case?"

Marina nodded. "I know of two."

One she preferred much more than the other; she had no desire to use the southern tunnel. But the manor...that could work. And if Aeric had left anything behind, he'd have done so on the third floor.

"Perfect," Ryder said.

Pirn was already chilly, and as they ascended the mountains, frost began to cover the foliage. In some places, sleet fell from the branches of firs and pines, making the already unforgiving ground slippery. Since Ryder knew the terrain better than Marina, she mirrored his movements as best she could.

One day, one step, one breath at a time.

After many steps and breaths, Marina lost herself in her thoughts, which filled her head like static. She feared what she'd see when they reached the Delve—*who* she'd see, if she could even make out the bodies. But that didn't stop her from walking and focusing on what she could control—on what was right in front of her instead of what lay miles ahead.

Raisel, Thora, Evren, Tover, Boris, Astra, Cal.

She was moving forward for them—and for those who were still alive. She had to. When her legs began to ache, she pushed harder, determined to get to the Delve. She'd walk until she couldn't anymore, and then, if she needed to, she'd crawl.

Silently, they picked their way through mountain passes and forests, scarcely stopping to rest and eat. Marina loomed behind Ryder, lifting her eyes every so often to observe the stiffness in his shoulders. His head was buzzing with thoughts too, she realized, and she left him to them.

The chill deepened as the sun set, but it didn't stop her from sweating through her sweater. Whatever; she'd get rid of it and find a spare in the Delve. Instead, Marina paid careful attention to her boots, making sure she didn't step on sharp rocks or anything that might ruin them. She'd cleaned them well enough last night, but bits of leather had started to fall off.

They stopped for the evening in a gully halved by a stream swarming with fish. Ryder took the opportunity to catch a few, and while Marina felt utterly useless watching him, she was thankful for the food.

"How did you learn to do all this?" Marina asked as he started a fire. "Did they teach you in Altus?"

"I learned this as a kid. Grew up next to a river."

"And you taught yourself?"

"Taught myself a lot," he said. Marina thought she detected bitterness in his voice, but she tried to ignore it.

Ryder smothered the fire before they ate. He didn't want it to attract any ruemin, but at this point, Marina wondered if they'd be lucky enough to avoid them entirely. Offhandedly, Ryder had mentioned he hoped his capital armor would dissuade ruemin from attacking, but Marina had a feeling all he was trying to do was reassure her. As desperate as she was to believe him, they both knew ruemin would sense the Omnia if they got too close to her, and they'd quickly deduce that Ryder was helping her stay hidden from Kieron. But for now, the Admare Mountains were quiet. Still, they slept in shifts, pledging to start again come first light.

That night, huddled beneath her coat, the waves in Marina's dreams didn't come. In their absence, a cactus bloomed amidst a desert storm. Rain fell in sheets, and when it let up, daffodils sprang from the cactus's nettled arms. For a while, the desert was sunny, but the storms came again—*would* come again. No matter. The little cactus would stand strong through it all.

Marina, Marina, Marina. The voices morphed into music—guitar strings—and in the air, she could smell strawberries and cinnamon. The scent lingered when she woke and packed up, but it wasn't until they started walking that the realization hit her. When she halted, Ryder quickly said, "You okay?"

"Fine. I just...I realized something."

He raised an eyebrow at her.

"My dreams," she said. "They've changed, and not just a little. They were different. *New.*" When the confusion remained on Ryder's face, she said, "I had a real dream last night. One without waves."

Ryder didn't seem to understand, but she didn't mind. She was more concerned with what the change meant. As they resumed walking, Marina supposed the answer was simple. *She* was changing—*continuing* to change, just like she had in the Delve. Like she would until she took her final step and breath. There was no escaping it.

The thought evoked as much discomfort as it did hope. She let both feelings wash over her, resolving to accept every emotion and change from here on out.

Another first, Marina realized. For the first time ever, she accepted more than her storms and waves. She accepted the girl who came with them, barbs and all.

That was power. And it burned brighter than the sun itself.

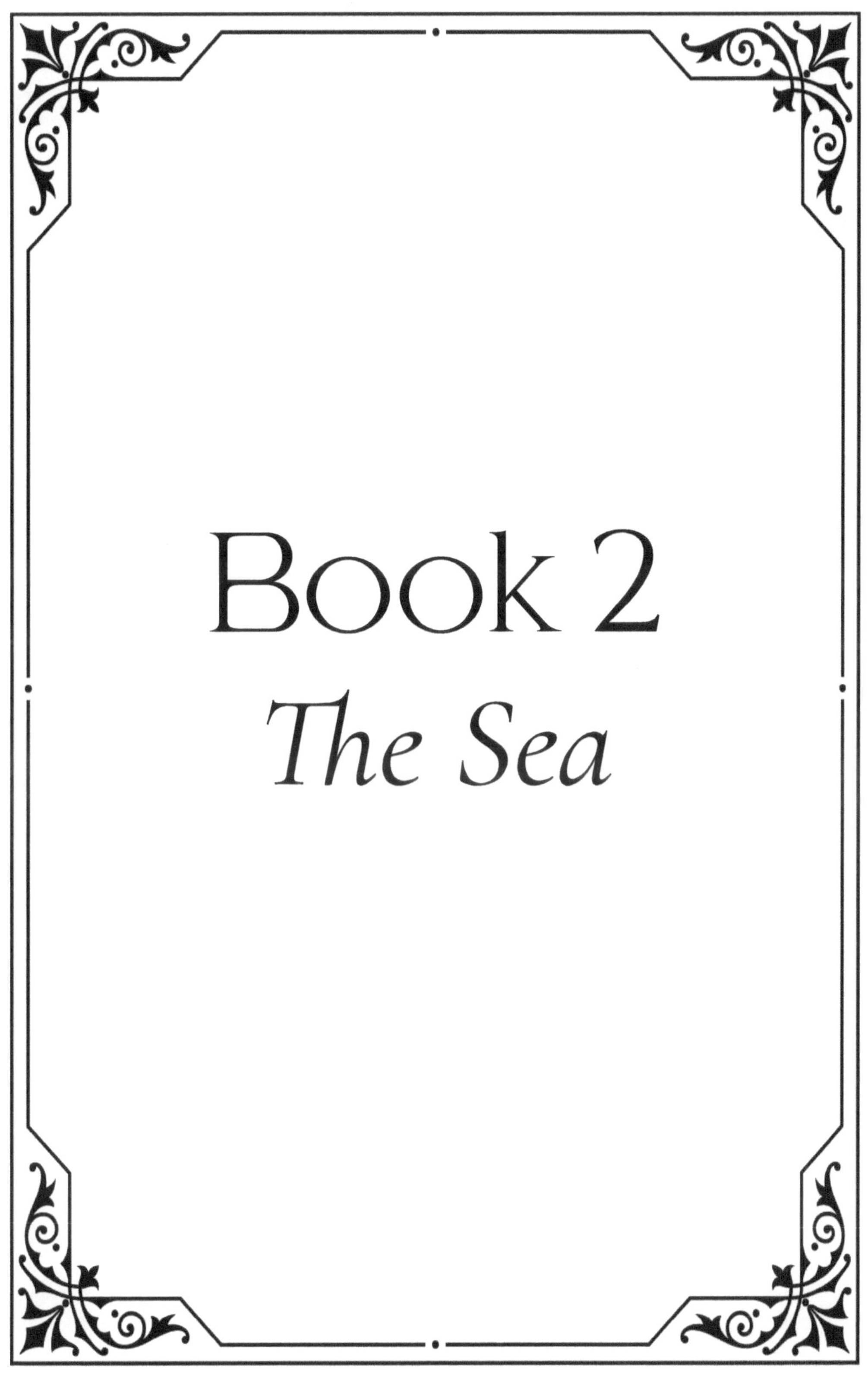

Book 2

The Sea

CHAPTER 1
Morning Stars

Death hung in the air. To distract herself, Marina watched the sky above the Admare Mountains, which glinted with dwindling stars. A few yards away, Ryder surveyed the dead, his hand pressed over his mouth and nose. The climate didn't do much to prevent the smell. It clung to clothing and armor, seeping through even the thickest fabric.

It had only been a few weeks since Kieron had attacked the Delve, and though Marina supposed the cold slowed decomposition, skin didn't do well exposed to the elements. Untouched faces, many of whom she didn't know, had turned ashen, eyes staring into nothing. Jaws rotted off others, and some were missing ears, lips, and noses—picked away by birds, no doubt. But most of them bore the wounds of ruemin—torsos punctured by fangs and limbs shredded by nails just as sharp.

One of these corpses is Boris. The thought—and the smell—made her nauseous. She crouched down and covered her face with her hands.

The last time she'd spoken to Boris, he'd been in the Delve's gardens. Cal had been there too. They'd seemed so happy around each other—as though they were family.

And now they were gone.

One day, one step, one breath at a time.

Only, it was hard to breathe when the air smelled so horrible. She tried another approach: *Raisel, Thora, Evren, Tover, Boris, Astra, Cal.* If she knew the others' names, she'd add them to her list. Who else was amongst the dead? The bumbling greenhouse worker she'd met on Double Moon, or perhaps the elderly cook she'd run into in the manor? She should've asked them their names. Dammit, why hadn't she asked their names?

"Marina," Ryder said. When she looked up, he added, "Think of how many got out."

She nodded numbly, then stood. *One hundred.* Maybe more. Of course, Aeric was probably still furious with her—not like she blamed him. And yet, she didn't regret what she'd done. Not after she'd given one hundred Elsudrans more time to flee.

But not Boris. And Cal...she hadn't even made it out of Altus.

"We don't have to look at them," Ryder said.

"I know," Marina breathed. She didn't add that she felt she had to.

One hundred people may've escaped, but close to an equal number died. The bodies had been spaced evenly in front of the Delve's northernmost entrance, which was no longer hidden by Aeric's glamour. The iron door once built into the face of the rock had been obliterated, and above it, painted symbols gleamed.

"What does that say?" Marina asked. It didn't hold the sheen most Elsudran letters did. It had probably been written by Kieron's soldiers, who had as much of a penchant for theatrics as he did.

"That's in Northern dialect," Ryder said. "I'm from the South, remember?"

She eyed him. That was bullshit. He knew what it said; he'd been there when it was written. He sighed when he realized he hadn't convinced her.

"May their bodies never return to the sea," he read, "as punishment for their sins. May sunlight sear their flesh, cleansing them of treason. Let the dead remind the living: this is the reckoning of thieves. If you follow in their footsteps, you, too, will burn."

Marina's stomach sank. Cal had said as much—that the losing sides in war were left to rot in the sun rather than being sent out to sea, as was Elsudran custom. She'd mentioned this warning too, left behind by Kieron and meant to deter others from keeping the Omnia from him.

Ryder grimaced. "If we're going in, let's get on with it. I'm gonna be sick if I have to smell this any longer."

He was right; it was wretched. The stench filled her mouth just as much as her nose, and she eagerly followed Ryder through the iron door.

The guilt on her face must've been obvious, though, because Ryder said, "The dead don't care whether we stay or go. Trust me."

The smell faded as they made their way into the Delve, and by the time they reached the northern border's watchtower, the air was no longer unbearable. If anything, it was merely...stagnant.

The light outside, stronger now that the sun had started to rise, streamed in through the watchtower windows, dancing off what used to be glowing panels—now blown to bits.

"We destroyed the power grid when we attacked," Ryder said, "so it'll be dark."

His voice shook, and when Marina glanced at him, she thought she saw tears in his eyes. If she did, he shook them away, but the regret on his face remained.

Ryder's demeanor had changed since they'd fled Altus. No longer was he Kieron's smug, dutiful guard. He was a traitor. But that didn't seem to be what unnerved him. As he looked out the watchtower window, eyes flicking over the mountains and trees in the distance, his lips quivered.

She didn't know what to say or feel. He'd killed some of these people himself, and seeing the bodies made it so much harder to forgive him. She wanted to—it would make everything easier—but she couldn't. Not fully. Judging by the look on his face, he couldn't either. And yet, the impulse to hate him for what he'd done was as strong as the one that came after—the one that understood he'd only been trying to survive. She knew Ryder's story: that of a young man desperately searching for the person he loved, only to realize too late that very person had fled to safety without him. Pierce would never forgive himself for what he'd done, and Marina didn't know if—or when—Ryder would let go of the grudge he held.

But who was she to pass judgment, when just a few seasons ago, she'd wanted to abandon this entire realm to save herself? She hardly had a moral scale of her own to weigh Ryder and Pierce's deeds to, so she decided not to at all. She didn't have room for that kind of conflict. All she could think of was *now*—this very moment, and those just ahead—and when she took in Ryder's drawn lips and shiny eyes, she whispered, "You would've been killed if you'd refused." Softer—perhaps to reassure herself too—she added, "Having to do horrible things doesn't make you a horrible person."

Ryder wiped at his eyes. "Sure as shit doesn't make me a good one."

Though her chest hollowed, she didn't say anything else. She'd learned quickly that Ryder preferred to work through things on his own. Once or twice, she'd tried to reassure him that she'd vouch for him when they found the others, but he'd brushed her off. Of course, it was really Pierce he dreaded seeing, but Marina didn't dare bring that up. She knew better than to prod that festering wound.

Ryder cleared his throat, then flicked on his voco's flashlight. "Shall we?"

Marina turned on her own, then nodded. Together, they descended, holding their wrists out in front of them and straining to see past the beams of light. Their flashlights certainly weren't weak, but they were nowhere near as strong as the Delve's floodlights, and as they came to the bottom of the border stairwell, Marina realized how different the caverns looked in the dark. She could barely make out the stalactites that hung above them, and though she knew the Delve's layout well enough, it took her some time to reorient herself as they took the hallways down to the plaza.

She couldn't imagine what it had been like for those still in the Delve when Kieron's soldiers got in. And Ryder...what had it been like for *him*? He'd never told her, but he'd mentioned looking for Pierce among the dead. Had he done that for her or himself?

She didn't ask him. They trekked through the Delve quietly—mechanically—gathering remaining weapons in the south before hitting up the manor. Though Ryder wasn't fond of the idea, Marina convinced him to accompany her to the east and west too. She wasn't sure how long it would take to find Candens Inlet, and she couldn't bear leaving the Delve without having covered all their bases.

She forced herself to focus on collecting supplies, finding she much preferred mindless scavenging to the flurry of emotions simmering within her.

This had once been a place of people—of light and life, even if it was underground. Now, it was silent. Dead. Even the plants in the eastern gardens had wilted now that the power was out. Luckily, storage yielded some canned soup and vegetables, which Marina and Ryder filled a few bags with before heading back to the plaza.

She knew Ryder didn't want to waste any time, but she couldn't help herself when she stopped by the sea cavern's entrance. Even from the plaza, she could see the glow the water gave off. When she set her bags on the ground and peered inside, her throat tightened.

"This was where I woke up," she said, "after I was brought here."

After *she* brought *herself* here.

Though it had only been a few days, Exorsus lingered like a distant memory. She hadn't told Ryder exactly what had happened, but she knew he could sense the changes she'd undergone.

Exorsus. She still couldn't fully fathom it. A maker, a watcher, a void beyond the sea... it was, in many ways, the closest thing to a god the sister realms had. It didn't intervene, perhaps, but it saw. She'd used the Omnia like a key to access the doorway that led beyond, and like the first Keepers, she'd come into contact with a kind of power even the Omnia couldn't compete with. Not omnipotence, perhaps, but enough power to manipulate the tapestry of time as it pertained to her—to fully accept the Omnia and stifle Kieron's ambitions. At least for now.

She'd emerged from Exorsus feeling different. Stronger. Whether or not the change was mental, she could feel the power brewing in her body. She could feel yearning too— yearning for the things she'd given up. Her mom and dad. Gemma and Hank. The people she could've seen again, had she chosen a different path—had she harnessed the power of Exorsus to give her back her old life. But she hadn't.

She accepted her choice, but that didn't stop the emotions from taking their course. They ran through her in waves and brought tears to her eyes.

"I met Cal here too," she added.

Ryder smiled sadly—faintly—and when she reached for her bags, he said, "No hurry."

She appreciated how patient he'd been with her lately. The journey from Pirn to the Delve had already taken half a day longer than expected, and it hadn't been because of Ryder. Marina had never walked that far before, and after a while, she'd started needing more breaks. Thankfully, the urgency Ryder felt leaving Altus had faded upon reaching the Delve and realizing it was empty. Anyone behind them was a day or two out, which meant they had enough time to collect themselves, physically *and* mentally.

Marina leaned against the archway, listening to the lapping water. And clicking... there was distant clicking too.

She spun around, muscles stiff. Ryder heard it too. The sound echoed throughout the plaza and reverberated off rock walls. It wasn't coming from the sea cavern but from one of the stairwells. *Click, click, click.*

"The western one," Ryder breathed, then swore. "We avoid them *all* the way here..."

Marina angled her flashlight across the plaza to the western stairwell and let power crest at her fingertips. Her momentary shock faded, replaced by wild fury at the beasts that lingered in the shadows—that had brought suffering to Sundra and now were *here* because of Kieron, feeding on souls and wreaking havoc as they hunted down those Kieron considered threats. *A mutually beneficial partnership,* he'd called it.

Her anger turned visceral, and the moment Marina caught sight of the tall, scaled figure at the bottom of the western stairwell, rage careened from her hands in a blast of light—so bright the plaza lit up as it whizzed past the fountain. The flashlights on their vocos flickered violently, like the buzzing in Marina's head. She didn't enjoy the feeling, but she accepted it. At the very least, it made the Omnia's power easier to pull from.

At one point, she'd thought of the Omnia as a leech, but now, she regarded it more as a temporary friend. One that gave her abilities a boost, so long as she protected it. And protect it she would—from Kieron *and* the monsters he loved so much.

The light hit the ruemin above its hip, and Marina wasn't sure if the popping she heard was from breaking bone or the tines that jutted from its throat, clicking wildly as the light died down. Its screeches filled the caverns, and when it started toward them again, it limped. Luckily, there was only one, and now it was wounded. Still, it was an uncomely sight: covered in scales, arms hanging below its knees, nails as silver as its eyes.

"Thief," it croaked—*click*—its nostrils flaring as though it sensed the Omnia.

Marina raised her arms again, but Ryder said, "Wait."

He snapped his helmet on, and though the ruemin recoiled, it continued limping toward them. Even on injured legs, it moved quickly and towered a good foot above Ryder.

Marina's heart skipped a beat. "What are you doing?"

"It has something I want." Ryder unsheathed his sword, then muttered, "No way I'm wasting bullets on a straggler."

Marina tensed as the ruemin repeated, "Thief." *Click.*

She met its hungry gaze, her lip curling. One ruemin didn't pose nearly as much of a threat as multiple did. The moment it lunged forward, Ryder's sword met its neck, and Marina watched as its head went flying into the basin of the fountain.

The ruemin's body slumped to the ground, fingers twitching. Marina imagined the others—hundreds of miles away, perhaps—screaming as though they'd been beheaded too.

A chill ran down Marina's spine as she glanced at the ruemin's nails, shining under Ryder's flashlight. He'd decapitated it just above the pronged appendage on its throat, and as he bent down and began cutting away at it with his dagger, she realized *that* was what he'd wanted. When he got it free, he wiped the tines off and placed the appendage in his pocket. Marina neared the fountain, where the ruemin's head floated in shallow water.

"Why do you want that?" she asked.

Ryder retracted his helmet, shrugging as he approached her. "Might be useful. It was for Vaughn, at least."

Marina's heartbeat grew sluggish at the name. She had no idea if Vaughn was still alive, and she was even less certain how she'd feel if he wasn't. Last she'd seen him, he was bleeding out because *she'd* ripped off his arm. She hadn't made the decision consciously; all she'd been able to think about was protecting Cal, Ryder, and herself. If Vaughn hadn't intercepted them in that godforsaken courtyard—if he hadn't called out for hordes of ruemin with the spare appendage he carried—Cal would've made it. She wouldn't have had to take down the tunnel, and she wouldn't be another name on Marina's list.

On second thought, Marina *hoped* Vaughn was dead. It was a cold, unsettling feeling, but it was better than guilt, and in some way, it fueled her.

"Do you think there are more?" she asked, nodding at the ruemin's body.

"The others would've been close if they were. This one probably wandered in through the north and got separated." When Marina relaxed, Ryder nudged her. "If I'd known you could light the place up on your own, I wouldn't have used my flashlight."

Marina laughed weakly. "My stamina needs work." Bursts of power were useful, but they weren't sustainable. Even Exorsus couldn't make her invincible, and as the back of her head began to ache, she yielded to her human nature and sat at the fountain's edge.

Ryder's grin tightened. "Something tells me you'll have plenty of practice."

Absently, Marina nodded, peering once more into the fountain. The ruemin's eyes remained open, staring up at shadowy stalactites. She followed its gaze, imagining what the sky above looked like—the sky the dead stared into, which danced with the ghosts of morning stars.

CHAPTER 2
Made and Broken

Water still worked in the manor, and Marina couldn't get enough. She showered until her fingertips pruned, then changed into a fresh set of clothes she'd found in her old room's wardrobe. Ryder, who'd cleaned up before her, was sitting at the base of her bed when she emerged from the bathroom. He held his palms out in front of him, the sweat on his brow illuminated by his voco's flashlight.

"What are you doing?" she asked.

"Practicing." Light flickered at his fingertips, then faded. "And failing."

"That doesn't look like failing to me."

"You should've seen what I used to be able to do. Couldn't shoot a lance of light, but I could generate it for more than half a second. Guess I hoped it'd help, being close to..." *The Omnia,* he meant. Ryder gestured at her, then shrugged.

Marina sat beside him. "You're being too hard on yourself."

Ryder responded with a grunt, then went back to rearranging their things. They'd found a few more bags to store supplies in, and as he began sorting through them, Marina scanned the room. There wasn't much that was useful, minus extra clothes, but they'd still gone through everything. Ryder had even found a hooded coat for Marina.

"You're going to need it," he'd said. "Your hair's a memorable shade."

He'd found sunglasses for himself in one of the barracks too. The news of their appearances had probably spread throughout Elsudra now, and soldiers would no doubt be on the lookout for a woman with reddish-brown hair and a man with distinct eyes.

One blue, the other green. Pierce had spoken so fondly of Ryder's eyes. How would he react when he saw them again?

If he saw them again. They still had to make it to Candens Inlet.

You will. You have Ryder.

She felt rather useless, putting all her faith in him. But he knew the quickest routes to take and the best towns to recuperate in before heading south. For what it was worth, her memory of the Delve wasn't half bad, and she'd scored them some weapons and medicine.

She wanted to feel thankful for all the supplies they'd found, but gratitude was hard to come by, especially when every room in the manor had been torn apart.

They'd been in and out in under a day, Ryder had said. Kieron, having had it out for Aeric more than anyone else, hadn't spent much time in the Delve. After the massacre, he'd had his soldiers sweep the sections for any useful information, then left when they'd come up empty-handed.

When Ryder spoke of it—of the people he'd killed, even if he'd tried to do it quickly—pain flickered in his eyes. When the pain subsided, bitterness rose in its stead, and he struggled to hide it.

Marina was no better. With every room they passed, the sickening feeling in her stomach grew until it became nauseating to simply breathe.

When she'd first come here, she'd hated the Delve—hated the way the manor halls were more disorienting than the caverns themselves, and how no matter where she went, the lighting gave off the same artificial glow. But somehow, amidst all that hatred—amidst her escape plans and determination to learn Locus so she could rid herself of the Omnia— she'd grown to love this place. And now, she felt like she was mourning her home.

She'd tried to prepare herself for what she'd see when she got here, but actually seeing it was another matter entirely. She'd known what the entrance would look like, just like she knew each room they looked into would be as good as demolished. But every time she opened a door or peered around a corner, she felt like she was either going to be sick or cry. She must've done a bad job hiding the despair on her face because Ryder asked her multiple times if she was okay. All she could bring herself to do was nod, which Ryder clearly knew was a lie, but he didn't press her.

When looking through things became useless—and when Marina wasn't sure she could stomach much more of it—she and Ryder took the hallways down to the end of the second floor.

As they reached the door to the third floor, Ryder asked, "You say it's glamoured?"

"It *was* glamoured. But now that Aeric's gone..."

She put her hand tentatively to the knob, then creaked it open to peer down the stairwell. Only...there was no stairwell. There was just a closet, empty minus a few brooms lying against a wooden wall.

Marina took a step back. "This is definitely where it was." She pushed the brooms to the side, moving her flashlight over the wooden wall and checking for any indications of a door. There were none.

"On the bright side, nobody would've suspected *this*," Ryder said.

"It's not glamoured though. It can't be. Aeric isn't here to reinforce anything."

Ryder tilted his head. "Not everything needs to be hidden by a glamour." He collected the brooms by their handles, then tossed them into the hall. "Especially if the hiding place is easily overlooked."

Marina blinked at him, then breathed, "Behind the wall."

"You said you needed practice with your stamina."

She steeled herself, then gestured for Ryder to move behind her. It was a little trickier to summon sheer force without rushes of adrenaline, but not impossible. She did what she and Aeric had practiced so many times: acknowledged the unruly waves in her head, then opened the floodgates and let their power run free.

She was getting good at throwing light and force. Something about it was natural—exhilarating, even—and this one flew forward as effortlessly as the one in the plaza. The hallway lights, once deadened, flickered as her lance passed, and as it hit the wall, the wood cut sharply in half. The sound echoed throughout the hall, and when the darkened stairwell came into view, Marina let out a breathless laugh.

No magic—just drywall. They must've thrown it up before leaving through the third floor's tunnel. Perhaps that had been the cleverest choice; Kieron didn't know the third floor existed, and an old broom closet, void of any magical energy, was unassuming.

Ryder and Marina took the stairwell quickly. It was still a disorienting trek, but it no longer ended at a stone wall; instead, it widened into the familiar tawny hallway that led to Aeric's office. The tightness in Marina's shoulders eased when they entered, only to tense once more when she took in the state of the room.

Aeric's paintings littered the floor, all of them broken, and the rug once at the center of the room had been thrown face-down over the chaise. Next to it, crumpled paper and shards of glass covered the serpentine table, and it was only when Marina looked to the walls and saw the broken sconces that she realized where the glass had come from.

But Kieron hadn't found this place, which meant...

"How long will it take until Aeric forgives you for leaving?" Ryder asked wryly.

Marina's face went cold, and she lowered her flashlight so she didn't have to look at the mess. Aeric, despite all he was, didn't strike her as someone who'd lash out like this. His anger was quiet—simmering beneath the surface but never boiling over. Until now.

"Can you blame him?" Ryder said. "You'd handed yourself over, and he lost what he was sworn to protect."

She nodded in concession. If anything, she hoped he'd gone easy on Pierce and Ismene, who'd believed in her so deeply they'd broken rules for her.

But that was the path she'd chosen. They'd chosen it too.

One hundred people, she reminded herself. Whether or not they'd all made it to Candens Inlet, she wasn't sure, but at least they hadn't ended up like Boris and the others, rotting away in the Admares.

And...Exorsus. If she hadn't left, she never would've made her decision. Had it been the right one? She couldn't afford to grapple with that. She was *here,* and all she could do was move forward.

She took in the rest of the room. Now that the glamour didn't conceal the stairwell, it stuck out sorely. The stone floor caved in, forming a rocky mouth that plunged into darkness. She wasn't sure how deep into the caverns it funneled, but she knew where it led: to the sea, south of the Admares. Aeric had told her as much.

"How many days do you think it'll take us to get to Candens Inlet?" she asked.

Ryder shrugged. "If we follow the coast for a while, we can cut back through the mountains and find the closest town, then use their portals to get to the South. We'll make our way from there."

"You don't think Kieron could follow us, could he?" Marina asked. Her stomach flipped. "Especially if I just blew down that drywall..."

"That's why we're moving quickly," Ryder said. "Besides, I took the trackers out of our vocos in Altus, remember? And even if they *have* realized where we're headed and follow us to the Delve, we're still a day or two ahead. Once we reach portals, there's no saying where we'd go."

It didn't fully calm her, but Marina nodded anyway. She edged over to the shelves, sweeping her gaze along the old books and loose papers in search of anything useful. She wasn't sure what she was looking for, but if Aeric had left anything behind, he'd have done so here. The first time she found this room, she'd searched just as aimlessly, figuring she'd know what she needed when she found it. How ironic.

Ryder tossed his bags aside, then cleaned off the chaise and lay down on it. "Dibs," he said, then closed his eyes.

Meanwhile, Marina made an effort to flip through each book—determined to look everywhere, even if she found nothing. It wasn't until she peered atop the bookshelf that she realized Brenna's ring was gone. It would've been hard to miss otherwise; it was a massive thing, made to look like a plasma globe. Aeric had taken it with him, no doubt. That didn't surprise her, but it *did* spark her curiosity. Aeric had never told her much about the ring or why he had it. But it was obviously important enough for him to take.

"Ever heard of Brenna's ring?" she asked Ryder.

He didn't open his eyes. "As in 'Sorcerer of the Court' Brenna? I've heard of her portal. Guarded it too. But I've never heard of her ring."

"You guarded her portal?"

"For the Keepers, and later for Kieron," Ryder said. "Well...not the portal, exactly—just the entrance to the room the portal's in, which Kieron has made almost impossible to get to, let alone get inside of. When he took up residence in Altus, he heightened the security leading to the room—had a bunch of defensive technology built during the dead years in preparation, then incorporated magic when they ended. You can't even get there directly anymore without setting off alarms. Guards take underground tunnels instead."

"Why did he heighten security?"

Grimly, Ryder said, "My job wasn't to ask questions."

After a prolonged lapse of silence, Marina whispered, "How did you get in with him?"

She'd wondered it since meeting him but had been too preoccupied to genuinely ask. Even now, she said it carefully, unsure how he'd react.

When Ryder didn't answer, she twisted her head to look at him. He'd opened his eyes and was staring at her with a tight jaw.

"What?" she said. "I'm asking seriously this time."

"We just escaped. Can I get *one* day where I don't have to think about the man?"

Marina held his gaze. Their only source of light came from their vocos, but she could still make out enough of his expression to know he wasn't going to budge. Though she sighed, she acquiesced and turned her flashlight back to the shelf.

Ryder shifted. "What about you?" he finally whispered. "Did you really find Exorsus?"

Marina nodded, then figured if Ryder wasn't going to tell her about Kieron, she might as well fill the silence by telling him about Exorsus. She spoke as she wandered the room, explaining what Exorsus was, as best she could, and why the first Keepers had feared it so much. She told him how Exorsus had rejected Kieron because of what he'd done in Sundra —how he'd offered a piece of his soul to the ruemin, ensuring he wouldn't abandon them when he returned to Elsudra, only to damn himself to a life drinking their blood to stay alive. Even then, Exorsus hadn't recognized him as one of its creations and had lashed out at him when he'd tried to access it. Then, she told Ryder what Kieron had wanted her to do, and how she hadn't done it—how she hadn't just prevented him from obtaining the Omnia, but how she'd taken it from him herself.

At some point, Ryder got up and began conducting his own mindless search around the room as he listened. Though he seemed particularly unnerved by Kieron's dependence on the ruemin and the details Marina gave about *how* Exorsus rejected him—atrophying his fingers so badly he had to wear a glove to hide the damage—Ryder kept his reactions minimal. When she finished, he lingered by the serpentine table, silent.

"No wonder the ruemin call you a thief," he finally said.

A shaky smile tugged at Marina's lips, but it didn't stay. "Cal told me once that we may not be able to control the way of the world, but we can control the paths we choose. There might've been a thousand paths for me in Exorsus, but only two mattered, and only one was right. So I chose the best path I could, and now all I can do is walk it."

"Here's to walking it, then," Ryder said. He clicked open a tortoiseshell box, and Marina only half noticed him pull the brass instrument out of it. When he put it to his eye, she realized what it was.

"Don't!" she gasped.

Ryder jumped, dropping the device on the table. "What's wrong with you?"

"That's an—"

"Anteactus," Ryder said, annoyed. "Obviously. You realize *I'm* Elsudran, right?"

"The last time I put that to my eye, it made me delirious. Aeric said the government ones hold too much information to be absorbed in one sitting."

"I appreciate your concern, but this one's been destroyed." Ryder held up the anteactus and weighed it in his hand. "It's just a shell. The internal technology has been removed. There's something else inside."

She furrowed her brow. "Can you get it out?"

"Dunno. It'll be hard."

Marina's heart began to flutter. "How hard? Maybe we could—"

She paused when Ryder undid a screw on the top and tipped the anteactus over. A thinner instrument slid from its body and clinked onto the wood.

"I was kidding," he said.

Marina shot him a look as she approached the table.

"A whistle," she breathed. Only a few inches long, it was attached to a cable brass chain and wrapped in a note that read: *Use in the forest. Friends will answer.*

"Think it's from Aeric?" Ryder asked.

"Has to be," Marina muttered. How hadn't she thought of the anteactus? She gave Ryder a grin, then said, "Good job finding that."

"And you wonder why Kieron valued me," he said. He was joking, but that was good—good he was able to find some wry humor hidden amongst the horror of everything. Maybe one day, he'd satiate her curiosity and tell her how he'd made Kieron, of all people, trust him so implicitly. For now, jokes would do.

She turned back to the note, which glistened in the scant light. "Is there a forest near

Candens Inlet?"

Ryder made a face. "There is, but it's wetland. Absolute shit to travel through. I grew up in a nearby town, and nobody went there. Not unless they wanted to risk getting torn apart by alligators."

"Maybe that's why they chose it."

"Maybe. But there are few places to hide...unless you're a fish." He paused. "Or a bird."

"Do you think Aeric means a different forest?"

Ryder shrugged. "You know him better than I do."

Marina bit the inside of her cheek. Aeric wouldn't have specified the forest; he'd have been too paranoid that the note would be intercepted. But he clearly expected her to know—and judging by its hiding spot, this note *was* for her—which meant he had to be referring to Candens Inlet.

When she told Ryder, he sighed. "I hope you're right. The land is covered in swamps, and the trees are some of the tallest in Elsudra. Whoever these people are, they took full advantage of their environment, just like the Delve." He eyed her closely when he said, "Which means it won't be easy to find them."

Marina nodded at the whistle. "That's why we have this."

Something flickered in Ryder's eyes. "Right. 'Friends will answer.' But whose?"

"*Our* friends," Marina said when she realized what he was getting at. "I told you; I'm not going to leave you out to dry. I wouldn't be here if it wasn't for you."

"I know." Ryder nudged her dismissively, then turned back to the chaise.

She knew he was brushing her off—that he regretted even saying anything—but she couldn't drop it this time. She needed him to know. "I won't abandon you, Ryder," she said. "I promise."

This time, when Ryder smiled, his lips thinned. "You'll have to forgive me for being skeptical," he said. "That kind of promise has been made and broken before."

CHAPTER 3
Circle

The next morning, after a day of rest and food Marina hoped would give them enough staying power, they left. Part of her didn't want to leave, because she feared she'd never see the Delve again. Would anyone else come upon it, or would it remain as it was for centuries—lights permanently shut off, with only the dead to stand guard? But forward was the only way to go—*one day, one step, one breath at a time*—so she forced herself to leave, praying she'd remember the Delve as it used to be and not as it was now.

Ryder packed his armored suit instead of wearing it, then donned the clothes of an Elsudran civilian. Though he said nothing of it, Marina noticed his choice of a tunic, which had sleeves long enough to hide the burns on his hands. She hoped it would be enough. The scars of Kieron's followers covered entire palms—a mockery of the traditional Elsudran symbol and an ode to his regime.

The escape route to the sea was a long and narrow trek along hundreds of spiral stairs bordered by rock walls. Just when Marina began to think they *had* to have reached the bottom, the stairs would twist again, and eventually, she stopped guessing. When the stairs finally ended, they walked another half mile, maybe more, through a tunnel so dark and wet that when distant light caught Marina's eyes, she let out a sigh of relief.

The tunnel edged into a swale, which they followed toward the light. Marina could smell the salt before she saw the ocean, and by the time they reached the sand, eagerness pricked at her fingertips.

The ocean was just as she'd remembered it. The sun danced on the water, peeking through morning clouds. She'd seen the view from afar with Pierce, and now, she could finally see it up close. She kept her eyes on the sea as they walked but occasionally glanced up at the Admare Mountains, which towered above them, snowcaps sparkling.

According to Ryder, this was the only stretch of beach on the southern side of the Admares. Most of the range ended at cliffs, which plummeted hundreds of feet into the ocean below. But if they followed the coast until it stopped, then headed back north through the mountains for a short time, they'd reach a town called Tin.

"That's where I want to head," Ryder said. "Tin, then Inber, which is a small village just outside the forest that surrounds Candens Inlet."

Marina nodded. "Which town were you raised in?" she asked, desperate for something normal to talk about.

"Mossley."

"What was it like?"

"Boring. Full of farmland."

He clearly wasn't in the mood to expand. Ryder's silence wasn't cold like Aeric's, but it was easily as uncomfortable. That, and his shift in demeanor saddened her.

Though her feet ached, she quickened to catch up to him. "I haven't thanked you yet," she said. "Not really. And...I want you to know how much I appreciate what you did. For me *and* Cal."

He gave her a strained smile. "You're welcome." After a pause, he said, "And thank you for...what you did in Exorsus. I can't think of many people who'd have done the same."

Marina forced a smile in response, only because her throat was too tight to speak. She rubbed her stinging eyes, hating how easily she was brought to tears, then remembered what Cal had said to her months ago.

It's a strength. Such an incredible, beautiful strength—to feel so deeply.

That was who she was, and she'd promised herself not to fight it. Keeping that promise would be hard, but she'd be damned if she didn't try.

"You okay?" Ryder asked.

"Just thinking about Cal."

She looked back to the sea, wondering if come tomorrow's daybreak, she could access Exorsus like she had in Altus. She held the Omnia. It was all she needed—that, and her innate abilities. But the circumstances surrounding Cal's death belonged to *Cal*, not to her. Even the Omnia didn't give Marina control over anyone but herself in Exorsus, and she wasn't sure how much control that amounted to. The tapestry of time was ever-weaving, and she was but a single stitch.

She voiced her thoughts to Ryder, who gave her a wary look. "You can't change what happened, no matter how horrible you feel about it."

"That's...not what I was thinking."

It was kind of a lie. She wasn't sure what she'd been thinking, or if she'd been thinking anything at all, other than how deeply she missed Cal and how they'd almost made it.

Cal had almost made it.

"Cal's choice was hers," Ryder said. "Not yours, not mine—hers. And if Exorsus is as I understand it, nobody but her can change that."

"Do you think she would if she were given the chance?"

Ryder stared ahead, his eyes as desolate as the coast. "No."

A briny breeze washed over them, and Marina breathed with it. *One day, one step, one breath at a time.*

"Cal's death wasn't your fault," Ryder said when she didn't respond. "No more than it was mine or my voco's. It was the ruemins' and Kieron's...and her own. But she knew what her choice meant. Let her make it, and let the dead find peace." Softer, he said, "All you can do is move forward."

"If only it were easier."

Ryder nodded. "If only."

Marina listened to the crash of waves, hoping they'd give her some peace. Instead, all she could think of was the message Kieron's soldiers had left behind.

"Cal told me about what Kieron did to those who remained at the Delve," she said. "About how they were left out to rot in the sun. I just...I don't think it really hit me until I saw it. And I wish I could've done something for them, like..."

"Like what?" Ryder said when her voice trailed off. When she didn't answer, he said, "Stop tearing yourself apart."

"I could give you the same advice."

Though Ryder grimaced, he didn't respond. After a few moments, he muttered, "War is brutal." Dryly, he added, "Just ask Safira."

She pictured that tall, beautiful woman with a half-golden face, whose spirit wasn't comprised of waves like Marina's or fog like Aeric's, but smoke, thick and unyielding.

"What happened to her?" she asked.

"Other than the obvious? I know only what I've heard. At the beginning of the war, she was taken captive by a group of *rebels*—Kieron's words—who tortured her for days before she was found near death, with only half of her face intact. Most of them were sorcerers, who must've matched her pretty damn well because she didn't stand a chance."

"Holy shit," Marina breathed.

Ryder responded with a shrug. "But Vaughn saved her life, and the rest is history. People call her the mechanical woman, but rumor is she created that name for herself."

"Do you think she did?"

Ryder nodded. "Everything's an opportunity to Safira, just like Kieron. That name is her way of showing people what she'd survived and cautioning anyone against trying again." His lips twitched. "Safira's suffered, but she's made others suffer just as much. She was part of the court once, if you'd believe it. But she was quick to turn on them. If there was anyone she'd be loyal to, it's her old mentor."

Kieron. Ryder didn't have to specify for Marina to know. Safira and Aeric had been Kieron's students around the same time.

"Kieron recruited her when he returned from Sundra because she'd been one of his best students," Ryder said. "She idolized Kieron—some say even more than Aeric did—and shared his ideology too. Order, conformity, elimination of the Keepers...all of it appealed to Safira as much as it did to Kieron. The only difference was she was content with Kieron holding the Omnia and simply serving beside him. And when it came to serving Kieron, Safira was ruthless."

That didn't surprise Marina one bit, though it did send a shiver down her spine.

"But at the beginning of the war," Ryder continued, "Safira was captured by members of the court—sorcerers who were furious with her betrayal. From what I hear, even *Kieron* thought Safira was done for. But she survived...barely. After Vaughn ensured her recovery, she approached Kieron's enemies not only out of loyalty to him, but also vengeance for herself. She became head of Kieron's war department too—orchestrated massacres like the one that happened in Lewes."

The one Ismene's family was killed in, Marina remembered.

"She did some of that work personally, like when she went to one of our western cities—Sal—and targeted the inclined," Ryder said. "She'd go home to home and use psychometry to check essences, then round up anyone with even a hint of magical ability."

Right. Kieron sought to enforce complete homogeneity amongst the masses. He targeted anyone he believed might endanger his claim on the Omnia, minus himself and his chosen cohort of sorcerers—which used to involve Aeric, but now was down to only Safira and Vaughn. Ryder didn't need to specify what happened to those Safira rounded up. Everyone knew it, and Marina couldn't imagine the turmoil families went through trying to hide their inclined relatives, if they tried at all. Kieron didn't only eliminate the inclined, after all. Anyone who challenged him, discreetly or not, was a threat.

Traitors are an ever-growing weed that must be continually pruned, he'd told her in Altus.

It was what had ultimately driven Aeric to desert him—or, in Kieron's eyes, betray him. Now, it was Safira who Kieron intended to take his place. And once she did, she'd no doubt be on the lookout for a successor she could steal away when they were young and indoctrinate the way Kieron had indoctrinated Aeric. As harrowing as the idea was, Marina supposed if she were the parent of an inclined child, she'd rather they be pardoned and brainwashed than killed.

Ryder lowered his eyes to the sand. "Safira would find streets and squares with high numbers of inclined civilians, then have the soldiers release what we call 'lock bombs.' She liked them because they didn't destroy buildings or leave traces." He chewed on his lip, then said, "Lock bombs were rarely used before Safira because they're so cruel. They screw with people's mental clarity and disrupt the brain's ability to communicate with the body. Most people's bodies stiffen and weaken, but those hit the hardest can experience temporary paralysis—as though their limbs are locked in place. When Safira set the bombs off, anyone who might've been able to match her—either with weapons or magical talent —was so defenseless she could take on dozens of people herself. Sometimes, she'd kill them on her own. Mostly, she'd feed them to the ruemin."

When Ryder met Marina's gaze, he hastily added, "I never witnessed what Safira did. That was before I worked for Kieron. But...I heard stories. And the soldiers who were around to see it said the same thing: Safira liked the game. She liked it when everyone was so out of it that it was like playing with puppets. I've always wondered if that's because there was a time when *she* felt like a puppet—when she was at the mercy of others."

"That's horrible," Marina whispered.

"Well, it checks out. Kieron chose her because of her viciousness, and that viciousness made her the target of people who were equally as sadistic. Which, in turn, made her more ruthless than she'd ever been." His chin quivered. "It all runs in a circle, and those of us not lucky enough to escape it either die or become part of it."

Silence followed. This time, Marina surrendered to it.

CHAPTER 4
Red

Though the walk to Tin was shorter than the trek to the Delve, Marina felt as though it dragged on for an eternity. They stuck to the hard sand closest to the waves, but still, her muscles throbbed. On their way from Pirn, she'd tried to use conveyance to speed up the process, but it had only tired her out—especially because conveying with more than one body was immensely taxing.

She'd hoped that stopping to rest would help, but when they made camp on the backshore, her sleep was even worse. The waves in her dreams were nonexistent now. Instead, she dreamed of the dead—of their vacant eyes and rotting skin. Only they weren't arranged in a line; they were arranged in a circle, and Cal's body was at the center of it.

Cal hadn't been lucky enough to escape it—the pain, the violence, the grief. It had come for Astra and taken bits of Cal as well, and she'd yielded to it in the end, even if it was for a noble reason. But death didn't care if one was noble and brave; it took them all the same. And Cal wouldn't return to the sea either.

When Marina woke the next morning, her cheeks were wet with tears, and she found herself wishing her dreams were as they used to be. She packed to keep herself busy, and when Ryder woke soon after, they headed off. Though her legs still hurt, she refused to stop. All she could do was push forward, so she did, for the dead as much as the living.

After a while, walking became mindless. As the beaches thinned out and they made their way back in through the mountains—which weren't near as sharp and brutal as they were by the Delve—she lost feeling in her legs. Whether it was because of the cold or disassociation, she didn't care. At least they'd stopped throbbing.

The sun had just started to set on the second day when they reached Tin. It resembled Pirn in style, despite the fact that it was better off and drew in more people. It was strange seeing them walk around the streets and converse freely; they were nowhere near as invisible as people in Altus. But they minded their own, and Marina was happy enough to do the same.

Before they'd crossed the town lines, Ryder had put his sunglasses on, and Marina had covered her hair. They'd concealed their vocos too; the golden ones were unique to Altus and were bound to draw attention. It was impossible to keep their vocos hidden from everyone, though. Since they were used for payment just as much as communication and navigation—and since vocos belonging to the palace qualified for free lodging anywhere in Elsudra—they had no choice but to show them to the front desk at the nearest inn.

Tin was one of Elsudra's smaller towns, but Ryder made it clear they were at risk simply by showing up. Every region in Elsudra was likely under lockdown, he'd said, which meant nobody with civilian vocos could use portal systems or travel freely. They needed to strike a balance between appearing like civilians to some and guards to others, which meant their performances needed to be as cautious as they were thorough.

Luckily, the inn Ryder found was family-owned and as unfrequented as the one in Pirn. Marina waited in an alley outside while he booked himself a room, and though she didn't love the idea of waiting alone, she knew Ryder was right; a shrewd staff member might catch on if two young people showed up claiming to be undercover palace guards.

She wished she had the ability to alter their appearances. It would certainly make things easier. But Elsudran magic had its fair share of limitations, and even holding the Omnia didn't make her powerful enough to change physical matter. If she knew how to glamour, she could divert the path of light to conceal them, like Aeric did to the Delve's entrances. But he'd only explained the basics of glamouring to her; he'd never gotten the chance to show her.

Perhaps he'd teach her one day—if they found him, of course, and if he wasn't furious with her. By the time Ryder whisked Marina inside, she was so overcome with worries about Aeric that she hardly thought about getting caught. Luckily, Ryder was paranoid enough for the both of them. He'd waited until the front desk was empty, then snuck Marina to their room so quickly she'd hardly had time to take everything in.

Their room was quaint, but clearly meant for one person. When Marina glanced at the lone bed, Ryder quickly muttered, "Had to pretend I was alone, remember?"

She shrugged. Truthfully, she didn't care; she'd rather they keep people off their trail. Besides, Ryder only had one person on his mind, even if he never admitted it. And she'd never understood the big deal about sharing beds anyway. She'd never intended to use them for anything other than sleeping.

When Ryder realized she wasn't bothered, he grinned. "This might be the only time

I'm glad to share a room with someone like you."

She raised an eyebrow as he set their bags down. "Someone like me?"

"Someone who isn't smitten with me."

"God, you're arrogant. And I don't get smitten with anyone."

"Clearly." He took off his shoes and sat at the edge of the bed. "Should've seen the girl out front. She might've been easier to fool than the man in Pirn."

Marina stared at their bags for a moment. Though she knew it would annoy Ryder, she couldn't help herself when she asked, "You're sure nobody will suspect anything?"

"If my charm works the way I think it does, we're fine." He sighed when she gave him a look. "I told her I was a guard sent to Tin to covertly monitor the public's safety, and she has no idea you're here. Family-owned inns don't have great security."

"She didn't seem wary?"

"She thinks I'm here to keep people like her safe. I guarantee she's more scared of what she thinks I'm protecting her from."

"Us, you mean."

It seemed to amuse Ryder. "I imagine Kieron's propaganda department has already painted us as quite the monsters."

Marina crinkled her nose. "I'm surprised he has one."

"For someone who's terrified of people getting close to him," Ryder said, "he sure knows how to make them do his bidding."

The knot in Marina's stomach didn't budge. Her nerves must have been noticeable because Ryder sighed. "You badgered me in Pirn too, and nothing happened. You've been surrounded by Elsudrans who hold extreme opinions about Kieron. You'll realize the majority care more about living comfortably." He laughed without mirth. "It's safer to put blinders on in Kieron's Elsudra, and that girl out there is no different. Regardless of how she feels about Kieron's reign, all she wants is to stay safe."

"You think there's a chance she disagrees with his reign?"

"She won't say it out loud if she does. Not unless she wants her family arrested."

Marina tensed. Of course Kieron would make any kind of criticism illegal.

She nodded, but couldn't help herself when she repeated, "You're sure we're safe?"

"Well, no," Ryder said, scoffing. "I'm not *sure*. But I'm close enough to it to be able to sleep well, so shut up and stop worrying."

He got a laugh out of her at that. Pierce and Ismene had told her the same before—in much nicer ways, of course.

"I'm glad you're here," she admitted. "I don't know if I could've gotten us a room."

"Honestly, I kind of enjoyed it. It's been a while since I've been able to flirt with a pretty girl. Or boy."

Marina scoffed. "What's that supposed to mean? You never flirted with me."

"You want me to?"

"No," she said quickly.

This time, it was Ryder who laughed. "I did a little. Then you blackmailed me."

"Oh, right. That's more my style." Marina lay back on the bed and observed the beams on the ceiling. "I have used flattery before."

"Did it work?"

"Yes. And then it backfired."

Ryder was silent for a moment. "Ocot?"

She nodded. She couldn't bring herself to add his name to her list—not when he'd been part of the reason the Delve fell. But sometimes, she'd remember how terrified he'd looked when Kieron had slit his throat, and pity would rear its head.

"He was an idiot," Ryder said. "And Kieron never would've kept him around. He's too paranoid."

Marina frowned. "You say he's scared of people getting close to him. But *you* were close to him, and he trusted you."

Why? Safira and Vaughn made sense, but a young guard who'd spent the years prior training to protect the Keepers was a much bigger risk.

"You got in after Aeric left too," Marina continued. She knew she was pushing it, but after days of walking and only the occasional strained conversation, her curiosity ran rampant. "I bet Kieron was more paranoid after that."

"Not really," Ryder said. "Just angry. And maybe a little hurt."

"Hurt?" The words came out in a confused laugh.

Ryder remained straight-faced. "Kieron might be horrible," he said, "but he still has emotions. And even if he never said it, I think he'd wanted to rely on Aeric."

"You do know what happened when he realized Aeric was getting cold feet, don't you?" When Ryder shook his head, Marina whispered, "Kieron tried to have Vaughn destroy Aeric's mind—turn him into someone who couldn't think or rebel against him."

Ryder shrugged. "I guess he wanted the Omnia more."

The night brought a cool rain with it, and Marina woke to pale skies hovering above the mountains. The streets glinted with wet cobblestone, and the smell of pine flitted through the inn's hallways.

She'd slept well, which was a godsend. According to Ryder, they'd need ample energy once they made it to the South. The wetlands around Candens Inlet wouldn't be easy to trek through, and stamina was a must.

Ryder seemed considerably less rested, though. As they packed their things, he muttered about how much Marina had tossed and turned, and how she was perhaps the most violent sleeper he'd ever met. By the time they'd snuck out of the inn and began their search for somewhere inconspicuous to eat, he was in a horrible mood.

He seemed to lighten up a bit when they found a place. Luckily, there was nobody around—not even cooks. Elsudran eateries were nothing like the ones back home. Premade meals sat in glass cases that opened after payment via voco—or after confirmation that one had a golden voco and thus worked for the palace, which meant they could eat for free. That eased Marina's stress considerably since it meant there were fewer chances someone would see them and realize Ryder and Marina fit the descriptions Kieron had no doubt disseminated. But they couldn't be careful enough, and Ryder reminded Marina they needed to finish their breakfast quickly.

The food was plain but filling. The East didn't have the most luxurious dining options, but according to Ryder, it was the best region to recuperate in, being the least populated. Since it was only the two of them, Marina let her mind wander a bit. She might've woken well-rested, but her dreams still hadn't let up, and her head spun from them. She'd dreamed of Cal again, and then of Ocot and the four scouts Kieron had set ruemin on. There was blood too, seeping from throats and staining marble tiles.

Her mind was far away as she ate, and she didn't notice three others come into the eatery until Ryder swore under his breath. When she caught a glimpse of their armor, gold flashed before her eyes instead of red.

Shit. One of them—a woman not much older than Ryder—tucked her dark hair behind her ears. When Marina saw the burns on the woman's palms, she nearly choked on her food.

"We're civilians," Ryder whispered. He'd moved his sunglasses to his head when they'd started eating, and he quickly put them back on before pulling his sleeves over his hands. "That's all. Just civilians having breakfast."

Marina gave him a quick nod, then sheathed her hands under her sleeves as well, praying nobody would see her golden voco. She figured it'd be strange if they got up and left the moment another party walked in, but the more she observed the guards, the more she wanted to bolt. Even three were overwhelming. And why were they in Tin? Maybe guards really *had* been sent out to occupy every Elsudran city.

The oldest guard, a bald man with a circle-style beard, patted the back of the guard next to him—a young man with sandy-blond hair, a good twenty years his junior. None of them seemed on high alert; they weren't wearing their helmets, had their weapons tucked away, and kept their gloves off as they gathered food.

The old guard was the loudest. Even as they settled down at the end of the community table, he didn't quiet down. Occasionally, Marina was able to pick up on what he was saying, but most of it was cursing and jokes the other two were obviously pretending to laugh at.

"I'll tell you what," he said. "I'll take you to the shittiest restaurant in the North, and then you'll have to admit I'm right. It's like dining in a palace compared to the East."

"Only because the North is wealthier," the woman said, resting her cheek in her hand.

"So what? I'm still right." He laughed, then looked over to Ryder and Marina. Ryder tensed, but the man only grinned. "Hope any native Easterners don't take offense."

Ryder responded with a smile, and when the man shifted his gaze to her, Marina did the same. When they turned back to their food, the man said, "Where are you lot from?"

"Great, a fucking talkative one," Ryder breathed. When he turned back to the man, his demeanor softened. "East, born and raised."

The bearded man laughed loudly. "Look at me, making a fool of myself. You all have some good alcohol, though. Makes up for the food. Is it just the two of you today?"

He didn't wait for them to respond before pushing his food closer. The young woman and man exchanged glances, then followed suit.

Though Ryder maintained a casual air, Marina knew he was cursing internally. She was too. Random civilians were one thing, but Altus guards?

"Why are you in Tin?" Ryder asked, nodding at their armor.

"You haven't heard?" the young man said. "It's—"

"Mayhem in the capital," the bearded man interrupted. "Guards have been sent out to occupy every town and city in Elsudra. If I were you, I'd stay indoors for a while. Tin got an influx of ruemin last night too. Wouldn't want civilians caught up in that."

"Terrifying creatures," the young woman muttered.

Marina made fleeting eye contact with her and forced a nod of agreement, praying she hadn't paled. Ruemin could sense magical energy—like dogs catching a scent—and she held the very source of Elsudra's magic. Surely, her presence would be noticeable to them if they got close enough. Worse still, ruemin usually traveled in packs...

"What kind of mayhem?" Ryder asked. Subtle as it was, Marina could've sworn he pulled their weapons bag closer to him.

"The kind of mayhem that'll be starting rumors," the bearded man said.

"An assassination attempt," the younger man added. "We hear one of Kieron's closest betrayed him. Another guard—"

He cut himself short when the bearded man and young woman cut him a glare.

Marina almost laughed. *An assassination attempt.* Kieron's words, no doubt, to make it seem unprovoked. He probably didn't even need a propaganda department; he could spin the truth well enough on his own.

"I only mean...higher-up shit we don't have leeway to talk about," the younger man corrected. "Omnia's return and all."

"Right. And its new Keeper," Ryder said. "Crazy times we live in."

"That's why guards have been sent out to every region," the bearded man said, taking a sip of his drink. "We're keeping the peace until the thief is apprehended, and the traitor who helped."

"Only problem is," the young woman added, "we haven't the slightest clue what kind of person came back with the Omnia." She wavered. "Or what they can do."

Marina almost thought she detected a hint of warning in her voice.

"Not true," the bearded man said. "We were given the necessary information." His eyes landed on Marina, whose stomach soured. "Civilians were too, but you can't rely on 'em. So, we're here, and we're warning the general public to stay home, you two included. Where in Tin do you live?"

"A few blocks from the portals," Ryder said. "Guess we ought to get going then."

The bearded man gave him a smile. "I doubt you'd need sunglasses," he said. "Cloud coverage is nice today." Though his tone was even-keeled, there was a pointedness to it.

"Headache," Ryder responded smoothly. "I didn't get much sleep last night."

The man nodded absently, then shifted his gaze to Marina. "Your friend is quiet."

Marina shot him what she hoped would come across as a casual smile. "Sorry. I'm not a morning person."

"Why eat so early if you're not a morning person?"

She shrugged, her shoulders tight, then angled her chin at Ryder. "He is."

"Ah. He chose the place, I take it?"

"My friend can't make a decision to save her life," Ryder said. He scooped up the bag next to him, and Marina grabbed the ones near her.

The bearded man looked at her, expecting some kind of response, but Marina only nodded awkwardly at him. He didn't press her; he simply stood and offered two of his fingers to her. "Well, it's a pleasure to meet the both of you."

A test—to see if she knew Elsudran customs. Marina glanced at Ryder, then tapped two of her own on the back of the bearded man's.

There. See? Just an Elsudran civilian. She met the bearded man's eyes, which seemed to soften, and whispered a silent *thank you* to Cal.

For a moment, there was peace. Even Ryder seemed to relax.

And then, movement—so quick Marina didn't realize the bearded man had snapped a leaden cuff around her wrist until he pulled back.

She knew what it was immediately. A diminution cuff, meant to suppress her abilities. But the bearded man had only managed to get one on her, and she recoiled before he could grab her other wrist and see her voco. Not like it would've mattered. He already knew who they were.

Thoughtlessly, she summoned a burst of light with her free hand, but all it did was zap at her fingers and fade out.

No, no, no…

Even one cuff was enough to stifle her. The bearded man must've known that because he didn't waste time trying to pull out another. Instead, he drew his gun and pointed it at Ryder, then snapped on his helmet. The young woman and man beside him swung their legs over the bench, hands on their baldrics. Ryder eyed his bag, but the bearded man said, "Stop. Hands up. I need to see your palms."

"This is ridiculous," Ryder said. "Restraining a civilian? We didn't do anything."

"Hands. Up."

The silence that followed this time was cold.

"What did I say about us receiving necessary information?" the bearded man said slowly. "A young woman with auburn hair, and a man not much older with *very* distinct eyes. Distinct enough, I imagine, to need sunglasses to hide them." He paused, then said more sternly, "Put 'em up. Palms toward me."

Ryder stared at him, his lips a thin line. "Fine."

Marina almost thought she detected relief in the young woman's eyes as Ryder raised his arms, but Marina knew well enough to brace herself.

Everything happened in an instant. She wasn't sure how Ryder managed to get his hands on his gun, but once he had, he shot the bearded man straight in the shoulder. The bearded man clutched at his wound, then fired a shot of his own, but Ryder twisted violently aside to evade it.

The other two guards swore and drew their weapons, and Marina wasn't sure what went through her mind when she grabbed a glass on the table and smashed it into the young man's head.

He keeled over, holding his ear as the woman snapped on her helmet, then drew her gun and pointed it at Marina.

"Don't move!" she hissed.

It wasn't much of a deterrent. Kieron would've given them orders not to kill her, but

Ryder wasn't as safe. In a flurry of adrenaline, Marina slammed her body into the woman's, desperate to get her on the ground so Ryder would only have the bearded man to deal with. He'd hurt him, but the man's armor had protected him from the worst.

Marina's heart beat wildly in her ears as her vision narrowed. The bearded man had known who they were, but she wasn't sure if the other two had been as certain. They were caught off guard, and the young woman's shock was useful. She writhed under Marina for a moment but eventually managed to get out from underneath her.

With the damned cuff, she was useless. The young man, still swearing and bleeding, came to the woman's aid, helping her up and tackling Marina to the ground when she tried to stand.

"Stay...down," he ordered. The side of his face was wet and red, and he was obviously disoriented. His fingers danced around his collar for the button to his helmet, but before he could press it, Marina kneed him in the stomach.

He groaned, his hand falling away from his neck. She tried to knee him again, but he held her legs down, and with the woman's help, they kept her pinned.

Another shot sounded, followed by a crash as the bearded man slammed into a bar table at the side of the room. Something small hit Marina's shoulder—a key.

"Use it!" Ryder shouted.

Marina tried to free one of her hands, but the young man grabbed the key before she could—and one of Ryder's bullets went straight through his head.

The young woman shrieked, shielding herself as blood splattered her helmet. Marina grasped at the key, kicking the woman aside as she tried to reach for it. But she wasn't trained—not in combat, or defense, or anything but a bit of magic. The woman was quicker than she was, and she somehow managed to get her knees on Marina's shoulders, blocking her from reaching the key.

"I won't hurt you if you let us go," Marina pleaded. "Just let us go, please."

"Shut up," the woman hissed.

She didn't seem to find any enjoyment in this, but she wasn't going to give in either. She was on orders, and she'd follow them until the end.

Desperate, Marina began squirming wildly under the woman to get free.

"I said *don't move*." She dug her knees even harder into Marina's shoulders. "Keep moving and I'll knock you out."

Ryder was too preoccupied to come to her aid; the bearded man was a practiced soldier, and he put up a good fight despite his bullet wound.

The young woman's helmet gleamed in the artificial light. Even though it was gold, all Marina could think of was ruemin scales, and suddenly, she felt as though she were back on the Admare's frost-covered ground, pinned by a monster instead of an Elsudran. Back then, she didn't have the skills—the magic—to defend herself. So, Marina did what she'd done with the ruemin: she screamed.

The woman's hand clamped over her mouth, and when Marina felt her fingers against her lips, she bit down.

A crunch sounded, followed by a howl, but Marina kept tugging with her teeth as the woman's thumb came undone from her hand. Blood filled Marina's mouth, but she didn't stop until the finger was no longer attached.

The woman's scream filled the room, and though Marina prayed she'd pass out, she stayed on top of her. She dropped the key, then punched Marina in the side of the head.

A thousand stars danced throughout the room as Marina's gut roiled, but she had to act. The woman was in shock, which gave Marina more than enough time to reach up and press the button at the side of her armor. The moment the woman's helmet retracted, Marina scooped up the key and jammed it into the cuff's pinhole.

Now she could see the woman's face. When the cuff fell from Marina's wrist, the woman paled. Fury cracked through Marina and careened from her hands. The woman flew backward, slamming into the table. There, she twitched and went to right herself.

Make it quick.

The woman wouldn't stop fighting. None of them would until the other party was dead—or, in Marina's case, captured. Marina's arms went wide, and then there was red, pouring from the woman's throat and dribbling from her mouth. Maybe that was mercy.

She wasn't sure what kind of damage she'd done—it was quick and heedless—but when the woman slumped to the ground again, Marina knew she was dead. A stupor overtook her, just like with Vaughn, only this time, it was worse.

The bearded man groaned loudly, glancing at the woman's body and giving Ryder half a second's respite.

It was more than enough. Ryder shot him again in the chest, sending him to the ground. In a blinding instant, he was on him, hands at the bearded man's neck. The moment the man's helmet retracted, another one of Ryder's bullets went through his head.

Silence followed. It wasn't cold or calm; it was numb.

Marina stared at the bodies, all covered in blood—as red as the corpses in her dreams.

CHAPTER 5
Alibi

Distant screeches of ruemin cut through the air. Marina could hear them from outside, but she had no idea how close they were. She prepared to bolt, only to gawk at Ryder when he rushed to the woman's body and began to type something into her voco.

A message of distress, Marina quickly realized. As she neared him, she was able to make out what it said: *Requesting immediate support in Tin. Host and traitor located, two soldiers down. Ruemin eliminated traitor, host wounded me and escaped. Situation critical.*

Marina gasped when he entered their coordinates. "Why would you—"

"Needs to seem real," Ryder breathed. "Trust me."

That hardly explained anything, and it certainly didn't make her feel any better. But he'd gotten her this far...he couldn't betray her now. Could he? She didn't have much time to consider it. Ryder released the woman's limp wrist and yanked Marina out of the eatery. The screeches had grown louder, which was enough to send civilians into their homes and leave Marina and Ryder alone amidst deserted sidewalks and streets.

"We need to move before anyone sees us," Ryder said as he pulled Marina's hood back over her head. His shoulder was bleeding, but he didn't seem to notice. "Portals. *Now.*"

Though her head pounded, Marina kept up with him. By the time they reached the portal courtyard, she felt like she was going to collapse. More screeches reverberated through the air, followed by clicking.

Where were they? Could the ruemin sense the Omnia even if they couldn't see her?

She whirled around to face the street behind her, jumping when the southernmost portal flickered to life. Ryder grabbed her wrist and positioned her voco over the console, which now registered two travelers, then said, "*Go.* I told you; they can't get through."

Marina nodded rapidly, following Ryder's lead as he touched his bare hand to the portal's mouth. In an instant, the screeches cut off, and the icy cobblestone transformed into a courtyard that smelled of sweetgrass and muck.

Before Marina could take in her surroundings, Ryder jerked her away from the portal. When she blinked at him, stunned, he said, "Didn't want to risk you touching it."

The portal was fading but still active, its mouth like light dancing at the bottom of a pool. Marina watched it before turning back to Ryder and scoffing. "I wouldn't have."

Ryder didn't respond until the portal had died down fully. "Still," he said through a sigh. "Portals recognize flesh. If you'd brushed even a finger against the light—accidentally or not—it would've activated and sucked you right back to Tin." He shook his head. "Doesn't matter. We're in the clear now."

"What did you do back there with the soldier's voco?"

She must've sounded a little accusatory because Ryder grimaced. "Death is the best alibi," he said. When Marina raised an eyebrow, he added, "I'm one of Kieron's biggest threats right now. If he thinks I'm dead, I'm safer. Both of us are. Kieron's soldiers won't be on the lookout for two people anymore. And they won't anticipate you getting far since you don't know Elsudra."

"You don't think soldiers will look for your body?"

Ryder's lips twitched into a smile. "Ruemin tend not to leave bodies. Not unless they're instructed otherwise."

For half a second, Marina felt guilty for nearly assuming the worst. But Ryder didn't seem offended by it; he simply shrugged, then winced at his shoulder and said, "Welcome to the South."

"Are we in Inber?"

"Mossley. It was the first town I could think of. Besides, after what just happened, it's best to throw people off as much as possible. We'll stay here for an hour or so, then use another portal system to get to Inber."

Though Marina wanted to get to Candens Inlet as quickly as possible, she knew it was better to be safe than sorry. Luckily, Mossley had no shortage of hidden marshes they could wait in. A river ran through the town, and pockets of water sprang up around it. They found a spring-fed pond surrounded by rocks and trees, then sank to the ground at its edge and collected themselves.

They washed their faces and hands, sorted their belongings, then filled their flasks with water and some iodine they'd found in the Delve. At the height of her adrenaline, Marina hadn't noticed the lingering taste of blood in her mouth. Now she did, and it took her several minutes of washing her mouth out before she didn't feel nauseous.

When the taste finally subsided and she didn't feel so sick, she turned to Ryder and nodded at his chest. "Are you okay?"

Ryder nodded, but it was so unconvincing that Marina made him remove his shirt so she could see the damage.

"Just grazed by a bullet," he said when her eyes widened. "I'll be fine."

As much as he tried to play it off, his wound didn't help his case. It looked like a fiery comet—a chunk of blood and ripped skin, surrounded by mottled lacerations. Though Marina thanked the heavens the bullet hadn't embedded, the damage still looked painful.

"The guard might've been a good fighter," Ryder said, "but he was a lousy shot."

"It still needs treatment. Which bag has medical supplies in it?"

Ryder nodded to one of the smaller ones, and Marina got out some gauze and tape. She used the rest of their iodine to clean his wound, then patched it up.

"I'd try to heal it, but I haven't been taught," she said. "I don't want to make it worse."

"Don't worry about it." He paused, a weak grin on his face. "Nice try, using the wound as an excuse to make me take off my shirt."

"Shut up, Ryder. I'm not in the mood."

"I'm *joking*. We'll be fine. We made it this far, and we'll get to Candens Inlet today."

She leaned back on her heels. "Are you not upset by what happened?"

"I'd be more upset if I was dead and you were back with Kieron."

Marina's chest tightened. She didn't know how to respond to that. Instead, she looked around. "Where is everyone?"

"Mossley is rural, like Tin and Inber. Better if we stick to less populated areas. Cities like Altus probably have guards stationed at every portal system, and something tells me you've had your fair share of killing for the day."

The sun flared on the pond. Marina stared at it to distract herself from her brimming tears. Ryder put his shirt back on, trying not to move his shoulder, then whispered, "You'll get used to it."

Killing, he meant. She wasn't sure how she felt about that—how she was *supposed* to feel. She tore her gaze from the water as Ryder stood. He was good at masking his pain, but not perfect. When his shoulder moved, he flinched, and Marina couldn't help but wonder how far he'd be able to get even if he pushed himself.

They stuck to backroads and fields, which Ryder said would lead them to one of Mossley's seldom-used portal systems.

"In better circumstances," he said, "I would've liked to show you around Mossley. It's surrounded by farms and has a great view of the river."

"I thought you said it was boring," Marina muttered. They'd made their way to an empty field buzzing with midges, and she shook one off her cheek.

"Boring isn't bad. I'd like to see Elsudra go back to being boring instead of...this." This time, when he winced, Marina couldn't tell if it was because of his shoulder.

She ran her palms over the tall tips of grass. Memories of Tin still lingered like a fresh nightmare, but talking helped. "Why did you decide to move to Altus?"

"Because I knew what I excelled at." Ryder took a measured breath, and Marina supposed he, too, was distracting himself when he said, "I grew up in a community home with kids who didn't have guardians. Most went on to become farmers or something similar, but I didn't want that. I wanted to serve in the capital. Plus, the benefits were good. Free food, housing...all of it. Of course, only the best stayed in the program, but I knew that wouldn't be a problem for me."

Cautiously, Marina said, "Pierce told me you showed him up the first day you arrived." When Ryder turned to look at her, his expression blank, she added, "He spoke fondly of you."

"He thought I was dead," Ryder replied flatly. "Most people speak fondly of the dead."

Marina opened her mouth but ultimately decided to stay silent. It wasn't her place, and even if it was, she had a feeling Ryder didn't want her input. Instead, she kept her eyes on the silhouette of the Admare Mountains.

By the time they reached the portal system, Marina's head and jaw ached so badly that she struggled to keep her balance. She tried to stay hydrated, but water didn't do much to curb the pain. Both of them were slower than usual, and she prayed it wasn't a long walk from Inber to their destination.

Inber was smaller than Mossley, but it looked similar. The horizon hadn't changed much either; Marina could still see the Admares as they swept across the vista and touched the sky. The air, however, had grown more humid, and the roads they took swarmed with bugs. It was as miserable to take in her surroundings as it was to withdraw into her head, so she focused on her steps instead.

One at a time, she told herself.

If she let herself mull over what had happened in Tin or fret about what *would* happen when they reached Candens Inlet, she'd break down. Guilt, coupled with overwhelming nerves and a pulsing headache, made for quite a bad combination, but since Ryder was still walking—still pushing forward, despite his wound—she forced herself to do the same.

They stopped to rest and eat only once, and when the Admares began to fade out, Ryder said, "We're getting into swamp territory now. When we head into the forest, watch where you walk. If anything non-Elsudran moves, kill it."

The smell of buttonbush faded, morphing into decay that worsened with the heat and turned the ground into mud. The water here wasn't clear like it was by the river in Mossley; it was murky, lined with slick-trunked trees and gnarled branches.

She'd prepared for this. In the Delve, she'd swapped out her ballet-pink combat boots from home with an old pair she'd found in storage. Ryder had made quite the fuss that she was taking up space by putting her boots in one of their bags, but she'd dismissed him. She wouldn't leave them behind, and she certainly wouldn't subject them to the forest peat.

For half a second, she considered teasing Ryder and forcing him to admit she was right—the mud had ruined their shoes—but held her tongue when she saw his face. As the green farmlands and blue skies faded to brown, the confidence he'd been clinging to faltered—so much that Marina reached for his hand. He seemed surprised, but he didn't pull away, even as the scars on his palms brushed against her skin.

Occasionally, the croak of a frog or rustling leaves broke the silence. Marina kept her eyes on the ground, terrified she'd step on an alligator. She didn't see any, but Ryder had mentioned them, and she knew the animals well enough—Elsudra or Georgia, they blended into their surroundings and tore legs off unsuspecting victims.

That would be ironic—death not by ruemin or Kieron, but by alligator.

Every once in a while, however, she'd shift her gaze from the brackish waters to the world above, obscured by trees she'd never seen the likes of. They shot up hundreds of feet, their tips making the sky look like a sheet of moss.

She nodded at the bag they'd placed the whistle in. "Think we can use it?"

"Don't see why not," Ryder said.

They stopped near a tree covered in a tangled thicket of vines, and Ryder rested against its trunk as Marina took out the whistle. She put it to her lips, her hands shaking—from fatigue or nerves, she wasn't sure—and blew.

The sound cut sharply through the air, and for a moment, it seemed even the insects stopped buzzing. She blew again, praying this would work—praying she'd made the right choice by coming here.

Friends will answer. She blew again. And again.

"These 'friends' are mighty silent," Ryder said through his teeth.

Marina swore. "You wanna try?"

"Hurts a bit to breathe at the moment, so no."

Her ears began to ring. "What do we do if nobody answers? Die here?"

"Exorsus, you're dramatic. Give it a few minutes."

It was painful to wait, but since there wasn't much else they could do, she conceded. She counted the minutes, then blew again. Still, nothing. They trudged forward, then tried in another spot. A symphony of katydids answered them.

"This is almost comical," Ryder said.

Marina rotated the brass beneath her clammy fingers, then raised it to her lips.

Ryder cut her off. "Listen."

The soft chirping of birds flitted throughout the trees, followed by clicking.

Marina's heart almost stopped. Only...the clicking was weak.

Ruemin?

Ryder put a finger to his lip, then drew his gun.

Shit. "Do you think they can hear the whistle's frequency?" she whispered.

Ryder shook his head. "Aeric wouldn't give you something that would attract danger."

When he began moving toward the sound, Marina caught him by the arm and widened her eyes at him.

"I think it's trapped," he whispered.

She blinked at him, straining to listen. The clicking was followed by distressed cries and the sound of groaning trunks.

"If it's trapped, that means *people* were around to trap it," Ryder added.

"And if it's not?"

"Then we kill it and move on."

It took a fair amount of courage, but Marina followed him. They weaved through a small creek, which led out to a clearing encircled by bald cypress.

A net hung from one of the smaller trees, suspended a few feet above the ground and writhing violently. Light glinted off silver nails that clawed at the mesh but failed to rip it. Marina could barely make out the entangled ruemin until she squinted.

"I'll bet they leave it for the alligators," Ryder said through a laugh. "Smart."

"Then you're right...people are around," Marina said. Her head buzzed as she eyed the ruemin, then lifted the whistle and blew it again. They had to hear it. They *had* to be close.

The ruemin moaned, then clicked again, so pathetically Marina almost considered putting it out of its misery. Instead, she took another breath, angling the whistle at the trees and praying its sound would reach every cranny of the forest.

This time, when she blew, the trees rustled. The ruemin twitched, a mess of scales and silver, then let out a screech as figures burst through the trees.

There must've been fifty, maybe more, all dressed in armor the color of underbrush. But one was familiar—a muscular man who retracted his helmet, revealing closely cropped gray hair and deep brown skin.

Marina let out a gasp, her knees threatening to buckle as she locked eyes with Florin.

CHAPTER 6
Exceptions

She'd seen Florin shocked before, but not like this. He approached her slowly, as though he wasn't sure what he was seeing.

"We came alone" was all she could think to say.

Something flickered in his eyes. He made a gesture for his soldiers to stand down, but he was cautious enough to keep a few guns pointed at Ryder—just in case.

"I'm not under duress," Marina said quickly. "Ryder...he helped me. Have someone do psychometry on me to confirm. I'm telling the truth."

"Neva," Florin said to another man. "Get Neva."

"Where's Aeric?" Marina asked. "Is he okay? What about Pierce and Ismene?"

"All okay." Florin repeated it a few more times, and Marina yielded to the tears that fell down her cheeks. "Nobody's followed?"

"Not...not that we know of."

Florin nodded. "I believe you," he continued, his voice a whisper, "but someone else needs to confirm you're trustworthy. When that's done, we'll get the two of you to safety."

Despite the guns pointed at him, Ryder stayed calm. Before one of the soldiers could take his weapons by force, Ryder had already dropped his own gun and held out his bags— a peace offering of sorts, which Florin seemed to register.

More orders were thrown about as soldiers dispersed, but instead of watching them, Marina observed the ruemin. Nobody paid mind to it; even as it clicked and screeched, soldiers brushed past it, parting only when a middle-aged woman entered the clearing.

She was around Marina's height, with ivory skin, deep-set hazel eyes, and chin-length hair—as sandy-blond as the guard Ryder had shot in Tin. Red flashed before Marina's eyes, and she desperately tried to shake the memory away. It wouldn't budge.

"This is Neva," Florin said as the woman approached them. "Leader of the sanctuary here and ally to our cause."

"More of a well-wisher," Neva said through a taut smile.

Marina wasn't sure what that meant, but she returned Neva's smile anyway.

"You're the Marina we've heard so much about?" she asked.

Marina nodded. "Ryder and I...we escaped Kieron. And—"

"Best if I see it myself," Neva said, sternly but politely.

Marina extended her arm. "By all means."

Though Neva's grip was warm, her essence felt much more like Aeric's. It was cold but bright, and in the presence of the Omnia, it sparkled.

Snow...Neva's spirit was snow. A gentle flurry danced atop Marina's waves—quick and elusive, but not quite as fluid as water or fog. Marina could tell it took effort for Neva to orient herself, but she managed well enough. Sleet rained into the sea, and Marina could sense Neva's curiosity at the Omnia—at the light beneath the water that burned as brightly as the sun. Marina stilled her waves, then let her memories wash over them.

Georgia. The Delve. Altus. Marina could feel Neva's demeanor change as she witnessed Exorsus, but she didn't pull back or raise her shields, and when the flurry faded, she made it a point to dissect every last bit of Neva's reaction.

Neva, however, remained passive as she shifted her gaze to Ryder. "Now you."

Though Ryder hesitated, he extended his arm.

Watching psychometry take place from the outside made Marina realize just how quickly it occurred. Neva's hand rested on Ryder's wrist for only seconds, but judging by the look on her face when she pulled back, Marina knew she'd seen more than enough. This time, it was harder for Neva to conceal her shock. Whether it was due to Ryder's damaged essence—the likes of which Marina could only imagine—or the things he'd done, Marina wasn't sure. Still, Neva nodded to the soldiers and said, "Let them up."

Marina couldn't stifle her sigh of relief. Florin, too, relaxed considerably. When they began moving, Marina reached once more for Ryder's hand. His fingers wrapped around hers, and when she was the only one within earshot, he whispered, "Thank you."

～

The Delve's inhabitants had burrowed below. Here, they hid amongst the sky. Elevators built into trunks of wide trees materialized in response to soldiers' vocos, and Marina's awe overpowered her frayed nerves. Even Ryder could barely drink it in fast enough. Though his lips remained parted on the ascent, he didn't speak—not until they reached the top, and even then, his words left him in a breath.

"Exorsus."

Exorsus, indeed. The sky, no longer obscured by a canopy of green and brown, glinted with the first hints of evening stars. If she reached high enough, perhaps she could touch them. It was a rather silly thought, but she'd never felt as close to them as she was now.

The settlement spanned in all directions, built on the stilts of a wooden village that hung over the wetlands. Marina peered over the railings, but the ground below was so far away she could scarcely see it. A strip of blue spanned the horizon, and Marina could've sworn she heard the distant cries of seagulls.

"We have sorcerers glamour the thickest trees below us, which keeps our hideaway hidden and secure," Neva explained. "Still, I've found it's best to look straight ahead, especially if you're squeamish this high up."

Ryder certainly didn't seem to be. He looked down as they walked, squinting through the cracks in the wood.

The network of walkways and wooden structures made as much use of trees as the Delve had of rocks. Small buildings had been built into trunks so intricately that it almost seemed like nature had made them, not Elsudrans. Gnarled branches and roots supported every pathway, some on different levels—all miles above the forest floor.

"The trees are enormous," Marina breathed.

"Some of the most ancient in Elsudra," Florin said. "Our ancestors built this place, but it was long forgotten after the first Keepers."

Neva's lips tugged upward. "Not by everyone."

She gestured for them to follow her into a circular dwelling—a common room, Marina supposed. Massive windows ran from the floor to the ceiling, letting in light that filtered in from the trees outside. Shadows of branches and leaves filled the pinewood floor, as though the room was meant to feel as though it were part of a tree itself.

As the four of them settled at a trestle table, Marina observed the ceiling, where string lights hung from beams. They looked so similar to the ones in the Delve that Marina's eyes began to sting. She averted her gaze, turning instead to the buffet table near the door, where a dozen empty wine glasses glinted in the light.

"I'll have the two of you directed to an apartment in a bit," Neva said. "We're more cramped than we used to be, but we've made do by having people share units."

"Thank you," Marina said. *For accepting the Delve. For saving them.*

"I want to speak to both of you about what I saw in your memories as soon as I've had time to mull things over." Neva looked to Florin, then added, "None of us expected this."

"We didn't expect you to escape," Florin clarified. "We were preparing to send troops to Altus." He and Neva exchanged a tense glance, and Florin's tone was stonier than usual when he added, "But we ran into roadblocks when it came to mobilization."

Marina couldn't help but notice Neva's jaw tighten.

"Well, we're here," Ryder said when the silence grew uncomfortable. "And we could use a trip to the healers."

Neva nodded, but before she could respond, the door opened again.

Marina wasn't sure how, but she knew who it was before she turned to look. Perhaps it was the stiffness that overtook Neva or the curt footsteps; either way, when Marina locked eyes with Aeric, she burst into tears.

She knew he hated when she did that, but she didn't care—not about his reaction or the others'. All that mattered was that they were safe. She and Ryder had found them, and now they could move forward.

"I'm sorry" was all she could say. Some kind of frenzy must have overtaken her, because she stood, pushed her chair aside, and hugged him. "I'm so sorry," she repeated. "I'm sorry I left, but I'll explain everything. I'll tell you what happened…it all makes sense now…all of it…"

She kept rambling, and when she felt Aeric's hands on her shoulders, she let go. She braced herself for his anger—for that ice-cold rage that made rooms freeze over—but none came. Though his tone was as sober as ever, it wavered ever so subtly when he said, "You're here. That's what matters. Just…just sit down."

It wasn't a command—not like it had been when they'd first met. If anything, there was an edge of exhaustion in his voice. Defeat, even. It might've shocked her had the circles under his eyes not been so dark. She searched for words as they sat. Another apology brewed at her lips, but when Aeric's gaze landed on Ryder, she changed course.

"I have to make something clear," she said. "Ryder got me out of Altus. He's the reason I made it here. Neva confirmed all of this through psychometry." Though she was speaking to Aeric more than Florin or Neva, she looked at all of them when she said, "He's on our side. If he wasn't, I wouldn't be here."

Silence followed, but Marina didn't try to define it. It was Ryder's reaction she focused on, and when he softened, her tears threatened to resurface.

Neva leaned back in her chair and brushed her thumb across her lips. "One hundred and three people," she said to no one in particular. "That's how many we've made room for, not including the two of you. I'm not averse to helping, but our supplies are limited, and not everyone who came from the Delve is inclined. Originally, our sanctuary was meant for those being targeted due to their abilities. We've made exceptions." She paused, and only then did her eyes meet Marina's. "But it's clear we aren't the only party who's made exceptions as of late. For that, you're welcome here." She folded her hands and stood.

"Take time to settle in. I'll make sure you find your lodgings and receive adequate care. We'll convene at a later time."

One hundred and three. The number lingered in Marina's head as Neva left the room. Not one hundred...one hundred and three.

She pressed her hand to her stomach and closed her eyes, letting it sink in.

Safe. They were safe.

She found some momentary peace behind her closed lids, but it was interrupted just as suddenly by red—by slit throats and Cal's choked voice.

Let me do this, Astra.

It could've been one hundred and four. Maybe one hundred and five, if Boris had made it too...

She wrenched her eyes open, forcing herself back.

"Aeric, I need to tell you—"

"You need to see the healers," he said. "Then we'll talk."

Marina glanced at Florin, then at Ryder, who nodded and said, "You do. Your face."

She put a hand to her aching jaw, then conceded.

She'd expected Aeric to be furious with her, and though she was relieved he wasn't—not outwardly, at least—she realized why when she and Ryder arrived at the infirmary. When Marina peered into a mirror above the washroom sink, she hardly recognized the girl who looked back. The side of her face was black and blue, and as gaunt as it had been when she'd arrived in Elsudra months ago.

Her feet were covered in blisters too, which the healers treated. One of them—a woman with wavy hair the color of wenge wood and bright, angular eyes—applied ointment to her heels, then ran her hands over a cut on Marina's calf, reducing its size by nearly half. Marina watched her as she worked but was too exhausted to ask what she was doing. Healing was a slow and methodical practice, and by the time the woman finished, it didn't hurt as much to walk.

The lodgings were dispersed about the settlement, and after the healers finished with Ryder, Florin directed them to a communal room with a few beds, each of which had a trunk at the end for personal belongings. The room was unoccupied, so Marina chose a bed by the window and placed her boots beneath it.

"While you were with the healers, Neva made a comment about moving people to make room for us," Ryder said as he settled on a bed. "Couldn't help but feel like she wanted me to know it was a nuisance."

"Things seem...tense," Marina said. She glanced at the door to make sure it was shut. "Neva said she was a well-wisher, not an ally."

"Not everyone is as intent on taking Kieron down as the Delve. Some people would rather just protect themselves." Ryder paused. "But she saw your memories. Saw *Exorsus*. Maybe it'll push her to make another exception."

Marina rested her head—which still ached, but not as horribly—on the nearest pillow.

Letting people into her sanctuary was one thing. Perhaps Neva had made the choice because more soldiers meant more protection. Besides, she couldn't turn away one of Elsudra's top generals, and she certainly couldn't turn away the Sorcerer of the Court. But mobilizing her people—putting them in undue danger for a cause she wasn't sure would succeed—was a far riskier gamble.

Neva may be open to change, but facing Kieron was one hell of an exception to make. And judging by the strained cautiousness that lingered between her and Aeric, Marina worried even Exorsus didn't have the power to sway her.

CHAPTER 7
Not a Burden

The next couple of hours were a blur of showers, food, and fresh clothes. Florin brought them vocos as gray as the swamp water beneath them, which Marina eagerly took. As elegant as the ones from Altus were, she was happy to see them go.

Though she wanted to look for Pierce and Ismene, she focused first on Aeric. He was present when she and Ryder returned to the common room, and though she knew it was hasty, she pulled him aside and said, "You need to see."

They stepped out onto a balcony that overlooked trees and wooden buildings, leaving Ryder and Florin in the room. When Marina glanced at Ryder, he gave her an encouraging nod, then turned back to Florin, who was making quite a concerted effort to not look at Ryder's palms.

The air was less humid this high up, and Marina let it wash over her. She took a breath, then held her arm out to Aeric. "Explanations won't do it justice."

He beheld her with a look she couldn't read, and Marina couldn't help but remember that day in the Delve's dining room. She wondered if he was thinking of it as well—of how severely he'd terrified her with psychometry, even if it had been necessary.

It was necessary now too—perhaps more so—and when Aeric rested his hand on her wrist, she let her shields fall.

She wasn't sure how long they stood there, silent and dazed, but when Aeric removed his hand, his eyes shined.

The first thing he said was, "You accepted it."

She nodded. "I'm sorry I left. Sorry I didn't listen." Her voice broke. "I'm sorry for more than that too. I'm sorry for blaming you when I first came here. You aren't the reason I hold the Omnia...I'm the reason *you* have to oversee it. And I'm sorry I put this burden on you—sorry I told the Keepers to—but you're the only person..."

Aeric shook his head and leaned against the balcony. "It's not a burden." Silence followed, and when he straightened, he whispered, "You shouldn't have had to make the choice to begin with. And you shouldn't have had to endure Kieron."

Marina looked off to the side, her gaze brushing over the hundreds of trees below them. "Well, we're here now," she said. "We've made it this far."

Aeric didn't respond. His expression was blank, as though he was still struggling to let everything sink in. "What you learned in Exorsus about time—about it being a blanket—Kieron now knows this too," he finally whispered. "He understands Exorsus as well as us."

Marina's stomach flipped. She'd tried to shield her memories from Kieron upon leaving Exorsus, but he'd matched her closely. She could still feel his shaking hands on her forehead—the flames that danced atop her waves and searched for weakness. If it hadn't been for Ryder, he might've been successful in getting through entirely.

Cautiously, Marina asked, "Does that worry you?"

"It..." Aeric stopped himself. "No. It's just something I need to think about."

She wasn't sure what he was getting at—Kieron was still after the Omnia, with or without this new knowledge—but she wasn't inclined to push him. That, and a familiar voice sounded from within the common room, beckoning her inside.

Florin and Ryder were still there; Neva too. And...

"Marina!"

Ismene flung herself toward Marina, tears streaking down her face, and suddenly Marina was sobbing all over again.

"How...how did you get here?" Ismene stammered. She released Marina to look at her face, then embraced her once more, still crying. "We've been so worried. I've barely slept since you left...all I could think of was what we'd done...what *you'd* done...oh, Exorsus, I can't believe you made it back..."

"Thank you," Marina breathed into her hair. "Thank you, thank you."

She repeated herself several more times, still clinging to Ismene. She'd barely collected herself by the time she pulled away, and when the door opened once more and Marina saw Pierce, she broke down all over again.

Neva must think I'm a mess, she thought, but she hadn't cared before, and she didn't care now. Pierce rushed toward her, his eyes as wet as her own, and his voice shook when he said, "I knew it wasn't goodbye."

Marina wrapped her arms around him, trying not to cry and failing miserably. She wasn't sure how long they stood there, but when Pierce finally pulled back, his movements were slow and disoriented.

Marina glanced at Ryder, who regarded Pierce with an expression she couldn't read. Aeric had reentered the room too; he sat at the table's head closest to the door, an impatient look on his face. Neva watched them all closely, her gaze so sharp and assessing that for half a second, all Marina could think of was Gemma.

Pierce took a step toward Ryder, then another, and Marina's head began to buzz. Instinctively, she reached toward Ismene, whose eyes were as wide as her own.

But before Pierce could open his mouth, Ryder shifted to face Neva and said, "I imagine it'd be best if we get down to business."

Calm. Dismissive. As though he didn't know who Pierce was.

Pierce looked like he'd just caught the flu. His eyes glazed over, and when he took the seat next to Aeric, his gaze shifted to his feet.

Ismene glanced at Marina but didn't say anything as she sat next to Pierce.

There was only one chair left—between Florin and Ryder—which Marina took, trying her best not to react. Ryder stared ahead, a muscle feathering in his jaw.

Neva, thank goodness, broke the silence by saying, "Business here continues as usual. While I'd like to meet to discuss what happened in Altus, I also find it important that I underscore my goals."

Aeric tapped his finger on the tabletop. "Which are?"

"The same as they have always been," Neva replied evenly. "Preservation of this sanctuary and my people. I might have let the Delve in, but that doesn't mean I'd like to meet its fate. I wasn't part of the Keepers' plans, and I don't intend to be. While I can supply you with weapons, I cannot supply personnel."

Her position wasn't surprising, but Marina's heart sank all the same.

Aeric bristled, and Marina could sense a terse response forming at his lips. Before he could utter it, however, the door to the common room creaked open.

A girl, no older than ten—in her first quarter, as Elsudrans would say—lingered at the threshold, watching them from behind thick-rimmed glasses. The frames were made to look like rays of a sun, and when she tilted her head, they caught the light, glinting off her coiled ebony hair and deep brown skin. Around her neck, she wore a familiar device that had been made into a necklace. An anteactus, Marina realized. It was gold like her glasses and shined just as vibrantly.

Neva nodded at the girl. "Can this wait, Yolie?"

"I just wanted to know if I could join." Yolie's voice was small but clear.

Though she softened, Neva shook her head. "Not now. We're dispersing for the night anyway." She looked back to the table, her gaze shifting from Aeric to Marina to Ryder. "We'll meet here tomorrow. Noon, perhaps?"

"For what, exactly?" Aeric said. "If your stance is unchanging, there's nothing to discuss, and I'd sooner meet with Florin to decide how to move forward."

"Happenings in Altus concern us too," Neva responded testily. "Especially now that we're harboring the Omnia's host."

Aeric stiffened but didn't respond. When he stood, the rest of the table followed, but before he could leave, Ryder said, "Aeric, can we speak?"

Marina didn't know whose reaction to observe: Aeric's, Ryder's, or Pierce's. Her eyes darted between the three but settled on Yolie, who stared at all of them just as intently.

Aeric seemed surprised by the question but responded with his usual curt nod. Ryder relaxed, then put a hand on Marina's shoulder and said, "See you later."

Though she wanted to ask him what he wished to speak to Aeric about, she bit her tongue and nodded. Ryder strode from the room without so much as a glance in Pierce's direction, and the others filed out until only Marina, Ismene, and Pierce remained.

Pierce stared at the floor for a moment, then braced his hands on his knees and stood.

"Pierce," Marina whispered.

He wavered, and when he turned to look at Marina and Ismene, his eyes were wet.

"Are you okay?" Ismene asked.

"Fine."

"Don't go," Marina said. "I haven't seen you in weeks."

"If I stay any longer, I'm going to break down."

The silence that followed was fragile, and when Marina spoke, she did so softly. "Then break down. But stay with us."

Pierce's chin quivered as he lowered himself back to the table. He put his head in his hands, and just when Marina thought perhaps his tears wouldn't come, his shoulders began to shake.

"I shouldn't be surprised," he finally said. He rubbed his face and made a sound Marina could only interpret as a humorless laugh. "And I shouldn't be acting like this. Not after what you've gone through."

His eyes, dull and red, met Marina's, and her chest ached. "You were right about Ryder," she said. "And if you two hadn't done what you did for me back in the Delve, he wouldn't be here now. That's something, isn't it?"

Pierce nodded, but more tears ran down his cheeks. "Thank you for believing in him."

Though Ismene seemed hesitant, she reached out and wrapped her hands around Pierce's. She didn't say anything about Ryder, but she did whisper, "Reconciliation is a long, slow path." There was something different in her tone—something she tried to push down, but bubbled up anyway. Ismene wasn't the bitter type, but judging by the tightness in her eyes, Marina knew she was fighting the feeling.

Aeric and Florin had planned to leave her for dead, Marina thought. *Of course she's upset.*

"These past few weeks have been horrible," Ismene whispered, more to Marina than Pierce. "Aeric's reaction to your decision was terrifying."

Marina held her breath, but dared to ask, "How?"

"We thought he'd kill us both," Pierce muttered, then gave another choked laugh. "I tried to tell him about Ryder—tried to tell Florin too—but neither cared. Florin had to talk Aeric down, but that didn't stop Aeric from threatening us. And once he'd finished threatening..." Pierce's voice faded. "I never thought I'd see someone like Aeric break so severely. Honestly, that might've been the scariest part."

"He didn't think you stood a chance against Kieron," Ismene said. After a long pause, she added, "But we did. And we were right."

Now it was Marina's chin that quivered. "What happened after?"

"We left...with more people and more time," Ismene said. "There were some who volunteered to stay behind—mostly the elderly, who worried they'd slow us down, and some sentries."

"Boris," Marina breathed.

Pierce nodded. "And Dane. They knew it'd be suicide, but Boris said he'd rather die with a clean conscience than live in guilt about Ocot. Dane must've agreed." He looked once more to the floor, and Marina could barely make out his words when he said, "As for me, I fled. Again."

The pain in Marina's chest was becoming too much to bear, and since she could think of nothing else to say, she whispered, "Ocot's dead."

Pierce met her gaze, wide-eyed. Even Ismene uttered a sharp breath.

"What *did* happen in Altus?" Pierce finally asked.

Marina put her fingers to her lips and exhaled. "I don't know where to start."

Ismene peered out the nearest window, observing the night sky that hung above the treetops. When she looked back at Marina, she shrugged. "From the beginning."

CHAPTER 8
Chamomile

Marina's voice was raw by the time she returned to her room. She'd told them everything—every detail, down to Ocot and Cal—and when she'd cried, they'd cried too, unable to fathom how they'd possibly piece themselves back together again. But they would. They had to. *One day, one step, one breath at a time.*

Ryder was already in bed when Marina turned in. She knew he wasn't asleep, but he didn't react to her, probably because he didn't want her to press him about Pierce. She hadn't planned on it; that wasn't her battle to fight. Instead, she retreated to the bathroom and washed up, then fell asleep the moment her head hit the pillow.

Sleep came easier now than it had in quite some time, but Marina's dreams were as tumultuous as ever. Cal visited her again, clumps of her hair falling out and into Vaughn's palm. Vaughn closed his fingers around the raven strands, and his laughter began to morph into screams. Bones popped and tendons snapped as his arm came undone from his body, then hit the ground thumb-first. Suddenly, it wasn't Vaughn at all, but the guard from Tin —her hand a fingerless stump.

When Marina woke, she felt sick to her stomach. What she wouldn't give for just one night of waves.

The morning drudged on from there. Breakfast was served in a communal dining hall at the center of the compound, nestled above a cluster of swamp gums that made the air smell of eucalyptus. A fair number of people filled the tables, and their eyes all shifted to Marina and Ryder. Thankfully, the attention seemed to unsettle Ryder as much as it unsettled her, and they decided to bring their breakfast back to their room.

Ryder didn't say a word as they ate. When their vocos chimed with messages from the infirmary instructing them to stop by, he let out a heavy sigh and pushed his plate away, muttering something about how his pain medication suppressed his appetite.

It was a shitty lie, but Marina didn't call him on it. Instead, she offered to bring his plate back to the dining hall, which seemed to relieve him. Not enough to change his demeanor, but enough for Marina to notice. She knew he dreaded seeing Pierce, and after yesterday, Marina had a feeling Pierce was just as anxious. He hadn't been in the dining hall either. Back at the Delve, he'd have sought her out. Ismene was noticeably absent too.

This wasn't like them. She'd expected Aeric to be hard to find—he always was—but Pierce and Ismene were different. Ryder was different. None of them were acting like themselves. She knew it was stupid to wish they'd be like they used to, especially given everything going on, but she missed Pierce's playful banter and Ismene's cheeriness. And though it used to grate on her, she missed Ryder's smug smiles and sarcastic comments. He was just as sullen on the walk to the infirmary as he had been during breakfast.

Tucked away between two trees and surrounded by a garden of medicinal herbs, the infirmary was far enough away from the dining hall and other communal areas to limit noise. Distant voices skimmed over the canopy, and when the healers finished with her and brought Ryder in, she listened to them as she walked the gardens.

The plants were smaller than those in the Delve and less colorful, but it was a garden all the same. When she bent down to observe a small patch of white and yellow flowers, a voice closer than the rest said, "That's chamomile."

The voice might've startled her, had it not been so soft. When Marina lifted her eyes to the figure a few patches away, the little girl with golden glasses smiled at her.

"Yolie, right?" Marina said.

Yolie's smile widened. "Does your home have chamomile?"

Marina glanced at the flowers, then nodded. "We put it in tea."

"Us too." Though Yolie stood and edged a few steps closer to Marina, she kept her distance. "I feel more awake around you. Neva says that's because of the Omnia."

Gently, Marina said, "You can come closer."

"You're not scared?"

"Of what?"

"Elsudrans," Yolie said.

Marina couldn't help but smile. Obviously, Yolie hadn't been wary at all—just considerate. "I used to be," Marina admitted. "But not anymore."

"Neva says you escaped Kieron."

Somehow, Yolie's voice made even Kieron's name sound pleasant. Marina's gaze flicked over to the infirmary building as she said, "I had help."

"The guard with burns on his hands," Yolie said. "The healers said he got lucky—no ballistic trauma, just a graze wound."

Marina watched her pick one of the flowers and twirl its stem between her fingers. "How do you know?"

"I like to watch them work," Yolie said. "Some of them got annoyed at first, but then Neva told them they couldn't turn me away. Only rules are the patient has to agree, and I'm not allowed to pester anyone with questions. But that's okay. I learn on my own."

She was talking to herself at this point, observing the flower between her fingers with curiosity.

"How do you know Neva?" Marina asked.

"She's kind of my mom. Not really, just kind of."

Marina didn't ask Yolie where her biological mother was; she had a feeling that wasn't the kind of question Yolie wanted to answer. Instead, Marina said, "I like your anteactus."

"It used to be my older brother's. He couldn't do psychometry like me, so he said this was the next best thing."

"You can do psychometry?" When Yolie nodded, Marina blinked at her. She was so young. Didn't children have weaker grasps on their magic? "Can you shield too?"

"That's the easy part."

A laugh escaped Marina's lips. "Not for me." Even Aeric hadn't learned to properly shield until he was a teenager.

"Everyone has things they struggle with. That's what Neva says." Yolie cast the flower back into its patch and wiped her hands on her shirt. "I don't like generating force."

Marina tilted her head. "Maybe I can help you." She paused, then added, "If you promise to let me in on anything you learn from the healers."

Yolie's eyes lit up. "I could teach you to glamour too if you don't already know. I can't do living things yet, but inanimate objects are easy. Neva says I can glamour as well as two sorcerers put together. When the dead years stopped and the other sorcerers started glamouring the compound from below, I almost got her to agree to let me help. But then things got more dangerous, and now she won't budge." Before Marina could ask what she meant by that, Yolie added, "I've kept practicing on my own, though. I have a few tricks I could show you."

"I'd love that." The sound of the infirmary door opening caught Marina's attention, and before Yolie could respond, Ryder was at Marina's side, gesturing to his voco.

"It's noon," he said. "Best get going. We've an interrogation to attend."

"I don't think Neva's going to *interrogate* us," Marina said.

"Not you, maybe." He glanced at Yolie. "Bit of a coincidence running into you again."

Yolie's glasses glinted in the sunlight. "Not really. I followed you both here."

Ryder snorted. "Why?"

"Because I've never been this close to a Keeper, which makes her interesting," Yolie said, tilting her head at Marina. When her gaze settled back on Ryder, she added, "And Neva told me to stay away from you, which makes *you* interesting."

Ryder stiffened. "Of course she did." He didn't say anything else before turning on his heel and leaving.

Yolie didn't seem to think much of it. She faced Marina, unbothered, and said, "You should come to the observatory. That's where I like to practice magic."

"I'd love that too." Marina peered down the walkway at Ryder, who clearly wasn't going to wait for her, and gave Yolie an apologetic smile. "Soon, okay?"

Yolie nodded, and Marina hurried to catch up with Ryder. When she reached him, she could think of nothing to say but, "Apparently there's an observatory."

Ryder pursed his lips. "How exciting."

Marina bit back a groan. Her dreams, coupled with Neva's reluctance to provide aid, left her head foggy—much too foggy to deal with this. Of course, Neva's reluctance was understandable, and so was Ryder's mood, but it frustrated her anyway.

"I don't think Yolie meant to upset you," she whispered.

"Obviously not. I'm not mad at a kid."

"Is it Neva? Because I bet with time—"

"It may surprise you to realize this, Marina, but I was well aware before we came here that people wouldn't immediately trust me. And I don't blame a single one of them. So stop trying to make me feel better."

The bite in his tone brought Marina to a halt. "Don't be a smart-ass." When Ryder turned to face her, she crossed her arms. "I know you're stressed, but so am I. You think I'm happy to come here and realize we're hard-pressed for aid? That everything we've done may not matter if we don't have enough people on board?" Her breathing grew hitched. "And Cal..."

Ryder put his hand on her shoulder. "It'll matter."

Marina nodded. "I'm not going to push you into anything," she said gently. "But don't pull away. You're part of this, and we need you. *I* need you."

"You aren't alone. You have Aeric and Pierce and the rest."

He flinched at the name, but he hadn't said it bitterly. Still, Marina made sure he heard every word when she said, "You matter too."

CHAPTER 9
Silent Alarms

Neva, Florin, and Aeric were already in the common room when Marina and Ryder arrived. Ryder had been spot-on about an interrogation; Neva launched herself into questions the moment they sat down, dissecting every detail about Kieron, Altus, and what she'd seen in their memories.

Marina tried her best to answer, but after a while, her head pounded so severely she could only bring herself to give one-word answers. Ryder, too, spent most of the meeting rubbing his temples and recounting everything mechanically. Neva was harder on him, as he'd suspected. Marina tried to back Ryder, but in the end, it was Aeric who said, "Everything they tell you, you already know. Unless you've changed your mind about providing aid, I suggest we adjourn so the future may be discussed instead of the past."

Neva bristled but clamped her lips shut when a man entered the room. He was around Neva's age, perhaps a bit older—medium height, with dark, curly hair that grayed at the sides, a sharp nose, and umber skin. He smiled at them, then sat next to Neva and rested his chin in his hand. At first, Marina thought he was wearing a silver glove, but its metallic shine indicated otherwise.

She wasn't sure why—she knew it was a prosthetic—but the image of Kieron's gloved hand popped into her head anyway. She cursed internally. The two were *not* the same. She shifted her gaze to the man's face, which was soft and kind.

"This is Lars," Neva said to Marina and Ryder. "One of my most trusted confidants and a longtime friend."

The warmth in Neva's voice and the sudden flush in her cheeks made Marina wonder if Lars was more than a friend. Neva wouldn't have made it obvious either way; she kept a firm hand on her formality when she said, "He's been caught up with everything."

"So please, continue," Lars said. His voice was mellow but clearer than a clarion. "I'm nothing but a shadow."

A grin tugged at Neva's lips. "More than a shadow. We owe this sanctuary to him."

"I have a knack for preparedness is all," Lars said. "My family has lived in the South for decades. My father knew of this place, and his father before him, but we kept it under wraps. Easy to do, I suppose, when most people avoid the swamplands."

"Why do they avoid them?" Marina asked.

"Alligators tend to be overactive here," Lars said. "More so than anywhere else, at least. And these ones don't shy away from Elsudrans." He raised his metallic hand. "Lost my hand to one when I was a boy. It made its way into Inber, and I was in the wrong place at the wrong time. Thankfully, my mother shot it before it could swallow the rest of me."

Marina glanced at Ryder. He'd mentioned alligators, but he hadn't underscored how aggressive these ones were. On second thought, perhaps he'd omitted that information on purpose. Even now, he seemed determined to avoid her gaze. Instead, he nodded at Lars and said, "You're from Inber?"

"I am," Lars said. "But I've traveled since then."

"I'm from nearby—Mossley." Though Ryder spoke smoothly, Marina couldn't help but notice the hesitance in his voice.

"Seems you've traveled as well." Lars's eyes flicked to Ryder's palms, which Ryder quickly sheathed in his sleeves, but Lars didn't react. Instead, he turned to Marina and said, "As have you. Perhaps the farthest of us all. Thank you."

Marina found it rather inconvenient when her eyes began to sting. She thanked the heavens she could suppress them, but she still had to clear her throat before speaking. "Thank *you* for letting the Delve in."

"It was a shock to learn our Sorcerer of the Court had been alive all along," Lars said. "And even more of a shock to see him overseeing the Keepers' wishes."

Marina kept Lars's gaze as she said, "They chose wisely."

Though Aeric didn't react, something flickered in his eyes. Ryder gave Marina a soft smile, which emboldened her. She turned to Neva. "So...*have* you changed your mind?"

Neva laced her fingers, then took a measured breath. "I'm sorry."

Marina's heart dropped. She wasn't sure why; she'd expected that.

"If the information we've received from Ryder—as well as our own intel—is correct, that means Kieron outnumbers us five to one," Neva said, "and minus those from the Delve, our soldiers aren't trained nearly as well."

"But most of you have at least some level of magical ability," Ryder said, "and, if I had to guess, better morale. Some of the people fighting for Kieron are only doing so because they'll be killed if they refuse." He said it pointedly—to Neva most of all.

"Maybe," Neva said. "But if I send soldiers off to fight battles they're grossly underprepared for, then not only have I lost good people, but I've also put the rest of this sanctuary at risk. Come the day there's a threat against us, we won't stand a chance."

Aeric's hand tightened around the rim of the table. "And you think you'll stand a chance if Kieron remains in power?"

"I need to be careful with the gambles I make," Neva said, an edge to her voice. "We are one of the most at-risk groups in Elsudra. So when I weigh the costs of sending people we need off, I don't do so lightly. We've remained hidden this long, and I don't intend to expose us now." When she turned to Marina, she softened. "What you did doesn't go unnoticed. But I also cannot, in good conscience, send people off to die out of sheer hope."

"We aren't a fighting group," Lars added. "The Delve was made by the military for the military. The bulk of our people are regular citizens. Some inclined, perhaps, but having those abilities doesn't automatically make one a warrior. You seldom see a Lewes-educated healer go on to fight soldiers from Altus." He leaned back in his chair. "I'm afraid our help comes in the form of sanctuary, not war."

Florin, who previously seemed to have been lost in thought, broke his silence when he said, "Full-on war may not be necessary."

Neva raised an eyebrow at him. "A few days ago, it seemed to be."

"A few days ago, Marina wasn't here with us," Florin said, "and our only goal was to get her back. A more traditional route may've been warranted then, but now, things are different. We don't need to resort to the reckless attacks we saw when Kieron returned from Sundra."

Marina wasn't sure if that frightened or relieved her, but she didn't particularly care at the moment; it was Neva's reaction that mattered.

It was Lars, however, who chuckled and said, "If it's assassination you're proposing—"

"We'd end up like sorcerers did before the dead years—bodies hanging throughout the capital," Neva interrupted. "Altus swarms with Kieron's soldiers, and Kieron himself stays in the Pale Tower, which, according to our new informant"—she cocked her head at Ryder —"is guarded by hordes of ruemin. Even an assassination attempt is too big a risk."

The Pale Tower. Ryder had mentioned that before. It was where Kieron disappeared to, hidden from the world he wished so desperately to rule. If he was paranoid enough to isolate himself, then he knew he wasn't invincible. That alone offered Marina some measly hope, but not enough to suggest anything.

She hated how useless she felt here. Military tactics and assassination attempts weren't her strong suits and likely never would be. What *were* her strong suits? Generating force and bursts of light?

Perhaps she'd been foolish to think she'd be able to do this. If she was overwhelmed now, how the hell would she ever live up to the expectations of the Keepers—expectations she'd imposed on herself?

Like an angry wave, heat rushed through her, sending her heartbeat into a frenzy.

Stop. Breathe. One at a time.

Florin's voice roused her. "I'm not proposing assassination. Not right now, at least." He paused and folded his hands. "Previous attempts have been foiled because Kieron was well protected—by ruemin more than anything. If we can find a way to strip him of this safety net, he'll be vulnerable."

The heat within her pricked at her skin, and Marina placed her palms on the cool table before saying, "But there are hundreds of them in Elsudra, aren't there?"

"Our best guess is a little over a thousand," Florin said. "Maybe fewer. But only *one* came through the portal with Kieron."

Whether or not it was purposeful, everyone's eyes shifted to Aeric.

"Brenna's portal?" Marina asked. She didn't know why, but she lowered her voice to a whisper when she said, "The one Aeric hijacked?"

Aeric's lips thinned. "Technically, I—"

His voco cut him off—not with any chimes or alarms, but with lights. In fact, all of their vocos seemed to have gone into a frenzy.

Marina shot a wide-eyed look at Ryder, who was clearly as confused as she was, then at Aeric, whose jaw was tighter than usual.

"It's okay," Florin said quickly. "No need to panic. Business can carry on as usual, so long as we keep our noise to a minimum. Whispering will do."

Neva wasn't quite as calm. Her hand flew to Lars's shoulder, and her voice left her in a breath. "Yolie…"

"Is safe," Lars said. "She's probably—"

"In the infirmary," someone else interrupted. The door had cracked open, and a willowy woman slipped inside. She looked familiar—her hair dark like trees deep in a forest, and her eyes lively, if not a bit worried.

Lars grinned, but it was strained. "Exactly what I was going to say."

Neva rested her forehead in the palm of her hand. "Thank you, Elta."

"She's with the other healers," Elta said. "One of them sent me a message. Nothing to worry about."

That was who Elta was—the healer who'd treated the blisters on Marina's feet and tended to the cut on her leg. She couldn't have been much older than Ismene and Cal.

Marina grew lightheaded. Why did she have to remember Cal now, when she was already overwhelmed? The light on her voco flashed again, and Marina wondered if it had grown brighter. Did anyone else notice that? *All* the lights had grown brighter. And the silence…somehow, it was more deafening than screams.

Though she didn't expect it to, Ryder's voice grounded her. "What are the lights for? And when do they stop?"

"They're alarms," Florin responded. "There aren't rock walls here to suppress sounds, so silent alarms are smarter. The lights signal for people to get inside and stay there until the flashing stops." He paused, looking at Ryder more than anyone else when he said, "Kieron is increasing his troops' presence in most towns. He's had a small unit stationed in Inber that conducts sweeps of the swamplands every so often, but their schedule is unpredictable."

Silence followed, which Ryder broke when he said, "I was unaware of this."

Florin gave him a subtle nod, but Neva only frowned.

"Yet you knew to take the backroads to get here," she said.

Before Marina could process Neva's implication, Ryder scoffed. "You saw my memories. You know I'm not hiding anything."

"I didn't say you were."

Ryder's mouth tightened. "I didn't *know* anything. I made an educated guess that backroads were safer. Anyone with a modicum of intelligence would've done the same."

Either Marina was imagining it, or the corners of Aeric's lips twitched upward.

"The soldiers don't have a clue we're up here," Elta said when the silence grew too tense. She shot a hesitant smile at Marina and Ryder. "We're too high up, and we have glamours. They were just reinforced this morning."

"Any particular reason Marina and I weren't told about these alarms when we arrived?" Ryder asked. "Seems important." There was an edge to his voice, and he didn't bother to hide it.

Marina almost shot Ryder a warning glance, but Neva beat her to it.

"This is new territory for us," Lars said. "The past season has been one of change, and we're still adjusting. The alarms had never warranted use until halfway through Aragonite —a week or two after the Delve arrived here, actually. Kieron's soldiers had never had reason to come this far south before."

"My contacts have gone silent too," Neva said testily. "The last messages I received were in early Aragonite, and they spoke of soldiers swarming towns, ripping apart homes, dredging damned rivers…it was worse than it'd been when Kieron returned from Sundra. I had no idea what caused the chaos until the Delve showed up. It all came together after that: the increased ruemin run-ins, the unanswered messages...everything."

So *that* was what Yolie had been referring to when she'd said things had gotten more dangerous. Marina's stomach soured. She'd known Kieron had attacked the Delve, but she hadn't fathomed how extensive his search for Aeric had become. And it *had* to be Aeric he was searching for. He'd had the Omnia's host with him until just a few days ago, after all, which meant there was only one person he'd been missing.

Ryder had said as much—that it was Aeric who Kieron had wanted to find when he'd destroyed the Delve. It only made sense that Kieron would continue his rampage across the realm—that he'd tear apart Elsudra to find the one person he couldn't seem to let go of. Aeric knew it too, no doubt. Though he didn't so much as flinch, Marina could detect the shift in his demeanor. She wondered if it was noticeable to Neva and the others.

She wasn't sure how long the alarm lasted, but nobody spoke. Florin must've realized Neva wouldn't be receptive to what he had to say at the moment; he remained silent until the flashing stopped.

"This is what I mean," Neva finally said, her voice still a whisper. "We're more at risk now than we've ever been. Even the sorcerers who maintain our glamours can't go below without worrying about running into troops and blowing our cover. Day, night...it doesn't matter when they go out. The threat is always there. Some days, there's nothing; others, the alarm goes off several times. Yesterday and today have been mild, in truth."

Ryder shifted. "How many soldiers make up the unit?" When Neva raised an eyebrow, he didn't try to control his tone. "My job didn't involve planning sweeps of other regions," he snapped. "I wasn't made privy to that knowledge. I didn't talk to generals or attend high-level strategy meetings. I was Kieron's glorified messenger, nothing else."

When he side-eyed Marina, she opened her mouth to back him up. Lars, however, spoke first.

"Our estimate is ten," he said calmly. "It's a small group."

Neva stood. "And it would only take one to alert Altus of our presence and send in hundreds more. A squad is just as dangerous as an army." She shook her head, noticeably pale. "We'll reconvene this evening. I need to go check on things."

Marina supposed she meant Yolie. But Neva didn't give anyone a chance to ask her what she meant; she left quickly, and though Florin sighed, he didn't try to hold her back. Lars left soon after.

Still dizzy, Marina turned to Aeric. But before she could ask him—or Florin—about whatever they'd planned to propose to Neva, Aeric said, "We'll speak later. Try to rest."

And then, like that, he left too. Florin didn't hang around much longer either.

Marina leaned back in her chair. What a ridiculous suggestion. Aeric knew rest was seldom possible for her, especially now. But he clearly didn't want to entertain any of her questions, and she was much too exhausted to follow him and demand answers.

Ryder put his head in his hands, and Marina didn't fight the numbness that settled in. Maybe *that* was a form of rest.

"How's the gunshot wound doing?" Elta asked gently.

Ryder barely lifted his head. "I've suffered more permanent injuries," he muttered.

Marina shot Elta an apologetic look, but she didn't seem put off by Ryder's mood. "How about we go get you two something to eat?" she said. "There's not much a good meal can't solve."

Though Ryder still didn't look up, Marina managed a smile. It was robotic—perhaps a bit detached—but it was something. She stood, then tugged on Ryder's arm, which got him to stand.

Perhaps both of them needed someone else to make decisions for the time being, or perhaps they were just too weary to turn Elta down. Whatever the reason, they followed her from the room like aimless children.

❧

Marina tried to stay present, but even the sunlight didn't snap her out of her stupor. All she could think about were flashing lights and the world below, teeming with soldiers in golden armor.

She came to a bit when she found Ismene in the dining room, picking at her food with a similarly blank expression. Elta seemed more than happy to accompany them, and though Ryder groaned as Marina dragged him over to the table, he didn't resist—not after confirming Pierce was absent.

Would they go on like this forever? Hiding in their rooms to avoid each other and eating meals alone?

Well, at least Ismene was out and about. When she saw Marina, she brightened. She greeted Marina and Elta, and though she was leery of Ryder, she remained polite. Luckily, Elta was as peppy as Ismene, and the two warmed up to each other immediately. When Ismene started going on about the compound's library—a hint of her old self in her voice—Marina found it easier to focus.

"I found a section specifically for books about healing, just like the ones my parents used back in Lewes," Ismene said. She turned to Elta. "I can only imagine how many you've had to read."

Elta blinked at her. "You know I'm a healer?"

"I've tried my best to learn about everyone here," Ismene said. "Makes me feel more at home. Helps me pass the time too, especially since I don't have near as many duties here as I did in the Delve."

Elta chuckled. "I'm flattered you consider me a healer. When I first arrived, I'd only dabbled in medical magic. But they had a shortage of healers here, so I did my best to help." She shrugged. "Some of the other healers don't consider me as well-versed as them, but I make do."

"You did a good job on my wounds," Marina chimed in, trying to match Ismene's and Elta's cheeriness. She glanced at Ryder, hoping he'd at least murmur his agreement, but he only stared at his food.

"I'm glad to hear it," Elta said. "Especially since the majority of my training happened during the dead years when I didn't have my magical abilities to rely on."

Ismene shook her head. "Such a miserable period. You wouldn't believe how many times I had to see the healers for something as simple as a paper cut."

Though she and Elta laughed about it, Marina's stomach churned—especially when Elta said, "I thank Exorsus every day that the Omnia returned to us. Twelve years of stagnancy was enough to drive me mad."

Twelve years; the equivalent of five back at home. But that was still a long time for the world to effectively stop—for magic and life energy to cease and for Elsudrans to blindly await the day their realm's beating heart returned. And now she held the Omnia. *She'd* made that choice. She prayed to God—to whatever power might be listening—that it had been the right one. Perhaps she'd have prayed to Exorsus, had she not known its true nature. Even if it heard her, it wouldn't answer.

She tried to listen as Ismene and Elta spoke—Ryder nodded along too, though Marina had a feeling he wasn't really listening—but for some reason, all she could think of was the eatery in Tin. Perhaps it was because the dining hall here resembled it: large communal tables, a buffet of food at the side...maybe Altus guards would find this place too.

Stop. Breathe. One day, one step, one breath at a time.

Kieron had told her that even if he hadn't known about the Delve, he was well aware of other hideaways. Was the Candens Inlet sanctuary one of them? No...it couldn't be. If that were the case, he wouldn't be having his soldiers conduct sweeps of the swamplands below. He would have destroyed this place the second he found out about it, especially given the kind of people residing here.

It was interesting seeing so many inclined Elsudrans in the same place. Occasionally, someone would summon water into their glass. A middle-aged man sitting a few paces from the buffet even refilled his plate without moving a muscle. A woman with a baby sat at a table in the corner of the room, light sparking at her fingertips, and a laugh bubbled at the baby's mouth.

"Cordelia," the mother sang. "My little Cordelia."

My Rina. My little Rina.

Marina's eyes began to burn.

"She was pregnant during the dead years," Elta said, noting where Marina was looking. Marina kept her gaze on the baby, determined not to cry. "Gave birth right when they ended."

The baby suckled at a red pacifier, which she released when she laughed. Before it could hit the ground, her mother's fingers twitched. The pacifier fluttered mid-air, dancing between them and sending the baby into another fit of laughter.

"Can't fathom being pregnant that long," Ryder muttered.

As off-handed as the comment was, a smile tugged at Marina's lips. "You're lucky you'll never have to deal with that."

He gave her a wry look. "Don't act like *you'd* ever get pregnant. You have the maternal instincts of a snake."

Though Elta and Ismene exchanged a glance, Marina burst out laughing. It surprised her, but she welcomed the unexpected boost in mood, especially when Ryder grinned. There was amusement in his eyes too—amusement that seemed to come and go in waves.

Maybe this time he'll hold on to it.

And then, the amusement faded.

Or not.

Ryder tensed as Pierce set his tray down next to Ismene and Elta. He was mindful about where he sat—directly across from Marina, diagonal to Ryder—and when he spoke, he looked at nobody in particular.

"Hope you don't mind," he said.

Marina and Ismene stumbled through awkward greetings, and Marina did her best to not glance at Ryder.

He was stubborn—too stubborn to get up and leave right away. Instead, he took a slow sip of water.

Elta clearly picked up on the friction, but she played it off by introducing herself to Pierce and asking where he'd grown up.

Pierce did a horrible job reining in his emotions, but he managed to respond to Elta's question and even asked her a few of his own. Marina tried to listen as Elta told Pierce about how she'd always wanted to work in Altus, but the lingering unease squelched her attempts at cheeriness.

"I grew up in Kalendus," she said. Then, to Marina, she added, "It's a city in the West.

I served on the council for a few years, overseeing day-to-day operations."

"Kind of like Ismene," Marina said, praying the compliment would lighten things up.

Ismene's face reddened. "My work was done on a much smaller scale."

"I bet it wasn't too different," Elta said through a shrug. "Managing people, taking charge of the things nobody thinks to take charge of...something tells me you were great."

Ismene smiled. "Kalendus is an impressive city."

"I'd be prouder of it if it didn't remind people of Kieron," Elta said. Her lips twitched, and she shot a hesitant glance at Marina. "It's where he was raised. Nowadays, it's hard to associate Kalendus with anyone but him."

Marina couldn't help but side glance at Ryder, then at Pierce. Elta clearly regretted bringing up Kieron because she quickly tried to change the subject.

"That's how I met Neva," she said. "Her work brought her to cities all over the realm, and I had the pleasure of welcoming her to Kalendus. I swear, she should've served in government herself. We're lucky to have her here."

Marina almost asked what Neva's job had been before everything happened, but she couldn't find her voice. The enmity in the air had grown suffocating—so suffocating even Elta surrendered to it.

Pierce eyed his food as though he was waiting for Ryder to say something, but Marina knew Ryder wouldn't speak first.

Pierce must've too, because when the silence came to a fester, he pushed his tray away and looked Ryder in the eyes. "I'm so sorry," he rasped. "You don't know—"

"I *do* know," Ryder said stiffly. "I just don't care."

"I only hoped...it's been so long."

"Yes. Twelve dead years and nearly four seasons. I counted."

Pierce's throat bobbed. "I did too. And I thought of you every day..."

"I have enough of my own mistakes to contend with, Pierce," Ryder said, his jaw tight, "most of which started after I stayed in Altus looking for you." He stood. "But what's done is done. It's best for everyone if we keep our interactions to a minimum from here on out. Business casual."

Marina tensed as he scooped up his food tray and prowled off. Silence lingered in his wake, even heavier than before.

"That went...better than I thought," Pierce whispered.

Ismene and Elta shifted uncomfortably in their seats, and since Marina could think of nothing else to do, she said, "One day at a time."

Pierce only lifted his eyes to hers and nodded.

CHAPTER 10
A Hundred Pawns

Pierce stayed with them as they ate, even though he didn't eat anything himself. Elta fetched some pastries for the table, which Marina supposed were mostly meant for Pierce, but he didn't so much as look at them, so Marina and Ismene took a few instead.

The rest of lunch was strained. Elta probably thought they were a terribly morose bunch, and since Marina couldn't bear for that to be the first impression they left, she made it a point to ask the three of them to show her around.

Elta seemed hesitant at first but agreed when Ismene made it clear she wanted her to come. Pierce didn't seem to mind either way, though he stayed uncharacteristically quiet as they meandered the wooden pathways. When he'd shown her around the Delve, he'd talked nonstop, and she'd been the silent, brooding one. Now, she tried to match Ismene's and Elta's energy, but it felt forced.

Despite being half the size of the Delve, the Candens Inlet sanctuary harbored nearly five hundred people. They had enough space, even with the growing numbers, but unlike the halls in the Delve, one couldn't walk far here without passing someone. People seemed to know who she was; most gave her friendly nods, and a few went out of their way to greet her—to thank her.

For what? Kieron was still breathing, and his presence loomed over the sanctuary.

She swallowed the urge to say, "Don't thank me yet," and instead accepted their gratitude, though it was clear they didn't quite know what they were thanking her for. To them, it was simple: she held the Omnia. They didn't seem curious how or why. But maybe that was better. If she failed, they wouldn't know she'd taken on this burden purposefully.

Stop thinking that. Stop thinking you'll fail.

Her commands did precious little to stop the thoughts, so she instead forced herself to breathe—to walk with Pierce, Ismene, and Elta, one step at a time.

Some of the walkways ended in round balconies overlooking miles of thick, waxy leaves. Up here, the sky was clear, and so blue that the ocean paled in comparison.

They stopped at a balcony nestled between the library and some small apartments, empty minus a gray cat perched on the railing. It watched the trees with chartreuse eyes, then shifted its gaze to them as they approached.

Ismene brightened, then nudged Pierce. "Your friend joined us."

That got a smile out of him. "Always popping up outta nowhere, isn't he?"

Marina blinked at the cat. She hadn't seen many animals in Elsudra, minus birds and ruemin. But birds were a dime a dozen, and the ruemin didn't count. "Whose is it?"

"Nobody's," Elta said. "He made his way up here during the dead years, and we couldn't bring ourselves to kick him out. He doesn't have a name, though."

"I call him Ash," Pierce said softly.

Marina snorted. "*Very* creative."

Pierce rolled his eyes, but his smile widened a bit. "Shut up. It suits him."

"Ash is quite fond of Pierce," Ismene said. "We've started timing how long it takes for him to show up when Pierce is around."

Marina tilted her head. "Can animals be inclined?" She'd never thought of it before.

"Not like Elsudrans can," Elta said. "But I've heard of some with an affinity for water."

"Ash definitely doesn't have those talents," Pierce said. "Doesn't have many talents at all, I'm afraid. He's just...Ash."

"Well, he's very handsome," Marina said.

"His one redeeming quality." Pierce's smile faded. "That, and he doesn't hold grudges."

Marina and Ismene shared a glance, but before either could respond, Pierce rattled off some excuse about needing rest. Marina didn't push him to stay—not when his eyes began to shine. When he left, Ash hopped from the railing and slinked after him.

Once both were gone, Ismene sighed. "I've never seen him like this." She leaned against the railing. "We share a room, and when we first arrived, it was him trying to make *me* feel better. Now, he hardly talks."

Elta shifted her balance between her feet. "I take it Ryder and Pierce knew each other before everything happened?" When Ismene nodded, Elta rubbed her palms together. "That's...unfortunate."

"It'll take them time to adjust," Marina said. Hesitantly, she added, "It'll take us *all* time to adjust. Things are tense with Neva too."

Elta didn't respond right away. When she did, it was clear she was searching for the safest words. "It's been a lot," she said. "Especially recently, with troops so close. She and

Lars spent the dead years overseeing this place, and there's nothing scarier to Neva than the possibility we might be found."

And now, given the Delve's presence, that possibility was more likely than ever. A sudden heaviness settled on Marina's chest. "I'm sorry," she whispered.

"It's not your fault," Elta said. "Your home was attacked. You had to find a new one." She glanced at Ismene, then back at Marina. "If there's one thing most Elsudrans can agree on, it's that losing your home—losing loved ones—is one of the worst pains imaginable." Her chin trembled, but she steadied it. "That's part of the reason I tried to learn more about medicine when I got here. I wanted to heal people, even if I could only treat the physical wounds." She paused. "But I didn't completely abandon politics. I work with Neva from time to time, and I'd be willing to talk to her—about this or anything else. If you think it would be helpful, that is."

Marina stared at her. The offer seemed genuine, but Marina couldn't help herself when she asked, "Why would you?"

The question came out more skeptically than she'd intended, but Elta only smiled.

"I'm thankful for this place," she said, "but I don't want to stay here forever. I want my world to go back to what it was—or perhaps grow into something better. And if I have faith in any group to get rid of Kieron, it's Aeric and Florin...and you." When Marina knit her brows, Elta added, "I heard what you did for the Delve. Anyone who gives themselves up to Kieron *and* manages to escape him has my vote. Especially if we hope to see the end of this horrible reign one day."

Marina's heart fluttered. She didn't know what to feel: honored that Elta considered her someone worthy of investing faith into, or terrified of not living up to it. Regardless, she figured having Elta on her side would be helpful.

"I might take you up on that," Marina said.

It would be helpful, of course, if she knew what the hell Aeric and Florin wanted Neva to provide aid *for*. At the moment, she had no idea what they were planning. The more she thought on it, the angrier she became. Aeric knew she hated the unknown—that she couldn't bear being kept in the dark—but he'd left without telling her anyway.

Rest. That was what he'd told her to do. Rest, without knowing what it was they were going to try to convince Neva of. Rest, though there was a strong possibility that no number of carefully crafted plans would sway Neva's decision.

Aeric doesn't want me to rest, Marina thought. *He just doesn't want me to badger him, like always.* She clenched her fists, then closed her eyes against the breeze that flitted through the leaves and forced herself to breathe alongside it.

Florin had made it clear he didn't have assassination in mind. But he *had* mentioned the ruemin…and portals. Brenna's portal, specifically.

She tilted her head, then asked, "How do portals work?"

Ismene and Elta exchanged a glance.

"You come from a realm without them?" Elta asked. When Marina nodded, she said, "They're programmed to recognize beings of our genetic makeup. That's why the moment any part of our flesh touches the light, the portal activates an internal mechanism that pulls us in and brings us to our destination." She shrugged. "Some people touch their hands to the portal's mouth; others simply step through with their hands and arms slightly in front of them, granted they've removed anything covering their skin. There aren't any rules on how to travel through portals—as long as it registers some flesh, it'll work."

"But what's that got to do with Neva?" Ismene asked.

"Florin mentioned them today," Marina said. "But he was interrupted by the alarm before he could expand, and then Neva cut our meeting short." She paused, then added, "And Aeric brushed me off before I could ask him."

Ismene pursed her lips. "Not surprising." There it was again—that undercurrent of bitterness in her voice. She covered it up with a stilted chuckle, then said, "I wish I knew more about the intricacies of portals, but I took them for granted back when I had the freedom to travel."

"Same here," Elta said. "I think most Elsudrans took their old life for granted."

After a moment of silence, Marina asked, "Does it matter how much of you touches the light?" When Elta frowned, she added, "Ryder told me even a finger brushing against the light will take you back where you came from."

"Never touch an active portal unless you intend to travel," Ismene said. "That's what my dad always said."

"They stay active for a few seconds after you arrive as a buffer," Elta explained, "in case you make a last-minute decision to go back the way you came. But Ryder's right; the moment any part of your body touches the light, you'll be pulled in. The physics of going through portals is different from going through a doorway. Your entire body goes one place at the same time. You can't linger over the threshold, just like half your body can't exist in one place while the other half exists somewhere else." She grinned wryly. "You'd be dead if that were the case, and portals don't recognize dead bodies."

Marina considered for a moment. "So they only recognize living beings?"

"Living beings from the sister realms, to be precise," Elta said. "But they're designed to take anything that's attached to us through as well. Wouldn't want people to arrive without their clothing or belongings."

"Portals are quite particular," Ismene said, then giggled. "On the rare occasion that I'd travel with my family, my sisters and I would try to game the system by going through at the same time. We hoped it would only register us as one person and wouldn't make us pay. But they'd shut down and force us to swipe our vocos before we could get through."

"Well, the government's not doing their job if they don't demand at least some of your money," Elta teased.

Ismene rolled her eyes, but her smile widened. "They take what they can from us."

Before she could decide against it, Marina blurted, "What about Brenna's portal?"

Elta's and Ismene's smiles faded.

"What about it?" Ismene asked.

Marina lowered her voice to a whisper. "How does it work?"

This time, Elta wasn't so quick to answer. She glanced sidelong at Ismene, who'd started fiddling with a strand of her hair. "I never saw it," Ismene said. "When I worked in Altus, it was locked away in the palace basements and guarded around the clock. Only the Keepers and the Sorcerer of the Court had access. When Kieron returned from exile and brought the ruemin with him, everything happened quickly. I only remember being escorted to safety by palace guards, and we were told what happened *after* Kieron had lost the battle for Altus and fled with Aeric." She chewed her lip nervously, then said, "But... from what I understand, Brenna's portal works like our intra-realm portals. At least...it does now that it's no longer unidirectional." She brought the strand to her lips, then sighed through it. "But I have a feeling that portal didn't require vocos to activate."

"Fitting," Elta muttered. "People only get free passage when they're exiled."

A nervous laugh bubbled at Ismene's mouth, but she suppressed it. "Brenna's portal wasn't made to help people get around," she said. "It was made to get *rid* of people. But I think you know how that turned out."

Marina's stomach flipped. She imagined every Elsudran knew how that turned out, especially now that the ruemin were here. And they were only here because Kieron had brought them with him upon his return from exile—because Aeric had hijacked the portal to bring him back, just like Lars had said.

Elta seemed eager to get back to showing Marina around the compound—either that or she wanted to change the topic—because she made it a point to start the tour back up. The three of them meandered a while longer, but Marina was so deep in her thoughts that eventually Elta gave up. She and Ismene fell in line with each other, talking about the gardens, and though Marina walked alongside them, she was too distracted to join in.

If Brenna's portal worked like the Elsudran portals, then it could only recognize living beings from the sister realms—beings like Kieron. He might have lost a piece of his soul in Sundra, but his blood still flowed; that was obviously enough for a portal to recognize him and pull him through. But if the portal couldn't recognize ruemin—if it wouldn't activate at their touch—then what had Kieron done? Brought each one through with him?

No…Florin had said only one ruemin came through with Kieron.

A shiver snaked down Marina's spine. One ruemin had come through, and somehow, the rest followed suit—quickly, like Ismene had said. Now there were hundreds, slinking through every Elsudran city and hiding in the aspen-shrouded Admares.

Aspens. What was it Cal had said back at the Delve?

They're a little like aspen trees. Of course. Kieron didn't need to bring more than one ruemin through—not when they were all connected. Whatever intangible root system held them together clearly stayed intact in Elsudra. But that connection couldn't stretch across the thresholds of realms, which meant when one ruemin passed into Sundra…

They'd all go with it. It only made sense. The same way she couldn't so much as brush a finger across an active portal's mouth and stay where she was, the ruemin couldn't exist in both Elsudra and Sundra when they were part of the same entity. That had to be why Florin had said only one came through with Kieron.

Which meant *that* was how they were planning to bring the ruemin out.

She wasn't sure of the plan's technicalities, but that had to be the basis of it. What else could Florin have been alluding to?

Marina's chest tightened. If the alarm hadn't gone off and Aeric hadn't dismissed her, perhaps she wouldn't be making guesses on her own, scrounging up knowledge where she could and praying it would give her measly insight. She'd done that back in the Delve. Aeric knew that, and he'd *still* rebuffed her. Clearly, old habits died hard.

She was tempted to try to find him and Florin before the turn of the evening and ask if her suspicions were correct, but she didn't want Elta and Ismene to think she was rude. Luckily, Elta had an upcoming shift at the infirmary, and it didn't take long before she parted. She said something to Ismene, who broke into a smile, then nodded at Marina.

"I hope Neva warms up," she said. "But if she doesn't, I'll try to help where I can."

"Thank you," Marina breathed as she walked away. She turned to Ismene, who was still smiling, and asked, "What did she say to you?"

Ismene bit her lip. "She invited me to the gardens. Said she works there and would love to have me join."

The tension in Marina's shoulders eased a bit. It was clear Ismene felt lost here—that she missed having a purpose. Maybe the gardens would help with that.

Though eagerness to find Aeric pricked at her fingers, it faded as she and Ismene made their way to another balcony. The afternoon sun wasn't so direct now, and its light shrouded the canopy in gold.

"How are you doing?" Marina asked after a few moments.

The question seemed to surprise Ismene. She fiddled with her voco, then shrugged. "Same as everyone. Better now that you're safe. And this region is beautiful, isn't it? I traveled once to the South before when I was young, but never this far…"

She lost her voice along the way, and only when Marina held her gaze did she say, "I've tried coming to terms with it. But I don't think I've been successful."

It. What else could she mean, if not the fact that she would have been left behind?

"I always knew there was a possibility the Delve could be compromised," she said, "but there were so many ways it could've gone—so many worst-case scenarios—that those of us who weren't sentries were never explicitly told what to expect. I guess it turns out that was intentional." Her voice was a whisper, and even then, she struggled to steady it. "Aeric and Florin were making the best choices they could, given the circumstances. I don't blame them. I know they didn't want to leave anyone for dead. But…I suppose it all feels horribly familiar."

Gently, Marina asked, "How?"

"I told you about my parents," Ismene said. "About how they'd abuse the trust of their daughters for their own benefit. I ran away from it—to Altus, where I wouldn't be a pawn in someone else's game. But I never escaped the game. I just started playing a bigger one." She stared at her hands. "It didn't matter how devoted I was—to my parents or Elsudra. It didn't matter how hard I worked or how faithfully I served. I was always disposable. Just another pawn." Her face twisted, but her eyes didn't water. "Aeric's barely spoken to me since we've arrived. Now that he doesn't need me, I might as well be invisible."

"He…has a lot on his mind," Marina said.

"I know." Ismene rubbed temples. "I'm sure I sound ridiculously bitter."

"No. Of course not, Ismene. You have every right to be upset."

For perhaps the first time since Marina had known her, Ismene didn't try to lessen the tension with a smile. "I jumped from one horrible cycle to another, didn't I?" she said. "And the worst part is, I wasn't the only one. A hundred others didn't make it out of the Delve. A hundred pawns."

Marina's heart sank. She couldn't help but remember how she'd once abused Ismene's kindness to get back at Aeric. She'd treated Ismene the same way everyone else had: as a pawn. Her voice shook when she said, "I'm so sorry."

"Don't be. If you hadn't gone to Altus, I…" Ismene bit down on her quivering lip. "I'd rather endure this terrible game than no longer be around to play it," she said once she'd steadied herself. Softer, she added, "And thanks to you, I'm still around."

CHAPTER 11
Head of the Snake

It wasn't evening when Marina returned to the common room, but Aeric and Florin were already present. She figured they'd probably waited until everyone else filed out to reconvene just the two of them, which annoyed her about as much as the way they stopped talking when she walked in. Whatever. The silence gave her room to speak.

"You're planning to sacrifice someone to pull the ruemin back into Sundra," she said, not bothering to phrase it like a question.

After another bout of silence, Florin let out a half sigh, half laugh. "That's the gist of it." His lips edged into a grin as he glanced at Aeric. "I had a feeling Neva, Lars, and Ryder would put it together, but not a non-Elsudran."

Aeric frowned. "How *did* you figure that out?" he asked, though it sounded more like an accusation. "You have no idea how portals work."

"Actually, I do," she said. She sat at the table, directly across from Aeric and Florin. "I asked around."

Aeric's gaze hardened. "Who—"

"I asked the same person I always ask when you don't give me information."

Aeric must've realized she meant Ismene because he relaxed ever so subtly. Still, his words were clipped when he said, "We don't need this getting out, even to people like Ismene. What we say stays in this room."

He probably wouldn't react well if she told him she'd also asked Elta, but she hadn't planned on admitting that. Instead, she shrugged and said, "Technically, you didn't *say* anything. And if you hadn't been so eager to brush me off, I could've asked you instead."

Aeric pinched the bridge of his nose but didn't respond.

"What I don't understand is how you'd *keep* the ruemin in Sundra, especially if Kieron could just as easily bring them back again," Marina said. "The portal is still bidirectional, isn't it? Do you plan to hijack it to only go one way again?"

"No," Aeric said flatly. After a pause, he added, "I told you this back at the Delve: I didn't hijack the portal. I hijacked something that powered it."

Marina blinked at him, but before she could say anything, he reached into his pocket and pulled out something small—something that glowed in the light when he put it on the table. A ring with a center stone made to look like a plasma globe.

The breath left Marina's throat in a gasp. Was that...?

"Brenna's ring," Aeric said. "When she passed away, Kieron inherited it. When he was exiled, *I* did." His eyes rested on the ring for a moment before shifting back to Marina. "Brenna had made it to resemble her spirit—thousands of tendrils of electricity. When she created her portal, it served another function. Every portal has an internal mechanism that makes it work—a blend of magic and technology. With our intra-realm portals, the mechanism powers when Elsudrans pay with their vocos and indicate the city they wish to travel to. Once it's on, even the slightest touch of living flesh causes the magic to activate, and the portal—"

"Sucks a person in and transports them to their destination," Marina said eagerly. She couldn't help but glance at Florin when she said it. She might be a non-Elsudran, but she wasn't *entirely* ignorant, thanks to Ismene and Elta.

"More or less," Aeric said. "But Brenna wanted complete control over her portal—a mechanism she could keep near her at all times and turn on and off at her will. She knew her portal was dangerous; if someone brushed against it while it was on—a guard, or worse, a Keeper, for instance—they'd be pulled into Sundra and locked on the other side. So she used her ring to control the portal's properties, from its unidirectional nature to whether or not it was active. And it was the *ring* I hijacked."

Marina squinted at the center stone. The tendrils inside it must have been as thin as strands of hair—each one as purple as the ring itself and so vibrant they looked like little strikes of lightning.

"How did you hijack it?" she asked.

This time, when Aeric's eyes landed on the ring, he didn't look up. "I manipulated its magic and technology so the mechanism was always on," he said slowly. "Then, I removed a barrier Brenna had implemented that prevented her portal from running *to* Elsudra. With that barrier gone and the portal constantly active, one could move in either direction unhindered." His voice trailed off, and when he still didn't raise his eyes to Marina or Florin, Marina's throat tightened. She knew Aeric regretted what he'd done, and though she tried to think of something to say—some placation that would ease his guilt—she couldn't muster any. She wouldn't have needed to, though. When the door opened, Aeric finally looked up.

Neva and Lars entered the room, the former's brow as knitted as it had been when she'd left earlier. When she saw the ring, her grimace turned into a scowl.

So she knew it was here—knew what it *was*. Interesting.

Neva didn't say anything as she sat at the table, but Lars made it a point to smile at the three of them. When Ryder slipped inside a few moments later, Lars smiled at him too.

Ryder was still in a bad mood from lunch, even if he patted Marina's shoulder as he sat next to her. She didn't dare ask him how he was doing; his energy was obvious enough.

She couldn't help herself, however, when she turned to Aeric and asked, "Why do you have that?"

She'd wondered about it for a while—since she'd first seen it in the Delve. But back then, she hadn't known Brenna's ring powered her portal. Now, she was even more curious, but it wasn't Aeric who answered her.

"As it so happens," Florin said, "that pertains to the matter at hand."

"And is part of the reason why Kieron has increased the presence of his troops," Neva added coldly.

Aeric held Neva's gaze, his voice stiff as ever. "Which is why our priority is to get rid of it. Pending your agreement to provide aid."

Neva pressed her lips together, but Florin made it a point to speak before she could. Mostly to Marina, he said, "Brenna's ring, much like anything that relies on the Omnia's magic to function, lost its abilities during the dead years. Her portal, too, died down— became an empty archway like our Elsudran ones. But when the Omnia returned, her ring...came back to life, so to speak. Which meant her portal did too." He folded his hands. "As it stands, Brenna's portal is perpetually active—an open hole in the basement of the palace. But it is *Elsudran* magic that keeps it—and the ring—in the state they are. If the ring were to pass the threshold into Sundra, its magic would cease, the same way the Omnia lay dormant when it was cast out of Elsudra. And if the magic imbued into Brenna's ring no longer exists, her portal stops working, and the hole closes."

No buffers. No turning around. Just a deadened portal and the nightmares it forever locked away. Marina's heart skipped a beat.

Florin unclasped his hands, then plucked the ring from the center of the table and held it up to the light. "Of course, a ring can't pass through a portal on its own. An active portal won't recognize anything that isn't alive. It won't recognize ruemin either."

Lars's lips twitched, but he didn't smile. "Which is why you plan to use an Elsudran to take the ring *and* a ruemin through." When Florin nodded, he said, "We figured that's where you were headed with this."

It didn't seem to perturb anyone, though—the thought of using some random Elsudran as a sacrificial lamb. It might've disgusted Marina had she not been met with a worse realization: it didn't bother *her* either. Not like it should. She tried to justify it by reminding herself what this plan would achieve, but it didn't do much.

Aeric turned to Marina. "The existence of this ring poses a threat to Kieron. He needs the ruemin here in Elsudra—needs their blood to stay alive. Without them, his days are numbered." Though he straightened, Marina couldn't help but notice he'd paled. "Kieron took the ring back from me when he returned from Sundra, then tried to destroy it. He knew if the other side apprehended it, they could do exactly what we're planning now, which would cripple him irreversibly. But he couldn't."

Marina raised an eyebrow. "What do you mean?"

"I might have disabled certain parts of the ring," Aeric said, "but Brenna had done her due diligence to make sure it couldn't be destroyed entirely. It's heavily shielded with the same magic we used in the Delve, then fortified with technology to make the shields last— technology *she* created specifically for her ring. Brenna was considered one of the most talented Sorcerers of the Court for a reason."

Marina remembered reading that. Of course, Brenna's talent had come with consequences. The ruemin weren't *her* fault, but her portal was how they'd got here.

"Nobody had ever tried to destroy her ring before," Aeric continued, "and Kieron had underestimated how well Brenna had shielded it. Since he couldn't break or disable the ring himself, he only had one option."

Aeric made it a point to address Marina, but she knew he could feel Neva's sharp gaze. "I knew eventually Kieron would amass a following strong enough to overtake Altus and return to the palace," he said. "And once he was there, he'd no doubt grab some random guard—or perhaps an unfortunate civilian—and force them through Brenna's portal with her ring, shutting the portal down and making it so there was no way the ruemin could be brought out of Elsudra. I made certain he couldn't do that." He made fleeting eye contact with Neva before looking down. "When I...left him," he said, his voice a touch lower, "I stole the ring and took it with me."

No wonder Kieron had been so desperate to get into the Delve—not just to find Aeric, but to find the ring. And now that the ring was *here*...

They were at an even bigger risk. Marina glanced at Neva, who was still scowling.

"If someone—anyone—passes through Brenna's portal with her ring *and* a ruemin," Florin said, "we'll have knocked out a significant number of problems. The ruemin will go out the way they came in, and the portal will be sealed. This will make Kieron vulnerable.

Whether he dies from assassination or his own waning health, we'll avoid full-scale war."

Marina's ears began to ring. In a way, they were planning to do exactly what Kieron would have done had he still had possession of the ring. The only difference was they wanted to lock the ruemin on the opposite side. But they still intended to sacrifice someone. What did that make them?

It all runs in a circle, she thought. Just like Ryder said.

"This is where we'll need help," Florin said, to Neva and Lars more than anyone else. "Five of the Delve's scouts—neither inclined nor trained in undercover rescue missions—already managed to get into the palace, which means it's possible. They were caught, yes, but they got in."

His voice faltered, and Marina's hands tightened around the arms of her chair. Not just caught. Killed.

That's on you, Kieron had said.

It's on me.

Somewhere in the distance—no, in her head—clicks sounded, and when she winced, Ryder wrapped his hand around her wrist.

"If we send out a small group," Florin continued, "comprised partially of sorcerers with a knack for glamours, we'll have a better chance at getting in and staying unnoticed."

That made sense. Cal's group hadn't had the ability to conceal themselves with magic; Florin's would. Thankful as Marina was for glamouring, she couldn't help but fear it too. Could someone be here now, lingering in the shadows? Could Kieron?

You're being paranoid, she told herself. *Glamours can be sensed. If anyone were here, Aeric would've already detected them. You're safe.*

She repeated it to herself—*safe, safe, safe*—but found little solace. When her paranoia faded, a new worry arose. Glamours could indeed be sensed by seasoned sorcerers, and to some extent, even ruemin. Regardless of whether their group concealed bodies, magical energy would linger. Only diminution cuffs could conceal that, and that was a double-edged sword because one couldn't wield magic with them on.

When she brought up her concern, Florin gave her a tight-lipped smile, as though he'd already thought of that. But it was Aeric who said, "The ruemin aren't astute enough to know exactly where magical energy is coming from unless it's directly in front of them. They may sense a higher concentration of magic near you because of the Omnia—the difference between a dull ember and a solar flare. But you won't be going, and in Altus, there's more than enough magical energy to muddy their senses."

Marina relaxed. It certainly wasn't heroic to dread returning to Altus, but she did.

"As for glamours," Aeric said, "those can go unnoticed even by sorcerers if they aren't actively looking. When Safira sensed the Delve's, it was because Ocot had tipped her off."

"And when I sensed your glamour to the Delve's third floor," Marina said, somewhat absently, "I was looking too."

She'd mostly been speaking to herself, and she certainly hadn't meant it as a slight, but Aeric bristled anyway. "You get the picture," he said. "If the group goes in covertly, it lessens the chance someone will be keeping an eye out for their glamours, which lessens the chance the glamours will be sensed at all."

"If you provide a few such sorcerers to aid us, all we'll need is a single ruemin and one of Kieron's guards," Florin said to Neva. "The latter should be doable, especially with Ryder's help. And you all have a knack for catching ruemin."

Ryder was going? The tension in Marina's shoulders, which had started to ease, swelled once more. She glanced at Ryder, who she figured had already agreed to this or expected it because he only nodded. It made sense; he'd guarded Brenna's portal before, which meant he knew the measures Kieron had put in place to protect it—and, more importantly, how to circumvent those measures.

"We *had* a knack for catching ruemin," Neva corrected. "We don't maintain our nets anymore. Not with the sweeps going on. Soldiers seeing old nets is one thing; locals could've put them out during the dead years. But new nets would raise suspicion."

Marina thought she detected an air of accusation in Neva's tone—*another inconvenience caused by Kieron's hunt for the Delve,* she seemed to be saying—but Florin didn't react to it. Gentle as ever, he said, "Your old nets still work. And worst case, we'll track a ruemin down ourselves. They're not hard to find."

When Neva nodded, whatever tension Marina had detected faded.

"Once you catch a ruemin," Marina asked, "how will you get it to Altus?"

"We can use intra-realm portals for that," Florin said. "Same rules apply—the only difference is the hive-body isn't getting stretched across different realms, which means we can bring the lone ruemin to Altus without moving the rest. Kieron's soldiers were notorious for doing that to spread the ruemin across the realm quickly."

He spoke evenly, as though he was recounting something from a history book. Maybe that was the only way he could bear to talk about the horrors of Kieron's war—as though it were all a tragedy of the past, not worth staying angry over. Sometimes, Marina wondered if that way of thinking was how he kept such a level head.

"The sorcerers we recruit will also need to know dissolution magic," Florin continued. "That way, once we take a ruemin from the nets below, we can permanently sedate it so it doesn't fight back or summon others."

"Might also be useful with whichever guard we collar," Ryder added wryly.

Back at the Delve, Aeric had mentioned dissolution magic—magic that debased the mind, rendering the victim no more than a puppet. Kieron had wanted Vaughn to do that to Aeric, hadn't he? Marina didn't dare clarify, though; not in front of the others, at least. Besides, at the moment, she was more curious about the ruemin.

"Why can't a dead one be used?" she asked. "Brenna's portal won't recognize a ruemin anyway, right? That's what we're using one of Kieron's guards for. Isn't a guard enough to activate it?"

"It's not for the portal," Florin responded. "When a ruemin dies, its connection with the larger entity breaks, like a limb having rotted and fallen off a body."

Or an aspen tree dying and detaching from the root system, Marina thought. It made sense, even if she wished it wasn't the case. Using a dead ruemin would make things much easier.

"This is why we need sorcerers," Florin said. "Two or three—who know some combat, preferably—to accompany Ryder...and myself." He was looking directly at Neva now, and his words were slow and clear. He wanted her to know he didn't intend to send random people off on a possible suicide mission—that he believed in this plan enough to go himself. Did Altus scare Florin like it scared her? Did it scare Ryder? Marina couldn't be sure. They were much better at concealing their emotions than she was.

Neva frowned. "That's a very large ask," she said. "Good at glamouring, practiced in dissolution, and familiar with combat. There are only two sorcerers in this compound who fit those qualifications, and we need them here." She didn't expand; she simply angled her chin at Aeric and added, "You already have a sorcerer who everyone knows is adept at glamouring, and who I'm sure is more than competent at dissolution magic. Why try to recruit others to do what he could?"

Florin shook his head. "If we're going to do this, we need to reduce the likelihood of being caught."

"We've reached a stalemate with Kieron," Aeric said. "If there's anything he hates, it's the idea that he's on equal footing with anyone. I'd like to play into that. If I call a diplomatic meeting with him—one with only the two of us, in a neutral place—then he'll have reason to leave Altus."

Marina's stomach plummeted even further. It was already unbearable to think of losing Ryder and Florin, and now losing Aeric was also a possibility. And yet, she couldn't help but remember what Aeric had told her in the Delve—how when Kieron had realized Aeric was getting cold feet, he still couldn't bring himself to have Aeric killed. He'd tried to have Vaughn subdue Aeric instead. Maybe Aeric was betting on Kieron having retained some of his sentiment.

Lars raised an eyebrow. "That's assuming Kieron agrees."

"He'll agree," Marina muttered, loud enough so everyone could hear.

Aeric shared a knowing glance with her. "If I bluff," he said, mostly to Lars and Neva, "and make us out to be more desperate than we are, he'll accept my invitation to speak compromises—not because he intends to, but because at the moment, he needs leverage. He'll play along for his own gain, as is his way."

And if Aeric himself was proposing they meet, Marina thought, Kieron would be even more likely to accept.

"In that time, we'll have already sent people into Altus," Florin said. Then, mostly to Marina, he added, "With our intra-realm portals working again, travel in Elsudra is quick. It could take Kieron mere minutes to get to and from Altus, which is why Aeric needs to stall him as our mission is happening. The longer he can keep Kieron out of the capital and away from the palace, the more time we'll have."

Marina glanced at Aeric, whose face was drawn.

"And if everything goes according to plan?" Neva asked. "Then what?"

"The head of the snake will be vulnerable," Florin said, "and we'll have a better chance at chopping it off."

He set the ring back on the table. Neva stared at it for a moment, then looked to Lars, who gave her a subtle eyebrow raise.

Neva sighed, then said, "I sympathize with your cause. But we need our sorcerers here —especially those with talents for glamouring. We aren't a military facility like the Delve. We aren't Altus either; we don't have the materials or the people to make high-tech weapons. We're barely getting by. Our glamours require daily reinforcement, and that's not counting the fact that we're now adjusting to a population increase. And while I'm sure you don't intend to stay in Altus longer than necessary, surely it would take more than a day. Not the palace mission, perhaps, but the entire ordeal itself."

Florin didn't argue with that. Instead, he said, "I intend to be quick once we're in the palace. Aeric can't stall forever. But how long it takes us to get out will depend on the state of the capital, which will descend into chaos if we're successful. Kieron's soldiers will act fast. I'll do what I can to ensure we get out safely."

Neva tilted her head. "And can you guarantee my sorcerers *will* get out safely?"

Florin must've known that was somewhat of a rhetorical question, because he simply said, "No, I cannot."

"You cannot," Neva echoed pointedly. "So at best, I only have to deal with about a day of weaker glamours—of keeping my other sorcerers below longer and working them harder to compensate for what we've lost, all while knowing the end result won't conceal us nearly as well as what we had before. At worst, we *never* go back to what we had before, and I've lost not only two gifted sorcerers, but also two members of this sanctuary."

Florin's response was immediate. "At best, the risk you and your people have taken results in the elimination of ruemin from Elsudra, and the—hopefully swift—death of Kieron. Which means you'll no longer need glamours or this sanctuary at all."

Neva was quiet for a moment. "Or," she said, "the risk my people and I take results in the compound being found by the soldiers in Inber *before* you see your mission through, and we all die anyway." She rubbed her temples. "We are working with limited personnel, just as you are. Sorcerers who glamour are in high demand nowadays, and we're using every last one of them."

Every last one of them? That wasn't true. Marina raised an eyebrow. "Yolie mentioned wanting to help glamour the compound." Though she knew it was brash, she added, "And she told me you said she could glamour as well as two sorcerers put together."

She regretted it the moment the words left her mouth.

Neva's eyes narrowed. "Yolie isn't an option," she said, her voice whetted to an edge. "She's a *child*. And with the recent sweeps—"

"It was a suggestion," Aeric interrupted coolly.

Marina's face heated, and she clamped her lips together. At the moment, it seemed anything she said either drew attention to her non-Elsudran ignorance or stoked already simmering tensions.

Florin, luckily, was good at smoothing things over. He spoke as gently as ever when he said to Neva, "I know we're asking a lot, and I don't expect an immediate answer. I plan to send undercover scouts into Altus to gather information about everything from the portal to activities that take place in its vicinity. Ryder has given us valuable insight, but there's no saying the additional changes Kieron has made to palace security these past few days. We need to be as prepared as possible before Brenna's ring gets anywhere near her portal."

Again, Neva tensed, but Florin had anticipated it. "I won't send my scouts out until I've gone over the mission with you in as much detail as you feel is warranted," he said. "I'm committed to the safety of this compound. I won't give anyone the go-ahead until you've approved the plan. My hope is that this preparatory period will give you more than enough time to consider our proposal."

Before Neva could respond, Lars put his hand on her arm. "A reasonable request," he said. He nodded at Florin. "We're on your side. We want the same world you do. But the people we look after are a high-risk bunch. I'm sure you can understand our hesitance."

Florin bowed his head. "That, I do."

When he stood, so did Neva and Lars.

That was it? Wait? Marina figured it was logical enough, but she couldn't help herself when she turned to Aeric. "What am I supposed to do?"

"Continue training with me," Aeric said. "We'll pick up where we left off. Even if this plan goes smoothly, there's no saying what Kieron will resort to in the event he realizes his time is limited. I'd like you to be as strong as possible, just in case."

Though Marina nodded, her stomach plummeted. "In case Kieron needs to be faced directly, you mean?"

"Maybe. There are many ways this could play out, but in all scenarios, your magical strength could very well be what saves you."

Marina nodded again, her hands clammy. She waited until everyone else was either heading to the door or too preoccupied to hear before pulling Aeric aside and whispering, "If he *does* need to be faced, I wouldn't do it alone, would I?"

She'd been so bold in Exorsus—so bold with Kieron. That boldness had long burned off, and now, the thought of him made her blood run cold. She'd face him if it came down to it; she *had to*, lest she sought to reduce her decision to nothing. But that didn't mean she wasn't terrified. He'd already gotten past her shields in Altus. Who was to say he wouldn't overpower her again?

Though Aeric's voice was as cool as always, the ice in her core melted a touch when he said, "Never."

CHAPTER 12
Hill by the Sea

Instead of heading back to her apartment that evening, Marina set out to find the observatory Yolie had mentioned. She knew she wouldn't be able to sleep, and Ryder was still in a mood, so she decided to let him have their apartment to himself for a bit.

It didn't take her long to find the observatory. There was only one domed building, nestled so high that even the tallest trees strained to reach it. Its staircase was old and creaky, spiraling around perhaps the largest trunk she'd ever seen and ending at a landing that overlooked the entire compound. From above, the wooden pathways looked like a web interspersed with trees. The breeze from earlier had died down, and now, the air was humid like it would be in Georgia before a storm. A soft pitter-patter sounded on the stairs behind her, and Marina's skin prickled in anticipation of rain. When she turned to face the sound, however, chartreuse eyes stared back at her.

She might've gasped had she not been so out of breath from the climb. Ash watched her curiously, his tail swishing against the wood.

"Hi," she whispered. She knelt, expecting Ash to bolt. But he obviously wasn't wary of people because he came up beside her and rubbed against her legs. His coat felt like silk, and the tightness in her shoulders eased as she ran her fingers along it.

When she went to open the observatory's door, he stayed at her feet. Was she allowed to let him in? For some reason, Neva didn't strike her as a pet person, and Marina didn't want to upset her any more than she already had. Ash, however, seemed determined to follow her because he slipped through the moment Marina cracked the door open.

It was dark inside, which didn't seem to bother Ash. Marina, however, had to rely on dim lights embedded in the wall to find her way. The room itself was less a room and more a cylindrical chamber, and for a fleeting moment, Marina felt as though she were back in the Delve. A ramp spiraled down to a platform at the center, and sky-facing telescopes had been placed at every landing. She angled her head up, figuring the ceiling would be plated like the patrol-tower windows in the Delve. How else could they observe stars? She squinted to make out a fixture on the ceiling, but the low light made it impossible to see clearly. She grasped the railing as she descended, blindly stepping forward until...

"Marina?"

This time, when chartreuse eyes cut through the darkness, golden glasses followed. Yolie stood at the center of the room, Ash in her arms.

"Did you bring the cat here?" she asked.

"Should I take him out?"

Yolie made a movement Marina could only interpret as a shake of her head. "I shut him out before because he was distracting me. But he can stay."

Her glasses caught a tendril of light, but Marina could still barely make out the rest of her. "What are you doing?" Marina asked.

"Practicing," Yolie said. "Is that why you're here?"

"I just wanted to see the place. Only, I can't see too much."

"That's my fault." Yolie set Ash down, then clapped her hands. The lights brightened, shrouding the room in blue. "I like it to be dark when I do magic. It helps me focus."

Marina smiled at her. "Fancy seeing you again today," she joked. She glanced at the floor, where flowers of all kinds had been arranged in a circle. "Are those for magic?"

Yolie scooped a few up. "No. I just think they're pretty." She handed Marina a yellow chrysanthemum. "You should put this one in your hair." When Marina placed it behind her ear, Yolie grinned. "I'm glad you came. I thought maybe you were just being polite."

The possibility didn't seem to upset Yolie, but Marina's heart still sank. "I really did want to come," she said. "I would've come sooner, but today has been..."

When her voice faded, Yolie gave her a knowing look. "You'll get used to the alarms," she said. She frowned. "Well, unless you're like Neva. Then you might not."

"I think she's mostly worried about you," Marina said.

Yolie rolled her eyes, and Marina chuckled. Despite looking like a child, she reminded Marina of a teenager. If it hadn't been for the dead years, she really *would* be one.

"I'm sorry if Neva seems mean," Yolie said. "I promise she's not always."

"She doesn't," Marina said. "Just overwhelmed." *And understandably so.*

"She's gotten worse since the troops started coming through. She used to let me come here whenever I wanted, but now, she says I have to stay in my apartment at night." Yolie caught herself, but it was too late. Sighing, she said, "Could you not tell her I was here?"

"Our secret," Marina said.

"Thanks." Yolie gave her an absent smile, then sat on the ground beside the flowers. Ash came up behind her, pressing his body against her back and purring.

Marina sat across from her. "What are you practicing?"

"Oh, loads of things. I like to bend light, but it's more fun when the stars are out."

"How do you see the stars from here?"

"The ceiling." Yolie giggled when Marina looked up. "Not now. Come back when it isn't cloudy. Then I'll show you. Besides, it's more fun to practice glamouring when you have good light to work with." She paused, then added, "If you still want to."

When Marina nodded, Yolie's smile widened. Marina supposed it could get a little lonely here. Come to think of it, she hadn't seen anyone Yolie's age yet.

"How many kids live here?" she asked.

Yolie plucked a few more flowers from the floor and began to put them in her own hair. "A couple. I'm one of the youngest, minus Cordelia. Most of the kids are in the first part of their second quarter, but they're boring. Plus, none of them can do magic well."

If anyone else had said it, Marina would've thought they were being arrogant. But Yolie didn't sound arrogant at all—just matter-of-fact.

"Why aren't there more people your age?"

"A lot of inclined kids were killed before the dead years."

Marina's lips parted. Why the hell had she asked that? Of course the answer was going to be horrible. But Yolie seemed rather desensitized to it all; she only shrugged and said, "Kids aren't good at controlling their abilities, which makes them easy targets. I'm good at it, though. Neva says that's probably why I was never caught. But that's not the reason."

She knew she shouldn't press, but Marina couldn't help herself when she asked, "What *do* you think the reason was?"

"My brother," Yolie said. "His name was Ronan." Her fingers brushed against the chain her anteactus hung on. "We used to have our dad around, but he died a couple of years before the war. It was only me and Ronan for a while. But then the war started and our town got invaded." Her lips twitched. "And then the mechanical woman killed him."

The mechanical woman. Marina's heart skipped a beat.

"Safira?" she asked. When Yolie nodded, she said, "Which town?"

"Sal. It's in the West. That's where I grew up, on a hill by the sea."

Ryder had mentioned Sal—the western town Safira had destroyed.

"A hill by the sea sounds beautiful," Marina said gently. She couldn't help but think of her own home back in Georgia. Her chin quivered. "I'm sorry about your family."

Yolie chewed on her lip. "If they were here, they'd want me to use my abilities to help protect other people. Ronan especially—I'm sure of it. But Neva doesn't listen when I tell her that." She shrugged, then went back to fiddling with her flowers. Since Marina could think of nothing else that would lift Yolie's spirits, she asked her to explain glamours.

It seemed to work. Marina had already learned about the basics of glamours back at the Delve, but she didn't mind hearing it again. Apparently, Yolie had learned the rules of glamouring from Neva but had quickly surpassed her. Marina wasn't surprised; Yolie clearly excelled at magic that required a high degree of calculation.

Once a glamour was cast, it tended to stick on its own, given reinforcements by the sorcerer. Even though Yolie couldn't glamour living, moving bodies yet—most sorcerers were never able to, apparently—she seemed more than certain it was possible for her. Marina wished *she* had that kind of confidence. At the moment, she wasn't even sure she'd be able to glamour inanimate objects. Still, she tried to listen. Maybe if she learned how to glamour, she could help the sorcerers glamour the compound, which would make Neva more likely to help the Delve.

The more Yolie spoke of glamours, the more Marina realized how much talent Neva was wasting by refusing to let Yolie help. She understood Neva's anxiety, but more than that, she understood Yolie's frustration. There was nothing more terrifying to Marina than the possibility that she herself would be useless in this fight. But Yolie's skill level wasn't what was holding her back. In a way, Marina wondered if that was worse—if it made Yolie feel even more useless. She didn't lack the ability to help; she lacked the permission.

Perhaps, under different circumstances, Neva would be easier to persuade. If the unit in Inber were no longer a threat—if they were no longer conducting their unpredictable sweeps—then maybe Neva would at least consider letting Yolie help glamour. It wouldn't be a permanent thing...just long enough to make up for any sorcerers who'd leave for Altus with Florin. If anything, the Delve could ease some of the burden they'd placed on Neva.

Marina hadn't realized she'd spaced out until Yolie tried to have her glamour a flower. Since she didn't want to make it obvious she'd stopped listening, she gave it her best shot —and another, and another.

On her umpteenth failure, Yolie said, "Trust me, it's easier to glamour in better light. That's why you have to come back when the stars are out, okay? Besides, you still need to show me how you generate force."

Marina nodded, then let out a wry laugh. "You'd think being the Omnia's host would make me a little better at these things."

"Being slow at some things doesn't mean you aren't talented. It just means it takes a little longer for your talent to show."

A smile tugged at Marina's lips. "Did Neva tell you that?"

"No," Yolie said, then patted Ash's head. "I came up with that on my own."

CHAPTER 13
Everything Beautiful

The rain began the next day, heavy and unyielding. Marina and Yolie stayed up through the small hours, which Marina had a feeling Neva wouldn't be too happy about, even if Yolie had claimed she wasn't tired.

Marina wasn't sure when she returned to her apartment and fell asleep, but by the time she woke, it was well past noon. Ryder's bed was empty; he wasn't in the dining hall either, and *nobody* was outside. She didn't have to meet Aeric until that evening, which gave her precious little to do other than listen to the rain. But she couldn't do that without thinking of Georgia—of that night outside the coffee shop and the months that followed—so she decided to nap to pass the time, which was a bad idea.

Her dreams had been mild that night—she hardly remembered them, though she could feel Kieron's presence in each one—but now, she dreamed of Altus. She walked the crenellation that overlooked the sea, but when she tried to peer through an embrasure, a severed head peered back at her. There were five of them, and when Marina realized they belonged to Cal and her unit of scouts, she woke with a jolt.

Ryder sat at the edge of his bed, taking off his shoes. Droplets of water fell from them, forming a puddle by his feet. "Did I wake you?"

Marina propped herself up on her elbows and shook her head. "Where were you?"

He bit the inside of his cheek. "With Aeric."

"Everything's okay, right?"

Ryder gave a strained smile. "Fine. I'm just speaking to him about my abilities." He made it a point not to look at her as he slid his shoes under his bed, then mumbled, "And how to regain them."

"Does he think you can?"

"He does." Ryder lay back on his bed. "He just says it'll take a while, and it may not be as easy for me as it used to be." With a little more vigor, he added, "It's fine. None of my combat skills took a beating; that's what matters. I'd rather be able to slice someone up than generate a spark of light."

His voice shook, but Marina pretended not to notice. She leaned against her headboard, listening to the rain batter the windows. Her conversation with Yolie lingered at the back of her mind. "Yolie told me Safira killed her brother."

Ryder let out a long breath. "Can't say I'm surprised."

"It happened in Sal." She scoffed. "What kind of monster kills *kids*?"

"The kind of monster that works for Kieron." This time, Ryder's voice didn't shake; it broke. He wasn't referring to Safira.

Oh, shit. Marina's heart dropped. Had he...?

She faced Ryder fully, a flush in her cheeks. "I meant Safira specifically."

"I know. But you're not wrong."

She couldn't leave it at that. "Safira kills out of belief. You—"

"The reasons why I killed don't take away the fact that I did. I took civilian lives as frequently as Safira, and that's why Kieron kept me around. I was the kind of monster he could rely on."

A chill overcame Marina—one lodged so deep in her chest that even breathing didn't make it go away. For a while, they lay in silence, listening to the ceiling creak.

Eventually, Ryder said, "I wonder if it drives Florin insane to think of relying on me if this mission happens. Guess he figures I don't have the luxury of switching sides anymore."

Marina turned on her side. "He clearly trusts you not to abandon us. Isn't that good?"

"Not trust—desperation." Ryder lowered his voice. "The manpower here is pathetic. I meandered about the barracks yesterday, observed what I could. These soldiers can't hold a candle to the Delve's, and this place has nowhere near the same kind of technology."

"From what I've heard, it sounds like the people here had to pick up multiple jobs," Marina said, thinking of Elta. "Lars was right. This is a sanctuary, not a military facility."

And Florin must be grasping at straws. The chill in her chest worsened.

"I don't understand why Florin and Aeric didn't try to execute this plan after the dead years when we were still in the Delve," she said.

It would've been a better bet, would it not? They would've had more soldiers, and they wouldn't have had to rely on Neva's agreement to provide aid.

"They need more than one willing sorcerer to see this through," Ryder said. Wryly, he added, "Besides, something tells me they were a little in over their heads after the dead years ended."

It took a moment for Marina to realize what he meant. When it clicked, she let out a hitched breath. "You think I'm the reason?"

Her stomach coiled. Had she really caused *that* much trouble? Maybe she had. Maybe Aeric and Florin had been so occupied with her—with the confusion she'd brought and the messes she'd made—that they hadn't the ability to put this plan in motion.

"You had your own worries then, I take it," Ryder said. "You wouldn't have known."

And Aeric wouldn't have told her—not when she'd spent her first season in Elsudra so determined to leave.

Ryder shifted uncomfortably. "I doubt you were the *only* reason, Marina. These things are never simple. Ask Florin and Aeric if it bugs you so much." When Marina put her head in her hands, he said, "Hey. I didn't mean to stress you out."

"I'm not stressed."

"Bullshit. You're always stressed." Softer, he said, "We'll get the ruemin out of Elsudra somehow. Besides, we have the ring *and* the Omnia's host."

"And Kieron has a massive army and way better technology," Marina muttered.

"Yet we managed to escape him." When Marina glanced at him, he gave her a weak grin. "And if we get rid of the ruemin," he added, "he'll be at an even bigger disadvantage."

It was a long shot, perhaps, but at least it was something.

If Florin's plan worked, how would the ruemin leave Elsudra? Would they be pulled into Brenna's portal by some nonexistent wind—dragged across the regions, flailing and clicking—or would they blip into nothingness? How had they come *into* Elsudra?

When she asked Ryder, he grimaced. "I didn't see it happen. I just know that's why the palace's lower levels look the way they do."

Like a storm had destroyed them. Marina remembered how different the palace basement looked from the halls above. The cracked walls, the toppled columns...she'd wondered what had caused so much damage.

Ryder had told her once that Kieron loved his theatrics. Marina supposed Kieron had found it rather fitting to return to Elsudra in such a violent way—to let the ruemin destroy what they could as they fled with him...and Aeric.

Aeric had surely witnessed the ruemin come into Elsudra, but the thought of asking him made Marina feel queasy. She didn't want him to relive that for her sake. Besides, what did it matter how the ruemin had come—how they'd leave? As long as they went back to Sundra, locked behind a lifeless portal, she could live with her curiosity.

"If only Brenna's portal were like Exorsus," Marina said. "If it recognized souls instead of bodies, it might've turned Kieron to dust before he could get through."

"Would've saved us suffering," Ryder said. He paused, then laughed mirthlessly. "Our great, united army. What a joke. It broke apart the day Kieron returned."

Thunder reverberated through the clouds, and the panes on the windows rattled.

"Some soldiers had secretly pledged fealty to Kieron before his exile and joined him the moment he returned," Ryder said. "They had ruemin on their side, but we had the numbers. After Kieron lost the battle for the capital and went into hiding, his numbers grew. His strength had always been his ability to get others on his side, especially when people were already discontent with the way Elsudra was. So he gained traction—lots of it —and became a massive threat. The court was horrified when they finally had to face just how upset so many Elsudrans were. But I guess everything beautiful cracks eventually." Softer, he added, "And all the ugliness beneath is finally laid bare."

Marina thought of Altus—of its shining golden buildings and the shanties just miles away. One of those shanties had been where Evren had raised Aeric. Marina couldn't help but remember how sick she'd looked in Aeric's memories, and how Kieron had used her death to stoke the flames of Aeric's hatred for the court—how he'd made sure to remind Aeric she would've lived had she the means to seek help. And maybe he'd been right. The court had been selfish and the Keepers out of touch, but...

"They had to have been better than *Kieron*," she whispered.

"Undoubtedly," Ryder said. "But that doesn't make them saints." He tapped his foot against his bed's baseboard. "Even then, I stayed loyal to the court and the Keepers longer than most. Fought on their side until their side was no longer. But somehow, I don't think any of that will sway public opinion of me. Whether I disregarded my loyalty when Kieron first came back or whether I waited several seasons...none of it really matters in the end, does it? Because I still did the things I did."

Marina waited until he met her gaze before whispering, "I think it matters."

Ryder was silent for a moment. "After the dead years started," he finally said, "and Pierce and the rest abandoned Altus, I figured I could either die for people who probably wouldn't fight for me, or pledge my loyalty to someone who would."

"Yourself?"

Ryder nodded. "Only...now I'm here, and I've found something better to pledge my loyalty to." He watched the rain outside, then shrugged. "Maybe Neva will too. Aeric left for a meeting with her and Florin after the two of us finished up. He seemed confident she'd let Florin send scouts out."

Marina knit her brow. "Did he say why?"

She wasn't surprised when Ryder shook his head. She was surprised, however, when he said, "Aeric told me he's never seen an essence as damaged as mine." Another mirthless laugh followed. "In a way, I think he was impressed."

Marina had no idea how to respond to that, but when Ryder sat up, so did she.

"You remember those corpses we passed on your first day in Altus?" he asked. "The ones hanging in the palace?"

She flinched. They were hard to forget—each one hanging from the crown of an archway, features so decayed they'd hardly looked real.

"That's the kind of shit Kieron does to people," Ryder said. "Guilty, innocent, inclined or not...doesn't matter to him. If they're a threat, they don't belong in his world, and he wants everyone to know it. He was worse during the dead years—so paranoid about the loss of his abilities that he became even more ruthless. So I did everything I could to make him think I was an asset, even if I knew that one day, I'd be found out and killed too." He stared down at his palms. "At the beginning of the dead years, a small group of Kieron's guards tried to assassinate him. They were young, and so optimistic it made them stupid. I knew there was no way they'd be able to hurt him without the ruemin killing them first, but I didn't tell them that. Instead, I encouraged their plan—concocted it with them. I'll give them credit; they got close. They attacked Kieron in the throne room, but before the ruemin could get to them, I'd already killed every single one—every bright-eyed soldier who thought they'd be a hero. And I made sure Kieron saw me do it."

He curled his hands into fists, hiding the burns. "That was the first time I felt a piece of me break. And I wondered if that was the only way I could live—if I broke myself down so much that by the time the Omnia returned and Kieron could use psychometry, he'd see me the way I wanted him to."

And it had worked. Marina's chest hollowed, and though she wasn't sure how Ryder would react, she got up and sat beside him. Ryder's shoes hadn't dried yet, and Marina watched the droplets fall silently to the wood.

"I tell myself I'm lucky," Ryder said. "There were too many soldiers for Kieron to sift through all their memories. Even Safira and Vaughn couldn't help offset the burden. The sheer number would've been too much for three people to absorb. So they'd only check essences, just to make sure nobody else was inclined. And by the time I got close to Kieron, I'd crafted such a convincing mask that he'd grown comfortable." He shook his head. "But no matter how much I tell myself I'm lucky for surviving, I don't feel it. Not when surviving has made me forget what living is like."

Silence followed. Though Marina wasn't sure why, she couldn't help herself when she asked, "What did Kieron do after you killed those guards?"

"He had me hang up their bodies in the palace," Ryder said. When Marina blinked at him, he gave her a tearful smirk. "Who'd you think the corpses were?"

CHAPTER 14
A Blanket

Whatever read Ryder had gotten on Aeric ended up being right. Neva agreed to Florin's request to send his scouts out, and on the last day of Aragonite, they departed. It was a small group—fewer than a dozen, all under orders to take different routes to not draw attention—comprised entirely of the Delve's people. Marina knew Neva had her own scouts, but she wasn't willing to send them to Altus, and nobody pushed her.

The alarms went off several more times that week, each one as unpredictable as Neva had said. Sometimes, they flashed while the compound slept, and Marina would overhear soldiers whispering of it the next day. Other times, they'd start up in the middle of lunch or dinner, reducing the lively chattering in the dining hall to scattered murmurs.

Even worse was the fact that Marina's unease lingered when the lights stopped flashing. All she could think about was what the scouts would find, or whether or not they'd return at all. One night, she'd gotten so worked up about the possibility of them being intercepted—of Kieron using psychometry on them and uncovering the sanctuary— that Ryder had attempted to calm her in perhaps the worst way possible. He'd sat her down in their room, then told her rather plainly that the scouts carried capsules of poison with them—that they'd agreed to swallow them if they got caught. Psychometry, after all, couldn't be done on the dead.

He'd realized what a horrible idea that was when Marina broke down.

When she wasn't worrying about the scouts, she was worrying about Neva. As long as Kieron's soldiers remained stationed in Inber and combed through the swamplands on erratic schedules, there was no way she'd agree to provide aid. And if she ever *did* agree, then what? Ryder, Florin, and Aeric would go off on possible suicide missions?

She tried to focus on small steps—on improving her magic and mulling over ways to convince Neva. She considered talking to Elta, but Marina only ever saw her in the dining hall, and when Elta wasn't answering random people's medical questions, she was talking to Ismene. The two of them brightened when they spoke to each other, and Marina couldn't bring herself to put a damper on the mood—especially when she had no idea what Elta could say to Neva that would help.

So she funneled the bulk of her energy into training with Aeric. In addition to the common room, the compound had spare rooms Neva let them use, which significantly lessened the pressure. Marina couldn't stand the thought of other sorcerers watching her flail as she struggled to cast glamours.

And struggle she did. Glamours were as hard for her as shielding, which, of course, made Aeric all the more eager to focus on them. He had her start by glamouring cups, but she couldn't wrap her head around the physics of it all. Diverting the path of light away from the object to make it effectively invisible sounded simple enough, but actually doing it was near impossible. She had no idea how Aeric and Yolie were so good at it.

On particularly rough days, her mind would flit away, shutting out the room and Aeric's impatience. He was much better than he used to be—but by no means perfect. At times, he'd mutter something under his breath, and when Marina called him on it, he'd act like he'd said nothing.

It didn't help that the headspace she attended sessions with was heavily dependent on Pierce and Ryder. Unless he was training with the other soldiers, Pierce spent most of his time meandering about with a sullen look on his face, Ash at his heels. Ryder, on the other hand, refused to train unless Pierce was absent.

Marina and Ismene made it clear they wouldn't get involved—Pierce responded with an "I understand" and Ryder with an "I didn't ask"—but their moods cast such a pall over things that Marina was tempted to force them to talk. Though she felt selfish thinking so, she had a feeling her training would improve if they did.

She did her best not to let circumstances sway her, but the seeds of regret she tried so hard to push down grew anyway. She knew her parents would want her to continue on even when things were hard—to remind herself *why* she'd chosen this path. But sometimes, when the compound slept and the sky was a tapestry of stars, she'd curl up by one of the balconies and cry. She missed them so much it hurt.

"Marina."

Eyes fluttering, she turned to Aeric, who stood gripping the edge of a table. "What?"

"If you're not going to listen, then you're wasting my time."

She glanced at the cup next to his hand. "I heard what you said."

"Did you? Repeat it, then."

Dammit. She shrugged. "Just to...glamour the cup."

"Not even close."

Marina rubbed her temples as he took a seat across from her. "We've been going at this for hours," she said. "I've hit a roadblock."

"You're preoccupied. This always happens when you aren't immediately successful."

"Not *always,*" Marina mumbled. She looked back to the cup, wondering what it had been like for Aeric to learn glamouring. Kieron had taught him, no doubt.

Kieron. The thought of him being able to glamour himself—hiding in plain sight—popped back into Marina's head.

"You don't think Kieron knows where we are, do you?" she asked.

"If he did, you'd already be back in Altus, and the rest of us would be dead." Aeric paused. "Or as good as."

As horrible as it was, Aeric's confirmation relaxed her as much as it could. They were still safe. But how much longer until they weren't?

Her head was becoming quite the bother. She was used to it, but before Exorsus, she'd gotten a break from it when she slept. Now, even her dreams wouldn't leave her be.

"Do you think Florin's plan will work?" she asked.

Aeric rested his chin on his hand. Pointedly, he said, "I hope. But I don't know. None of us can know for certain."

That was a logical answer. But she hadn't wanted logical. She'd wanted reassurance. Aeric knew that, of course. "All we can do is what's in our power," he said, "and all that's in our power is now. Which brings me back to glamouring—"

"But we're still banking on Neva's agreement to provide aid, aren't we?" When Aeric sighed, she said, "How did you two convince her to let the scouts leave?"

Aeric's hand moved to the base of his forehead. "If you're tired, we can stop." When Marina eyed him, he added sharply, "We were honest with Neva about the stakes."

"What do you mean?"

Aeric opened his mouth, then closed it again. It was a rare sight—to see him at a loss for how to respond. Eventually, he said, "Our goal hasn't changed, and I need not give you more reasons to catastrophize."

Her stomach flipped. "So there *are* reasons to catastrophize?"

"This is what I mean."

The urge to snap at him swelled up inside her. She let it flow like an angry wave—let it foam and thrash, then settle down when she didn't give in. Instead, she took a breath, then calmly said, "Unknowns make me catastrophize. You're not helping by shielding me from information."

She almost expected Aeric to protest—or perhaps to dismiss her, like he so often did—but instead, he took a lengthy breath and said, "The day you and Ryder arrived here and I saw your memories, I told you I believe Kieron realizes his conception of time was wrong. Do you remember?"

Marina knit her brow. "Yes."

Only she'd been so caught up with everything else that she hadn't given it much thought—or perhaps she simply hadn't fathomed how it could be serious. Truthfully, she still couldn't fathom it; she wasn't sure whether she should be worried about where Aeric was headed, or ashamed that she didn't already know.

"I didn't want to worry anyone," Aeric said, though Marina knew he meant her. "Not before I'd fully processed Exorsus. But once I did, I realized...perhaps we *should* worry."

Marina's breath, which she thought she'd been controlling, caught in her throat.

"Your experience in Exorsus made it clear that events across time and space are woven together, for lack of better words," Aeric said. "Evidently, Kieron didn't know this until he saw your memories. The last Keepers destroyed their ancestors' archives when he returned from Sundra, so any information he hadn't found before his exile was no longer around for him to steal. If the first Keepers *had* mentioned the nature of time, Kieron wouldn't have known. But then, he breached your shields. He witnessed Exorsus, the same as you did."

Aeric hesitated for a moment, as though he couldn't bear what he was about to say. "Kieron is an opportunist," he continued quietly, begrudgingly, "and this knowledge—this truth about Exorsus—is a potential opportunity. If he comes to access Exorsus, he could theoretically warp time to such a high degree that it folds in on itself, creating a loop he has complete control over—one that restarts at his death and cements him as the Omnia's eternal host. Not a ruler. Not even the sun itself. A *god*. He'll never have to risk the Omnia by moving it down a line of successors like the Keepers had. It will be with him—always."

Before Marina could let that sink in, Aeric hastily said, "This is a theory, not a certainty. But since *I've* wondered about the possibility, Kieron undoubtedly has too. And it's the potential that worries me." He paused, then only somewhat to her, added, "Time as a line may only move in two directions, but time *isn't* a line. Not in our realms, at least. It's a blanket. And a blanket can be folded."

Silence followed, heavy and suffocating. For some reason, all Marina could think of was what she'd seen in the anteactus back at the Delve. What she'd *felt*. It hadn't been her fear, but that of the first Keepers, who'd been so terrified of Exorsus that they'd stripped away their descendants' identities and died wallowing in regret.

Only, it wasn't Exorsus they'd feared. Not really. They'd feared what someone could do if they accessed it.

Marina's chest constricted, sending shooting pains through her body. She'd fought Kieron as hard as she could, but he'd matched her too closely. How were they ever supposed to defeat him if she couldn't even keep him out of her head? And what Kieron had learned...he'd only learned it because she'd been weak.

She should've fought harder. Better. She should've *been* better.

She put her head in her hands. Maybe it was best if she couldn't comprehend the possibility—best if it all remained a theory.

"As it stands," Aeric said, "Exorsus rejects Kieron—a saving grace for us. But even if it doesn't recognize him as one of its creations, it recognizes the Omnia, and if he comes to hold it, he'll have access because *it* does. He told you himself: Exorsus wouldn't devour the Omnia. If he holds it, it will be his shield." He folded his hands, knuckles white. "Kieron was after the Omnia before he knew this, but I believe his motivation has only doubled since your time in Altus. If he was determined then, now he's—"

"Hell-bent," Marina breathed. She quickly realized Aeric didn't know what that word meant, but it seemed he chalked it up to Earth-lingo because he didn't question her.

"This was what Florin and I discussed with Neva," Aeric said. "We made it clear that this matters for all of us—that if she desires the survival of her people, walking the line of neutrality will give her the opposite. If we don't do everything in our power to snuff out this threat, then we're setting ourselves up for failure, because the threat isn't going away. If anything, it's getting larger. The longer we wait, the more likely Kieron is to find you and force you into Locus."

"I wouldn't give in," Marina said weakly.

"That's easy to say when you're safe," Aeric said. "Easy to say when your friends are. But if Kieron found Pierce and Ismene, say, and dangled their lives over your head, you'd find yourself in the same predicament you were with..."

He cut himself off, but Marina knew the name that lingered at his lips.

Cal.

He'd seen those memories—seen her give into Kieron not once, but twice. First with performing Tempus, then with summoning Exorsus. He'd seen the ruemin tear into the scouts and the lock of Cal's hair Kieron had placed in Marina's hand. And he'd seen her crumble under it all.

Aeric was right. Kieron would find a way to make her give in. That's what he did— what he excelled at.

"If he takes the Omnia from you, he will solidify his control over Elsudra—only now, it might not be for some brief, historical stint, but for *eternity*. And if he cannot, he will set his sights on destroying this world and everyone in it. Loss is not an option to him."

Marina wrapped her arms around herself, but her body had gone so numb she could scarcely feel anything. Technically, Aeric hadn't been lying; their goal was still the same. But the consequences of not achieving it were much worse.

"Thankfully," Aeric added, "hearing this swayed Neva to let Florin send out scouts."

Marina considered for a moment. "If the soldiers in Inber weren't an issue anymore, do you think it would be enough to get her to provide aid too?"

"Florin and I have...discussed the possibility," Aeric said slowly.

"With Neva?" Marina asked. When Aeric nodded, she tilted her head at him. "And?"

"She wasn't thrilled with the idea. But she wasn't opposed to it either." He paused. "It's not as easy as slaughtering them. If it were, we'd have already done it. News of a massacre—a fight of any kind—would reach Kieron, which would eventually lead him to us. Whatever we did would need to be bloodless."

"What if we hid the bodies?"

"How do you think Kieron and his generals would react to the sudden disappearance of a unit?" Aeric mused. "That's just as dangerous. The moment messages stopped coming in, they'd realize. Our best bet is to keep the soldiers exactly as they are—stationed in Inber, running patrols through the town—but to...*remove* parts of their memories, making them forget their orders to sweep the swamplands."

"That's possible?"

"It's a form of dissolution magic," Aeric said. "Sorcerers may not be able to plant or fabricate memories, but they can remove them—*dissolve* them. But it's difficult to do and seldom practiced."

"You know it, though, don't you?" The question was rhetorical, but her heart sped up anyway when he nodded. "There must be others here who do too." Before she could decide if it was smart, she added, "Would you be able to teach me?"

"I could explain," Aeric said, "but the only way to learn is by doing. That's why so few people know dissolution magic—in *any* of its variations. Delirium inducement too. Those kinds of magic require the sorcerer to practice on others, and I've never heard of anyone consenting to be practiced on."

"I could practice in Inber, then." Aeric didn't respond—not like she gave him much room to. "The end result would be wiped memories, so it doesn't matter if a soldier sees me, right? We'd have to wipe the memories of our presence anyway. Besides, you've been trying to teach me all kinds of magic so I'm as prepared as possible for whatever comes. Dissolution magic can't possibly be an exception. And if this gives me the chance to help... or maybe not help, but to learn magic that might let me help *later*, then—"

"I didn't say no," Aeric interrupted.

Marina blinked at him. "You mean...you'll consider it?"

"It might surprise you," he said, "but I've *already* considered it. Dissolution magic is a critical skill and this may very well be the time to learn it. But this mission is a risk, and when I brought up your involvement, Florin wasn't amenable to it."

Marina had a feeling he was choosing his words carefully. She chose hers carefully too, and even then, she wasn't sure they were the right ones. She wasn't sure if pushing this was smart because, if she was being honest with herself, accompanying them on this Inber mission sounded like hell. But she couldn't stop herself. "I might not be perfect at magic," she said, "and I know I'm not who you expected the Omnia's host to be. But I'm trying. And I want to learn what I can so I can help—now *and* in the future."

Aeric's eyes flitted to the nearby window, where he watched the clouds beyond the panes. "I plan to speak to Florin again soon," he said after a few moments. "I'll let you be part of the discussion."

The tension in Marina's shoulders eased. "Thank you. That's all I ask." Her heart fluttered, but she steadied her voice when she added, "In Exorsus, I made a promise to the Keepers. I have to do what I can to keep it—to be the person they hoped I'd be."

Aeric's gaze finally met hers. Though she expected a multitude of responses, she didn't expect the one he gave her.

"You already are."

CHAPTER 15
Broken Things

On the fourth day of Calcite, the sun finally peeked through the clouds. There were more people out because of it, and for the first time since it had started raining, Marina and Pierce met up. They made a trip to the library—a quaint room of wooden shelves stuffed to the brim with well-loved books. Some were about magic, which Marina took, and though Pierce perused with her, he didn't seem interested in any. He didn't talk much either, but after they left and Marina asked about his training with Florin and the others, he brightened a little.

When it was clear he was in a halfway decent mood, she dared to ask, "Has Florin said anything about his scouts?"

"Not to me," Pierce said. "But I wouldn't be surprised if he hasn't heard from them. It'll take some time for them to gather the information they need."

"Does he seem confident, at least?"

"He doesn't seem *scared*, which I guess is about as good of an indicator as I'll get."

They passed a cluster of apartments built between cypress trees. The leaves glittered with dew, and the smell of wet wood lingered in the air. Pierce put his hand out, catching small droplets. "He *did* tell me he plans to have Ryder go to Altus with him."

Marina focused on her breaths, directing them evenly through her mouth. If she was this nervous about Florin's scouts being in Altus, she had no idea how she'd handle it when Ryder left. And Pierce...she wasn't sure he'd fare any better, even with everything going on.

"Neva has to agree to everything first," she said. She hesitated, then added, "But if she does, I wouldn't worry. Ryder and Florin are good soldiers, and they'll be accompanied by sorcerers. They should be okay."

In truth, she was trying to reassure herself more than Pierce, but it didn't work, and

Pierce didn't seem to hear her. He gazed absently at the fog hanging above the trees, then murmured, "I told Florin I could go too."

Marina stopped in her tracks. "What?" When Pierce only glanced at her, she said, "No, Pierce. Ryder and Florin are already going. I can't..."

Can't risk losing you too.

"No need to freak out," Pierce said. "Florin turned me down. And something tells me Ryder wouldn't have been happy to know I was coming."

"You don't need to go."

"Perfect. I'll be just as useless as I was in the Delve. Maybe more so." Pierce gave a hard smile to the ground, then shook his head. "Let's say it all works out. Then what? Kieron resorts to endgame tactics, so you and Aeric have to finish him off? I'd get to worry about the two of *you* instead. And the whole time, I'm stuck here, training for fuck all..."

"You're helping protect this compound."

"I'm doing what I did in the Delve all over again. Nothing."

A chill skirted through the trees and over walkways. Marina hugged her books to her chest, then whispered, "It's not nothing."

Pierce's lips twitched. "I know. I'm just feeling sorry for myself. Ignore me."

She gave him a nudge with her shoulder. "Never."

He softened a little. "I didn't even ask about *you*. How's training with Aeric?"

"It's...good."

She didn't think the day would ever come when *that* was her answer. But even if her progress with glamouring was rocky, she wasn't as hung up on failures as she used to be. Every step was an improvement. Aeric had started to vary their training with other lessons too, both related and unrelated: making shields, manipulating light...even a bit of healing.

Of course, he'd also had her practice combat skills. He taught her how to channel force through shadows in addition to light—the difference, he explained, lay in one's conceptualization of the energy and, as a result, how that energy manifested. Visualizing light made it easier to channel energy into a rigid form, ideal for sharp blows or pinning an opponent down. Visualizing shadows, on the other hand, yielded flexibility—best for binding or constricting enemies. While some sorcerers could manipulate light with fluidity, they were rare—people like Brenna. Even *Aeric* found it difficult.

Marina didn't mind that practice much, even if she preferred the straightforwardness of light. What she did mind, however, was practicing disintegration and pain inducement. A few nights ago, Aeric had pushed her to cut open cups of water—an exercise not unlike slitting throats. Marina was successful with it, but afterward, all she could think of was Ocot. She'd dreamed of him, writhing about on the palace floor, but in her dream, Kieron hadn't been his executioner—*she* had.

Her mood had been even lower in the days that followed, so Aeric eased up on the combative skills. Still, Marina couldn't help but wonder why acts of magical violence came so easily to her. Generating force, tearing off limbs, inducing pain, breaking things...it was intuitive. *Natural.* What did that say about her, especially when she was taking so long to learn glamouring? Aeric had tried to ease her turmoil by telling her if she eventually did end up wielding dissolution magic, her talents might be suited for it. She wasn't sure how she felt about that.

Though she tried to keep her updates on the lighter side—for Pierce's sake, if nothing else—it didn't stop her from thinking about it. It didn't stop her from thinking about what Aeric had said about Kieron either—what he believed Kieron would do if he ever *did* come to hold the Omnia. She could hardly fathom it: an eternity of no progress, no innovation, no *nothing* but Kieron's reign. Of course, Kieron had never sought progress; he'd prefer to stay in a stagnant present, clinging to the Omnia for dear life, wiping out any possibility he'd ever lose it. And if he couldn't, he'd try to take the world down with him, just like Aeric had said.

How did time loops even work? Marina figured *she* wouldn't exist in Kieron's eternity; he'd have already taken the Omnia from her and killed her before entering Exorsus. Perhaps that was one small mercy. But what about everyone else? Would he find and kill Aeric and the others at the beginning of every loop, damning them to endless failure and death? Even the dead years couldn't compare to such a hell.

She didn't dare mention any of this to Pierce. Aeric didn't need to swear her to secrecy. He and Florin had already told Neva and Lars; whoever else they decided to let in was up to them. Marina had no desire to stoke further fears.

Her fear, however, was another issue entirely. It rattled in her head and clawed at her gut, chipping away at her until she could hardly think of anything else. Walking became mindless, and she didn't realize where they were until she reached the door to her and Ryder's apartment. Pierce, who'd clearly been as lost in his own head, tensed when he registered where they were. Marina offered for them to sit outside instead.

They found a nearby balcony to settle down at, but it didn't stop Pierce from glancing back at the apartment.

"Is it only the two of you?" he asked.

Marina nodded. She tried her best to sound unbothered when she asked, "Where are you and Ismene at, by the way?"

"A couple blocks down. We share with two others—Hollis and Zora. They grew up in Lewes, so Ismene gets along well with them."

"Ismene gets along with everyone."

Pierce made a murmur of agreement, his gaze absent. To take his mind off Ryder—or perhaps to take *her* mind off Kieron—Marina went back to talking about her progress with glamours. Of course, it seemed to bore Pierce a bit, but when she confided in him about how hard it was for her, he gave her a smile reminiscent of the ones he'd given her in the Delve—gentle and encouraging.

"You'll get there," he said. "You always do."

For some reason, hearing that from him alleviated some of the tightness in her chest, which, at this point, she'd started to think was permanent. Of course, she should've known the relief was destined to be short-lived. Before she could respond, the flashlights on their vocos went into a frenzy.

Pierce swore. "We'll hunker down in your apartment, I guess."

Marina nodded, praying it wouldn't be long. Sometimes, the alarms only lasted for a few minutes, but a couple of days ago, they'd continued for over an hour.

She had no idea how to react to the sweeps. The initial anxiety had burned off, but she had a feeling she'd never truly get used to them. She was more similar to Neva than Yolie in that regard.

She and Pierce slipped inside the apartment, shooting each other glances. Pierce took a seat on the trunk at the base of Marina's bed, then rested his elbows on his knees and his head in his hands. He looked up a few seconds later, however, when the door opened.

Ryder already looked flustered, but seeing Pierce made it even worse. His lower lip curled as he said, "Of all the places you could've waited out the alarms, you chose *here*?"

Marina gave him a look, but she had no idea if it communicated what she intended. She was feeling a thousand different things at the moment, and she wasn't exactly in the headspace to warn Ryder to back down.

"We were nearby," Pierce said hastily. "But...I can leave."

"And risk drawing attention to your movement or sound?" Ryder grimaced but shook his head. "Too dangerous. I don't know when the glamours were reinforced last. Just leave once the alarms stop."

Pierce murmured in agreement, paler than usual as Ryder sat at the foot of his bed. For a while, no one spoke, but the silence was so cold that Marina didn't care if she made things awkward by breaking it.

"Has anyone been able to get a pattern on the soldiers' schedule?" she asked.

"The pattern is that there's no pattern," Ryder said through a sigh. After a pause—and a glance in Pierce's direction—he added, "Florin's been able to make guesses, but there's a margin of error. I hear they've set up camp right where Inber ends and the swamplands begin. They go into town most days, but every so often, they conduct sweeps here." He scrubbed a hand across his face. "I swear I heard them outside. Their voices, their movements...like they're right beneath us. Typical of Kieron's soldiers. It's always about making their presence and power known."

Tension lingered in the air, which Marina broke cautiously when she asked, "Have you heard anything else from Florin?" *Like his thoughts on getting rid of them?*

Ryder shook his head. "The scouts seem to be taking up a lot of his mental energy."

"Were you just with him?" Marina asked.

"No. I was coming back from seeing Aeric."

Pierce, who'd been staring at his voco with glazed eyes, lifted his head and blurted, "You're seeing Aeric?"

Ryder's mouth tightened. "Training with him."

"For what?"

"My shooting skills," Ryder said sarcastically. When Pierce remained silent, he scoffed. "Magic, obviously. My abilities have taken a hit. He's helping me get them back."

Pierce shot Marina a wide-eyed glance. "They...they did?"

"Turns out working for Kieron doesn't bode too well, especially when you have to damage your own essence to survive," Ryder said.

Though it disturbed her a little, Marina couldn't help but fantasize about dropping bombs on the soldiers. It'd punish them for making her live through this.

Pierce pressed his fingers against his eyes, and when he lowered them, he whispered, "I...I had no idea."

"Altus got worse during the dead years," Ryder said stonily. "You'd know, had you not turned tail and run. I, on the other hand, have these to remind me." He flashed Pierce his palms, and Marina wasn't sure if he intended to make Pierce feel guilty or scare him away. Or maybe it was simply Ryder's attempt to remind Pierce who he'd become and the shame he carried.

Pierce swallowed, then nodded. "I know. I'm...sorry."

Ryder gripped the edge of his mattress. Now that he'd started, he couldn't stop. Fire simmered in his eyes, leaking onto his expression and into his tone. "How long did it take Marina to convince you to let her leave the Delve so you and the others could flee? A couple seconds? Or did you desert on the spot?"

"That was *my* choice," Marina said. When Ryder's eyes met hers, she gave him another look. *Please don't bring me into this,* she begged silently.

She understood Pierce's frustration about being useless. She felt much the same. There was nothing she could say or do that would make things right between them—not without inserting herself into a fight that wasn't hers and crossing a dozen lines.

"In Altus, she told me you'd vouched for me," Ryder said.

"I...I did."

"And you told her I could help her escape."

Pierce watched him warily. "Yes. And...you did. I can't thank you enough."

"I don't need your gratitude," Ryder snapped. "I helped Marina because *I* wanted to. You had nothing to do with it. Though I did find it funny how quickly you'd let her leave the Delve, and how you seemed to think the moment I realized you two knew each other, I'd drop everything to run off and find you."

Marina ran her hands through her hair. These godforsaken alarms...the lights were going to drive her crazy. She covered her flashlight with her sleeve, hating how stuffy and claustrophobic this room felt—how she wished the soldiers below would leave so she could get air. With every flash, a new worry plagued her. Neva's reluctance. The danger that had followed the Delve here. The extent of Kieron's hold on Elsudra. The way he'd broken her down in Altus. The way he'd broken Aeric down over the course of so many years. The way Ryder had broken *himself* down to survive.

But Kieron didn't care if people broke—not if it got him what he wanted. He didn't care if he broke himself, like he'd done to his soul in Sundra. He'd leave behind a world of broken things if it meant the Omnia was his.

"I didn't think that," Pierce said breathlessly. "That wasn't my—"

"Twelve years," Ryder hissed. "I had twelve dead years to think about how quickly you'd left me. Now you're here, in my room, and ironically, I want nothing more than for you to do just that."

"I...I don't..."

Ryder held up his voco, which had stopped flashing. "Leave, Pierce."

Marina blinked to clear her vision, then glanced at her own voco. She hadn't even registered that the alarms had stopped.

Pierce closed his eyes, then nodded. When he stood, his legs shook.

Marina stood too. "I can come," she said weakly. "I need air."

Neither of them heeded her.

The fog had burned off, and the sun beat down on their heads as they stepped outside. Marina shut the door slowly, then turned to Pierce, desperate to say something.

It wouldn't have mattered, though. He'd already walked away.

CHAPTER 16
Weathervane

Marina threw herself even deeper into training. It was one of the few things she could control. She knew what she couldn't control: Neva, the scouts, Pierce and Ryder, or even Ismene, whose usual sunny demeanor had darkened ever so subtly. As much as Ismene smiled when she saw Marina—as cheerily as she spoke of her trips to the herbal gardens with Elta—a kernel of sadness resided in her eyes, and with it, what she'd said to Marina out on the balcony. *Just another pawn.*

Marina tried to replace those words with Cal's advice—with reminders that all she could control was the paths she chose. So Marina chose to train. She'd yet to glamour a whole object, even if she'd made minor strides. But everything else was coming along nicely, and by the middle of Calcite, Aeric commented on the progress she was making.

Sometimes, she'd run into Yolie. Once or twice, they sat outside and practiced magic together, but Marina hadn't yet found time to return to the observatory. That, and the sky in the South was cloudy more often than clear, and Yolie insisted the stars needed to be perfect before she showed Marina what they looked like. Instead, they hung around the gardens, attempting glamours on small flowers. Marina showed Yolie how to generate force too, and though her blasts were on the timid side, Yolie didn't shy away from the challenge. But those moments—the happy, lighthearted ones—were few and far between. Most often, the noise in Marina's head was so overpowering she could scarcely focus, let alone glamour. Still, she funneled her anxiety into hours of practice and reading, hoping that as her skills improved, her fear—and her dreams—would take on a milder nature.

They didn't. Sometimes, they'd be so bad she'd wake up crying—loudly enough to rouse Ryder. He was a good sport about it; he comforted her when he could and sat with her when he couldn't. But she knew he had his own shit to sort out, so whenever possible, she'd escape to the balconies and let the breeze lull her into calm.

The one perk about being outside at night was the air. It wasn't as humid as it was during the day, and the breeze carried with it the smell of eucalyptus. Whenever the clouds parted, Marina would try to count the stars, but she rarely got above ten before another cloud obscured them. One night, she made it to fifteen, only for her focus to be sullied by lights coming from the main common room.

The door was shut, but one of the windows must've been open because Lars's and Neva's voices flitted into the night air. Though she knew the respectable thing to do would be to turn around and return to her room, she inched closer.

"...a bloody weathervane," Neva was saying. "It worries me. He's partially why we're here to begin with—why we can't so much as scavenge without running into ruemin. I don't want to throw our people into a fight he played a hand in starting."

*Aeric...*they were obviously talking about Aeric.

"Do you really think, after everything, he'd change course a second time?" Lars mused. It sounded like a rhetorical question, but Marina couldn't be sure.

"I don't know. It's hard for me to glean anything from him."

"The girl's easier to read," Lars said carefully. "She seems to trust him."

"Yes, but she also banked on Kieron's closest guard to help her escape."

Marina's jaw tightened. That hadn't been some impulsive decision. Neva knew that; she'd seen her memories. But the skepticism in her tone ran deep anyway.

Lars chuckled. "He did, didn't he?"

Thank you, Lars. He seemed to at least be considering their proposal.

"I will back you, as always—to present a united front, if nothing else," Lars continued. "But you and I both know we've no chance of surviving long if Kieron succeeds, and nobody can stay hidden forever. Maybe it's high time we take a risk. What better group to do so with? They have trained soldiers—better than ours could ever be—and one of Altus's generals is with them. If they've done anything, it's proven themselves to be credible."

Neva didn't respond to that. Marina wished she could see her face; at least then, she'd have some small idea of what she was thinking.

A moment passed—then another—and in a whisper, Neva said, "You remember the stories people told during the dead years, don't you? Of the savior who'd one day come?"

"Children's stories."

"Maybe. But they gave people hope." Neva lowered her voice even further, and Marina had to hold her breath to hear. "That girl is a great many things: persistent, talented, and in some ways, ruthless. But she's also young, inexperienced, and terrified—far from the savior we anticipated."

Marina closed her eyes and inhaled through her nose. She couldn't fault Neva for an accurate observation.

Silence followed. When Lars spoke, there was a hint of amusement in his voice. "Tell me honestly, Neva," he said. "Did you ever think there was such a thing?"

⌁

Marina returned to her room shortly after, determined to avoid the kind of awkward run-in she'd had with Aeric and Florin in the Delve. Her bed creaked as she climbed into it, and she fell asleep counting the stars outside her window.

She dreamed of Gemma and Hank that night. It was the most normal dream she'd had in a while, but Kieron's presence still lingered. When Gemma's blue eyes morphed into *his*, she woke up—still tired, but unable to fall back asleep. She decided instead to pick up where she left off—counting stars until they disappeared into the periwinkle sky.

At sunrise, she retreated to the bathroom and took a long shower, mulling over what she'd heard Neva say. Strangely enough, it wasn't what she'd heard about herself or Ryder that upset her. It was what Neva had said about Aeric.

Neva might've caught bits and pieces of Aeric's memories from Marina's, but she clearly hadn't seen enough to realize who he truly was. And no number of memories would ever compare to facing Kieron in the flesh.

Of course, she'd once viewed Aeric exactly as Neva did. A traitor. A *weathervane*.

Perhaps Aeric was as fearful as she was of the future. If they succeeded, would the public accept him? Ryder was probably just as scared. Even without Kieron, the scars on his palms would never fade—permanent reminders of the person he'd had to be.

One day, one step, one breath at a time. For all of them.

When she returned to the room, the sun had risen above the hills, casting ribbons of light onto the floor. Her boots, which shone more orange than pink, peeked out from underneath her bed. Since she had precious little to do, Marina relaced them. The trek from Pirn to the Delve hadn't been kind to the leather, and she couldn't help but wonder if there was some type of magic that could fix them. She considered asking Aeric. He'd probably view her request as trivial, but she couldn't bear the thought of her boots falling apart. If they did, she'd have nothing left of her parents.

Her head buzzed as she fiddled with the laces. She was only halfway through when her voco chimed, waking Ryder. He shot her a look, but before he could blame *her* voco for waking him, his chimed as well. He went to listen, but Marina had already jumped to play her own, heart thrumming as she listened to Florin's message.

"Come to the common room after breakfast," he said. "The scouts are back."

CHAPTER 17
Quiet Tension

More than five Elsudran weeks had passed since the scouts had left—five weeks of radio silence and wary hope. Marina wasn't about to wait until after breakfast to hear the news. She'd rushed from the room before Ryder could so much as get out of bed. She knew she'd get to the common room early, but she'd rather wait there. She wasn't hungry anyway.

She figured Florin had probably been much too busy to debrief them via voco, but she wished he'd at least given them a rundown. She couldn't bear not knowing what the scouts had found—*if* they'd found anything.

Lars was the only person in the common room when Marina arrived, and he must've noticed the anxiety on her face, because he said, "If what I hear is true, the scouts were successful, and they gathered all the information Florin hoped they would." He leaned back in his chair, a tendril of sunlight glinting off his metal hand. "More importantly, they all returned. I hope that eases you."

Marina put her head in her hands, forcing herself to breathe evenly. When she looked back up at Lars, she said, "Thank you."

"All I know is what I've heard from Neva," he said. "Of course, she does tend to be accurate." He paused. "I feel I haven't properly thanked you yet. If what Neva tells me is true, you've made quite the sacrifice. Elsudra will forever be in your debt."

Not if Kieron wins.

She cursed herself for jumping so quickly to that. Why couldn't she just accept Lars's gratitude?

"Of course," Lars continued, "I don't think many Elsudrans will ever know enough to appreciate what you did. Aeric and Florin have underscored the importance of keeping our knowledge of Exorsus a secret. Neva and I can't help but agree."

Well, at least they'd all found *something* to agree on. "That's probably best," she said.

Lars gave her a subtle nod. "Either way, I'm honored to be one of the few who knows. If there's anything we can do—"

"Help us," Marina blurted. "What I did won't matter if Kieron succeeds. And I worry he might if we go at this alone. If you or anyone else could help with glamouring, Brenna's portal could be shut down in a day, and the ruemin would be gone."

It was fanciful thinking, perhaps, but Lars didn't argue against it. He only smiled and said, "I'd volunteer myself if I could, Marina."

She raised her eyebrows. "You can't glamour?"

"I don't wield magic at all."

Marina's lips parted. Hadn't this sanctuary been built specifically as a hideout for inclined Elsudrans?

"It's not that I don't have the potential," he added, studying the confusion on her face. "I just never chose to build on it."

That shocked her even more. She'd never considered the possibility that an Elsudran with magical leanings would refuse to capitalize off them.

"Do you mind if I ask why?" she ventured.

Lars shrugged. "My parents sent me off to Lewes when I was a boy to study. They said I had the potential to be a healer. But I didn't wish that for myself. Truthfully, I'd always dreamed of living on a farm. And when I saw the way magic was exploited by our government and the court, I grew even more disenchanted."

"Which is exactly why I chose him to stand beside me." A different voice—Neva's. She shut the door behind her, then sat next to Lars.

"Because I embrace taboos," Lars quipped.

"Because prestige doesn't motivate you," Neva said.

Marina went still for a moment. Before she could decide if it was smart, she said, "I didn't want to learn magic either when I came here. But it was for a different reason." Though she was speaking more to Lars than Neva, she made sure Neva heard her when she said, "I didn't trust Aeric. And I didn't want to fight a war I blamed him for starting."

Remember what I showed you, Neva. Remember how—why—I came around.

"But then," she continued, slow and deliberate, "I realized the man I'd once viewed as traitorous and dangerous and untrustworthy was really just loyal. Maybe overly so. And then I met Kieron, and I came to understand how severely he'd manipulated Aeric's loyalty—how he'd taken everything that made Aeric good and weaponized it." She shifted her gaze to Neva. "Kieron did the same to me. He learned who I was, and he used it to control me. I almost broke under it."

Neva tilted her head. "But you didn't."

And Aeric did, her eyes seemed to say.

"I endured Kieron for weeks," Marina said. "Aeric endured him for years. If he could withstand that and still come out the man he is today, then there's no one I'd rather fight beside."

Neva kept her expression blank, but she glanced sidelong at Lars. Before either could respond, the door opened. Florin and Aeric entered, the former's eyes alight.

"I'm sure the news has already circulated," Florin said, "but we've received quite the detailed report."

A hand wrapped around Marina's shoulder, and she looked up at Pierce, who took the seat beside her. "Florin said I could come," he whispered, as though justifying it to himself instead of her. He shrank a little when Ryder walked in, but the two made it a point not to look at each other.

Once everyone was seated, Florin said, "The security surrounding Brenna's portal is heightened, but that was expected. The room it's in is protected by a draining shield, and the halls leading to it are riddled with defenses. That means the only way to access it is through underground tunnels—exactly as Ryder described." He turned to Ryder. "You continue to be an asset. My scouts verified everything you told me, minus the specifics of the tunnels, which only you know. Better yet, I don't foresee Kieron making any changes to his defenses, given your standing in the capital."

Marina didn't realize what Florin was talking about until he said, "That's another important piece of information my scouts picked up: rumor in Altus is that Ryder is dead. The distress message sent from the Tin soldier's voco summoned backup to the East, and the fact exact coordinates were sent out solidified the lie further."

Rather smugly, Ryder raised his eyebrows at Marina. She narrowed her eyes back at him, but Ryder had been right. Death *was* the best alibi.

"Whether Altus is completely convinced, I can't be certain," Florin said, "but unless ruemin are waiting for more victims or are given explicit rules, they're notorious for prowling off with food, so the lack of a body wouldn't be surprising. At the very least, my hope is this news has made Kieron less intent on making drastic changes to security out of the fear that Ryder's a threat. He'd have been more likely to direct his attention elsewhere —like finding a foreign girl who had to navigate an unfamiliar realm alone."

All eyes locked on her, then shifted to Ryder, who seemed happier than usual, all things considered. He might've sent the message to protect himself, but it had panned out well for the rest of them too.

"As for operations in the palace basements," Florin continued, "the scouts came back with fairly detailed information. I'll continue to review it over the coming weeks so the sorcerers who accompany us can prepare accordingly."

He sounded confident about the sorcerers coming. Had Neva finally agreed to supply personnel? Before Marina could ask, Florin said, "I should also note that I've received a thorough report on the schedules of those who work near the portal." He hesitated, then added, "Including Vaughn."

The blood drained from Marina's face. When she finally got her voice to work, she rasped, "Vaughn's alive?"

"His arm has been replaced, and he's guarded now," Florin said. "But yes, he's alive."

"Let me guess," Ryder said. "His arm is golden, like Safira's face. They do love that color in the capital."

Marina put her elbows on the table, then pressed the heels of her palms to her eyes. She had no idea how to feel—how she *should* feel. Should she be glad she hadn't killed Vaughn, or worried he was still a threat?

"We'll need to know Vaughn's schedule too if we're to avoid him during the Altus mission," Florin said. "Again, I plan to go over this with the soldiers—and sorcerers—who accompany us."

Marina turned to Neva. "You've agreed?"

Neva didn't respond. Instead, she flicked her eyes over to Florin, who said, "Almost."

"We've reached a compromise," Aeric said pointedly. "And I promised I'd let you be involved in discussions, did I not?"

Marina knit her brow. "Inber?"

Though Neva nodded, she said, "But I need to make myself clear: I am not forcing anyone's hand. The sorcerers I have in mind will be given options, not orders. Likewise, the vocos your group brings will be traceable to the Delve. I want there to be no way this gets back to us."

"Which we've already agreed to," Aeric said.

Neva held his gaze before saying, "There are only two sorcerers here, besides Aeric, who know both glamouring and dissolution magic, and who are strong enough to help weather the effects of the draining shields. They also have some combat experience, albeit limited. I'm willing to give them the choice to be part of *both* the Inber and Altus missions. Whether or not they accept is up to them."

She pressed her lips together and inhaled through her nose, but she didn't expand. Florin clearly didn't expect her to. Rather quickly, he said, "Their names are Hollis and Zora. A smart couple—raised and educated in Lewes."

Pierce perked up. Though he spoke timidly, especially with Ryder so close, Marina could sense his excitement when he said, "They room with me and Ismene."

Florin gave Pierce a knowing smile. "Neva plans to talk to them today and give them time to think everything over."

Marina wondered if that was why Florin had let Pierce sit in on the meeting—because he hoped Pierce could sway Hollis and Zora in ways Neva wouldn't.

"They're two of our best glamourers," Neva said. "Heavily involved in technology too, Zora especially. I understand that's an important part of your plan in Inber."

Marina glanced at Florin, then Aeric. "What *is* the plan for Inber?"

Aeric gave her a look that clearly meant *we'll discuss it later.* Florin only grimaced.

Some nameless anxiety overtook Marina, but she swallowed and nodded.

"I'd be remiss not to stress how substantial a risk this is for us," Neva said. "If Hollis and Zora die on either mission, we've lost two sorcerers who we rely on for glamours. Their talent speeds up our daily reinforcements considerably, and other sorcerers depend on them to fix weak spots."

Neva glanced at Lars, who gave her a soft smile. As imperceptible as it was, it seemed to calm her. "But I realize circumstances are dire," she continued to Florin more than anyone else. "And if Inber is successful—if the swamplands drop out of the soldiers' search route—then I can deal with what I hope will be a temporary absence as Hollis and Zora head to Altus with you. Especially if you don't see that mission taking longer than a day."

"The Altus mission won't be as quick as the Inber one," Florin said, "but when that time comes, I give my word to you and your sorcerers that we'll work through every technicality. For now, we'll focus on Inber—on getting through it safely and extinguishing our most pressing threat."

Neva nodded stiffly. That signaled the meeting's end, apparently, because it wrapped up from there. As people began to rise from their chairs, Marina had to fight to hold her tongue. She wanted to say something to Neva about having Yolie help glamour to offset Hollis and Zora's absence during the Altus mission—about how it was shortsighted to not at least *consider* using someone willing and able to help—but Neva had already reacted poorly to that suggestion once. That, and right now, Marina was more concerned with the quiet tension hovering between Aeric and Florin, which was as rare as it was unnerving. She had a feeling it had to do with her involvement in Inber.

Neither of them said anything about it. Aeric was among the first to leave, followed by Neva and Lars. Florin parted soon after, only to be stopped by Pierce before he could reach the door.

"You're sure you don't need me for the Inber mission?" Pierce asked.

"We've discussed this," Florin said. "I'm keeping the group as small as possible to minimize the chance of detection." He paused, then added, "You're needed here. Hang around your apartments today. See who you run into."

Hollis and Zora, he meant. Though Pierce agreed, Marina could see the word gutter in his eyes—*useless.*

Marina rested her chin in her hands as the others filed out, expecting to think about Inber, but instead thinking about Vaughn—about how silently he'd fallen to the ground when she'd ripped his arm from his body, and how his hand still hadn't let go of the ruemin's bone-like appendage.

"I spoke to some healers the other day."

Marina looked up. Pierce wasn't speaking to her, but to Ryder, who lingered by the door, his face drawn.

"I just...you mentioned your scars," Pierce continued, "and I figured maybe they'd be able to reduce their appearance—"

"I never asked you to do that," Ryder said flatly.

Silently, Marina begged Pierce to leave it be, but she knew he wouldn't.

"I wanted you to have options," Pierce said. "I thought...maybe it would help."

Ryder laughed mirthlessly. "You think I wouldn't have asked the healers myself if I wanted them to fade?" He shook his head. "I don't run from things, my scars included. They don't need erasing."

Pierce barely reacted when Ryder left. He stood motionless for a few moments, then turned to Marina and gave her a tight-lipped smile.

She could see the pain in his expression—pain he was trying so hard to push down but was unable to. He seemed to have almost resigned himself to it.

CHAPTER 18
Products of Nature

Aeric stayed true to his word about involving Marina in discussions. As the sun set that evening, he sat down with her and Florin, who was indeed reluctant to include her on the Inber mission.

It was probably the most she'd ever seen Aeric and Florin butt heads, but she'd gone into the meeting prepared for it. Florin was mostly concerned with the integrity of the mission, and he didn't sugarcoat his thoughts about Marina accompanying them.

"At the very least, it slows us down," he'd said. "At most, it compromises us and puts not just her and the Omnia, but *all* of Neva's sanctuary, at risk."

Aeric had been equally as bullish, much to Marina's surprise. It occurred to her then just how important learning dissolution magic was. There was too much at stake for her *not* to learn, Aeric argued, and he seemed to think it was likely she'd need it eventually. She hadn't been ready to try her hand in the Delve—and even if she had been, it would've entailed practicing on an innocent person—but now she was, and they didn't have the luxury of waiting for the perfect time for her to learn.

It wasn't until Aeric underscored dissolution magic's use in combat that Florin gave in. Inducing amnesia or sedating a person could allow Marina to escape without killing. If she *did* need to kill, there was something to be said for cleaner, quicker deaths. Simply touching someone's skin could grant Marina access to their essence, and if she was strong enough, she could obliterate them from the inside out within seconds. Though the idea unsettled Marina, she agreed with Aeric. If she was to protect the Omnia, she'd need to know more than slitting throats and tearing off limbs.

Of course, in Inber, the goal was merely to sedate—and, if she was wily enough, to erase specific memories. If she failed, Aeric would be there to finish what she started.

But even with Florin's agreement, he and Aeric stressed that Marina's inclusion on the Inber mission was subject to whether or not she agreed to rigid rules.

The plan was to take place at night, under the cover of darkness. Florin's scouts had confirmed ten soldiers in the unit—including a squad leader in charge of sending reports to superiors in Altus—and night was when the largest number would be off duty. They were also less likely to complete a sweep then. But chances were never zero, so Florin decided to kick things off by having his soldiers conduct sweeps of their own. When the swamps were cleared, Florin, Aeric, Hollis, Zora, a few soldiers, and Marina would depart.

Florin's scouts had already located perimeter defenses around the camp, which could detect conveyance in addition to normal movement. Luckily, they had the tools needed to dismantle them. After a small portion of the defenses were down, Aeric, Hollis, and Zora would infiltrate the camp's command center and watchpoints—glamoured, if needed, to prevent anyone from seeing them. There, they'd use dissolution magic on the soldiers, wiping memories of the swamplands—orders and previous sweeps alike—along with the event of dissolution itself. Once they'd done that, they'd target those who were sleeping.

It became abundantly clear, however, that the plan wasn't limited to a single mission. If all went well with the dissolution magic, mentions of swampland sweeps would drop out of reports sent to Altus. This would stir up questions, no doubt, if not result in officers coming to the South to inquire directly.

That was where Zora came in. Before inducing amnesia on the squad leader, Aeric planned to temporarily incapacitate him, giving Zora time to take the squad leader's voco and clone its software to one of the Altus vocos Marina and Ryder had brought, creating a decoy. After extracting the tracker from the squad leader's voco and placing it in the decoy, Zora would swap the two, and they'd pocket the original voco to take back to the compound. Aeric would then wake the squad leader, conduct psychometry to obtain any authentication phrases the squad leader used in his messages, and finish with dissolution.

It seemed like a crazy plan, but if Zora and Aeric did their jobs correctly, the squad leader would remain unaware. Evidently, the squad leader *also* wouldn't know that the messages he sent to Altus thereafter were actually being sent to a burner voco in Candens Inlet—messages that would be repurposed to include reports about the swampland sweeps, then sent off to Altus using the original voco. Neva's technicians would play the role of intermediary between Altus and the squad leader, placating officials in Altus while responding appropriately to the squad leader himself.

Of course, all of this was dependent on Hollis's and Zora's agreement to come. If they *did* agree—which Florin didn't seem too concerned about—Aeric, Hollis, and Zora would locate an occupied tent on the outskirts of the camp, and once they'd done what they needed to, Marina would take on the last soldier: someone who was sleeping, and who consequently wouldn't have their armor on or weapons at the ready. Even then, Aeric refused to let Marina do it alone. He'd accompany her, and the others would be nearby in case of an emergency.

Marina's first inclination was self-consciousness—she wasn't *that* incompetent, was she?—but she knew Aeric and Florin were right to be cautious. As easy as combative magic was for her, she wasn't a soldier. If something went wrong, magically or otherwise, she'd need backup.

And according to Aeric, plenty could—and likely would—go wrong.

Dissolution magic was one of the more delicate kinds of mind magic—prone to error and nearly impossible for an amateur sorcerer to get right. It required finesse as much as it did a willingness to risk hurting someone. In its most extreme forms, it was capable of dissolving an entire essence, the results of which ranged from vegetative states to death.

Seasoned sorcerers, however, knew how to destroy just enough to subdue a person—to bring about blunted affect and compliance. That process required a sorcerer to smother someone's essence with their own, putting a damper on the victim's consciousness. The victim would remain awake but weak; conscious but unresisting. A puppet whose strings could be pulled by anyone in any way.

It came as no surprise to Marina when Aeric told her that Vaughn was unparalleled when it came to that kind of dissolution magic—even better than Kieron himself—which was why Kieron had wanted him to conduct it on Aeric.

Other forms of dissolution magic were far less severe. If sorcerers targeted memories instead of the essence itself, they could induce a selective form of amnesia. This required attention to detail and precision; a single misstep could result in the wrong memories being dissolved—or worse, parts of the essence.

The possibility scared Marina—even more so when Aeric underscored the fact that disintegrating parts of a person's spirit was worse than simply damaging it. Damage could be repaired, but what no longer existed couldn't be brought back.

Aeric ended their conversation by making Marina promise to surrender if things went wrong—to let him intervene in whatever way he found fit and to neither question him nor object.

She'd promised.

Their discussion kept her awake that night and plagued her well into the morning. She met Ismene, Elta, and Pierce in the dining hall for breakfast, and though she tried to engage in small talk, she couldn't.

As cautious as Florin was, it was clear he didn't want to wait around any longer than necessary. He planned to deal with the Inber unit before Calcite's end, pending Hollis and Zora's agreement. Luckily, Pierce had talked to them and seemed optimistic.

Marina tried to share in his optimism, but her head was loud this morning. Thoughts of dissolution magic twisted into thoughts about Kieron and Exorsus—about the world Elsudra could become if he got what he wanted. When Ismene and Elta spoke of their work in the gardens, all Marina pictured was what they'd look like if Kieron burned this place to the ground. When Pierce spoke of the progress Neva's soldiers were making under Florin's guidance, hundreds of dead bodies flashed into her head—rotting beneath the sun.

It was only when Pierce tapped her shoulder and whispered, "You have a friend," that she really came back to the present.

Yolie stood at the corner of the dining hall, clutching her breakfast tray. She looked smaller than usual—probably because she was the only child in the room. When her eyes met Marina's, she smiled hesitantly, and Marina waved her over.

She brightened as she approached, then took the seat closest to Marina. Pierce, Ismene, and Elta gave her gentle smiles, but all Yolie did was tilt her head at Pierce's untouched food and say, "Are you going to eat that?"

Pierce glanced at his tray. "Want it?"

When Yolie nodded, he pushed it to her. She piled his fruit onto her plate, then said, "You're the one the cat likes."

Pierce chuckled. "Haven't seen him in a while, actually."

"He's elusive," Yolie said matter-of-factly. She looked at Ismene, then said, "Your aura is strong. What form does your essence take?"

Ismene smiled. "Wildflowers."

"I bet that's why Elta likes you so much," Yolie said. When Elta's face reddened, a smile tugged at Yolie's lips. "She *loves* gardens."

Marina knit her brow. Was it commonplace for everyone in Elsudra to know the form their spirits took? She'd never realized her own—not until she'd come to Elsudra and Aeric had done psychometry on her.

She asked, and Elta—who seemed intent on speaking before Yolie could add anything else—told her most Elsudrans developed a good sense of theirs in early childhood. Every being in the sister realms had an essence, but the presence of magic in Elsudra made it easier for Elsudrans to conceptualize their own, regardless of magical ability.

Marina hadn't appreciated just how unique essences were. They could be similar, but never identical, and Elsudrans went to great lengths to teach their children that every essence was a product of Exorsus—that marginal magical abilities or lack thereof didn't curtail a spirit's beauty. How that played out in practice, Elta said, wasn't always so idealistic. Marina remembered Aeric saying he'd have likely remained in poverty if it hadn't been for his abilities—abilities his mother had used to get Aeric in front of Kieron when he was a boy.

Mostly, though, whether solid or fluid or somewhere in between, one's essence was a source of pride—a reminder that Elsudrans were products of nature, like all of Exorsus's creations.

Though Marina tried to listen as they spoke of their own essences—Pierce's was moss, apparently, and Elta's was copal resin—all she could think about was Ryder and what he'd had to do to himself to survive. And if Kieron won this fight, then nearly everyone here would live out their days in hiding—terrified their essences would mark them as a threat to Kieron, who wouldn't hesitate to snuff them out.

It was a sickening thought, and Marina's ears began to ring. She barely heard Elta ask, "What form does yours take?"

Marina blinked to clear her vision. "Sorry?"

"Your essence. I don't think you've mentioned it."

Somewhere in her mind's eye, Marina could see her waves. They rose and fell, one after the other, and she breathed with them.

When her head stopped spinning, she said, "An ocean."

"That's fitting for the Omnia's host," Elta said, smiling warmly. "Eventually, maybe you'll return it to ours."

The comment stuck with Marina throughout the rest of breakfast. Though the noise in her head didn't give her much ability to focus, it still gnawed at her as they finished up. When Pierce left, Ismene and Elta offered to show Marina the gardens behind the dining hall. Yolie accompanied them, but since these gardens were solely for food production, she resorted to rearranging the flowers in her pockets.

"She reminds me a little of Thora," Ismene said.

A few yards away, Yolie stood with her palms out, bending the sunlight so it reflected off the flowers' petals.

"She's very good at magic," Marina added. "Half of the things she knows, even Aeric didn't learn until he was much older."

"Have you introduced the two of them?"

"Aeric and Yolie?" When Ismene nodded, Marina shrugged. "I hadn't thought of it. Something tells me Aeric would brush me off. He's been preoccupied lately."

"Times may be different," Ismene said, "but the job of a Sorcerer of the Court has always been to train magical savants. And if you say she's good at magic, I think you may be wasting an opportunity if you don't."

"I agree," Elta said. "In another world, that girl could've been a Sorcerer of the Court."

"You should tell that to Neva," Marina muttered.

When Elta and Ismene exchanged a glance—which seemed to have become a habit for them, Marina realized—she told them about Neva's reluctance to let Yolie glamour.

"Even if the Inber mission is successful, she'd *still* rather risk weak glamours while Florin's group is in Altus," Marina said. She lowered herself to a nearby bench and rubbed her temples. "I'm open to offering myself as help," she added. "I just...don't know how much help that would amount to."

Ismene sat next to Marina. Gently, she said, "Maybe Neva will change her mind once the unit stops being a problem. Set your sights on one thing at a time."

Elta plucked a leaf from a nearby peppermint plant and smoothed it with her fingers. "My offer from earlier still stands. Once the Inber mission is completed, I can talk to Neva about Yolie. Hearing it from someone she knows a little better might help."

"You can try," Marina said, "but from what I gather, she doesn't even listen to Yolie." She scrubbed her hands across her face. "And this is assuming the Inber mission works, let alone happens at all. Florin wants to do it as soon as possible, but we don't know if Hollis and Zora have agreed yet."

"They will," Ismene said.

"How do you know?"

"Because I was there when Pierce spoke to them. I heard what he said." Ismene chewed on her lip. "Hollis and Zora hold grudges of their own against Kieron. They had family in Lewes, like me. And they know where we're headed if this turns out badly."

No, they don't, Marina thought. Ismene didn't either. They thought they knew, but the reality was so much worse.

The potential reality, she reminded herself. *It's only a theory.*

Theory or not, what difference did it make? If Kieron could come into contact with Exorsus upon possession of the Omnia, there was no saying what he'd be able to do. Some possibilities Marina couldn't bear to think of.

She tried not to, but distractions were hard to come by. Watching Yolie rearrange flowers or listening in on Ismene and Elta's lighthearted conversations didn't do it. When Marina caught sight of Ash in the gardens and summoned him onto her lap, she prayed maybe that would relieve some of her stress. But no matter how mindlessly she petted him, the heaviness in her chest wouldn't fade.

She must have had quite the tortured expression on her face because Elta approached her and held out a fresh peppermint leaf.

"The scent eases anxiety," she said when Marina frowned at her. "You need it."

If she didn't feel like she was going to suffocate, Marina might have laughed at that. She eagerly took the leaf and held it under her nose.

One breath. Then another. After a few times, breathing got easier.

"Thank you," Marina whispered. Perhaps she'd take a leaf to Inber—she'd certainly need it. "Can I keep this?"

"All yours," Elta said. "Bring a bunch back to your apartment, if you'd like. We have more than enough."

When the noise in her head died down, Marina managed a smile. "Maybe I'll ask Yolie if she'd like to meet Aeric. Neva might not agree to it, but I guess we'll cross that bridge when we get there."

Ismene considered for a moment. "You think Neva would say no to that too?"

Marina shrugged. "Neva and Aeric don't seem to have warmed up to each other. I don't think she trusts him."

"I happen to remember someone else who didn't trust Aeric," Ismene said, "and *she* came around."

CHAPTER 19
Peppermint

The peppermint leaf worked wonders, and Marina found herself in a much clearer headspace later that day. She was half convinced Elta and Ismene were angels—not only did Elta stop by her apartment in the afternoon with a fresh bunch and a cup of peppermint tea, but Ismene's prediction about Hollis and Zora turned out to be correct. When Ryder returned from training with news that Hollis and Zora had agreed to help, Marina almost cried out of relief.

Ryder admitted it was, in part, talking to Pierce that had swayed them.

"Guess he mentioned your sacrifice," Ryder said. "Not the specifics—just that you made one."

Some of the tightness in Marina's shoulders lifted. "I'm glad he helped."

"Yes," Ryder said coolly. "He's very good at getting people to do things, isn't he? He only lacks the capacity to do such things himself."

The tightness came back. "That's not fair, Ryder," she said.

"Careful throwing that word around. You'll start to realize nothing is."

Marina glowered at him. "Don't lecture me about *fair*." She clamped her lips shut before she could say anything else—before her words could bore into the wound Ryder refused to tend to. Instead, she took the bunch of peppermint from her bedside table and put it to her nose.

Despite giving her a look, Ryder didn't ask what she was doing. Instead, he rested his feet on the headboard of his bed and stared up at the ceiling. "I hear Hollis and Zora have a seedy past."

"How so?"

"Nobody knows for sure, but it makes sense. No normal sorcerer knows dissolution magic." When Marina flinched, he said, "They're not the only people here with ghosts. They want a better world as much as the rest of us." He paused. "I volunteered to come to Inber too, but Florin's intent on keeping the group small. I wanted you to know I asked... to help protect you and the others."

Despite everything, that made Marina smile. "I appreciate that."

Ryder returned her smile with a tight-lipped one of his own. "You'll be safe," he said. "Florin will be there to oversee everything, and Aeric won't let anything happen to you."

"A lot rides on protecting the Omnia," Marina said. She smoothed the peppermint leaves with her fingers like Elta had done. The texture helped as much as the smell.

"Not the Omnia," Ryder said. "You." When Marina raised her eyes to his, he added, "You know that look Neva gets when Yolie is mentioned? Aeric gets the same one when *you're* mentioned. He'd burn the world down if it meant keeping you safe."

For some reason, that didn't make Marina think of Aeric so much as it made her think of Neva. Shame rushed through her. She shouldn't have pushed Neva so hard to let Yolie glamour—shouldn't have challenged her in front of everyone when it was clear how consumed Neva was with keeping Yolie safe.

After some time, Marina whispered, "I don't want anyone to burn the world down for me." She set the peppermint bunch back down. "All I want is to be the person the Keepers hoped I'd be. I want to help you all fight for a better world—the kind where people don't have to hide or damage themselves to survive."

Ryder's chin quivered, but his voice was even when he said, "The kind where one man hoards power for eternity, you mean?"

Marina blinked at him. "You know?"

Silence followed, which Ryder broke with a sigh. "Florin told me."

"Did he tell anyone else?"

"Don't think so." He sat upright. "He told me I should know—said you, Neva, and Lars did. Or maybe he just wanted to make sure I knew the true stakes so my loyalty didn't waver later on." The wry look in his eyes faded. "I gather Aeric's pretty sure about this theory of his."

"He's not the type to rattle off theories unless he's certain," Marina said.

"Figured as much." Ryder sucked on his cheek. "So Kieron takes the Omnia, enters Exorsus, and creates a loop that...what, begins again at his death?"

"And starts when he's in Exorsus, probably," Marina said.

A repeating pattern within the landscape of time—a pattern *he* controlled.

"I'd be dead by then," she muttered. Strangely enough, her stomach didn't turn to lead at the thought. Probably because, in Kieron's eternity, not dying was so much worse.

"If that happens," Ryder said, "I plan to die too. By my own hand or someone else's, I don't care, but I'll be gone before he accesses Exorsus." He shook his head and laughed mirthlessly. "Fuck survival. There's no way I'm living in this eternity of his."

❧

Following Hollis and Zora's agreement, Florin set a date: the first day of Calcite's eighth week, which was coming upon them soon. Marina and Aeric's training became wholly focused on dissolution magic, and though she couldn't practice it herself, that didn't stop Aeric from explaining everything to her. Mostly, he underscored the importance of exercising restraint—of dissolving singular memories and nothing more.

Marina remembered when she'd done psychometry on Florin back in the Delve after the alarms had gone off—how her distress had caused her waves to thrash about in his essence, and how she'd pulled back before she could do damage. But she'd still felt the potential brewing within her—the kind that could take away every memory and perhaps even the spirit itself.

While dissolution of the essence could work while a victim was unconscious or asleep, targeting memories required them to be awake. The same rules applied with psychometry; memories simmered beneath the surface of an essence, rising only when the mind and body were active. Targeting a sleeping soldier, then, was simply to ensure they were unprepared—so that armor and weapons were within arm's reach instead of on the body.

In the days leading up to the mission, Marina felt herself wavering. At times, she wondered if she should tell Aeric she couldn't do it. But then the alarms would go off, and she'd watch as people scattered like ants, retreating indoors and praying the glamours did their job. The flashing lights solidified her determination as much as they heightened her fear. She'd remind herself why she was doing this—the importance of what she was learning, and how if she wanted to be the person the Keepers yearned for, she'd need to become the kind of sorcerer Aeric was. The kind *Kieron* was.

And so, she learned the intricacies of dissolution magic—listened as Aeric told her to harness and control the power of her waves. She attended meetings where Florin outlined the mission and agreed when he told her that the most important rule she needed to follow was staying close to either him or Aeric the entire time—unless, of course, the two of them were incapacitated, in which case she was to convey as quickly as possible back to the sanctuary, worrying only about herself. No matter how many times Marina reassured herself that wouldn't happen, the possibility made her feel sick.

Meeting Hollis and Zora helped distract her. Despite the rumors Ryder had heard, they were a kind, rather unassuming couple who spoke with fondness of their days in

Lewes. Zora was a petite woman around Aeric and Neva's age, with dark eyes and spiked hair. Hollis was only a few years older, if Marina had to guess, and Zora's opposite in almost every way. He had a fair complexion—blond hair and nearly colorless eyes—with a stocky build and a tendency to move and speak slowly.

In some ways, they reminded Marina of Gemma and Hank. Zora was talkative, often interrupting or poking fun at Hollis, who was impossible to ruffle. Even the day before the mission, when everyone else was quiet and on edge, Zora made jokes and laughed loudly. Her confidence was contagious, and it managed to ease Marina's nerves just enough to be noticeable.

Still, when the sun set on the first day of Calcite's eighth week and they prepared to depart, Marina placed a peppermint leaf in her pocket.

CHAPTER 20
Glass House

They left in the final moments of twilight, all donning armored suits. Marina was surprised Neva had extra to provide them with, but she was grateful all the same—wearing the suit made her feel safer, and it would help her blend in more than her normal clothes. She spent a few minutes fiddling with the helmet, which made her jump the first time it snapped in place. Behind it, she could see everything clearly. In fact, whatever material the goggles were made of helped her see in the dark too.

Though Florin and the three soldiers he brought as backup carried weapons, he didn't bother supplying her, Aeric, Hollis, or Zora with anything. They could do enough damage on their own.

The sounds in the swamplands amplified at night. How were they supposed to hear anything when the crickets were so loud? On the other hand, the chirping muffled their footsteps as much as the damp ground did, and the vegetation was abundant enough that anyone moving through it would cause rustling.

Of course, that could alert them to danger as easily as it could give them away. The Inber unit was undoubtedly trained when it came to listening for approaching danger.

Florin's soldiers might've confirmed the swamplands were clear, but Marina still couldn't help but feel like *they* were the ones being hunted. Eventually, she decided to put all her faith into Florin because her endless cycle of worries was as unhelpful as it was suffocating.

Florin and his soldiers led the way, adept at moving both swiftly and quietly. Zora, too, was agile enough to maneuver past branches and evade pockets of mud, and Marina tried to copy her movements. She wasn't surprised Aeric moved quietly—it had always been one of his fortes—and though Hollis wasn't as sure-footed, he picked his way across the marshes effectively enough.

Since she'd taken backroads with Ryder, Marina had no idea what the camp setup would look like. One small mercy was that the swamplands were flat, which hindered the Inber unit's ability to claim an elevated vantage point. Still, they'd made do, and according to Florin, had stationed themselves next to a pond that edged into the forest—large enough to provide protection for more than half the camp, while also functioning as a mirror that reflected foliage and provided visual camouflage. Not counting animals, they didn't have to worry about outsiders infiltrating the camp from the water.

Florin led them to a wetland thicket at the edge of the pond farthest from the camp. A blanket of mist hung over the water, which was as comforting as it was eerie. If she squinted, Marina could make out one or two tents at the pond's shoreline. Farther in the distance, she swore she could see faint lights from Inber itself.

The thicket was well-hidden, full of gnarled trees and bushes so thick they hardly needed to rely on the mist to conceal them. But that didn't stop Marina's paranoia from running rampant. Even if the soldiers weren't a threat, the swamp itself was. She could only imagine the kinds of snakes that hid in the bulrush, and the freshwater was a breeding ground for alligators. She hadn't seen any, but alligators were masters at hiding in plain sight—and from what Lars had said, it was obvious the ones here weren't as scared of people as the ones in Georgia were.

And ruemin...they were around here too, no doubt. She wasn't sure what was worse. At least the armored suits' helmets scared the ruemin. Maybe that would keep them away.

Marina's heart sped up anyway, so she took the peppermint leaf from her pocket and inhaled. She could still catch the scent through the helmet, even if it was less potent.

Breathe. One at a time.

It was obvious Florin and his soldiers had already identified the camp's blind spots and the best places to infiltrate from—and more obvious that Aeric, Hollis, and Zora had been previously informed of the details—because they left the thicket as quickly as they arrived in it. As resolute as they were to get this done with, Aeric still took time to pull Marina aside and whisper, "Keep your eyes on Florin until we're back. Do only what he tells you to, nothing more."

All Marina could bring herself to do was nod. And then, like that, they were gone.

Conveyance, Marina realized. Once they'd dismantled perimeter defenses, conveyance was clearly their best bet at getting into the camp undetected. Conveying across the pond would have been optimal, but space didn't stop existing when one used conveyance; the water would react, and sound would surely draw attention.

Whatever path they were taking to get in, Marina figured she'd learn about it soon enough. But for now, she'd keep her eyes on Florin and try to breathe.

She reassured herself that if something went wrong, Aeric, Hollis, and Zora would simply convey back to the thicket, or perhaps even the sanctuary itself. Florin and his soldiers couldn't escape so easily, but Marina had a feeling they were more than capable of managing without sorcery.

They'll be okay. Just breathe.

Waiting had never been her strong suit, but here and now, surrounded by unfamiliar sounds and the unknown, it was agonizing. After a while, watching Florin became an obsessive practice. She monitored his movements—every glance to his voco, every look he shot his soldiers—and even once the darkness had fully set in, she kept her eyes glued to his silhouette.

Even with the night-vision goggles, the darkness heightened Marina's paranoia. The trees were so tall and thick that starlight couldn't make its way to the forest floor, and the faint lights from Inber had long since faded. The crickets' chirping blended with the low drone of cicadas, and Marina had no idea if the insects were really getting louder or if it was all in her head.

Every so often, the screen of Florin's voco would light up. She strained to see the digital messages he was getting, but the screen's light was on its lowest setting. It was only when he nodded to her and the soldiers that breathing got easier. She didn't know exactly what the nod meant, but it had to be something positive.

After half an hour, maybe more, Florin leaned closer to Marina and said, "Soon."

Soon. Soon, they'd return—and she'd try her hand. The simultaneous mix of relief and panic was so overwhelming that she directed all her attention back to watching Florin and inhaling the peppermint leaf's scent. It was starting to lose its potency, but that didn't matter. They'd be back at the compound in an hour or two, and Elta would give her a new bunch. The thought kept her grounded, and when Aeric, Hollis, and Zora returned, she maintained a level head.

This was no joyous reunion—no smiles were exchanged, no congratulations given. Aeric approached Marina directly, his voice quieter than before. "We're finished, minus one soldier—around your age and size, asleep in a secluded tent. That's who you'll take on."

He spoke quickly but clearly. Hollis and Zora were to stay with Florin and the soldiers in the thicket, but if something happened, Aeric would send Florin an emergency alert on his voco—in which case Hollis and Zora would convey in with Florin and the others to provide backup.

"Since we're doing this quickly, I will convey you in myself," Aeric continued. "The moment we arrive, you will enter the tent with me and wake the soldier. After I restrain them, you will wield dissolution magic to the best of your ability, and I'll check after to ensure you didn't miss anything. Are you ready?"

At this point, all Marina could do was nod. There was no turning back. She'd do what she could—*learn* what she could—and Aeric would be there to help if she needed it. She steadied her hand as she placed the peppermint leaf back in her pocket, and when she nodded again, Aeric took hold of her arm.

The world blurred.

Aeric's landings were smoother than hers, which Marina figured was another reason he'd wanted to convey them both. They landed at the pond's shoreline, where clumps of hemlock sprouted from the waterlogged soil—the flowers as thick and white as the mist. They thinned out by the nearest tent, where a bundle of weapons had been placed by the unsecured door. Clearly, whoever slept in that tent hadn't placed the weapons there themself. It didn't take Marina long to realize Aeric, Hollis, and Zora had done it when they'd handpicked this tent for her.

It was rather humbling how deliberate they'd been. The tent was inhabited by only one soldier, who didn't so much as stir in her sleep when Marina and Aeric entered. She was young, from what Marina could see—probably in her early twenties.

It made sense. Even if this soldier knew how to fight—which Marina was certain she did—she was around Marina's size and stature, likely fresh out of training. Though her armor lay at the foot of her bed, there was no way she'd have enough time to put it on. She was outnumbered and unarmed.

Still, Marina's hands shook as she took off one of her gloves and tucked it under her belt. Her hand felt horribly vulnerable as she extended it, but skin-to-skin contact was necessary, and there was no way around this.

No turning back, she reminded herself.

A breath. Waves up. Her hand neared the girl's shoulder, which was covered in tresses of dark hair.

Dark hair...like the soldier in Tin.

She shook the thought away, only to have Cal's face follow suit—strands of raven hair falling in front of her eyes.

Not now. Don't do this now.

She wasn't going to let her mind win. It could throw a thousand unwanted images at her, and she'd ignore it. All that mattered was her waves and the power they held.

Marina braced herself as she tapped the girl, prepared to enter her essence the moment she woke up. The girl stirred, but her eyes didn't open.

Come on. Wake up.

She almost glanced at Aeric, but before she could, the soldier jumped up, brandishing a dagger. Marina had no idea where she'd gotten it from—probably under her pillow, or perhaps she'd been sleeping with it attached—but she swung it so hard and fast that it scraped against Marina's helmet. The sound it made was grating, but it didn't do any damage.

Marina's body acted before her mind. She lurched backward before the girl could swing again, then flicked her eyes to the soldier's hand. Inducing pain was instinctual, and the moment the soldier's hand spasmed, she yelped and dropped her dagger to the ground.

Thank *God* the soldier wasn't wearing armor. It was a measly bit of relief, but it emboldened Marina. The soldier had to have known reaching for her blade was fruitless, but she tried anyway. Before Marina could induce pain a second time, Aeric had already knocked the soldier off her feet.

It had all happened fast, but Marina didn't waste time recovering. The moment Aeric had the soldier pinned to the ground—his hand pressed over her mouth—Marina dove toward her and made contact with her forehead.

It wouldn't have mattered if the soldier had tried to scream or fight, because now, the world was waves. They crashed into a canyon made entirely of agate stone—glassy towers of red, blue, and brown rock that spanned the girl's essence. Getting to the heart of the canyon was easy; as mighty as the rocks were, they were as good as paper when it came down to it. Marina maneuvered through nooks and crannies, where memories were neatly tucked away. Recent ones were of humid days and quiet nights, which Marina swept past. She knew which memories she needed to target, but finding them was harder than she'd expected. The rocks formed a labyrinth, and there was a memory around every corner—smiles exchanged during training and laughter shared around small fires. The other soldiers weren't just coworkers; they were friends.

This girl's memories...they were so *normal*. Marina wasn't sure what she'd expected. Perhaps she'd anticipated the callousness of a soldier fighting for Kieron's side—the drive of a girl training to preserve such a hideous regime. But there was none of that.

Did the soldier truly understand who she was fighting for? She didn't seem cruel. Ignorant, maybe, and young, but not cruel.

It didn't matter. Her job wasn't to question the soldier's morality. And so, the moment Marina's waves came into contact with a cluster of memories set in the thick of the wetland forest—when she heard orders from the squad leader pertaining to schedules and sweeps—she steeled herself and let her waves crest.

Dissolving memories, she quickly realized, was much different than getting through mental shields. When she'd slipped past Florin's redwoods and Aeric's fog, her intent hadn't been to destroy anything. Whatever fissures she'd formed had been on their shields —mere extensions of their essence. Once she'd gotten inside, she'd only watched.

Now, she was shooting in the dark, completely unaware of how or where to start. Even with the Omnia—with the light of a thousand suns that danced alongside the ocean current—she wasn't sure how she was supposed to *erase* memories.

She tried anyway. Seawater engulfed the memories—once, twice, then a third time.

Washing them away, Marina thought. *That's all.*

Only...something else had dissolved with the memories. Chunks of rock.

Somewhere an immeasurable distance away, Marina's heart rate skyrocketed.

Slow down. Be careful.

It was too late for that. Pulverized agate fell into the water—a small portion of the canyon, perhaps, but still too much. Marina tried to steady herself as she resumed her search for the other memories, but seeing the rock disintegrate sent rushes of panic through her, and her waves reacted.

It was like navigating a glass house. Every time her waves so much as lapped against a memory, nearby rocks broke into fragments and withered away. She desperately tried to pinpoint what needed to be dissolved—there had to be more memories about swampland sweeps, and she still hadn't erased the soldier's immediate memories, which, all things considered, were among the most important to get rid of. If the soldier remembered *this*, their mission would be for naught. Maybe it *already* was for naught. The canyon had started to crumble, and Marina could feel bits of the soldier's essence dying.

No, no, no...

She had to let go. She'd done enough...Aeric could finish it. But drawing back was as dangerous as moving forward. It didn't matter how hard she strained to steady her waves. Whatever pulsed through them—adrenaline, power, or a mix of the two—made them uncontrollable. The cracks she'd already caused weakened the entire essence, and its foundation was starting to crumble.

Desperately, Marina tried to fix what she'd done—washing her waves over the rocks, praying they'd stick back together—but nothing worked. If anything, it only made things worse. The stone crumbled, beautiful colors turning to dust before dissolving entirely.

Marina knew the damage was severe before Aeric grabbed her arm and yanked her out of the soldier's essence, but seeing it was worse.

The soldier lay with her eyes open, chest rising and falling softly. Saliva dripped from her mouth, and her lips had turned blue. She wasn't dead, but she was about as close to it as one could be. There was no fixing this.

It's on me.

Marina looked to Aeric, eyes wide, but his face was drawn. Slowly, he stood, and when she did too, he said, "What happens next is my decision. Whether or not you watch is yours."

Before she could respond, he picked the dagger up off the ground, then took the soldier by her wrists and dragged her limp body from the tent. For a moment, Marina wavered, wondering if perhaps it would be best to just stay and let Aeric do what he planned because he was already going to, and whether or not she watched didn't matter.

But it *did* matter. It mattered because she'd done this, and though she was too numb to feel guilt at the moment, she knew it would come eventually—knew it would torment her like everything else did, only it would be a thousand times worse if she hid from the consequences.

She slipped out of the tent, her arms wrapped around her body as Aeric placed the soldier at the water's edge. He was quick—emotionless, though Marina figured he had to be—as he scattered dirt on her clothes and face. It wasn't until he ripped away a piece of her pant leg, however, that she realized what he was doing.

Aeric positioned his hand over the soldier's calf, and when he bent his wrist upward, her leg twisted. Marina's head grew light, and she knelt down in case she passed out.

She wasn't sure exactly what kind of attack he was staging. As he inflicted puncture wounds on the soldier's leg, Marina figured the most likely was an alligator. Or maybe his goal was to simply maul her body so badly that the others would have no reason to think a person had done it. These were swamplands, after all, and Lars had made it clear how unforgiving they were. But a broken leg and bite wounds weren't severe enough to throw off suspicion, were they?

She regretted it as soon as she thought it. Aeric put his hands to the soldier's neck, and when the sound of crushed bone and ripped flesh cut through the air, all Marina could think of was how glad she was that the crickets were so loud.

If the soldier hadn't already died, she would soon. The base of her head had been flattened and half of her neck was gone, exposing vertebrae and a mess of structures Marina couldn't pinpoint. Not like she'd have tried to. At the moment, her focus was elsewhere—on the voice in her head that repeated the same phrase over and over.

It's on me.

CHAPTER 21
Annihilation

Marina felt nothing as they returned to the sanctuary. She felt nothing as Pierce and Ismene greeted them, overjoyed, and nothing as Neva, for perhaps the first time since they'd come here, thanked Aeric and Florin.

She felt nothing the rest of the night too, but she knew where it was headed. It would fade as she slept, and the guilt would be there to tear her apart in the morning.

She expected her dreams that night to be of opened throats and crushed bone, but instead, they were of laughter. Light, carefree laughter that bubbled from the mouth of a person Marina knew nothing about—a person she would *never* know anything about, other than the fact she'd fought for Kieron and had an essence made of agate.

Marina desperately wanted to focus on the former. So what if the soldier had been young and naive? So what if she'd had friends and family? She'd fought for Kieron's side— the side that sought to extinguish all threats to Kieron's reign and would slaughter Neva's sanctuary in a heartbeat if they found them.

But Ryder had fought for that side once too. So had Aeric. And no matter how hard Marina tried to convince herself that those two were more complicated, she couldn't.

She assumed Aeric had told Florin what had happened after they'd returned, but she wasn't sure about the others. Ryder seemed to pick up on her mood the next morning, but he didn't comment on it. Instead, he told her that, all things considered, Florin was in decent spirits. The mission had worked, and Zora had successfully swapped the vocos. Florin intended to keep an eye on the unit and assess for signs of internal discord, but he seemed confident they'd continue their duties in Inber and leave the swamplands alone.

Marina knew Ryder was exaggerating to make her happy—Florin couldn't be in *that* decent of spirits, considering what she'd done—though perhaps Florin was simply relieved he'd secured two good sorcerers to join him in Altus, whenever that mission was set to happen. She couldn't think of that now. She couldn't think of anything but the soldier.

She expected Aeric to cancel their training that night and was disappointed when he didn't. There was no way she'd be able to focus on glamouring.

He'd clearly anticipated her headspace, though, because he started by telling her that they were now entirely in charge of which of the Inber unit's reports got sent to Altus—or, more fittingly, which ones didn't. Their burner voco had already received an emergency message from the squad leader, who seemed more than convinced the soldier's death was due to an animal attack. Aeric didn't go into many details, but it was obvious Altus had briefed the unit on the threat of swampland predators before they'd departed. This made Neva's technicians' job easy. They'd placate the squad leader by sending him run-of-the-mill instructions on how to mitigate the risk of future attacks, then underscore the importance of continuing with town patrols and not getting bogged down by bureaucratic procedures related to the deceased. By downplaying the incident and steering the unit away from potential investigations, they'd maintain control of the narrative.

Aeric remained levelheaded as he told her, and Marina realized how prepared he'd been for her to mess up.

"But I didn't expect the damage to be so severe," he admitted. "And I didn't expect it to happen as quickly as it did. I thought I'd have time to pull you out before you did anything permanent, then take over and fix things myself."

Was that supposed to make her feel better? She had no idea with him. He'd told her once before that she had an innate ability to destroy things, and he seemed to be saying the same thing now.

"Does the type of magic that someone's good at say something about who they are as a person?" Marina asked. When Aeric's eyes met hers, she tensed. *Please say no.*

"Maybe," he said, and her chest constricted—not because the answer surprised her, but because it confirmed what she'd already thought. Aeric observed her, then added, "But how they use their talents says more."

Marina stared at her hands. "I take forever to learn things like glamouring, but I never needed to learn how to destroy glamours. When it comes to dissolution magic, I don't struggle with dissolving—I struggle with *not* dissolving. I annihilated an entire essence within seconds, killed a soldier in Tin intuitively, and tore Vaughn's arm clean off on my first try." She laughed bitterly. "Kind of fucked, isn't it?"

"Vaughn is a sadistic man responsible for the torture and death of hundreds of Elsudrans," Aeric said, "and you tore his arm off to save your friends' lives and escape." He tilted his head. "I, on the other hand, excel at calculative magic, and I used my talent to hijack Brenna's portal and let Kieron and the ruemin into Elsudra—which resulted in the deaths of so many Elsudrans even Vaughn cannot compete. Tell me, which is more *fucked*?" After a bout of painful silence, he added, "You may have a knack for violent magic, but that doesn't make you bad."

Marina put her head in her hands, then murmured, "I'm sorry for what happened. For making you do...what you had to."

"I've done worse."

She raised her head to look at him, but he was as deadpan as ever. How he managed to hide his emotions, she'd never understand. She knew he wasn't indifferent to the suffering he'd caused; she'd seen his memories—felt what he did.

"We're responding appropriately, and there's no use ruminating over what's done," he continued. "As long as we can appease the unit until the Altus mission, the compound will remain safe." When she didn't respond, he added, "We were successful last night, Marina, even if some of it wasn't pretty. And you've learned a great deal about dissolution magic. You have the strength needed to kill someone, and while I know you don't want to hear this, that could save you. When it comes to less severe forms of dissolution, you know where your deficit is. You're too heavy-handed. Next time, you'll tread lighter. Go slower."

Marina flinched as her eyes started to burn. "I don't think I can do that again."

"You might not have a choice."

This time, Marina didn't need to guess whether or not he was trying to make her feel better. Though the thought made her stomach curdle, she wondered if perhaps she'd been too brash in Exorsus. She didn't regret what she'd done—she was glad she'd destroyed Kieron's chance to take the Omnia—but perhaps holding it herself wasn't the way she was meant to help.

Maybe she had the ability to improve her skills—to increase her precision with mind-based magic, learn glamouring...all of it. But did it matter? They were running on limited time. They couldn't stay here forever and wait for her to perfect every skill.

But what if she helped in a different way? What if she put the Omnia somewhere better? Back in the Delve, she'd wanted to use Locus to sever the Omnia from herself and give it to Aeric, but Aeric had made it clear the ritual might be her end. It was finicky— even riskier than dissolution, she imagined, and she obviously didn't have a knack for finesse. That, and she had no idea how long it would take Aeric to teach her.

Only...she didn't need Locus when she had something better. Something more powerful. She'd accessed Exorsus before, and even now, she could feel the ability in her veins—that which sang with the Omnia's magic and was strong enough to open the door to what lay beyond. In Exorsus, she wouldn't be constrained by Locus's rules—wouldn't be limited to moving the Omnia between only those with the ability to agree. She could give it back to the ocean like Elta had said in the dining hall.

She dared to voice her thoughts to Aeric, whose aloof mask faltered when he raised his eyebrows. The room grew so silent that even through the thick walls, Marina swore she could hear the trees rustle outside.

"One day," Aeric finally said, "that might be an option. But not while Kieron lives."

"But he can't enter Exorsus," Marina said. "It devours him. While I hold the Omnia, there's still a risk he could force me into Locus. Even worse, there's a chance last night could happen again—that I could mess up and put everyone in danger. If the Omnia were in the sea, there's no way he'd be able to get it back."

"Not on his own," Aeric said. "But Kieron doesn't do things on his own." He lowered his voice, even though they were the only two in the room. "The first Keepers accessed Exorsus without holding the Omnia themselves, even if it took them seasons. Kieron told you this, remember?"

Marina nodded, then tilted her head. "Except the first Keepers were four of the most powerful sorcerers in Elsudra."

"That doesn't mean others can't do what they did," Aeric said. "Never assume the past can't be repeated just because what happened was an anomaly. It *always* can be. Accessing Exorsus and taking the Omnia from water was possible for the first Keepers. That means it would be possible for other equally powerful sorcerers, and Kieron happens to keep two such sorcerers by his side. He didn't choose Safira and Vaughn randomly. He knows what they can do—what they *would* do for him."

A chill ran down Marina's spine.

"Kieron knows how to access Exorsus now," Aeric continued, "and together, the three of them could very well do what the first Keepers did—even if it took them as long or longer. Then, Kieron would have Safira or Vaughn enter Exorsus and take the Omnia from water themselves. After that, he'd be free to rely on Locus again. Only this time, the Omnia's new host would consent."

Marina blinked at him. "How are you so sure they'd be that loyal?"

"Because I once was." Though he held her gaze, his voice was weak when he added, "I would've gone to the end of the world for him. In some ways, I did." His lips twitched. "Safira and Vaughn are the same, maybe more loyal. They aren't only following Kieron; they're following his ideology as well. That's exactly why he handpicked them. They're powerful enough to aid him while not desiring what he does, and they've already proven how far they'll go to uphold his regime."

Marina knew Aeric was right. Safira had demonstrated her devotion to Kieron several times over. And there was no version of Elsudra, minus Kieron's, where Vaughn could engage in the kinds of horrific experiments that had gotten him kicked out of Altus in the first place. Kieron had mentioned spending years trying to convince Vaughn to join him, and that Vaughn had only agreed when Kieron had given him an offer that proved his reign would be different.

Kieron certainly *had* handpicked his three sorcerers. One driven by reverence, one by opportunity, and one by love.

Even now—even though Aeric had abandoned Kieron—Marina could *still* feel his love for him. It was broken and withered, defined more by pain than warmth, but it followed him. Haunted him. And she knew Aeric hated himself for it.

The pit in Marina's stomach rose until it clawed at the back of her throat, though she wasn't sure if the feeling was because of last night or because of what Aeric had said. Maybe both. Maybe, despite all their similarities, guilt was what truly made them alike.

Aeric was practiced at keeping his guilt from overflowing—more so than she was, at least. He cleared his throat, then said, "When it comes to Kieron and his fanatics, the only answer is annihilation. We need the Omnia's host on our side for that to happen." He hesitated, but there was no uncertainty in his voice when he added, "And though it may disturb you to your core, Marina, annihilation is what you're good at."

CHAPTER 22
Willow Leaves

Even though the idea of sending Hollis and Zora to Altus plagued Neva, she didn't renege. The success of the Inber mission seemed to ease tensions between her, Aeric, and Florin. It didn't eliminate Neva's anxiety about the Altus mission, of course, but it seemed to help—to know Aeric and Florin had the compound's safety in mind too.

It helped even more that Hollis and Zora were eager to go to Altus. In the days following the Inber mission, they worked with Florin from sunrise to sunset. Ryder joined them, and while Marina knew he dreaded returning to the capital, he didn't mention it. Instead, he threw himself into preparation, and since it seemed to take his mind off everything else, Marina tried to follow his example. She trained whenever she could—with and without Aeric—and when she wasn't practicing, she was reading. Mostly, she focused on glamours, desperate to succeed at magic that wasn't violent. But understanding light and shadows was still hard for her—as hard as learning how to divert them—and with every failure, she realized how right Aeric was. She *was* good at annihilation.

If she didn't think about the soldiers in Inber or Tin, perhaps she could find comfort in that. After all, what Aeric had said to her hadn't been an insult. If anything, it'd been a vote of confidence. Hadn't it?

She tried not to ruminate on the past or the future, though she was tempted to. On days when even training couldn't distract her, she'd seek out Pierce, Ismene, or Elta. But strangely enough, it was Yolie whose presence grounded her. Sometimes, the two of them would spend hours watching the sun reflect off the canopy, and whenever they settled down to practice magic together, it never felt like a chore.

When Pierce wasn't busy, he would spend time with them. Yolie seemed to enjoy his company, partially because wherever Pierce was, Ash tended to show up too. As for Pierce, he had his own reasons for seeking out distraction.

As Double Moon neared, however, distraction was harder to come by. Florin wanted the Altus mission to happen at the beginning of Pearl, but that could only be set in motion if Kieron agreed to Aeric's request to meet outside the capital—which meant they needed to successfully contact Kieron before Calcite's end.

Neva's technicians planned to use the remaining Altus voco—the one that hadn't been used as a decoy—to reach the palace. Once enough messages were sent through, they believed Kieron would pick up on his personal line, especially if the messages were from Aeric. Since the voco no longer had a tracker, it was a safe way to keep the compound undetectable while also prompting Kieron to respond himself. Everyone was confident about this, and Marina wasn't inclined to question Elsudran technology—it was different from Earth's, after all, in a way that was neither modern nor archaic.

Even with the technicians' assurances about location anonymity, it was obvious the idea unsettled Aeric. He was determined to go through with it, but when he told Marina the call was set to happen during Calcite's ninth week—which started the very next day— his eyes turned glassy. And yet, he didn't object when Marina said she wanted to be there.

Time was moving quickly. In Georgia, it would've been July, which Marina only knew because Ismene had helped her align the Elsudran calendar on her new voco with the calendar back at home, just like she'd done in the Delve. Last Double Moon had been in February. If Aeric's call was successful, Florin, Ryder, Hollis, and Zora would head out in only a few weeks.

For now, she'd try to focus on the present, because it was all she could do. It helped that the sun was out, which Yolie said was the best weather for collecting foliage. Marina and Pierce joined her for a walk around the compound as she picked low-hanging leaves and placed them in her pockets. She liked making things out of them—a hobby she'd picked up from her brother.

"He made me a doll out of willow leaves once," Yolie said.

Pierce scooped up Ash, who'd been lingering at his heels. "He must've been talented."

Yolie nodded. "He tried to sell some after our dad died, but it wasn't enough."

Marina's heart sank. Perhaps it was because she couldn't stop herself from thinking of Aeric's mother, who'd tried with pottery what Ronan had with dolls.

Evren. One of the many names on Marina's list. And now *Ronan* was too.

"He tried everything," Yolie continued, her eyes downcast. "He'd find any job he could, sell things he'd made...none of it worked. So eventually, he started stealing, even though he hated it. One day, he stole from a merchant who lived in our town. She sold clothes and fabric to other regions. All he'd needed was shoes. He never stole *anything* he didn't need. But she caught him."

Marina almost offered consolation but clamped her lips shut when she realized Yolie was smiling. Instead, she asked, "Who was the merchant?"

"Neva." Yolie picked a eucalyptus leaf and held it to her nose. "She gave him the shoes, and when he told her he knew how to make things, she offered him a job. He was great at it." She shrugged. "Ronan didn't trust her at first, though. He thought she'd send us to a home for children without guardians. Plus, he was in his second quarter, so he could take care of us both well enough. But Neva promised she wouldn't send us out of Sal. And when she realized I could wield magic like her, she helped me learn." She folded the leaf and placed it into her pocket. "But then, a year later, the mechanical woman came to find people like me and Neva. She almost found us, but Ronan...he saved us both."

Yolie's lips trembled, and she didn't say anything more. The heaviness in Marina's chest swelled into flames, bringing a flush to her face. Yolie hadn't deserved that. She hadn't deserved any of this. Neither had Ismene's sisters, or Cal and Astra, or Boris and Dane, or Pierce's father. Was there anyone in Elsudra who *hadn't* lost someone in this war?

So much for distraction. Now, all Marina could think of was those who'd died—who would continue to die if things didn't change. The past and future wouldn't stop plaguing them until Kieron was gone.

If she couldn't think about the present, then perhaps she'd focus on the possibilities the future would bring—not suffering and war, but something better.

Marina watched as Yolie manipulated a tendril of light that reflected off her glasses, then remembered the conversation she'd had with Ismene and Elta. Perhaps, in another, better world, Yolie would've been one of Aeric's students.

"Would you like to meet Aeric?" Marina asked.

Though Pierce raised an eyebrow, Yolie didn't react much. She simply looked up at the trees and said, "Neva says he worked with Kieron."

"Not anymore. Now, he wants him gone as much as we do."

"Why do you want me to meet him?"

"Because you can do things most people can't. You have a pretty special talent."

Yolie considered for a moment. "Ice follows him wherever he goes. Every room he's in feels...colder."

Pierce laughed. "Fair assessment."

"Aeric's nice when you get to know him," Marina said. She paused. "Nice-*ish*." When Yolie didn't respond, she added, "You don't have to meet him if you don't want to."

"Of course I want to." She pulled her gaze away from the trees. "When would I?"

Marina shrugged. "How about this evening?"

She had a session with Aeric tonight, but she knew neither of them would be in a great headspace—not with the lingering call coming up. That, and the pit in Marina's stomach hadn't budged since Inber. It had only been a few days, but she couldn't stop thinking about it. She didn't want to bring it up to Aeric again—he had enough on his mind, and he'd made it clear how useless rumination was—but she couldn't bring herself to tell anyone else. Partly, she worried she wouldn't be able to explain what had happened without breaking down. But another, far more selfish part of her feared the response. If she told Pierce, Ismene, or Ryder, what would they think of her? She'd pushed to go on that mission, only to mess up severely and force Aeric to resort to drastic measures. She was judging herself harshly enough. She didn't need others to do the same.

Perhaps *that* was truly why she wanted to introduce Yolie to Aeric—because she was desperate to do something good that would offset the horror she'd caused in Inber. If Aeric saw Yolie's potential and something good came of that, maybe the burden on her conscience would be lifted.

When Yolie nodded, the pit in Marina's stomach eased.

It's a selfish reason, she thought, *but at least Yolie might benefit from it.*

"Don't you think you should talk to Aeric before springing Yolie on him?" Pierce asked. "Something tells me he doesn't like surprises."

"Asking Aeric is a risk I'd prefer not to take," Marina said.

Yolie giggled. "I feel the same way about Neva."

Well, that settled it, Marina supposed. The idea seemed to excite Yolie, but by now, Marina knew *anything* having to do with magic made her light up. Yolie spoke of it with optimism, and when Marina brought up healing, she offered tips on how to start small— beginning with wilted flowers seemed to be her preferred method of practice.

"When you get better," she said, "you can move to animals and Elsudrans."

They spent the rest of the afternoon together, learning about healing. Pierce was just as interested as Marina, and Yolie had no shortage of knowledge. Most of what she'd learned, she'd picked up from Elta and the other healers. Marina asked if healing magic could be used to repair her old boots, only to receive the rather disappointing answer that it couldn't. Healing relied on the regenerative nature of life energy, apparently, which only living things had.

Even so, hearing Yolie talk about the intricacies of magic gave Marina hope. If people like Yolie were to be part of the future, then it was a future worth fighting for. And no matter how horrible the road to get there was, not taking it would be so much worse.

CHAPTER 23
Spun Gold

Since Marina knew Pierce was right—Aeric wasn't the type to respond well to surprises—she had Yolie wait outside. She didn't plan to ask Aeric; she simply planned to give him a second or two to prepare. But when she slipped inside the common room, where they'd been training the past few nights, Aeric wasn't alone.

He sat with Florin, who smiled at Marina as she entered. Nothing seemed to be the matter, but Aeric was paler than usual.

"What's wrong?" she blurted.

"I don't know why you always expect things to be wrong," Aeric said stiffly.

Florin was quick to reassure her. "All is fine. I figure since Calcite's ninth week begins tomorrow, we'd best not waste any time. The technicians have readied the Altus voco, and tomorrow morning, Aeric will make the call."

Marina flinched. She'd known the call would be soon, but she hadn't anticipated it being *this* soon.

Maybe now wasn't the best time to introduce Aeric to Yolie. But when Florin left and Aeric rested his forehead at the base of his palm—when the pit in Marina's stomach reared its head again—she said sternly, "I'm going to introduce you to someone."

Aeric lowered his hand. "I don't have time—"

"It can cut into our training. I'll practice overtime if you want me to."

She knew Aeric wasn't going to be happy with her, but since she had a feeling he was going to spend the rest of the night worrying himself sick—same as her—she pushed the door open and gave Yolie a nod. Yolie had been kneeling by a raised bed of marigolds, and she placed a few of the fallen flowers in her hair before walking in.

"Please just say hello," Marina whispered to Aeric, who narrowed his brow but stood.

She'd warned Yolie that Aeric may not be in the mood, but Yolie didn't seem to mind. When she entered, Aeric shot Marina a look.

"You want me to meet a child?" he asked, annoyed.

"A talented child," Marina said.

Yolie sat in one of the common room chairs, tilted her head at him, and said, "My dad was tall like you. But he smiled more."

Aeric kept his eyes on Marina. "I know who Yolie is. If this is about convincing Neva to let her glamour during the Altus mission—"

"It's not," Marina interrupted.

"But if you can convince her, I promise I'll be the best student you've ever had," Yolie added eagerly. She sat upright, glasses glinting in the light.

Aeric bristled. "Who said anything about you becoming my student?"

"Isn't that your job?" Yolie asked. When he didn't respond, she said, "You're Sorcerer of the Court."

"I'm not—" Aeric cut himself off. "I don't have time to train anyone new."

Yolie shrugged. "I can already do pretty much everything, minus making force. But Marina's been showing me how. You wouldn't need to train me *that* much."

When Aeric frowned, Marina said, "I told you, she's talented."

"She's a child," Aeric said. He didn't lower his voice. "Children are overconfident."

Yolie smirked, then glanced up at the string lights and extended her hands. The bulbs brightened, and tendrils of threadlike light seeped from the sockets—slithering through the air and weaving around the room until they reached her fingers. She twirled the light around her hands as though it were spun gold, forming something of a cat's cradle that she held up to show Aeric.

Fluid. Flexible. As effortless as twisting strings. Hadn't Aeric said few sorcerers were talented enough to manipulate light like that?

"I learned to do this years ago when I lived in Sal," Yolie said. "Neva says most people can't manipulate light until their second quarter, and she says almost *no one* can bend it like I can." She raised her eyebrows, then released the strands and watched them flit back to the ceiling.

Aeric opened his mouth, but before he could respond, Yolie said, "I'm not done. Look." She pointed to the buffet table near the door, where the once-empty wine glasses now overflowed with water. "I would've done wine," she said, "but we don't have a lot, and Neva gets mad when I summon it from the kitchens."

She stood and approached the buffet table, then ran her hands along the top, legs, and box apron. With every movement of her fingers, parts of the table faded—and then the

glasses themselves—almost as though she were erasing bits of matter from the universe. But she wasn't; she was simply diverting the path of light and shadows, so precisely that the water in the glasses—which caught light differently than the wood—faded too.

Marina gawked at her. She'd seen Yolie glamour before, but she hadn't seen her glamour something that complicated. Aeric was clearly impressed too—impressed enough, at least, to not make a snide comment as Yolie nodded at her glamour, returned to her chair, and said, "I'm not overconfident. I'm just good."

Marina's spirits lifted enough to allow for a laugh.

"You're right," Aeric said. When Yolie beamed, he continued, "But your talent makes training all the more necessary. Skills like those should be meticulously cultivated."

Was he implying he *would* train her? Had her demonstration actually swayed him?

"Well, Neva's already taught me everything she knows," Yolie said, "so maybe after Kieron's gone, you'll have more time."

Marina's heart skipped a beat. Yolie had said it nonchalantly, as though they were obviously going to defeat him—as though it was a matter of time before everything was normal again.

She wasn't sure if that kind of faith made her feel better or worse. If they failed...

Stop. Focus on the now. That's all you can do.

She directed her breaths through her nose, watching Aeric.

Before Aeric could respond, however, Yolie turned her head to the door. Marina had left it cracked open, which in hindsight probably hadn't been smart, because Neva had clearly been nearby and overheard them. She leaned against the jamb, arms crossed, as she used her foot to push the door open wider.

Marina tensed, only to realize Neva didn't look upset. If anything, she looked amused.

"Every time you demonstrate your skills," she said to Yolie, "I realize how good you've gotten." She nodded at the glamoured buffet and added, "I expect you to take your glamour down. I haven't the patience to do it myself."

Yolie smiled and rolled her eyes. "I will." After a brief moment of silence—and a glance at the glamoured buffet table—she added, "But you admit I'm good."

The subtle smile on Neva's face twitched when she realized what Yolie was getting at. "I'm not letting you glamour the compound. Not with the—"

"There are no sweeps," Yolie said. She nodded at Marina and Aeric. "Not anymore."

Neva shot her a warning look. "I know that. But the squad is still nearby, which means the risk is still heightened. We've talked about this."

"Not recently," Yolie argued. "And I'd only do it until Hollis and Zora get back from Altus." When Neva's lips thinned, Yolie said, "You can't keep everything from me. I know what's going on."

Neva shifted her gaze to Marina and Aeric—but mostly to Marina. "Did you mention this to her?"

"No," Marina said quickly. She turned to Aeric for backup, but he was sitting down again, pinching the bridge of his nose and looking terribly irritated.

"Nobody mentioned it to me," Yolie said. "I overhear things, especially when I'm bored—which is a lot."

Neva pursed her lips. "We got through the dead years without glamours. Now that the squad isn't actively passing through, we can weather a day or two with weaker ones."

Only it's not the dead years anymore, Marina thought. *And Kieron isn't just looking for Aeric and the ring now. He's looking for the Omnia too.*

She kept her gaze on Aeric, but she wasn't sure what for; he was too consumed with the lingering call to argue with anyone, and even if he wasn't, he probably wouldn't fight Neva on this. She'd already agreed to so much.

In some slapdash attempt to ease the tension, Marina turned to Yolie and said, "I'm still learning to glamour. If you keep giving me tips, maybe *I* could use them to help glamour the compound while Hollis and Zora are gone."

In a way, she hoped it would placate Neva and Yolie as much as she hoped it would placate herself. She already felt useless when it came to the Altus mission, and after Inber, she was desperate to prove her abilities could result in more than destruction.

Apparently, Aeric thought *now* was a good time to respond. He lowered his hand, then said sternly, "No. You're not doing that."

Marina shot Aeric a look, her jaw tightening. She wasn't sure if he was implying that she was bad at glamouring or that she was the Omnia's host and needed to stay in the compound when he wasn't there to look out for her. Regardless, it bugged her.

Yolie fiddled with the hem of her shirt as she whispered, "Giving tips isn't the same as actually helping."

Well, so much for *that* suggestion. Marina didn't bother pushing it further.

Yolie, however, wasn't as quick to give up. "Everyone keeps saying how desperate Kieron is to find the Delve's survivors," she said. "Doesn't that make strong glamours even *more* important? Besides, I'd only be down there for a few minutes. I'm really fast."

"It wouldn't be a couple minutes," Neva said sharply. "You're talented, Yolie, but these glamours are large and complex. It's not the same as glamouring a buffet table. It's not even the same as it would've been glamouring the Delve. We don't have rocks to conceal us; we have trees—moved by wind and subject to all manner of changes throughout the day. Something as simple as a leaf falling contributes to the deterioration of glamours. You know this. You've witnessed sorcerers spend an hour below on a day with good weather. You've heard them talking about how frustrating it is to start from scratch every time they go back down. More than that, you've heard my reasons for why I *don't want you doing it.*"

"But—"

"We're not having this conversation." Neva gestured at the glamoured buffet with her eyes, then repeated, "Take it down," before leaving.

Yolie sighed, then dismantled her glamour as smoothly as she'd put it up. She didn't say anything as she left—she simply reached into her pocket and produced a hydrangea, which she placed on the common room table.

"She really *is* talented," Marina told Aeric once they were alone.

"Talented or not, it's up to Neva to decide how she'll protect her sanctuary," Aeric said stiffly.

"I know that." Marina sat in the chair next to him, then said, "I meant in general. It was Ismene's idea to introduce the two of you, you know. I think she's onto something. Yolie really would be a good student. Someday, at least."

"Don't pester me about this again," Aeric muttered. But his eyes were on the flower, and Marina noticed.

Though training was stilted, she and Aeric got through it. And when Marina turned in for the night and fell asleep, she dreamed of glamours, flowers, and light that looked like spun gold.

CHAPTER 24
Unstable

Far more people were present for the call than she'd expected. Florin, Ryder, Hollis, Zora, Neva, Lars, and a few technicians gathered around the trestle table, and though Marina grew lightheaded when she saw the Altus voco Aeric would use, she was thankful they'd let her sit in too. Neva even had some people stationed outside the common room so nobody would interrupt, and when Aeric came in—pale and obviously short on sleep— she locked the door.

Florin made it clear that if the call didn't successfully go through today, they'd try again tomorrow. And the next day, and the next. He didn't seem to think it would take long for Kieron to pick up. Neither did anyone else. Kieron might not pick up for anyone, but he would for Aeric.

Aeric knew it too, no doubt. Marina figured that was why he looked so sick.

"Let's hope we get lucky," Florin said wryly. He nodded to a technician, who explained to Aeric that the messages would be intercepted by palace staff before being directed to Kieron. They probably wouldn't answer, but that didn't mean Aeric wasn't being heard.

As eager as Aeric seemed to be to get on with it, his hand loitered over the voco before he finally picked it up. Marina had taken the seat beside Ryder, and when he wrapped his fingers around her wrist, she realized how badly she was shaking.

Breathe.

"Kieron," Aeric said. His hands shook too, but his voice was calm. "This is Aeric."

When silence followed, he tried again—and again, and again, just like Florin had said.

"This is Aeric," he repeated for the umpteenth time. "I'm calling you on a—"

A burst of static sounded from the voco. More silence followed, but Aeric picked up where he left off.

"Kieron, this is Aeric," he said again, and Marina closed her eyes.

She had no idea what she wanted to happen. Kieron answering was as unsavory as him not answering. She couldn't think about anything, save the static on the voco and the fuzziness in her head.

Ryder's grip tightened.

"Kieron," Aeric continued. "This is—"

"Aeric."

Marina's eyes flew open. Had she imagined that? No, she hadn't; everyone else had gone dead silent. Neva pinched her lips together, and beside her, Lars's face was drawn.

The static began to clear.

"Aeric," Kieron repeated. "What a *surprise*."

Aeric stared at the voco, and for the life of her, Marina couldn't tell what he was thinking—or if he could summon the courage to respond. From the corner of her eye, she could see Hollis and Zora exchange wide-eyed glances.

A painful moment passed before Aeric said, "Can you hear me?"

The voco adjusted, and suddenly, Kieron's voice filled the room so evenly it almost sounded like he was there with them. "Clear as day."

She was going to be sick. But she couldn't stop listening; she was here, and she needed to see this through. Ryder stared at the edge of the table, his jaw tight.

"I can only guess you're not calling alone?" Kieron mused. His voice sounded tinny. Before Aeric could respond, he said, "To what do I owe the honor?"

Aeric pressed his lips together before answering. "I want to propose a meeting. Just the two of us."

The line was silent for a moment. When Kieron finally spoke, Marina knew he was smiling. "Did she find you?"

Aeric glanced at Marina. "Yes."

"I'm surprised she made it," Kieron said. "Especially since those who helped her escape from Altus seem to have met fitting ends. What a waste."

Despite everything, Ryder smirked.

Aeric didn't comment on that, which Marina figured was the smartest thing he could do. Any hint that Ryder was alive could ruin everything. Instead, deadpan as ever, Aeric said, "She was wounded and demoralized when she found us. Her disposition has only deteriorated lately. At the very least, you and I can agree this is a dangerous state for the Omnia's host to be in—one neither of us wants to see worsen."

Kieron clicked his tongue, then laughed mirthlessly. "So you call me on an untraceable line using Altus technology, from whatever new hole you and she have found to hide in, and you propose the two of us meet." When Aeric didn't respond, Kieron said, "I can't help but sense accusation in your tone, Aeric. I kept Marina safe in Altus, *and* I gave her perhaps the best choice she's been given since she came to Elsudra. She still chose to flee—to put herself and the Omnia in danger."

Aeric inhaled steadily through his nose. "And this is precisely why I want to meet." He paused. "She's never going to be as powerful as our Keepers thought. No amount of training will make her that way. If we continue on as we are, we'll be locked in a stalemate for the foreseeable future, and her headspace will continue to get worse."

"Until my people find yours," Kieron said.

"*If* your people do." Aeric's voice was sharp, and some of Marina's nerves burned off, replaced by pride. Aeric, it seemed, was refusing to shrink.

More silence, followed by Kieron's sigh. "You know, I really did miss your voice, Aeric. It's been so long. And as much as I'd love to see you in person, I'm not naive. I know that you know there is only one solution for me, and it cannot be reached with worthless meetings and arbitrary compromises."

"Is that a risk you want to take?" Aeric said. "You only found the Delve because one of our own betrayed us, and we've taken measures to ensure that isn't a possibility anymore. Worst case, we'll remain where we are and wait you out."

Kieron chuckled. "Wait me out? You seem to think I'm going to die soon. Come now, Aeric, I'm not *that* old, and Elsudra is not that large. And things have funny ways of falling into my hands."

The tension in the room came to a boil, but Aeric refused to let it burn through his icy mask. Coolly as ever, he said, "Or she checks out sooner, taking the Omnia with her."

Marina's heart skipped a beat, but Aeric didn't give her—or Kieron—much time to stew on that. "Even if you find her again and get her back to Altus alive, there's no saying whether she'll be able to complete Locus," Aeric continued. "You know better than anyone it requires a sturdy mind to keep the Omnia protected. The Keepers had that; Marina doesn't. She can barely get through training given the state she returned in. Do you really think she'll be able to complete Locus without shattering?"

He shot her a look, but Marina nodded at him to continue. *This* was his bluff, and she had to admit, it was a good one. Kieron knew Marina's head. He'd seen it. It was believable to think she'd broken down after fleeing Altus. If Locus truly was as fickle as everyone made it out to be, then having her do it would be like playing with a bomb. And if she exploded, she'd take the Omnia down with her.

Still, Aeric's bluff brought about a pit in her stomach. Even if she mastered the finesse of mental-based magic—which, after Inber, seemed like a long shot—she'd still need to master her psyche. And though she hated to admit it, that seemed even more unlikely. As far as she'd come, she was still *her*.

"You can use every tactic at your disposal to force her to perform it," Aeric continued, "but you cannot force her to be successful. Your plan to pressure the Keepers until they complied might've worked with them. But Marina was hanging by a thread before Altus, and after what happened, she's barely hanging on at all. Whatever games you played with her—whatever horrors she witnessed when she fled—have crippled her. This could end with *everyone* losing, and it brings me back to the stalemate we've reached."

"A shame," Kieron said after a few moments. "She seemed so certain of her decision."

Exorsus flickered into Marina's head. She *had* been certain. She still was, even with the fear and regret...wasn't she?

Aeric grimaced, but he didn't falter when he said, "She's unstable. You and I both know it. At this point, the Omnia is vulnerable, and if it takes damage, none of this will matter. Surely, we can agree on that."

Unstable. The word rang in her ears.

The bluff had truth to it—that's what made it so good. Even after Exorsus, she could feel the storms that lingered within her. She rode them out as best she could, but what if they became too much again? The potential lived within her, didn't it?

At the moment, her emotions made sense. Everyone was as perturbed as she was, after all. But she'd always felt as though she was kneeling on the precipice of stability and instability—that at any moment, her storms could take a turn for the worse and the progress she'd made would come crashing down. It had back in Georgia, and even if she was managing to keep her head above water right now, she knew the way her mind worked. If things ended badly, she worried that no number of breaths could keep her from becoming exactly the person Aeric spoke of.

Silence followed again, longer and more painful than before. When Marina began to wonder if Kieron's voco had disconnected, he said, "Is she there with you?"

Aeric's response was immediate. "No."

"You're going to need to work with me, Aeric." The condescension Marina knew so well had seeped into Kieron's voice. "I'm inclined to accept your request if I know you're not lying, and she did indeed find you."

Aeric held his hand up to Marina—not like she was thinking of saying anything either way. "I'll have her brought here, then," he said, then kept his hand up for a few minutes.

Kieron waited too, the voco's static a faint buzz in the background, and when Aeric gave Marina a nod, she cleared her voice. Still, it shook when she spoke, but she supposed that was fitting, given everything Aeric had just said about her.

"Kieron," she rasped. "I'm here."

"Marina," Kieron said cloyingly. "I hear things have not gone as well as you *or* the Keepers hoped. I tried to tell you what a horrible decision they made, but you refused to listen. You threw away a miracle, and look where it got you."

Marina didn't respond, but she had a feeling Kieron wasn't waiting for her to. She assumed he was speaking to Aeric when he said, "I accept your request, provided that you accept mine."

Marina's heart beat in her throat. Florin's brow creased, and Neva leaned closer to the table as Kieron said, "Marina must come with you."

Aeric froze. Though the others shared looks, Aeric only stared at the voco. "Why?"

"Does it matter?" Kieron said. When Aeric didn't respond, he added, "You don't have to accept. Granted, if you don't, the meeting will be called off, but it's still up to you."

Aeric's lips thinned. "I'll ask again," he said stiffly. *"Why?"*

"What makes you think you're in any position to demand my reasoning? You're the one who called me." At Aeric's pause, Kieron said, "We're meeting to discuss the Omnia and its host, are we not? As such, I think it makes sense that the Omnia's host is present."

"She has nothing to add," Aeric retorted. "This is between the two of us."

"It's between the three of us or none of us," Kieron said. "Nobody else will accompany you except a small number of rank-and-file soldiers—rules I will abide by also." Again, he repeated, "Nobody else." After a lull, he impatiently added, "These are my terms. Make your choice and do it quickly. I won't be picking up again."

This time, Aeric exchanged a glance with Florin, who grimaced but said nothing. What other option did they have? In order to direct Kieron's attention elsewhere, they needed him in Lewes, and if Kieron refused to meet unless they agreed to his terms, there was only one way forward.

Aeric turned back to the voco. "I assume we'd come with diminution cuffs as well?"

"But of course," Kieron said. "I wouldn't put it past you not to make this meeting as regimented as possible."

Aeric pinched the bridge of his nose. "We will uphold all the traditional rules of an Elsudran armistice. The keys to our cuffs will be swapped before the meeting, and the city we choose will be—"

"Uninhabited or evacuated. I know the rules, Aeric. I taught you them."

Aeric's gaze met Marina's, and for a moment, she didn't see him as he was now, but as he was so many years ago—wary-eyed and unsure. She gave him a nod of confidence—of trust, though she didn't think it would do much.

She was wrong. Aeric's voice was as sure as ever when he said, "Then she'll come."

CHAPTER 25
Diplomacy

They decided to meet in Lewes on the last day of Pearl's third week, which meant the Altus mission would be set in motion that same day. As of now, they had roughly five Elsudran weeks, and Florin didn't let a day go to waste. As the rest of the compound prepared for Double Moon, he met with Hollis, Zora, and Ryder. Marina wasn't sure exactly what they did, but Ryder often returned from meetings so tired that Marina didn't want to bug him by prying. Florin also assembled ten of the Delve's soldiers—a number Kieron had agreed to as well—to accompany Marina and Aeric, but he planned to deploy another dozen to wait outside Lewes. Best-case scenario, they wouldn't be used. Worst case, they'd stave off any incursions.

Elsudran armistices were sacred, but Kieron wasn't one to play by the rules even if he swore he would, and his insistence on Marina's presence sparked paranoia. It was possible Kieron would attempt to take Marina *and* Aeric hostage in Lewes, but Florin hoped the enforcements on both sides would be enough to deter any fighting.

Even so, there were a hundred ways Kieron could double-cross them—the two most likely being fake diminution cuffs and Safira.

Florin didn't seem to worry as much about the former, though he did plan to equip one of his soldiers with an extra set of keys to both Aeric and Marina's cuffs. It was noncompliant, perhaps, but this was Kieron they were dealing with, and Florin made it clear they wouldn't use the keys so long as Kieron's side didn't attack.

Where Florin and Aeric seemed most worried was when it came to Safira. Wherever Kieron was, Safira was almost always nearby, and though Kieron had promised to only bring ten soldiers, neither Florin nor Aeric believed him. He'd been so adamant about ensuring both sides arrived only with common foot soldiers. Worst case, he could be stringing them along so he could overmatch them.

As for Safira, she was adept at hiding in the shadows of cities, waiting for the opportune moment to rain hell on her enemies—be it with the lock bombs Ryder had mentioned, more soldiers, or her own magic. Luckily, lock bombs took a few seconds to go off, and Safira would need to give Kieron time to prepare before releasing them, which meant they'd have time too. The same went for extra soldiers or swooping in herself; Aeric and Marina would have time to remove their cuffs, then summon force fields, launch attacks of their own, or simply—and perhaps most preferably—convey out of the vicinity.

Marina and Aeric's training pivoted in the week that followed to focus specifically on the Lewes meeting. Florin often joined them, and together, he and Aeric outlined not just potential scenarios and how to react, but how *Marina* was to act.

Aeric had pawned her off as unstable to Kieron, which meant she needed to sell it— not too much, of course, but subtly enough to ease suspicions on Kieron's part. Marina didn't think that would take much acting. Whenever she thought of Inber, or Tin, or the scouts in Altus, or the way Ocot had looked before he'd died, or what Cal had said to her before going into that tunnel, the gaping hole in her gut threatened to spill over and out. Luckily for her, she'd never been good at hiding her emotions.

Of course, the rules about how she'd need to act came second to all the other rules, which Florin and Aeric drilled into her head.

Don't speak unless spoken to. Agree with everything Aeric says. If it's a lie, pretend it's not. Don't react. Don't respond. Don't indulge him.

Though the thought of seeing Kieron again sent her heart into a frenzy, Marina much preferred it to staying behind. Having to wait out Aeric's meeting and Florin's mission at the compound—with no indication of how things were going—would've been torturous.

Pierce and Ismene weren't happy about the recent developments, but they didn't harp on it. For her sake as well as their own, Marina could tell they were taking great pains to focus on small things, like the upcoming holiday.

As it turned out, Elta liked to decorate as much as Ismene, and on the morning of Double Moon, Marina awoke to lights wrapped around trees and woven across wooden walkways. And though the usual voice at the back of her head still badgered her like it always did—reminding her what had happened in Inber and what *might* happen in Lewes —she managed to keep it at bay.

In truth, she was a little nervous for Double Moon; she hadn't had a true day off in quite some time. After a week of Lewes preparation, Aeric had Marina shift back to focusing on glamours. Once or twice, she'd successfully glamoured something small, only to lose her progress the next day. One night, she'd grown so frustrated that she'd chucked the cup Aeric wanted her to practice on across the room. He'd simply sighed and summoned it back to the table.

But today, Aeric was absent. Even here, he found ways to be a ghost, and Marina figured he'd be impossible to find with all the celebrating going on. Ryder didn't come around either, but she knew where he was; this year, even Double Moon didn't stop Florin from scheduling trainings and meetings.

She spent the morning with Pierce, who spoke of Double Moon in Altus and vowed this time next year, they'd finally get to celebrate at home. They ran into Yolie too, who was especially giddy—the sky was clear today, which meant the view from the observatory would be perfect. When Marina and Pierce agreed to watch the night sky with her, she became even more ecstatic. She disappeared shortly after to find Ash—since the cooks always made a little more food on Double Moon, he tended to slink around the kitchens— and Marina tried to soak up as much of the lingering excitement as she could.

Today, she told herself, *you'll focus on Double Moon and nothing but that.*

After all, she'd never actually seen the moons before. That was something to look forward to, wasn't it?

Maybe. But she'd trade it for string lights and petals—for one hundred more people alive to celebrate. This year, when the moons rose above the Delve, only the dead would look upon them.

Focus on today, Marina.

People-watching helped her stay present. After breakfast, she and Pierce met up with Ismene and Elta, then grabbed a bench at one of the balconies. While Pierce went off to fetch them all cider, Marina observed small groups and tried to make out what they were saying. She felt like a bit of a snoop, but it was interesting to watch inclined Elsudrans interact freely. They all had varying levels of ability. A few summoned drinks for their friends, and a group of children a few years older than Yolie seemed to have made a game out of manipulating the path of a eucalyptus leaf. They sat in a circle, hands under their legs, each kid competing for control over the leaf and squealing as they pushed it toward one of their friends. When it brushed against a girl's cheek, she accused the others of cheating, then sat on the outside of the circle. It was an ingenious way to practice, Marina thought, even if it wasn't entirely fair. The same boy kept winning, which made it pretty obvious his innate skillset trumped the others.

"You're spacey today, even for you."

Marina blinked at Pierce, then took the drink he held out to her.

"She's people-watching," Ismene said, giving Marina a gentle smile. "A good way to familiarize yourself with everyone."

"If you can remember faces, I guess," Pierce said. "I'm shit at it."

Ismene certainly wasn't. She knew who everyone was, and as people passed, she whispered their names to Marina and Pierce. One particularly large group clustered around Neva and Lars, who stood over by the drinks, and Ismene was able to name every single one of them. Cordelia's mother—her name was Lana, Ismene said—cradled her child as she spoke to Lars, placing the red pacifier in Cordelia's mouth when she began to fuss.

"I knew your memory was good, but I didn't realize it was *that* good," Elta said.

Ismene giggled. "Remembering people has always been my talent."

"Another reason you'd do well in government," Elta said. When Ismene shook her head, she said, "I'm serious. Knowing who people are is the first step to diplomacy."

Apparently, Elta had mentioned this more than once, and though Ismene playfully shrugged it off, Marina could see how her eyes lit up when she thought about it. When Marina and Pierce voiced their agreement, the light grew.

"You *should* think about it," Elta said. "People like you are needed in government—the kind who aren't solely in it for themselves. It'll be even more important if we ever get the chance to rebuild. And it doesn't hurt that you know how to command a room."

Pierce chuckled. "Let me guess: Ismene took over decorating and refused to rest until the lights were perfect?"

Ismene waved her hand at Pierce, but her lips edged into a smile. She exchanged a glance with Elta, but it was different than usual—it wasn't out of shock or curiosity, but out of warmth. Playfully, Ismene said, "Hanging lights and navigating politics are two very different things."

"You could stand to be less humble," Elta said. "You ran an entire manor back at the Delve and you worked alongside the Sorcerer of the Court. Didn't Aeric ever thank you?"

Ismene didn't answer, but her smile faded.

"You should demand it of him one day," Elta said. When Ismene crinkled her nose, Elta eyed her. "I'm not kidding. Demand what you deserve."

When Ismene's gaze flitted to her feet, Marina's heart sank. "Elta's right," she said. "You made a big difference." Though she almost decided against it, she added, "You were one of the few people who kept me sane when I first arrived."

Ismene's smile returned, but it wasn't as bright as it had been. Though she stayed cheery throughout the rest of their conversation—joking with Pierce, exchanging warm glances with Elta, and shooting Marina smiles—she couldn't hide everything. Granted, neither could Marina. When Pierce caught her watching Neva for the umpteenth time, he gave her a nudge.

She wasn't sure what it meant. At first, she thought he was telling her to stop being so obvious, but when she met Pierce's gaze, she realized what he was saying.

Diplomacy.

Perhaps seeking Neva out would be worthwhile—not to ask anything of her, but to thank her. To show her that the Delve was grateful for her sanctuary and her help.

Ismene, Elta, and Pierce agreed to accompany her, which lessened Marina's nerves. Still, her heart beat a little faster as she wove past the circle of kids and the people that scattered the walkways.

Neva noticed her before she approached, and though Lars continued conversing with a few others, it was obvious he did too. Marina loosened her shoulders, straining to appear relaxed as she bid Neva a happy Double Moon and said, "I wanted to thank you...for everything. For taking on such a huge burden."

Neva's brow twitched but didn't furrow. "I suppose I should thank you too—for helping ease one of those burdens," she said slowly.

Marina tried to smile through the knot in her stomach. She knew Neva was talking about Inber, but she had no idea if Aeric and Florin had told her what had happened to that soldier. They probably had. Besides, Neva was no doubt aware of the messages her technicians were intercepting.

Marina cleared her throat. "I'm glad I could help." She glanced at Elta and Ismene, who'd joined Lars's conversation, then at Pierce, who gave Neva a polite smile of his own.

Neva took a sip of her drink. "I never thought the day would come where a general, two sorcerers, *and* Kieron's old guard would be working together, but here we are."

"Only because you reconsidered." In the quiet that followed, Marina could hear the leaves rustle. She shifted her gaze to the canopy—to the branches that were as thick as the Delve's stalagmites—and said, "I know I'm not the person everyone expected would return with the Omnia, but I want you to know how determined I am to help."

She turned her smarting eyes back to Neva, then to Lars, who'd stopped talking and now faced the two of them. Someone else had joined them too—someone who'd clearly been but an earshot away.

Yolie held Ash tightly in her arms, stifling his attempts to wriggle out of her grip. "I'd like to help too," she said.

Neva put a hand on Yolie's head. "You don't need to—as we've discussed. And put the cat down. He looks miserable."

Yolie sighed, then loosened her hold. Ash jumped from her arms and made a beeline for Pierce, who scooped him up.

When Yolie's gaze didn't let up, Neva said, "I don't know how many times I need to make my position on this clear."

Yolie put her hands on her hips. "Ronan would want me to help."

"Ronan would want you safe."

"Right," Yolie said. "He'd want me to be protected. By good glamours."

When Neva groaned, Lars said, "We've lost enough children in this war. Soldiers aren't the only danger below."

"I'm not scared of ruemin," Yolie protested. "Or any other creature."

"I am," Lars said. "And you'd do well to be too. Your job is to stay here."

"I *would* stay here, technically." Yolie angled her head at Lars. "I wouldn't be traveling to a different region, would I?"

When Marina felt herself smirking, she clamped her lips together. As ridiculous as she felt Neva was being—and as passionately as she wanted to side with Yolie—she'd come here to thank Neva, not push her.

Elta, however, hadn't come with that intention. She glanced at Marina and Yolie, then turned to Neva and said, "I've been meaning to ask—how *are* we planning to account for Hollis and Zora's absence? They're in charge of a large portion of our glamours."

"We didn't have glamours during the dead years, and nobody found us," Neva said.

"But Kieron's soldiers weren't stationed as closely as they are now," Elta said. "The squad may not be conducting sweeps anymore, but their presence is still a risk, isn't it? Let's say one stumbles too far into the forest and we don't have sturdy glamours to conceal us. Then what? A good number of the Delve's soldiers are accompanying Marina and Aeric to Lewes, and while we might have our own, I can't exactly speak for their skillset. I'd think Hollis and Zora's absence would require more caution on our part, not less."

Lars raised his eyebrows at Neva, who frowned and said, "If we had the resources available, we'd use them."

"I think you *do* have them," Elta said gently. After a moment's thought, she added, "I also happen to know a bit about glamouring myself. I'm not nearly inclined enough to make them on my own like Yolie can, but I'm able to add finishing touches to glamours that already exist. If I take over what Yolie starts, she wouldn't need to be down there as long as the others." She paused. "You and I are of similar ability, Neva. You could come too—to help me *and* to stay close to Yolie while she's down there."

Neva's lips parted, but she didn't respond.

"Our work might not be as pristine as Hollis and Zora's," Elta added, "but it would be something. And that something would make us much safer."

Marina blinked at Elta. She might've hugged her, had there not been so many people around. Judging by the way Neva hesitated before answering, it was clear she was at least considering Elta's proposal. Still, when Yolie tugged on her arm, eyes wide, Neva said, "It's one thing to send adults down there. But a child—"

"I'm *not* a child," Yolie argued. "If it weren't for the dead years, I'd be in my second quarter."

Another bout of silence passed, but this time, neither Neva nor Elta broke it.

"I'd be willing to go down there too," Pierce said. "I can't glamour, obviously, but I can make it my mission to protect Yolie while she works." He gestured to Marina with his chin. "I have some experience being a bodyguard, and I'm one of the few soldiers from the Delve who isn't going to Lewes. I'd love to help in *some* way."

Marina's heart skipped a beat—even more so when Neva looked to Lars, whose frown had turned into a quizzical smile, and then to Yolie, who was nodding furiously.

But it was Elta who seemed most determined to see this through. Marina wasn't sure if it was because she'd promised to speak to Neva if Marina needed it, or because she also saw the way Neva's love for Yolie clouded her judgment. Maybe it was both.

"I know you want to keep Yolie safe," Elta said, "but she'll be safer if our glamours are fully functioning. She won't be down there long—not if the two of us take over after she gets us started. And who better to protect her than the son of one of Elsudra's generals?"

The corners of Pierce's mouth tugged upward.

Silence followed, but it wasn't strained. And yet, it was only when Lars put a gentle hand on Neva's shoulder that Neva said, "I'll think on it."

CHAPTER 26
Two Constants

Neva's answer hadn't been a yes, but it was still a miracle—one Marina profusely thanked Elta and Pierce for as they headed to the observatory that evening. Yolie was even more excited than she'd been in the morning, and for the first time since Inber—perhaps longer—Marina didn't feel like she was forcing a smile.

It was still light out when they reached the observatory. Since Yolie refused to open the ceiling until the moons were out, they relied on Ash for entertainment. He really *was* attached to Pierce; he spent an hour on the floor beside him, nuzzling up against Pierce's side and purring. After some time, Marina and Yolie occupied themselves by switching between glamour practice and generating force, relying on Ismene and Elta for moral support—and occasionally Pierce, whenever he wasn't entirely distracted by Ash.

When it came to force, Marina had Yolie start with her emotions—not with quieting them, but with feeling them, then funneling their power into lances of light, electricity, and compressed air. It seemed to work; Yolie's bursts grew stronger each time she had a go, and when she rested, they'd switch to glamouring, pressing on until Marina was at least somewhat successful.

Switching from teacher to student was a nice way to divvy up practice and make it less tiring. Yolie wasn't as strict as Aeric, and she didn't mind when they got distracted or took breaks. At one point, when their practice meandered, Yolie let Marina peer into Ronan's anteactus, which was far simpler than the one in the Delve.

Still, there were hundreds of memories embedded in the device—*Ronan's* memories. Most were of Sal, overlooking a glittering bay, but a few were of their family. Their father was a tall, lean man whose warm smile had been passed to Ronan and whose bright eyes resembled Yolie's. There were other, more recent pictures too—of a textile mill, fabrics, and some of the things Ronan had made. Neva was in a few of them, and she was smiling. For some reason, that struck Marina the most.

Ismene and Elta looked through the memories too, and even Pierce got through a few before Ash pawed at the device and sullied his focus.

If there was one thing Yolie liked speaking of more than magic, it was Ronan. It was obvious she'd adored him—*still* adored him. Marina couldn't help but think of Cal and Astra, or Ismene and her sisters. Ismene seemed to be thinking the same thing; when Yolie told them of games she'd play with Ronan, Ismene's eyes grew misty.

At one point, the talk might have brought tears to Marina's eyes as well, but tonight, there was only determination. It fluttered in her chest and stoked a fire beneath her heart, so intense that when Yolie suggested Marina try to glamour Ronan's anteactus, she didn't back down. She practiced as she listened, thankful Pierce, Ismene, and Elta were as eager to share memories as Yolie was. They were great with her, and it was obvious they enjoyed Yolie's company as much as she enjoyed theirs. Pierce made Yolie laugh, and Ismene put forth the same motherly demeanor she'd had when Marina first arrived in the Delve.

All of them were so *good*. Good friends, good people...and they deserved the world. They deserved not to reminisce about old Double Moons, but to experience new ones—to live without fear and forget the horrors of Kieron's reign. And so, Marina practiced, running her fingers over the natural curves of the anteactus and letting the shadows do the rest. She swathed the brass in scant light, her intuition guiding her as much as her mind, and when she successfully glamoured one section, the rest followed suit.

A trill rose in her chest. She could see the subtle sheen that covered the anteactus, but from where the others were sitting, it was entirely hidden in folds of light and shadow.

Yolie shrieked when she noticed. "You did it!"

This was more than the occasional cup or flower. She no longer cared how long it had taken her to learn; several weeks, several years...what did it matter? She'd learned it, and even once she removed the glamour, she could feel the potential bursting at her fingertips.

That was what it felt like to pass a learning curve: ecstasy. Marina hardly noticed Yolie run to the side of the room as she glamoured the anteactus once again, this time quicker and smoother.

Was there anything more exhilarating than magic? It filled Marina's head and veins, dancing and singing in her blood. She'd hold on to this high as long as possible, and from across the room, Yolie gave her a knowing grin.

"This is even better," she said.

She flipped a switch below one of the sconces, and the ceiling retracted. Brightness flooded in, springing from every crevice of the ceiling's fixture and shrouding the chamber in pools of starlight.

No—of moonlight.

The moons hung above the observatory, each one at an opposite end of the sky, so bright that the stars around them faded. They must've been three times larger than the moon back home, maybe more. Or perhaps she'd never been this close to the sky before.

She could see every crater—every speck of red and orange amidst the silver—and between them lay tendrils of stars, spread out so far and wide it looked like the moons were reaching out to each other, falling short of a touch.

Cal had said she liked to see the moons; finally, Marina understood why. She'd never seen the sky so alive—so balanced. A thousand constellations couldn't compete.

Pierce seemed far more intent on watching Marina and Ismene's reactions than the moons themselves. It was only then Marina realized Ismene hadn't seen them at all when she lived in the Delve. She wasn't sure what was worse: having never been blessed with the view, or having it so cruelly snatched away.

The tears that ran down Ismene's cheeks glinted silver, and she watched the sky before finally turning to Marina and saying, "I *knew* you'd get to see them in person one day."

Marina reached out and squeezed her hand. This was a glimpse into Elsudra—not Elsudra under Kieron, but Elsudra as it had been for thousands of years before him, and what it would be regardless of how this fight ended. The moons would rise every year— two constants in a world of unknowns—and that was enough to bring Marina peace.

They watched the sky for hours. Even when their eyes grew heavy and Yolie dozed off on the floor next to Ash, they drank in every last bit of moonlight. Elta figured out how to adjust one of the telescopes, and they took turns peering through until the moons were no more than silhouettes in the sky.

CHAPTER 27
Old Rage

Marina drew her hand flat in the air, the last bit of moonlight curling beneath her palm. Yolie had turned in hours ago, but the rest of them couldn't sleep. Instead, they'd found a quiet balcony near Marina's apartment that had a good view of the horizon. Elta parted before the sun rose—someone had drunk too much during the ceremony and called, asking for medicine to ease their headache—and now that it was just Pierce and Ismene, Marina felt as if they were back in the Delve. Only here, there was sky, and they huddled on one of the benches as they watched the moons descend.

"You'll see them next year," Pierce said once they'd disappeared behind the hills. "We'll get to do this all over again."

Marina rested her chin on the railing post. "I can't wait."

The sky turned from periwinkle to pink, and in the distance, doves began to coo. Morning mist hung so thickly above the walkways that Marina could scarcely see the other apartments, but when she heard her door open, she knew it was Ryder. He smiled when he saw her but stopped when he made eye contact with Pierce. Ismene was still looking out at the canopy—she didn't realize Ryder was there until he said, "Stay out late, did you?"

Marina nodded, pretending not to notice when Pierce shifted his gaze to his feet. "Very late," she said. "Where were you yesterday?"

"With Florin and the others." He put his hands into his pockets, squinting through the mist. "It's Pearl now, so we only have a few weeks before we head out."

The tranquility from last night melted away, piling into acid that gnawed at her stomach. Why did he have to remind her?

The look on her face must've been obvious because Ismene turned away from the view and said, "I have confidence in Florin. A good team is heading out."

A *great* team. What if they didn't come back?

Marina tried to breathe through her nose as Ryder shut the door. "Are you going to meet with Florin now?" she asked.

He shook his head. "Just getting food." He glanced at Pierce, who'd shifted his gaze to the horizon.

Marina half nodded. "I'll...see you later, then."

Ryder gave her a smile, but she could see through it. She hated how eager he was to leave, but for some reason, she hated it more when Pierce turned and asked, "Did you get to see the moons?"

Ryder stiffened, but surprisingly enough, he stopped. "They're hard to miss."

It wasn't that Pierce was trying, but that he didn't seem to know when *not* to. Part of Marina understood his desperation, but another part wished he'd leave it be and wait for Ryder to come around on his own. The last couple of times they'd spoken, it had gone terribly. Did he really expect *this* time to be any different?

He must have, because he forced a smile and said, "Small joys, right?"

After a painful bout of silence, Ryder scoffed. "Okay, Pierce." It was only when he turned down the nearest walkway that Pierce stood.

"Ryder," Pierce blurted. "I'm *trying.*"

For a moment, Marina wondered if Ryder wasn't going to respond at all. He wavered, then turned, his eyes so red even the mist couldn't hide them. "Maybe you should stop."

"I can't." Pierce's hands shook by his sides, but he steadied them when he repeated, "I *can't.* I don't know if I ever can."

"I'm going to eat," Ryder said tersely.

When he turned again, something in Pierce cracked. Marina could feel it—the horrible, hopeless fire that blazed in his gut and cleaved his chest in two.

"What will it take?" Pierce pleaded. "I made the worst mistake of my life the day I left Altus, and it's destroyed me every day since."

Ryder halted. This time, when he turned, he did so slowly. "You don't know what it means to be destroyed," he said, drawing out every word. "You have no idea."

Pierce put his hands up. "Fine. Maybe I don't. So tell me."

Ismene edged closer to Marina. At this point, there was really no way to leave without looking like an ass, so the two of them remained where they were, stiff-limbed and silent, and Marina prayed this wouldn't escalate the way things had with Ocot last Double Moon.

But Ryder exercised more restraint than Ocot. Even as his jaw tightened and his breathing quickened, he took his time before responding. "What do you want to hear, Pierce? That I can find it in my heart to forget everything, even though I stayed in Altus to look for you when I should've left just as quickly?"

"I tried to justify what I did," Pierce said weakly. "We were so angry with each other. I thought you hated me—that you wouldn't have come even if my dad *did* get you in, which I knew he couldn't, because the Keepers almost didn't let *me* go. I told myself I couldn't turn down my spot because going was the only thing that would've brought my dad peace. And I thought maybe you would go back to Mossley, or somewhere you'd be safe." His voice broke. "But mostly, I was scared and selfish, and there's nothing I can say that will change that. I made an unforgivable choice, and I spent the dead years paying for it."

"You didn't pay enough."

Though Pierce spoke cautiously, there was an edge to his voice that he couldn't fully conceal. "We've *both* done terrible things to survive. Don't act like I'm the only one."

Ryder shook his head. "You think I don't know that? You think I don't spend every day thinking about what a horrible person I am and how I don't deserve forgiveness either? You think I don't see all the people I killed every time I shut my eyes? That I don't hear them begging when it's quiet?" He wiped at his eyes, which glistened with tears. "I'll always see them, and I'll never forgive myself—just like I won't forgive you for abandoning me. I'm a horrible, hateful person who will live the rest of my life in shame, wondering if things could've turned out differently if I hadn't stayed to look for someone who'd already abandoned me."

Some quiet rage had settled over Ryder, and Marina could've sworn even the mist stopped moving. It was worse than any outburst he could've had—worse than yelling, or swearing, or pulling an Ocot and tackling Pierce to the ground—because it was *old* rage. It had taken years to build up, and if it had been hot and violent at one point, it had long since frozen over.

Maybe Ryder would never come around. And maybe Pierce knew that. Maybe he'd accepted the fact that he'd never be forgiven and instead sought punishment.

"Do you want to know how *I* spent the dead years after you'd broken our promise?" Ryder continued. His voice was so low he hardly sounded like himself. "Do you want me to tell you about the ways I proved myself to Kieron? About how I slaughtered innocent people in front of him, or how I broke myself down so much that I started to view it as just another job?" He laughed mirthlessly. "Or what about how I was among the first to raid the Delve—how the lights were off when I went below, and how every time I killed someone or left them wounded for the ruemin to eat, I wondered if maybe it was you? I'd try to listen to their screams, praying I didn't recognize the voice. When I saw the bodies lined up outside and realized you weren't among them, I almost cried. You have no idea how relieved I was that you were safe—and how *angry* I was. I hate you for making me go through that, almost as much as I hate myself."

Ryder's lips began to shake, but he didn't stop. "I hate you for leaving me. I hate you for being the reason I stayed in Altus, looking for you like I was some lost dog. I hate you for being part of the reason I had to go to such lengths to survive—proving myself to a man who would've killed me instantly if he'd figured out how I'd been born, regardless of how close I got to him or how many people I killed."

Tears fell down Ryder's cheeks, pooling at his chin, and he let out a sound that was somewhere between a breath and a sob—so unlike him that Marina's chest hollowed.

"But do you want to know what made me hate you the most?" Ryder continued. "All those years I was in Altus, I still loved you. Every fucking second." He let out a hitched breath. "No matter how angry I was—no matter how much I hated you—I couldn't stop loving you."

Marina could hardly make out what he was saying, but when Pierce stepped closer to him, tears in his eyes, Ryder's voice sharpened. "Don't touch me," he snapped. "Stop trying to make things better. They won't get better. I've had to spend so long just surviving that I've forgotten what it feels like to live, and I've accepted that. I don't need you trying to change things, or begging for my forgiveness when I can't even forgive myself."

Marina turned her head away from them and focused on a gnarled tree a few feet beneath the balcony. When it grew blurry, she closed her eyes. She cursed herself for crying—it really wasn't helpful, and at this point, Ismene seemed to be the only one with her head on straight—then yielded to her tears when she thought of the bodies outside the Delve.

"I'm sorry," Pierce said hoarsely.

Ryder scrubbed his hands across his face. "I know you are. We're both sorry—so sorry it feels like we're drowning in it. And none of it will matter because we can't change what we've done. There's only one thing you can do."

Marina opened her eyes to Pierce, who was nodding rapidly. "Anything."

"Stop trying."

The words landed like physical blows, and though Pierce flinched, he accepted them. He nodded again, and when Ryder finally left, he let him go.

CHAPTER 28
Risks

The first weeks of Pearl were quiet. No alarms, commotion, or emergencies. Though Florin's scouts kept an eye on the Inber unit and Neva's technicians continued to intercept and manipulate messages, their web of deception seemed to be holding. But that didn't ease the tension in the air, and oftentimes, Marina couldn't tell where it came from. The upcoming Altus mission was an obvious source of stress, but the hostility from the morning after Double Moon hadn't burned off either. Pierce was seldom in good spirits, though it was obvious he was trying to put on a happy face. And Ryder...well, he didn't try. His mask had long since come off, and he had no intention of putting it back on.

Marina tried to find joy in the little things—like showing Aeric how she could finally glamour consistently or watching Yolie grow confident about generating force—but it was hard, even more so when Pearl's third week came about.

Sometimes, Yolie would sit in the common room as Aeric and Marina trained, and while Aeric made it clear her presence was a distraction, he didn't kick Yolie out. He did threaten it, though, especially when Yolie piped in with tips of her own. After that, she'd started whispering her tips to Marina instead.

Truthfully, Marina liked Yolie's presence. As the Altus mission neared, Aeric grew more austere and Marina more overwrought, and Yolie was a welcome distraction.

Aeric seemed to realize this too. One night, he integrated Yolie into a lesson entirely of his own accord. Yolie was elated until she realized the lesson was on draining shields. When she began to protest—draining shields made people feel sick, and glamours were *so much more fun*—Aeric gestured to the door, and she backpedaled quickly. After that, she listened intently as he explained how some shields were layered with magic that, when touched, sent the nervous system into disarray and caused symptoms akin to the flu.

The shields were aptly named; draining was precisely what they did, albeit indirectly. With the nervous system in shambles and the body struggling to recuperate, one's energy —and thus ability to wield magic—was depleted. Nobody could overpower draining shields alone, which was why they were used in prisons—and, of course, why Kieron had relied on them to keep Marina contained in her room at the palace.

It was a reminder Marina didn't need. Worse still, when Aeric told Marina and Yolie to dismantle a draining shield he'd made, Marina had to force herself not to mentally check out. She'd tried so hard *not* to think of Altus, and interacting with a draining shield was a surefire way to bring back memories she preferred to avoid. But according to Aeric, the effects wouldn't be as bad this time around. When two or more people made contact with a draining shield, their bodies would form something of a series circuit, lessening the toll and increasing the likelihood they could dismantle the shield together. There were weaknesses in every design, he said, and sensing those weaknesses could go a long way.

And so, Marina rallied—which seemed to inspire Yolie—and together, the two of them tackled Aeric's draining shield. Granted, it was much smaller than the ones in Altus, which was largely due to how difficult they were to make. Even then, by the time they succeeded and the lesson ended, Marina's head ached.

Yolie stayed after and taught Marina how to soothe a headache on her own, which was easier than dismantling a draining shield and far less tiring. Oddly enough, Marina was in decent spirits as the night came to an end; it was *Yolie* who was uncharacteristically quiet. After Aeric left, Marina coaxed her into admitting what was wrong.

"It's the second night of Pearl's third week," Yolie whispered. "I didn't think it would come so fast."

Marina tried to ignore the knot in her stomach. Two days remained until she and Aeric left for Lewes—until she saw Kieron for the first time since Aragonite. She could scarcely imagine how terrified Aeric must be.

"It's only a meeting," she said, though she knew she sounded nowhere near as calm as she'd intended.

"No, it's not," Yolie murmured. She pulled a chrysanthemum from her pocket, which she began to pick apart. "Florin thinks the mechanical woman might be there." When Marina gave her a look, she said, "Walls are thin here. I overheard soldiers talking."

Of course she did. And with Neva no doubt preoccupied this week, Yolie had likely flown under the radar more than usual.

"They don't know for sure," Marina responded. "They only want to be prepared."

Yolie hesitated before whispering, "If she is there, I hope someone kills her."

Silence followed. Obviously, Yolie cared less about Kieron than she did Safira. It made sense. To her, Kieron was yet another faceless name thrown around by Neva and the rest. But Safira...she'd seen Safira—knew the things she did.

Yolie ran her fingers over Ronan's anteactus, her eyes still on the flower. When she looked up, her eyes red, the neutrality Marina was trying so hard to hold on to faded.

"Sometimes, I think..." Yolie's voice trailed off, but Marina didn't prod. She only waited—waited as Yolie brought the anteactus to her cheek, cradling it like one would a baby, then said, "I think it's my fault Ronan's dead."

For some reason, when Yolie's gaze met hers, Marina didn't see her eyes; she saw Cal's. Or maybe it was the guilt she saw—so enduring that it didn't matter whose it was.

Marina's chest constricted. "Of course it's not."

"You don't even know what happened."

"But I know you, and you could never be at fault for something Safira did." Marina gave her a sad smile. "I lost my parents not too long ago. I used to think it was my fault too. Sometimes, I still do."

Ronan's anteactus glinted in the light, and all Marina could picture was her boots— old and fraying, but as important to her as Ronan's anteactus was to Yolie. Since she could think of nothing else to say, she told Yolie about them—about how her parents had given them to her, and what her dad would say when she wore them.

Girly and tough. Just like my Rina.

The words rang in her head—*my Rina. My little Rina*—but they didn't make her chest heavy. Not like they usually did. Yolie told Marina about her own father's nicknames for her; he'd called her the names of different flowers every day, and when he'd passed, Ronan had picked up the habit.

"Only Ronan didn't know as much about flowers as my dad," Yolie said, "so I started collecting them, and we'd learn their names together." Her lips edged into a small, shaky smile. "I guess I never stopped."

She smoothed her pockets with her hands, barely looking up when the door creaked open and Neva peered in.

"It's late," Neva said—but not sternly. "We're going to shut off the lights soon."

Yolie wrapped her arms around Marina before parting, and though Marina wasn't entirely sure what Neva would think, she returned the hug. And yet, when Yolie left the room, Neva smiled at Marina.

She'd seen that smile—not the tight kind Neva gave during formal conversations, but the one in Ronan's memories. For someone who could make a room as icy as Aeric could, Neva's smile was warm. Comforting, even.

"I haven't heard her open up to someone like that since her brother," Neva said.

Marina blinked at her. She wasn't sure how to feel about Neva's admission to eavesdropping, but she'd be a hypocrite to judge Neva for it. She'd snooped on Neva's conversation before, after all, and Yolie was right: the compound's walls were thin.

When Neva sat beside Marina instead of leaving, it became noticeable how relaxed she was. As much as she could be, at least.

"She's needed a friend," Neva said softly. "Or perhaps an older sibling."

Marina returned her smile. "I enjoy her company."

"Sometimes, when I hear her talk but don't see her, I..." Neva shook her head, then gave a half laugh, half sigh. "I realize she isn't the child that entered the dead years. None of the children are, of course, but Yolie especially. She's like her brother in that way. Both of them—wise beyond their years." In the common room's dim light, Neva's eyes shined. "I'd love to witness the person she becomes."

After a few moments, Marina whispered, "She'll become someone very special."

"Only if she's given the chance to," Neva said. "And in this world, she won't be given it." She rested her chin on her knuckles. "Lars often tells me I found peace during the dead years—in the stagnancy of it all. I brushed him off, only...when the Delve arrived here, I realized he was right. Change can go one of two ways, and the possibility of bad change scares me more than none at all."

"It scares me too," Marina said.

"I know. But *you've* moved forward. Even when it meant leaving everything else behind." Neva's gaze rested on Marina, though Marina couldn't discern the emotion in it. "There's bravery in that—in seeking change even if it means taking risks." She paused. "I've never been one to take risks."

Marina chuckled weakly. "Honestly, Neva, neither have I."

"But you have. And though his past still unsettles me, so has Aeric. And Florin. And the rest." Neva frowned at her feet. "I've started to wonder if I'm the only one not taking those risks—and if I'm holding Yolie back from her future more than I'm protecting her."

Marina was careful to limit her reactions to that. Gently, she asked, "Is that why you agreed to send Hollis and Zora to Altus?"

"Partially. The Inber mission helped. I don't doubt the Delve's intentions."

Marina's stomach sank, but Neva didn't say anything else about it—thank goodness. Instead, she stood, straightened, and said, "But the Inber mission isn't why I'm letting Yolie help with glamouring."

Now, it was a little harder to conceal her emotions. Marina gawked at Neva. "Really?"

"Briefly," Neva said hastily. "Elta was successful in convincing Lars, and the two of them have been badgering me since Double Moon. They told me I was being irrational—

that Yolie would be protected, and Elta and I would take over after she got a glamour started. Then Lars asked if the only reason I was so adamant about Yolie staying above wasn't to protect her, but to protect *myself* from the anxiety I'd feel if she went below." She chuckled wryly. "He's always had a gentle way of calling me out. But maybe I needed it. And just now, I heard you and Yolie speak, and for a moment, it sounded like she was talking to Ronan. I remembered how much of a difference he'd made in her life—how he's part of the reason the two of us are here today."

Her chin began to quiver, and Marina didn't pry. She still didn't know what had happened in Sal, save the horrors Safira had brought. The same hatred that boiled in Yolie's eyes when she spoke of the mechanical woman flared up in Neva's now, and yet it was truly grief that settled over the room like a heavy blanket.

Neva didn't buckle under it. "As much as it will pain me, Lars is right. I can't hold Yolie back because of my own anxieties." She closed her eyes and breathed, then said, "You took a risk when you accessed Exorsus. Ronan took a risk too—for me, perhaps, but mostly for Yolie. And he'd never forgive me if I didn't let her take risks of her own."

CHAPTER 29
Wholeheartedly

The conversation stuck with Marina for the rest of that night and well into the morning. There had been so much she'd wanted to add—to reassure Neva of: the risk would benefit the safety of the compound, Pierce would watch over Yolie for the short time she was below, Neva and Elta would be there the entire time...and yet, she knew anything she had to say had already been said a hundred times over by Lars and Elta.

She'd wanted to seek the two of them out and thank them for persuading Neva, but the day before the Altus mission was hectic. Marina didn't see Ryder, Florin, Hollis, or Zora until well into the evening, and she'd spent most of the day with Aeric, going over the plan for Lewes in excruciating detail.

By the time everyone met in the common room, Marina was exhausted. Luckily, both Elta and Lars were present, and though Marina couldn't pull them aside without drawing attention to herself, she shot Elta a glance that she hoped would portray her gratitude. Perhaps she'd properly give her thanks when she returned from Lewes.

If. The little voice in her head had harped on that word these past few days—*if* they returned, *if* they were successful, *if* this didn't all go to shit and reduce the risks they'd taken to nothing.

The evening started out as a final meeting called by Florin but soon dissolved into something less formal. By the end of the night, all that was left to do was pick up new vocos. Before Florin had sent his scouts to Altus, the technicians had hijacked old vocos from the Delve to bypass the portal systems, allowing for movement between cities despite Kieron's lockdown. Lars had later suggested they do the same to everyone's vocos as a precaution.

"They're in the works," he said. "Technicians said they should be done in a few hours, but I'm sure they have plenty at the ready now. Might as well start collecting them."

Dismissively, Aeric waved a hand at Ismene, who stood next to Pierce and Elta. "Ismene...go get the vocos from the technicians."

Ismene's mouth tightened. Marina understood why, of course. Was this the first time Aeric had so much as spoken to her since arriving here? Judging by the look on Elta's face, Marina figured it probably was. Elta opened her mouth but clearly decided against whatever she'd planned on saying; she shut it promptly and gave Ismene's arm a squeeze. Though Marina was equally tempted to call Aeric out, she held her tongue too. Aeric was terribly out of sorts tonight. Ismene must've noticed as well; she only nodded.

Pierce seemed to catch on, however, because he offered to fetch them himself. Though Marina figured it was partially for Ismene, she had a sneaking suspicion it was also to get away from Ryder. The two hadn't spoken since the morning after Double Moon. Ryder had said everything he'd wanted to say, and true to his word, Pierce had indeed stopped trying.

Ryder relaxed a little once Pierce had left, but tension was still high all around. Minus Lars and maybe Florin, who always seemed to have their heads on straight, Marina wondered if perhaps *she* was one of the calmest. Though the pesky voice in her head continued to hound her with unknowns, her fear wasn't crippling. She figured she'd probably expended all her energy worrying these past couple of weeks.

Either way, she was glad to be as levelheaded as she was, especially when Ryder sat beside her and said, "You're handling this well." He smirked. "Or is it that everyone else has finally risen to meet your level of anxiety?"

"Funny," she said. "Be careful in Altus, Ryder."

"And you in Lewes." His wry smile faded. "Don't let Kieron toy with you. He'll try."

"I know." Marina looked over to Aeric, who was speaking with Florin. She and Aeric were set to leave a few hours after Florin's group, and when Marina overheard them talking about sending confirmation messages upon their arrival, she swallowed hard. "If this works, do you think Kieron will know the moment the ruemin are out of Elsudra?"

Ryder grimaced. "If this works," he said, "*everyone* will."

She'd figured as much. Perhaps she'd witness Kieron's reaction when he registered he'd been played for a fool. The thought was as beguiling as it was scary. The realization that his time was limited would surely make him desperate and violent—another reason Florin had decided to send more soldiers with Marina and Aeric. The soldiers accompanying Marina and Aeric had been trained with retaliation in mind, and those to be stationed outside of Lewes were equally prepared.

"When will they catch a ruemin?" Marina asked. "It hasn't been done yet, right?"

"Not yet. Florin plans to have some of his soldiers go down in a few hours and check the nets. Ruemin don't exactly flock to the swamplands, but there's bound to be a couple down there. And Neva seems to think the old nets are working well enough to catch at least one." He shrugged. "If we can't find one in a net, we'll hit up the outskirts of a town or two. They tend to linger close to potential prey."

He sounded confident about that. Still, Marina couldn't help herself when she asked, "How are *you* feeling about tomorrow?"

"Terrified." Ryder tapped his knuckles on the table, then said, "But hopeful too. More hopeful than scared. We'll get the ruemin out of Elsudra one way or another. For Cal."

For Cal. For Astra. For Ismene's sisters. For everyone whose death had come at the hands of those monsters. Marina's eyes began to sting.

Since they were heading out before dawn, Ryder decided to turn in early. Pierce returned as he left, and the two passed each other without so much as a glance in the other's direction. She knew it hurt Ryder as much as Pierce, but she didn't say anything as Pierce set the vocos down on the table. Hollis and Zora stopped by briefly to grab theirs, and once Neva and Lars had left, Pierce and Ismene bid their farewells to Marina.

"We'll see you soon," Ismene said, her chin wobbling.

"It's not goodbye," Marina whispered.

Pierce embraced the two of them. "It never is. We'll be here when you return."

It was still painful to hug them, though—to part, even if they didn't plan for it to be permanent. But as calm as she kept herself, she couldn't stop the unknowns from eating at her. They were eating at Aeric too. As Pierce gave Florin a parting hug, tears lining his eyes, Marina kept her gaze on Aeric. He sat motionless at the table, his mouth resting on his fist. Once Pierce and Ismene left, he broke his stillness by shooting an icy look at her.

"I expect to meet you here *on time* tomorrow," he said. "Understood?"

As the night progressed, he only grew terser, and Marina figured tomorrow wouldn't be much better. She simply nodded and resigned to tiptoe around his impatience until they returned.

If you return, the voice in her head reminded her. And yet, for some reason, it wasn't the future she found herself dwelling on as Aeric left. When only she and Florin remained in the room, she hastily said, "Can I ask you something?"

Though Florin raised an eyebrow, he nodded.

"This plan with Brenna's ring...was there a reason you couldn't move forward with it back in the Delve?"

When Florin hesitated, Marina kicked herself for asking. But she knew it would've been impossible for her *not* to ask. She hadn't forgotten what Ryder had alluded to back in Aragonite, after all—that *she'd* been part of the reason Florin and Aeric hadn't been able to see this through earlier.

Florin's silence confirmed it. But when Marina flinched, he shook his head.

"It wasn't only you," he said. "At the end of the day, it was smarter for us to stay underground and maintain the Keepers' lie that Aeric was dead. This plan requires a team of more than soldiers—one that can work to reduce threats on *all* fronts as much as possible. We had a few healers in the Delve, but only one person knew glamouring and dissolution magic, and that was Aeric." Softer, he added, "When magic returned to Elsudra, we considered going at it alone—Aeric, myself, and a few soldiers in one group— but that was a risk already heightened by Kieron's presence in the palace. If things had gone wrong and Aeric had died, not only would the Delve's glamours have disintegrated, but the Omnia also would have been even more vulnerable than it already was."

Though Florin didn't say it out loud, Marina knew what he was thinking. With the Omnia's return being such a shitshow, it had clearly been a risk they couldn't take.

"I'm sorry I made things so difficult back in the Delve," she said. She'd figured she should apologize to Florin at some point, and now seemed like a good time.

But Florin only chuckled. "It wasn't easy," he admitted. "But do you know what stuck out most to me and Aeric in those early days?"

When Marina raised an eyebrow, Florin said, "Your determination. Once you'd set your sights on learning Locus, you did everything in your power to achieve that goal. And even now that your ambitions have pivoted, you approach them wholeheartedly. That is the kind of Keeper we need on our side, Marina—the kind whose devotion we can rely on. And after what you did in Exorsus...I have no doubt that we can rely on yours."

In the hours before dawn, the swamplands sang with cicadas and frogs. Ryder's confidence about finding a ruemin hadn't been misplaced; it took some searching, but the soldiers eventually found one in a net not far from the Inber unit's camp. Hollis and Zora subdued it quickly, then left from there with Florin and Ryder—all glamoured. The sun had barely risen by the time Marina and Aeric headed out.

It was hard to leave, especially as she said goodbye to Yolie. As eager as Yolie was to help with glamouring—and as happy as she'd been that Neva was going to let her—it was obvious she didn't want Marina and Aeric to go. Neva and Lars were around to see them off too, but they didn't waste time with sentimentalities. Marina wondered if it was easier for them to treat the mission that way—as though it was a minor errand that would last but a day, and then everything would be right again.

Of course, it didn't feel trivial at all. Florin had chosen the best of the Delve's soldiers to go to Lewes, and they'd departed the night before donning so many weapons that it looked like they were heading off to battle. Only a few remained in the morning to escort Marina and Aeric, as militant as they were heavily armed.

The plan was to convene outside of Lewes, then have the soldiers sweep the city and make contact with Kieron's troops before the meeting occurred. It was all so strictly arranged that Marina worried she'd be screamed at if she stepped out of line, so she made it a point to stick close to Aeric. He wasn't much better than the soldiers; he remained silent as they trudged through the wetlands, head down and eyes so dark he looked as though he were walking toward his death.

What Florin had said to her kept Marina going. She tried to walk with purpose—wholeheartedly, though her stomach soured more with every step. She kept her hands in the pockets of her coat, where she'd placed a few fresh peppermint leaves. It was the least she could do to calm herself.

Since they couldn't risk running into the Inber unit, they took the same backroads out of the swamplands that Marina and Ryder had taken into them. From there, they trekked to the outskirts of Inber and found a vacant portal system, which the soldiers still scouted before clearing it for use.

All the portal systems looked the same, Marina realized. A pedestal built into a fountain stood at the center of a circular courtyard, surrounded by four archways that led into nothing. When a soldier hovered her voco over the fountain's console and selected a city, the northernmost archway came to life—a veil of light hanging over what was once air. Whatever the technicians had done to the Delve's vocos had clearly worked.

"We're heading to a northern town near the Notlis Mountains, east of Lewes," she explained to Marina. "That'll make it seem like we aren't coming from the South. When we leave, we'll go back the same way."

Marina tried to listen, but all she could focus on was the soldier's hair. It was bright red, like Boris's. Had she known him? Did she know where he was now—up in the Admare Mountains, rotting beneath the sun? Was that where she'd end up? Was it where they'd all end up? So much for being calm last night. Now, she was going to be sick.

No, you're not. You're going to see this through. Wholeheartedly, like Florin said.

She forced herself to hear every word the soldier relayed to her, then followed her instructions exactly. Once everyone had synced their vocos with the console, they stepped through the portal, then did the same in the town they were using as a red herring.

The climate in the North was milder than in the East and South. The air neither pricked at Marina's skin nor made her sweat, and once they reached Lewes, the smell of pine and wildflowers tinged the air.

She remembered Ismene saying that Lewes was nestled below the Ulaex Mountains, and from the portal system at the edge of the city, Marina could see the range clearly. It wasn't as long as the Admares, but it was just as tall, and so green that the sky paled in comparison. If she squinted, she could make out streams and waterfalls that cascaded down hills and pooled into rivers.

Marina focused on the water as a few soldiers departed, finding it was one of the few things that calmed her—that, and her peppermint leaves, which she took out when her breathing grew too shallow. After a sweep of the city, their soldiers planned to meet Kieron and *his* soldiers. Apparently, they were to stay with Kieron to confirm the legitimacy of his cuffs and make sure he didn't remove them. A few of Kieron's own were headed to Marina and Aeric to do the same. At least, that's what the redheaded soldier told her. Marina's heart pounded at the thought of golden-armored soldiers.

There was a paved trail that led from the courtyard into Lewes, but Marina couldn't bring herself to look down it. Neither could Aeric, apparently, who sat at the edge of the fountain with his head in his hands. When his voco chimed with an incoming message, he made it a point to move far enough away so Marina couldn't hear.

She had a feeling it was Florin, who was probably already in Altus, but she supposed Aeric didn't want her hounding him with questions because when he returned to the fountain, he didn't look at her. He simply nodded at the redheaded soldier, who lifted her own voco to her lips. After that, everyone went back to being silent. Though it couldn't have been any longer than thirty minutes, waiting felt as torturous as it had in Inber. After some time, even peppermint stopped helping.

It was nearly noon now, and the sun beat down on them—so bright and wild its reflection on the water burned her eyes. When Kieron's soldiers arrived, their armor shone even brighter. Before they reached the courtyard, Aeric approached Marina.

"When we reach Kieron, I talk," he said. "You follow my lead, like we've discussed."

Kieron's soldiers were quiet and curt, though Marina preferred that to talkative. They watched as the redheaded soldier placed diminution cuffs on Aeric's and Marina's wrists, and when she handed them the keys, they pocketed them without a word.

The walk into Lewes was just as silent. Since Marina knew eyes were bound to be on her the entire time, she retreated into her head.

Raisel, Thora. Their names came first—a reminder of what had happened in Lewes. Though it was truly a deserted city, it wasn't entirely dysfunctional. Somewhere in the distance, she could hear a clock tower bell, marking the turn of the hour. She forced herself to walk, repeating the names at every peal.

Raisel, Thora, Evren, Tover, Boris, Dane, Ronan, Astra, Cal.

CHAPTER 30
Ants to Sugar

The bell continued to ring until they'd made their way into the center of the city. At some point, there would've been more people around to hear it, but now, its chimes skirted through empty streets and past abandoned buildings.

Marina had expected Lewes to be a wasteland, but it was nearly as untouched as Altus. Stone pathways wove about shops and market squares, dotted with chairs and tables. Some had fallen over, but for the most part, things looked untouched. Garden plazas built between buildings overflowed with flowers, and a few more portal systems—surrounded by beech trees that rustled in a quiet breeze—popped up as they walked.

Perhaps that was why Ismene had loved the gardens in the Delve and why she spent so much time tending to flowers in the sanctuary. Perhaps it reminded her of home.

Lewes's residential areas were peaceful and vacant too, and it wasn't until they reached the clock tower itself that the scenery changed.

If the ruemin had been sent to target civilians, Kieron's soldiers must've been sent to destroy specific buildings. As they passed piles of ash, she remembered Pierce telling her how books had been burned. These had to be libraries or schools—places with knowledge Kieron sought to erase.

Of course. He'd had his soldiers leave buildings untouched unless they were places of progress—of education and innovation. Of *magic*.

"Lewes's School of Medicine," the redheaded soldier muttered. Marina wasn't sure if she was speaking to her, but when she twisted her head to look beyond the clock tower, her gaze met charred stone and dilapidated archways.

A few blocks from the clock tower, surrounding a portal system outside another set of shops, guards in golden armor stood waiting. To keep herself from panicking, Marina counted them. *Ten*—the same number that accompanied her and Aeric. The number Kieron had promised. He very well could have another group waiting at the outskirts like they did, but for the sake of this meeting, each side had the same number.

What about Safira? She could be anywhere—behind buildings, in alleyways, or on the other side of one of the portals. Florin and Aeric hadn't understated those possibilities. But obviously, if Safira was nearby, she wouldn't make it easy to spot her.

The paranoia—or perhaps it was simply her general fear—clearly took its toll. Marina could feel the blood drain from her face, but as they approached the courtyard, she didn't try to calm herself. She was supposed to look unstable, wasn't she? That was the story Aeric was selling. Luckily, it wasn't hard to bring out that side of her.

Marina tried to peer into the courtyard, but she couldn't see Kieron from behind the golden-armored soldiers. As she got closer, she released her grip on the storm in her head —just enough so it was noticeable.

Safira's lock bombs were the easiest to fret about. Florin and Aeric hadn't shut up about them these past few weeks, not like Marina blamed them. According to Florin, Safira had relied heavily on them during the war. Why use magic when technology could do equally as much damage?

Damage...like she'd done to the guard in Inber. Irreversible, reprehensible damage. How many people would she kill before this ended? *If* it ended? And if it did, would she be strong enough to move on, or would she wreak the same havoc on herself? How horribly ironic it would be—to live through all of this, only to be her own end. How *fitting*.

She hadn't truly let herself spiral in quite some time. Even now, she was unsure how far she should go. Because she *could* go further if she let herself. She had it in her. She was good at it: spiraling, chipping away at her sanity, destroying the progress she'd made...

Too far, Marina. You're going too far.

Only, it seemed to pay off. When the golden-armored guards parted to reveal Kieron, her eyes were filled with so many tears that it took her a while to make him out.

The first thing she saw was his smile—then his gray teeth, sickly skin, and blue eyes. Marina side glanced at Aeric, who clung to his icy stare. She couldn't help but sense the young boy who cowered beneath it.

Strangely enough, Kieron didn't speak as they approached. It was unlike him to let someone *else* start the conversation, but when Aeric's jaw tightened, Marina knew it was another one of Kieron's games.

The shift in Aeric's demeanor may not have been noticeable to the soldiers, who stood only paces away, arms clasped in front of their shining baldrics, but it was noticeable to Marina. Noticeable to *Kieron*. For a painful, silent moment, Aeric said nothing, and when he finally did speak, his voice was low.

"Thank you for meeting us," he said.

That only made Kieron smile more. "You can do away with the formalities, Aeric. It's only me." His eyes shifted to Marina, lingering on her before moving back to Aeric. "It's been so long. You don't look any different. A bit grimmer, perhaps, if that was ever possible. But I suppose that comes with treason."

When Aeric didn't respond, Kieron looked back to Marina and frowned. "These past few seasons have been hard for you, haven't they? I can only imagine. I'm so sorry about the loss of that scout. I know she was your friend."

Cal. Marina's heart dropped to her stomach. She shifted her gaze to Kieron's hands. Though her vision was still a touch blurry, she could see the glove he wore on his left.

When Kieron realized where she was looking, his fingers twitched. "We found her body," he said smoothly. "Or, at least, *pieces* of it. It was buried amongst the rubble, covered in sewage. Her face wasn't recognizable, but her hair was. Vaughn got good use of the parts we managed to salvage."

Marina began to see spots in addition to tears. It'd been less than a minute since the meeting began, and Kieron had already provoked her. Not like she was surprised; of *course* he'd brought up Cal.

You don't know what we're doing here, she thought, clenching her teeth as she raised her eyes to meet Kieron's. *You won't know until the ruemin are gone, and then you'll realize. You'll realize you're losing.*

Aeric's voice was sharp. "I suggest we speak about what we came here for."

Kieron continued looking at Marina, dissecting every inch of her expression, only to turn back to Aeric when he couldn't get anything. "I'm all ears."

"We need to find a compromise," Aeric said. "Going on like this will result in nothing but failure for us both."

"So you've said," Kieron mused. "A stalemate. That's what you think we've reached?"

"What else would you call it? Neither of us is winning; we're just waiting for the next turn of events. I meant what I said about Marina. She won't be able to do Locus, even if you force her."

"You underestimate her. She performed Tempus beautifully."

"Tempus is different."

Kieron's smile faded. "So you wish for me to give up, do you? To abandon decades of work, all because the girl can't get her head on straight?" He chuckled. "No, you know I'd never do that. You know I'd never compromise. So tell me, why are you here? And be honest. You know I hate lies."

Aeric's posture weakened. Marina imagined it had been quite a while since someone had spoken to him with that tone, but Kieron did it so easily—so effortlessly—that Aeric couldn't help but react. Though he maintained an even tone, his voice was a touch softer than usual when he said, "I realize it is preferable for you to think I'm lying, but even you cannot ignore the fact that Marina wasn't who our Keepers expected. Are you so blinded by the Omnia that you'd risk damaging it?"

Kieron's eyebrows rose. "I'd have to disagree with you. Marina is exactly who the Keepers expected, as it was *she* who answered their call. Their error, as I realize now, wasn't that they failed to interpret Tempus, but that they threw their faith into lost causes."

He wasn't only talking about her. He was talking about Aeric too. Two lost causes, chosen by the Keepers because *she'd* guided their hands.

She hurled a thousand silent curses Kieron's way. She knew what he was trying to do —the doubt and fear he was trying to stir up. Anticipation pricked at her fingers. When the tides changed, his smug comments would be wiped from his tongue.

Finish this, she begged Florin and Ryder, Hollis and Zora. *Get the ruemin out. Close Brenna's portal.*

Were they in the palace now? How far had they gotten?

When Kieron faced her, her chest constricted. *Stay calm. Stay emotionless.*

"What do you say, Marina?" he asked.

Throat tight, she whispered, "About what?"

"About Locus. Do *you* think you could perform it?"

"I wouldn't."

Kieron clicked his tongue. "That's not what I asked."

He took a step toward her. Though Aeric tensed, he didn't move.

Still, Kieron noticed. He held up his wrists, flashing his cuffs. "I don't intend to do anything," he droned, "except look upon an old friend."

Another step. In the afternoon sun, his skin gleamed like wax.

"An old friend," he continued, "who I feel I know as well as you, Aeric." He angled his chin at Marina. "It pains me," he said, "to think that the two of the people I understand most in this world are so determined to see me fail. It pains me even more to know how desperately they lie."

Aeric opened his mouth, but Kieron spoke first. "You think you can fool me by saying she's too far gone to do Locus?" he said. "Think you can present her to me a little teary-eyed and expect me to throw my hands up and surrender? I know what unstable looks like for her. I saw her memories too. If I took her back to Altus as she was and forced her to agree to Locus, she'd perform it eventually—just as flawlessly as she performed Tempus.

She has a knack for pushing through, even when she's in shambles."

That was, perhaps, the strangest compliment she'd ever received, though she didn't think Kieron intended it that way.

"That's a risky assumption to make," Aeric said. "Especially when it comes to Locus."

"As I told Marina once, I'm not opposed to risks if they get me what I want," Kieron said. "Evidently, neither are you. You traveled all this way to meet with me—to *lie* to me—so I've no doubt you understand that sometimes, risks are necessary." He took a deep, satisfied breath. "But I don't intend to take her back to Altus. Not yet. I don't need to. Be it a day or a year, she'll come. Everything falls into my hands eventually."

Though Marina could tell Aeric was trying to remain unruffled, he looked away when Kieron's eyes met his. She had to give it to him, though; he was still able to make the temperature around them drop when he said, "And then what? When the Omnia *falls into your hands*, what happens? You'll access Exorsus and attempt to go on like this forever? Squashing out rebellion for eternity?"

Kieron laughed through his nose. "I wish I could say I'm surprised you made that leap, but I suppose you know me as well as I know you."

"I'm not wrong, then."

"No. You're not."

It took Marina a few seconds to realize what they were referring to. Aeric's theory about what Kieron would do once he could access Exorsus—about the eternal loop he'd create—was a theory Kieron had thought of too. And Kieron saw no point in denying it.

The breeze sharpened, and Marina's chest constricted again, sending shooting pains to her shoulders when she tried to breathe.

"You might think it mad, but if I'm right, it would be best for the Omnia," Kieron said. "Its safety would never be risked again—it would no longer be passed down a line of successors whose passion for Elsudra may not burn as intensely as mine. Safira would have been a fine Keeper, but there's no one in this realm who cares as deeply about the Omnia as I do. And as much as I admire Safira's iron fist, even she cannot placate the ruemin as effectively as I have."

In a way, Marina thought it remarkable how fervently Kieron justified his role as the Omnia's host. She could tell by the way his eyes flashed when he spoke. She'd noticed it before—this belief he held that he and the Omnia were one and the same.

"There was a time when I thought *you* were as devoted to this realm as I am," Kieron added, his gaze locked on Aeric. "When you showed your weakness, it nearly destroyed me. Safira has proven herself to be of much stronger mind, but how could I ever know for certain? Now, I can bet on never having to find out—that there's a chance the Omnia and

I will become eternally bound, as we always should have been."

This time, it was Aeric he took a step closer to. "I meant what I said about everything falling into my hands," Kieron continued. "Time and time again, people come to me—like ants to sugar—and they give me what I need. It happened with the sentry who led me to the Delve, and then it happened with Marina herself."

When Marina's hands threatened to curl into fists, she flattened them against her legs.

Don't let Kieron toy with you, Ryder had said.

Ryder...thinking of him was another thing she couldn't do. The more she wondered where he was and if he was safe, the less she could breathe.

"Then, I ran into another wall when she was in Altus," Kieron said—slowly, as though he was intent on keeping them here and making them hear every word, "and I couldn't for the life of me figure out how I'd motivate her to perform Tempus. But soon after, five scouts arrived, desperate to be heroes. And one of them was her friend."

Breathe, Marina. One at a time.

"Even before all this bother," Kieron continued, "things had a funny way of coming to me when I needed them most. Years ago, I failed to convince one of the brightest sorcerers in Elsudra to work with me. I wanted him on my side when the time came, but politics had left a sour taste in his mouth. He'd been ousted from the palace for his alternative methods of scientific inquiry, and though I promised I'd let him practice as he saw fit, he didn't believe me. For years, I badgered him—offered him wealth and power—but nothing worked. I needed to *prove* I wasn't like the rest."

Vaughn...he was clearly talking about Vaughn. Back in Altus, Vaughn himself had alluded to being ostracized by the capital healers because of his medical experiments and proclivity to collect his victims' hair. Marina's ears began to ring.

"But then," Kieron said, "a sick woman and her inclined son arrived at the palace. She begged me to train him, and though childrearing wasn't what my job entailed, I figured— at the time, at least—I'd need a successor eventually. So I made a deal with her: I'd train the boy if she became my peace offering." He put his hand into his pocket, and when he removed it, he held something that shone in the sunlight.

Marina blinked at it, then at Aeric, who remained frozen as Kieron placed whatever he was holding into Aeric's palm. Now that it was closer, she could make it out—a lock of long hair, just as golden-brown as Aeric's.

"A few seasons later, she died in a medical experiment," Kieron whispered—slowly, as though he wanted to draw out the moment as long as possible. "As for me, I'd gained an ally in Vaughn. And the boy...he'd fallen into my hands too."

Aeric stared at the lock of hair in his palm, his eyes glazed.

But...hadn't Evren been sick? Hadn't she...?

Marina's body went cold. All those memories Aeric had shown Marina where Kieron pawned Evren's death off as a tragedy—all those times he'd kindled Aeric's hatred for the court by reminding him she could've lived had the elite not been so selfish—had only been half of the truth. Evren had been as much a victim of poverty as she had of Vaughn. Of *Kieron*. Of course Kieron waited until now to make this known. He could've told Aeric at any point—or he could've kept it hidden forever—but that wasn't his way. Every move he made was a calculated ploy to break the other side down at the right moment.

Say something, Marina begged Aeric. *Show him you won't break.*

But Aeric said nothing. Was he shutting down?

He couldn't. They were here for a reason. Kieron's game wouldn't matter when they pulled the board out from beneath him. They only had to stick this out a little longer.

"Even recently," Kieron continued, "talk of Brenna's portal was being stirred up amongst my soldiers. This was unusual, so I deployed my network to pinpoint where the talk was coming from. We tracked it down to a small group who, after days of surveillance, we realized weren't soldiers at all, but *scouts*, who we followed to a hidden sanctuary in the southern swamplands."

The gasp began at the bottom of Marina's spine. By the time it moved to her throat, it had gone silent, so she stood there, gaping at Kieron as he smiled. He wasn't looking at her, though. He was looking at Aeric, who still stared at the lock of hair in his palm.

"My officials suggested bombing it, but we couldn't do that without destroying precious cargo." Kieron's gaze shifted to Marina, the sight of which made her stomach twist. "But then, things worked out like they always do. Next thing I know, I'm receiving a call from Aeric, of all people, so desperate to get me out of the palace that it didn't take me long to make an educated guess why, especially given the talk your scouts stirred up. I knew you were going to try something with Brenna's ring at some point, but I didn't know when—until you so much as told me." He shook his head in mock disappointment. "But I needed Marina out of the compound, and Aeric...you *agreed*. And while you've both been here, traveling all this way to rattle off your lies and helping me stall, my forces have swept in and completed a bit of deforestation."

He seemed to find it quite funny. Or maybe it was Aeric and Marina's reaction he found funny, because now, Aeric wasn't the only one who failed to rein in his emotions. Marina had never seen him like this—face void of color, eyes wide...even when the Delve was about to fall, he'd clung to his composure. Now, the mask he'd worn so well was crumbling. And Kieron drank in every second of it.

"I'm sure Safira will give the group you sent into Altus my regards," he said. "She's been charged with detecting any attempts at breaching our security, magical or otherwise. And thank Exorsus she was. If she hadn't been aware of this, your group may've gone unnoticed. But I have no qualms when it comes to Safira's competence, and I imagine your people have already been apprehended, which means Brenna's ring is also back in my possession. And I thank you for that—I really do. I've been meaning to get rid of it for a while. It poses a threat to the ruemin."

The redheaded soldier had her helmet on now, but Marina could pinpoint her voice. Still, she had no idea what the soldier was saying. Was she talking to them or Kieron? It didn't matter...she'd pulled out her gun and was pointing it in Kieron's direction.

Before Marina could get her bearings straight, Kieron held up his hand. His soldiers had their weapons out in front of them now too, but Kieron didn't seem flustered.

"If you attack me," he said, more to Aeric than anyone else, "then it will be *you* who broke our promise of amnesty, and I will give my forces full freedom to do whatever they can to protect me—and the Omnia."

If he looked at Marina when he said it, she didn't notice. Her tears blinded her, but she strained not to make a sound—not to gasp, or scream, or say anything, because she'd been told not to indulge Kieron...

But she *was* indulging him. It was too late.

Even with all her worrying and usual pessimism, she hadn't anticipated *this*. It wasn't only Ryder she may lose, or perhaps had already lost. It wasn't Florin either, or Hollis and Zora. Now, she'd lose Pierce and Ismene too. And Yolie...

Finally, Aeric's eyes met Kieron's. But Aeric didn't respond; he only raised a shaking hand to the soldiers, who put their weapons down.

Kieron straightened, then sighed. "I appreciate that you were running on limited resources and time," he said. "Given the circumstances, it's commendable what you *were* able to do—your stunt in Inber especially. But Exorsus, Aeric. For always being ten steps ahead, you were so far behind on this one that it almost disappointed me. I thought I raised you better." In the light, his teeth shined like his eyes. "An ant to sugar indeed."

They hadn't just been played for fools now—they'd been played for fools ever since Florin's scouts had returned. Even worse, the entire time Neva's technicians had been posing as the Inber unit's squad leader, Altus had *known*, but they'd feigned ignorance anyway. They'd waited—*Kieron* had waited—for the right moment. And like everything else, that had fallen into his hands too.

Marina thought she heard the redheaded soldier say something else, but at this point, she wouldn't have been surprised if her brain was playing tricks on her. Maybe this whole thing was a trick, or maybe it was another nightmare, and soon enough, she'd wake up to streams of light coming in through her apartment window, illuminating her boots.

Her boots. They were probably gone too, and with them, the last of her parents.

What would her world look like without the ones she loved? Without the people she'd given up everything for?

It would look like nothing. And Kieron knew it.

"Let it be known that I abided by all the rules of this meeting," Kieron said. He turned from them, then approached the pedestal at the fountain. When the northernmost portal lit up, he gestured to his soldiers. "I did not have my people attack yours, nor did I attempt to take the girl by force."

In the distance, the redheaded soldier ordered something again. When her hands wrapped around Marina's arms, she barely reacted. She only looked at Aeric, who stared at Kieron with a look she didn't bother to decipher.

"I look forward to the next time I see you," Kieron said warmly. "Both of you."

She didn't see him step through the portal. She didn't see anything because her vision wasn't just blurry—it was nearly black, so eddied by spots that the rest of her senses faded with it.

CHAPTER 31
The Unbidden Figure

There was no use for diversions or red herrings now. They traveled directly back to Inber, then passed the town line and made their way through what was once the Inber unit's encampment—now completely deserted.

Had they been evacuated? Or worse, had they joined Kieron's additional troops in the forest to take down the compound? Marina imagined they'd enjoy that. The unit had to know by now what had really caused their fellow soldier's death, and they'd probably jump at the opportunity for revenge.

The Delve soldiers shouted orders at each other as they racked their guns and rushed into the forest.

"We'll get them out," the redheaded soldier said as she undid Marina's cuffs. Marina wasn't sure if she'd used the extra keys or if Kieron's soldiers had returned the original ones. They probably had—yet another reminder that Kieron had followed all the rules and *still* taken them down.

It was only when her cuffs fell to the ground that Marina snapped out of her daze. She moved toward the mouth of the forest, but Aeric's hand wrapped around her arm before she could make it a single step.

"Don't," he said.

"They're *in there*," she protested, trying to wrest her arm from his grip.

Though Aeric was clearly shaking, his voice was firm. "Stay here."

"His soldiers may still be there! They may be slaughtering them!"

Slaughtering Pierce, Ismene, Yolie, and the rest. Children and adults, inclined or not... they could all be dying. She'd chosen to hold the Omnia so she could protect Elsudra—staying out here now would be a betrayal. She had to do something.

"Then our soldiers will face them," Aeric said. "Not you."

Marina twisted away from him. "They *can't* kill me! That's exactly why Kieron wanted me in Lewes. If I go in now, none of his troops will lay a hand on me. And if they do...if they do, I'll rip them to pieces..."

"Marina—"

Her vision narrowed again, and though she knew she was verging on hysteria, she couldn't stop the rage from rising to the surface—couldn't stop her waves from curling in her head, brimming with violent power. She turned and ran, wondering if Aeric could stop her.

Either he couldn't or he didn't, because her body kept moving—feet sinking into the marshy ground, mud seeping into her shoes. She kept going until smoke curled around her lungs, then used conveyance when she realized she was moving too slowly. When she saw the first of the fallen trees, she came to a stop.

The redheaded soldier noticed Marina, but she didn't order her to turn back. She didn't need to. Kieron's soldiers were long gone.

They'd bombed the trees; that much was obvious. The larger ones hadn't fallen, but their trunks were blackened, beset by cracks that cleaved deep into their cores. Smaller trees—still the size of redwoods, maybe larger, with jumbled roots and disintegrated leaves —had fallen into the swamp water, and those on dry land sizzled with low-burning flames.

The smoke stung her eyes, but she refused to close them. Buried amongst piles of charred trees were the planks of wooden walkways, and Marina tried to look for bodies— for someone who may still be alive. The glamours must've fallen to the ground with the trees, or perhaps the bombs had been strong enough to rip them apart too.

"People!" one of the soldiers yelled.

More orders followed suit, and when Marina whirled around to see where they were heading, she came face to face with Aeric.

She went to brace herself, but he put his hands up in surrender.

He didn't need to say anything. She knew he wasn't going to force her out now he knew Kieron's troops had left. Even if he'd had something to say, she wasn't sure he could get himself to. His face was drawn and vacant, and when his eyes began to water, she knew it wasn't because of the smoke.

He took in the destruction, his chin lowered to his chest and his hands limp, and when his gaze settled on something a few yards away, Marina couldn't help but follow it.

Something small and red peeked out from beneath a pile of wood, and though she couldn't see it fully, she knew it was a pacifier. Near it, buried deep in the rubble, a woman's hand lay opened, and a few paces from that, a soldier gently wrapped something small in a charred blanket. He retracted his helmet, his shoulders heaving as he let out a long, silent sob. Slowly, he touched his forehead to the blanket, lips trembling as he whispered something. Maybe it was prayer. Maybe it was something else. Marina didn't know. She didn't know where he was taking the little bundle either when he disappeared into the brush—perhaps to the nearest body of water he could find, even if it wasn't the ocean. She didn't have room to wonder. All she could hear in her head was a mother's voice. Lana's voice.

Cordelia. My little Cordelia.

The rage pricking at her fingertips settled, and Marina's legs buckled. Her knees hit the ground, sobs wrenching out of her, and when Aeric knelt beside her, he still said nothing. He only wrapped his arms around her.

Maybe this all *would* make her unstable. Then Kieron would never be able to make her do Locus, and he'd only have himself to thank because he'd pushed her to this point. He'd left her with nothing, and in return, she'd give him exactly that.

"Aeric! Marina!"

The voice cut through the air, and with it, a figure. She could hardly see who it was, but when Aeric pulled her up and the figure embraced her, Marina knew it was Pierce. Her ears rang so loudly she wasn't sure what he was saying, so instead, she focused on blinking away her tears. As her vision cleared, she could better make out the figures in the distance—one of whom had golden glasses.

When Yolie saw Marina and Aeric, she let out a high-pitched gasp and broke from Neva and Lars. Neva didn't stop her; given the way Neva held one arm to her body, it was clear something was broken, and she wasn't about to waste energy trying to keep Yolie at her side. Lars, too, probably realized it wasn't smart to rush after her, because he stayed beside Neva, supporting her despite his own limp.

Yolie bounded over fallen trunks, passing through clouds of smoke that caught bits of sunlight. She didn't slow as she reached Marina, and when she collided into her, Marina nearly lost her balance. Yolie buried her face into Marina's shoulder, coughing and crying, and for some reason, that was what brought Marina off the ledge.

Yolie. She had to be strong for Yolie.

The soldiers escorted a group of about fifty—maybe more—which seemed like a large number until Marina remembered the compound had harbored nearly five hundred people. She frantically searched the crowd for Ismene's long, dark hair, nearly collapsing when Elta parted from the mass of bodies, her hand tightly intertwined with Ismene's. Ismene's eyes widened, and she began to run, pulling Elta alongside her.

They'd made it out...but how? If this group was comprised of the only survivors, it couldn't have been a coincidence.

No...no, it wasn't. Marina still hadn't gotten a handle on her hearing, but Aeric was obviously thanking Pierce—not just offhandedly, but profusely.

Pierce...he'd done something. Was he the reason they'd lived? She still couldn't hear properly. But Pierce was crying...if he'd saved them, why was he crying?

Perhaps because so many hadn't been saved, like Cordelia and Lana and the children Marina had seen on Double Moon—children whose names she couldn't remember, or perhaps had never learned. Maybe that was best; her list only seemed to keep getting longer, and she wasn't sure it would ever stop.

Her body was numb when Ismene reached her, and she couldn't feel Ismene's arms when they wrapped around her. All she could think of was Ryder, Florin, Hollis, and Zora. Would their names be next?

It finally registered with Marina. *That* was why Pierce was crying. It had to be. Aeric must've said something to him about the Altus mission. Pierce's shoulders were shaking and his face was as contorted as Marina imagined hers was.

"We need to get out," Neva said when she reached Aeric. Now that she was closer, Marina could see how unnaturally her wrist bent. Her voco hid some of the damage, but it, too, was cracked and dented.

Neva didn't seem keen on fixing it, though. She refused to wallow in the destruction around them—all she focused on was moving forward.

"I know people in the West," she continued, fighting hard to steady her voice. It broke anyway. "Most of them live in Tolsea. We...we can go there."

"You're sure they're still around?" Aeric asked, but he didn't sound like himself. His voice was broken.

"Do you have any other ideas?"

Aeric clearly didn't because he only responded with a nod of agreement.

Marina swallowed what she wanted to say. Even if this worked, how long would they remain hidden until Kieron found them again? Until he *killed* more of them?

Would this all stop if she gave herself up? It was a shameful thought, but she couldn't ignore it. Maybe she'd made a mistake accepting the Omnia, and she should give it up now before it could get worse. Maybe fewer people would die if Kieron got what he wanted.

No. *No.* She couldn't succumb to that kind of thinking. That was exactly what Kieron had been planning with the Keepers—to induce so much pain across Elsudra that they figured it would be more humane to give in. It was what he was doing now.

This wouldn't stop if she yielded. It would only get worse, and it would last for an eternity. Kieron had confirmed it. The pain would only end once he was gone.

But for now, she needed to focus on getting out—on the next couple of steps.

A few of the soldiers volunteered to stay back and continue searching the forest for more survivors. Neva, Aeric, and Lars immediately launched themselves into logistics. Everyone's vocos had been hijacked by technicians to bypass the portals—*thank God for Lars,* Marina thought—and they figured they'd reach Tolsea safely if they traveled in batches small enough to avoid attention.

Though Aeric seemed as intent as Neva and Lars to move forward—to plan rather than flounder in the horrors around them—he looked so broken that watching him became painful. Pierce, too, was struggling to hang on, but he forced himself to move. Only then did Marina realize he was clutching a bag at his side. Something inside squirmed against the fabric, but she didn't have time to focus on it.

Somewhere in the distance, she could hear shouting.

It came from one voice, which steadily grew louder. Marina couldn't make out who it was so much as she could make out its direction. The voice didn't belong to one of the survivors; it cut through the northern trees, which meant this person had made their way into the forest from Inber.

Neva and Aeric spun toward the sound, their arms up as though they were ready to rip apart an Altus soldier. The redheaded soldier rattled off commands and held her gun out in front of her, preparing to face the unbidden figure that careened through the brush. Only...it wasn't an Altus soldier.

It was *Ryder.*

Marina's senses faded again, then came back in a burst when Pierce let out a cry. Was this a dream? Was Ryder real?

Yes...he was. He was real, and he was alone—covered in so much blood and sweat that, if it weren't for his eyes, she may not have known it was him.

She didn't see Florin, Hollis, or Zora with him, but she couldn't think about what that meant. Ryder was shouting at the top of his lungs—shouting at them to *go, run, get out.* At first, Marina couldn't make out what he was saying because he hardly sounded like himself. But as he got closer and she realized what he was going on about, three things became abundantly clear.

One, Florin's mission had failed, just like Kieron had said.

Two, Kieron's soldiers had retreated before the bombs went off so Kieron could send in something worse. Or maybe it was simply that he found it poetic to take out the remaining survivors with the very beasts they'd sought to banish.

And three, it wouldn't matter if they ran.

The ruemin were already here.

CHAPTER 32
Only Once

When the first *clicks* sounded, all of Marina's muddled emotions condensed into fear so sharp she was almost thankful for it. At the very least, it got her moving. Something resembling electricity cracked through her veins, sparking life into her senses. Finally, she could see and hear clearly—maybe a little too clearly. This was the kind of fear that made every color much too bright and every sound unbearably loud.

Of course. Why have soldiers face the survivors—especially those who had abilities similar to Neva's, Aeric's, or hers—if ruemin could do the job as well, if not better?

But Kieron's soldiers and the ruemin had one thing in common: they were all on strict orders to bring her back to Kieron, which meant none of them would kill her. Even the ruemin, wild and unpredictable as they were, could sense the Omnia, and they were smart enough to know the soul it had attached to wasn't theirs to suck dry.

Aeric must've known that too. Or perhaps he'd known Marina wasn't going to retreat with the rest of the group, who the soldiers had herded into a circle like scared goats. He came up beside her, and the moment the first ruemin sprang into view, he made a sweeping motion with his arms and cleaved its body in half.

Ryder, who'd been only a few paces from it, jumped out of the way, but that didn't stop the ruemin's blood from splattering the side of his face. As quick as the ruemin's death had been, Marina could hear dozens more in the distance—their screeches echoing through the trees.

No. Not dozens. *Hundreds.*

How many ruemin had Florin estimated were in Elsudra? A thousand, maybe fewer? Kieron couldn't possibly have sent all of them. Or maybe he could have. This group was his biggest threat, no doubt. He'd do everything to crush it.

Pierce shoved his bag into Ismene's arms, then pushed her in the direction of the soldiers. Neva grabbed Yolie as well, yanking her off Marina and ordering her to join the rest of the group.

"Go!" she shouted.

Protests bubbled at Yolie's mouth but died down when Lars pulled her away.

Half of the soldiers formed a protective wall around the group, and the other half began making their way out into the trees, helmets on and weapons at the ready.

This time, it wasn't one ruemin that rushed toward them. It was hordes of them—screeching so loudly almost everyone went to cover their ears.

And then the gunfire started.

Ruemin dropped like flies, but every time one went down, two more emerged. They hurtled over logs and through singed leaves, cowering for only seconds when another got hurt, then leaping forward with vigor. As hard as Marina prayed for them to stumble into traps, she knew those had been destroyed as well.

Ryder shot a few with his gun, and when it stopped firing, he threw it aside and unsheathed the sword at his hip. He clutched the carbon hilt, limbs shaking violently, and when Pierce came up beside him, he didn't move away. Instead, he snapped on his helmet, which made the ruemin closest to them quail.

Pierce was wearing an armored suit too, thank goodness, and his baldric held more than enough weapons. When a ruemin pounced at them, he shot it in the torso, then again in the face before it could recover. Another followed, and unthinking, Marina's arms widened. The ruemin's head split in half as though someone had taken a sword to it, sending scales and blood flying. Some of the innards catapulted toward Pierce, but he had his helmet on before they could make contact with his face.

Each time a ruemin died and the others recoiled, it gave them a second's respite. The soldiers began ordering the survivors to move forward, but there were more ruemin than people, and when another cluster came storming through the trees, chaos erupted.

There were too many. When two ruemin jumped onto a soldier and took him down, the circle of people disbanded. Screams sounded—not from ruemin, but from Elsudrans—and in all the commotion, Marina couldn't make out where Ismene and Yolie had gone.

She didn't have time for that. A pack of four barreled toward her, but before Aeric could tear them apart, she'd already flayed them herself. At the height of her adrenaline, it felt natural, just like the rest of the violent skills she'd so easily come to possess.

Good. Right now, she was *proud* of her ability to annihilate—to bring ruemin to their knees before tearing scales from their bodies. Though exhaustion swept in, it wasn't as bad as it used to be. It set her off balance, perhaps, but it didn't stop her from fighting.

Ryder, however, wasn't doing well. He'd obviously been injured—by ruemin or Kieron's soldiers back in Altus, she wasn't sure—and when a ruemin swiped at his arm, he nearly lost hold of his sword.

He staggered, but righted himself, then hacked the ruemin's head off so forcefully that his blade got stuck in its skull.

The ruemin uttered a collective wail, but by the time their pain had passed, Ryder still hadn't managed to free his sword. He was bleeding too, so badly Marina worried he may pass out. When the ruemin made a beeline for him, Marina widened her arms...

...and slammed stomach-first into the ground.

Scaly hands held her down, nails glinting in the streams of light that poured through the demolished canopy. She tried to move, but the ruemin—there had to have been more than five of them—had her in such a bind that her limbs were useless. She tried to tear one apart with her eyes—she knew she could do it—but it grabbed the back of her head and pressed her cheek into the ground before she could.

"*THIEF!*" it yelled. Its mouth was so close to her face that the following *click* sent a sharp pain through her ear.

Aeric...where was Aeric? She couldn't see him through her periphery, but she could see Ryder, who'd been knocked down like her. She tried to scream, but the ruemin on top of her were so heavy that all she could do was gasp.

The ruemin on Ryder must've found the button on his collar—the one that kept his helmet on—because it moved to press it, holding Ryder's arms down with its legs. When Ryder's helmet retracted, it let out a throaty cackle and raised its nails to his exposed face.

But it never came down on him. Before it could so much as move a finger, Pierce body-slammed into it, sending the ruemin flailing and clicking into a nearby pond, where it wrestled with Pierce in the shallow water. For a moment, Marina thought it had him submerged, but when Pierce's gun sounded and the ruemin's head jerked back, she let out a cry of relief.

Pierce rushed back to Ryder's side, but Ryder was already up and lunging toward the ruemin on top of Marina. He tackled one off her as violently as Pierce had, then jammed a dagger into its eye.

If the other ruemin screamed, Marina didn't hear them. Another burst of force, zapping and buzzing with electricity, sent three more flying off her. When she could finally move her head, she looked up, expecting to see Aeric.

She met Yolie's eyes instead.

Yolie stood with her hands out and legs planted wide, but before any of the ruemin could come at her, Neva jumped in front of her. Despite only having one good hand, she managed to generate force of her own. A lance of light shot from her palm, coming down on one of the ruemin so hard that its body popped like a bug under a shoe. Its entrails seeped from its gut, and the others paused long enough to hold their stomachs as though their organs had been exposed as well.

Marina turned onto her back, focusing on the few ruemin closest to her long enough to slit their throats. With a rapid movement of her finger, a good five or six collapsed, choking on the blood that poured from their necks. She wasn't sure if it was her dizziness or fear, but as they clawed at their throats, Ocot's bloody body flashed before her. And then the scouts—the middle-aged woman, the limping man—torn to pieces by ruemin.

It's on me.

She tried to pull herself up, but the forest was spinning so intensely that all she could see were patches of green and brown.

Her stamina might've been improving, but it wasn't perfect. Neva had overexerted herself too, and her injury wasn't helping. When a lone ruemin launched itself at them, however, Marina's vision returned with a jolt.

She wasn't sure what she was thinking, other than that the ruemin wouldn't kill her, because she threw herself toward Neva and Yolie. The three of them crashed to the ground, Marina shielding their bodies with her own and bracing herself for another attack.

It never came. The ruemin barely made it another step before light careened into it— far larger than Neva's. In an instant, Aeric had the ruemin on its back, and though he was yards away, he chopped its head from its body like Ryder had with his sword. When another hurtled toward them, Aeric sent shadows to its neck. Rapidly—so rapidly Marina barely registered it—the ruemin's head twisted to the side, and Marina was unsure if the *crunch* she heard was its vertebrae breaking or its appendage shattering. Whatever it was, it angered the others. Clicks and screeches followed cries of pain.

The ruemin were only going to keep coming. Marina rolled off Neva and Yolie, then grasped Neva by her shoulders. "Convey out," she demanded. "We have to leave. There's no stopping them."

Neva nodded, hoisting Yolie up. "Tolsea," she sputtered. "Go to Tolsea." Her gaze darted about, and Marina realized she was looking for others. "Only once," she breathed.

Marina knew immediately what she meant. She only had enough reserves to convey once, and then she'd be useless.

Pierce must've overheard because he began to shout, "Take him!"

This time, it took Marina a second to realize what Pierce was going on about. When she saw him wrench Ryder—who'd collapsed next to a pile of ruemin—off the forest floor, her heart all but stopped. Ryder's eyes fluttered, and he'd lost so much blood that Pierce had to drag him over to Neva.

"Take him!" Pierce repeated.

Neva wrapped her arms around Ryder's waist, then ordered Yolie to do the same.

"Lars..." Neva rasped.

"We'll find him," Pierce said quickly. His helmet muffled his voice. "Go!"

Neva was obviously determined to get Yolie out. When her eyes landed on Marina, all she said was: "Tolsea."

Before Marina could nod, the three of them were gone. As tempted as she was to worry whether they'd make it out of the forest and find the closest portal system, she knew it'd do little good to focus on that. Instead, she and Pierce sprinted to Aeric, who'd just killed another couple ruemin—and who was clearly beginning to lose his strength as well. Either he'd overheard them or he remembered what Neva had said earlier because he took off toward the largest group of people, Marina and Pierce in tow.

They had to step over bodies to get to them—some soldiers, most from the original group of survivors who'd now never make it out of this forest—and once they reached the crowd, Marina caught sight of Ismene. She clutched Pierce's bag to her chest, choking on a sob when Marina rushed toward her.

Before Marina could reach her, however, a ruemin leapt from one of the trees. She couldn't make out its target—not until its nails came into contact with Ismene's face.

A scream followed—not Ismene's, but Elta's. Ismene had already fainted by the time she hit the ground, but before the ruemin could bore into her, Aeric threw himself at it. He tackled it off her, then rammed it into the trunk of a fallen tree.

The ruemin shrieked but jumped back at Aeric. Strangely enough, it didn't try to slash at him with its nails or tear into him with its teeth. If anything, it tried to pin him to the ground. Had the ruemin been ordered not to kill Aeric too? Had Kieron meant what he said about wanting to see *both* of them again?

Either way, the ruemin's reluctance to harm Aeric made things easier for him. He wrapped his arms around its neck—right below its wildly clicking appendage—and twisted its head to the side. A *crack* sounded as the ruemin's neck broke.

Marina wasn't sure if he'd done it with magic or with his hands, but she didn't particularly care. She and Pierce stumbled over to Ismene, who lay curled around the bag, which was now writhing violently. Elta had knelt beside her and was running her hands across the gash on Ismene's face, but Ismene had been cut deep. The blood kept flowing, staining the forest floor red. It was a blessing, Marina thought, that she wasn't conscious.

Another blessing: the ruemin seemed to have let up a little, and though the soldiers still kept their weapons out, she wondered if perhaps the worst had passed.

"Can anyone convey?" Marina asked desperately.

She glanced at Elta again, who let out a whimper and said, "I...can't go more than a couple of paces."

Marina opened her mouth—*it's okay*, she wanted to say. *Ismene needs you. Focus on her—* but her mouth was dry. Luckily, whatever Elta was doing to Ismene's face seemed to work; the bleeding had stopped, at least for the time being.

Still, Elta froze when rustling sounded from above.

The soldiers immediately pointed their guns up, and the remaining group braced themselves. For one beat of silence, then another, they watched the trees, eyes trailing up the blackened trunks of still-standing monstrosities.

And then, leaping from the branches like they had from the Altus battlements, ruemin rained down on them.

The first shot that sounded didn't come from a soldier; it came from Lars, whose aim wasn't perfect, but precise enough to hit a ruemin in the shoulder. Screeches echoed about the forest, and more gunfire followed.

Wherever Lars had come from, Marina was grateful, but he couldn't do much with a gun. Nobody could. The redheaded soldier managed to take down a large group in one go, but when the ruemin nearby recovered, they set their sights on her. One sprang from a branch and landed on top of her, followed by another pack, and Marina didn't see the rest.

Everything was happening so quickly that she couldn't get her bearings straight. A few feet away, a man around Aeric's age hurled a measly bit of light at one of the ruemin, which barely stunned it. It took less than a second before the ruemin bore into him.

Aeric pulled Marina up. "We need to take as many as we can and *get out*."

He was right. Each of them could only convey once, just like Neva. They didn't have enough energy—or time—to come back.

Elta helped Ismene up, who clearly couldn't stand on her own. She came in and out of consciousness, eyes fluttering one moment, then rolling back into her head the next. Aeric grabbed the two of them, then some other soldiers, but he obviously wasn't going to leave before Marina.

Perhaps it was good that they didn't have much time to think about who to take because it would only make things harder. Marina reached out for Pierce, then shouted at Lars to wrap his arms around her. Lars lunged toward her, but before his hand could reach hers—before he could get so much as a few feet in front of her—a scaled body launched itself at him. Lars hit the ground, flailing as the ruemin's fangs sank into his chest.

Someone screamed. Maybe it was Lars. Maybe it was her. Marina couldn't tell. The forest was spinning again, this time slowly. Her vision was all over the place—blotches of green, brown, and red—but her hearing was fine, and Aeric's voice was loud and clear.

Go, he was saying. *Go. Leave him. He's gone.*

But Pierce had told Neva they'd find Lars. There'd been a promise in that—that they'd bring him with them.

It didn't matter. Only getting out mattered. Aeric was right. So Marina wrapped her arms around those nearest to her, holding Pierce the closest because if she lost him too, she might lose herself. People began to realize what was happening, and they started screaming. Begging. Pleading to be brought.

Aeric and Marina managed to grab hold of a couple of other survivors and soldiers, but at this point, conveying was going to take so much energy Marina wasn't sure either of them could take any more bodies.

"Go!" Aeric yelled.

The forest blurred. Clicks reverberated through the air—clicks and screams and tearing flesh—but Marina did as Aeric said. She conveyed as far as she could, determined to reach the mouth of the forest.

She almost got there. Her body gave out near the pond that had once bordered part of the Inber encampment, which meant they were close to the town line. Marina released her grip on Pierce and the others as she struggled to steady her breathing, but before she could wrap her arms around them again, a scaled body jumped from the underbrush.

Marina heard it—the clicking, the gunshot, the screech—before she saw the ruemin itself, but Pierce was quicker than she was. He was quicker than the ruemin too, and his bullet went through its neck before it could reach them. The ruemin screamed again, then launched itself into a series of broken wheezes. It clawed at its throat, where its bone-like appendage had been almost completely severed, and before it could regain its wits, Pierce shot it in the chest. The ruemin stumbled back, then crashed into the water.

It was dead before it landed, but it didn't float there limply. Instead, its body thrashed as another set of scales—more gray than black—broke through the surface of the water. Silence followed as the water rippled, then calmed, but Marina didn't give herself time to process any of it. Before another ruemin could come hurtling at them—or before whatever had pulled the dead ruemin under could resurface—she reached out for Pierce and the others, then tried to convey again.

Only once.

She couldn't go any farther—not in the state she was in. Conveying with another person was already far more taxing than conveying alone. Adding others, even a small number, was a recipe for disaster. She'd sent her nervous system into disarray, and when she tried to step forward, her legs buckled.

The group once hanging onto her caught her before she could fall, but it was Pierce who swung his arms around her waist and dragged her forward.

"The portal system is close," he said, or perhaps it was someone else; Marina's hearing was failing now too, and it waxed and waned with the rest of her senses.

She let Pierce take the lead. They reached a clearing—or, at least, she thought they did. The world was so jumbled that all Marina could see was the color of the grass and sky.

Blue and green, like Ryder's eyes. He'd made it...he'd made it, but Florin, Hollis, and Zora hadn't. And Lars...he hadn't made it either, along with so many others. Though her emotions were blunted, Marina still felt the hole in her chest—the one she'd felt after Cal had gone into that tunnel.

They weren't coming back.

In the distance, she thought she heard soldiers throwing commands at each other—at the survivors, who now couldn't have been more than ten in number—and though she wasn't sure where it was coming from, she thought she could hear Pierce's voice too.

"We're so close," he said. "C'mon, only a few more steps."

Maybe she was imagining it. But someone was swiping her wrist over a console, and when the air changed from humid to mild, she knew they were no longer in the South.

Wherever they were, the weather was pleasant. A gentle breeze like the one in Lewes caressed her cheeks, and when the ringing in Marina's ears came to a crescendo, the breeze lulled her to sleep.

CHAPTER 33
Enemies of the Realm

This sleep was different—dreamless—and when Marina woke, the air smelled of oil and dust. It took her a few moments to realize she was lying on a pile of folded fabric instead of a bed, already soiled from the blood and dirt on her body.

Somewhere very far away, she could hear music. A guitar. Whoever was playing knew Fleetwood Mac songs. When they began to pick the chords to "Landslide," she knew the music wasn't coming from a distant place at all, but from her own head. She wasn't sure how long it took her surroundings to sharpen, but she refused to move until it did. When the world stopped spinning, she rolled onto her side, eyes trailing across a concrete floor. A story above, humming machinery interrupted the music in her head, but the ceiling was so thick she wasn't sure if she was imagining that too.

No less than a second after she'd pushed herself up, a hand wrapped around her arm, keeping her steady. It took Marina longer than she'd expected to locate the person beside her, but it seemed she'd lost all emotion; when she met Pierce's eyes, she didn't react.

They'd obviously made it to Tolsea, but she didn't care. They must've found someone Neva knew too—probably someone who'd worked as a merchant, like her. What else could this place be if not a textile mill? Rows of empty looms and metal machines stretched out across the floor. Every so often, one would creak, as though it were begging to be used.

Marina hadn't expected *that* to bring her emotions back, but she supposed something had to. Those untouched machines would probably stay in this basement forever, never fulfilling their purpose. When she began to cry, Pierce hugged her.

"We're safe," he said. "It's okay."

She didn't respond to that. Instead, her gaze flitted over to a pile of fabric at the other end of the room, where Neva and Yolie lay sleeping. Even through her tears, Marina could see Neva's face—wet from tears of her own. She knew about Lars, no doubt. Now, she had to grieve him, alongside hundreds of others.

The pain in the air was unbearable. To distract from it, Marina tried to take in the rest of the room, focusing on what she saw instead of what she felt.

There was a fair amount of space, but not much privacy. Curtains hung from portions of the ceiling, but other than that, the space was wide open. A few soldiers stood at grime-coated workbenches, taking inventory of weapons, and nearby, a small group sat in a circle, eating. They spoke in whispers, as though they were worried the machines running upstairs wouldn't drown out their voices.

On the wall across from the workbenches, several mats had been laid out—a person on each of them. Most looked pretty bad; bandages covered faces and limbs, and they moaned as they fell in and out of sleep. When Marina saw Ismene, who was one of the few wounded who was actually awake, she figured each of these people must've been a victim of the ruemin attack.

Except Ryder. His wounds had come from Altus—perhaps from Safira herself. He lay on a mat next to Ismene, his breathing labored but consistent. Every so often, Ismene would peer at him, as though she was worried his pulse would stop. Elta sat beside them; she'd check on Ryder too, but her attention seemed just as taken up by the others—Neva included, though her wrist didn't look as bent as it had earlier.

Was she the only healer who had survived? It sure seemed like it. Dark circles lined her eyes, but she was meticulous about making the rounds and checking up on each of the wounded. Every so often, she'd kneel down and peer into a bag beside Ismene as well.

Mindlessly, Marina's hands flitted to the pockets of her coat, searching for the peppermint leaves. They were still there, but they'd dried out, and when she went to touch them, they crumbled. She scooped what little she could from the insides of her pockets, then stared at the dried, broken pieces that clung to her clammy fingers.

When Pierce said something, Marina shook the fragments from her hands and shifted her gaze to him. He looked at her for a moment, then repeated himself.

"Ryder...brought back Brenna's ring," he whispered. "It's with us."

Marina blinked at him. When the realization hit her, it did so in waves, rushing through her veins and bubbling at her mouth in gasps.

And yet, Pierce didn't seem as relieved. His face contorted, and he ran his hands across it as though he hoped that would stop his tears. "It was Florin...he's the reason," Pierce said. "He's the reason we have Brenna's ring and they don't—the reason Ryder came back at all. Ryder said it himself. Hollis and Zora were dead, and Safira was closing in on them...so Florin gave Ryder the ring, then held off the soldiers and Safira by himself. He gave Ryder enough time to get out."

He couldn't control his tears now, and the story came pouring out alongside them. The mission had gone smoothly in the beginning—so smoothly that Florin, Ryder, Hollis, and Zora had managed to infiltrate the palace grounds within an hour of their arrival in Altus. But they'd never reached the inside; Safira had sent out drones before they could. The drones couldn't identify glamours, but they were equipped with thermal cameras that also registered body mass, composition, and a slew of other factors. As useful as glamours were, they could only conceal physical matter, not get rid of it entirely. And when it came to things like bodies, the heat they emitted could give them away. Unsurprisingly, Florin had expected this and had cautioned the group to avoid the drones, even if it meant taking alternate routes to get into the palace.

The trouble was, Safira had expected *that*. Unbeknownst to them, she'd prepared to use the drones strategically—to corral them into a place where they could be easily attacked. That was when the guards and ruemin were sent out, and Safira had followed suit. She'd detected the glamour itself within minutes, taking out Hollis and Zora before setting her sights on Florin and Ryder.

Hollis and Zora had put up a good fight, but they weren't nearly as strong as Safira and all the soldiers she had on her side. In the end, neither was Florin. But Ryder seemed to believe that Florin knew he wouldn't be returning to the South, and he gave Ryder two things before he died: Brenna's ring and time to escape. How exactly Florin had done it, Pierce didn't know, but it had worked, and Ryder made it back in time to realize the ruemin had been sent in to target the remaining survivors. Despite having suffered severe injuries in Altus, he'd still scrambled to warn them and help fight.

"They're heroes," Pierce croaked. "They're heroes, and it still doesn't matter, because I'll never see Florin again."

He began to cry harder, and since Marina could think of nothing else to do, she leaned forward and hugged Pierce. He rested his head on her shoulder, his sobs dying down as he whispered, "You need a shower." When Marina pulled back, Pierce chuckled tearfully. "You smell like blood and dirt."

She didn't have the energy to respond to that. Plus, she figured he was right—grime coated her hands, and she knew her face wasn't any better—so she let Pierce lead her to showers at the far end of the basement. Her body was still weak from conveying so many people, but luckily, she didn't have to walk for long. The basement itself wasn't much more than a wide hall interspersed with columns and those depressing, unused machines, and though the bathrooms and showers were neither large nor luxurious, they offered privacy and running water. Marina imagined they used to be used for worker hygiene, or perhaps safety purposes. Whatever the reason, running water was a solace she tried to cling to.

Marina couldn't muster the energy to cry as she washed, so she focused on wiping the dirt off her skin. That was all she could do. Take one step forward, then another—go through the motions and pray one of them would matter.

As she stood beneath the showerhead, she thought of redwoods—the kind that had formed Florin's essence. Tall and strong, but gentle too. She tried to close her eyes and picture them, but stopped when she began to see the smoke of Safira's essence, edging in and smothering the trees.

Florin was gone, along with Hollis, Zora, Lars, and so many others. As horrible as Marina felt when she considered the silver linings, she couldn't ignore her relief about Brenna's ring. Florin hadn't just given Ryder a chance; he'd given them *all* one. That was cause enough to be relieved, even if it felt like an inapt emotion. They'd lost, perhaps, but they hadn't lost everything.

Pierce found her a fresh set of clothes and something to eat, which she thanked him for, though her gratitude felt useless. No number of thank-yous, apologies, or tears could bring Florin back. Next to Tover, Florin had been the nearest thing to a father Pierce had ever had. He'd been Aeric's friend too—or, at least, he'd been closer to Aeric than Aeric let most people get.

Aeric...where was he? When Marina asked Pierce, he pointed to the far corner of the room, where the majority of the curtains had been set up to section off sleeping spaces. Most were open, revealing rows of chintz and velvet people had arranged into beds, but the one at the far end had been drawn.

"He's going to need time," Pierce said softly. "Neva too."

Marina glanced over at Neva, whose brow furrowed as she slept. She couldn't imagine the hell Neva was experiencing. This morning, she'd had a home and hundreds of people to fill it. She'd had Lars. Which made Marina feel even more callous when she whispered, "I don't think we have time."

Pierce pursed his lips but didn't respond. He knew she was right. How long could they hide out here before Kieron found them? The fact that they still had Brenna's ring likely made him more determined, and this time, they didn't have a glamoured compound and a slew of soldiers to protect them.

Marina lowered her voice further when she asked, "What happened before the bombs went off? Aeric was thanking you in the forest."

Pierce's chin quivered, and he took great pains to steady it before saying, "I wouldn't have noticed if I hadn't been down there...if I hadn't gone with Yolie while she glamoured."

Marina stared at him for a moment, but Pierce didn't wait for her to ask anything else

—not like she'd expected him to.

Kieron's soldiers had likely placed the bombs right after Aeric and Marina had left Inber. But they obviously hadn't wanted to detonate them until Aeric and Marina were in Lewes—and more importantly, until Florin, Ryder, Hollis, and Zora were in Altus. If Florin had caught wind of what was happening—if the bombs had gone off before they'd reached the palace and he'd been alerted by Neva or Lars, or any number of potential survivors—he would've known an attack was waiting for them too, and he would've turned around before Safira could apprehend them.

So Kieron's soldiers did what Altus in general seemed to be quite good at: they waited. But come late morning, the glamouring began, and Pierce had gone down with Yolie, Neva, Elta, and the rest.

It had been little things, Pierce said, that tipped him off. Apparently, certain bombs had a smell—scarcely noticeable to someone untrained, but acrid enough to set off alarm bells in a soldier. It'd been part of Pierce's training back in Altus, and Tover had gone the extra mile to ensure his son remembered how to identify military-grade ones. More than that, the animals were acting strange.

"Birds were scattering," Pierce said. "My dad used to tell me animals can sense danger before we do; they're some of the best alarm bells. So when birds started leaving trees, and when the air started smelling like chemicals...I knew something was wrong."

He wouldn't have noticed if he'd been up in the compound, he admitted. Glamouring took place just above the ground—high enough to avoid leaving traces of magic on the forest floor, but low enough to meticulously cloak any telltale shadows or markers that could signal the compound's presence.

Pierce seemed to think the bombs must've been positioned roughly around that area. Since the compound was so expansive, the explosive yield would've needed more lateral than vertical force to take the entire thing down. Of course, he'd never seen the actual bombs. He'd gotten Yolie, Neva, Elta, and the other sorcerers to the ground as quickly as possible. Elta had called the technicians, hoping they'd trigger the alarms, while Neva and Pierce had called Lars and Ismene—and as many others as they could.

"Lars and Ismene were among those who got a head start," Pierce said. His voice had grown ragged, but he pushed on. "By the time the technicians triggered the alarms, it was too late. Everything happened so fast, and most people couldn't reach the elevators before the bombs went off."

And it still hadn't mattered—not for Lars and the other victims of the ruemin. But that had been Kieron's intention. Take the majority out first, leave the rest for the ruemin.

For a moment, all Marina could think of was how good it would feel to kill Kieron. If she and Aeric left now, maybe they could get into Altus—slaughtering Kieron's soldiers until there was no one left to protect him. And then they'd slaughter Kieron too. The rage that filled her was so wild that for a moment, Marina wondered if it was possible. It was freeing to bask in the impulse, but it was just that: an impulse—one that flitted away when Pierce spoke again.

"Lars was right," he said. "The compound wasn't made to be a military facility like the Delve. It was only made to hide people. And it would've continued hiding them, if..."

His voice trailed off, and Marina didn't urge him to finish. She knew what he'd say—what he was thinking. She was thinking it too. Everyone probably was.

Barely two seasons. That was how long it had been since the Delve had arrived in Candens Inlet—since Neva had let them in, though Marina knew she hadn't wanted to. Two seasons before a sanctuary that had survived twelve dead years came crashing down. All because Kieron had tracked the *Delve's* scouts.

What would she say to Neva when she woke? Apologies would mean nothing. Neva probably hated them. And perhaps she should. Her goodwill had been repaid with hundreds of her people dead—buried under trees and torn apart by ruemin.

The grief was palpable. It hid in the crannies of the room, staining the walls and bringing a heaviness to the air that the machines groaned under. Even those asleep felt it.

Ismene had dozed off by the time Marina and Pierce approached Elta, but like everyone else in the room, she, too, didn't sleep soundly. Stitches ran from her right eyebrow to her left cheek, and when she moved, she uttered labored breaths.

When Elta saw them, Marina braced herself—for anger, or tears, or silence. But Elta only rushed over to Marina and pulled her into a hug, which was almost worse because it pushed Marina closer to breaking down again.

She held her tears in, and although her lips quivered when she spoke, she kept her voice steady. "I'm so sorry," she whispered.

Elta only nodded, then looked to Ismene. "The scar will be minor," she said gently. "It doesn't look like it now, but soon enough, it'll barely be noticeable. She was up and talking a few minutes ago, which is a good sign."

"What about Ryder?"

"He hasn't woken up much," Elta said. "He took a falchion to the leg and a bullet to the chest, but his armor did its job. He has a bruised lung and a nasty cut, but not as dangerous as it might've been without protection. I'll be able to heal it."

Marina glanced at the others on the mats, all asleep. "What about them?"

"Some will be all right." Elta paused, and though Marina could tell it pained her, she added, "Some have a hard night ahead."

Marina forced her chin to steady when it started to tremble. Before she could respond, however, the bag beside Ismene—the one Elta had been peering into—moved.

Hadn't that been the bag Pierce carried back at Candens Inlet?

"What *is* that?" she asked.

Despite everything, Pierce managed a trembling smile. When he bent down and opened the flap, a gray paw swiped at him.

"He's a little spooked," Pierce said, "but he came out in one piece." He glanced at Ismene. "Guess she saw him before she reached the elevators—grabbed the poor thing and stuffed him in a bag."

Marina's eyes widened. Getting out of the wetlands alive had already been a miracle. Leave it to Ismene to go out of her way to save Ash. "Do the others know?"

"They're preoccupied, and Ash refuses to come out of the bag, so...not yet."

A smile tugged at Marina's lips. It was fleeting and worn, but she savored it. "Think Neva's contacts will be okay with a cat staying here?"

"They have too much on their minds right now to worry about Ash," Pierce said, then lowered his voice. "They're a family—they own the textile mill. Neva almost had to beg them to harbor us. Honestly, I think they only agreed because they were scared Aeric would kill them if they didn't." He tried to laugh but failed. "Either way, they said they could only risk a few nights, and then we'd have to leave."

Marina's stomach dropped. "Where would we go?"

Both Pierce and Elta were silent. Eventually, Elta said, "Wherever Neva thinks is best. She knows a few places, I think. Maybe some other people who might help us."

She didn't sound sure—not in the slightest.

"That's life for enemies of the realm," Pierce said. "Can't stay in one place too long."

Marina raised her eyebrows. "Enemies of the realm?"

"Kieron's words. It's what he's telling civilians, at least." Pierce tried to scoff, but it came out more like a whimper. Even once he'd cleared his throat, his voice wobbled. "Us and anyone who helps. Which means while we're here, we're putting a family in danger."

At this point, Marina's stomach couldn't sink any lower, and nothing she'd say would make much of a difference anyway. She looked back at the drawn curtain in the corner of the room, and Pierce noticed.

"I don't think Aeric's in the headspace to be a leader right now," he said.

Marina bit her lip. "Think he'll kill me if I try to talk to him?"

"Give him the night. But after that, you should try." Pierce paused, then gave Marina a tight-lipped smile. "Call me crazy, but you might be the only person he'll respond to."

CHAPTER 34
Lost Causes

The night took three people. Elta didn't seem surprised when she checked their pulses the next morning, but she still couldn't hold back her tears when she reported the deaths to Neva and Aeric.

It was the first time since the Candens Inlet massacre that Marina had seen Aeric—when he emerged from behind the curtain to get rid of the dead. It was a messy process, and this time, Marina decided not to watch.

There were now barely over a dozen survivors. Marina tried to remind herself that if it hadn't been for Pierce, there would be even fewer, and if it hadn't been for Florin, perhaps Ryder wouldn't be here either. But looking on the bright side felt impossible, and more than that, foolish. There was very little to be optimistic about. But Brenna's ring was still with them, which meant hope remained. They couldn't let it go to waste. So when Aeric hadn't reemerged by early afternoon, Marina decided to go to him instead.

Knocking on a curtain felt stupid, but she did it anyway. She did it again when he didn't answer. After the third time, she figured he'd have shooed her away already if he didn't want her there, so she cracked open the curtain and stepped inside.

Aeric sat on a bow-backed chair, slumped forward so that his forearms rested on his legs and his hands were out in front of him. He held something golden-brown that shined in the minimal light.

"Is that...?" Marina stopped herself before she could ask the worst question possible.

Aeric's fingers curled around the lock of Evren's hair. "What do you want?"

He was really straining to hold on to his icy mask, but he should've known at this point that she wouldn't have cared either way. It didn't work on her like it used to. Though her throat tightened, Marina refused to succumb to tears. Instead, she straightened and said, "We can still move forward with the plan, can't we? It just...might look different."

Aeric gave her a look, then put the lock of hair into his pocket. "Take a look out there and tell me how eager you think Neva will be to find volunteers this time."

"I could be a volunteer. So could Pierce." Though Aeric shook his head, Marina pressed on. "People will rally. We have to. We don't have time—"

"Leave, Marina. We'll discuss this later."

Heat flushed through her. She spun around and slipped past the curtain, then found a chair and dragged it across the concrete so loudly she knew heads were turning. She didn't care. She continued dragging it—pressing on even though she was still weak and the chair felt ridiculously heavy—until she was back in front of Aeric. She positioned the chair in front of his, closed the curtain again, then sat down across from him and crossed her arms.

Aeric gave her a cold look. "This isn't the time to push me. You and I are weak from conveying so many people, and the others are equally as worn down—some even worse. *Everyone* needs time. We'll discuss this—"

"No," Marina interrupted. "We don't have time to discuss this later. We only have now. You could be invisible in the Delve and at Candens Inlet, but not here." She paused, searching for the right words. There weren't any. "There's no other option. We have to continue with Florin's plan."

Aeric remained silent. It wasn't his usual, calculated silence, though. It was empty.

"We'll kill him," she said. "We'll kill Kieron for doing what he did. We'll kill Vaughn and Safira too, after we get rid of the ruemin. Florin's plan can *still* work."

Spasms sent twitches to Marina's fingers, but she stopped herself before trying to persuade him again. Instead, she whispered, "Are you okay?"

She'd never asked him that before—never considered he'd *want* to be asked. But when his eyes met hers, she wondered if everyone else had always assumed the same thing.

The question seemed to catch Aeric off guard. After a moment's thought, all he said was, "If we don't succeed, you should know that you've already done so much for Elsudra. Our Keepers would have been proud of you."

Her heart sank. "Don't say that. We *have* to try. I'm still willing and able to help, just like I promised the Keepers. But I can't do it on my own. Maybe the two of us could face Kieron and focus on the ruemin after, or—"

"I don't know if I could."

"You could. You..." Marina stopped herself. He hadn't meant he didn't know if he was capable of facing Kieron; he'd meant he wasn't sure he could bring himself to kill him.

"You once told me that you felt like a marionette," Aeric said, "but nobody has ever been more of a marionette than I. Even now, I crumble under Kieron's games, and he knows it. Why do you think the idea of taking the Omnia from you scared me so much?"

"But you left him. You cut your strings. You're not his puppet anymore."

"It's not that simple."

Marina nodded. "I know," she whispered. Though she figured it would be similarly unhelpful, she added, "I'm so sorry about Florin."

Aeric's eyes flitted to his hands, as though he half expected to see the lock of Evren's hair. When he didn't, he stared at his palms absently.

"We were already working with scant resources back at Candens Inlet," Aeric said. "We had minimal technology and very little time. We were in a beleaguered situation then...we're in an even worse one now. Portals are being guarded around the clock by soldiers, and soon, we'll run out of hiding places in the city. Tolsea may be large, but it isn't infinite, and neither are Neva's contacts."

"If it's inevitable that they're going to close in on us, then it means we need to work faster," Marina said desperately. "We need to try again, for Florin and everyone else. I meant what I said about volunteering. I could go to Altus." Though her stomach dropped at the thought, she pushed on. "Even if we could find a way out of the city, we could—"

"All I can think about is keeping you and the Omnia away from Kieron," Aeric said. "Bringing you to Altus would so much as put you in front of him. That's not an option."

"Do we have others?" This time, when Aeric didn't respond, Marina reached out and grasped his wrist. "I'm not going to stop fighting until this is over," she said. "I know our chances don't look good, and I know that even if they did, the world after is just as scary."

She could sense it meant something to Aeric—his demeanor changed, even if subtly.

"It's scary to me too," she continued. "Victory, defeat...all of it. I don't know where I'm headed, other than forward. But I can't stop now. We can't stop. Please, move forward with me. I can't do this without you."

Aeric looked up at the ceiling, his eyes lingering on the cement. When he nodded, he didn't lower them.

✄

That evening, Ryder woke long enough to eat something and scowl at Ash, who'd grown comfortable enough to emerge from the bag and decided to lay at Ryder's feet. Pierce also lingered nearby, but Ryder didn't turn him away.

At some point, Marina knew she should speak to Neva too, but Neva wasn't in the basement with them. Elta said she'd gone above to speak with the family who owned the mill. Though it was clear she was trying to hide it, she couldn't conceal her anxiousness.

But it was Yolie who worried Marina most. She hadn't moved from her pile of fabric, and when she wasn't sleeping, she'd sit with her knees to her chest and her head pressed into the crook of her arm. Marina wanted to check on her, but Aeric had finally emerged from the curtain—permanently, it seemed—and started speaking with the few soldiers still around. She couldn't help herself as she eavesdropped on their discussions about obtaining more supplies, finding portal systems and alternate routes out of Tolsea, and the presence of a few smaller towns nearby that might not have as many soldiers present. But Kieron's soldiers were bound to be around every corner, and their group was in no position to evade or confront them if it came down to it. Tolsea had its fair share of backroads that led out of the city, but those were closer to the outskirts—at least, that's what the soldiers were saying. Just when they'd started to discuss how long it would take before they'd be ready to risk traveling that far, Neva reentered the basement, paler than usual.

Aeric noticed immediately. He watched Neva as she whispered something to Elta, and his eyes remained on her as she approached the table he and the soldiers sat at. Marina crossed the room in seconds, heart in her throat, but Neva didn't so much as glance at her when she said, "We need to leave by dawn tomorrow."

One of the soldiers—Marina heard someone refer to him as Ivo—cursed.

"Tolsea got an influx of soldiers this afternoon," Neva continued. Her voice was hoarse and broken. "And there's talk in the city that she will be coming too. Nobody knows when, other than soon. Tonight, maybe."

She? Marina furrowed her brows, but her heart skipped a beat anyway. Why did she have a horrible feeling that "she" meant...

"Safira will turn every building inside out until she finds us," Neva whispered. She shot a look at Yolie to make sure she wasn't listening. "If she was sent here, it means they must know we're in the city, or at least have suspicions."

"How?" Marina said, half to herself, half to Neva. "The portals in Inber were vacant when we left through them, weren't they? And we got here so quickly..."

"His soldiers are everywhere," Neva said. Tears lined her eyes, and her voice shook. "If they didn't see us, then civilians might've."

Ivo shook his head but didn't seem to dwell on it for long. He motioned for people to start packing, and once the other soldiers had left the table, Aeric said, "There's no possibility we can stay a little longer?"

It was obvious he only asked out of desperation. But desperation ran amok down here; it hung in the air, as thick as the grief.

Neva didn't react well to it. Her jaw pulsed as she wiped at her eyes with her good hand. "No. There's no possibility. I've twisted myself in knots making exceptions for all of you, and this is where it's gotten me and my people."

When she glanced around the room, she could no longer hold back her tears. She threw a withering glare in Aeric and Marina's direction, then hissed, "I'm taking no more requests. Not when your last one got four hundred Elsudrans killed. And Lars…" Neva's chin shook violently, but she steadied it long enough to say, "I've half a mind to leave with the rest of my people, who have a much better chance blending in than the Sorcerer of the Court and a Keeper."

She couldn't even refer to them by name now, apparently. Though Marina knew Neva wasn't thinking clearly, she couldn't help but bristle.

Aeric, too, had never been one to respond well to anger, even if Neva's made sense.

"We have soldiers," he said coldly. "From the *Delve*."

"You can take them," Neva said. "I've no doubt you'll get them killed too."

Marina had no idea who she was talking to—Aeric, probably, though Marina couldn't help but feel like some of it was directed toward her. Regardless, Elta must've overheard, because she quickly approached Neva and put a hand on her shoulder.

"We'll pack, Neva," she said. "All of us. We need this whole group to survive."

"Given the track record, this whole group *won't* survive." Neva closed her eyes, lips pinched as she breathed. "I should never have acquiesced to your demands. I should've done what I knew would help keep my people safe." When she opened her eyes, she narrowed them at Marina and Aeric. "But perhaps I was as ill-suited to be my people's leader as you two have been in your roles."

Marina's head and body went silent. *Lost causes,* Kieron had called them.

Something flared up in Aeric's eyes—something Marina couldn't pinpoint. It wasn't cold, the way so much of his anger usually was. If anything, it burned.

"I will not have you blame Marina for the failings of plans she did not spearhead," Aeric said, his voice low.

"You're right," Neva said. "If I blame anyone, it should be you, Aeric. Because if there's anyone here who has failed in irreversible, unforgivable ways, it is you."

The insult hurt Marina more than the one Neva had directed at her. She looked to Aeric, who she expected to say something back—something that would cut Neva even deeper, as was his way. But he only nodded at Neva as she left. A silent acknowledgment, Marina supposed, that he agreed.

CHAPTER 35
No Room to Feel

Marina never met the family who'd let them stay two nights in their mill. In a way, she wondered if that was best. She wouldn't have known what to say to them anyway—to thank them or apologize. Words weren't coming to her like they usually did, so she stayed silent as they left the mill's basement and ventured into the brisk city air.

They left when it was still dark out, an hour or so before sunrise, breaking into smaller groups that would draw less attention. Even then, Aeric glamoured the groups before they departed—each one comprised of a few people linking their arms together to keep them moving at a similar pace within the glamour. Marina had tried to watch him while he worked, and though her head was all over the place, she'd still managed to pick up on some of his techniques. They'd be good to know come the day she'd have to glamour living things instead of simple objects.

Actually *being* glamoured felt like being wrapped in a curtain of air, shadows, and light. If a sorcerer was good enough, the living things they glamoured could move freely, given that they were careful enough and didn't purposely try to break through it. Thankfully, Aeric was more than good enough. Marina had suggested using shields too—if only to provide additional layers of protection—only to learn that shields were even more finicky to use when moving for extended periods of time. Unlike light and shadows, which could be gently bent, hard walls of air were inflexible.

Even if shields had been feasible, she wouldn't have been able to help. Before they left the mill's basement, Aeric had her put on diminution cuffs. According to Aeric, it hadn't been as necessary that she wore them in the textile mill's basement since it had been underground and insulated. When it came to concealing magical energy, that was about as effective as the cuffs themselves. But now they were at ground level, and if ruemin were nearby, the cuffs would prevent them from detecting anything. Marina couldn't argue with Aeric's logic, but she still hated wearing them.

She tried to focus on the positives to keep herself from spiraling. There weren't many. At the very least, Neva's anger seemed to have faded. If anything, she'd decided to focus solely on getting them to the next location, and if she truly did intend to split up the group, she wasn't going to do so now. Of course, Marina didn't think that was really her intention, and Elta seemed relieved they had soldiers with them, especially since they needed people to help carry the wounded.

Neva had given them directions to a warehouse she hoped they could use; any other potential hideaways were too far to reach in a single go, especially with the wounded. The warehouse she spoke of was in the middle of the city and not far from the textile mill, which made it a good option for a temporary stay. But given the quality of Aeric's glamours, they couldn't see or follow Neva, which meant they only had her word to rely on. Even with Elta's insistence last night that everyone stay together, Marina couldn't help but feel paranoid. If Neva wanted to, she could take off now with Yolie and the others, and that warehouse she'd mentioned might turn out to be nonexistent.

Aeric seemed to have thought of that too. There were three groups total: his, Elta's, and Neva's, and Aeric made it a point to mix those in each group so that Neva couldn't go anywhere without taking people from the Delve, and vice versa.

They stuck to alleyways, pausing every time they heard a noise, no matter how distant. Sometimes, Marina swore she heard voices, but she couldn't be sure. The sound the breeze made as it skirted over awnings and around corners was terribly lifelike, especially when her senses were heightened.

But they kept walking—kept pushing forward until they reached the warehouse Neva had described. Marina could sense Aeric's relief, even if she couldn't see him, as they slipped inside through a backdoor that had been poorly boarded up.

The warehouse didn't belong to anyone—not anymore, at least. After Aeric removed everyone's glamours, he got to work on the warehouse itself, concealing any signs of their presence as best he could. And because Marina could think of nothing else to do and no other ways to help, she watched. Once Aeric finished, he had Marina help him make the finishing touches on a few glamours. The city streets had been devoid of ruemin, which meant she didn't need to wear the cuffs—at least for the time being.

It didn't feel like training, even if Marina knew it was. Aeric was so wrung out he could barely offer remarks on her progress or ways to improve, and Marina felt much too sick to solicit them. The sinking feeling in her gut worsened when she learned that Neva had initially expected to find someone here—an old colleague she'd worked with. He'd been a merchant like her, and he'd had an inclined son.

They hadn't come to Candens Inlet, and Neva had no idea if they'd found sanctuary somewhere else or if they'd been killed. If there was any solace to be found, it was that Neva knew the warehouse well. Amidst broken pallets and decaying boxes, she uncovered what looked like a metal jar with a glass top. Marina watched her as she flipped a few switches on it, then set it on a fold-out chair.

It flickered for a few moments, and the glass began to emit a weak light that resembled a screen. Neva was the only one watching it—Aeric was more concerned with scouring the warehouse for holes in the walls or entrances, and everyone else was busy rummaging through supplies. Yolie had curled up in a nearby corner next to Ismene, who whispered to Elta as she laid out mats for the wounded.

Cautiously, Marina approached Neva. When Neva didn't glare at her, she said, "Is that a projector?"

Neva nodded. "We can get better news through it than we can through our vocos. I'm hoping the city updates civilians about military activity so we know when Safira arrives... if she hasn't already."

Marina knelt beside Neva. The text on the screen carried a shine, similar to the books that were built to be read in any language. Whatever channel Neva had it on was just intermittent updates, but none of them mentioned anything other than portal system shutdowns and a newly imposed curfew.

"They might omit specific information entirely," Neva said after a few moments. "Especially if they think we're monitoring the news." She rubbed her hands down her face. "Before Kieron, individual cities were in charge of the news they broadcasted. Now, Altus is. Back when Safira came to Sal, we didn't know until well after she started conducting her...business."

Neva didn't need to go into detail. Safira's business involved death—and few were better at it than her.

"I'm so sorry, Neva," Marina whispered. "I know it doesn't mean anything now, but I'm so, so sorry. We never intended—"

"I know you didn't." Neva's jaw tightened, and she squeezed her eyes shut—probably to try to stifle the tears. "What I said yesterday about you...I said it out of anger. And what I said about Aeric—"

"Was correct."

Marina shifted to face Aeric, who'd come up behind them and watched the screen with glazed eyes.

Neva didn't respond to that—she didn't try to refute it. She only pursed her lips and stood. Marina did too.

"I *have* failed in irreversible, unforgivable ways," Aeric continued, his voice low and unsteady. "And you are not the one who needs to apologize." His lips trembled, but he stilled them when he said, "I'm sorry, Neva—for everything. For Lars. For your people. For all of this." He turned to Marina. "And I'm sorry to you too. I could live my whole life making amends, and it would never be enough."

Marina blinked at him. She knew it was hard for Aeric to apologize, but this wasn't discomfort—this was despair. And it nearly broke Marina to see it.

"I don't have room to hold a grudge," Neva said. "I have no room to feel anything clearly because all I can think about is keeping her safe." She tilted her head at Yolie, who was resting her head on Ismene's lap. "A few days ago, she was as safe as she could be, considering. Now she's hiding in Tolsea like we did in Sal, knowing the woman who killed her brother might kill her too." She looked up at the support beams on the ceiling—another attempt to stop her tears, Marina supposed—then braved making eye contact with Aeric again. "I know you didn't intend for that. I know you'd take back all the mistakes you've made if you could. But that doesn't make forgiveness any easier."

"You don't need to give it," Aeric said.

For a long, drawn-out moment, Neva was silent. Finally, she said, "We'll focus on survival. All of us. And if we make it through, perhaps apologies won't feel so trivial."

She knelt back down, eyes glued to the screen, and Aeric gave Marina no more than a sidelong glance as he moved back toward the soldiers. Since she didn't know where else to go, Marina settled down next to Ismene and Yolie, then leaned her head against the wall.

"He...apologized," Ismene said. "To you and Neva."

Marina nodded, and only then did she notice the askance look on Ismene's face. Immediately, she knew where it came from.

When Ismene realized she wasn't doing a good job hiding her emotions, she quickly said, "It doesn't matter. Like Neva said...apologies are trivial. We need to survive first."

"That doesn't mean you don't deserve one," Marina replied.

Ismene forced a smile, then squeezed Marina's arm. "There are more important things." She muttered something about wanting to help Elta with the wounded, then gently moved Yolie's head off her lap and made her way over to the mats where Elta was helping Ryder walk. Pierce lingered a few paces away, Ash in his arms.

Her stomach couldn't sink any lower at the moment, but Marina didn't focus on her own emotions. Instead, she tapped Yolie on her head and whispered, "How are you?"

Yolie only shrugged. "Okay."

"You don't have to lie."

Yolie sat up, then gingerly reached for an old satchel, which she pulled toward her. She opened it, then dumped the contents into her lap.

Ronan's anteactus—or, at least, what was left of it. Though the lens didn't look much different than usual, the rest of the device was in such a sorry state that if Marina hadn't known about Ronan's anteactus to begin with, it might've taken her a while to realize what it was. Cracks ran up the brass, and whatever internal mechanisms and magic it had relied on clearly wouldn't work again.

"I don't remember when it happened," Yolie whispered. A choked sound bubbled at her mouth. "Probably...probably while we were escaping. Or when the ruemin came."

Marina's chest grew heavy. "Oh, Yolie," she said. "I'm so sorry."

Ronan's anteactus, her boots...Kieron's troops had destroyed lives *and* memories in that forest. She had a feeling that would be an additional victory for him. Her heart quickened, so intensely that she could feel it pound in her head as well as her chest. But she needed the reminder—the reminder that they were still alive, and Kieron hadn't taken that from them yet.

She'd woken in this city groggy and defeated, which made the clarity she'd come to possess all the more surprising. Of all the times to break, she would've expected now. But she wasn't breaking. If anything, her breaths felt sharper, as though every fiber of her being was hell-bent on seeing this through. And Ronan's broken anteactus added yet another drop of fuel to this ever-burning fire.

Tears fell from Yolie's eyes onto her lap. "When I was sad, Ronan used to tell me to talk to him about it. He said if I shared my sadness with him, it wouldn't hurt so much. But now he's gone, and so are his memories...and what he did won't matter if Neva and I die here."

Marina opened her mouth, then closed it. She wanted to tell Yolie they wouldn't—that they'd all make it out of this and no more lives would be lost—but she couldn't bring herself to. Instead, she scooted closer to Yolie and said, "You can share your sadness with me. I'm not Ronan, but maybe it'll help anyway."

Yolie thought on it for a moment. "The rules are we *both* have to share something. That's what Ronan would say. Otherwise, it's not really sharing."

Though Marina hesitated, she eventually nodded.

It got Yolie to perk up a little. "You first." When she extended her arm, she said, "You can do psychometry. Ronan couldn't."

She couldn't back out now—not when this seemed to be coaxing Yolie out of her shell. So Marina rested her hand atop Yolie's wrist and let her shields fall.

CHAPTER 36
Ronan

Yolie's essence didn't come with a temperature. Marina couldn't feel it the way she could feel Neva's, Aeric's, and Kieron's. But oh, she could *see* it.

The light of a thousand stars rushed into Marina's essence, glittering atop the water so wildly that it almost matched the light beneath her waves—the light of the Omnia, which seemed to flicker in response to Yolie's presence. Marina realized Yolie had never told her the form her spirit took, but even if she had, words wouldn't have done it justice. When the starlight dove beneath the water, it brightened, but it obeyed the flow of the current and let Marina choose what to show it.

She let Yolie see fragments of her life in Georgia and but a droplet of the storms she carried with her. When that rainy night in August flickered into view, she shrouded it in waves, blurring the memory just enough so Yolie would understand.

One day, one step, one breath at a time. She let Yolie hear those words too, hoping she'd find them useful. She showed Yolie bits and pieces of the Delve, then bits and pieces of Altus—trying her best to keep Safira out of the memories. Still, she didn't sugarcoat things, and she even showed Yolie glimpses of Exorsus. She could feel Yolie's spirit brighten with curiosity, but never did she try to see more than what Marina showed. When Marina finished, Yolie didn't remove her hand, but instead let Marina's waves rush forward and into *her* mind—into constellations as endless as Marina's sea, so bright she wasn't sure which memory to focus on.

But Yolie was equally adept at shielding as she was at psychometry, and she guided Marina expertly through walls of light and into a cobblestone alleyway.

They were in Sal. Though it was night in Yolie's memory, the outline of every building was swathed in a golden haze—as were Neva, Ronan, and Yolie herself. Neva stared at the ground, her brow furrowed and dotted with sweat.

It was the middle of the war, only a day after Safira had entered Sal. The awareness hit Marina in a gust, as did the panic—*Yolie's* panic. Neva had come to their house in the middle of the night, telling them they had to go and barely giving them enough time to pack their things. Every portal system was surrounded by Altus guards, so they wove through the city instead, attempting to reach the outskirts and head to the South on foot.

Ronan—who couldn't have been any older than sixteen, Marina thought—tightened his grip on Yolie's hand, his eyes darting about the shadows. Like all Elsudran cities, the streets in Sal were narrow—used solely as pedestrian walkways. It might've been easy to hide in the back alleys, but Altus soldiers were everywhere; they'd taken up every theater, communal lounge, and municipal building in the city.

Sal was similar to Lewes and Altus, Marina realized—or perhaps Yolie was, in some way, telling her. Like many cities near water, it had a higher number of inclined citizens, which made Kieron all the more eager to target it. They'd ridden the coattails of hope for too long, and now, it was clear Neva knew there were no other options. They had to flee. Which, of course, made their current predicament all the more harrowing.

Neva cursed through her teeth and put a shaking hand to her head. She was looking at bodies, Marina realized—two, to be precise, both dressed in Altus golden armor, palms branded with Kieron's sigil. The first lay in a slump, throat slit, but the other was barely recognizable; his head had been cleaved in two, and his skin hung from his face like peeling wallpaper. Yolie...*Yolie* had done that. She'd flayed him.

Yolie whimpered. *"He...he said he'd report us for breaking curfew. And then they'd find out what we can do."*

She'd made such a horrible mistake. The first guard had been killed by Neva in a way that didn't indicate magic, but the second made it clear someone inclined had done the deed. It had happened quickly. The guard had put in a call to Safira, and before he could finish his message, he was dead. Yolie couldn't bring herself to feel remorse—not when he was in this city to kill people like her and Neva. But the guards' vocos had trackers, which meant Safira already knew where they were.

Neva gestured wildly for Ronan and Yolie to start moving again, but they barely made it ten paces before voices brought them to a halt. They flitted down both sides of the alleyway, growing in tandem with echoes of boots—and the clicking of heels.

Marina could pinpoint that sound anywhere. It reverberated off buildings, and while Marina had no idea how Safira had arrived so quickly—she figured conveyance, but even then, she must've been *somewhat* nearby—she knew there was no way they could talk their way out of this. Neva knew it too. She cursed, her eyes darting about. The nearest shops were dark and locked, and nobody was stupid enough to let strangers into their home after curfew, so Neva took Ronan and Yolie by their arms, then conveyed to another alley. She didn't know where to go, and she could only convey so far without losing breath, but she didn't stop. She conveyed another three times—all short distances—transporting them from alley to alley until she found an abandoned shop, which she whisked them inside of.

It was a bakery—one Yolie knew. Her dad used to buy them treats from it on Double Moon. It had been owned by a nice elderly woman who'd had some minor talents in magic. Sometimes, she'd glamour pastries to entertain the kids.

She was gone now. Gone because of Safira—because of the soldiers in gold suits with burns on their palms. Pastries rotted in display cases, and tables had been broken.

They crouched beneath an opened window, trying to get an idea of where the voices and footsteps were coming from. Neva had obviously pushed herself beyond her limits; she was pale to the point of sickness, and her limbs shook. She couldn't convey them out of here—not in her state. The voices grew louder, and Marina wondered if every nearby alley had been infested with soldiers.

"I can try," Yolie whispered. "Or I could glamour us."

Neva shook her head. "Too risky. You haven't been taught conveyance, and you don't know how to glamour living things yet."

It wouldn't have mattered either way. Soldiers had already reached the alleyway near the bakery and begun shining their voco flashlights through every window.

"Just call her," one of them said. "She'll be able to detect anything we're missing. And if not, have the damned ruemin sweep the streets."

Another one laughed. "Or detonate lock bombs."

Neva cursed again under her breath. If Safira was on the lookout for magical energy, even glamours wouldn't protect them—if Yolie could make them at all. And if ruemin or lock bombs were used, they'd have even less of a chance.

Ronan must've known that because he was outside in an instant. He'd gotten up so quickly that Neva didn't notice until Yolie lunged forward.

Neva had her by her waist before she could reach the door.

"Don't," she hissed, then covered Yolie's mouth so she couldn't call for her brother.

The soldiers must've been nearby; Ronan's voice was loud when he said, "I did it."

The soldiers obviously hadn't seen where he'd come from, because one of them swore. "Sneak up on another group, boy, and you may get your head blown off."

Another soldier, his voice a stern growl, said, "Did what?"

Yolie squirmed again, but Neva didn't relax her grip. She tilted her head up, arms wrapped around Yolie, her lips moving without sound. A prayer, Marina realized.

"I killed those guards," Ronan said. *"They attacked me. I was defending myself."*

Silence followed. After a few moments, someone *else* said something—someone who'd just arrived, her heels clicking as she approached.

"You killed both of them?" Safira asked coldly. *"Why?"*

Marina couldn't see her—*Yolie* couldn't—but her voice was as distinctive as ever.

"It was self-defense," Ronan said. *"I swear it."*

Neva's prayer quickened. Marina tried to make out the words she was mouthing, but all she could glean was, *"Exorsus, please..."*

The clicking of Safira's heels grew louder. *"Why self-defense? Are you inclined?"*

"Only slightly," Ronan lied.

"Only slightly," Safira echoed. *"And yet, you were able to flay a grown man."*

"I've...I've never done anything like this before," Ronan said. *"And I'm exhausted...I couldn't do it again. It was only because I was defending myself. Please, let me go. I won't be a threat."*

Ronan had to know she wouldn't let him go. He had to know this was futile. But if he could paint himself as the culprit, Safira would have no reason to go hunting for others.

Eventually, Safira said, *"Let's see how inclined you are. Extend your arm."*

She was going to do psychometry on him. But if she did—if she saw Ronan's essence and realized he was lying—she'd know he was trying to protect someone.

Ronan must've been thinking the same thing because a gunshot sounded. Neva's hand flew to her mouth, and when she went to peer into the bag beside her—the bag Ronan had taken the gun from—Yolie sprang out of her grip and up toward the window.

She only saw a glimpse of it. Safira clutched her wounded shoulder, and when Ronan charged at her, she made a movement with her hand. Blood began to pour from Ronan's face and neck, but before Yolie could see any more, Neva pinned her to the ground.

"Lower your shields," she hissed. *"Lower them, Yolie."*

A scream bubbled at Yolie's mouth, but she couldn't find her voice.

"Lower them," Neva demanded again, and Yolie gave in.

A flurry of snow whisked into her mind, and when the cold lulled her to sleep, she didn't fight it. The cold swarmed about Marina too, and when she found her body again and met Yolie's teary eyes, she let out a pained sigh.

Yolie remained silent, but Marina could fill in the gaps herself. Safira must've believed Ronan was indeed the inclined suspect—either that or she'd been too preoccupied with her injury to continue the hunt—because Yolie and Neva had made it out of Sal.

No wonder the memory was so potent now. Yolie must feel like she was living through Sal all over again. Even worse, Marina could feel Yolie's guilt, which was as bad now as it had been in the memory. If it hadn't been for Yolie's mistake, perhaps Ronan would've made it out too. Whether or not it was her fault didn't matter. She'd always think it was.

Marina knew the way it felt—the way no number of reassurances would ever ease the guilt. So she didn't offer any. Instead, she remained silent as Yolie pushed her glasses up and rubbed at her eyes, then closed the satchel with the fragments of Ronan's anteactus and whispered, "How am I supposed to remember him now?"

Marina waited until she knew her voice would be even before giving Yolie's forehead a tap. "Through here," she said, then pointed at Yolie's heart. "And there. Through all the nicknames Ronan called you, like your dad did, and the things he liked to do, like making dolls out of leaves. All of that is him. And you carry it too." Heart fluttering, she added, "I remember my parents through songs."

The corners of Yolie's lips twitched. "Songs like what?"

"You wouldn't know them. They're from my home."

A moment of silence passed between the two of them before Yolie said, "Sing one."

The temptation to refuse rose to the surface before Marina remembered what she'd done in Exorsus. She was no longer the girl who forbade herself to sing; she'd broken that cycle. She looked around the room. The walls were thick, and if she whispered, only Yolie would hear. So, Marina pointed to the translator in Yolie's ear and said, "Take that out."

She wanted Yolie to hear the words untranslated, even if she didn't know what they meant. She'd have a good enough idea. Music was powerful that way.

Yolie slipped the tube out of her ear, and whatever hesitation Marina had felt flitted away when she noticed that Yolie didn't seem as preoccupied with Ronan's anteactus. Singing wouldn't put it back together, and in a way, Marina felt it was as trivial as apologies. But that was all they had: small, slow fixes—tiny steps in the right direction, even if they seemed insignificant in the grand scheme of things.

And so, Marina sang.

The words to "Landslide" came just as easily as they had in Exorsus, and though Yolie didn't understand their meaning, she seemed taken up with the melody. She listened intently, eyes wide and lips parted.

It was easy enough, Marina thought, to keep her voice low enough not to draw attention, but harder to keep it steady. The lyrics reminded her of all the changes she'd weathered as of late—the path she'd carved for herself in Exorsus, and how important it was to walk it, even if she feared where it would lead.

When she finished, Yolie readjusted her translator, then wrapped her arms around Marina. And for a while, the two of them sat there, breathing in tandem. From the corner of her eye, Marina caught a glimpse of Neva, who was still kneeling by the projector—but who wrenched her gaze from it long enough to throw a tearful smile Marina's way.

CHAPTER 37
Solar Flare

By midday, Neva had given up watching for citywide updates. Even if there had been any—which there weren't—the projector kept malfunctioning, and they didn't have the resources to fix it. Worse still, they'd started to run out of food and medicine. After some deliberation about safety, a few of the soldiers decided to take on the role of scouts and make covert trips around Tolsea to accumulate supplies and information. They left separately, wearing civilian clothes and carrying nothing but easily concealed weapons.

It was hard to watch them go—to not know if they'd come back, or worse, who they might come back with in the event they were followed. Florin's scouts had been followed, after all, and this time, they were at an even bigger disadvantage.

They could either sit in silence and worry about it or consider how to move forward, and Marina chose the latter. Thankfully, so did Aeric.

The original plan had been shattered, but pieces of it could be salvaged. What Florin had said about the head of the snake needing to be vulnerable remained pertinent, and the fact that they had Brenna's ring meant targeting the ruemin and shutting down the portal was still possible.

Of course, this time, the plan would have to look different. They didn't have easy access to ruemin anymore—no nets, no sanctuary to retreat to if a ruemin uttered a distress call and summoned others before it could be sedated. Despite the fact the palace prisons swarmed with them, simply grabbing one had never been an option. With so many ruemin in such close quarters, the likelihood they'd be cornered and attacked skyrocketed. They needed a way to lure a small number to Brenna's portal, then wield dissolution magic on one and kill the others before any could cry out for their packmates. And if anyone knew how to lure ruemin with specific calls, it was Vaughn.

He'd said as much back when Marina was in Altus—that he'd put in a great deal of work sensitizing the ruemin to his sound, which he'd clearly been successful with. According to Aeric, he wouldn't have been able to summon them to attack Marina, Ryder, and Cal if they hadn't recognized his frequency. Doubly interesting was the fact that ruemin didn't solely screech to alert others; they had a variety of calls they communicated with, and some were more peaceful.

If dissolution magic could be wielded on Vaughn to turn him into something of a puppet—which, ironically, was what Kieron had wanted Vaughn to do to Aeric—then he could be coerced into summoning a few ruemin into the portal room, where Vaughn wouldn't be the only one waiting. After that, all they needed to do was to leave one ruemin alive before throwing it—and Vaughn—into the mouth of Brenna's portal.

When Florin's scouts had gone to Altus, they'd gotten a good idea of Vaughn's schedule, which wasn't variable. He preferred working during the night, and thus spent the hours from dusk to dawn in his laboratory, not far from Brenna's portal. But palace security was as heightened as it had ever been, and Vaughn was guarded. If he was to be the linchpin in their plan, that meant they'd need to dispose of anyone protecting him.

Aeric planned to bring two soldiers, one of whom had to be Ryder—the only person who knew how to get around the security guarding Brenna's portal. Luckily, Ryder was still considered dead in Altus. His armor had concealed his identity, and he'd waited until he got back to the swamplands before taking his helmet off. Even then, he'd only done so to reveal his face, ensuring there was no doubt about who he was. As for Safira, she knew one of Florin's soldiers had escaped with the ring, but she didn't know who that soldier had been.

Marina wondered if that had been another reason why Florin had made sure Ryder could escape—so that Ryder could maintain his alibi and return to Altus without Kieron anticipating the leverage his knowledge gave them.

Since Ryder was one of their most valuable assets at the moment, Aeric had Elta shift most of her healing focus toward him. Marina could tell Elta was uncomfortable neglecting the others, so instead, she worked longer and harder.

In addition to Ryder—and another soldier, if they could recruit one—Aeric needed someone who could help him dismantle draining shields and maintain his glamours. When Marina asked why the latter was necessary—Aeric would be around to maintain his own glamours, wouldn't he?—he didn't answer her. When *she* offered to help, he said something dismissive about her lack of talent with glamouring, then changed the subject.

At the moment, Aeric seemed most concerned with dissolution magic. Though he wouldn't have admitted it, Marina had a feeling he *wanted* to be the one to wield it on

Vaughn. It wasn't like he had much of a choice either way; Aeric was the only remaining sorcerer who knew dissolution magic—or, at least, knew how to wield it without completely obliterating an essence. If Vaughn was going to be both their tool to lure a ruemin *and* activate Brenna's portal, he needed to stay alive. Until he got to Sundra, of course, at which point the ruemin would probably tear him apart. Marina hated how satisfied that made her.

Though Marina figured she'd be pushing it if she brought up her involvement, she couldn't help herself. But Aeric brushed her off—again. He hadn't solidified the group who'd go with him yet, and his primary concern seemed to be making sure Safira was indeed in Tolsea.

"It's vital she is," he said, "or at the very least, that she's not in Altus."

It took Marina aback. She hadn't expected him to be *hoping* for Safira's presence in the city, but perhaps it made sense. There was no way to lure Kieron from the palace now, but Safira's absence could make it easier for them to target Vaughn and the ruemin.

Aeric didn't confirm his thinking, though. He gave Marina an absent look and said, "Remind me—how often did Kieron tell you he drank ruemin blood?"

Marina knit her brow. "Daily, I think," she said, trying to remember what he'd told her out on the merlons.

With but a daily glass, I can keep myself from withering away. Of course, it wasn't the blood he needed so much as it was the part of his deadened soul that existed within it.

It seemed to amuse Aeric—as much as he could be amused right now. Kieron's quid pro quo with the ruemin bound him to them forever. Even in his eternal reign, Marina imagined he'd still rely on their blood to sustain himself—on doses of his deadened soul, which he drank like medicine.

"Good," Aeric said. "The more frequently he requires a drink, the quicker he'll weaken if he doesn't have access."

Marina shifted nervously in her seat. There weren't any tables in the warehouse, but Neva had found more fold-out chairs, which they made do with. Aeric, however, couldn't seem to decide whether he wanted to sit or stand, and alternated between both several times each minute. Seeing him absent and unfocused was one thing, but *restless?* It was terribly uncharacteristic, so Marina did her best to balance out his nerves by remaining as calm as possible. If things worked out, perhaps they could go back to their usual roles, and she'd be the nervous one while he'd settle back into laser-focused aloofness.

"Kieron likely keeps stores of ruemin blood," Aeric continued. "Probably enough to last him weeks. Florin and I considered the possibility, but we figured any stockpiles Kieron *did* have would prevent him from growing irrational if our plan had worked. Even with the ruemin gone, if he thought he still had time to find you and leverage Locus, he would've been less likely to resort to whatever madness he might've had he realized his defeat was inevitable. But we're running on borrowed time now, and we no longer have a sanctuary to hide in." He gripped the back of his chair, knuckles white. "If we're going to do this, the snake needs to be decapitated immediately. We cannot risk Kieron gathering his stockpiles and fleeing—biding time with Safira and his soldiers so he can target us again and take you hostage—or worse, resorting to endgame tactics Elsudra won't be able to recover from."

"So Kieron—and anything or anyone keeping him alive—needs to be annihilated immediately, is what you're saying," Marina said. Aeric wavered, then nodded. "And *that's* where I come in?" she added cautiously.

She already knew what Aeric's answer would be, but when he shook his head, she felt like she'd been punched anyway.

"Why not?" she pressed. "You said it before. Annihilation is what I'm good at."

Aeric's tone brooked no argument. "I don't want you in Altus. There's a possibility we won't be successful. If we aren't, I want you as far away from Kieron as possible. Besides, if Safira is indeed in Tolsea, your presence *here* would be more useful to us than if you were in Altus."

Marina eyed him. "So I'm bait?"

"I don't care what you call it. Safira is looking for both of us—and Brenna's ring—but it's the Omnia's presence that will keep her tethered to Tolsea. *Your* presence. This city isn't like Altus—it doesn't have anywhere near the number of glamours, shields, and magic-made technology needed to offset the Omnia's energy. Ruemin will be able to sense an unusual concentration of magic, which means you won't blend in as well as you would in the capital. Even worse, we're currently at ground level. Our previous sanctuaries weren't, which helped distance you from the ruemin and insulate your essence." Marina must've paled, because Aeric added, "I've said this before: even if ruemin can sense a higher concentration of magical energy, they aren't shrewd enough to know where it's located unless the source—in this case, the Omnia's host—were standing directly in front of them."

Right—the difference between a dull ember and a solar flare. But keeping a solar flare hidden was no easy feat, and those sanctuaries they'd once relied on were now nothing but rubble and ashes.

"As long as the ruemin continue sensing spikes in magical energy, Safira will stay in Tolsea," Aeric said. "She won't leave until she's found what she's after...unless something more pressing calls her back to the capital."

In the dim light, the circles under Aeric's eyes had grown even more severe. But this was the most present he'd been today, and Marina wasn't the only one who noticed. Neva lingered nearby, listening, and though Pierce and Ismene had busied themselves helping Elta tend to the wounded, the three of them were clearly listening too. Even Ryder, who sat against the wall with his eyes half-lidded and Ash on his lap, wasn't asleep; Marina could tell by the way he grimaced when he heard Safira's name.

"If our plan with Vaughn works and Florin's initial goal to lock the ruemin in Sundra comes to fruition, Safira will know immediately," Aeric said. He didn't bother to lower his voice—in fact, Marina had an inkling he wanted Neva to hear this. "More importantly, she'll know Kieron is in danger, and that's enough for her to abandon Tolsea and get back to the palace. If we can string her along here until the ruemin and Vaughn are gone, then my group can get into Altus without her as a threat. When she finally does arrive to protect Kieron, I can set my sights on both of them."

Marina's stomach churned. "Both?" She didn't mean to challenge Aeric's abilities, but as talented as he was, so were Safira and Kieron. And Kieron might have soldiers come to his aid too.

"You forget Kieron doesn't want me dead," Aeric said flatly. "I may not hold the Omnia, but I'm important to him in other ways. Even if he abandons his sentimentality, he won't do so without hesitation, which I can use to my advantage."

Marina was silent for a moment. "What about *your* sentimentality?" she finally asked, quietly enough that any eavesdroppers wouldn't hear.

Aeric knew what she meant. He'd said it himself, hadn't he? He didn't know if he'd be able to take Kieron down. She wanted him to admit it—that he might need help. But all he said was, "I'll do what I need to do."

Aeric lowered his gaze, and a sudden chill overcame Marina. She wasn't sure how, but she knew what he was thinking, even if he didn't voice it. Perhaps it was the vacancy in his eyes—vacancy that reminded her of months spent in her empty house back in Georgia, contemplating what it would be like to fade into the shadows and become nothing.

Aeric was more than willing to go down if it meant bringing Kieron and Safira with him. But it wasn't only that. Regardless of whether he died in a fight or by his own hand, Marina had a feeling he didn't intend to make it out of Altus at all.

CHAPTER 38
In Times of Crisis

The clarity Marina had held to these past few days blurred. This was more than Florin's plan. Aeric didn't *want* to step into a brighter future. He didn't think he had a place in it. He'd alluded to it before—maybe not in so many words, but clearly enough for her to know what he intended. Had this come from the conversation they'd had earlier? Had Aeric figured that the only way to live with killing Kieron was to *not* live afterward? And was that another reason why he didn't want her in Altus—because he planned to die either way and didn't want her to go down with him?

She didn't know what to think, or say, or do. When the soldiers returned early that evening and confirmed Safira's presence in the city, she felt even more conflicted. Given their current situation, this plan could very well turn out to be a coup. But confirmation the mechanical woman was nearby sent everyone into a fit of paranoia—one that flared up when the warehouse creaked or when they thought they heard unfamiliar voices outside.

If Safira was searching for magical energy, even their glamours were a risk. Though glamours were harder to pinpoint than most other forms of magic, they still tried to rely on non-magic options as much as they could. Neva found tarps they used to conceal the windows, and Aeric did his best to limit his glamours to only the most visible entrances. He even insisted Marina put her diminution cuffs back on. Luckily, she carried the key.

The threat of detection would only last until the ruemin were gone and Safira subsequently hurried back to Altus. Aeric didn't seem to think it would take long—this game of cat and mouse they were playing with her. He intended to lure Safira to the capital one way or another, and it was obvious he'd stop at nothing to make sure she didn't come back, even if it meant he wouldn't either.

He never said it. Ivo volunteered to accompany Aeric and Ryder, and despite all their discussions, Aeric never once mentioned his plan to die in Altus. But he didn't need to.

The truth lingered between Aeric and Marina, unspoken. Marina now knew why Aeric needed someone to upkeep his glamours once he left the group, and when he began seriously considering the sorcerer they'd take with them, she figured this was her best chance to insert herself and prevent the worst from happening.

"Maintaining glamours isn't nearly as hard as making them," she argued, "even if they're on living things. If you get it started, I could—"

"You're not coming," Aeric said for the umpteenth time. "Your role is here, keeping Safira in Tolsea until chaos in Altus summons her back to Kieron's side. You know this. I don't have time to entertain your arguments."

"I'm not..." Marina took a breath, then steadied her voice. "There aren't many people left with the talent to maintain glamours. The wounded need Elta, and..."

She almost added something about Yolie being a no-go, but she held her tongue. That was obvious enough; simply mentioning Yolie could very well be the push Neva needed to abandon their group entirely.

Aeric gave her a look. "So instead, you want to risk going—overturning one of the key parts of this plan—all so you can try to force me to leave Altus with you or so you can insist on confronting Kieron and Safira with me."

It sounded desperate and idiotic when he said it out loud, which Marina knew it was. But what was she to do? Agree to stay in Tolsea and let Aeric see his suicide plan through?

"You're not coming," Aeric repeated.

"Then who—"

"I will."

Neva's voice. Marina turned to face her, and when she looked back at Aeric, she realized he hadn't expected that either. She hated the relief she saw in his eyes, and though she knew her emotions were unreasonable, she wanted to snap at Neva to stay out of it—to stay here and protect Yolie, and to let Marina go to Altus because nobody else would try to keep Aeric alive. And why should they? If he insisted on it—if there was a chance he could successfully take Kieron *and* Safira down—what did the loss of his life matter?

Evidently, it only mattered to Marina. Neva's concern, as Marina expected, was Yolie.

"If successfully infiltrating Altus and taking out the ruemin is the surest way to get Safira out of Tolsea, then it's a risk I'll take," Neva said. She glanced at Yolie, who had moved beside Ryder and was petting Ash.

"Are you sure you can maintain glamours on *living*, moving things?" Marina asked, praying her answer would be no.

"If I practice once or twice before we leave, I'll make do," Neva responded. "If I fail, then I'll use conveyance—at least to get us to safety."

"What about your wrist?" Marina asked, grasping at straws.

"Elta did a good job with it," Neva said. "It's sore, but I can move it fine."

Now desperate, Marina said, "What about draining shields? Florin said—"

"I'm aware," Neva said, a bit more sternly than before. "I'm capable of helping with those too. Aeric and I will be able to dismantle any."

"Good," Aeric said. "That's...that's good. Thank you."

Based on the relief in his voice, he'd clearly been praying for Neva's accompaniment all along. Marina cursed internally, then looked to Yolie, hoping she'd overheard and would jump in and try to stop Neva from leaving. Not like she'd be successful; Neva had already made up her mind, and she'd made it up *because* of Yolie. And so, as Neva and Aeric began to discuss when they'd leave, Marina listened, her head numb and eyes gummy. Neva seemed as intent as Aeric was to do this soon—they had a narrow window of time, and every minute they stayed increased the likelihood Safira would find them.

Worse still, when the sun set that evening, Tolsea's breeze carried screeches of ruemin with it. The soldiers guessed they were coming from the nearby forests, but the ruemin would make their way into the city soon enough. Hearing the echoes of their screams was enough to worry both Aeric and Neva, who planned to have the group leave again in the hours before dawn—preferably to find somewhere below ground, where the ruemin and Safira would be less likely to detect them. That was where Marina and the rest would stay as Aeric, Neva, Ivo, and Ryder left for Altus, glamouring themselves and heading on foot to a nearby, smaller town where guards were less likely to patrol every portal system.

Neva knew one more person in the city—Shaw, she called him. He was a merchant who lived on the outskirts of Tolsea with his partner, Yuna. Neither were inclined, which meant they wouldn't have had reason to flee the city, and moreover, Neva had worked with Shaw for years. The way she spoke of it, they seemed to have been good friends—good enough that Neva seemed confident he'd receive them. At least, she hoped he would.

But staying in the warehouse—with its poorly boarded-up windows and glamours that could draw attention—was more dangerous than seeking out Shaw, and with Yolie's life on the line, Neva was even more determined to get them somewhere safer.

Perhaps she also hoped Yolie would find more peace in a basement as opposed to an abandoned building. Whenever she thought she heard a distant screech or clicking, Yolie would burst into tears, burying her head in Neva's stomach and muttering not about the ruemin, but about the mechanical woman.

With all the stress, Marina had no idea how to confront Aeric without creating waves —waves they had neither the time nor resources to weather. She trusted Aeric's plan, even if she hated the parts of it he refused to speak of, so she stood by as he assigned Pierce the responsibility of overseeing the group's safety—more specifically, Marina's safety. She occupied her spinning head by packing with Ismene and Elta, and when Ryder practiced putting weight on his leg by doing laps around the warehouse, she and Pierce lingered nearby to help if he needed it.

She tried to ground herself by learning the names of the people who comprised their group—or perhaps, in a way, she felt she needed to.

In addition to Pierce and Ryder, five soldiers had survived: Ivo, Kins, Gian, Esther, and Elm. They'd served in the Delve, but Pierce didn't know them well. They'd worked closer to Florin than they had him.

Not counting Elta, Yolie, and Neva, only four others from the sanctuary had made it out of the wetlands. There was Wren, an older woman who'd lost her adult son in the Candens Inlet massacre, and Jace, who'd worked as a cook. Blaine knew a lot about the technicalities of magic, though his talents failed to reach the level of Neva, or even Elta. Adela was the youngest, minus Yolie—sixteen or seventeen, if Marina had to guess—but had barely woken up since they'd arrived in Tolsea. A ruemin had badly mauled her shoulder and taken a large chunk of her torso, and late that night, she succumbed to her injuries and became the newest name on Marina's list.

Elta took Adela's death the hardest, and even Ismene—who'd slept these past few nights next to Adela—was much too distraught to tell Neva and Aeric. So Marina did. She figured they'd have noticed soon enough, but if it took the burden off Elta, she wanted to help. One fewer thing for her to stand around and feel hopeless about.

She knew what Aeric was thinking as he disposed of Adela's body—knew, despite the guilt that tore him apart, he was also relieved there was one fewer wounded person to worry about transporting. Still, it was hard not to worry about getting everyone to Shaw's safely, and rest didn't come easy for anyone. Marina got a few hours of sleep in, only to wake when it was still dark and be overcome by grief—for Adela, Lars, Florin, Hollis, Zora, and so many others. She squeezed her eyes shut, trying to fight the feeling that she was sinking—into the ground, into herself, into nothingness.

It was a different kind of torture—waking in the dead of night to stirring bodies and groans of old crates, which formed monstrous silhouettes amidst the shadows. But she soon realized it was voices that had woken her. As hard as they tried to whisper, they were too close to her to be silent.

Pierce was saying something about sifting through Elta's bag to find pain medication.

"No," Ryder said. "She barely has any left. I'll be fine." A pause lingered between the two of them. Finally, Ryder added, "Thanks, though."

His voice wasn't strained, and though Marina felt guilty eavesdropping, she couldn't stop. It was better than rotting in grief and fear.

For a while, they were silent. Ryder said something about Ash, and Pierce admitted to slipping him scraps of food from his own meals. When Ryder laughed, Marina's heart fluttered. Was this their first real conversation since the morning after Double Moon?

"Marina's handling everything...well," Pierce said. Though Marina faced away from them, she could feel their eyes on her. She didn't dare move a muscle.

"It's like your dad always said," Ryder replied. "In times of crisis, the calmest are those you'd least expect."

Marina wasn't sure if that was an insult or a compliment, and she didn't feel calm at all. But she didn't care. They were *talking*, and it wasn't tense.

Pierce chuckled sadly. "He did say that, didn't he?"

More silence followed. This time, it was Ryder who broke it. "I'm sorry about Florin."

A nearby crate creaked.

"It's not on you," Pierce said.

Ryder cleared his throat. "Back at the compound, he told me you were one of the first people she trusted. You and Ismene."

"Well, Ismene's a given."

"It wasn't Ismene I was surprised about." There was an edge of playfulness to Ryder's voice, and though it was weak, he held to it when he said, "I think Florin was trying to play matchmaker or something. Must've picked up on the tension between us."

Pierce hesitated before whispering, "Did it work?"

Marina heard Ryder shift, probably to face Pierce. "You got me out of that forest," he said. "I'm thankful for that. And I know you regret what happened before the dead years. You're not the only one who carries that burden." He took a deep breath. "In Altus, my life flashed before my eyes. And not the way it usually does in a fight—in a way that signaled the end. Don't think I've ever experienced that before. But...you were part of what I saw."

Pierce didn't respond, and Marina wished more than ever that she could flip onto her side and watch them instead of just listening. Of course, it was probably safer to stay facing the opposite direction, especially now that her eyes burned with tears. Seeing them would only make her more emotional.

"But I don't want to lie to you either," Ryder continued. "I don't know if I can bring myself to forgive you—or me. It's all...too much."

Pierce's voice was soft. "I know."

Ryder considered for a moment, and Marina couldn't help but feel a change in the air when he whispered, "But that doesn't mean I don't want to try."

CHAPTER 39
Valuable

They had only stayed in the warehouse for a day, but the city looked different when they emerged. Streets and alleys lined with blockades made getting to the outskirts harder, and several blocks from the warehouse, windows and doors had been marked with symbols she couldn't read. Marina looked to the high walls, expecting to see golden-armored soldiers lining them, but there were none.

She didn't question it; truthfully, she was too concerned with moving carefully to question much of anything right now. If someone bumped into something, or if a weapons bag rustled in a way that was a touch too loud, they might give themselves away. Plus, Marina had no idea what kind of technology Elsudran soldiers from Altus might have. So she did what everyone else was doing: she kept her eyes down and prayed Aeric's glamours would hold out until they got to Shaw's.

When she'd escaped Altus with Ryder, she'd put her faith in him—hoping he'd know the city layout and thanking the heavens he was a trained fighter. Now, she found herself relying just as heavily on Aeric, Neva, and the remaining soldiers in the group. The diminution cuffs she wore felt heavier than usual, and Marina kept one hand in her pocket where the key was, ready to undo them if she needed to. But then she'd hear distant screeches followed by clicks—which she'd fool herself into thinking weren't from ruemin but from Safira's heels—and the cuffs would feel less like a burden and more like a shield.

The warehouse and textile mill had been closer to the heart of the city, which meant they had a long walk ahead of them to get to Shaw's. Tolsea was Elsudra's largest city—even larger than Altus, apparently, and getting out of the capital had already taken what felt like an eternity. Kieron also hadn't planned for Marina and Ryder to escape, and those initial moments of shock had given them time.

They weren't so lucky now. But glamours were their best bet, and they were keeping up a good pace. Since Marina couldn't see her feet or the others in her group, she focused on the road ahead of her—and when it got hard to do that, she focused on the fabric of Aeric's coat and the warmth of Ismene's hand.

Ivo, Ryder, and Pierce stood on the outside of Marina's group, which made her feel a little safer. In fact, Aeric had positioned soldiers on the outside of all three groups, each one clad in armor and portable weapons. They walked for some time, weaving through whichever alleys they could find that weren't blockaded. As they left the congestion of what Marina assumed was the heart of the city, the blockades thinned out.

Of course, Tolsea didn't have much of a heart at the moment. She didn't expect there to be crowds out this early—and given the current state of Elsudra, she figured most people wouldn't want to risk meandering roads and running into soldiers or ruemin—but even when they'd left the textile mill, she'd spotted light coming from distant windows. But the windows here were dark, and the streets were so quiet Marina thought she was hearing things when buzzing cut through the air. She might've continued thinking it was all in her head if Ismene's grip hadn't tightened. She felt herself being tugged to the left by Aeric too, over to an awning at the side of a nearby building.

"Don't panic," he whispered. "Just follow."

Marina knew what he was talking about when a drone materialized—small and silver, gliding through the air so fluidly that Marina was surprised Aeric had noticed it at all. Ivo, Ryder, and Pierce had noticed it too; though she couldn't see them, she could feel them stiffen as their group of six pressed up against the door the awning hung over.

But where were the others? Kins, Elta, Blaine, and Elm were part of one group, and Yolie, Neva, and the rest were part of the other.

Every group has soldiers, she told herself. *They'll notice.*

Her attempt to reassure herself was useless, especially when she remembered the drones Pierce had mentioned—the ones equipped with the cameras Safira had used back in Altus. They couldn't identify glamours, but they could identify body heat, and given the number of people in each group, there was bound to be a lot of body heat to detect.

They could duck out of sight when possible, using things like awnings to conceal anything the drones might pick up, but what if another passed by when there was nowhere to hide? Worse still, what if Safira was using the drones to herd their groups like she'd used them to herd Florin's? Marina almost whispered her concern to Aeric but refrained. He knew what Safira had done in Altus; surely he anticipated her moves here.

The drone didn't seem to locate anything, much to Marina's relief. It whirred as it moved to the end of the alley, then turned the corner and disappeared.

They started walking almost immediately. Everyone held their breath, listening for more, but the streets had gone silent again.

There was no way of knowing if the other two groups were taking the same routes. Neva had given them directions to Shaw's, but Tolsea was a maze of a city. Winding streets ended at flights of stony stairs, which led to corridors, back alleys, and closed shops.

If Tolsea weren't on lockdown, Marina imagined it would be lively—perhaps even a little crowded. She tried to think about that as they walked—about what it might be again. People filling the streets, shop doors open...maybe music would play.

She was thinking of guitar chords when they made it to a narrow alleyway. *E flat, A minor, F sharp*...and gunfire.

If she'd let her instincts take over, she might've dropped to the ground—which would have been the worst decision ever because it would have messed up Aeric's glamour. But clearly, not everyone understood that.

A ways away—at the far end of the alley where the gunfire had started—Marina could make out a group of people. Two soldiers in gray armor, a wounded man, two women, and a little girl with golden glasses.

Marina's heart jumped to her throat. Only one shot had been fired, but it had hit the man. Jace, Marina realized. He knelt on the ground, hands clasped over his thigh, as Gian and Esther went to sling their arms around him. Wren lingered with her hands over her mouth, and a few paces away, Yolie clung to Neva.

Their glamour had probably broken the moment the bullet hit Jace and he fell to the side. But the gunfire wasn't over—a few yards above them, a drone hovered in the air like a wraith. Now that the glamour had disintegrated, it didn't need to rely on their body heat.

Even if she'd tried to scream—which she wouldn't have—her mouth couldn't form the words. Beneath the camera, which looked more like a silver eye, several more gun barrels locked on the group.

Neva was quicker. She didn't reach out for Wren or anyone else; perhaps even a few steps would've taken too much time, or perhaps she wasn't thinking of them. Instead, she wrapped her arms around Yolie and conveyed across the alley, slamming into Aeric and Marina's group. Their own glamour fizzled out as they fell to the ground, and from the spot they lay, Marina could see rounds of bullets mow down Gian, Esther, Jace, and Wren.

Before she'd so much as processed it, three more drones descended into the alley—and now, they were heading in their direction.

Aeric jumped to his feet and made a wide motion with his arms, his gaze locked on the closest drone. Marina expected him to shred it to pieces like he had the ruemin, and though he hit it squarely, causing it to spin into the side of a building, the drone quickly righted itself. It was dented, perhaps, but still working. Whatever material the drones were made with seemed to withstand bullets too. Ivo—at least, she thought that was who it was, but it was hard to tell with his helmet on—managed to put a hole in the camera of one, but that didn't stop the drone's guns.

Its first shot sliced into his chest. More followed, riddling his armor with so many holes that eventually, the bullets could reach his skin. Ivo had already hit the ground by then—limp but still breathing. Marina tried to reach out for him, praying his armor had saved him, but before she could make contact, Aeric grabbed her by the shoulders.

She knew immediately that he was going to convey. In a wild rush of adrenaline, Marina lunged forward and wrapped her arms around Ismene, Pierce, and Ryder.

"Ivo's still alive," Marina said desperately, hating her diminution cuffs.

Aeric didn't listen. He simply lifted his voco to his mouth, then—loudly enough so Neva could also hear—said, "Eastern alley."

Neva pulled a sobbing Yolie closer to her, and the two were gone within seconds. And then, the world blurred. Marina clung to the others, praying wherever they landed would be void of drones. She wasn't sure how far Aeric went—or how far he *could* go, given how long they'd already walked and how exhausted he probably was. Though she figured a large chunk of it was due to adrenaline, Marina's limbs shook when they landed in another alley.

Luckily, Neva and Yolie weren't far behind. They stumbled a few paces, then caught themselves. Neva had her hands on her knees, her labored breathing broken by silent sobs, and Yolie stood beside her, crying just as quietly. Marina's chest hollowed when she thought of Yolie's memories—of the terror she'd felt in Sal, and how similar this was to it.

"Aeric!" someone whisper-shouted.

Elm rounded one of the nearby corners, followed by Elta, Blaine, and Kins.

The relief hit Marina in waves. *They got Aeric's message. They lived. Thank God, they lived.*

"We heard gunfire," Elm said. "They're going to sic ruemin on the wounded if they're still alive. We need to—"

"We'll go," Aeric said. He was shaking too, Marina realized.

"We're...we're not far from Shaw's," Neva managed. She wiped at the tears on her face. "But it's too far for me to convey."

"Two groups now." Aeric's voice was breathless but firm. "I'll re-glamour. If a drone targets a group and someone is too wounded to continue, leave them. Keep going."

Pierce, Ryder, Elm, and Kins—the only remaining soldiers—nodded immediately, and though Elta and Ismene exchanged wide-eyed glances, they didn't protest.

Marina's stomach sank. Aeric didn't need to specify that those rules didn't pertain to the Omnia's host, which didn't relieve her near as much as it made her feel like a liability.

But she didn't say anything as Aeric began dividing people up. Instead, she swept her gaze across the alley walls. There was nothing to take cover under if a drone showed up now, which meant all they could do was move fast and pray the alleys ahead had more options.

Aeric glamoured Pierce, Neva, Yolie, Blaine, and Kins first, then glamoured everyone else in his group. They'd barely reached the end of the alley before screeches cut through the air, and Marina knew Elm was right. If Ivo and the rest were still alive, they wouldn't be for long. But they kept moving—no looking back, no hesitation.

The drones, unfortunately, were equally determined. One turn into an intersection revealed a dozen more, some so close to the ground that even hiding under awnings wouldn't help them. Marina had no idea if soldiers were manning the drones or if they were advanced enough to work on their own, but whatever the case, the device's lens locked on them immediately.

The first drone that fired hit Elm—right in the leg where Jace had been shot. Though Elm didn't fall to the ground like Jace and ruin the glamour, Marina knew where he'd been standing. That, and a small section of Aeric's glamour had been disrupted by the bullet; from it, she could see Elm's armor. But Elm kept moving. Maybe his armored suit had protected him from the worst, or maybe he was better at pushing past the pain. Whatever it was, they continued on despite the fact the glamour on Elm's side was slowly dissipating. It was weaker now, and if Aeric didn't fix the hole, it would come undone in minutes.

A couple yards away, another drone came to a halt, hovering in the air and preparing to shoot at a seemingly nonexistent target.

Pierce's group, Marina realized. And not just anyone in Pierce's group—when the drone began to fire, it targeted one of the soldiers Aeric had positioned on the outside. *Pierce.*

What little order they'd managed to regain dissolved when the bullet hit Pierce's leg and part of the glamour came undone. Marina could hear Yolie's strangled cry as the drone refocused and fired another shot. This time, it sent Pierce flying backward, and the rest of the glamour unraveled.

Pierce hit the ground like Ivo had, and though Marina strained to see where he'd been shot, her vision had grown foggy. Beside her, a helmeted soldier—Ryder—gasped.

The drones...their targets were purposeful. Their cameras allowed them to avoid anyone who might be Marina or Aeric—firing nonfatal shots with the intent to dissolve glamours so they could get a more precise read on who they were attacking.

Kieron's words rang through Marina's ears again, so real she almost thought he was standing next to her: *I look forward to the next time I see you. Both of you.*

Now that the glamour around Pierce's group had dissolved, the drones weren't aiming for legs. Finally, they could go in for the kill.

Ryder made a sound—a whimper, which Marina had never heard him make before. He knew the rules, but it was *Pierce* who was wounded. Pierce who might die. When Ryder began to move toward Pierce, Marina snapped.

She didn't remember the next few moments—didn't remember jamming the key into her cuffs and conveying over to Pierce, then throwing herself in front of him. She tried to generate a shield of air around them, but she was exhausted and it was weak.

Luckily, she didn't need much of a shield. Though the drone's gun had already gone off, it jerked away when it registered her, sending its bullet to the side. A narrow miss, but a miss all the same.

Pierce swore. "Marina..."

She looked down at her leg. Apparently, the bullet *hadn't* missed them. But before she could get too in her head about the blood gushing out of her shin, Aeric had already pulled her up and snapped the cuffs back on her. She realized why when she heard the screeching again—this time, closer. But it wasn't fear of the ruemin that coursed through her; it was fear of what Aeric was yelling to the others.

Run, Aeric was saying. *Just run. Don't let them track you.*

And then he wrapped his arms around her.

He couldn't re-glamour them. There was no time. But...everyone else was supposed to *run?* He wasn't about to run. He was about to convey...and this time, only with her.

How were Pierce and Elm supposed to run with wounds? Ryder couldn't run very far either—he was still limping. And what about Yolie? Would the drones really attack a young girl? Of course they would. If Safira was in charge of them, they'd attack everyone mercilessly. And if the ruemin were as close as they sounded, they would too.

Marina began to struggle—begging Aeric to let her take off the cuffs so she could help convey people. The ruemin could run faster than they could, and there was no way everyone would get out in one piece. Right when she thought she was getting through to him, Aeric put his hands on her head. Fog seeped into her essence, and with the cuffs, she couldn't raise her waves to keep him out.

Safira had done this to her—snuck into her essence and knocked her out. Aeric was doing the same thing. He was making it so she couldn't protest or take up valuable time.

But what about the others? They were valuable too.

Not as valuable as the Omnia's host. No—not as valuable as *the Omnia.*

As Marina slipped into foggy nothingness, a bit of her old self rose to the surface— the girl who had wondered if holding the Omnia would be the end of her. And though Aeric's fog was nowhere near as suffocating as Safira's smoke, the helplessness Marina felt was worse.

CHAPTER 40
Last Resorts

No doors. No windows. The floors and walls were made of concrete, and the fabric Marina lay in wasn't as nice as the ones in the textile mill. They smelled musty, and the air was even worse. But she had more pressing concerns than the state of the cellar they were in. Though sitting up made her ears ring—and her shin felt like it was being attacked by an ice pick—she couldn't bear not knowing who was in the room with her.

She met Yolie's eyes first—golden glasses shining in the dim light—and let out a breathless cry.

"We're okay," Yolie said. Her voice was frail, and she was clearly sugarcoating things.

At the moment, it seemed like Yolie was the only person up. How had she made it out? Neva couldn't have conveyed her, and from the looks of things, she'd taken a beating out there. Neva lay with a damp cloth over her face, covered in sweat, and a chunk of skin on her arm had been torn off—by ruemin or bullet or something else, Marina didn't know.

Beside her, Elm sat next to Pierce, who leaned against the wall with his eyes closed. Elm didn't look too bad, minus his thigh and torso. He pressed a cold pack against his bare skin, which was covered in fresh bruises—probably from the one or two bullets that had made contact with his armor. Pierce was bruised up too, and his leg was covered in bandages and clean fabric. His shin was wrapped—same as hers—and so was his thigh.

Ryder was awake. Ironically, he was now one of the healthiest people here. He and Ismene, at least, who knelt beside a sleeping Elta. Ismene held Ash in her arms, which, under different circumstances, might've made Marina laugh. That cat sure managed to live through a lot. Maybe he'd be the only member of the group to make it out of this alive.

Marina's gaze shifted to Elta's face, and whatever humor she'd salvaged upon seeing Ash disappeared. Of everyone here, Elta was in the worst shape. Her waist, chest, and half of her face were covered in bandages—once white, now red—but that didn't seem to be what concerned Yolie. She kept glancing at Elta's arm, which was dressed below the elbow in bandages that weren't stained red, but pale green.

"A soldier shot her," Yolie whispered. "Not with a normal bullet...with a poison one. Elta was still awake when we got here and helped me get it out, but Blaine says he thinks it's infected. And Ryder says those bullets emit gases that spread the infection if you don't take them out quickly enough."

Like the bullet Ryder had shot Kieron with in Altus. Marina's stomach soured.

"Do you think you got it out quickly enough?" she asked, fearing the answer.

Yolie was silent for a moment. "I don't know."

Tears began to sting Marina's eyes, and she looked up at the ceiling to curb them.

"Blaine and I have been healing everyone," Yolie said. She glanced at Blaine, who was hovering over a bucket in the corner, pale and clearly nauseous. "Well, mostly me. But Blaine's been washing the bandages, and he's good at giving tips."

Absently, Marina's gaze flitted to Aeric, who lay passed out at the end of the room. Second to Elta, that shocked her most.

"He conveyed a lot of people to Shaw's. All at once too," Yolie said.

Marina blinked at her. That couldn't have been good for him—and judging by the looks of things, it hadn't been. They had to have been miles from Tolsea's outskirts. How he'd done it without killing himself, Marina had no idea.

Yolie's voice was barely a whisper now. "He grabbed you, then Neva and me. But he couldn't leave without the rest. And Kins..." Yolie averted her gaze, then pushed up her glasses and rubbed her eyes. "Kins took down a drone, but his bullets ran out, and then the ruemin came. He told Aeric to go...so Aeric did." Her chin trembled. "I heard a bomb go off before we left. Neva says we have a couple more with us...but they're only a last resort."

Bombs meant as last resorts...like the kind Cal had used to take down the tunnel and ruemin in Altus. Marina expected that to either fill her with grief or to simply make her go numb. Instead, all she felt was rage. She wasn't sure for what or whom. Kieron, Safira, and Vaughn, obviously. All the soldiers who fought for them, and the officials who sent them out into cities. Anyone manning those drones. The ruemin. Hell, she was even mad at Aeric for not letting her help convey. She could've shared the burden with him, even if she wouldn't have made it as far. Maybe she could've gotten Kins out. Now Aeric was weak —overexerted, which wasn't a normal state for him—and he only had himself to thank.

She was mad at herself too, for assuming Aeric was going to take her and abandon the others—for being so quick to think of him as this unflinching pragmatist because that was who he'd been at the Delve, and as deeply as Marina hated it, she understood *why* he'd be that way. But it wasn't just that. As much as she fought the feeling, she was angry because of the choice *she'd* made—for accepting the Omnia. She wasn't the person the Keepers thought had responded to their calls. She wasn't strong enough to take Kieron down, and at this rate, she'd probably never be.

Was this where things were destined to end? In Shaw's dank cellar, filled with the wounded and hidden beneath a city controlled by Safira and ruemin?

All she could think to do was cocoon herself in old coats, blocking out the hum of the fluorescent bulbs that lit the cellar and praying everything would stop hurting so much when she woke. But that was never how things worked.

She didn't sleep for long. Nobody seemed to, though they didn't have to worry about sleeping in shifts anymore. It was hard to sleep with everyone in such close quarters, and the first thing Marina woke to was Ismene consoling Neva. It took Marina a while to make out what they were saying, but she picked up on it when Neva mentioned Jace. She said more—something about how she should've shielded her group or targeted the drone, but all she could think of was fleeing with Yolie.

"You had only a second to make a decision," Ismene whispered.

"I deserted the others," Neva said through tears. "Wren lost her son, and now she's dead too. Gian and Esther...they were trying to help Jace. I didn't help any of them. I left them to be finished off by ruemin. My people...people I'd known throughout the dead years. People I was supposed to protect."

Since Marina didn't have room to process Neva's guilt—not when she carried so much of her own—she turned her eyes to her voco and tried to distract herself. It was afternoon now on the third day of Pearl's fourth week. Back at home, August would've just begun.

One year. It had been almost a year since the accident—since her family had been taken from her. Come the end of Pearl, would she be alone all over again?

The fear didn't stifle her. If anything, it moved her, and when she realized Aeric was awake, she sat beside him. She planned to speak first—to say something about the Altus mission, maybe, or to thank him for not leaving the others behind—but he beat her to it.

"I told you to leave the wounded."

Marina glanced at Pierce. "You know I couldn't."

"You took off your diminution cuffs, piqued the ruemins' senses, and got yourself shot in the leg." It was obvious he was straining to steady his voice. "What if the drone hadn't adjusted quickly enough? What if it had shot you somewhere fatal? Your only job is to protect the Omnia."

"I'm still alive, aren't I?"

Aeric's lips thinned. "Don't do that again."

"I can't promise that," Marina said. "I can't abandon people. There's no way—"

"I can't lose you," Aeric snapped. When Marina blinked at him, he said, "*Elsudra* can't lose you. If you die and the Omnia follows suit, our realm is done for. Kieron will know he's lost his chance and will resort to endgame tactics. Even eternal dead years won't stop him from seeking revenge. You cannot be so frivolous with your life."

He was one to talk, considering this unspoken plan of his to die in Altus. Obviously, he'd argue that wasn't the same thing. But his concern wasn't solely about the Omnia—that much was clear. It was about her too.

"It's been almost a year since I lost my parents," Marina said. Aeric only gave her a look, but she continued. "You know what that did to me. You saw it when I arrived in the Delve. More than that, you *personally* know how the loss of family can destroy a person. Everyone here does." She gestured to Neva with her head—then to Ismene, Pierce, Yolie, and the rest—steeling herself before she whispered, "Do you plan to die in Altus?"

That got him to respond, though his voice was unsteady. "That's off-topic, Marina."

"And *that's* not an answer."

"I can't control what happens in Altus."

"What about after? What if, by some miracle—despite our losses—things work out? Do you still plan to give up?"

Aeric's silence said enough.

"You saved people out there," Marina said desperately. "You took them to Shaw's, even though you could've left with just me. Do you not plan to at least *try* to save yourself too?"

Aeric spoke quietly, but Marina knew other people could listen if they wanted to. "My initial plan *was* to leave with only you. You'd already drawn the ruemin closer by removing your cuffs and disobeying orders, and you were so out of sorts that nobody in their right mind would have let you make decisions. But the Altus plan would've been endangered if Ryder and Neva were no longer around, so I risked conveyance—even though I knew conveying that many people such a long distance would hurt me. Now our plan is set back by a day, maybe more, so I and everyone else can recuperate, and all the while we'll pray Safira doesn't find us. Happy?" He shook his head. "I didn't make the choice out of goodwill."

"Right, because goodwill isn't how you operate," Marina said sarcastically. "But that doesn't explain why you took those who aren't necessary to the Altus plan."

"Maybe I knew losing them would've left you in shambles, which *also* makes us vulnerable," Aeric responded. "Or maybe I needed to alleviate some of the burden on my soul, even though at this point—after Florin and everyone else who has died because of me —I think it might kill me anyway. Maybe I wanted to do one good thing to balance out all the horrible things I've done, which means I didn't save them for them, but for *me*. Is that the answer you're looking for?"

Though she could tell Aeric was fighting with everything he had to remain calm, a tear slipped down his cheek. When he opened his eyes, more followed.

It caught her off guard. Her breath clung to her throat, and this time, when she opened her mouth, no more words would come. She knew Aeric was running on fatigue and adrenaline, which was perhaps the worst combination, but she hadn't expected this.

After some time, she said, "Is that why you want to die? Because you think you deserve it?" She knew she'd worded it bluntly, but when Aeric's eyes met hers, she knew with even more certainty that her suspicions had been correct. Softer, she added, "A year ago, I felt the same way about myself. Then I came here and changed. I forgave myself. I forgave you too, though I know you never asked me to. Because that's what family does."

Aeric scoffed weakly. "How would I know?" He didn't give her time to formulate a response to that. "You deserved so much better," he said.

Though her throat was scratchy, Marina's voice was surprisingly clear when she said, "So did you." She sighed. "I wish I could ask you to stay for you. But since I don't think I can, I'm asking you to stay *for me*. Don't go to Altus looking to die. If it happens, so be it, but don't give up. Fight to stay—to see what comes after."

"I'm sorry" was his only response.

"Then *prove it*." She didn't try to lessen the impact of her tone; she let it land hard enough that Aeric lifted his eyes to hers. "Prove it," she repeated. "Prove it by staying. Prove it by being someone I can count on. You said you couldn't lose me—well, I can't lose you either. You want to alleviate the burden on your soul? Don't abandon me. I told you I can't do this without you, but I wasn't just talking about Kieron. I wasn't just talking about now." The scratchiness in her throat had become unbearable, and her voice wasn't nearly as clear as it had been moments ago. She could only manage a few more words before she became unintelligible, so she chose them carefully. "Now *and* after."

She'd made the right choice, it seemed, because whatever remaining ice Aeric clung so tightly to faded. It wasn't so much that she could see it, but that she could *sense* it. Whatever warmth flickered between the two of them made her wonder if perhaps a fire had always been burning under his ice—if perhaps, in some way, his emotions were wild and overwhelming like hers, but that had only made him more intent on smothering them with cold.

It didn't matter. All that mattered was Aeric's nod, which wasn't angled at the ceiling this time, but directly at her. "Now and after."

CHAPTER 41
Pillar

Marina met Shaw that evening. He was a wiry man with eyes that darted about the room, and though he smiled at Marina when he spoke to her, she could tell it was forced. He was nice in the way a scared dog was—as though he feared doing the wrong thing could get him punished.

He wasn't far off base, Marina thought. He was walking a dangerous path—one that grew all the more apparent when his partner, Yuna, came to visit them holding a baby. It took effort not to think of Cordelia.

If there was any solace to be found, it was in the safety of the cellar. It was hidden beneath a basement, which made it hard to find and provided better insulation than the textile mill, so Marina didn't need to wear diminution cuffs. But sensing magical energy wasn't the only way Safira or the ruemin could find them. They wouldn't be safe forever.

All they had to do was make it a few days. Aeric and Neva planned to leave for Altus at the start of Pearl's fifth week, which was two days away—later than they'd initially thought, but they hoped the extra day would give them more time to gather their strength. Elm volunteered to take Ivo's place, but with his injuries, Aeric worried he'd only slow them down. Instead, he told Elm to stay behind—to heal with Pierce and to help protect the group if it came down to it.

Aeric, Neva, and Ryder it was, then. The rest would remain here, hidden beneath Shaw's mansion. Neva knew the layout well. She'd attended parties with Shaw and Yuna before the war had started, and she'd been close enough to Shaw to be his houseguest on other occasions. There was a fire escape above the cellar—nestled in the corner of Shaw's basement—that would allow them to leave the mansion covertly. From there, they'd head out of Tolsea on foot, then find a smaller town nearby where portal systems wouldn't be as heavily guarded.

That evening, Neva funneled her energy into practicing glamouring people, and Marina learned alongside her. Even if she was going to stay in Tolsea with everyone else, Marina couldn't bear not knowing the basics. If Safira *did* find them, she and Yolie would be the only sorcerers who knew glamouring. Blaine had a lot of tips—many of them useful—but he couldn't apply them himself. Still, he was eager to help, mostly because he needed to distract himself from the wounded, who Yolie was now caring for on her own.

Though no amount of practice would make it so Neva could start her own glamours, by the end of the night, she'd successfully maintained the ones Aeric made—and hers were strong enough to persist through movement. Marina's weren't as sturdy, but she *could* start her own, which gave her some hope. Mostly, they practiced on Ismene and Blaine, who could move around well enough to test them.

Of course, Marina was even better at taking glamours down—not just hers, but Neva and Aeric's too. She tried to tell herself that was okay—that if Safira found them, destroying things might protect her most—but at this point, reassurances were useless. She hesitated the next morning when Yolie asked her if she wanted to practice healing, then accepted when she realized it might be her only distraction.

Yolie helped Marina heal physical wounds first, like the one on her shin. After that, they turned to practice on Pierce, whose leg was still causing him pain. Mostly, Marina practiced the basics, then had Yolie take over when it came to more complicated parts. For simply observing healers and learning herself, Yolie was quite proficient. Marina managed to get the hang of some things too, and she found it pretty amazing how quickly magical healing—especially when used in tandem with medication and dressings—could speed things up. She tried not to wonder if healing could've been used on Ivo and the rest had they been taken here too. Instead, she focused on those who *were* here and resolved to let the rest of her emotions surface later.

By early afternoon, Elta had woken up. Her larger injuries weren't worrying—Yolie had managed to stop the worst of the bleeding, and now all Elta could do was wait—but the bullet wound on her arm was another story. As much as magic could stave off simple infections, more severe ones required medicine as well—medicine they no longer had. Worse still, Elta had come down with a fever in the night. She kept a calm head about it, but the infection wasn't getting better, and at this point, she and Yolie were mostly preoccupied with slowing the spread.

Since Marina knew her presence would likely be more suffocating than helpful, she instead practiced mental shielding with Pierce and Ryder. It felt more like distraction than practice, but it was better than sitting idly and fretting about Elta.

Besides, it was the first peek Marina had gotten at Pierce's essence—which truly was moss, just like he'd said, and as strong as Florin's redwoods when it came to keeping her out. She overpowered them eventually, even if Pierce held her off long enough to boast about it. But it was Ryder's essence Marina braced herself for. Not because she was worried about what he'd throw at her, but because she wasn't sure she was ready to see it.

It used to be sand, he told her. But his sand had hardened into clumps, as though Ryder had tried to make it resemble rock. When Marina first saw it, she thought of the soldier in Inber—of the beautiful agate stone she'd so effortlessly destroyed. But Ryder's sand wasn't smooth. It wasn't fully rock either, though she suspected at one point, it might've looked that way. Here and there, the clumps dissolved into grains, and she knew he was fighting hard to regain his old essence—to rip off the mask he'd once worn and try to remember what he'd hidden.

Marina only hovered when she pushed past Ryder's shields. Even then, she didn't stay for long, and when she pulled back, she said nothing of it to Ryder. She knew he wouldn't want her to, and more than that, she didn't know what she'd say. In fact, it seemed *nobody* knew what to say about anything. It was easier to let the day pass and do what they could to get through it—to heal and train, to prepare for Aeric, Neva, and Ryder's departure. By nighttime, the reality of what Neva had agreed to do hit Yolie, who became inconsolable. As much as Neva tried to comfort her, Marina could tell Yolie's state was taking a toll on Neva too. So Marina pulled Yolie aside and began to teach her songs.

She was surprised when it worked. After some time, Yolie had calmed down enough to teach Marina songs of her own. Ismene and Elta joined—though Elta was too weak to sing, she listened, and every once in a while, a smile would tug at her lips.

Ryder was busy helping Pierce circle the room and put weight on his leg, which Yolie seemed to have done a fine job healing. The two of them walked the perimeter, and when they got tired of that, they began to dance. It wasn't dancing so much as it was swaying—putting weight on one leg, then the other—but they leaned against each other all the same, listening to the hushed songs and savoring what they could.

After a while, Yolie curled up next to Elta and Ash and dozed off, and since Ismene refused to sing on her own—"Not unless you want your ears to bleed," she joked—Marina began running through the list of all the songs she'd sung back at home. She chose the ones that sounded best when she whispered, finding herself rather pleased with how many she remembered and how naturally they returned to her.

As always, Ismene was an unabashed cheerleader—asking for more songs and telling Marina she loved the sound of her voice. Pierce chimed in with jokes about Marina's vocal flair offsetting her "absolutely horrendous dancing skills," which got a laugh out of Ryder.

Seeing Ryder smile like that for the first time in so long was enough to make Marina's night. She was glad they were able to salvage some peace in the cellar, even if it was temporary. Marina had a feeling it was just that—the temporary peace—that made Ryder press his lips to Pierce's at the end of one of her songs. Marina clamped her lips shut as she exchanged a smile with Ismene.

Pierce's eyes fluttered when Ryder pulled back. He kept blinking, as though he was trying to figure out whether or not the kiss had been real.

"You always used to make that face," Ryder said.

Pierce shook his head. "You can't do that. It'll only make it harder when you leave."

Ryder laughed through his nose, then whispered, "Don't deprive me of my small joys."

Apparently, that was enough to persuade Pierce to lean forward and kiss him.

When Marina and Ismene giggled, Ryder turned to Marina and said, "Who told you to stop singing? It's the only thing keeping me sane right now."

For a moment, she only blinked at him. When a smile crept onto her lips, it didn't feel as weak as she expected it to.

And so, without the hesitation she'd grown so used to, Marina sang.

The night chugged on restlessly. Once Aeric, Neva, and Ryder's discussions had run dry, Aeric pulled Pierce aside and laid out a whole host of rules. With Ryder gone, Pierce and Elm were in charge of the group's safety. If neither Aeric, Neva, nor Ryder returned from Altus within two days, they could assume the plan had failed—in which case, Pierce and Elm's responsibility would be getting Marina out of Tolsea, as far from Safira as possible.

Now that she was able to listen in on every conversation, it became abundantly clear to Marina that some of this discussion had occurred back when Florin was around. Florin and Aeric might've had faith in the initial Altus mission, but they hadn't been certain of anything. Despite running on limited resources and even more limited time, they'd still considered hypotheticals. Most of them had been rather broad—general ways to keep Marina and the Omnia away from Kieron at all costs—and Marina began to wonder how things might've looked if Neva *hadn't* had contacts in Tolsea. Would Aeric have taken only Marina and found someplace else to hide? No...that wouldn't have worked; Aeric was too cautious to risk heading to Altus on his own, especially when backup could mean the difference between success and failure, and certainly not if it meant leaving Marina without protection.

Regardless, Marina had a feeling Pierce and Elm had already been told to prioritize her safety over everyone else's—though, at this point, there was no way she would leave

Yolie, Ismene, and the rest behind. She suspected Neva knew this, but she wasn't sure how much it comforted her.

Neva seemed to place most of her trust in Blaine, who Marina learned used to be a property appraiser before he'd fled to Candens Inlet. He'd worked mostly in the North and West and had become familiar with cities in both regions. More than that, he had knowledge of seldom-traveled areas and potentially neglected properties they could turn to. In that way, Pierce and Elm needed Blaine—and if Blaine was loyal to anyone, it was Neva, and subsequently Yolie.

Marina hated these unspoken divisions about as much as she hated knowing all of this would only be a problem if things went wrong in Altus. But when Shaw visited again that night with news that troops had expanded into the suburbs, interrogating everyone from business owners to families, Marina knew Aeric, Neva, and Ryder would be eager to leave before the sun rose. Shaw said he thought they had about a day, maybe two, before the soldiers made their way to his neighborhood, and it was obvious he wanted *everyone* to leave as soon as possible. If there was any silver lining, it was that the troops seemed to be moving slower than he expected, which he chalked up to Tolsea's size.

Aeric and Neva didn't tell Shaw where they were going. Instead, they pretended like they were heading out, glamoured, to get a read on the soldiers and Safira, as well as to look for ways to escape the city on foot instead of relying on the guarded portal systems. They omitted the fact that Neva knew Tolsea as well as she knew Sal, and she'd already settled on a few back routes soldiers would either overlook or not know of. They promised Shaw they'd return the following evening, and the full group would depart then. That way, when soldiers came knocking on Shaw's door, the enemies of the realm would be gone.

At this point, promises were nothing more than pacifying lies. So when Aeric made Marina promise she'd prioritize the Omnia's safety over her friends' lives, she did so without a fuss. Whether or not he believed her, Marina had no idea.

"Remember what you promised the Keepers," Aeric responded. A careful choice of words, no doubt. But Aeric didn't give her room to comment on it; he nodded curtly at her, then added, "If we leave while you're asleep, then this is goodbye."

He was so wrung out Marina couldn't tell if he was trying to sound emotionless or if he simply couldn't muster anything. Still, she glanced around the room—where everyone was either settling down or already asleep—then reached for Aeric's wrist and whispered, "And remember what you promised me. Now *and* after."

All he gave her was another curt nod. He said nothing else as he moved to his corner of the room, and though Marina expected to retreat deep into her head before falling asleep, when she returned to her pile of fabric beside Ismene and Elta, all she could focus on was Ismene's face.

Ismene's lips had parted, as though she were on the verge of saying something. Elta noticed too, even though her eyes were half-closed. She turned her head toward Ismene, then whispered, "Are you okay?"

Ismene didn't answer. Instead, she put her hand to Elta's forehead and asked, "How's your fever?"

Elta grimaced. "It's not going anywhere. Not until we get medicine, at least." Wryly, she added, "Answer my question."

Ismene hesitated. "I'm fine."

"Bad liar," Elta said softly. She winced as she adjusted her position against the wall, and when Ismene went to help her, Elta lowered her voice further. Still, Marina could hear every word. "Demand what you deserve."

Slowly, Ismene stood. Marina had seen that look in her eyes only once before—back in the Delve, after Marina had weaponized what Ismene told her in confidence to get back at Aeric. Now, all the things Ismene had been stewing over for weeks narrowed into anger, though she kept her voice low when she reached Aeric. Of course, she had to know by now that low voices didn't matter here.

"You're leaving tomorrow," she said. "Even then—even after more than two seasons—I still don't get a single word?"

Marina glanced at Elta, who watched wearily but intently. Aeric, who'd previously been sitting, stood immediately—clearly uncomfortable with Ismene looming over him.

"You want a goodbye?" Aeric asked. It was obvious the question was meant to sound condescending. At least, Marina thought it was, though it was equally likely Aeric wasn't in the headspace to monitor his tone.

"It's not what I want," Ismene said. "It's what I deserve." When Aeric only stared at her in response, Ismene's chin began to quiver. "I've tried so hard not to hold anything against you," she continued. "As much as it killed me to know I would've been left behind in the Delve—as much as it tore open old wounds—I understood why you and Florin had to make that choice. When I was ignored by you in Candens Inlet, I shook it off because you were preoccupied with more important things. I justified everything because I know you're shouldering a burden no Elsudran should have to shoulder. But now we've been in the same space for days, and still, nothing. Twelve dead years working together in the Delve, another year weathering the Omnia's return, and I might as well be a stranger to you." Her eyes had lined with tears, but none of them fell. "Maybe it was wrong of me to think I was anything more. Maybe I was nothing but a pawn to you, and I'll have to make my peace with that."

Whatever impatience Marina thought she'd seen in Aeric's face disappeared. If she wasn't mistaken, Marina could've sworn what Ismene said had hurt him. But when Marina remembered what Ismene had said to her out on the balcony in the compound—when she thought of how Ismene would wilt when Aeric was mentioned, or how deeply destroyed she'd looked in the Delve when she'd learned of Aeric and Florin's plan—she wondered if maybe it needed to.

"I don't need a goodbye," Ismene said. "I just need *something*."

Aeric was silent for a moment. Then, slowly, he said, "You don't deserve something, Ismene. You deserve everything." Ismene blinked at him as he continued. "But since I can't give you that, I gave you nothing."

This time, it was Elta who eyed Marina, and despite how tired and beaten down she was, there was satisfaction in her eyes—as though this was the response she'd expected.

Ismene certainly hadn't expected it. Finally, her tears fell—and more followed when Aeric said, "You were my pillar during the dead years, just as much as Florin was. I never said it. I couldn't...and I knew you wouldn't ask me to. When we planned to flee the Delve, I thought of nothing but the Omnia, and I pushed down my concern for you—my concern for anyone we planned to leave behind. I told myself it was the only way, even if that way was heartless. Even if it made me no better than Kieron, who'd treated those around him like pawns if it meant achieving what he intended to."

Ismene shook her head. "You're not Kieron. I've never thought that."

"You'd be justified if you did," Aeric responded. "You'd be justified in being far angrier with me than you are now. But that has never been your way, and when I say I am so glad you're still here with us, Ismene, I do not say it lightly. Elsudra needs someone like you." He closed his eyes, and when he opened them, they shined. "That does not change what I've done to you—or, perhaps, what I haven't, out of fear anything I'd do would never be enough. And so, what I give you now won't be what you deserve, because the truth is, I'll never be able to give you that." He put his hands on her shoulders and whispered, "I'm sorry. Thank you. And—"

Before he could finish, Ismene put her hand up. "Don't," she said, and she glanced ever so subtly at Marina. "This is not goodbye."

CHAPTER 42
The Mechanical Woman

Before the sun rose beyond the concrete walls, Aeric, Neva, and Ryder gathered their things and readied to leave. Marina had dozed off once or twice that night, but her sleep had been restless, and so had everyone else's. Even now, the smallest bit of noise made her stir, so when Shaw's footsteps echoed as he descended into the cellar, she opened her eyes. He was saying something, but it sounded friendly. Friendly enough, at least. Still groggy, Marina listened.

"You shouldn't rush," he said. He must've been talking to Neva, because he added, "Especially since your arm hasn't fully healed."

"It's a minor wound," Neva responded. "We'll be okay. We're already indebted to you and Yuna, and I don't plan to be here any longer than we need to."

"Still," Shaw said. "You're my friend. I thought about it a lot, and...I can't bear to force you out and jeopardize your safety."

Perhaps it was the way Shaw's voice broke at the word "friend"—whatever it was, Marina's stomach flipped. She propped herself up on her elbows, eyes adjusting to the cellar's light as she tried to make out Shaw and Neva.

Aeric stood nearby, brows furrowed as Shaw added, "Aeric is still recovering too. I was speaking to Yuna about how it's a bad idea for you to leave in the state you're in."

Aeric's response sounded as skeptical as Marina felt. "I appreciate your concern," he said, "but we're not going far." He didn't so much as glance at Neva, who nodded along with the lie. "Last night, you estimated *a day or two* before they'd reach this neighborhood. Now you're suggesting we wait?"

"They're farther out than I thought," Shaw said quickly, "and I wouldn't want to make you feel like you have to leave before you're ready." He rubbed the back of his neck. "We hear news from our neighbors…they know people in other areas. The interrogations have been taking them a while, which means we could have a week before they get here."

Something about this wasn't right. But Aeric didn't jump into justifications about why they should leave now—about why every second they stayed here put them in more danger, especially considering Marina and the rest were already going to be here longer.

Instead, he remained silent as Shaw said, "It was Yuna who convinced me. Said it wouldn't be right if you left now. You could all use more time to gather strength—"

"I heard you the first time," Aeric said.

Marina and Neva glanced at Aeric, but neither of them cautioned him to back off. An expression Marina couldn't discern had settled onto Neva's features too; as hard as she clung to neutrality, her eyebrows narrowed and her jaw tightened.

Shaw forced a smile. "I know. I'm sorry. It's been a lot. Being a new father, I mean. Especially with all…this going on." He laughed sheepishly—or, at least, he tried to. But his voice was weak when he said, "She's only a few months old, my baby girl. Tiny, precious thing. I've never felt love like this. But I expected that. It's the fear that's caught me off guard. I can't fathom anything happening to her. Her *or* Yuna."

Neva cast a hesitant look at Yolie, who had curled up that night beside Pierce and Ash and hadn't moved since.

"You know what I mean," Shaw said when he noticed. His breathing had grown hitched, and his eyes shined. "You…you understand what it's like to care for someone who isn't yourself. Someone who needs you—who you'd do anything for."

When Shaw's eyes began to water, Aeric's demeanor grew even icier. "Why did you come down here, Shaw?"

Shaw opened his mouth, but no words came out.

Why was he stalling? And why was he pushing to prolong their stay when, just last night, he'd been so unsettled by the news of interrogations? Concern for their safety didn't have a place here—not when Shaw had Yuna and his child to look after.

Unless the safety of Yuna and the baby was dependent on Aeric remaining *here*. After all, it wasn't only Marina and the Omnia Kieron wanted back in Altus. At the moment, Brenna's ring was still a threat to him—one he hadn't yet eliminated—and Aeric possessed it. Aeric, who Kieron had said he planned to see again—who Safira was searching for as much as she was searching for Marina.

Marina's stomach dropped when she realized Aeric was thinking the same thing.

"I'll ask again," Aeric said, his voice cold. "Why did you come down here?"

Shaw's voco began to chime, but he covered it with his hand. "That's…probably Yuna." When Aeric stepped closer to him, he hastily said, "I…truly, I only wanted to tell you that

Yuna and I don't mind you staying here another day. We—"

Aeric cut him off before he finished—not with words, but with a lance of light that sent Shaw stumbling into the wall. Before Shaw could right himself, Aeric had him by his neck. Neva gasped as loudly as Shaw, but Aeric kept him in place and snarled, "Did you bring them here?"

"No," Shaw choked. "No...never. I—"

"Shaw," Neva said, her voice low. "What did you do?"

Hearing it from her made Shaw break down. Tears ran down his face as he muttered, "I...I have a baby girl." He repeated it—again and again until it became impossible to understand him. Eventually, he managed, "I'm so sorry. They said they'd pardon anyone harboring your group as long as we came clean, and I...I couldn't stay silent. I couldn't risk it. They'd kill me if they found out on their own...they'd kill my family. Please know that. You have to know that."

"*I* could kill you," Aeric hissed. "*I* could kill your family. Did you think of that?" His voice grew colder when he added, "Tell me where they are, or *I'll kill your family*, Shaw."

Neva said something, but Aeric wasn't listening. He wrenched Shaw from the wall, then slammed him back into it so hard that Marina almost cried out.

"Please," Shaw choked. "Please..."

The room pulsed in Marina's vision, but from the corner of her eye, she could still see Elm, Pierce, and Ryder, who'd already snapped their helmets on and were throwing weapons together. Ismene had scooped up Ash and was helping Elta stand, and a few paces away, Yolie stood near Blaine, her eyes wide.

Another lance of light shot from Aeric's hand into the wall beside Shaw's head. Aeric must've been two inches from Shaw's face when he barked, "Where are they? Why haven't they come yet?"

"They told me...told me to make sure you were here when they arrived," Shaw said, choking on his tears. "I'm sorry. My baby girl—"

This time, Aeric yelled louder than Marina had ever heard him. *"How close?!"*

"Already here," Shaw sobbed when his voco chimed again. "She's already here."

Safira. The blood drained from Marina's face. Soldiers were one thing. The mechanical woman was another.

Shaw fell to the floor when Aeric released him, hands on his head as he choked out apologies. He rambled on some more—said something about how they would've found them anyway, and he hadn't had a choice—but nobody was listening.

Their plan was crumbling before them, but nobody seemed to care about that at the moment. Right now, they had to get out.

Glamouring people, especially multiple of them, would take up precious minutes—minutes they didn't have. Had Safira entered Shaw's home already?

Shaw's voco kept ringing. Every chime sent him into another fit of sobs, and in any other circumstance, it would've been pitiful. But this *wasn't* any other circumstance. Safira was here, and he was the reason why.

His blubbering, too, was becoming unbearable. They needed to get out—away from this wretch of a man and this enclosed space before *she* found a way in...

"The fire escape," Neva said. "Up above, in the basement. We'll use it."

Her voice must've snapped some sense into Shaw, who stood and turned toward the cellar stairs. Before he could climb them, however, a lance of light slammed into his temple. This time, when he collapsed to the floor, he stopped crying.

Marina gawked at Aeric, who kept his hand extended until he was sure Shaw was down. For half a second, Marina wondered if he'd killed him, but Shaw's chest rose subtly.

"Move," Aeric ordered.

The next minute was a blur—scrambling up the wooden steps, then passing through an equally musty basement to the fire escape Neva had mentioned. Aeric had Marina in diminution cuffs before they got there, and he stuffed the key in the pocket of her coat. Then, he pulled her hood over her hair like Ryder had done in Tin.

Marina braced herself as Aeric scaled the ladder and blew the hatch clean off with another lance of light and air—larger than the one he'd used to knock Shaw out.

Gauzy sunlight streamed in through the hole. Though it once would've tempted her, now she dreaded leaving the safety of the basement.

But it wasn't safe. Not anymore. If they stayed, they'd be little better than rats backed into a trap. So she climbed, following Aeric, Neva, and everyone else into an alleyway at the back of Shaw's mansion. And it truly was a mansion—it towered above them, complete with mansard roofs and marbled balconies, all vacant.

Marina's palms brushed against weeds that peeked out from the uneven asphalt, and she listened—for rustling, or voices, or the clicking of Safira's heels.

Nothing. The alleyway was silent. Even so, Yolie clung to Neva, murmuring something unintelligible. It took Marina a few seconds to make out "the mechanical woman."

Everyone was in a horrible state, but Elta looked the worst. She gasped as she stood, unable to straighten without wincing and covered head to toe in sweat. Ismene and Blaine supported her as they moved, both holding guns in their free hands. Marina had no idea if they knew how to use them. Given the way Ismene's hands shook, she didn't think they'd manage precise shots, but some form of protection was better than nothing.

Ryder, Pierce, and Elm were at the front of the group, moving so quickly that when they skidded to a stop at the nearest corner, Marina slammed into them.

Drones began to fire, showering down onto the street in front of them. Shrapnel went flying, shattering windows and littering the pavement. That's when the voices started—distant but distinct orders coming from unfamiliar mouths. Wherever they were, they were near. When screeches cut through the air alongside them, all hell broke loose.

Ryder fired a few shots at the drones before turning back the way they came. Marina figured he was aiming for the cameras, but she couldn't be sure. She couldn't be sure of *anything* right now—where the soldiers and ruemin were, how close Safira was, or if it was too late to escape. So instead, she focused on her feet—on moving with the group as quickly as possible and shielding her ears from the gunfire. But it wasn't drones or guns that met them at the opposite end of the alley.

Ruemin came from the rooftops, taking chunks out of masonry as they scaled walls and balconies. In an instant, Marina was back in Altus as ruemin descended the hillside—back in the swamplands as they rained down from trees—only this time, she couldn't flay them. But Aeric could; he took out a couple, and Neva severely wounded one, but it wasn't enough. When it came to hordes, killing a few only bought them seconds to run.

They stuck to the alleys behind homes, but these ones were bigger than they were at the center of Tolsea. From above, Marina imagined their group looked like ants—running in a maze with no clear exits, turning into dead-ends, and trying not to step into the light. Every time a ruemin screeched or a click sounded behind them, Marina ducked, unable to see clearly enough to know how far away they were.

And Ismene...where was Ismene? Marina couldn't see her anymore. She couldn't see Blaine or Elta either. She whirled around to where ruemin were still climbing down walls, but she didn't see dead bodies. Before she could feel relief at that—if any was possible at the moment—several ruemin hit the ground and began to sprint toward their group.

This time, the world blurred before Marina felt Aeric's arms around her. He'd taken Pierce, Ryder, and Elm too—a small enough group, but he still couldn't convey them far. He said something to Neva before he left—something Marina was much too disoriented to make out—and when they landed in a nearby square, Marina could still hear screeching and footfall.

Where were Neva and Yolie? *Oh God, please be okay...*

Before she could panic, Neva and Yolie appeared in the square, stumbling over a curb. When they righted themselves, Neva shot a frantic look at Aeric. "Where are—"

"Don't know." Aeric's hand wrapped around Marina's wrist as he pulled her forward. "Can't see them. Keep moving."

She could tell it scared Aeric as much as Neva—to have lost Blaine, Ismene, and Elta

—but he knew time was ticking, and they needed to get out of Tolsea soon. All Marina could hope was that Blaine knew where to find a backroad to get out of the city. He knew the West, didn't he? He had to have worked in Tolsea, and even if he didn't know it as well as Neva, his knowledge could be enough to get Ismene and Elta out.

Since she'd panic if she considered the alternatives, Marina convinced herself that was true. For now, they needed to focus on moving, like Aeric had said.

Buildings with shuttered windows and locked doors loomed over them, throwing long shadows onto the cobblestones. Every so often, a shutter would part, and Marina swore she saw eyes peering through.

Instead of asphalt, the pavement on the outskirts of Tolsea was made from paving stones as periwinkle as the early morning sky. Marina focused on the color as they prepared to make their way out of the square, but the churning in her gut didn't wane. If anything, it had gotten worse. Perhaps it was because of the air, which had grown chalky.

Everyone else noticed too. Aeric came to a halt first, and though Ryder, Pierce, and Elm kept their guns up, they too stopped walking.

The air wasn't just thick—it carried a bitter odor.

Aeric's grip tightened on Marina. Beside them, Yolie whimpered as she pushed up her glasses and wiped at her tearing eyes. Pierce came up behind Marina and Aeric, his mouth open, but before he could say anything, the sound of metal interrupted him.

Something small clanked over the little grooves in the paving stones as it traveled. It moved quickly, and Marina didn't see the canister until it bumped against her foot. Whoever was controlling it—wherever they were—had known who they wanted to target, because three more followed, each one barreling in *her* direction.

And then, in less than a second, the canisters exploded.

Neva's knee-jerk reaction was clearly to protect Yolie because she wrapped her head in a bubble of air. But the bubble was small, and it didn't stop Yolie from flying backward.

Marina hit the ground too, blood roaring in her ears as Pierce fell beside her. He was lucky; the helmet on his armored suit protected him. As for her, the fumes had already filled her lungs.

She tried to summon a protective bubble of her own, but it was too late. Even if she'd reacted sooner, it would've been useless with her cuffs on. She cursed at them, blinking to clear her eyesight, but whatever she'd inhaled left her so disoriented she could hardly move. Even if she weren't wearing the cuffs, there was no way she could wield magic now.

Of course. Neva had reacted so quickly because of what had happened in Sal. These were the bombs Ryder had told her about—the ones Safira loved so much. What did he call them? Lock bombs?

The streets had filled with so much fog that Marina could no longer see the periwinkle paving stones, and with every inhale, her head spun. She didn't know Aeric had come up beside her until he pulled her up, and even then, his figure was blurry. It *was* him, wasn't it? Nearby, another helmeted soldier helped Pierce up.

Aeric stumbled—or maybe it was her—as he pulled her forward. He hadn't inhaled as much of the fumes as she had, which she thanked the heavens for. If he had, they *definitely* wouldn't escape this.

Only...Aeric *wasn't* planning on escaping. He found a shop only a few paces away, which had an elevated porch that hung a few feet off the ground, then pushed her under it. He pushed two others under with her as well. Soldiers. He gave one of them a ring with a gaudy, electric center stone.

"You three...stay *here*," Aeric hissed. He moved his hands over them—once, twice, then a third time. He was glamouring them, but Marina couldn't remember why. Who were they hiding from?

No matter. It was peaceful under the porch—dark and cold and perfect for sleeping— and Aeric's glamour felt like a blanket on top of them. He added something else; it wasn't heavy like a glamour, but hard, like a wall of air. *A shield.* He was shielding them too.

One of the soldier's arms wrapped around Marina. She tried to move to look at him— not like she'd be able to see him—but her body didn't respond.

"Don't move," he said. Ryder. His voice shook. "Stay...stay calm."

She *was* calm, though. Calmer than he was. Calmer than Pierce, too, who didn't say anything, but Marina could feel him—shaking, and huddled so close to Ryder that it had to be him.

It was kind of Aeric to choose them to be with her. He really *was* kind, even if he acted like a jerk sometimes. But she did too, so she couldn't hold it against him. Perhaps she should thank him. She opened her mouth, but Aeric was already speaking—not to her, but to Pierce and Ryder.

"Remain with her," he ordered. "Protect her and the Omnia, *no matter what.*"

Protect her from *whom?*

Vision spotty, Marina watched as Aeric stood and walked back to the center of the street, where the remnants of fog had died down. He wasn't as sure-footed as he normally was, but at least he could walk. At the moment, she was totally paralyzed.

Stupid. She should've acted quicker. She should've taken off her cuffs and shielded herself the moment the air started to smell. Now, she was no better than a puppet.

A puppet...that was why Safira did this. Because she didn't want anyone to fight back.

Safira. Right. *That* was who they were hiding from. But Marina couldn't see her; the street spanned out before them, wide and empty minus Aeric, Neva, Elm, and Yolie.

Marina's heart quickened, and whatever daze she'd been floundering in receded. Yolie should be here with them. She couldn't protect herself from Safira...she was too young. Would she end up like Ronan?

She went to pull herself from under the porch, but her limbs wouldn't obey. So much for Ryder telling her not to move; she couldn't if she tried. But her senses and thoughts were sharpening, and she could make out the faint *click, click, clicks* that echoed off the buildings. The clicks didn't come from ruemin, though Marina knew they were near. These came from *heels*.

Yolie rushed over to Neva, surprisingly agile compared to everyone else, which Marina had to credit Neva for. But Neva hadn't protected herself from the fumes as well as she'd protected Yolie. She tried to push Yolie away, but her movements were jittery.

"Go, Yolie," Neva urged her.

Please. Go. Run. Find somewhere to hide.

Yolie didn't obey. She wrapped her arms around Neva, protesting when Elm grabbed her by the arm and tried to pull her back. But he wasn't doing too well either, and he couldn't contain Yolie. Even if he could've, it was too late.

It was *always* too late for them. Florin's plan had failed because Kieron had caught on sooner. Their new plan had failed because of Shaw. And it was too late now because the mechanical woman had found them.

CHAPTER 43
Now and After

The sun had risen, and it beat upon Safira's hair and face so intensely that when she emerged from around one of the corners, Marina had to squint. As Safira neared Aeric and Neva, however—dozens of helmeted soldiers in tow, followed by even more ruemin—her smile was unmistakable. The fleshy side of her face dimpled, and the metallic half glinted as though it couldn't contain her pride.

Of *course* she was proud. She'd found them, and she'd probably find Marina too. Safira was as good at sensing glamours as she was at playing this sick game of hers. No matter how hard they fought, Aeric and Neva had to know she had the upper hand.

Marina's daze continued to fade, and with it, her fume-induced calmness. Now, she was descending into full-blown panic, but she couldn't do anything except breathe, and even then, her chest was tight. There she lay, unable to move or speak or do anything but acknowledge how uneven Safira had made this playing field. The fumes had died down, but Aeric, Neva, and Elm still couldn't stand without swaying.

The mental effects of the bombs didn't last long, but the physical effects—the severing of the brain's ability to communicate with the body—persisted.

Safira's eye swept across the street. Evenly, she said, "Have you glamoured her, Aeric?" When he didn't respond, she raised her eyebrow. "I know you weren't able to get her out of Tolsea in the state you're in."

Neva pushed Yolie behind her. This time, Yolie didn't fight her.

Come on, limbs, Marina begged. *Move. Please, please...*

If she could, she'd break away from this glamour, take off her cuffs, and help them. She knew Aeric would be angry with her, but they needed the help, and she'd evaded both Kieron and Safira before.

What did it matter? She *couldn't* move. Her arms and legs were useless. It made no difference how hard she tried or how intensely she prayed. All she could do was watch.

Safira rolled her neck, chains and sprockets shining in the afternoon sun, then nodded at her soldiers and the ruemin. "You know the rules. Keep him alive; kill the rest. I'll find the girl afterward."

Him. Aeric, obviously. He realized too, because the moment the gunfire started, he jumped in front of Neva, Yolie, and Elm and swathed a shield around their bodies.

A single shield could only do so much, and Aeric was still running on low reserves. When his shield of air faltered, Elm began firing—at soldiers, at ruemin...whoever he could get to. Marina had to give it to him: he took down two ruemin and a soldier. He might've targeted Safira, but she'd wrapped herself in a shield as she waited for the gunfire to stop.

This was worse than any nightmare. At least she could wake up from those. This was a hell so enduring that even squeezing her eyes shut didn't stop the torture. The gunfire went on for ages, and when it stopped, it took quite some time before Marina could open her eyes again.

Elm had fallen. His armored suit had withstood most of the damage, but he was too injured to stand. Impending doom descended on Marina, and when the soldiers stopped firing, ruemin sprang forward.

Aeric flayed three of them before they got to Elm's body, but eventually, he must've decided it was useless because he focused all his energy on shielding Neva and Yolie.

Still behind her own bubble of air, Safira watched as the ruemin bore into Elm.

That's on you.

Kieron. Marina felt like he was breathing down her neck, and her pulse skyrocketed. Now she was in the throne room, witnessing the ruemin tear apart those scouts.

Elm had been from the Delve. Maybe he'd known them. And now he joined them.

When a ruemin screeched, Aeric's force field faded once more. He put his hands on his knees, breathing like a wounded animal, trying—and failing—to regain his energy.

Neva wasn't doing well either. She kept trying to prod Yolie away, but her movements were clumsy. Safira, however, stood straight as she lowered her force field. She held up a hand to her remaining soldiers, and when they stepped back, she widened her arms.

Aeric shot up, hands out, as he deflected with a lance of light whatever attack she'd hurled their way. It buzzed and popped as it flew toward Safira, and this time, Yolie took the chance to run. She bolted to a stairwell in between two larger buildings, then crouched, her knees to her chest and hands over her ears.

One of the ruemin noticed and began prowling in her direction, but before it could get within a few yards of Yolie, Neva had decapitated it.

The others howled over Elm's body, teeth dripping with his blood as they recovered from the pain of Neva's attack. Marina expected Neva to target them too, but she'd already overexerted herself, and now she could hardly stand. She hurled a weak burst of light in Safira's direction, which Aeric must've considered the perfect opportunity. When Safira went to deflect it, he made a motion with his fist.

The sound of groaning metal echoed throughout the street as Safira's hand flew to the mechanical half of her face. For a moment, she stood there, fingers dancing along the grooves in her cheek. When she lowered her hand, Marina could make out a dent so large that Safira's face looked uneven. What was once both beautiful and terrifying was now just the latter, and even the soldiers near Safira quailed as their guns flew out in front of them.

She didn't give them time to shoot, though. Instead, she extended her arm toward Neva, who went to shield herself but was too late.

Too late, too late, too late.

Marina writhed against her paralysis as Neva fell to the ground, blood oozing from the side of her head. Though her chest moved, her breathing had grown shallow. Marina retreated into the darkness behind her closed lids, praying for this all to end.

Here she was—the Omnia's host, no less—hiding beneath a porch while her friends fought a fruitless battle. She should be out there helping. Now she had to watch them die.

"Safira!"

Marina's eyes flew open at Aeric's voice. He'd gotten Safira and her soldiers' attention too. Even the ruemin, who were still picking Elm apart—*his soul...they're devouring his soul* —lifted their heads long enough for the sunlight to reflect off their silver eyes.

Aeric steadied himself. Slowly, he reached into his pocket and pulled out a gray shell.

Marina knew what it was immediately. A bomb—not the kind Safira used, but the kind Kins had. The kind *Cal* had.

No. No, you can't. You can't, Aeric. Now and after. You promised me, now and after...

But this was his last resort. He couldn't fend Safira off with magic—not in his state.

No, no, no...

"No," Safira hissed, then jumped at Aeric as he pressed the pin and threw the bomb.

A lance of light shot from Safira's hand and hurtled toward Aeric. His arm flew up to send it off course, but he was disoriented and everything was happening quickly. The lance hit him in the temple—right where he'd struck Shaw—and Aeric hit the ground.

Every bone in Marina's body screamed as gunfire resumed. Only...the sound wasn't coming from guns. Aeric's bomb popped as it went off—again and again, each one louder than the last. He'd thrown it directly into the mass of ruemin, but Cal had been right when she'd said this kind of bomb covered a lot of ground.

The entire square erupted, and after a while, Marina didn't know if she was closing her eyes or if she'd gone blind. The shield Aeric had covered her, Pierce, and Ryder in might've protected their bodies, but it did nothing to dim the bomb's brilliance. And yet, Marina could've sworn she'd seen Safira throw herself onto Aeric, who lay unconscious beside Neva—could've sworn Safira had summoned her own shield, which caught fire as the buildings did.

For some reason, despite the shrieking ruemin and screaming soldiers, Marina thought of Safira's essence. Smoke. That's what the bomb would leave when it finished wreaking its havoc—when the flames died down. Marina hoped that when Safira saw her soldiers—limbs blown from their bodies, intermingled with the inky blood of ruemin— the smoke would horrify her.

She knew it wouldn't.

If anything, *Marina* was the one whose horror consumed her. It was all she felt: horror as her vision returned to her, as she searched the stairwell for Yolie and couldn't see her, as the bombs stopped and the smoke died down, as bodies—golden-armored and scaled alike —littered the pavement. When the decking of the porch she lay under cracked, all she could do was pray Aeric's shield would protect them from the worst.

It seemed to, even as bridging and beams came down. Marina didn't feel like anything was broken, but she was in such a state that she figured her brain was probably blocking the pain. That, and her focus was on the square. Though she had to peer through fallen joists, she could still see it.

When Safira lowered her shield and stood, she started cursing. Most of her soldiers lay motionless, and all of the ruemin did. Even with the soldiers' armor, those who'd been hit the hardest were still missing parts of their bodies, and the ruemin had been completely torn apart. Some heaved as they lay amongst blood and organs, and all Marina could think of was how similar to bugs they looked—mangled messes of bent legs and flattened torsos. As their clicks died down, she looked to the little that was left of Elm's body, then again to the golden-armored soldiers. Only three soldiers had survived, or at least were conscious, and they pulled themselves up shakily.

Safira bent down and clasped a pair of diminution cuffs on Aeric's wrists, then swore again as she rifled through his pockets.

"It's not here," she said, her voice so low and garbled that the soldiers—now loitering near her—exchanged glances. Even with her shield, Safira hadn't made it out without injuries. The fleshy side of her face was scratched up, and judging by the way she held her stomach, she'd been hit by something.

This time, when Safira rattled off curses, she didn't filter herself. She kicked a nearby empty gun before straightening and swearing again. For someone who was as aloof as Aeric, seeing Safira like this was jarring. Only then did Marina realize that Kieron had probably been furious with her for letting Brenna's ring get away—and that this was her chance to fix her failure in Altus.

Safira pointed at Aeric and gestured for one of her soldiers. Aeric...he was still breathing. That alone was enough for Marina to hold on to her sanity, even as the soldier hoisted Aeric up.

"Bring him to Altus," Safira ordered. "When you get there, tell Kieron I'm still searching for her and the ring." She paused. "None of you saw anything?"

The soldiers shook their heads. The fog must've been too thick for anyone watching to see Aeric hide her, which was a minor miracle. But Marina knew Safira wouldn't stop looking, and when she found her, she'd find the ring too.

"Go," Safira said.

The soldier holding Aeric hesitated. His torso was bleeding, Marina realized. In fact, all of them were in pretty bad shape. With Safira's dented face and the soldiers' armor damaged, they were hardly the threat they'd been minutes ago.

Safira motioned for another soldier to help, which left only one with her. He was in the best condition, but by the way he moved, Marina could tell he'd been badly bruised.

"I'll call in backup," Safira said. "And tell him not to worry. The girl was hit the worst; I made certain of it. She won't be a threat."

The soldiers didn't question Safira. They responded by hooking their arms under Aeric's. Before they set off, Safira put her hand on Aeric's forehead, and Marina could only guess she was either confirming unconsciousness or inducing it herself. The two guards transporting Aeric were in no state to fend him off if he woke, and there was no way Safira would risk him escaping.

Any amusement Marina might've felt observing the sorry state of Safira's soldiers dissipated when they began to drag Aeric away. She tried to move—she couldn't let them do this...she couldn't let them take him—but her paralysis wouldn't yield, even as the soldiers rounded the corner with Aeric.

Safira's hand brushed across the dented half of her face once more, but she quickly composed herself.

"She can't be far," she said to the soldier. "Sweep the nearby blocks, then check if the drones have picked anything up. I'll contact Altus."

Safira was still holding her stomach, and the soldier noticed. After nodding, he said, "If you need to go back, I can—"

"No," Safira snapped. "Go. Obey orders."

The soldier nodded again, then racked his gun and limped out of the square. Finally alone, Safira removed her hand from her stomach and held her bloody palm out in front of her. She grimaced, her gaze lingering on her voco before trailing to the stairwell.

At first, Marina was relieved she'd gotten distracted—that she hadn't yet summoned backup to Tolsea—but the relief came to a grinding halt when she realized what Safira had been distracted by.

Nearly every structure in the square had been damaged. But not the stairwell. Amidst cracked foundation and pummeled stone, it was as good as untouched. It had clearly been shielded...by someone inclined.

Yolie.

No, no, no...

Safira lowered her hand. Then, slowly, she picked her way over bodies and approached the stairwell. Before she could reach it, however, one of the bodies moved.

Neva. She'd rolled onto her stomach, and despite her head wound, managed to pull herself up. What felt like a thousand bursts of electricity careened through Marina's body, sending her heart into a frenzy.

Why didn't you play dead, Neva? she wanted to scream. *You should've played dead!*

She wouldn't have. Not when Yolie hid in the stairwell—when Safira would no doubt kill her before resuming her hunt for Marina and the ring. But Neva didn't hold much power at the moment, and she knew it.

It didn't stop her from trying. The moment Safira realized she'd moved, Neva's arms widened. A bubble of air materialized around Safira, but not soon enough—a gash had formed at her throat, cutting through chains on one side and skin on the other. Marina's heart all but stopped as Safira wrapped her hand around her neck, then moved it out in front of her and studied the blood on her fingers. The wound was worse than the one on her stomach, and Safira's hand shined red in the afternoon light.

Neva had done damage, perhaps, but not enough to be fatal. Safira's bloodstained hand curled, and Neva stumbled back—one step, then two, then several more.

When Neva hit the ground, blood seeped from more than her head; it poured from her throat too, in the same spot she'd attacked Safira. And after a few agonizing seconds— each one so long it felt like an eternity—Neva stopped breathing.

CHAPTER 44
Starlight and Smoke

Someone screamed. Was it in Marina's head?

No...it was real. It was Yolie.

Too late, too late, too late. The words tormented Marina as Yolie stepped out of the stairwell. It was too late for Aeric. Too late for Neva. Too late for Elm. And now, it would be too late for Yolie.

Marina almost expected Yolie to rush to Neva's body, but she didn't. She faced Safira full on, her glasses shining as vividly as Safira's face. Though her voice shook, Yolie was loud and clear when she said, "You killed my family." She choked on a sob but didn't break down. Instead, she glowered at Safira and repeated, "You killed them."

Safira wiped away the blood trickling from her neck, then regarded Yolie with an irritated look. She'd been hoping for Marina, clearly, only to be confronted with a child.

Don't do this, Yolie. Please don't do this.

"You killed Ronan and Neva." Yolie continued repeating their names as she edged toward Safira, who put up her hand in warning.

"Be smart," Safira rasped. "I can make this painless, or I can make it much worse."

Yolie stared at Neva's body for a moment. Then, slowly, she lifted her teary eyes to Safira, who was obviously struggling to steady her breathing.

The damage Aeric and Neva had done to Safira had weakened her—not enough to render her unconscious, but enough to matter. Was that why Yolie was taking this risk? Or was she so consumed by grief that she wasn't thinking clearly?

It was the latter. From where she lay, Marina could see it in Yolie's face—the rage and sorrow that aged her a hundred years and left her with hatred so mind-numbing that Marina wondered if Yolie didn't care what this risk resulted in.

When Yolie widened her arms like Neva had, Safira staggered back. But before she could return the blow, Yolie had already wrapped herself in air. Safira cursed, then angled her head sharply at Yolie.

Yolie must've torn at her wound because Safira's hand flew back to her neck. When she recovered, she cleaved through the center of Yolie's shield, then sent a cluster of shadows her way. Like Vaughn's, they purled and rippled so thick over the paving stones that Marina imagined she'd pulled them from every cranny and crevice of the surrounding street. They pooled around Yolie's ankles, sending her down.

Marina thought she heard Ryder curse beneath his breath—though it could've been Pierce, or perhaps it was all in her head—as Yolie hit the ground on her side. She turned on her back as the shadows swathed at her feet, her gaze darting to the rooftops. One of the shadows entwined about her neck, constricting with so much force that when Yolie began to gasp, Marina's eyes flew shut again.

She couldn't watch this. It was too much. Her panic had deserted her, and now, there was only helplessness. It swelled out and poured over, and even if some miracle granted her the ability to move again, Marina wasn't sure she could bring herself to.

The gasping stopped.

Yolie...no, no, no...

Marina squinted across the street, bracing herself to see Yolie's dead body—vacant eyes behind thick glasses and limbs as stiff as the corpses in the Admares. Only...Yolie was very much alive. Her arms were up, and they were pointing at *Safira.*

Flashes of white and gold began to caper across every inch of metal on Safira's face and neck. It was as though Yolie had stolen a beam of light from the sun itself, then directed it toward Safira, who covered her remaining eye with her hand. It may not have blinded her, but it certainly stunned her. The shadows waned, and the moment Yolie wriggled free, she stood and threw more light Safira's way.

No...not just light. *Force.*

Force—like the kind Marina had taught Yolie back in the sanctuary. The kind she'd told Yolie to funnel her emotions into.

Safira's hands flew out, but Yolie had still caught her off guard. Dumbfounded and pale from blood loss, Safira dug her heels into the ground and formed a shield with her arms. A gray, billowing cloud dropped like a curtain in front of her, tinging the air with acrid odor. *Smoke,* Marina realized. Safira must've shielded herself with air; either that or whatever metal her throat was made out of wasn't affected. Yolie began to cough, but she kept on—pulling the light from every streetlamp, from the afternoon sun, and perhaps, in some ways, from the stars that comprised her essence.

Starlight and smoke collided—violently, wildly—and even when Yolie's legs gave way, the force continued pouring from her hands as she cried out their names.

Ronan and Neva. Ronan and Neva. Ronan and Neva.

Every ounce of power in Yolie's body burned—not for herself, but for those who'd been taken from her.

The sobs that eddied Yolie's screams nearly broke Marina, had it not been for the strength in them—for the will and grit that set fire to even Safira's smoke. When the curtain of gray dropped, Yolie's light threw Safira to the ground. But she didn't stop. She stood and neared Safira, still yelling their names—*making* Safira hear them.

On and on she pushed, white light coming down on Safira so hard that the golden half of her face began to pop from her skin. In the distance, Marina thought she heard gunfire, but she couldn't be sure. The sound of metal coming undone from Safira's face was louder than Marina expected it to be, and after a couple of grueling seconds, it broke from her skin and went flying. It skidded across the stones—a mess of chains and metal—and after that, there was only the crunch of bones and flesh.

Yolie *still* didn't stop—not until she knew Safira was dead. Even then, she persisted for another minute, maybe more. When she finally lowered her arms, she collapsed onto the stones beside the mechanical woman.

A few spots of light flickered in protest, glinting off Yolie's glasses and Safira's hair.

Eventually, they faded too.

CHAPTER 45
Return to Us

At the height of noon, Tolsea's air hummed with a gentle breeze. It skirted around buildings and weaved through alleyways, then dipped beneath the porch and brushed against Marina's skin.

She wasn't sure how long it took her to regain control over her body. Even once her limbs could move, every muscle shook. Ryder and Pierce edged out from under the rubble, then lifted the wooden beams off Marina and pulled her out.

As Pierce helped her sit, Ryder scooped up Yolie and brought her over to them. When Marina saw her eyes flutter, she let out a broken, tearless sob.

She could make sounds now, but she couldn't speak. Thankfully, Ryder could, because he lifted his voco to his lips and sent out calls to Ismene, Elta, and Blaine, praying someone would return his messages. He could walk without stumbling too, and he began pacing about the dead, searching them for anything they could use.

It was automatic for him, Marina realized—or perhaps treating it like a task made the pain easier to weather. He came across some additional weapons on the soldiers, then scoured Safira's pockets until he found the key to Aeric's cuffs. Even then, he kept circling the dead like a vulture. He clearly wasn't going to leave until he'd picked them clean, which Marina figured was resourceful, albeit a bit morbid. If anything, she was glad he could stomach being so close to so many freshly dead bodies, because she wasn't sure she could. Every time she glanced at Neva, the cracks in her chest deepened.

Since it was impossible not to look at the bodies that littered the street, Marina focused on Safira, hoping at least *that* would give her some small sense of victory.

It didn't. If anything, the sight was so harrowing it almost made her sick.

Even from where they sat, Marina could see the damage on Safira's face. Only half of it remained, as broken and caved in as the metallic portion that lay across the street. Her eye had been pushed back into her head, so bloodshot that her iris gleamed red—blood staining a pool of sea green. Her nose bent unnaturally, and her once high cheekbone had been snapped in two.

Yolie uttered a labored breath from beside them. She was unconscious but still alive, and that's what mattered. Marina couldn't help but wonder if she was more powerful than all of them—than Aeric and Kieron and all the magical savants in Elsudra.

Either way, she wouldn't be fighting again. They'd make sure she got to safety, then…

Then what? There was no one else to finish Florin's plan, and Marina couldn't bear to go into hiding again and leave Aeric at the mercy of Kieron.

Remember what you promised the Keepers, Aeric had said.

She might've sworn to protect the Omnia, but she'd sworn it for Elsudra. For the ones she loved. She had to protect them. Who else would?

She'd gone to Altus once. It seemed there was nothing left to do but make that choice again. But this time, she wouldn't be there to buy anyone time. She'd be there to do what Florin, Aeric, and Neva could do no longer. The ruemin, Vaughn, Kieron…all of this had to end. Because of Yolie, Safira was gone. One fewer threat to stand in their way. An iota of hope flickered in Marina's chest.

As unfathomable as trying to finish things was, it was equally impossible for Marina to think about going back into hiding. The others couldn't blend in with her present. She couldn't do that to them. But what would she tell Pierce and Ryder? If she could talk, which she couldn't—her mouth still felt like it had been jabbed with numbing needles—she wouldn't know what to say.

She didn't have to settle on anything now; nearby voices demanded her attention.

Ismene sprinted toward them, Blaine and Elta in tow. It was only when she got within a couple feet that Marina could see her clothes and face, covered in specks of blood.

Before Ismene could say anything—before Blaine and Elta could so much as stop walking—Ryder said, "Are there any soldiers nearby? Any ruemin?"

Blaine shook his head, then gawked at the corpses that crowded the square. When he spoke, he sounded like he always did—quiet and a little amused. "I think you got most of them," he said.

"Aeric did that," Pierce replied. "But Safira had two of her soldiers take him to Altus."

Ismene took that the hardest. Tears welled in her eyes as she cradled Ash, who she'd wrapped in her coat. Though he wriggled, it was clear he'd mostly given up.

"Safira was going to call for backup," Ryder added. "But she never got to. She sent one of her soldiers off—"

"I killed him," Ismene whispered, then wiped her cheeks with the back of her hand.

Even Marina, whose head was still fuzzy, blinked at her.

"After we got separated, the three of us tried to make our way to backroads on our own," Ismene said. "Then the sound of bombs sent us fleeing for cover, and when we emerged, the city was so...silent. We thought you'd been killed." She glanced at Marina. "Or taken." Her chin trembled when she added, "We tried to keep moving, but we ran into a soldier. He must've been hit by the bomb because his armor was badly beaten up. Blaine stunned him, then I..."

When her voice faded, Elta—weak, but present enough to smirk—said, "Ismene shot him. Multiple times."

Blaine lowered Elta next to Marina. For a moment, Elta quietly surveyed the dead. When her eyes filled with tears, Marina knew she'd seen Neva. Blaine noticed too, then made a noise so strangled Marina couldn't tell if it was a moan or a cry.

Pierce and Ryder took on the burden of explaining what had happened. Though Blaine and Ismene listened, Elta's gaze remained on Neva. It clearly took pains for Elta to return her attention to the group when they finished, but she did. She assessed Yolie first —she'd overexerted herself and had taken damage to her throat, but nothing permanent— then turned to Marina.

"Give her water," Elta told Blaine, who pulled a beaten flask from his bag. Apparently, it helped flush out the lock bombs' toxins.

Marina drank sloppily, but she managed to get everything down. It took an additional few minutes before she could stand, but eventually, her senses returned.

"Safira must've summoned all her soldiers to her when she found you," Blaine said, "because the portal system near us is empty. We should use it while we have the chance. I know a few places we can go."

Thank God. Oh, thank God. If even a small group of Safira's soldiers had survived the bombing, any hope of getting out of Tolsea would be lost. And yet, despite how eager she was to leave this wretched place, Marina remained motionless as Blaine scooped up Yolie— as Elta gingerly lifted her bandaged arm and put it around Ismene's neck. When they started moving, Marina couldn't bring herself to follow. Pierce noticed; he came up beside her and said, "I can help you."

She shook her head.

It took a few moments for the realization to dawn on Pierce, but when it did, he held her gaze. Understanding lingered between the two of them—warm and quiet enough to make time feel like it had slowed down.

Pierce made a small gesture to Ryder, who caught on too. Perhaps he'd been thinking the same thing, even if he hadn't mentioned it. Perhaps all three of them had.

Running was no longer an option. Pierce reached into the pocket of his armored suit, then pulled out what Aeric had given him. Brenna's ring.

When Ryder noticed, he turned to Blaine, Ismene, and Elta. "We won't be coming."

Blaine only stared at them. Ismene, however, blinked back her shock. "Why?"

"We're going to finish this," Pierce said.

Ismene and Elta exchanged a glance.

"Go," Marina managed. Her voice was raspy, but it was working, at least. She looked to Yolie, who was still out—eyes squeezed shut and breathing deeply. "Go to safety."

"Marina..." Ismene started. She clamped her lips shut when Marina's eyes met hers.

Slowly and unsteadily, Marina stepped toward her, then put her forehead to Ismene's. "Let me make this choice," she whispered.

For a second, they were back in the caverns beneath the Admares, coming to terms with the risk she was about to take. Ismene must've remembered that Marina had begged the same of her back then, and her response didn't change. Her eyes clouded with tears, but she kept her wits about her when she nodded. "Okay."

Tension flooded from Marina's muscles like water from a dam, and this time, tears fell. Her arms, thank goodness, worked well enough to wipe them away. At least Ismene wouldn't fight them; it would only make this harder.

Elta, however, wasn't as easily convinced. Though it took strength for her to speak, she didn't hold back her reservations. "This wasn't the plan," she said. "What happens if the three of you don't make it out?"

Marina looked at her feet for a moment. "The Delve. Tin. Candens Inlet. Tolsea. His people have found us every time. And every time, people die. The same thing will happen wherever we go next. We have to try to end this."

Elta blinked back her tears, and Marina half expected more protests. But Elta was as weak as ever, and in the direct light, Marina could see the beads of sweat that dotted her pale forehead and the glossiness in her eyes. And though the bandage on her arm hid most of the damage, what little skin peeked out had turned from white to dark gray. Elta knew it—knew the chances of finding medicine were low, and if this didn't end now, she may not live to get help. Her eyes lingered on her arm, then moved to Ismene, who gave her a weak nod. When Elta finally beheld Marina, all she responded with was a trembling, tight-lipped smile.

"I know you're not asking our permission," Ismene said after a few moments. "I know you'd leave anyway. But I only have one request." She looked at Pierce, then Ryder, then Marina. "Please...whatever you do, return to us."

CHAPTER 46
Unwelcome Visitors

Goodbyes lasted only seconds. Pierce embraced both Ismene and Ash, and Marina planted a small kiss on Yolie's head, who barely stirred.

Return to us, Ismene had said. They would. They had to.

Ismene's group departed first—to the South, Blaine had said—and once Ryder and Pierce confirmed the streets and portal system were clear, they approached the console by the fountain. Blaine had told them of a church on the outskirts of Altus that had been abandoned when the war started. Even better, it was in an isolated area and had a belfry they could camp out in for the night.

Pierce and Ryder seemed to know of the church, but it was Blaine who gave them clear-cut instructions on how to get there. Ryder, Pierce, and Marina would travel to a small town at the edge of a lake outside Altus, then follow Blaine's directions to the belfry on foot, where they'd spend the night. The next morning—after resting and finalizing their plan—they'd head out to reach the palace by evening. After that...

She'd think about that when they got there. Now, she needed to move. To step. To *breathe.* There were only three of them, perhaps, but they had all the needed skills. She could wield magic, Ryder knew the palace, and both Ryder *and* Pierce could fight, if it came down to it. Which it probably would.

One day, one step, one breath at a time. That's it. All they could do was move forward and remember who they were fighting for.

There were so many names on her list now. Too many. Marina prayed it would come to an end—that no more would be added. Still, she repeated them as they traveled. It helped replace her fear with anger. With *determination.*

When Kieron *did* learn what had happened to his troops—to Safira—Marina hoped it would sucker punch him. Now, the woman who'd killed and hunted for him could no longer do his bidding. One by one, his puppets' strings were being cut, and soon, there'd be no one left to hide behind.

⁓

They arrived in a northern town just outside of Altus, which was bordered by water in the east and trees in the west. From there, they moved into the most wooded areas they could find, sticking to seldom-trekked roads until small signs signaled their entrance into Altus.

"I asked you once to put me out of my misery if we ever returned here," Ryder said to Marina, "but now, I think there's a chance someone else may do the honors."

Had they not been standing at the edge of Altus, Marina *might've* smirked at that. But right now, she couldn't bring herself to laugh. Pierce couldn't either.

Ryder grimaced, then said, "We should be close to the belfry. But we're still entering Altus, and we can't risk being seen by anyone. I hope your glamouring has improved."

Marina uncuffed herself, praying Aeric was right about Altus making it easier for her energy to blend in. She spent several minutes mirroring what she'd seen Aeric do and what she'd practiced in Shaw's basement: folding light and shadows, which she swathed them in until they were hidden. Even then, she kept adjusting it as they walked, which meant she had to keep her cuffs off. She prayed there weren't any ruemin in these woods.

On the other hand, if they did come across ruemin, perhaps they could knock one out and have it ready before reaching the palace. That way, they wouldn't have to rely on Vaughn—wouldn't have to rely on *her* to use dissolution magic on him, which terrified Marina more than summoning ruemin. But glamouring and transporting a ruemin sounded like hell, regardless of whether it was sedated. Even her *current* glamour was fading—tendrils of shadows unraveling from the blanket she'd tried so hard to wrap them in. She had them stop a few times to touch it up, but of course, that required movement. When she fixed one bad spot, two more popped up, and eventually, Marina had them pick up the pace so they could get to the belfry before her shoddy work wore off completely.

Glamouring three fully grown people, Marina thought, was near impossible. At least, it was for her. How did Aeric do it so well? And how had Hollis and Zora kept four people *and* a ruemin glamoured for so long?

One day, one step, one breath at a time. She repeated it to herself as the woods thinned out and they made their way around the base of some hills, then traveled the rest of the way through fields. Ryder would whisper directions, and Marina did her best to make sure their feet stayed in line with hers. They continued straight, and when Marina could see the ocean on the horizon, the belfry appeared in the distance.

The church itself was surrounded by a worn-down fence, which groaned every time the sea breeze skirted through its cracks. Once they'd made their way around back and Marina let the glamour fall, Ryder knocked some pickets down so they could slip through.

"You stand watch, okay?" Pierce said, then eagerly left to help Ryder find a way in.

Since being on heightened alert was a rather natural state for her, Marina supposed it wouldn't be too difficult to keep an eye out for anything. Besides, this place was as well-hidden as Blaine had said—protected on one side by the sea and on the other by a small set of hills. The closest houses were just beyond those hills, or back by the forest, closer to the portal system. If there was anything she should be worried about, it was ruemin. But everything was quiet. It should've been calming, but it was only eerie. That, and the silence made room for thoughts about Neva and the rest. To keep them at bay, Marina tried to point out the things she could see: the broken fence, the unruly weeds that sprouted up and around the base of the building, and the small patches of flowers. Bee balm grew in clusters, and yellow flowers beside them glowed in the setting sun.

Daffodils. Gemma had told her once that her parents had put a vase next to her crib when she was a baby. Marina's eyes began to sting.

Don't break down, she commanded herself. *Keep going. Gemma and Hank would want you to. So would Mom and Dad.* Still, her chin quivered, but she got over herself when Ryder signaled for her to join them at the side of the church. He and Pierce had found a broken window and managed to remove the boards covering it up.

Relief flooded through her, partially because they'd finally be able to get out of sight, but mostly because she needed to stop looking at the daffodils.

They scouted the premises once more before they hopped over the sill, then searched the church's interior before finding the stairwell to the belfry. Pierce and Ryder kept their weapons out in front of them, and though Marina remained just as vigilant, no amount of anxiety could stop her from drinking in the beauty of this place. Every wall was covered in paintings—not of people or deities, but *water*, brimming with sunlight. Blue, green, and white pooled over beams and pillars, crafted in the same style as the architecture in the palace, then fizzled out at the top of the stairs like waves upon the shore.

The bell itself seemed to resemble the sun. It sat outside the chamber, painted in gold so bright that the louvers surrounding it glowed. Beyond the tower, the horizon glittered in blue, and the real Elsudran sun—the one she'd seen for the first time at the Delve's southern border—had almost finished its descent.

Pierce came up beside her and set his weapons on the ground. "They used to ring this four times a day. You could hear it from anywhere in Altus."

"There was one in Lewes too," Marina said, though she figured it probably hadn't been attached to a church. "But that one rang."

"This one will too. Soon." Pierce gestured for Marina to follow him out to the bell, nodding at Ryder when he warned them to be careful.

They peered through a louver facing the ocean, breathing alongside each other as they watched the sun disappear. They could see almost the entire bay, across from which was a curved spit of land Pierce said was called the Antlers. From the belfry, they did indeed look like the horns of a stag—long and tangled bursts of rocky hills sprouting from the sea.

"Sometimes I think I'm still home," she whispered. "Especially when I see the ocean."

Glints of the sun's rays danced in Pierce's eyes. "Elsudra may not be where you were born," he said, "but it's your home too. It always will be."

"Even if I fail?" Marina's voice broke when she said it, and as hard as she tried to watch the ocean, she couldn't distract herself enough to stop the tears.

"If that happens," Pierce whispered, "you won't be failing alone." He wavered, then tapped the ground with his foot. "When I first met you, all I wanted was to prove myself. I'm sure that doesn't come as a surprise. Ocot made my intentions pretty clear."

Marina chuckled tearfully. "He didn't have the noblest intentions either. Nor did I."

"Yours were justified. But me...I only wanted to show everyone I was more than Tover's son. And I thought if the Omnia's host thought highly of me, others would too. But it didn't take long before I no longer cared about any of that. You were my family. You and Ismene...and now, *that* one too." He cocked his head toward Ryder, who'd clearly been eavesdropping because he grinned. Pierce wrung his hands before adding, "So when I say Elsudra is your home, I mean it."

Throat tight, Marina whispered, "I'm glad you found me in the sea cavern."

"Me too." His smile twitched, then faded. "It's strange to think that the last time I was in this city, I was fleeing it."

Marina turned from the view and faced Pierce fully. "You're not fleeing now."

Pierce didn't respond, but he didn't need to. For a while, the two of them soaked in the view. Ryder joined them, and they did what they could to admire the sunset. But the gravity of the situation—of what might come tomorrow—wasn't lost on them. When Pierce pulled Brenna's ring from his pocket and held it to the fading light, Marina figured they might as well run through Aeric's plan once more so they were prepared. Pierce and Ryder seemed to be thinking the same thing, and they didn't protest when she spoke of it. By the time they finished talking through everything, starlight winked on the ocean.

The plan was simple but daunting. If they headed out in the morning, they'd reach the palace by evening, which was also what Aeric had planned to do. The palace gates had a schedule: once at dawn and once before sunset, they opened to let soldiers on daytime and

nighttime patrol swap places. Since there were bound to be soldiers passing through the gates, conveying everyone into the palace grounds was more dangerous than glamouring. And so, Marina would risk glamouring living things—*it's not a large group...only the three of us,* she tried to reassure herself—and they'd slip through.

Not counting Marina's glamours failing, Pierce and Ryder seemed most worried that ruemin would sense the Omnia's energy. They mostly crowded the prisons, not the front of the palace, but since Marina wouldn't be wearing cuffs, there was a possibility she'd catch their attention. Thankfully, they'd be operating in Altus, and if what Aeric had said about the amount of magical energy in the capital was true, then Marina had better odds of blending in. Either way, all they could do was what they already planned to: remain aware, and if anything attacked them, kill it immediately.

Once they got *into* the palace, things changed. Apprehending Vaughn was their first order of business, and they couldn't kill him. If there was one thing that worried Marina more than glamouring for so long, it was what she had to do to Vaughn. She couldn't make the same mistake she'd made in Inber.

You're too heavy-handed, Aeric had told her. *Next time, you'll tread lighter. Go slower.*

She had no idea if she could—no idea what Vaughn's essence would look like, or if she'd even be able to get through, no less force him into compliance. Targeting memories was one thing, and she hadn't been successful at that. How the hell was she supposed to smother Vaughn's essence without annihilating it?

She almost said something to Pierce and Ryder but decided against it. She couldn't bear to talk about Inber, and there was nothing they could do to help her. All she could do was follow Aeric's advice—tread lighter—and try not to kill Vaughn and ruin everything.

If they made it that far, they'd rely on Ryder to get them to the room with Brenna's portal, then force Vaughn to lure ruemin to them. Ryder seemed to think most of the ruemin would come from the prisons—the scanner that unlocked for guards also registered the ruemins' nails, which meant ruemin could get in and out as they pleased—and they would be eager to follow a sound they were familiar with.

The rest of the plan was fairly self-explanatory, despite being much simpler in theory than in practice. The odds weren't lost on any of them, of course, as was the fact that there were no other options. But they'd made it this far. That had to count for something.

After a while, rehashing everything became useless, so they tried—and failed—to sleep. Ryder gave up first and headed downstairs around midnight, and for about half an hour, Marina helped ease some of the lingering pain in Pierce's leg. Eventually, Pierce went downstairs to check on Ryder, so Marina turned her attention to her shin. It wasn't too bad—bruised, and sore if she pressed on it—but she continued soothing it anyway. When she grew bored of that, she soaked in the view. She watched the starlit sky, practicing glamours on herself and rejoicing when they stuck.

Pierce and Ryder returned in the small hours with cans of food they'd found stored in a pantry at the back of the church, but it was obvious that wasn't all they'd been doing. Pierce's hair was messier than usual, and the sweat on their brows glistened in the dim light. As horrible as Marina felt, she couldn't help but smile when she saw them shooting glances at each other. She forced herself to eat some canned peaches and drink water, which was all she could stomach at the moment. As she ate, the tune to "Landslide" played in her head, and she let herself get as lost in that as she had the view outside the belfry.

She put her cuffs back on before she fell asleep. The biggest threat somewhere this isolated was ruemin, but if they didn't sense unusual energy, they'd have no reason to break into the church. If they did, Marina had a feeling Ryder and Pierce would hold them off long enough for her to use her key. But thankfully, the night was quiet, and when she woke, the sun had begun its ascent. Pierce slept beside her, and Ryder sat near one of the louvers, cleaning weapons and reorganizing their things. Since she knew she wouldn't be able to fall back asleep, she helped him take inventory. They had a fair number of weapons, but they were low on ammunition. Ryder didn't seem too worried about it—he and Pierce were more than competent with blades—and they had their most pressing items: a rope, which used to be Florin's, Marina's cuffs, which they planned to use on Vaughn, and the key to the cuffs Aeric now wore, which Ryder gave to Marina. By the time they'd finished checking for everything, the sun had made it above the hills.

"We'll head out soon," Ryder said, and though it made Marina's stomach flip, she was glad to go. The less time she had to drown in anticipation, the better. She helped Ryder pack everything up to distract herself, and soon enough, Pierce had woken too and lent them a hand. Before they left, Marina gave the bell a parting glance. It slumbered in its spot—a golden giant waiting to be woken—and she wished she could hear it ring.

Ryder noticed where she was looking. "I agree with Pierce. It'll ring again one day."

"I hope so," she whispered.

"I know so," Pierce said. "We're not a bad team, the three of us. We haven't lost yet."

No, they hadn't. But the ruemin were insidious, and the only real threat to them was Brenna's portal. Which meant Kieron wouldn't make it easy to get to. Head foggy, Marina muttered, "Ruemin means *unwelcome visitor* in Sundra. Kieron told me that once."

Pierce exchanged a glance with Ryder. For a few seconds, the three of them watched the bell, which shone more silver than gold in the dim sunlight.

"That settles that, then," Pierce finally said. "Let's get these unwelcome visitors out of our home."

CHAPTER 47
Leap of Faith

They stuck to the woods on the western side of Altus, and by the time houses began to materialize, Marina already had the group glamoured. It was around noon now, and the hard light and shadows cast by buildings helped her. She tried to strike a balance between meticulousness and obsession, vigilance and fear. All she could do was apply what she'd learned, fix the mistakes, and move forward, one step at a time.

Her glamour held up as they made their way into the heart of Altus; perhaps she'd needed a bit of rest and food. Though the streets were as empty as always, they stuck to alleyways, figuring no amount of cautiousness was too much.

Like the bell, perhaps one day, these streets would come alive too. When the ruemin were gone, and when Kieron and his followers were no more than distant nightmares, maybe people would find freedom in a city that used to be theirs.

If, the voice at the back of her head whispered. *Not when.*

She bristled at that voice, then let it wash away and refocused on her glamour, which was still intact. Maybe *when* was more likely than *if.* And if it wasn't, at least they hadn't fled. At least they'd tried. She couldn't tell what Pierce and Ryder were thinking, but she could feel their presence. They were tense beneath her glamour, but they kept walking until the houses around them grew grander and the sun dulled.

They stopped only a few times, finding places isolated enough to rest and refuel as quickly as they could. Still, by the time evening came and Marina saw the palace's golden gate in the distance, she could feel exhaustion settling in. If her fatigue won, the first thing to go would be her glamour, which made her even more mindful of it. When she caught sight of guards surrounding the palace entrance—dressed in gold as bright as the gate itself—her adrenaline spiked, and a new burst of energy careened through her.

She'd never seen the palace from the front. The gate had been built into the base of a hill, and atop a massive perron, the castle itself stood against a sky of emerging stars. At faint touches of the sun, its edges blurred, almost as though a halo had been placed atop towers and hoardings. How many of those were filled with soldiers? Could *Kieron* be watching from one of them?

When her heart quickened, she focused once more on her steps.

Your glamour is intact, she told herself. She'd just touched it up a few blocks away.

But it was getting hard to maintain, and no number of reassurances could stave off the fatigue. Why did glamouring living things have to be so damned hard?

They were close, though...that was good. Once they were inside, they could find some hidden place for her to collect herself again. She only had to hold on a bit longer.

The guards stationed at the gate stood like gargoyles, barely moving until the sounds of heavy footsteps filed in from nearby streets. Ryder had clearly known the right time to come; it took only a few minutes before the gates opened to let the soldiers in. Marina could hear them exchange words with the others, though it was mostly greetings. Casual—like the Inber soldier's memories. Of course, if they noticed the three of them, they'd probably try to kill Ryder and Pierce on sight.

Focus on walking. Nothing else.

Ryder had taken over now, and instead of mirroring her footsteps, she and Pierce tried to mirror his. That was a bit harder because Marina had to anticipate how he'd move and bend the glamour to fit his strides. He was really being mindful of his steps, but every so often, Marina would get the horrible feeling that her glamour would fade anyway and soldiers would notice. Worse, Ryder seemed intent on falling in place with those moving toward the palace. He wanted to keep up with the flow of traffic, which was a smart idea —*if* she didn't trip up.

She hadn't yet. They kept enough distance so as not to slam into anyone, but didn't stray too far. Once they'd slipped through the gate, they moved off to the side, thankful the perron was big enough to avoid the line of heavily armored guards that moved upward in single file. As tempting as it was to hold her breath, Marina forced herself to inhale and exhale at every step.

Every so often, the perron leveled out, flanked on both sides by pathways and smaller staircases that wound around the hill. At this point, Marina and Pierce had put all their faith into Ryder, who pulled them off the stairs and onto a trail that led away from the front entrance. She realized why when she glanced at the palace doors. Guards had to clock in with their vocos in order to be allowed entrance, and there wasn't near as much room for them to sneak in like they had at the gate.

She might've been glad to stop climbing the stairs had the trails winding around the palace not been even harder to trek. She strained to keep the glamour around them, but monitoring both it and six moving feet put pressure on more than her mental energy. Her muscles quivered too, and eventually, she resorted to squeezing Ryder's and Pierce's wrists to get them to slow down.

Even with her adrenaline, she couldn't hold out much longer—not with all three of them. But Ryder had anticipated that, and he whisked them into a courtyard surrounded by yew trees. Across it, Marina could see another set of stone stairs that led down around the other side of the hill. She knew this courtyard. This was where she'd ripped Vaughn's arm off. And down the stairs...

"Let me do this, Astra."

For a moment, Marina thought Cal was right in front of her. She shook the voice away, but it was harder to breathe now, and her glamour was going to fail any moment. They moved toward a particularly thick cluster of trees, which Marina hoped would hide them as she collected her energy, but stopped in their tracks when a door atop a flight of stairs opened.

A guard—a bit older than the three of them—whistled as he took the steps, hands in his pockets and gaze on the trees.

Shit. Marina felt as though she were dangling off a ledge, seconds away from falling. Her ears started to ring, but she kept her hold on the glamour as he passed by.

He came to a halt. For half a second, Marina thought he detected them—a stupid fear, really, because he wasn't a ruemin, and Kieron certainly wasn't in the business of hiring seasoned sorcerers as soldiers—but the young man kept his eyes on the trees, then sighed contentedly against the breeze.

Dammit. You idiot.

She couldn't do this—couldn't keep her glamour swathed over all three of them. The sun was setting too, which changed the nature of shadows and light, which she had to control for. How did Aeric manage all of this so effortlessly? He didn't even need to be that close to his glamours for them to stay intact. She'd never match his talent—not with this. She didn't have much time to think about that; her concentration was wearing thin. Removing herself from the glamour would lessen the burden, and at this point, it was either that or let the entire thing fall. She broke free from Ryder and Pierce's grips, trying not to imagine the horror flooding through them as the guard opened his eyes.

The guard didn't have time to lift his voco. Marina's hand moved of its own accord, and after that, everything was red.

All he'd been doing was watching the trees. Yes, he was one of Kieron's guards, but he'd been minding his own just the same. And now he was dead—like the soldier in Inber—because she was better at killing than anything else.

"You had to," Ryder said. Either he'd broken from the glamour too or it had failed anyway—regardless, she could see him and Pierce now.

"I'm sorry," she whispered. Her heart pounded in her head.

"Don't be." Ryder crept over, then slipped the guard's voco off his wrist. "We lost the only palace voco we had last time. Couldn't take them off bodies in Tolsea either—others might've noticed and caught on to us. Now, we don't have to worry about finding one."

Marina didn't mention that her apology hadn't been for him and Pierce.

You can't think about it. Keep moving forward.

Ryder and Pierce pulled the guard's body over to the thickest cluster of trees, then covered it up with some fallen branches. Pierce mentioned taking the armored suit along with the voco, but the front was covered in so much blood that he abandoned the idea.

"Can you glamour us again?" Pierce asked her. As gentle as he tried to sound, he couldn't hide the urgency in his voice.

He relaxed when Marina nodded. She took a few seconds to rally her energy, then funneled her every thought into manipulating the evening light.

She'd needed a break—that was all. She'd kept them glamoured for miles. In any other circumstance, it would've impressed her, but she set her sights on only *this* moment—on the steps they took as they scaled the stairs. She kept everything intact as Ryder tapped the voco to the door, and once they'd slipped inside, the weight on her shoulders eased.

She remembered this place too. They followed the antechamber and tunnels to more sets of staircases, and when the palace evolved into hallways she couldn't place, she whispered a thousand silent thank-yous to Ryder for coming with them.

In addition to Safira's absence, another blessing was how far the lower levels of the palace were from the halls above. Ryder knew the best places to go to ensure they didn't run into anyone, but even if he hadn't, these new shadows helped bolster her glamour. When they came upon a central chamber, empty minus two stairwells, she knew where they were again.

Instead of leading them to the prisons on the right, Ryder pulled Marina and Pierce down the left stairwell, which ended at a long corridor darker than the prisons themselves. Fissures ran up the walls, and if Marina squinted long enough, she swore she could see scratches in the stone, as though claws had been raked across them. The basements had clearly never been fixed after the ruemin came into Elsudra, and at this point, Marina knew Kieron too well to wonder why. Every stone was a reminder. A threat. No one but Kieron had ever returned from Sundra, and he wanted everyone to know it.

The palace was so different down here. Up above, open terraces welcomed the sea breeze, and during the day, every inch of the sun's light made its way in. Here, there were only a few unreliable bulbs that flickered as they passed.

Now, there were a bit too *many* shadows and not enough light, which put yet another strain on her glamour. Oh, how she hated glamouring. If everything turned out the way they hoped, she'd never glamour again.

When voices flit down the corridor, however, Marina changed her mind. She hated glamouring, but she *loved* glamours. She clung to hers with all the strength she could muster, praying it would stay up as the voices grew louder. Though she could feel Ryder and Pierce stiffen, they didn't stop walking. If there was any solace to be found, it was that the voices were unfamiliar and few in number. Guards, probably.

She was right. The corridor turned into a chamber, empty minus two guards standing in front of aluminum doors. Marina knew the doors led to Vaughn's laboratory before Ryder squeezed her hand. Down another corridor, adjacent to the one she'd emerged from, Marina could hear more voices, but they were distant enough not to send her into a panic. Here and now, it was two against three. That was doable, wasn't it?

What *did* nearly send her into a panic, however, was the thought of Vaughn behind the laboratory doors. Or perhaps—and this was even worse—Vaughn wouldn't be there at all. Maybe Kieron was onto them the same way he'd been onto Florin, and he'd stationed dozens of guards inside the laboratory. Maybe he was there himself. But Ryder and Pierce were intent on moving toward the guards, and Marina knew if she freaked out and tried to pull them in the opposite direction, the glamour would fall and they'd be screwed anyway. So she took a leap of faith, praying Ryder and Pierce knew what they were doing, and when they moved away from the glamour, she didn't hold them back.

The glamour fell like a blanket, and Ryder had the first guard in a headlock before he could register them. Maybe the guard *never* registered them. Ryder jerked his head to the side, and the guard's eyes went blank. Pierce was on the other in an instant, knocking him flat on his back. Somehow, the guard had managed to get his hand on his gun, but before he could fire it, Pierce pinned his arm to the floor. Ryder lunged forward and pressed his hands over the guard's mouth before he could call out.

Marina's voice left her in a breath. "Wait. Keep him down."

Pierce and Ryder exchanged wide-eyed glances, but they kept the guard in place. Before he could get his bearings straight, Marina's hand was on his forehead.

As hard as he fought, the poor man really didn't stand a chance. His spirit was made of branches—intricate, perhaps, but powerless in the face of Marina's waves.

Her worries—thank goodness—had been unfounded. Security measures had indeed been heightened all around, ever since Marina had fled Altus with Ryder, and these guards had been stationed in front of Vaughn's laboratory purely as a precaution.

Though Marina supposed this guard didn't know much beyond orders he'd been given, whatever he *did* know could help them. She continued sifting through his memories, collecting what she could.

Marina confirmed her most pressing concerns first: nobody in the palace seemed to know Vaughn was a target. He'd conducted business as usual until yesterday, when the soldiers arrived with Aeric. Kieron had put him under Vaughn's watch, but Aeric had yet to gain consciousness—which meant psychometry was impossible at the moment.

"Soon," Vaughn kept saying. *"He'll wake up soon."* And then he'd leave for an hour or two, and when he returned, he'd give the guards a smile—not a nice one, but the kind that made their blood run cold.

News of Safira's death had reached the palace quickly, and rumor was Kieron wanted to see what had happened in Tolsea through Aeric's memories. Though the palace guards who'd transported Aeric to Altus claimed Safira had still been alive when they'd left, Kieron had insisted on obtaining what he could from Aeric before letting Vaughn use dissolution magic on him. Regardless, it became abundantly clear to Marina that almost everyone in the palace thought *she'd* killed the mechanical woman.

Good. Marina would much rather Kieron think it had been her. That way, he wouldn't have it out for Yolie.

Another good thing: Vaughn wasn't in his laboratory at the moment. But he'd return soon, and when he did, there needed to be two golden-armored guards present, same as when he'd left. Outside, Pierce had mentioned taking the guard's armored suit. Now, they had two suits to take—if this second guard's death was as clean as the first's.

It would be. Though she couldn't bear to think about what she was doing, Marina let her waves thrash and convulse—let them annihilate every last branch in sight.

I'm sorry. I'm so sorry.

She wasn't sure if the guard could sense her apologies, but it didn't matter. By the time she'd removed her hand, he was already dead.

CHAPTER 48
Her Puppet

If Pierce and Ryder were surprised by what she'd done, they didn't voice it. Instead, they dragged the guards' bodies into the laboratory, and Marina kept watch while they swapped their gray armored suits with the golden ones.

They agreed with Marina's thinking; it would be easiest to attack and subdue Vaughn if they could corner him inside the laboratory. Once Pierce and Ryder had their suits on, they positioned themselves in the old guards' spots. It was impossible to tell who they were with the helmets. Even Marina had a hard time telling them apart, but Ryder was a touch taller than Pierce, which gave him away. Vaughn, however, would have no idea.

"We'll be loud about opening the door when he returns," Ryder said. "The moment he's inside, we'll put cuffs on him. Once he's restrained...Marina, you know what to do."

No, I don't, Marina wanted to say. *I don't know if I can do this. I might kill him.*

The laboratory doors closed before she could decide if she should say anything. The guards' bodies had been placed in the corner of the room, and since Marina couldn't bear to look at them, she directed her gaze elsewhere.

The laboratory wasn't as dark as the surrounding corridors, but it wasn't bright either. A maze of shelves lined concrete walls, occasionally ending at a long table filled with tools she couldn't name. Vaughn clearly prided himself on staying organized; every inch of the room had been cleaned and tagged. None of the labels carried a sheen, so she couldn't read any of them. She supposed they were Vaughn's personal notes.

Either way, she wouldn't have been interested. It was the glass cabinets at the far end of the room that caught her eye. They stood next to a thick curtain that sectioned off part of the room and reminded Marina of the textile mill. If she listened hard enough, she could hear a hum in the air.

These weren't cabinets—they were refrigerators. They didn't look like the ones back in Georgia, but the glass was cold to the touch, and every shelf held a vial filled to the brim with violet liquid.

Ruemin blood. Aeric had said Kieron likely hoarded it. This had to be what these vials were full of. But for some reason, it wasn't the refrigerators that held Marina's attention. Whenever she glanced at the curtain, her stomach turned to knots and her heart beat so fast she could scarcely feel it. The nagging sense that she needed to look—not later, but *now*—wouldn't leave her be.

She strained to listen for Ryder and Pierce's voices, but she didn't hear anything. Silently, she approached the curtain, hands shaking as she grasped the fabric and wrenched it to the side.

Almost immediately, her hands shot out in front of her, ready to deflect an attack.

Then, slowly, she lowered them.

A long table jutted out of one of the walls, shining in the overhead lights. Machines and glass shelves surrounded it, but all Marina could focus on was the man on the table.

Aeric looked exactly as he had in Tolsea, which might've relieved her, had it not been obvious how deeply unconscious he was. For a fleeting moment, Marina feared he was dead, but when she came up beside him, she could hear him breathing.

Safira had induced unconsciousness on Marina once, and she'd been out for days. She had no idea when Aeric would wake up, but it was obvious Vaughn hadn't wanted to risk anything; Aeric's ankles, wrists, and torso had been secured to the table with metal restraints. His voco had been removed too, and when Marina lifted up the sleeve of his coat, her hand brushed against the diminution cuffs Safira had put on him.

She knelt beside the table, searching fervently for a release button. If Aeric *did* wake up, he wouldn't be able to free himself on his own. When she found it on the underside of the table, she rejoiced—even more so when she pressed it and the restraints came undone.

The relief faded, however, when she stood, her gaze trailing to the shelves by the table. There were only a few, each made of tempered glass and smaller than the refrigerators. But Vaughn had made good use of the space. Each was filled with locks of hair.

Marina's hand flew to her mouth. She didn't have room to relish her small victory— not when the pain that existed behind the glass was so palpable.

These were people—*had been* people, with lives and dreams. But not to Vaughn. He viewed them the way Safira had viewed her victims: as puppets.

The hair was coded by color—blonds, browns, reds, and grays—and every lock had been tagged as meticulously as the tools in Vaughn's laboratory. She couldn't make out the symbols on these labels either, but she knew what they were. They were names.

One of the darkest locks of hair, which had been placed at the front of the shelves, drew Marina to it. It was familiar—not just its color, but its shape and length too. The tag that had been tied to it was marked with only three symbols, but Marina didn't need to understand Elsudran letters to know what it read. She knew this hair. She'd seen it so many times—falling over angular features, dangling above a polished cutlass. She'd held this lock once too; Kieron had used it as a threat.

Cal. Marina's vision began to spot. Kieron had said it himself—they'd given what they could of Cal's corpse to Vaughn. It didn't surprise Marina that Vaughn viewed Cal as his own, but it angered her so deeply that she felt it in her core.

It was painful to keep the rage from boiling over. She wanted it to shoot from her fingertips, destroying Vaughn's trophies before she turned to the vials of ruemin blood. Instead, she funneled the urge into something else—something more powerful than anger. It stirred within her as she pulled the key to Aeric's cuffs from her pocket, then unlocked them and placed the key in Aeric's palm. As she folded his fingers over it, she prayed he'd wake up soon and know they were near. With her breath in her throat and vision narrow, she readjusted the curtain, then crept over to the door. And then, she waited.

She wasn't sure how long—probably only a few minutes. When the knob jangled and Pierce's voice cut through the air, Marina pressed herself against a nearby wall and put her hands out, every wave in her head at the ready. But it wouldn't have mattered either way, because the moment Vaughn stepped into the room, Ryder had him on the ground.

Before Vaughn could make a sound, Ryder's hand was over his mouth. Pierce shut and locked the laboratory doors, then threw himself next to Ryder to help him keep Vaughn down. Light careened from Vaughn's hands and into Pierce, who went flying back.

Ryder's hand remained over Vaughn's mouth as he wrenched off his voco and threw it to the side. That was smart; now Vaughn couldn't summon help. Ryder went to secure the diminution cuffs, but Vaughn began to writhe so violently Marina worried he wouldn't be able to get them on. She sent a wave of force toward Vaughn's head, hoping she'd stun him. But Vaughn had anticipated her attack because he covered himself in a shield of air, the sudden appearance of which pushed Ryder back and separated the two of them, giving Vaughn time to wriggle free.

Ryder cursed as Vaughn jumped to his feet. Marina cut through a sliver of his shield, only for another burst of light to shoot from Vaughn's hands—*both* of them.

Ryder's suspicions about Vaughn's arm had been correct; it was indeed as gold as Safira's face, and in the flickering light, it glowed as vividly as the palace gates. Marina's eyes darted to his mechanical fingers, which weren't smooth and round like Lars's, but long and pointed like the ruemins'.

Fitting. For some reason, that only angered her more. She launched a wave of force at Vaughn. When he only stumbled back, she body-slammed him to get him to the ground.

Vaughn wasn't a big man by any means, but physical strength wasn't her forte either, and Marina had no idea how long she could keep him down. In the corner of her eye, she could see Ryder moving toward them with the cuffs, but when Vaughn began to flop around like a fish, she knew she couldn't let another second go to waste.

She braced herself, then dug her fingers into Vaughn's wrist. Flesh met flesh, and the world grew dark. She'd wondered what Vaughn's essence would look like, but she hadn't anticipated the thick, slimy liquid she was met with. Like her waves, it curled and rippled as it shot up around the barriers of his mind. But this was no seawater. This was *tar.*

Though her waves put a dent in Vaughn's shields, she couldn't get through as easily as she had with the guard. Swells of inky black devoured her water, and after a while, the tar began to take on a reflective shine. Was she making *any* progress? The second a hole formed, it closed up—sealed by tar even thicker than before. When the tar started to bubble, Marina's waves retreated and the room materialized once more.

With a quick jerk of his arms, Vaughn broke through Marina's grip and put his hands on her head. His metal fingers entwined about her hair, which jarred her enough for him to send what felt like a hundred lightning strikes through her skull.

No, not a hundred. That would've killed her, and Vaughn knew that. Whatever he'd done, it was enough to make her vision go black. When she regained it, everything was blurry, and she could hardly hear Pierce and Ryder. She stared at the lights on the ceiling, which had been sent into such a frenzy that it looked like they were dancing above her. For half a second, she imagined they were stars, glinting amidst an all-white sky.

The buzzing in her head subsided when Pierce's arms wrapped around her, and though she felt like a rag doll as he pulled her up, she was able to stand. She leaned against him and listened to his heart, which his armor muffled—or perhaps her hearing wasn't all there. But Ryder's voice was loud and clear when he said, "Cuffs are on. Do it *now.*"

She wasn't sure if it was because of rage or adrenaline, but her focus returned with a jolt. She took a breath, then wrapped her hand around Vaughn's wrist.

As fervently as his tar bubbled, it couldn't rise now that the cuffs weighed down his essence. Still, Marina met resistance when she flooded his mind—not from him, but from herself. Vaughn's memories were much like his spirit; all of them felt the same. Clinical, ordered, and meticulous, like the locks of hair he kept. Not everyone could give him hair, but he looked upon all of his experiments with fondness. It was they, after all, who kept him company and taught him things other healers were too high-minded to explore.

She tried to ignore the memories—tried to push past the feel of his essence—as her waves smothered the tar. Every time it remerged, she'd throw more water onto it—again and again, determined not to let it breathe.

Tread lighter, Marina reminded herself. *Go slower. Don't repeat Inber.*

Between each swell of waves, Marina waited to make sure she hadn't done irreversible damage. It wasn't the most thorough method, but since destroying Vaughn's essence was a risk she couldn't take, Marina leaned on caution. She wasn't erasing or dissolving; she was simply watering down his essence until it was malleable.

Marina ran through what Aeric had explained, pulling what little she could from her previous experience. This was a different type of dissolution...but it wasn't impossible. She wondered how it felt for Vaughn to be on the receiving end of an experiment. Right now, *she* was in control, not him. And when she was finished, Vaughn would be a puppet. *Her* puppet. Her tide filled Vaughn's essence, and when she started to feel him drowning in it, she pulled back.

Vaughn's eyes were glazed, but he was still alive, and she knew he was present. Somewhere, deep down, he was aware of what she'd done—that she'd been *successful.*

Marina could feel Pierce and Ryder's relief, and she dug for relief of her own—for pride. She'd done what she'd been so certain she couldn't. Aeric would be thrilled. *She* should be thrilled. But all she felt was deep, bitter hatred. She locked eyes with Vaughn, who couldn't react or speak, but who could hear—who could obey.

"Raise your arms," she commanded.

Slowly, Vaughn lifted his arms above his head.

Ryder made a sound that was somewhere between a scoff and a laugh.

Marina hardly sounded like herself when she said, "Lower them."

His arms got about halfway before his eyes widened. His mouth opened too, but Marina didn't give him a chance to say anything; she was back in his essence before he regained control. Wave after wave fell—once, twice, then ten times—until the tar was submerged again. This time, when she retreated, she turned to Pierce and Ryder. "I'll have to keep going back in," she said. "If I go too hard, I might kill him."

"Do what you need to," Ryder said as Pierce secured Vaughn's arms behind his back. "We'll go now. Stay behind me and do what I say."

Marina nodded. She lingered close enough to Vaughn that he was only a touch away—so he could hear her when she said, "I hope you remember the names of every person you've hurt. Because today, you will be dying for them."

CHAPTER 49
Tar and Water

As Marina quickly found out, Ryder had no intention of approaching the room with Brenna's portal directly. It would be preferable if they could, but just as Florin had said, defense systems filled nearby halls, making it impossible for soldiers and ruemin alike to get past without triggering alarms. It hadn't been like this during the era of Keepers; granted, the Keepers hadn't had reason to fear Brenna's portal like Kieron did now.

Kieron still had guards stationed outside the room, however, and they got there by taking a maze of subterranean tunnels—the ones Kieron had ordered to be built during the dead years, known only to his soldiers. Soldiers like Ryder.

That didn't mean they were completely safe. Once they emerged from the tunnels, they'd still have to deal with guards and the draining shield cast over the room's entrance. But if they could get inside, Ryder would be able to deactivate all the defenses, which would allow the ruemin they summoned to reach the portal unfettered.

Marina glamoured the four of them before they set off. Despite the way her hands shook when she made it, the glamour held up as they wove through corridors and reached what looked like a maintenance shaft. It was big enough for them to fit in, and where it ended, the tunnel began.

This tunnel was smaller than the one she and Ryder had trekked through with Cal. They had to go single file—Ryder first, his flashlight out in front of him, then Marina, then Vaughn and Pierce. As determined as Marina was to ensure Vaughn didn't emerge from his stupor, it got harder when she felt herself growing faint.

Hold on to the anger, she told herself. It was the only thing keeping her going. She thought of Cal—of Vaughn gazing upon her hair like a trophy, and how good it would feel when he met his demise. Cal would probably laugh knowing he'd died on the other end of

Brenna's portal, his remaining limbs ripped to shreds by the ruemin—his soul the last meal their species would have before they suffered for eternity.

For Cal. For Evren. And all the other people Vaughn had reduced to locks of hair.

They pushed on until they reached a fork in the tunnels. The left side looked like it had crumbled. Piles of rubble and slabs of rock lay haphazardly on top of each other, obscuring the view—if there was one at all. The tunnel opened up to the right, and though Marina felt a natural inclination to turn that way, Ryder stopped them.

"Left," he said. "We'll need to climb through."

"Through the rock?" Marina whispered.

"Doesn't take long." Ryder cocked his head to the right. "If you go that way, the floor will sense your movement and set off alarms."

The crevices in the rocks were small, but Marina managed to wriggle through after Ryder. Once she was on the other side, Pierce pushed Vaughn through, whose movements were so mechanical that Marina thought of puppets again.

Rubble formed a low ceiling—so low none of them could stand up straight. They remained hunched as they squeezed between rocks and ducked under low-hanging concrete, and when they slipped out from under the debris and a new tunnel widened before them, Marina found she could breathe a little better. She only got a second of peace before Ryder held out his arm and pointed to a stone on the floor.

"Pressure plate," he said. "There's more of them."

Marina swore. "Are you kidding me?"

"Kieron can't risk the wrong people getting to Brenna's portal," Ryder said.

"So don't step on the wrong stones," Pierce added wryly.

Ryder angled his flashlight down the tunnel, where all the stones looked exactly the same. "Keep listening to me and we won't get caught."

Pierce almost said something, but Vaughn's breathing—which had gotten louder—cut him off. It was enough to get Marina acting. She whirled around and grabbed his hand.

She could only do this so many times. Each swell she sent into Vaughn's essence was smaller than the last. Worse, she was growing weaker. She almost wondered if it would be easier to destroy the entire thing in one go. This balancing act required endurance and meticulousness, neither of which she excelled at.

Vaughn did. Even now, she could feel him fighting despite the cuffs. He couldn't overmatch her with strength, but Marina supposed his talent had always been a better fit for the long game. When she sensed him slipping under the weight of her seawater, she knew it would be temporary.

It was obvious Ryder and Pierce could sense her concern. When she pulled back, they got moving immediately.

The tunnel ended at several more forks, but Ryder knew which way to go. He'd obviously memorized the positions of the pressure plates too. Some weren't even on the floor, but on walls, which could be activated by simply brushing one's shoulder against it. They walked strictly in the middle of the tunnel, trying to make themselves as small as possible, moving alongside Ryder and stepping only where he told them to.

It was insane to think Kieron's guards had to memorize and navigate these tunnels—she didn't even want to think about what approaching this room head-on would entail—but Ryder was right: Kieron certainly hadn't skimped on security. Even when the last tunnel ended and Ryder flicked off his flashlight, Marina knew they weren't done.

They stopped at a corner, and Ryder held up his hand. Marina couldn't tell if he was signaling for them to stay put or telling them five soldiers were positioned by the entrance. He made another motion with his hand—not to her, but to Pierce.

"We'll deal with the guards," Ryder whispered. Then, to Marina, he said, "And you'll focus on making sure Vaughn doesn't resurface. Got it?"

He didn't wait for her to nod; he and Pierce left her at the corner, as good as alone.

Maybe it was worse than being alone. Vaughn stood beside her, no better than a walking corpse—though, to be fair, Marina preferred it to him being fully conscious.

Pierce had used a piece of their rope to tie Vaughn's cuffs together, which kept his hands secured behind his back. It was useful—a bit like a leash—but Marina still couldn't risk him regaining agency and trying to get away, so she wrapped her hand around his, prepared to face his essence again if she needed to.

His skin was thin and clammy, and whenever Marina thought too hard about the fact it was *Vaughn* she was touching, her lightheadedness returned.

Ryder and Pierce's golden armor must've caught the soldiers off guard because it took a few seconds before Marina heard a gasp. An unfamiliar voice said something but was cut short, followed by the sound of bodies hitting the floor.

What if it's Ryder and Pierce?

She held her breath, resolving not to check until a minute had passed. Just when she began to move forward, Pierce rounded the corner—his armor covered in blood—and took Vaughn from her. Ryder was behind him, and when he saw Marina's face, he gave her a look. "Your confidence in us is inspiring."

Pierce put a hand on Marina's shoulder and pulled her around the corner. "Top of our class for a reason," he breathed.

She almost said something about their injuries—Pierce's limp seemed a little worse, and though his armor bore no marks, Ryder couldn't move his shoulder without wincing—

but it wouldn't do any good to remind them. Instead, Marina followed them out into the light, where five guards lay in a pile of blood. Ryder and Pierce had mostly kept the mess contained, and it was clear they'd given the guards the cleanest deaths they could manage, but a few of them had no doubt put up more of a struggle.

"Do you have the energy to glamour?" Ryder asked. When Marina eyed the bodies, he said, "If the ruemin see it—"

"I do," Marina said, wishing Aeric were here. He'd be able to do this—the glamouring, the dissolution—effortlessly.

It took her a while to create the glamour—her reserves were running low, and it was starting to really worry her—but once she did, she covered up the bodies and blood easily. The pile was far enough away from the entrance that the ruemin probably wouldn't make contact with it, which was about as comforting as anything could be at the moment.

Marina turned her attention to the door itself. It looked a lot like the entrance to the prisons: made entirely of metal and surrounded by locking lugs. But the scanner in the middle of the door shined. The entire door did.

She'd expected this. And yet, her stomach still dropped when Ryder said, "We'll have to take off Vaughn's cuffs." When Marina paled, he said, "You can't dismantle it on your own, Marina. You know that. Multiple sorcerers have to work to break through these."

"But...what about you?" Marina asked. "Can't *you* help me?"

Ryder shook his head. "I might be inclined, but I'm no sorcerer."

Marina's heart began to pound.

Use the fear, she told herself. *Use the anger.*

Keeping Vaughn in check with cuffs on was difficult enough—and judging by the way his eyes were starting to flutter, Marina knew he was coming back.

She nodded at Pierce, who tightened his grip around Vaughn as he unlocked his cuffs. Before Marina heard them click, she'd already made contact.

Vaughn was tired too—her single saving grace. The tar rose, but not quickly, which helped her find her footing.

Tar and water could match each other, perhaps, but it wasn't just water she threw at him. She held an entire ocean, brimming with the Omnia's light. She only had to be strong enough to pull upon it. Vaughn was close to the Omnia too, but he wasn't its host. He might be able to manipulate its light with the cuffs off, but *she* was the sun itself.

You are my puppet. My waves are your strings.

"Put your hands on the door," she ordered when she pulled back.

Vaughn obeyed. The next few moments were mechanical. She put her hands next to Vaughn's, flinching when one of his metal fingers brushed against hers, then grounded herself and let the waves within her pool at her fingers.

"Help me dismantle the shield."

If she detected a hint of defiance in Vaughn's eyes, it faded.

Dizziness swarmed in quickly, but it wasn't as crippling as it had been when she'd gone at these types of shields alone. She prayed the shield would drain enough of Vaughn's energy to keep him weak. So far, it seemed to be working.

Of course, as Vaughn lost energy, so did she—and she didn't have much to lose at the moment. The door began to shine even brighter—not because of the shield, but because her vision had gone fuzzy. She locked her knees and pushed harder against the shield. This was what she was good at, wasn't it? Destruction?

No—*annihilation*. Sparks of light danced atop her fingertips, ravaging the shield from the center. If she could keep this up for a little longer, the whole thing would fall.

Beside her, Vaughn's breathing had started to accelerate.

Marina made a sound somewhere between a whimper and a gasp as Vaughn heaved— as his arms moved back, away from the shield...

Ryder grabbed Vaughn's wrists, keeping his palms on the door, then snapped, "Keep going. If you don't, I'll cut off your other arm."

Coupled with partial sedation, the threat seemed to work. Sweat dripped from Vaughn's brow, and bit by bit, the shield yielded—fizzling out until the effects weren't so severe. That didn't stop Marina from doubling over when it dropped. If it hadn't been for Pierce's and Ryder's grips on him, Vaughn might've too.

So much for treading lightly. At the moment, Marina could barely raise her own shields, no less smother Vaughn's essence.

"Recuperate," Ryder said. He snapped the cuffs back on Vaughn's wrists and shoved him toward Pierce. "I'll dismantle the security. You did good."

Well, Marina thought as she steadied her legs. It surprised her. The thought was so normal—a small, annoying sliver of her old self that, interestingly enough, didn't unsettle her. If anything, it helped ground her.

The pounding in her head died down as Ryder swiped his voco beneath the scanner and the door retracted into the wall. Once they were inside, he used a lever at the side of the door to pull it shut and began fiddling with a console on the wall.

The room wasn't much different than it had been in Aeric's memories, albeit far more dilapidated. Claw marks like the ones in the corridors ran down columns and defaced stone, and the light that used to make its way into the room through fissures in the ceiling was even brighter.

Only...they were below ground, and even if they weren't, it was the dead of night.

That didn't make sense until Marina lowered her gaze to the portal itself, where bends of light formed a veil that obscured the landforms beyond it. The portal's light glowed a soft purple, and whatever material peeked through the cracks in the room did too. The cracks almost resembled strikes of lightning—like the tendrils on Brenna's ring.

Marina wondered if, in a way, this room had been a piece of art to Brenna. The portal was no doubt the centerpiece. Had Vaughn's voice not disrupted her, Marina might've observed it a little longer.

"You...your voice," he said. He was talking to Ryder. "I...I know it. You're—"

Ryder continued working on the console, but Marina could hear the amusement in his voice when he said, "Heard I was dead, did you?" When Vaughn didn't respond, Ryder droned, "I have a knack for survival and even more of a knack for killing fuckers like you."

A breathy laugh—or perhaps it was a gasp—bubbled at Vaughn's mouth. "Doesn't matter," he rasped. "She's tiring out. She...she will, soon enough."

This time, it was Pierce who responded. As he pulled Brenna's ring from his pocket, he said, "Maybe. But you'll be dead first."

CHAPTER 50
Hunger

The gravity of the situation—of how far they'd already gotten—wasn't lost on Vaughn. He began to struggle against Pierce's grip as Ryder approached them, but he had to have known it was useless.

He did; it was why he switched his tactic. When Ryder rummaged through Vaughn's pockets and pulled out a wishbone—*the appendage he carries,* Marina realized as her vision adjusted—Vaughn sputtered, "You...you don't want to do this."

Ryder ignored him. "I've turned everything off," he said, mostly to Marina. He pulled the lever by the door again, just enough so it was cracked. "We need to lure them quickly, before anyone notices. Put him back under."

That was all the time she had to recuperate, apparently. As she neared Vaughn, he began to speak faster. "The shield took a toll on us both," he stammered. "You...you aren't practiced at dissolution. I can tell. Not thorough enough...and now you're weak too. You won't be able to—"

This time, Marina's hand met Vaughn's forehead, and the repulsion she felt at his essence died down when she realized she didn't have to listen to his rambling.

He was right, though; she *was* weak, and ample rest was a luxury she couldn't afford. While she managed to subdue Vaughn again, she knew her work was subpar.

She couldn't even fathom sedating a ruemin at the moment. Not in her state. Marina put her hands on her knees, breathing through her nose as Ryder shoved the appendage between Vaughn's lips. "Call for them," he ordered. "Calmly."

The sound that followed was nowhere near as hellish as the ruemins' screeches, but it wasn't pleasant either. It sounded like a mix of clicks and pops—cut short by a *crunch.*

Subpar work, indeed. One look in Vaughn's eyes was enough to know he was back—

conscious enough to bite the appendage in half and spit its pieces to the floor.

"I...won't," Vaughn breathed, throwing a glare at Ryder. "She can't...keep this up..."

The initial horror that flared up faded when Marina looked to Ryder, who laughed dryly. This time, he rummaged through his own pockets, producing the appendage he'd taken from the ruemin in the Delve.

"We have more," Ryder lied. "But if you break this one, I'll break your fucking ribs." Still, Ryder held the appendage at Vaughn's lips this time—far enough from his teeth to prevent Vaughn from biting it in half a second time—then looked to Marina.

"She can't," Vaughn repeated. "She should've gone harder the first time when she had the energy." He glanced sideways at Marina. "You were...too timid. Too afraid. Every time you went back in, you hurt yourself too. Now...now look at you."

The fact he was the one taunting her made Marina's face heat. But he should've known taunts didn't work on her—not like they had with Kieron. Not now. Her vision narrowed, and when she curled her fingers, Vaughn let out a gasp.

Safira had done this to her once, back in the throne room when Marina had tried to attack Kieron. Though the pain was short-lived, it was enough to fluster Vaughn. Fire blazed in her head—in her arms, her gut—and before he could recover, she was back in his essence a sixth time. This one, she decided, would be her last.

If only to prove she still had it in her, Marina didn't hold back. Her intuition took over, and rather than fretting about her reserves or reminding herself to be cautious, she put faith in her waves. When she trusted them and herself—when she held the reins but didn't confine them—her waves and her will aligned.

Ryder had already commanded Vaughn to summon the ruemin again when Marina pulled back, and this time, Vaughn didn't—couldn't—stop. He blew several times, each one calm, and when distant clicks flitted through the air in response, Ryder and Pierce rushed to the door.

"Don't help us," Ryder told Marina. "Don't waste more of your energy."

That didn't stop every ounce of Marina's body from going rigid as *click, click, clicks* echoed through the corridors outside. It took a while before the clicking neared, but when it did, Ryder pushed the door open a bit more, then flattened himself against the wall as long, silver nails entwined around the stile.

Marina knew ruemin preferred traveling in packs, but these ones were so close together that there were no breaks when they slipped into the room. It was like they didn't notice the others—or maybe they didn't think of separate ruemin as *others* at all. Two additional ruemin followed the first one inside, and when a fourth slinked in at their heels, Ryder shut and locked the door.

Marina had no idea if there were more beyond the threshold; four felt like too much already. She could tell the ruemins' senses had been spiked—because of Vaughn's calls, perhaps, but also because they were close to her. Either way, they didn't react to Marina and Vaughn. The moment the door clicked, they whirled toward Ryder and Pierce.

The first ruemin died the moment Pierce's sword met its neck. Pierce stumbled forward as he swung, and when he inhaled sharply, Marina knew the impact had hurt his wounded leg. Ryder's shoulder wasn't doing well either. He had to have suffered a blow outside with the soldiers; his movements weren't as fluid as they normally were, and though his blade met the ruemin's neck, it didn't cut through bone. Violet blood gushed from the ruemin's scales as all three screeched.

Marina's heart rate fell into a frenzy as she covered her ears, praying this room was soundproof. They couldn't risk drawing attention, which meant the sooner the last two ruemin died, the better. They only needed one, after all.

Her fingers twitched. She could manage to flay one of the others. It might be a little harder at the moment, but she was good at these things, and it didn't take her nearly as much energy as dissolution did.

Marina didn't have much time to make up her mind about disobeying Ryder. At the second swing of his sword, the ruemins' head came off. But the third ruemin recovered quickly, and it slammed its foot into Ryder's chest as it tackled him to the floor.

Within seconds, it found the button on Ryder's collar and began to push it wildly. When Ryder's helmet retracted, the ruemin grabbed him by the shoulders, then slammed his body into the ground so hard his head made an impact too.

"*LIARS!*" it screamed. *CLICK.*

It got in three blows before Marina made a motion with her hand. She expected the top half of its body to go flying, but all she'd done was make a gash in its torso. A wave of dizziness rushed over her as slimy intestines fell from the ruemin's stomach, and while she knew she had it in her to attack a second time, Ryder's warning wasn't lost on her. That was harder than she'd thought it would be, and it would be foolish to push herself further.

She didn't have to. When the ruemin doubled over, Pierce put a bullet through its head. He must've used a silencer because the shot didn't make a sound, but the remaining ruemin's screech certainly did. It cut through the air as its eyes darted about the room, unsure who it should attack.

It settled on Ryder, probably because he was already down. Ryder rolled out of the way before it could jump on him, and in an instant, Pierce's dagger met the ruemin's back —cutting deeply enough to wound it without killing it.

Somewhere far off, Marina swore she could hear more *clicks*. Since she couldn't bear to let the ruemin screech again and summon others, she shoved Vaughn toward Pierce and lunged toward the ruemin.

Her hand met its scaled torso, and somewhere in her mind's eye, she could see a fissure forming in a red sky. From it fell thousands of ruemin, so inexplicably connected Marina couldn't wrap her head around it. Every physical experience was shared amongst the others, but more than anything, the beasts shared hunger. They'd never known satiety—perhaps they didn't have the ability to know it—and so, they consumed.

These were memories, but they weren't memories in the way hers were. They were feelings, and when Marina tried to douse the ruemin's mind with her waves, she couldn't find a foothold. There was nothing here to subdue—no essence. There was only hunger.

She continued aimlessly throwing swells of water forward, hoping maybe it would put the ruemin to sleep, or at least overwhelm it enough so it was easier to overpower. It seemed to work, at least a bit. She knew it was possible. Hollis and Zora had done it, and so had Vaughn. Only, the three of them were practiced at dissolution, and as much as Marina loathed the words that came from Vaughn's mouth, he hadn't been wrong when he'd said she wasn't. Still, she fought on, desperate to subdue it as best she could, but she didn't get far before Pierce pulled her back.

She blinked at his sword, which he held hilt first, then gasped at the ruemin before her—knocked out and bleeding from the head. That was one way to do it.

"Was...making progress," she said, but her voice was so shaky that not much came out. Her body shook too, and Marina lowered herself to the floor, fearing she might faint.

"No more time," Pierce said, then pointed toward the door.

The far away clicks were much louder now, but it wasn't that which sent Marina into a panic. Nails raked against the metal door, and pounding followed.

"The ruemin are going to summon more," Pierce said quickly. "Guards too." He didn't help Marina or Ryder up. Instead, set his sights on Vaughn and the ruemin. Vaughn was still out of it, and it didn't take long for Pierce to wrench the ruemin off the ground and position it next to him. He used Vaughn's body the way one would a tree stake—pressed up against the ruemin's trunk to keep it on its feet—and though Vaughn's legs bent under the ruemin's weight, he remained standing.

Ryder wrenched himself off the ground, but he couldn't stand without help. He was too dizzy, Marina realized. Blood trickled down the back of his head and onto his armor, and his eyes fluttered as he sank back to the floor.

"I've got it," Pierce told them both.

"We're...so close," Marina whispered to Ryder—or maybe herself. "So close."

Close to getting the ruemin out of Elsudra and shutting down Brenna's portal, at least. Marina didn't want to think about what after would entail—how they'd get out of the palace, or if they would at all.

The pounding at the door hadn't stopped. If anything, it was getting worse. Marina looked desperately to Pierce, who'd jammed Brenna's ring onto Vaughn's finger.

Marina wasn't sure if that brought Vaughn back or if his consciousness had already started to return, but by the time his eyes regained alertness, it was too late. Something silver cut through the air, followed by rope falling to the floor.

Pierce recoiled as Vaughn stumbled backward. "Don't...don't move," Vaughn ordered.

Marina tried to stand, but her head was spinning and her legs felt like jelly. Even if she could, what good would it do? Vaughn had already freed himself.

Spots began to crowd her vision again, only they weren't due to fatigue. What had Vaughn used? He didn't have any weapons on him, and his cuffs were still on.

When another glint of silver split through the air, Marina got her answer. Without Vaughn to support its body, the ruemin slumped to the ground, but Vaughn kept its arm raised—silver nails dangling above his head. His limbs shook violently as he struggled to hold the ruemin up, and his words slurred together when he said, "They're coming." He angled his chin toward the door, where the pounding—the clicking, the scraping—had grown louder. "They'll...they'll get in soon. The door can't hold forever. And now only one of you can fight them off."

He shot a wild, desperate look at Pierce, but Pierce only scoffed. "Even more incentive to push you through. I don't need a rope to overpower you."

Vaughn's jaw loosened, and his shaking lips stilled.

"Don't believe me?" Pierce said. He unsheathed his dagger.

Slowly—almost apathetically—Vaughn lowered the ruemin's hand until its nails grazed against his neck. "I believe you."

This time, there was no flash of silver or splitting rope. There was only blood, pouring from Vaughn's neck.

CHAPTER 51
Live

Vaughn hadn't needed a weapon; the ruemin's nails were sharp enough. He'd known where to cut himself too, and exactly how deep, because the moment his eyes rolled back into his head and he hit the ground, he was as good as dead. Blood stained his golden hand, and on the other, Brenna's ring shone dully.

Had she been able to find her voice, Marina might've screamed. Ryder and Pierce, too, were silent as Vaughn's grip on the ruemin released.

The ruemin squirmed as though it were reeling from a nightmare, then slumped to the side. It was still breathing, but Vaughn wasn't. It didn't stop Pierce from diving toward Vaughn. Even Ryder regained a burst of energy, crawling over to them instead of walking, then clasped his hands over Vaughn's throat. Pierce began to give Vaughn compressions, each one more intense than the last. He retracted his helmet, preparing to administer rescue breaths, but stopped when he registered the blood that pooled at Vaughn's blue lips.

He was already gone. Gone...which meant the portal would no longer recognize him.

No. They'd controlled for so much. They'd done everything by the book. But Vaughn was dead anyway—dead because he'd known there was only one way to keep them from winning and sealing Brenna's portal for good.

Too late. The pounding on the metal door continued growing louder.

Ryder tried to stand again, but he was still disoriented, and he only got up halfway before his balance gave out. Marina covered her ears so she didn't have to hear the ruemin outside—so she could think about how they'd escape, how they'd protect themselves if she and Ryder couldn't move...

It was worthless. The ruemins' strength lay in their number, and Vaughn had known that. He'd known it was only a matter of time before they broke through. And now there was no way they could find a random guard, or regroup, or flee.

Too late, too late, too late. The pounding, the clicking...it was going to drive her insane. She couldn't stop staring at Vaughn's body either, which wasn't helping. Blood gathered around his head and seeped onto his oily hair. But his eyes...they looked the same as when he was alive. Vague, distant, and strangely prideful.

Of course he was proud. Even in death, he had reason to be. He'd won.

Pierce shoved the ruemin toward the mouth of the portal anyway, but when its body hit the bends of light, it didn't sink into it. Marina could hear a faint *zap*, as though it was brushing against a wall of electricity.

It was useless, but Pierce had known that. Aeric had said as much; Brenna's portal would only recognize living beings from the sister realms. Attaching the ruemin to Vaughn's dead body would do nothing, and it certainly wouldn't be able to pass through alone. But Pierce kept trying anyway. Kept failing.

The door began to groan under the weight of ruemin. There was no way the chaos hadn't alerted guards—no way the guards hadn't alerted *Kieron.*

"There...has to be a way out," Ryder muttered. "Has to...has to." He was verging on delirium—or maybe it was just desperation. Cruel, useless desperation.

Outside, the ruemin must've started flinging themselves toward the door, equally desperate as the three of them. Maybe they'd felt it when Pierce had knocked their packmate out. Maybe they'd come because of the screeches. Maybe...

None of it mattered. This was it. This was how it ended.

Marina couldn't feel her heart. Had it stopped beating? She rested a hand on her chest, searching for the sensation, but was met with nothing.

The door reverberated as an indentation formed, spreading across the surface like a ripple in a pond. Another followed, then another. When fractures spiderwebbed across the metal, Pierce's eyes trailed over to Vaughn's body. Stiffly, he approached it, then bent down and slipped Brenna's ring off Vaughn's finger.

Ryder was still mumbling to himself. "Barricade. We...can barricade..."

Pierce didn't respond. Instead, he stepped away from Vaughn and neared Marina. When he reached her, he knelt beside her.

"You are a force," he said, quickly but clearly. "I've known it since the day I met you. No matter what comes your way, remember that. You're stronger than it all."

She blinked at him. Either she was too out of it to process what he'd said, or she hadn't heard him properly, but her body reacted for her. A hole bore into her stomach, and her breathing shallowed as Pierce planted a kiss on her head. "I'm so very lucky to be your friend, Marina."

Ryder's mumbling stopped as Pierce approached him. Before he could speak, Pierce kissed him. "I love you," he said. "I always have. Both of you. And I want you to live long lives. You deserve that much."

The pounding on the door hadn't stopped, but Marina couldn't hear it anymore. She could hear Ryder though, as he rasped, "Pierce..."

Again, he tried to stand but failed.

The pit in Marina's stomach was an abyss now. It sunk into every organ and limb, and all she could do was watch Pierce as he put Brenna's ring onto his finger.

"Pierce," she gasped. Now she could feel her heart. "Pierce," she said again, but her voice was muffled by Ryder's.

"Don't," Ryder begged. "We can find a way...we can barricade. Just wait. *Please*, Pierce."

"They'll get in." Pierce's lips shook, but he sounded calm. "There's no other way."

"No," Ryder choked. "Pierce. *No.* Let me. I'll do it. I'll—"

Pierce kissed Ryder again, rendering him mute. "Don't just survive, Ryder. *Live.*"

Silence followed—silence that overpowered the pounding, the groaning metal, the hundreds of clicks outside—and it was so suffocating Marina couldn't get her mouth to work. She wanted to say *she'd* do it, but she knew it was worthless because her sacrifice would take the Omnia with her and plunge Elsudra back into the dead years. So instead, she listened as Ryder begged to be the one—watched as he stood, regaining some measly balance, either out of luck or willpower.

But Pierce was quicker. He evaded Ryder, who reached out to grab him, then swung his arms around the unconscious ruemin and dragged it toward the portal.

Ryder was screaming now. Over and over again, he screamed Pierce's name—pleaded with him not to go, tears pouring down his face as he stumbled in Pierce's direction.

Don't go, Pierce. Please...please, don't go. I love you. Don't leave me.

Marina wasn't sure if it was his voice she was hearing, or if her mind was playing tricks on her. She couldn't think. She couldn't form any words of her own. Would it have mattered if she could? Pierce wasn't listening. She extended her arms, fruitlessly trying to make contact with Pierce and hold him back. He noticed, then gave her a tearful smile.

Let me make this choice.

She'd begged it once of him and Ismene. And then Cal...she'd begged it of Marina too. And though Pierce didn't speak, she knew that was what he was saying.

But Marina couldn't let him go. She wrenched herself off the ground, hating her legs —hating her useless body and how fast Pierce was. Because before she or Ryder could reach him, Pierce stood in front of the portal, held the ruemin close to his body, and fell into the bends of light.

CHAPTER 52
Don't Go

This time, the silence that followed was as empty as it had been that night on the beach when the tsunami had come for her. Ryder's legs buckled, and from where he lay, Marina could see him screaming—his mouth opened wide, tears streaming down his tired face. When her body hit the floor again, she couldn't bring herself to move. There she lay, motionless—*useless*—as Brenna's portal began to pop and fizzle like a dying glamour.

Now, she could hear. *Clicking.*

When the metal groaned again, the door cleaved in two and snapped off its hinges. For half a second, Marina thought it was the ruemin who'd finally overpowered it, but whatever force had knocked down the door wasn't tangible. Still, she shielded her neck with her hands, and though Ryder continued to sob, he ducked too.

The world began to tremble.

With every quake, the stone walls blurred until they were nothing but projections—until reality itself bent to the force beyond the room.

She couldn't comprehend it. A baleful gust of silver erupted through the doorway, barreling into the room and toward the mouth of Brenna's portal.

Ruemin.

Marina could hear them screeching—the clicking of the bony appendages at their throat. They could fight as hard as possible—could claw at the air with their nails and try to scramble away, tearing down stones and columns as they went—but the portal had already recognized Pierce, and everything attached to him followed suit.

Connected in body, but not in mind. The ruemin were truly one. The portal swallowed them like a ravenous beast, sparks flying from beneath the archway and sending the air around them into a dance of purple and silver.

She wasn't sure how long it went on for. Seconds, minutes, and hours all felt the same —all as hollow as their victory. When the clicks died down into an echo, Brenna's portal gave one last flicker before dying out.

The archway remained, towering above nothing. In the distance, Marina could hear shouting and footfall. It got her moving. Somehow, she stood—gathered the closest weapons and bags, then stumbled over to Ryder, whose lips were still moving. When his voice finally worked, it sounded nothing like him.

"Don't go," he begged. "Don't go, don't go, don't go."

He kept pleading to the air—to the nothingness that filled the maw of Brenna's portal. He didn't even react when Marina tried to pull him up.

"We have to go," she rasped. The footfall grew louder. "We have to."

She helped Ryder stand, who leaned on her as they made their way back into the halls, where now, violent fissures had coaxed the walls closer to crumbling. He could hardly walk—not because of his dizziness, but because he was crying so hard. Still, they moved forward, adrenaline fueling them as they took turns Marina had never seen— hallways Ryder had deactivated security in, allowing them to reach Vaughn's laboratory in less than a minute.

They'd eliminated the guards in the basements, but more were coming. Up above, they were no doubt processing what had happened—realizing the ruemin were gone and that someone had cast them out. Marina could hear chaos echoing in the neighboring chambers, and by the time they slipped inside Vaughn's laboratory and shut the doors, it had reached the basements.

The guards would likely go to Brenna's portal first, where everything would finally register. Marina was certain it had already registered for Kieron. Even from the Pale Tower —if that's where he was—he could probably sense the ruemins' absence. And the moment the guards saw Vaughn's dead body, they'd be making their way to the laboratory. Perhaps Kieron had already mobilized the last of his loyalists to hunt her down. They had to suspect she was here now.

She locked the laboratory doors and pushed a table in front of it, expecting Ryder to help her, but he'd hit the ground again.

She'd never seen someone sob so hard. His body heaved as he cried—as he mumbled a plea that would forever remain unanswered.

Don't go, don't go, don't go.

Finally, Marina's tears fell too. She tried not to make it obvious she was shattering because Ryder already had. She needed to hang on for him. For Pierce.

If she could evade Kieron and his guards until daybreak, maybe she could access

Exorsus once more and release her hold on the Omnia for good. If she could give it back to the sea, Kieron would have no hope. Vaughn and Safira were gone—just like the ruemin—and now his time was limited. But daybreak had to be an hour away, maybe more. And even if it wasn't, how could she possibly reach the ocean without getting caught?

The palace rumbled, as though something deep in its foundation had broken. Marina's gaze trailed to the refrigerators at the end of the room, expecting the vials of blood to tremble in their racks.

But the refrigerators were gone. Demolished. Metal lay in clumps, as though someone had bent and twisted the casing until it curled in on itself, and glass shards stained with violet liquid littered the ground. Though she saw it, she didn't process it. She didn't have room to. Instead, she looked back to Ryder.

Don't go, don't go, don't go.

Gone. Everything was gone. The bad and the good. The ruemin. Brenna's ring. Pierce.

She'd never see him again. That soldier who'd found her in the sea cavern—who'd made mistakes, perhaps, but had always been so deeply *good*—was now nothing but a memory. It was because of him that the ruemin were out of Elsudra, and she'd never be able to thank him.

Another shockwave made the ground beneath Marina vibrate. She could feel herself starting to lose it. As tightly as she clung to her senses, she didn't know if what she was hearing and feeling was real. And when a hand wrapped around her arm—when she whirled around, expecting it to be Ryder but saw Aeric instead—she didn't know if her vision was tricking her too.

No...no, it wasn't. He was pale, but he was very much real.

He noticed her grief, and though perhaps he wasn't sure what had caused it, he didn't make her say it aloud. Instead, he let her embrace him—let her sob as the words in her head became nothing but dull whispers.

Don't go, don't go, don't go.

She buried her face into his coat, and when she peered around his shoulder at the bent metal and shattered glass, she realized Aeric had done it. If the way he shook hadn't told her, the rage in the air would have. She could smell it—as thick and sharp as the ruemin blood that stained the tiles.

When Aeric put his hands on her shoulders, she finally pulled back. Beside them, Ryder stared at the floor, his eyes glazed.

"They're gone," Marina whispered.

Pierce too.

Aeric seemed to know what she meant. He turned toward Ryder, whose voco had started to chime. If Ryder heard it, he didn't react.

Slowly and unsteadily, Aeric knelt beside Ryder and slipped his voco off his wrist. The chiming continued for another second, maybe less, before static interrupted it—before Kieron's voice echoed throughout the room.

"I'm sending this message to all palace vocos," Kieron said. His voice was ragged, and he failed to hide his own desperation—if he was trying at all. "But there is only one person I wish to reach." He paused, perhaps to regain the strength in his tone when he said, "Marina: I know you are here. I know you are listening."

Another blast—this one louder and more intense—rocked the room.

"Did you hear that?" Kieron said. "Those are bombs—the smallest we have. If I give the order, my army will release more, powerful enough to level Altus before the sun rises."

Marina's throat constricted. Aeric stared grimly at the voco, and even Ryder seemed to be listening. She could tell Kieron was shaking, but she didn't know whether it was from nerves or rage. "I am in the Pale Tower. For the next hour, my army will stand down. But if you—and only you—are not in front of me when that hour ends, I will have them bomb not just Altus, but *every* city in Elsudra. And it will be on you."

It's on me.

The blood drained from Marina's face as the line went silent.

Every city in Elsudra. Every innocent person—including Ismene, Elta, Blaine, and Yolie. She knew Kieron wasn't bluffing. Some members of his army might desert him now that the ruemin were gone, but others would be loyal enough to stay—to follow his orders until the end. And if she didn't go to him, he would ensure the end came for everyone.

Did he expect her to give into Locus immediately, or was he luring her to him for a fight—one she was too weak to win? When he defeated her, he'd probably leverage the same threats. Locus, or death for everyone in Elsudra.

Any hope Marina might've had to avoid Kieron's guards—to reach the sea, perhaps, or to outlast him until his stockpiles ran out—was for naught. He'd left her with no choice.

"I'm coming with you," Aeric said.

Ryder, who hardly seemed lucid, finally stood. "Me too," he said. He still didn't sound like himself. "I can...I..."

He was either hit by a wave of dizziness or grief—maybe both—because he sank back to the floor. When his eyes rolled back into his head, Marina knew he'd passed out.

"He can't," Marina said before Aeric could.

Aeric nodded and turned Ryder onto his side. His hair was matted with blood, and Aeric ran his hands over it. He couldn't do much, so Marina bent down and tried her best to heal the wound.

As she worked, Aeric said, "We have the hour. We shouldn't be hasty. I'll glamour Ryder so he remains hidden, and when the two of us set off, we'll do so cautiously."

He planned to convey himself and her as far as he could—he knew the Pale Tower well and preferred they reach it without Kieron's remaining soldiers seeing them—then glamour himself before they approached the entrance. There were bound to be guards, and while they wouldn't attack Marina, they might try to take Aeric out if they saw him.

Marina knew Aeric was right. At this point, all bets were off when it came to Kieron's sentimentality toward him. Right now, Kieron's only goal was the Omnia.

Minutes ago, Marina had thought her emotions would cripple her. Now, she could scarcely feel them. She acted mechanically. Found a flask of water in one of their bags and sipped it. Took a moment to let the pounding in her head die down. Watched as Aeric secured Ryder's helmet over his head—perhaps to protect his wound, which Marina had healed a little, or maybe to protect his identity. Aeric worked slower than usual, but he made good time, and the hour wasn't up yet.

Even so, by the time they prepared to leave the room, Marina was nowhere near recovered. But she could move forward, at the very least. She had to.

Grief, fear, anger, shock...they slept within her. Simmering. Waiting. As distant as the voice that echoed in her head, repeating the same thing over and over.

Don't go, don't go, don't go.

CHAPTER 53
All Great Wars

The palace was quiet, but not empty. Remnants of chaos filled the air, as heavy as the smoke that wafted in through the terraces. Marina could smell it as they conveyed through blurry halls and galleries, then landed in a cloister garth. They ducked under the peristyle, and once Aeric had glamoured himself, they wove around the back.

The Pale Tower was at the farthest end of the palace, nestled above the sea. She could feel Aeric behind her as she approached the stairwell, and together, they climbed.

From the stairwell's windows, Marina could see the ocean. It was the same color as the sky—deep blue, with streaks of red that danced across the surface. The sun lingered behind the horizon, but it hadn't risen yet. She could hear waves too, crashing against the hill the tower had been built into, and it invigorated her. She increased her tempo until she came to the top of the stairs, where four guards in golden armor stood waiting.

Marina wasn't sure if it was a coincidence or if it was supposed to be symbolic. Four—like the Keepers. She doubted Kieron was in the headspace to be symbolic right now, but the number wasn't lost on her. She thought of Four himself, and what she'd whispered to him in Exorsus.

What comes from the sea calls to the sea.

Her mother used to say that—that she came from the sea.

Helmeted and silent, the guards led Marina through ivory corridors. It was a maze back here; Aeric knew his way around, but at the moment, he was as good as nonexistent.

So *this* was where Kieron spent all his time. For someone who liked irony so much, Marina wondered if Kieron realized how ironic his own story was. Once a socialite Sorcerer of the Court using his silver tongue to entwine the elite in his web, he was now a faceless ruler hiding away in fear of his own mortality.

The door at the end of the hall wasn't glamoured, but it was locked. One of the guards approached it, then unlocked it with his voco and turned to Marina.

"Hands out," he said.

Marina only stared at him.

The guard produced diminution cuffs, then repeated, "Hands out."

She never decided whether she'd obey or try to fight instead. Aeric beat her to it. He'd come around behind two of the soldiers, then pressed the buttons on their collars. The moment their heads were exposed, they died—soundless and bloodless. Whether Aeric had used dissolution magic or something else, Marina wasn't sure.

Aeric was still glamoured when he targeted the third one, who pulled out his gun but never fired it. His armor caved in like the metal doors had, knocking him to the floor but not incapacitating him. A wisp of shadow twisted around his collar, so tight that the button snapped and his helmet came undone as well. Within seconds, the third soldier had died as quietly as the first two.

The fourth soldier, who had the most time to register everything, pointed his gun uselessly at the air.

"If you shoot, I'll kill myself," Marina said—mindlessly, thoughtlessly. "And then the Omnia will die, and *you* will be responsible for Elsudra entering eternal dead years. Imagine what Kieron would do to you."

She didn't know whether the guard bought her bluff—didn't know if it *was* a bluff. All she could think about was keeping things quiet and making sure Aeric didn't get blown to bits before they reached Kieron. When the guard lowered his gun, Marina didn't wait for Aeric to decide what they'd do.

This time, she conveyed—only a couple paces, over to the door where the guard stood. At the moment, that was enough to make her dizzy with exhaustion, but what followed was as natural as breathing. The world had barely unblurred before she'd undone the guard's helmet and put her hand on his head.

She never saw his essence. She didn't care what form it took or the memories it held. All she did was what she was good at: she destroyed.

Her anger flared up—a quick, fleeting snap of flames that bubbled beneath the surface of her waves—then fizzled back out when the guard collapsed.

Aeric unglamoured himself, and she met his eyes—only for a moment, but it was enough to get her moving again.

The door led to a holding room with thick carpets and glass tables. They trekked another flight of stairs—shorter and narrower than the last—and this time, there was no door hiding the room it led to.

Marina remembered it. She'd seen it in Aeric's memories. Pillars lined the walls, and a chandelier hung from the ceiling. Its crystals glinted in the soft light. Wide, open windows spanned the room, overlooking the indigo sea. At the center, sitting at a table with a glass of wine and a console, was Kieron.

His eyes didn't land on her—they landed on Aeric, who immediately blasted the console off the table with a lance of light. The lance was weak but effective, and the console shattered when it hit the floor.

Silence followed, empty and cold. Aeric didn't attack Kieron. Perhaps wielding so much magic so soon after he'd emerged from unconsciousness was taking its toll. Or, more likely, he couldn't bring himself to deal the first blow.

Strangely enough, Kieron didn't attack either. And neither did Marina.

Tired, pale, and quiet, the three of them took each other in. Assessing the threat. Deciding how to proceed.

Finally, a breathy sigh escaped Kieron's lips. "Is this how all great wars end? With the opposing sides at a table, drinking wine?" His gaze shifted to the broken console. "If you think that's my only method of communicating with my army, you're sorely mistaken. I can still initiate the destruction of Elsudra." He paused, and for the first time since she'd entered the room, Kieron beheld her. "But you're here. Not the way I intended...but here."

Where had her anger gone? If Aeric wouldn't launch the first attack, she wanted to. Kieron obviously wasn't in his element—she could see fear in his eyes, the same as she did that day in the throne room when she'd lashed out at him—but her body wouldn't move. It was almost as though Kieron was a bomb himself, and she worried her movement might set him off.

"I didn't think you'd come after what happened in Tolsea," he said to Marina. "That was where I erred. Now, the three of us are hanging by threads. But I have something the two of you don't. I have soldiers. Living, breathing soldiers you can't banish to another realm—who await launch orders, which only I can give. And I will give them. I will give them if you don't agree to Locus—to give me what is mine."

He didn't give Marina any time to respond, though she wasn't sure she would've. "I know you can learn it," he said, almost hysterically. "I know you're capable." He cocked his head at Aeric. "He does too. This is his biggest fear—you being in Altus. He knows Locus is possible for you, and he knows with even greater certainty that I can get you to comply. But this doesn't have to come down to a fight."

He spoke to Aeric when he said, "I don't want to hurt you, and you don't want to hurt me. So we'll stand down. We'll choose peace. That's all I've wanted."

If she wasn't verging on delirium, Marina might've laughed at that. He was desperate

—scared—and what he'd just said made that clearer than ever. He didn't give a shit about Aeric, and he'd certainly never given a shit about peace. He didn't know if he could win against the two of them, despite how downtrodden they were, and it terrified him.

Marina glanced at Aeric, expecting him to share her reaction—expecting it to fuel her and get her body moving again.

But Aeric's face was blank, and his eyes shined.

Kieron noticed too. "I still consider you my son," he said. "I still care for you, Aeric. We're family."

Family. That word hurt—and not just her. Aeric sucked in a breath as Kieron tilted the rim of his wine glass at Marina.

"She's not your family," Kieron continued. "Not like I am. She's not even Elsudran. What will happen if she continues to hold the Omnia? If I die? Not only to our realm but to *you*?" He pointed at himself. "I would never abandon you. If I took the Omnia—if I got her through Locus, which I know I can—then I'd use Exorsus to sustain myself. My loop may be smaller, but unending all the same. And you...*you* could join me. You were meant to. You still are, even if you've strayed."

Marina's muscles stiffened as she looked to Aeric, but he didn't heed her. For half a second, she almost worried he'd yield. Pain guttered in his eyes—pain and longing. But then he looked to her, and when he locked eyes with Kieron again, he shook his head.

Silence followed, which Kieron broke when he stood. Marina flinched as the legs of his chair raked across the flagstone.

"What has she ever done to warrant your loyalty?" he hissed. "I *raised* you. She's been a burden since the day she came here. And what of the rest of Elsudra? What have the people out there done that I haven't? Your mother was dead the day she brought you to me —dead because of the people who used her, then discarded her. She knew it; I knew it. Vaughn only accelerated the inevitable. I could've left you after, but I didn't. I cared for you. I *loved* you like you were my own. And this is how you repay me? By putting your faith into a foreign girl and keeping me from what's mine?"

Aeric held to the evenness in his voice when he said, "It's over."

Like dust, Kieron's rage settled, and he sighed. "Not yet."

He slipped his glove off his hand, but before Marina could take in his gray fingers, the crystals on the chandelier rattled.

Now, her limbs obeyed her. She raised her arms to throw out a shield, made stronger by the one Aeric threw alongside her. Whatever wave of force Kieron sent their way collided with a wall of air—enough to push them back, but not enough to make them fall.

Kieron didn't stop. He kept at them until he broke through the wall of air, but rather than raise another, Marina made a motion with her finger. Her waves were rough and jagged, and she imagined them careening from her fingers like knives. Instead of cutting through Kieron's skin, however, they made contact with another shield, as invisible as the force that shot from her hands. She could sense she'd cleaved through it, and she tried to cut through his skin again—to slit his throat, perhaps, like he'd done to Ocot.

She wasn't surprised when he deflected her attack. As much as she yearned to see him drown in his own blood like Vaughn had, she knew he wouldn't go down that easily.

Kieron wasn't as worn out as she and Aeric were, but this wasn't easy for him. He shook as he moved, and whether it was from weariness, age, or the fact that a sliver of his soul was now locked in Sundra, wielding magic taxed him.

He held up well enough, though. Each time an attack came his way, he deflected it and sent his own back at them. When Marina hurled a lance of light at Kieron, he sent it off course before it could hit him. It crackled as it whizzed toward the table, careening into the wine glass and sending it to the floor. The cup split in two, and wine splashed across the stones and seeped into the cracks. It looked an awful lot like blood—not thick and violet like ruemin blood, but dark red, like human blood. *Elsudran* blood.

The sight reminded her of the soldiers in Tin and the guard she'd killed outside the palace. It reminded her of those who'd been torn to pieces in Candens Inlet, and the scouts Kieron had set ruemin on to torture Marina and get her to bend to his wishes. And it reminded her of Pierce, even though she hadn't seen him die. All the same, she knew the ruemin had ripped him apart. His blood stained Sundran soil like Kieron's wine stained the flagstone. And his soul...they'd feast on his soul too.

A weight settled on her chest but was knocked from her when something slammed into her head. She hit the ground, reeling from the ache in her skull and cursing herself for getting distracted.

When Aeric lunged toward her, Kieron threw another burst of force at him, stopping him in his tracks. With his other hand, Kieron sent shadows toward Marina. She went to stand, but a tendril wrapped around her neck, holding her to the floor and constricting with all its might.

Safira had done this to Yolie. And Yolie...what had she done?

Aeric sent his own surges of force toward Kieron. While they sullied Kieron's balance, they didn't stop him from tightening the shadows around Marina's throat.

"Kieron," Aeric said. He wasn't begging him—he knew Kieron wouldn't listen—but his voice was shackled by desperation all the same.

"I said it's not over yet," Kieron hissed. His breathing was hitched. "Is this what you want? She dies, and the Omnia follows suit? Do you want that, Aeric? There is no Elsudra without me. There is no *Omnia*."

The pressure on her throat was unbearable. Flashes of golden light danced across her vision, and for half a second, Marina thought she saw Yolie's glasses and the constellations that made her spirit.

It was getting hard to breathe now, and the shadows that entwined about her throat weren't going to stop. Marina's eyes trailed to the ceiling, where the chandelier twinkled. Though her limbs ached, she lifted her arms and pointed them toward Kieron.

It was difficult to manipulate light before dawn, but color sprang from the crystals anyway. They weren't as vibrant as those Aeric had conjured as a boy, or as bright as the light Yolie had used against Safira, but it was something. It shot toward Kieron's eyes, flashing wildly enough to interrupt his focus. The shadows around her neck didn't retreat, but they loosened, and she tried to wriggle free.

The possibility of conveying out of them crossed her mind, but the shadows—if that's really what they were; they felt much heavier—comprised a spatial barrier. She couldn't convey out of the restraints Kieron had crafted any more than she could convey through doors and walls, which meant she needed to use brute force instead.

Brute force. *Of course.* She was good at that.

She let her waves rise and foam, then sent them toward the shadows with the strength of a furious tide. She knew it worked when air flooded into her lungs and the dark tendrils holding her down fizzled out.

She managed to roll to the side, her head clearing as she heaved great breaths. Air... she loved air. Loved the way it felt to breathe in—the way it could protect her.

The thought snapped her into motion, and she shielded her body as Kieron recovered. Which was smart, because the moment he regained his vision, he widened his arms at her.

The air surrounding her split, but Aeric was on Kieron before he could do anything else. Conveyance had obviously crossed his mind too, because he landed behind Kieron and wrapped his arms around his neck. Before Aeric could protect himself, however, Kieron threw his arms up and back, his palms facing Aeric's head. When a sharp lance of light cracked from his fingers and struck Aeric's forehead, Kieron managed to get free.

This time, it was Kieron who conveyed, but not to attack Aeric. In an instant, he had his arm around Marina's torso, and she cried out as he forced her to her feet. Light sparked at her fingers, but Kieron's hand wrapped around her wrists, keeping her palms angled toward the ground instead of at him.

He wrapped something else around her wrists too. Something leaden and cold. Even once she'd realized what they were—once she'd heard the snap of diminution cuffs— Kieron didn't release his grip. He kept his arm around her, then wrapped his hand around her neck. Marina cringed as his grayed, withered fingers made contact with her skin.

"Move, and I'll slit her throat," he warned. "The Omnia will take irreversible damage, and it will be over for *both* of us."

When Aeric froze, Kieron let out a breath. At first, Marina thought it was a laugh, but it was tired and desperate. She threw all her weight back onto Kieron, squirming as violently as she could, but it was futile. *Useless.*

She tried to kick him, but nothing she did weakened his hold on her. His hand lingered at her neck, prepared to draw blood if Aeric so much as moved a muscle.

How stupid had the first Keepers been to put the Omnia inside living beings? Perhaps greed and myopia were two sides of the same coin. They hadn't sworn oaths like their successors, and they'd let their desires rule them—fettering a gift from their realm and turning it into a curse.

Was this it, then? Was this the moment when the selfish desires of a few brought the world to its knees? If the Omnia were back in the ocean, Kieron couldn't threaten to destroy it. Not like he was doing now. But it was in *her*—in her soul, her essence—and she was as feeble and mortal as all the beings who'd held the Omnia before her.

Kieron's hand tightened around her throat, and for a moment, Marina wondered if he really *was* going to kill her. But when her vision faded and the world around her turned to flames and sea—when his wild, unyielding fire barreled toward her waves—she knew exactly what he was trying to do.

CHAPTER 54
Tsunami

Pain. That was Kieron's tried-and-true strategy, wasn't it? It had been his goal with the last Keepers to force them to consent to Locus, and now he was trying it with her.

"Kieron doesn't just use psychometry to obtain information," Aeric had told her once. *"He tortures people with it."*

Marina tried to raise her walls of seawater, but it was useless with the cuffs on—like standing with a weight on her back. Kieron went for the memory he knew first. In a murky spot of the sea, more gray than blue, a storm battered the curbs outside a closed coffee shop. There was another storm too—one she could feel all over again when she saw herself sitting with her knees to her chest, drenched and shaking.

"I can't do another day," she sobbed into her phone. *"Please, come tonight. This isn't going to stop. I can't stop them."*

Her episodes, she meant. Her storms.

Kieron didn't simply watch the memory—he stirred up the waters around it too, sending her waves into unrest. They were helpless beneath his fire—beneath the cuffs—and every gust of flames made the emotions worse, like she was losing control of them.

This wasn't dissolution magic; he wasn't dissolving or destroying anything. This was delirium inducement. She'd never experienced it before, but she knew what it was, deep in her bones. She could feel Kieron straining to evoke chaos without completely obliterating her senses. Whatever balance he struck was enough to keep her coherent but far more vulnerable to what she witnessed.

The memory was already painful. With the additional frenzy Kieron sent her waves into, it was close to unbearable. Any hold she might have had on her emotions slipped— any good sense she tried to grasp at withered away until she was completely at his mercy.

At the *memory's* mercy.

"We'll come." Her dad's voice. It cut out, then sharpened again, sending a thousand stabbing pains through her heart. *"We'll come."*

"I'm sorry," she said, then let out another broken sob. *"I'm trying so hard, but I hate being here, and they keep happening."*

"I know." This time, it was her mom who spoke. Her voice quivered. *"I know. It's not your fault. We're getting in the car now, 'kay?"*

Marina could feel her stomach drop from afar. Hopelessly, she tried to regain control of her body but failed.

"I want to drop out," Marina said. She scrubbed a hand down her face. *"I hate this."*

"Nothing triggered this one?" her mom asked.

"Nothing. Just being here, away from home, in a different environment. What's wrong with me?" Saying it made her cry even harder.

"It's how you are, Rina," her dad said. *"Chemicals, like the doctors said, remember? Gotta weather it. We'll figure something out."*

"You'll be home soon," her mom added.

No, I won't. Not with you.

Reliving this so vividly—while balancing on the precipice of delirium—was agonizing. Kieron knew it. When he removed his hand, he said, "Locus is your key to end this."

"Kieron," Aeric said. Now he was begging.

"Locus" was all Kieron responded with. When Marina kicked at him again, his hand flew back to her neck and flames sputtered into view.

"I want to go home." She wasn't outside the coffee shop anymore. She was in the Delve, sitting in Aeric's office after he'd tried—and failed—to coax her powers out of her. Instead, he'd sent her into a spiral. Not like it was that hard to do.

Though Marina knew time worked differently in psychometry—that this was all happening within the span of seconds—it felt so real and just as drawn-out as when she'd experienced it.

"Do you possess a modicum of self-control?" Aeric hissed. *"Of discipline? How do you expect to progress if you so easily shatter?"*

Unstable. Kieron's flames seemed to whisper it.

Aeric's voice sounded again, but this time, it wasn't from inside her head. The room came back into view when he said, "Even if she consents to Locus, she won't be successful if you keep torturing her. You'll damage her mind *and* the Omnia."

"Then let it be damaged. At least I'll have tried."

Who was truly unstable? Kieron would risk harming the Omnia if it meant there was even a small possibility he could hold it. If there weren't, he'd get rid of the entire thing.

When his flames rushed into her mind again, the memories came at her in droves. The middle-aged scout screaming as ruemin tore into her body in the throne room. The rotting faces outside the Delve. The burning trees and the lone red pacifier.

And then, a tunnel, and Cal's teary eyes.

"Let me do this, Astra."

The pain in these memories was even worse when they all came at her at once. She fought with everything she had, but the cuffs were stifling and the memories akin to nightmares. When Marina heard Ryder's voice echoing in her head—*"don't go, don't go, don't go"*—and she saw the empty mouth of Brenna's portal, she almost gave in.

Kieron must've sensed it, because he pulled back and repeated, "Locus."

Marina's eyes trailed to the tower windows. The stars had faded, and on the horizon, light from the ascending sun danced on the sea.

"Locus," Kieron said again.

All she heard was Pierce's voice. *You're stronger than it all.*

"You're going to end Elsudra if you keep on like this," Aeric pleaded. "You can't…"

"I *can*," Kieron barked. To Marina, he said, "Agree to let me take you through Locus—agree to try to perform it—or I'll make the pain worse. I'll kill you with it."

Marina looked up at him. "Then kill me with it."

Kieron's face twisted, and when his hand flew back to her neck, she felt as though a thousand shards of glass had pierced her skin. The pain inducement was almost as bad as the delirium, and when her memories returned with vigor, they flooded over her in waves.

Every horrible memory—all the darkest, most excruciating moments of her life—furled into a storm that pummeled her. In tandem with Kieron's raging fire and the delirium he wrought upon her spirit, it was strong enough to break her.

Yes, these memories hurt. They would never stop hurting. Kieron could make her relive them all, and perhaps it would be worse than physical torture.

But she would still rise.

Like the rays of sun beyond the windows, the ocean within her began to swell. Foam and saltwater warred with Kieron's fire—with the oppressive weight the diminution cuffs cast over her spirit—and deep beneath her waters, the Omnia's power pulsed outward.

Kieron tried to smother it. Every time her ocean rose, flickering with the Omnia's light, his flames pushed it back down.

People like you always break. He'd told her that once. He was telling her the same thing now, in far fewer words.

She answered him with names.

Raisel, Thora.

The Omnia fed her waves. When they crested, sea spray rained onto fire. Kieron held his grip defiantly, but his proximity to the Omnia couldn't match the power of actually holding it. And the diminution cuffs...they were *loosening.*

Maybe there was something more powerful than the talents her essence granted her. More powerful than the Omnia. It couldn't be held, but it could be felt. Remembered.

Evren, Tover.

She'd promised herself, not too long ago, that she'd accept every emotion. Even the painful ones. So if Kieron wanted her to feel pain, then feel it she would. She'd feel the agony and fear. She'd feel the grief.

After all, what was grief, if not love?

And she had loved—she *did* love—so very deeply.

When her waves shot to the sky, it was more than the Omnia moving them. Whatever it was—whatever force lay deep inside of her, only to be woken in this fleeting moment— it broke through the weight atop her essence. Somewhere in the distance, Marina heard the diminution cuffs clank to the ground.

Boris, Dane.

And now, her waves were free.

They shot up, throwing Kieron out, and when the room materialized, they kept rising. Aeric whirled to face the window, but Marina made it a point to lock eyes with Kieron, who'd gone slack-jawed.

Every inch of her burned so wildly that it overrode her exhaustion. And the emotions that had once slept beneath her surface—the memories Kieron had tried to torture her with—only made her stronger.

Outside, the ocean rose with the sun.

Lana, Cordelia, Adela, Wren, Jace.

It wasn't one thing that moved her, but everything. Every iota of her essence—her waves, the Omnia, and perhaps even her storms—came together as the sea beyond the Pale Tower rose. Marina widened her arms, one with the water as it licked up the hillside and reached its pinnacle at the opened windows.

Ivo, Kins, Gian, Esther, Elm.

Kieron hurled a force of light at Marina's head. Aeric obliterated it before it could reach her, then sent his own at Kieron, knocking him off his feet. Bedlam erupted as a giant, glittering wave crashed through the windows, cleaving pillars in two.

No. Not a wave. It was much too large. Much too powerful.

A tsunami.

It was her, and she was it—brimming with awesome, divine power that even Kieron couldn't challenge. Water flooded into the room, shattering the chandelier, but before it could sweep them up, Marina and Aeric slung their arms around Kieron. When Marina met Aeric's gaze, understanding lingered between them—calm, despite the chaos.

Hollis, Zora, Lars.

Kieron fought, but not hard enough. Within seconds, they'd submerged, and Marina closed her eyes. She trusted Aeric to restrain Kieron as the Omnia's power pulsed outward —as she used it to call forth the very thing Kieron both yearned for and was rejected by.

Ronan, Neva, Florin.

Evidently, Kieron realized what she was doing, and he must've feared it because he began to writhe against her grip. But her waters stifled him, and as Aeric held tight to Kieron, Marina called to Exorsus.

She could feel the power of the tide consume her—could feel it flow through her until her body was one with the sea.

Astra, Cal.

The waves around her responded. Kieron thrashed about violently, but Marina knew he was breaking. He'd tried so hard to hold the Omnia, but he never had. Never *would*. And Exorsus—the very thing he'd hoped would be his salvation—would be his end.

She could feel its presence. The darkness beyond was only a step away, and she needed to be the one to take it. She gathered all the strength she could—every emotion, no matter how deep, no matter how painful.

Pierce.

In a cold, foamy swell, the sea split in two.

And after that, there was only darkness.

CHAPTER 55
The Kind We Need

Darkness. Thick, velvety, and strangely peaceful. It was all Marina could perceive. But she knew Exorsus well, and like before, the first sense she regained was hearing.

Screaming. She could hear screaming. Not long after, she could see who it came from.

Kieron's body contorted in the darkness, as though he were a puppet at the mercy of invisible strings. The fingers on his already atrophied hand withered further until skin and bone became dust. He clawed at his arm as it, too, decayed—as everything that held him together rotted, then dissolved.

Beside her, Marina could see Aeric's eyes widen, and when Kieron began to scream louder, Aeric made a sound that resembled a whimper. Marina reached for him, but her limbs wouldn't make contact with him. It was as though he were right next to her and miles away at the same time, and all Marina could do was watch as Kieron crumbled.

It was the slowest torture imaginable. Marina knew time passed differently in Exorsus—that really, no time passed at all—but the screaming felt as though it lasted an eternity. Kieron sank to his knees as his legs disintegrated, gasping as his torso followed suit.

Exorsus presided absently over its creations, Marina supposed, but it didn't show the same indifference to what was *no longer* one of its creations. And thanks to Sundra—to the deal he'd made with the ruemin, which rendered him less than living—Exorsus no longer recognized Kieron as its own. It was devouring him—grinding him away as though he were a parasite that didn't belong in its universe.

Irony, Marina thought. Bitter, cruel irony, to be wrenched from existence by the very thing he wanted to control.

Kieron clutched his chest, his eyes darting about. Marina braced herself for his hateful gaze, but he didn't acknowledge her. He looked at Aeric, and only him, and as the skin near his mouth began to deteriorate, Kieron uttered his last word.

"*Aeric.*"

Kieron only said it once. And then, like ashes stirred by a nonexistent wind, his body blew into nothingness. A trail of low-burning fire followed—the last of his spirit, dwindling away.

Marina turned to Aeric, but the two of them were farther away from each other than before. When she opened her mouth to call for him, the darkness faded.

In its stead, ocean surrounded her.

She tried to call out, but she was alone, stranded in the midst of a sea with no anchor.

At first, she wondered if Exorsus had taken her there. But when the waves brought yellow petals with them—daffodils—she knew she'd brought herself.

This was the ocean where the Omnia was born. Where it should've stayed, if it hadn't been for mortals who sought the power of gods.

The first Keepers had woven the pieces of this tapestry long ago. She couldn't change what they'd done—couldn't change the oaths their successors agreed to swear, or all their years of blindness, however well-intentioned. But she could mend it. The first Keepers had taken the Omnia from the sea in Exorsus; and in Exorsus, she could finally give it back.

What a strange, fickle thing the tapestry of time was. In some ways, it wove itself, loosely guided by the choices of beings that comprised its stitches. But there was so much she couldn't do, so many people she couldn't bring back.

She wished she could. She wished she could control it all—not because of the power, but because perhaps it would ease her suffering.

That was the burden of her kind, wasn't it? Though she desperately wished she could change every part of the tapestry that brought her pain, she knew those weren't her choices to make. But that didn't mean she was choiceless.

For a short time, the Omnia had been part of her path. Now, it was time to let go.

She didn't need Locus. Not here.

One breath at a time.

A tide swelled from beneath her, bucking gently as though the waves were breathing alongside her. If she let it, could the ocean bring her home? It was a tempting thought—until she realized she didn't have only one home. Georgia and Elsudra meant everything to her, but one was a home of the past and another of the present. There were people in Elsudra who needed her.

She hesitated. They'd needed her when she held the Omnia. But if she gave it up, who would she be? The anxiety she'd been holding since last emerging from Exorsus washed over her—and with it, a voice. *Her* voice.

You'd be Marina. And that is enough.

She'd still have her waves—everything that made her who she was—and more than that, she'd have her family, broken and mending as it may be. She didn't need the Omnia to have those things.

She couldn't believe there'd been a time when she'd wanted to leave. This place—these people—meant the world to her. They *were* her world. But it didn't mean the hole within her wouldn't hurt when she thought of Georgia or of all the people—from Earth and Elsudra alike—she'd mourn. She wasn't sure she'd ever be able to fill those empty parts of herself. Even when she grew old, she'd still feel the longing and grief.

Maybe it was impossible for *anyone* to feel whole. But that didn't mean they couldn't heal. Ryder had said it before: *Anyone can heal, if they find something worth healing for.*

She had. She *would.* She'd told Gemma and Hank she was going to make a good life for herself; here in Elsudra, she could. But she needed them to know.

In Exorsus, she could feel all the paths she'd ever crossed weaving around her. Gemma and Hank were one of those paths, and though Marina couldn't see or hear the assurance she sent, she knew it reached them. How they'd respond, she wasn't sure. Perhaps they'd never understand what had become of her, or where she'd gone. But somewhere deep down, they'd feel her gratitude, and she prayed it brought them peace.

Now, she could move forward.

Four's voice echoed in her head. *The kind we need.*

She'd certainly try to be. For her family, for Elsudra, and for herself as well.

Water washed over her, calm and content, until she felt as free as the waves that made up her spirit. And as the Omnia flowed from her veins and into the sea, she did what her parents would've wanted—what had always been harder for her, and perhaps always would be, but what she'd continue to do no matter what.

She breathed.

CHAPTER 56

Home

On a sandbank beneath the palace, Marina woke to waves. They covered her legs in cool kisses, glittering with the light of the sun, now fully risen. For a while, she lay motionless, listening to the cry of gulls and watching the sea crash against the shore. She could taste salt on her lips—could feel the dewiness the ocean brought to her skin—but there was something different. Something *more*.

She felt lighter here, by the sea. She turned onto her stomach and curled her fingers around clumps of sand. A few paces away, Aeric pushed himself up onto his elbows.

When he saw her, a look she couldn't quite decipher flashed across his face. She stood and neared him, then sank back to the sand once she'd reached his side. For a moment, he only stared at her, then looked out at the ocean.

He could feel it too. The Omnia—nearby, and so much freer than it had been in a long time. It came with the breeze brought by the waves, and if only to test it, Marina summoned light at her fingertips. It wasn't the same as when she'd held the Omnia—it didn't come from within her so much as it came from around her—but she could still pull from it. Aeric's gaze drifted back to her, and for a while, he was silent.

And then his tears began to fall.

He put his head into his hands, crying without sound. His voice, too, was barely a whisper when he said, "I shouldn't mourn him."

Kieron. Marina flinched but didn't recoil. In a way, she understood. For so long, Kieron had been Aeric's family. No amount of victory could ever stifle that loss. There weren't any words that could make sense of the grief, and Marina didn't try to find them. Instead, she sat with him until his tears stopped. Once they had, he took another long look at the sea.

"You put it back," he said.

She nodded, eyeing Aeric cautiously. She wasn't sure how he'd react. But when he put his hand on her shoulder, all he said was, "Good."

A weight lifted off Marina's shoulders, and though her eyes brimmed with tears, she managed to hold herself together well enough.

Eventually, she'd have to leave this sandbank, but the gauzy veil that hung over her mind softened her emotions, and leaving would surely rip it off. Kieron was gone, but back at the palace, there was pain—pain and an empty portal.

Marina curled her knees to her chest and rested her chin on them, counting the waves that crashed to the shore.

One, two, three, four…

Together, they sat in silence, watching the ocean as reality settled back in. From their spot on the beach, Marina could see the crumbled Pale Tower, which clung to the edge of the hill like a vise. A few stones came loose, skidding down the rock face and falling to the waves below. Unperturbed, the sun rose on.

Finally, Aeric said, "We should go back."

One day, one step, one breath at a time. Her mother's voice gave her the strength to stand—to take her first step toward the palace.

Aeric stood, then hesitated. When Marina glanced at him, he said, "When you were in Exorsus…" His lips began to shake, and it took a great while before he spoke again. "I felt the Omnia back in the sea, but I didn't see you. I thought, for a moment, that you'd chosen to go home."

His eyes shined, and Marina wiped at her own. She couldn't help but wonder if she'd always be that stray soul caught between realms, trying to find a reason to move forward. But she'd gotten this far, and though she hadn't the slightest idea what she'd do next or how any of them would find the strength to carry on with all the grief they held, she didn't feel lost. Not like she had when she'd first come to Elsudra.

She looked out to the sea, breathing with each crash of waves—feeling the Omnia dance atop the tide and in the air. She wasn't sure if that brought her comfort or if it was something else, but the heaviness in her chest lessened when she said, "I *am* home."

CHAPTER 57
If Only

With the ruemin and Kieron gone, the inclined weren't the only people who came out of hiding. Previously outmatched soldiers and wary civilians came to Altus to help round up the rest of Kieron's loyalists. There weren't many left—most had laid down their weapons upon realizing they no longer had the ruemin on their side—but the select few who refused to renounce his reign met swift deaths.

In truth, Marina tried to stay far away from the fallout. She was surprised how many people had found sanctuary in the nooks and crannies of Elsudra, and though many of them—like Blaine—flocked across the realm to find estranged family members, some came to the capital looking to rebuild.

Ismene, Elta, and Yolie were among those who came to Altus. It was a hazy couple of days. Elta had taken a turn for the worse, and she was whisked off to treatment. Ismene had already been a mess, but when she'd learned of Pierce, she'd cried harder than Marina had ever seen her cry. For some reason, the fuzziness of everything left Marina's emotions blunted, and she hadn't shed a single tear. Instead, she'd consoled Ismene, numbed to her own grief. But she could feel it lingering, and every so often, Ryder's pleas assailed her ears.

Don't go, don't go, don't go.

Ismene coped by funneling her energy into taking care of Ash, who she'd brought to the capital, and when Elta emerged from recovery, Ismene's attention shifted to her. The healers had stopped the infection from spreading, but the flesh below Elta's elbow couldn't be saved. Her new hand resembled Lars's—smooth, rounded fingers and metal that shined in the light—and the prosthetic itself reminded Marina of an opera glove. Elta had chosen the color gold, but it didn't jar Marina like Vaughn's had, perhaps because Elta wore the color differently. On her, it was radiant. Hopeful, even. And Marina had a feeling that was why Elta had chosen it.

Elta was eager to rebuild without forgetting what had happened. On the day the healers discharged her from the infirmary, she and Ismene got to work spreading Pierce's name. In the seasons that followed, the two of them saw to it that every Elsudran knew what Tover's son had done—how he was responsible for the ruemins' eternal banishment.

Marina tried to spread the word too. Mostly, she hoped hearing people praise Pierce would bring Ryder peace, but she couldn't be sure. Last she'd heard, he'd locked himself in one of the palace apartments and wouldn't even let healers check on him. When she'd asked if she could visit, the healers had warned her against it.

It was Yolie she saw more than anyone, and that was because Yolie refused to leave her side. They needed each other, Marina thought—now more than ever. Yolie might've made a full physical recovery after Safira, but her longing for Neva was a wound Marina didn't know how to tend to. Yolie brightened when she played with Ash or practiced magic, but occasionally, Marina would catch a glimpse of her teary eyes and wish she knew how to help. How could she walk Yolie through her grief when she was so consumed by her own?

But she always left her apartment doors unlocked, and more often than not, she'd wake to Yolie snuggled up beside her in bed. Yolie had her own room—Aeric had seen to it —but she gravitated to Marina's whenever she got the chance, and Marina never turned her away. Sometimes, they'd lie awake in bed before the sun rose, teaching each other songs and manipulating light that streamed in through the curtains—light born of fading stars and a rising sun, and which eased their restless spirits more than most else could.

By the beginning of Olivine, Altus buzzed with activity. It was due, in large part, to Ismene and Elta. With Elta taking on the brunt of post-conflict reconstruction and Ismene gravitating toward newfound public relations, optimism in the palace rippled throughout the streets. People were hesitant but hopeful, which Marina supposed was the smartest response. Elta called it cautious optimism. If they continued on that way, perhaps they could limp their way toward recovery—toward rebuilding from all the lives lost during the war, and later, toward flourishing despite it all.

"We never dreamed we'd live in an age where the Omnia was back where it belonged," Elta said one evening. She stood on the palace steps with Ismene and Marina, which offered one of the best views in Altus. It had become a common thing for them—to spend evenings watching the sun set and the city lights sparkle beneath the stars. Tonight, Elta's eyes glistened, and she added, "Neva and Lars would be so happy."

Ismene squeezed Elta's shoulder, then Marina's. "Florin and Pierce would be too."

And Cal. And all the others. Marina turned her smarting eyes to the sea on the horizon. If she listened hard enough, she could hear gulls. Perhaps they, too, detected a change in the air. She could certainly feel it. When she looked inward, her waves no longer held the light they used to, but they'd retained their strength. In the midst of the ocean breeze, they responded, as though they knew the Omnia was near.

Ismene and Elta were some of the few Elsudrans who knew what the first Keepers had done and how vital it was their choices weren't repeated. The brunt of that responsibility —of keeping that secret—had fallen to Aeric, who'd publicly renounced his title as Sorcerer of the Court, vowing to protect the Omnia as it existed in water. Nobody knew what to call his job, but he seemed more content with it not having a name. When he offered to train Marina to take on the same role, she agreed—on the sole condition he'd train Yolie too.

Apparently, Aeric had already considered it, and when he'd accepted, Yolie expressed her excitement by littering his office with dozens of flowers. Though Aeric had told her to clean them up, Marina had caught sight of him failing to hide a small smile.

Once or twice, he'd said he thought Yolie's talent matched Brenna's. He never said it to her face, though, and he told Marina not to repeat it, claiming Yolie's confidence was high enough. Marina had told her anyway.

But it was Yolie's kindness, Ismene often said, that made her suited for such a job. Marina and Aeric were inclined to agree. In the middle of Olivine, before the tunnels Cal had blown down could be repaired, Marina proposed implementing palace gardens there instead. Ismene and Elta weren't the only people eager to start the project; Yolie was too, and when Altus received a shipment of seeds from nearly every city in Elsudra—far too many for the fledgling garden—Yolie had asked if the leftovers could be sent to Elsudrans who'd lost loved ones in the war. It was a small gift, she'd said, but flowers had been what kept her going, and she wanted others to have something like that too.

Yolie's request didn't surprise Marina. What did surprise her, however, was that it was Aeric who'd ensured the request was honored.

After particularly long days, Marina would walk Yolie to her apartments, knowing she'd end up in her room anyway, then retreat to the terraces to watch the ocean. She needed those moments of quiet, especially since it had barely been a full season since everything had happened. Some days, she was good at keeping the grief from spilling over. Other days, she wasn't.

Tonight, the grief filled her body like liquid lead. She fiddled with her voco—it was nearing the end of Olivine, which meant October would be around the corner in Georgia —then turned her attention to Ash, who pawed at the leaves of a drooping fern that sat in a ceramic pot just on the balcony's threshold. When he grew tired of that, he rubbed against her legs, purring until she gave in and sat down with him. He soaked up all the attention he could get, and for nearly half an hour, Marina mindlessly petted him. She was in such a daze that she didn't notice Ryder until he sat beside her.

Ash didn't seem fazed, but Marina had to swallow her gasp. Though Ryder gave her his usual roguish grin, it didn't hide the dark circles beneath his eyes. His voice wavered when he said, "That stupid cat is still here, I see."

Marina leaned forward and hugged Ryder, and his breathing shallowed.

"I'm fine," he said when she pulled away, as though he feared her asking. He repeated it, far less certain. "I'm fine."

He obviously wasn't fine, but neither was she, and Marina didn't see any reason to point it out. Instead, she pulled Ash onto her lap and said, "I miss you."

Ryder's lips shook, but he smiled. "Yeah, I miss you too."

Even the starlight couldn't bring life to his eyes. Against her better judgment, Marina said, "I've been worried. I haven't seen you in weeks."

"Don't be."

"Well, I am."

Ryder put his fist to his lips and exhaled. "The healers knock on my door a hundred times a day, asking me if I need anything to ease the pain. And they aren't talking about my physical injuries." He didn't meet her gaze when he muttered, "It's annoying enough. I don't need you doing it too."

Marina tried not to bristle. "I can't help it."

"Find a way to help it. I sought you out because I thought you'd be one of the few people who *wouldn't* badger me."

She stopped petting Ash. "Ryder..."

"I can't go two seconds without someone asking me if I'm okay when they damn well know the answer."

"I wasn't trying to be annoying."

Ryder stood. "I know," he breathed. "I know. I don't know what I was thinking, wandering around when it's so late. I should...should go to bed."

"But you just came."

Don't go, don't go, don't go.

Ryder's lips quivered. "Guess I need more space than I thought."

Space. *Isolation.* She'd done the same thing to Gemma and Hank; she'd turned them away and shook off their concerns. They'd been grappling with grief too, but she hadn't thought of that. Her own had been too painful.

"Are you sure it's a good idea to be alone?" she asked.

"Better than being hounded with a million idiotic questions."

The bite in Ryder's tone made her tense. Before he could leave, Marina abandoned all sense of caution and blurted, "I lost him too."

Her voice broke, but she maintained eye contact with him. He gave her a glassy stare, which, for some reason, she knew was the calm before the storm. She wrapped her arms around Ash, praying he wouldn't spook.

It was a good call on her part. Ryder slammed his foot into the ceramic pot the fern sat in, sending it to the floor. When it hit the marble, shards and soil went flying. The crash was so loud that Ash nearly jumped from her arms, and though Marina expected it to draw attention—from guards or staff or *someone* nearby—the hallways were as empty as they always were at night.

The silence that followed was torturous. For one moment, then another, neither of them said a word.

And then, Ryder began to sob.

He slumped to the ground, shoulders shaking as he cried into his hands, and though Marina wasn't sure how he'd react, she set Ash aside and scooted over to him.

"It's my fault," he choked. "It's my fault he's gone."

Helplessly, Marina said, "It's not."

"It is. It's my fault. I treated him so horribly at Neva's compound...I blamed him for everything. And if I hadn't guilted him for fleeing, maybe he wouldn't have felt the need..."

He didn't finish. His sobbing got worse, and Marina could no longer keep her own grief inside. Every beat of her heart made the hole in her chest larger until its darkness leaked onto her limbs, which were as useless as they were by Brenna's portal. She tried to put her hand on Ryder's shoulder, but she couldn't lift her arms.

When her own tears began to fall, she didn't fight them. It wouldn't matter if she did, anyway; they always won.

She cried for Pierce as much as she cried for Neva, for Florin and Cal, and for all the other names on her list. And her mother and father...she cried for them too because they were as gone as the rest—as gone as her boots and the memories she'd left in Georgia.

But the more she cried, the less severe the heaviness in her limbs became, and finally, she was able to wrap her arms around Ryder.

He didn't pull away, but he didn't return the embrace either. He just sat there—numb and distant, like a ghost.

Maybe that's all they were. Ghosts mourning yet another body that would never be cast out to sea.

Pierce would never be cast out to sea.

Ryder's head fell, and he rested it in her lap, repeating the same thing over and over again. "It's my fault...my fault he's gone."

"It's not," Marina said; or tried to say. She wasn't sure any sound came out. And even if it had, she didn't think Ryder would believe her. She could repeat herself a thousand times, and it wouldn't lessen the guilt and pain.

When she released him, Ryder put his hands to his face, only to pull them away just as quickly. At first, Marina wasn't sure why, but when he began scratching at the burns on his palms—violently, hysterically—she embraced him again because it was the only thing she could think to do. He cried onto her shoulder, and though she couldn't fully make out what he was saying, she caught bits and pieces.

"...a monster. Should've been *me*...not him..."

Marina pulled back again. She grasped Ryder's arms and made sure he was looking at her. "Don't say that."

"It. Should've. Been. *Me*." He let out a hitched breath. "The healers keep saying we've won, like it'll matter to me. Like it'll make me happy. But I didn't win. I lost in that room. And it's my fault."

She could barely see him through her tears, but she kept her eyes on him when she said, "That was *Pierce's* choice. He made it. You can't blame yourself."

Ryder's face crumpled. "What if...what if he's still alive in Sundra? We could...could get him back...Aeric could find a new way to reopen the portal...we could..."

He didn't finish. He fell into another fit of sobs because he knew, as she did, that the monsters Pierce had left with weren't the forgiving type. But he'd left with them anyway.

She remembered what Ryder had said to her on their way to Tin, and though her voice was weak, she whispered, "Pierce knew what his choice meant. He knew it...same as Cal. Let him make it."

And let the dead find peace.

Ryder put his head in his hands. "I can't stop seeing it. I'll never leave that room...that moment. I'll never stop thinking about ways I could've stopped him."

"You couldn't," Marina rasped. "*We* couldn't. And even if we could've, he wouldn't have wanted us to. You know that." When Ryder didn't respond—or move, or react—she took ahold of his wrists and pulled them away from his face. "Listen to me. It is *not* your fault. He made his choice, and he saved us. All of us."

Ryder's eyes met hers—the eyes Pierce had told her about, long before she ever knew Ryder's name. And though her throat was unbearably tight, she added, "We have to move forward. For Pierce."

Something silky rubbed up against her side, and before she could register it was Ash, he'd already approached Ryder. Slowly, Ryder put a shaking hand to his fur, which had taken on a silvery glow in the starlight.

"If only it were easier," Ryder finally whispered.

He'd clearly remembered their conversation too, because he gave her a weak smile, which she knew took all his strength to muster.

She returned it with a trembling one of her own. "If only."

CHAPTER 58
The Tide

Before dawn, when the city was silent, Marina could hear the belfry's bell ring. It was miles away, but its song flitted over hills and rooftops, then into the opened halls of the palace. It had taken three seasons to ring, and another two before she could listen without growing tearful. But in due time, the sound reminded her less of what she'd lost and more of what she'd gained.

Double Moon came and went, and it was as grand as she'd expected. Ribbons and lanterns hung from rooftops, and the palace opened its doors, beckoning all manner of people. Back in Georgia, it would have been around Christmastime, and after offhandedly mentioning the traditions to Ismene, Marina had come across a small fir placed outside the throne room, decorated with red and yellow flowers—Yolie's touch, she'd presumed.

On the day of Double Moon, Ismene and Elta announced an outreach program meant to connect with Elsudran citizens in a way the court had never deemed important. The two of them had been planning their announcement for months, and they'd clearly taken on a lot of responsibility—not just in the palace, but in Elsudran government as a whole. Sometimes, their ideas were so grand Marina wondered how they'd execute them all. But if Ismene and Elta were bullish on their own, they were unstoppable together, and Marina left the technicalities of politics up to them. People like herself and Aeric were much more content to work behind the curtain, but Aeric still emerged from wherever he vanished to on Double Moon to voice his approval for Ismene and Elta's work.

And yet, despite all the grandeur—despite the dancing in palace courtyards and the music that flitted throughout the city streets—the day had a somber feel to it. Everyone handled it in their own way. Ismene and Elta poured themselves into overseeing palace celebrations, then danced the night away together. Yolie clung to Marina's side, tidying up floral arrangements and teaching Marina the names of the flowers. Even Ryder had a drink before disappearing as quickly as Aeric had.

Later that night, once the moons had been seen and Yolie had gone to bed, Marina found Ryder in the basements of the palace, sitting in front of Brenna's empty portal. In the seasons that followed, she'd often find him there—a ghost lamenting the past, even if only for a few hours. She'd usually leave him be, but every once in a while, she'd sit with him in silence until morning.

They never spoke of it, though. During the day, Ryder stayed busy by training younger guards who wanted to serve Elsudra. Despite clearly thinking he was arrogant, they seemed to appreciate the talent he brought. His magic, too, improved a fair amount with Aeric's help. But Ryder seemed most at ease when he was with Ash, who grew as fond of Ryder as he'd been of Pierce. It was rare to see Ryder without Ash at his heels, and though Ryder claimed it annoyed him, Marina would often catch him dangling bits of light over Ash's head, stroking his fur as gently as Pierce had.

The palace felt different than it had when she'd first come. Now, it was lighter and safer and, in many ways, more beautiful than ever. But sometimes, at the turn of corners or in the middle of vacant courtyards, Marina's stomach would coil. The breeze that flitted through the halls would occasionally play tricks on her, bringing Kieron's voice with it, and sometimes she'd swear she could hear the *click, click, click* of Safira's heels or the ruemins' throats. On bad nights, the shadows in her room glinted with silver, and the silence morphed into desperate, useless pleas.

Don't go, don't go, don't go.

As best she could in those moments, she'd ground herself with breaths—or even the scent of peppermint leaves, which she often kept in bunches beside her bed—and though the feelings eased with time, she knew they'd never go away. Sometimes, the grief would mold together, and she'd have no idea who or what she was crying for. Her boots, perhaps, or the smell of strawberry-cinnamon cake and the sound of guitar strings. The way her dad would sing her name—*my little Rina*—or her mother's advice. Cal's raven hair. The warmth in Florin's voice. Neva's rare but powerful smile. Pierce's green eyes.

She could tell it was the same for Aeric. He didn't speak of Kieron, but she could see the way the memories consumed him, even if he covered up the pain with his wintry demeanor. But it eased around her, and even Yolie, who'd clearly started to view Aeric the way she had Neva. She had no issue defying or challenging him, and Marina came to enjoy training with them both. Though Aeric never admitted it, she knew he did too.

Recently, Yolie had started practicing conveyance. She struggled with it—something she clearly wasn't used to—but that didn't stop her from trying. Every time Marina visited the Pale Tower, she braced herself for Yolie's sudden appearance.

Somehow, Yolie *still* managed to catch her off guard. One warm Aragonite evening, when the smell of salt tinged the air, Yolie slammed into Marina so hard that the two of them nearly tumbled down the tower's winding staircase.

Marina summoned a force field, then swore.

"Sorry!" Yolie gasped. When Marina only stared at her, a smile tugged at Yolie's lips. "Maybe...*don't* tell Aeric I just did that."

Marina's heartbeat slowed, and she chuckled. "Our secret," she said.

"I'm getting better. I make way less mistakes than I used to."

"Way *fewer*," Marina whispered, then furrowed her brow when she noticed the sweat on Yolie's hairline. "How long have you been at it for?"

"A couple hours. I'd ask Aeric for tips, but he's annoyed with me."

"Why?"

Yolie grinned up the staircase. "Go see for yourself."

She conveyed away shortly after, and Marina took the stairs eagerly. The Pale Tower had been rebuilt so precisely that even the crystals on the chandelier looked the same as they always had. In the evening light, they glinted like stars. But the walls were different— not because of any changes in design, but because several paintings hung from the stone, each one an impasto landscape. Golden clouds amidst a night sky and a red sun looming over a deep blue sea caught her attention first.

Before she could observe the others, Aeric's voice sullied her focus. "She hung them on her own, if you'd believe it. Broke into my apartment and took them out."

Marina couldn't help but laugh. "Oh, I believe it."

She approached the table he sat at, which was littered with so many papers she had to move some aside to sit across from him. She glanced at a few. Most of them she'd already read, and given how thorough Aeric was when it came to training, she figured Yolie had too. Checks and balances to safeguard the Omnia were far more intricate than Marina had ever thought they'd be, but she'd come to enjoy the process. She wasn't the Omnia's host anymore, but she could still help protect what she'd spent so many seasons holding—what, in some ways, she viewed as a friend.

"You should keep the paintings up," Marina said.

He gave her an unamused look. "I never thought my job would entail dealing with a child's antics."

Marina laughed. "She's well worth the trouble she causes."

Though Aeric's expression remained sober, Marina could see the hint of a smile in his eyes. "She's not the only one."

At some point that evening, after Aeric had retired for the night and Yolie had found her way back to the Pale Tower only to fall asleep on one of the couches, Marina settled down by an opened window and watched the sun set. It had become a ritual these past few seasons, and on quiet evenings like these, Marina's thoughts wandered as freely as the sea beyond the palace.

Most often, she thought of Exorsus—of whether she was still powerful enough to access it like the first Keepers had. Her abilities hadn't changed much upon returning the Omnia, even if her closeness to the ocean affected them. She wasn't powerful enough to break through diminution cuffs, perhaps; she couldn't draw from the Omnia within her, but instead had to pull it from the sea, which now burned with the power of the sun. But there was something else that slumbered in her spirit, full of life and emotion, light and dark. Maybe it was the force that Cal had called a strength—that which made her feel the good and the bad so intensely. Whatever it was, she wondered if it could give her the power to part the sea at daybreak and step into the darkness beyond. But she never tried.

She'd grown better at making peace with the ghosts of her past. It didn't get rid of the grief, but it made it easier to handle. In the early days of their victory, when it had all still felt like a dream, Aeric had told Marina that—if she ever wanted him to—he could look into constructing a portal to her realm. But before he could tell her how hard it would be, or how it might not work, or how it carried a thousand risks, Marina had turned him down. Some doors were meant to stay closed.

She'd pretended not to notice his relief. In a way, she was relieved too—relieved she was able to leave her past behind her, and that she was moving forward like her parents would've wanted.

But she thought of none of that tonight. Instead, she thought of her dreams. They'd grown milder as the seasons passed, though she did have one more than the rest. In it, the tide edged its way onto beaches, then pooled into valleys and submerged mountains. Eventually, it rose so high that when it receded, everything was washed anew.

She wasn't sure why the dream brought her so much peace. Maybe it was because in the depths of those cold, salty waters, the sister realms were closer than ever. Or maybe it was the freedom water brought—so enduring that no number of oaths could stifle it.

Whatever it was, Marina knew one thing for certain: when she woke and looked out at the waves that spanned the horizon, she looked upon home.

Glossary

Anteactus: A device resembling a kaleidoscope that catches, reconstructs, and stores memories, then renders them into moving images. The breadth of memories stored depends on the intended use of the device: personal or bureaucratic.

Brenna's portal: Also referred to as the Sundran portal, this inter-realm portal connects Elsudra and Sundra. It was constructed by Brenna (a late Sorcerer of the Court and Kieron's predecessor). Brenna originally intended the portal to be unidirectional (flowing from Elsudra to Sundra).

Brenna's ring: A ring owned by Brenna, made to resemble her essence. Brenna altered her ring to function as the mechanism that powered her portal and controlled its properties.

Candens Inlet: An inlet in the South, surrounded by wetland forests. A group of inclined Elsudrans are rumored to have found sanctuary here.

The court: The wealthiest Elsudrans. Typically residing in Altus, the court leveraged its money and influence to dictate where and how magic was used. While not all of the court was inclined, many were; in Elsudra—specifically during the era of Keepers—those with magical talents tended to receive higher paying jobs and thus tended to accumulate more wealth. That said, members of the court who were not inclined still had substantial power over the use of magic.

Daughter Rituals: Locus and Tempus.

Dead years: A period of twelve Elsudran years, ranging from the moment the Omnia was sent from Elsudra to the moment it returned. Without the Omnia present in Elsudra, magic and life energy came to a halt. People did not age, give birth, or die of natural causes; however, unnatural causes (i.e. severe wounds that were not treated via external intervention) could be fatal.

The Delve: A network of caverns hidden beneath the Admare Mountains (a mountain range in the East). The Delve serves as both a military facility and hideaway for Elsudrans, specifically generals, soldiers, palace staff, and the Sorcerer of the Court—all of whom were handpicked by the Keepers to keep the Delve running before and after the Omnia's return. The facility itself was built during the era of Keepers over pre-existing tunnels used by early Elsudrans, who were searching for sources of water.

Double Moon: A holiday marking the end of the Elsudran calendar year, when the season Calcite turns to Pearl. On this day, two moons rise in the sky.

Elsudra: A small continental sister realm inhabited by just over one million people (Elsudrans). Like all the sister realms, Elsudra is a creation of Exorsus and was born from the sea (more specifically, a sliver of the sea that held the Omnia). Due to the Omnia's presence in water, early Elsudran communities attempted to settle near coasts and lakes. After the first Keepers came into power, magic in Elsudra was heavily controlled by the government and no longer a natural resource.

Era of Keepers: An era that began when the first Keepers took the Omnia from water and ended when the last Keepers sent the Omnia out of Elsudra. During this time, the Omnia—and thus all magic in Elsudra—was controlled by the government and the wealthy.

Essence: Also referred to as "spirit" or "soul," an essence is the nonphysical part of a living being that is the seat of emotions, character, and memories. Elsudrans (regardless of magical ability) have unique essences, which they can conceptualize via their mind's eye. Essences take the form of part of the natural world, and the degree of fluidity indicates the level of magical ability (i.e. an essence that takes the form of fog yields more magical ability than an essence that takes the form of snow or sand, whereas a strictly solid essence, like trees or rocks, cannot interact with magic). Regardless, all essences are a source of pride in Elsudra; they serve as reminders that everyone is a creation of Exorsus.

Exorsus: The creator of the sister realms, commonly referred to as "the beginning." While some Elsudrans believe it to be a mere creation myth, others view it as a sentient deity. Only the first Keepers knew its true nature.

Inclined: Shorthand for magically-inclined, an inclined individual has an inclination toward wielding magic. Those with unprecedented ability are referred to as sorcerers.

Keeper(s): Host(s) of the Omnia. By and large, this word refers to the descendants of four sorcerers who took the Omnia from water and became the first Keepers. Each generation saw four Keepers, who hosted the Omnia until their reign ended and they passed their quarters to descendants of their own. Upon obtaining their quarter, Keepers swore an oath that stripped them of identity and desire, ensuring the absence of corruption. While the first Keepers were uniquely powerful sorcerers, later Keepers varied in their degrees of magical ability (often little to none). After the last Keepers severed their holds on the Omnia and sent it from Elsudra, the realm underwent a period with no Keepers. Upon the Omnia's return, the new host is occasionally referred to as a "Keeper," albeit colloquially.

Locus: The ritual of movement, performed during the era of Keepers to transfer the Omnia between hosts. Central to Locus is the element of choice; the ritual necessitates the voluntary relocation of the Omnia from the giver(s) to the receiver(s). Participants must possess the capacity to both relinquish and accept the Omnia, respectively. As such, prior to the era of Keepers (when the ocean/water served as the Omnia's host), Locus could not be performed, as water lacks autonomy. However, after the first Keepers mysteriously came into possession of the Omnia, Locus became the established method for transferring the Omnia to the succeeding generation of Keepers. Notably, the outgoing generation of Keepers experienced irreversible damage to their essences and passed in the weeks following Locus's performance. Only the first Keepers survived Locus due to their adeptness in magically shielding their spirits, though they lived the rest of their lives weak. Subsequent to the first Keepers (whose magical abilities made them an exception), the responsibility of orchestrating Locus was assigned to the Sorcerer of the Court.

[The] Omnia: The essence of Elsudra itself, begot by Exorsus and responsible for energy and magic in Elsudra. Often referred to metaphorically as a sun, the Omnia's magic radiates onto everything in Elsudra; only some living beings, however, possess the ability to wield said magic. The Omnia itself requires a host, much like a heart requires a body to sustain it. Prior to the Keepers, the Omnia's host was the ocean (which connects to all other bodies of water in Elsudra). However, after the first Keepers came into possession of the Omnia, their line acted as hosts, leading to more centralized control of the Omnia.

Ruemin: An alien race of anthropomorphic, clawed, and scaled beings with prong-like appendages that jut from their throats. They communicate in an unknown language, roughly translated by Elsudran technology, and summon others by screeching and clicking. Ruemin come from a realm unrelated to the sister realms. Part of their peculiarity lies in their makeup, which resembles that of aspen trees; ruemin are connected by an intangible root system that functions as a unified entity, and thus each ruemin can feel the pain of another. While ruemin eat bodies, souls are what truly sustain them. Once they have devoured a spirit, a deadened version of it becomes an eternal part of the ruemins' larger entity. The word "ruemin" was first coined by the Sundrans. It means "unwelcome visitor."

Tempus: Commonly referred to as the ritual of guidance, Tempus is the oldest of the Daughter Rituals and is performed in a dream-like state. Historically, Tempus was performed during crises like war or famine to seek divine, albeit vague, guidance from higher powers, including possibly Exorsus itself. Sorcerers played a crucial role in overseeing and performing the ritual, which required immersion in water (Tempus requires maximal intimacy with the Omnia's host, which—in early Elsudra—was water). During the era of Keepers, however, only the Keepers could undergo Tempus, as they were the new hosts of the Omnia and thus possessed the required intimacy. While the Sorcerer of the Court orchestrated Tempus to compensate for the Keepers' lack of magical prowess, only the Keepers were partial to Tempus's guidance, received uniquely through dreams and thus inaccessible via psychometry. The Keepers' oath placed a variety of restrictions on the Keepers' ability to perform (and receive guidance through) Tempus. These rules were meant to prevent abuse of the ritual.

Sorcerer of the Court: Elsudra's most talented sorcerer, in charge of managing the Omnia. While the Keepers were considered mere figureheads in Elsudran society—absent from the public eye and discourse—the Sorcerer of the Court actively managed the allocation and use of magic. However, while the Sorcerer of the Court wielded ample power on paper, the court itself truly dictated Elsudra's magical infrastructure.

Sundra: One of the sister realms, related to Elsudra and Earth (and made by Exorsus). The Sundrans attempted to contact unrelated realms and accidentally let in the ruemin. A war ensued, bringing both species dangerously close to extinction. Eventually, the ruemin won and attempted to breed the remaining Sundrans to extend their food source. Rather than live like livestock, the Sundrans annihilated themselves. Elsudrans (notably, Brenna) constructed a portal that flowed from Elsudra to Sundra with the intent to leverage Sundra as a place to send Elsudra's most dangerous prisoners.